P9-DEJ-240

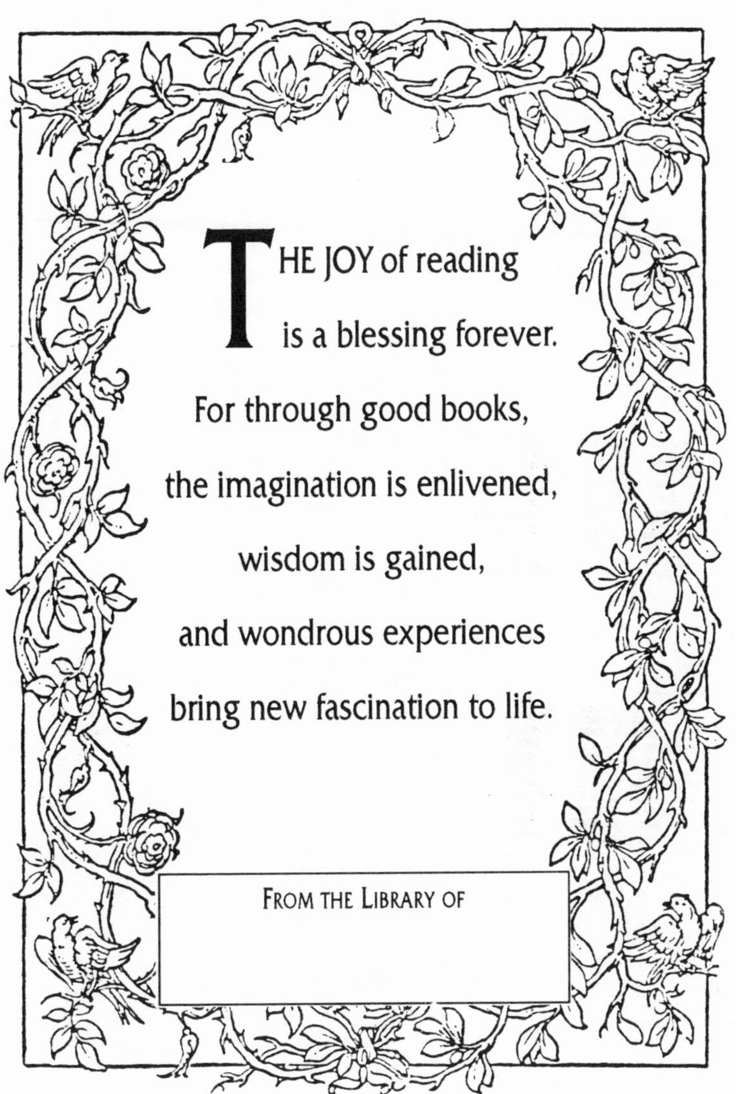
THE JOY of reading
is a blessing forever.
For through good books,
the imagination is enlivened,
wisdom is gained,
and wondrous experiences
bring new fascination to life.
FROM THE LIBRARY OF

EXCLUSIVE FAMILY BOOKSHELF 2-IN-1 EDITION

BOOKS THREE AND FOUR
OF
THE KENSINGTON CHRONICLES

WHO BRINGS FORTH the WIND

THE KNIGHT and the DOVE

LORI WICK

COMPLETE AND UNABRIDGED

WHO BRINGS FORTH THE WIND

Lori Wick

HARVEST HOUSE PUBLISHERS
Eugene, Oregon 97402

All Scripture quotations in this book are taken from the King James Version of the Bible.

WHO BRINGS FORTH THE WIND

Published by Harvest House Publishers
Eugene, Oregon 97402

Library of Congress Cataloging-in-Publication Data

Wick, Lori.
Who brings forth the wind / Lori Wick.
p. cm. — (Kensington chronicles)
ISBN 1-56507-229-4
1. Married people—England—Fiction. I. Title. II. Series:
Wick, Lori. Kensington chronicles.
PS3573.I237W49 1994 94-10718
813′.54—dc20 CIP

Printed in the United States of America.

94 95 96 97 98 99 00 — 10 9 8 7 6 5 4 3 2 1

First Combined Hardcover Edition for Christian Herald Family Bookshelf: 1995

For my grandmothers
Mabel Carrie Strebig and
EOline Elizabeth Johnson Hayes.
Thank you for the heritage of hard work
and boundless love.
I dedicate this book to you from
the bottom of my heart.

THE AUTHOR

Lori Wick, known for her warm pioneer fiction, now takes readers to fascinating lands across the sea in the Kensington Chronicles. Lori is the bestselling author of 11 novels, including *The Hawk and the Jewel*, *A Place Called Home*, *Whatever Tomorrow Brings*, and *Sean Donovan*. She and her family live in Wisconsin.

OTHER BOOKS BY LORI WICK—

A Place Called Home Series
- A Place Called Home
- A Song for Silas
- The Long Road Home
- A Gathering of Memories

The Californians
- Whatever Tomorrow Brings
- As Time Goes By
- Sean Donovan
- Donovan's Daughter

The Kensington Chronicles
- The Hawk and the Jewel
- Wings of the Morning
- Who Brings Forth the Wind

The Kensington Chronicles

DURING THE NINETEENTH CENTURY, the palace at Kensington represented the noble heritage of Britain's young queen and the simple elegance of a never-to-be-forgotten era. The Victorian Age was the pinnacle of England's dreams, a time of sweeping adventure and gentle love. It is during this time, when hope was bright with promise, that this series is set.

Prologue

LONDON
NOVEMBER 1852

"YOU'RE A BUFFOON, HENRY. I was a fool to have married you and an even greater fool to have given you sons. They're sure to grow to be just like you."

"Please, Ramona, please come back to me. Leave that man and return home. If not for my sake, then for William's and Tanner's. They need you."

"Get out of my sight, Henry, and take those brats with you."

"I'm sorry to disturb you, your Grace, but—"

"You forget yourself, Price. My brother, William, is the duke."

"I'm sorry, Lord Tanner, but your brother is dead. A fire at his London town house. Your wife was found with him. She died also."

Lord Tanner Richardson, Duke of Cambridge, woke with a start, sitting up in one violent motion. The bedclothes were drenched with sweat, and Tanner's chest heaved as he recalled the nightmares that so vividly portrayed his past.

The dreams hadn't changed in all these years. His mother's laugh was just as scornful, his wife's infidelity just as real. Bleakly content that he hadn't dreamt about either of them in ages, he threw the covers back and rose, ignoring his robe as he went to the window of his bedroom. The room was cold and the night dark, but his eyes still caught the images of bare trees blowing in the wind.

"Do you need something, my lord?" a voice spoke softly from the doorway.

"No, Price. Go back to bed." The duke's voice was cold, but the experienced servant knew better than to take this personally. The door was closed silently. It was some minutes before Tanner moved back to the bed.

Climbing back onto the mattress, he recalled the words his Uncle Edmond spoke during dinner.

"You need a wife, Tanner. You can scowl at me all you want, and even walk from the room, but it won't change the fact that you need another wife."

Tanner now gave a mirthless laugh as he settled the covers around him. If his uncle broached that forbidden subject again, he would stop him, even if he had to plant his fist on the older man's mouth to do it. He fell asleep telling himself that Edmond was wrong; he had no need of a wife, no need at all, none…

One

MIDDLESBROUGH, ENGLAND
MARCH 1853

ANASTASIA DANIELS SAT on the creek bank and stared down at the fishing line that lay undisturbed in the water. Four fish on another line lay at her side, but she'd set a goal of five and was not leaving the bank until she had them. However, her mind was beginning to wander. She pushed a stray lock from her face, wishing she had taken time to brush the honey-gold mass or at least secure it out of her eyes.

"Lady Stacy," a voice spoke from behind her, succeeding in drawing her attention from the surface of the water.

"Oh, good morning, Peters."

"Good morning, my lady. Breakfast is ready, and your grandfather is asking for you."

Stacy was on the verge of telling him she would come immediately when the pole twitched in her hands. She gave all her attention to the catch, and in just moments expertly pulled in a fat trout. She then turned to Peters with a huge smile that he found most contagious.

"Tell my grandfather I'll be right along."

Peters went on his way, and Stacy rose gracefully from the bank. The weighty line in her hand felt wonderful as she stepped lightly over the path and headed for the kitchen.

"Here you go, Mercy," Stacy nearly sang with triumph. "I think we'll enjoy these for lunch."

"I'll see to it, Lady Stacy," Mercy, the family cook, told her fondly. She shook her head with true tenderness as Stacy rushed out to clean up for breakfast.

Forty minutes later Stacy and her grandfather, Viscount Andrew Daniels, were finishing their morning meal.

"Did I tell you I caught five fish for lunch?"

"Five!" the old man exclaimed. "Why didn't you take me?"

"I went very early," she explained. "It took me forever, though. I must be losing my touch."

Andrew's only reply to this was a small grunt of disbelief.

"Peters says there's a letter here from London," Andrew commented.

"Oh, it must be Lucinda. Why don't we go into the salon, and I'll read it?"

Stacy began as soon as they were settled:

> The weather here is cold right now, but I can tell that spring is around the corner. It will be welcome as the cold gets into my bones these days as never before.
>
> I had two of Mother's pieces reset, the emerald and the ruby, and I'm hoping Stacy will be interested in them. They're quite lovely and up-to-date in style. I'll hold onto them until such a time as Stacy can view them herself.

Stacy stopped reading at that point, and after a moment her grandfather questioned her.

"Is that all she says?"

"No," Stacy admitted, the letter still in her hand. "She goes on about my age and birthday, both of which she has wrong."

"That's normal," Andrew muttered. "If she mentions your age, then she must have a bee in her bonnet about your coming to London."

Stacy said nothing to this, only sat quietly and watched her grandfather where he rested in his favorite chair. He returned her look, but she knew he saw little; his eyesight seemed to weaken daily.

"Read the rest, Stacy." The command was soft, but Stacy complied immediately.

> Stacy will be 21 at the end of October, and I can't believe she's never come to London. It's criminal of you, Andrew, not to let her come and try to make a life for herself here. I'm still angry with you that she had no coming out. It's time Stacy marry and start a family. I know you agree, but you're too stubborn to admit it.
>
> I'll forgive and forget all the past, however, if you'll allow Stacy to come next month and stay for the entire summer, from the first of May to the end of July. I won't settle for a day less. I've been begging you for years, and it's the least you can do.
>
> I await your letter. Please do not let me down, Andrew. Love to you and Stacy.
>
> Lucinda

Andrew listened as Stacy folded the letter and wished he could see her clearly enough to read her expression. He knew she would go in an instant if he asked her, but he wasn't certain she would tell him the truth as to whether or not she *wanted* to go.

From the time she was a little girl Stacy had hated confrontation or unhappiness of any type. Andrew was quite certain that she would walk on hot coals if she thought it would please him.

"Would you care to go to London, Stacy?"

"Would you like me to?"

The old man smiled. He had known very well she would answer his question with a question of her own.

"As a matter of fact, I think it might be a good idea," he said after a moment, keeping his tone carefully neutral. "I don't feel as Lucinda does, that you need to make a life for yourself there, unless of course you want to, but it might be a summer you would really enjoy."

"All right," Stacy agreed, but her voice told him something was wrong.

"You're worried about something."

"Two things, actually," she admitted. "I'm afraid Lucinda will be determined to marry me off."

Andrew nodded. Stacy was a tall girl, nearly six feet and with a statuesque figure. None of the local boys had wanted a wife, even one with the face of an angel, who towered over them.

"I'll set her straight long before you go," he assured her. "What else troubles you?"

"The train ride. London is so far away, and it frightens me a little to contemplate making the ride alone."

Andrew's heart sank. He had been hoping that she would be bothered by something plausible, such as London itself, so that he could with a clear conscience tell Lucinda she wouldn't be able to come.

He did not have the extra staff to send someone on the train with Stacy. However, just the week before his man, Peters, had told him the Binks were headed to London with their daughter Milly to shop for her coming out. He knew they would be delighted to have Stacy with them.

Careful to keep biased emotion from his voice, he told Stacy this. If Stacy believed he wanted her to go, she would pack that hour. If she sensed he was hesitant, nothing could draw her away.

In just a matter of words it was settled. Andrew dictated a letter to Stacy for his sister on the spot, informing Lucinda of his expectations for Stacy's trip. He also reminded his forgetful sister that Stacy was approaching her twenty-*second* year and that her birthday was at the *beginning* of October.

He sent Stacy to post the letter as soon as it was ready and then rang for Peters.

"How did she seem?"

"Fine, my lord."

"Not upset?"

"No."

"Her face? What was on her face?"

This line of questioning was quite common for Peters, so he answered without hesitation as he led his lordship to his bedroom.

"She looked thoughtful, sir. Not upset or overly excited, just thoughtful."

Andrew heaved a great sigh of relief. Next he would have to check with his cousin's young wife, Elena, for Stacy would be certain to visit her while in the village. If Peters had missed anything, Elena certainly would not.

Elena Daniels sat across the parlor from Stacy just an hour later and marveled, not for the first time, at her looks. She was like a Viking queen with her thick, honey-blonde hair that hung as straight as a line and her beautiful figure, neither of which Stacy seemed to be aware in the slightest. She carried herself proudly, and just looking at her, one would not guess how shy and timid she could be.

"So what do you think?" Stacy, who had told Elena all about the plans, wished to know.

"I think if you want to go, then you should." It sounded harmless to Elena, and she was able to answer Stacy calmly. She was just two years older than Stacy, but her marriage to Noel Daniels, who was 24 years her senior, along with the birth of two daughters, made her feel years older.

"I think Papa wants me to go, and I know it would make Aunt Lucinda happy," Stacy told her.

There goes that word again, Elena thought. *Stacy must see to it that everyone is happy.* When would she see that the only true happiness anyone could have was found in pleasing God?

"What about you, Stacy? Will it make you happy?"

Stacy's huge blue eyes were thoughtful. She knew she could be very honest with Elena, but wasn't certain she should be. She suspected that her grandfather would be checking with Elena as he always did with Peters.

If the truth be told, Stacy said to herself, *I would never leave Middlesbrough and the safe haven of Papa's home.*

She had never seen London with her own eyes, but the drawings and paintings she'd studied made it look very large and crowded.

"I think I've lost you," Elena commented, and Stacy was swift to apologize.

"I'm sorry, Elena. I was thinking of London and how big it must be. I'm to have three new gowns." Stacy's face took on a look of excitement. "I'm hoping Aunt Lucinda will approve of them."

"Will that be enough? Maybe you should wait and shop for a complete wardrobe there," Elena suggested.

Stacy looked doubtful. "I don't know if Papa can afford that."

"What about your dowry?"

Stacy sighed; she'd thought of that. "He would never agree. He's so certain that I'll marry someday."

"You could ask him."

Stacy's look of longing turned to one of fear. The question might anger her grandfather, and she would hate that.

"Would you like me to ask him?" Elena offered, accurately reading Stacy's mind. Quite suddenly Elena wanted Stacy's trip to London to be very special, and thought that an extra dress or two might help.

"No, Elena, but thank you for the offer."

Elena nodded. "I suppose you're wise to let it rest," she commented. "You'll need that money when you marry."

Stacy didn't reply, not wanting to contradict Elena. It wasn't that she was against marriage, but if the suitable young men Stacy had grown up with were any type of gauge, Stacy was probably right in believing that she would never be wed.

It was true that she was as sweet and lovely a girl as any man could hope to find, but her height was a definite disadvantage. Stacy had had numerous dreams of meeting a tall stranger who would not be put off by her height, but so far no such man had materialized. *Maybe in London*... Stacy let the thought hang.

Elena, who had noticed Stacy's thoughtful face but not commented on it, had her own thoughts about the men in London—men who might flirt with Stacy, making promises with their eyes that they never intended to keep.

Stacy had been raised in a sheltered world, one that made her very trusting. The thought of someone hurting Stacy was so painful for Elena that for a moment she couldn't breathe. Maybe it was best that Stacy not have those beautiful gowns.

Both women were pulled from their thoughts when Elena's daughters, Harmony and Brittany, suddenly entered the room. They were thrilled to see Stacy, who was one of their favorite relatives. After swarming into her lap, they begged their mother to let them stay with the adults for tea. All thoughts of London were put aside.

"WELL, WHAT DO YOU THINK?" Stacy asked of Hettie. Hettie Marks was the housekeeper for her grandfather, and had been long before Stacy was born. She had been like a mother to her since before her second birthday, when Stacy had come to live with her grandfather at Morgan, their centuries-old family estate.

"I think you'll do. Of course..." Hettie, who always had something negative to say, added, "I've no doubt the styles in London are quite different, and you might look like a country mouse."

"But I *am* a country mouse," Stacy reasoned quietly. Hettie could only shrug.

"You'll have to wait and see what Lady Warbrook has to say."

These words were thrown over Hettie's shoulder as she exited, leaving Stacy alone in her room. As soon as the door shut, the younger woman's eyes swung back to the full-length standing mirror.

She liked her new dress—in fact she liked all three of her new dresses—but the overwhelming feeling that they all looked the same hung heavy in Stacy's mind. When she had questioned the seamstress, a Mrs. Crumb from outside the village, the woman had assured her that the change in fabrics—

a light blue silk, a pale yellow satin, and a muted shade of red velvet—would disguise any similarities.

Stacy had taken her at her word, but now that the dresses were finished and ready to be worn, she wasn't so sure. Stacy stared at herself a moment longer and then shrugged much like Hettie had. There was little she could do about it now, and because she was going to be visiting a woman past her sixtieth year, Stacy assumed they would not be dining out each night of the week.

As she changed out of her dress, Stacy's mind wandered to her trip. She would be leaving in two days. Stacy let her thoughts drift into another world. A world where she was sought after. A world where a tall, dark man would fall in love the moment he lay eyes on her and want her to be his wife.

"But then he'll want you to live in London," Stacy, straightening suddenly, spoke aloud into the still room. "That won't do at all."

With composed movements, and working to bring her thoughts firmly back to reality, she pulled the hairbrush through her hair and then headed for the door to check on dinner preparations.

It simply won't do to stand about fantasizing when there is work to be done, Stacy told herself. Still, she was seeing a tall, faceless man bending gallantly over her hand.

Stacy's heart thudded with dread when it was time to say goodbye to her grandfather. Not an overly demonstrative man, Andrew Daniels surprised Stacy by giving her a quick hug. They were nearly of the same height, and Stacy had to force the words from her throat when he dropped a kiss onto her cheek and released her.

"Goodbye, Papa."

"Goodbye, Stacy. Write when you are settled."

"Yes, Papa." She stood quietly then and just looked at him.

Andrew stared in return. His vision was better today, and he could see the uncertainty and fear in her eyes. He kept his own expression bland.

"You're going to be fine," the old man spoke, wondering if he would be able to say the same for himself.

Stacy could only nod, wanting to believe him. It was such a childlike gesture that Andrew gave her another hug, this one quite lengthy and without words. When it was over, he stood quietly and watched her step into his ancient carriage. He stayed on the steps, not only until they disappeared from view, but until he could no longer hear the carriage wheels rolling or the sound of the horses' hooves.

Lucinda Warbrook, Countess Snow by title, surreptitiously shifted the locket-watch that lay on her bosom and studied the time. She'd done so every few minutes for nearly an hour.

"Stacy will be fine, Cinda," a calm male voice told her from across the room. Lucinda's chin rose.

"Of course she'll be fine, Roddy. She is a Daniels, and all Daniels are strong. I was merely straightening my lace."

Roddy Caruthers, Earl of Glyn and Lucinda's closest friend, eyed her with doubt. Lucinda met his gaze for only a moment before she relaxed and the two exchanged a smile.

"Would you like me to go to the train station and see what might be keeping her?" He'd offered to do this twice before, and both times Lucinda had turned him down. Now she looked as though she might be considering it.

"It's just that I have pushed this issue with my brother, and if anything should happen to Stacy before she even arrives—"

Lucinda broke off when Roddy stood. She was reaching for the bellpull so Roddy's coat and hat could be retrieved when the door opened. It was Craig, Lucinda's head servant, announcing Stacy's arrival. Craig closed the parlor door as soon as he'd had his say, and Lucinda looked at Roddy, a touch of panic around her eyes.

"What have I done?" she whispered.

"You've done exactly as you should, Cinda," Roddy assured her confidently, just as the door opened and Stacy entered.

Her face was washed with fatigue but nothing could disguise the sweetness of her smile or the lovely blue of her eyes. She stood quietly for inspection wearing the yellow satin dress, her hair pulled back in a youthful style.

Even as Lucinda approached, she thought both the dress and hairstyle too young for Stacy, but no matter; she would fix all of that. The older woman nearly rubbed her hands together in anticipation of dressing this magnificent creature.

"My dear Stacy," Lucinda spoke with genuine warmth as her arms surrounded the girl.

Stacy returned the embrace, surprised and strangely relieved to find that her aunt was just a few inches shorter than herself.

"How was the train?" Lucinda asked as she led her to the settee near the fire. The room was chilly, and Stacy welcomed the warmth.

"It went well. A bit cold at times, but Milly and I snuggled together for warmth."

"Milly?" Lucinda frowned in thought.

"Milly Binks," Stacy supplied. "I traveled here with her family."

"Of course. I remember now. She was coming to shop, I believe."

"Yes, for her coming out."

Roddy, having taken a chair, sat quietly and listened to this exchange with great pleasure. He'd known for years that Lucinda wrote her brother and niece regularly and gained steady replies in return, making this instantaneous friendship quite natural. What he hadn't been prepared for was Stacy's sweetness.

She was not some nauseating creature who feigned politeness or forced good manners; she was simply a very gentle woman who obviously found pleasure in small things, such as conversing with her elderly aunt.

"Oh, goodness," Lucinda's voice broke into his musings. "You're sitting so quietly, Roddy; I nearly forgot you.

"Stacy, this is my dear friend the Earl of Glyn, Roddy Caruthers. Roddy, this is my niece, Anastasia Daniels."

Roddy stood on this introduction, and with all the court manners of a prince, bowed low and gently kissed the hand offered him.

"It is a pleasure to make your acquaintance, Lady Stacy."

Stacy, who had begun to smile at the introduction, found her eyes growing round with surprise by the time her aunt's friend was finished.

"Have I said something wrong?" Roddy asked solicitously, his eyes sparkling with good humor.

"I don't think so," Stacy spoke softly. "I've just never heard Lady Stacy sound so grand. We're all quite familiar at home."

"Ahh." Roddy's voice was kind, a smile now in full bloom. "I think you will become comfortable with our formality very swiftly." His voice was so gentle that it put Stacy's doubts to rest. Stacy gave him a huge smile, one that Roddy returned, before Lucinda spoke.

"I've ordered tea for 3:00, Stacy, if you'd like to freshen up. You will stay, Roddy?"

"Of course, Cinda," Roddy accepted with a gracious nod of his head. He watched as his hostess took her young charge from the room.

Stacy silently followed her aunt up the wide staircase of the mansion, mentally figuring how many hours remained until bedtime. Near the top she was beginning to flag, but the idea of tea drove her on. Never had she experienced such a long day. The sights and sounds of the train stations, the train ride, and then London itself were nearly more than she could take.

Watching Milly and her family walk away at the train station after such a good journey of sharing and laughter had been harder than Stacy expected, but Lucinda's coachman was kind and just 30 minutes later Stacy had been relieved to walk into Lucinda's parlor and find it warm and homey.

Stacy was looking forward to her stay with her aunt, but she was not lulled into a false sense of security about this visit. She had seen a look in Lucinda's eyes that had told her her clothing was not acceptable. And there was more. Lucinda sported the same stubborn chin that her grandfather owned. He was a man who liked to have his own way. Stacy had no doubts that as warm and loving as Lucinda Warbrook might be, she would also possess a well-used stubborn streak.

"She's lovely, isn't she, Roddy?" Lucinda said after the tea service was cleared away and Stacy had asked if she could retire to rest awhile.

"Yes, she is," he agreed softly, gazing at the excited flush on Lucinda's cheeks and thinking how lovely she was herself.

Three years past her sixtieth birthday, Lucinda didn't look a day over 50. Her dark hair was liberally streaked with white, but it gave a softness to her face that not even her stubborn chin could hide. She had a temper and was fiercely protective of those she loved, but she was also wise, sensitive, and well liked among London's elite.

Roddy wondered briefly if Stacy had any idea just how fully her aunt intended to launch her into London society.

"She hasn't many clothes, and what she does have are all wrong for her, so I'm making an appointment with Angelica tomorrow."

"Does Stacy know that?"

"No," Lucinda spoke dismissively, "but all girls like new clothes."

Something on Roddy's face made her pause.

"Do you think she'll object?"

"I honestly don't know. She's nothing whatever like I expected. She's mature and quite accepting of her lot, I would say. I could tell she was uncomfortable in the red velvet dress she changed into for tea, but even at that I detected an underlying acceptance within her over the whole situation."

Nodding, Lucinda stayed silent, digesting what he'd said. Roddy was always so good at reading people. He never worried about putting his oar in as Lucinda did, but was content to sit back, listen, and observe. Sometimes he read the situation wrong, but Lucinda felt certain he'd hit the mark with Stacy.

No matter really, Lucinda thought. *Stacy will not have to be accepting of her situation any longer. I am here to see to that.*

It crossed Lucinda's mind that her niece might not care to have new clothes and attend every ball in London, but Lucinda quickly pushed the thought away. What girl wouldn't be thrilled with the summer Lady Warbrook was about to give her niece?

Three

STACY THANKED RAYNA, the personal maid Lucinda assigned to her, while carefully keeping a smile pinned to her face. When the door closed, leaving her alone, Stacy's hands moved to her mouth and she dropped onto one side of the bed.

She simply didn't know what to do. Her grandfather would be furious if he knew how many dresses Lucinda had ordered for her today. Stacy knew they would cost a fortune, money that her grandfather didn't have. She recalled the flash of anger in Lucinda's eyes when she mentioned this, and that had been enough to make Stacy hold her tongue.

It had done little to relieve her mind when Lucinda calmed down and explained quietly that the gowns were a gift. Stacy knew her grandfather would still not approve, and in a way she understood her grandfather's belief. Stacy often dreamed of finer things, but it seemed cruel to shower a person with beautiful articles of clothing they could never have again. Stacy was convinced that it was easier to go without your whole life than to live in opulence only to have it taken away.

Suddenly the room felt stuffy, and Stacy rose to go downstairs. A walk in the garden was sure to do some good.

An hour later Roddy stopped to see Lucinda, only to be told that she was taking a rest. He was on the verge of leaving his card and a note when Craig told him that Lady Stacy was in the garden. There was something akin to concern in the man's tone, causing Roddy to reconsider and make his way out-of-doors.

The weather was still a bit cool, but Stacy seemed immune to the conditions around her. She sat on a stone bench amid the budding flowers and stared into space toward the high stone wall that surrounded the yard. She found herself wishing for the green hills of Middlesbrough, where she could walk for hours without need of an escort.

Her mind was wandering among those fields when she heard a footfall. Glad for something to take her mind from home, Stacy turned with surprised pleasure to see Roddy.

"Good afternoon, Lady Stacy," he began. "Taking in this brisk afternoon?"

Stacy smiled shyly. "My room felt stuffy. I'm afraid I've hardly noticed the weather."

Roddy took a seat across from her and studied her. Stacy sat quietly under his scrutiny, searching her mind for some topic of conversation. She had never been very good at being witty or charming. She usually just said what was on her mind, but she didn't think her wardrobe an appropriate topic right then. Stacy was still groping for a subject when Roddy spoke.

"How was your shopping trip this morning?"

"Fine," Stacy answered a bit too brightly, and Roddy's brows rose in disbelief, causing Stacy's eyes to drop to her lap.

"Lucinda likes to shop," she spoke inanely, wishing that Roddy's gaze wasn't so penetrating.

"I take it that she bought you quite a number of dresses?"

"An entire wardrobe," Stacy admitted, looking miserable. "It was really very kind of her, but I just don't know what my grandfather will say when I arrive home with an entire trunk full of new dresses." Stacy did not know what prompted her to confide in this near stranger, but he was so kind and easy to talk with.

"Your grandfather doesn't care for your having new things?" Roddy's voice held no accusation, just deceivingly mild interest.

Stacy tipped her head to the side, searching for the right words to explain. As she did so her thick blonde hair fell like a curtain over one shoulder.

"My grandfather is a proud man, just as Aunt Lucinda is a proud woman. He wants me to have all that *he* can provide. Aunt Lucinda married well. My grandfather couldn't provide that many dresses for me if he saved for a year. And in truth, I can't think where I'll wear them. Some of the fabrics look fit for a princess."

"Did you explain that to Lucinda?"

"I tried, but she didn't look too happy about it."

Such a polite way, Roddy translated to himself, *of saying that Cinda became angry and Stacy immediately closed her mouth and backed down.*

"Has Lucinda told you all she has planned for the summer?" Roddy suddenly asked.

Stacy shook her head no.

Roddy nodded. "I think you may find that you will have ample opportunity to wear the dresses. As for your grandfather's reaction, let Lucinda handle it. You certainly won't be blamed for something over which you had no control."

Stacy sighed deeply. She felt caught between the hammer and anvil where her aunt and grandfather were concerned. To please one would displease the other, and that thought alone gave Stacy a headache. But her normal good sense took over then, and she told herself that Roddy was right.

"Thank you, my lord. You've been a tremendous help."

"You're most welcome, and I really wish you would call me Roddy. It's not as if I'm a duke," he added with a cheeky grin.

Stacy smiled in return but then looked worried. "I won't have to meet any dukes or duchesses, will I?"

"You might," Roddy told her. "Is that a problem?"

Stacy shrugged uncomfortably. "I just don't know what I would say."

"Don't say anything if you don't have to. And if you do find you need to reply, just be yourself. The London elite can be ruthless, but the only thing they could find to say about you is that you're the sweetest thing to arrive in decades."

Stacy chuckled softly at the compliment. "I think Aunt Lucinda is quite lucky to have Roddy Caruthers."

"I think so too," he agreed with her, another grin in place. With that he stood and offered his arm.

"May I escort you in to tea?"

Stacy accepted graciously, not even self-conscious that he was two inches shorter than her statuesque frame.

❧ ❧ ❧

"Did you give my letters to Craig?" Lucinda wanted to know. Over two weeks had passed since Stacy had spoken with Roddy in the garden, and during that time Stacy had been much easier about the wardrobe.

Now she was breakfasting with her aunt, and Lucinda was giving her the day's plans.

"I did give them to Craig. He assured me he would see to them," Stacy answered.

"Very good. Now, I wish to leave as soon as we've eaten. We've been invited to Andrea's, and I don't wish to be late."

Stacy nodded and continued with her meal. Her day-dresses had begun arriving just two days ago, and Lucinda had had the two of them out for tea both morning and afternoon since. Stacy had met more people in the last three days than she had in all her life.

They had all been kind, but Stacy could not shake the feeling that she was here on inspection. It put something of a damper on her outings, but most of the time she was determined to enjoy herself and go home rich with memories and experiences.

Every memory of home gave her a slight pang. She was truly pleased to be in London, but she missed her grandfather, Elena, Elena's girls, and Hettie terribly. When her feelings of homesickness threatened to overwhelm her, she thought of her dresses. They were the most beautiful she'd ever seen.

Stacy found herself feeling very pleased that Lucinda had not listened to her about her grandfather's wishes. Had she done so, she would not have been stepping out in London with clothes that made her feel as if she belonged. So often her words to Hettie about being a country mouse came to mind. Most of the time she still felt that way inside, but on the outside she knew she was at the height of fashion.

The dress she wore this day was a dark blue water silk of elegant simplicity. The neckline was high with a white lace inset. The same lace trimmed Stacy's three-quarter-length sleeves. The skirt was of a medium fullness, and the bodice accentuated the line of her waist and full bosom. As they climbed down from the carriage before Featherstone, Lady Andrea Brent's mansion, Lucinda felt a surge of pride in Stacy.

Featherstone sat on the Thames and was one of London's most talked-about residences. Stacy and Lucinda were inside, standing in the vast foyer, before Stacy learned that Andrea was a duchess.

"He said, 'The duchess will be with you in a moment,' Aunt Lucinda. Did he mean Lady Andrea?"

"Well, of course," Lucinda frowned at her. "What did you think?"

"I don't know. None of the other ladies I met this week were—" Stacy cut off her sentence when the servant reappeared and directed them forward.

He opened a door at the rear of the foyer and led them into a huge parlor. Andrea was inside and rose immediately to greet them.

"Come in, Lucinda." She greeted her with a kiss. "And you must be Stacy. Lucinda has told me so much about you." Stacy returned the spontaneous embrace, thinking that she liked Lady Andrea very much.

"Please sit down." Andrea indicated the chairs and continued to speak as they moved. "Your dress is lovely, Stacy. Something tells me the two of you have been shopping."

Lucinda looked so pleased that Stacy had to stifle a laugh. "We have been shopping," Lucinda announced proudly and went on to tell Andrea all they'd been about.

Stacy found herself quelling laughter again, this time at herself, when she remembered the quiet existence she believed Aunt Lucinda led. Why, the older woman had more friends than Stacy could keep track of! Stacy glanced up at Andrea to find her hostess's eyes on her. They shared a small, almost secret, smile, and Stacy had the impression that Lady Andrea could read her thoughts.

With an effort, the younger woman then concentrated on what her aunt was saying. She learned that they would be having tea with someone else the next day and then attending the Parkinsons' ball on Saturday night. The following Saturday it would be the Madisons' ball.

Stacy's eyes, having just been so amused, must have now shown her shock over this news. Both women smiled at her.

"You'll have a wonderful time, Stacy," Andrea assured her. "If your dress is half as lovely as it is today, you'll be the talk of the room." Andrea could see in an instant that she'd said the wrong thing. A moment later Stacy's words confirmed this.

"I don't want to be the talk of the room," she said softly, and Lucinda's voice was tight when she spoke.

"Honestly, Stacy, you would think you don't even like all the new things I've bought you or want to show them off."

"Oh, no, Aunt Lucinda," Stacy was instantly contrite. "I love my new dresses." Her answer was an honest one, but Stacy was far too timid to tell Lucinda she didn't care to be on display.

Lucinda, choosing to ignore Stacy's discomfort, nodded her stubborn chin as though she'd won the battle. Lady Brent was thankful that tea was announced. Neither of her guests noticed her scrutiny of Stacy's quiet face or her worried frown over Lucinda's control of the girl. Thankfully, tea-time passed smoothly.

Two hours later Andrea was seeing her guests to the door. The older women conversed as they walked, and Stacy was content to listen. All three of them were surprised when the front door suddenly opened and in swept the most beautiful woman Stacy had ever seen.

"Sunny!" Andrea cried and rushed forward to embrace the lovely chestnut-haired girl.

"Hello, Mum. Am I interrupting?"

"Of course not. Come and meet Stacy. You know Lucinda Warbrook."

"Of course. It's lovely to see you, Lady Warbrook."

"And this is her niece, Stacy Daniels. Stacy, this is my daughter-in-law, Sunny."

"Hello, Stacy." Sunny greeted her with genuine kindness. "I hope you're not leaving."

"Actually, we are," Stacy told her with real regret.

"My timing is awful." Sunny pulled a face that did nothing to detract from her lovely appearance. "At least I can walk you out."

This said, Sunny tucked her arm in Stacy's and began to chatter as they walked out the front door toward the waiting carriage.

"I think I know your cousin. Is her name Elena?"

"Yes," Stacy answered with surprised pleasure. "How do you know her?"

"We met a few years ago, just after she married your grandfather's cousin. She was in London for a visit, and I think she was expecting her first child."

"That would be Harmony. She's had another little girl since then; they named her Brittany."

"Those are lovely names. Do you miss Elena and the girls?"

"I can't tell you how much," Stacy told her fervently and then pulled a face of her own. "I also miss our home in the country. London is so huge and noisy."

"You forgot smelly," Sunny added.

Stacy laughed. "How could anyone forget that?"

"I prefer the country myself," Sunny told her as they walked. "Maybe you'll have a chance to visit Bracken while you're here. We would love to have you."

Stacy looked delighted and then uncertain. "I'm not exactly sure what Aunt Lucinda has in mind," she admitted softly.

The two older women were following slowly, so Sunny only had time to nod in comprehension and say just as quietly, "I think I understand. Lucinda must feel she's been given a live doll to play with."

Stacy laughed softly at the accurate description of her relationship with Lucinda and found Sunny grinning at her.

"I like you, Stacy Daniels," Sunny told her.

"And I like you, Sunny," Stacy barely had time to reply before being joined by Lucinda and Andrea.

Stacy thanked her hostess and climbed into the carriage without ceremony. As it pulled away, Lucinda commented on having just spotted the duke as he joined his wife and mother. Stacy wanted to question her on the spot, but Lucinda continued to speak.

"It had been on the tip of my tongue to ask Sunny if she was here with Brandon."

"Brandon?"

"Yes," Lucinda answered absently. "Sunny's husband, Brandon Hawkesbury, the Duke of Briscoe."

Stacy's eyes widened a bit, but Lucinda didn't seem to notice. Stacy was very quiet on the ride home.

Four

"WELL, WHAT DID YOU THINK of her?" Andrea asked of Sunny when they were finally alone.

"I think she's the sweetest thing I've ever met. And," Sunny paused for emphasis, "I know her cousin, Elena, who happens to be a believer. We met a few years ago, and she told me at the time that she was praying for Stacy's salvation. I find it very exciting that the Lord put us together, however briefly."

"Put who together?" Brandon asked as he joined the ladies and they went in to lunch.

Sunny explained her encounter with Stacy, and when Brandon prayed before they ate, he asked God to bless Stacy and give her further contact with Sunny.

They were halfway through the meal before Brandon commented cryptically on his mother's lack of enthusiasm.

"Over what?" Andrea wanted to know, thinking she'd been quite pleased over Stacy's visit.

"I was so excited about Stacy," Sunny admitted softly to her spouse, "that I forgot to tell her."

Andrea looked from her son to her daughter-in-law, and a slow smile pulled her mouth into a huge grin.

"I thought there was something going on, Sunny." She rose and kissed her cheek. "You have that special glow about you."

Brandon and Sunny exchanged a glance, one of love and sharing. The meal continued with a discussion about how old their first child, Sterling, would be when his younger brother or sister was born.

Stacy moved into the parlor at Lucinda's and collapsed into a chair. Her feet were throbbing, but she was as light-hearted as a child. She had survived her first London ball, and it had been the most exciting night of her life.

The ballroom and dining room at the Parkinsons' had been absolutely beautiful. Stacy needed only to close her eyes to see the lovely candelabras and hear the music play. She had danced for hours.

"I think she's asleep," Roddy commented as he came into the room and made himself comfortable.

Stacy's eyes opened, and she smiled. Lucinda had invited him in to rest by the fire.

"Sleepy, but not sleeping. I was thinking of the dance."

"I was thinking of it myself," Lucinda put in as she made herself comfortable across from Stacy, eyeing her maternally. "I think Lord Culbertson was quite taken with you."

"He's so nice," Stacy commented sweetly, "and he loves to fish," she added with enthusiasm, her blue eyes sparkling.

Roddy chuckled over Lucinda's good-natured groan.

"Is that all you spoke of?" the older woman wanted to know.

"Well," Stacy sat up straight and tried to think, wanting to please her aunt, "he told me about his horses, and I told him about Noel's stables."

"My dear Stacy," Lucinda's look was pained, "Lord Culbertson raises some of the finest horses in England."

Stacy's fine mood was deserting her. She tried to think of something else they spoke of that would pacify her aunt.

"He said my dress was pretty and my hair. And he didn't seem to mind that we were of the same height."

"But you spent most of the time discussing fishing?" Roddy asked gently.

Stacy nodded, looking miserable now. "I'm sorry, Aunt Lucinda. I hope I didn't embarrass you."

Stacy's look, that of a child who had disappointed her mother, was too much for the older woman. Lucinda's own look became a mask of shame.

"You could never embarrass me, Stacy. I couldn't have been prouder of you tonight if you had been my very own daughter. I'm sure Lord Culbertson was captivated."

Stacy looked uncertain, but she did feel a little better. "At least he wasn't a duke," Stacy added as an afterthought. "They still intimidate me."

"Why is that?" Roddy wished to know.

"I guess because the only one I've ever been acquainted with is rather mean. His wife is even worse. Each time I see them, they make me feel like some sort of country vermin. It makes me feel as though I've no right to be moving in their circles.

"Sunny and Andrea are certainly nice people, but it may take some time for me to get beyond their titles. I know it must sound silly to you, but I've no lofty aspirations. My grandfather is a viscount. I've always assumed I'd marry a viscount or a baron who led a simple life, and that's always been fine."

Lucinda did not look overly pleased with this news, but Roddy was able to catch her eye and with a slight move of his head, keep her hushed. Stacy, growing sleepier by the moment, didn't notice their silent exchange.

"Goodnight, Aunt Lucinda. Goodnight, Roddy; I'll be ready in the morning," she bid them softy as she stood. They returned her wishes for a good night and watched her exit the room.

"It's silly of her to be afraid," Lucinda said immediately, her tone impatient.

"Be that as it may, she is. I see no reason to try to calm her, since it's very unlikely that she will encounter many dukes."

Lucinda didn't seem very satisfied with his logic. She named the few eligible dukes out loud, all 80 if they were a day, until Roddy stopped her with a soft rebuke.

"Cinda! You don't actually have your sights set on a duke, do you?"

"No," she admitted. "In fact, I think Lord Culbertson might do very well for Stacy, and he's a marquess."

"He's also old enough to be her father." Roddy's voice was dry.

"Well, we might not be able to be so picky," Lucinda nearly snapped.

"Why must she marry at all?" Roddy questioned, not at all put off by her bad humor. His question only gained him a quelling look, one that amused him more than anything else. A moment's silence passed before Roddy suggested the only young, single duke he knew.

"There is always Lord Richardson." Roddy worked to keep his face bland while Lucinda's flushed with anger.

"Don't be ridiculous! He's the biggest cynic in all of England and all wrong for Stacy." Lucinda's foot beat a rapid tatoo on the floor. Roddy watched her for a moment and then stood with a lazy stretch.

"This conversation has worn me out. Remind Stacy that I'll be here at 10:00 sharp for our ride."

With that he leaned over and pressed a soft kiss to Lucinda's brow. Her anger melted at his tenderness, and even though no more words were said, their eyes held for just a moment before Roddy crossed the room to the door.

"Oh, Stacy, that color is beautiful on you," Lucinda complimented her the next morning when Stacy entered her bedroom wearing a pale yellow riding habit with a white blouse and short jacket.

"Thank you. I think this one must be my favorite."

"Roddy's head will swell when he's seen in the park with you."

Stacy smiled shyly without answering. Lucinda patted the side of the bed, and she took a seat.

"Are you having a good time with me, dear?" Lucinda's eyes were eager.

"Oh, yes, Aunt Lucinda. It's been wonderful." Stacy hesitated before going on. "Are you pleased with me?"

Lucinda's answer was to tenderly cup Stacy's soft, rosy cheeks in her perfectly manicured hands and place a gentle kiss upon her forehead. Stacy was very touched by the gesture and was surprised to see tears in Lucinda's eyes. The older woman busied herself with her bedclothes to cover the fact, but Stacy had seen them nonetheless.

"Aunt Lucinda?"

"Yes, dear." Lucinda's voice held a catch.

"May I ask you a question?"

"Of course." She cleared her throat and finally looked up.

"Why have you never married Roddy?"

Lucinda's eyes, which had first held expectancy, became very thoughtful, but she wasn't long in answering.

"He's never asked me."

Stacy tipped her head to one side. "But you love him?"

"Yes" was the serene reply. "I have for years."

Stacy nodded, feeling closer to her aunt than ever before. Silence passed for a moment, a gentle silence with no hint of strain or awkwardness, before Craig knocked and announced that Roddy had arrived for Stacy.

"I'm probably the most envied man in the park today," Roddy commented from the back of his horse. Stacy smiled.

"Aunt Lucinda said your head would swell when you were seen with me today," Stacy admitted and then looked swiftly at Roddy to see if she'd offended him with Lucinda's words. On the contrary, his shoulders were shaking with laughter.

They rode on in silence for a time. Roddy took them down one of his favorite paths. They were halfway to the other side when they passed another group of riders. Stacy recognized a few from the Parkinsons' ball and smiled, but in her mind the entire event passed without exception. Not so for Roddy. Stacy glanced over to ask him a question and found his handsome face in a fierce frown.

"Are you feeling ill, Roddy?"

"No. I'm just always amazed at the ton's propensity for gossip."

Stacy stared at him uncomprehendingly.

"I take it you didn't hear that remark concerning you and me?"

Stacy shook her head no.

"Well, then, we'll let the matter drop."

Stacy nodded in agreement but was troubled by his words. It was a pity really that her friendship with Roddy had to be put in a sordid light, because it simply wasn't so. He was only a few years younger than Lucinda and like a father figure to her. Even if her heart had moved to romance where he was concerned, in her mind he belonged to Lucinda. Stacy sighed softly and did her best to do as Roddy suggested.

"I don't believe you've heard a word I've said," Lord Edmond Black complained to his nephew as their horses stood off the path in a small copse of trees. "But I'm going to say it again. I think those horses are a good investment, and I think you should look into it."

Tanner glanced at the older man for an instant, but his eyes swung swiftly back to the woman riding through the park with Roddy Caruthers. Something tightened in his chest as he watched her smile at her companion, something he hadn't felt for years.

Edmond was talking again, so Tanner turned and tried to pay attention, but almost immediately, as though they couldn't help themselves, his eyes sought out the girl once again. This time he watched her until she disappeared from view, wondering absently how long her hair might be, and about her relationship to Caruthers.

"Tanner!"

Tanner's handsome head swung slowly back to his uncle. The look he gave the older man was one of pure boredom. "I'm listening, Edmond."

Edmond grunted with irritation. "You were doing nothing of the kind. You were watching Lucinda's niece."

"Lucinda Warbrook?"

"Certainly." Edmond's voice was still testy. "Daniels is the girl's name. Her grandfather is Andrew Daniels, Viscount Claremont. She never had a coming out, but she's here for the summer and Lucinda is dressing her like a princess and introducing her all over town."

Tanner listened intently, something he was not prone to do with Edmond. Edmond loved to gossip, and Tanner simply didn't care to hear about everyone in London. However, this tall-looking girl in the yellow riding habit captivated him.

"Now as I was saying..." Edmond began again, as their ride resumed, but Tanner's mind was still elsewhere.

The younger man had just remembered the invitation he had received to the Madisons' ball. He usually hated those affairs, but the thought of possibly seeing Lucinda Warbrook's niece was enough to make him reconsider.

Five

THE NIGHT OF THE MADISONS' BALL, Stacy was dressed long before Lucinda. She sat before the dressing table mirror and thought how lovely the emerald necklace looked with her green dress. Lucinda had done a wonderful job choosing the new settings for the family stones. In fact Stacy had already worn the ruby last week.

When Rayna finished stacking her hair high atop her head, Stacy walked downstairs to wait in the parlor with Roddy. She wondered in some amazement at how many hours he had stood in this parlor waiting for Lucinda to appear over the course of the years.

"Oh, my, Roddy," she commented as she came in. "You look very dashing tonight." Stacy moved to where he stood near the mantel and kissed his cheek. They had grown closer almost daily, and small touches were now customary and warm.

"Thank you, my dear." He accepted the compliment with a sparkle in his eye.

Stacy's grandfather had never been a demonstrative man, and now to have Roddy here to pat her hand or cheek and to accept her embraces and kisses was more special to Stacy than she could have put into words. It didn't cause her to miss Andrew Daniels any less, but it added a warm dimension to her life that she'd never before experienced.

Stacy and Roddy talked for the better part of an hour, both beginning to think that Lucinda was never going to make an appearance. Roddy's coach was waiting when she did come, however, so they were swiftly on their way.

"The Madisons are an old family," Lucinda explained on the way. "They have several daughters and one son. I would advise you to get to know him, but I think he's a bit of a libertine and a little young for you."

Stacy smiled in the darkness of the coach interior. Her aunt was forever out to see her married. Her grandfather had told Lucinda in no uncertain terms not to push this point, but Lucinda did as she wished.

"Now don't hesitate to dance with Lord Culbertson. You did well at the Parkinsons' ball; however, you must always watch who you're seen with. I want you to enjoy yourself, but spending even a few moments with the wrong person could ruin your chances." Lucinda's voice was now severe.

This time Stacy didn't feel like laughing. She wished with all of her heart that it was easier for a young woman to stay single, so that every union could be one of love. But this simply wasn't the case. Her honest desire was to marry, but at this moment Stacy wondered if she would ever meet the man of her dreams. She was comforted by the fact that she knew her grandfather would never force her. The thought made her sigh unconsciously, and Lucinda's voice came sharply from the other side of the coach.

"Did you hear me, Stacy?"

"Yes, Aunt Lucinda," she answered obediently, and the rest of the ride was made in silence.

The ballroom was crowded when they arrived, but Lucinda and Roddy were old professionals when it came to this type of entertainment. Stacy was more than willing to follow their lead, and within moments of coming to the edge of the dance floor, Stacy was swept out into a waltz.

She didn't catch the name of the man dancing with her, but she answered all of his questions and detected a gleam of disappointment in his eyes when he learned that she would not someday be the heiress to a fortune. Not until she arrived back at Roddy's side did Stacy begin to wonder if some of the young man's questions might have been out of order.

The next hour passed in much the same fashion, Stacy going from one partner to the next, some young, most old. She tried to ignore the fact that even if her hair hadn't been piled high atop her head, she would still be taller than most of them. The room grew very stuffy, and Stacy felt delivered when Roddy pressed a glass of punch into her hand.

The glass was on the way to her mouth when she spotted him across the ballroom—the tallest, most handsome man Stacy had ever seen. He was dressed all in black, and she stared at him because she seemed incapable of doing anything else. His own eyes were on her, and for the space of several seconds Stacy simply couldn't look away.

"Drop your eyes!"

The low, furious words came to Stacy's ears, but thinking they couldn't be for her, she didn't heed them. A fierce yank on her arm, one that nearly spilled her punch, finally brought her to her senses. She looked down to see Lucinda glaring furiously at her.

"I said, drop your eyes!"

"Oh." Stacy was startled and instantly contrite. "I didn't realize it was you, Aunt Lucinda. I'm sorry."

Stacy seemed to be at a sudden loss, her hands all aflutter as she changed her glass from one hand to the other. Lucinda wondered if she might not have overreacted and felt compelled to make amends.

"Here, give me your glass." Lucinda's voice was brisk now, but not angry. "Go to the retiring room and fix your hair. There's a good girl."

Stacy complied, but she honestly couldn't feel her slippers as they moved on the carpets. It was a comfort to find the retiring room empty. Head in the clouds, Stacy stood before the mirror and took in her flushed cheeks and dazed eyes. No wonder Lucinda had sent her from the room. Her own image faded as once again her mind's eye saw the man in black.

Can a person really be so drawn to someone after just one look? Stacy asked herself, and then her heart lifted. It didn't matter if no one else had ever felt as she did. He was the most wonderful man she'd ever seen.

"I wonder who he is." This was spoken out loud as Stacy's brow lowered in concentration.

Two young ladies chose that moment to enter the room, and Stacy swiftly turned and entered one of the booths. She wanted some time to herself. She came to her senses some five minutes later and knew she would have to return to the ballroom or Lucinda would miss her.

And who knows, Stacy told her heart as she moved toward the dance floor. *Maybe you'll spot him again.*

An hour and a half later Stacy knew that if she didn't get some fresh air she was going to be ill. It was dreadfully warm, and the young man who had promised her a glass of punch had left and never returned. She hadn't spotted the man in black again, but from across the way she could see Lucinda and Roddy talking with Lord Culbertson. Stacy was simply too warm to push her way through the crowd in order to join them.

With movements that were as subtle as she could make them, she moved toward the balcony doors. They were closed but thankfully unlocked, and Stacy drew in a huge breath of cool night air the moment she was outside. The breath nearly stuck in her throat, however, when a deep male voice addressed her from out of the darkness.

"I wondered how long it would take you to join me."

Stacy gasped as she spun and saw a man leaning lackadaisically against the stone railing, close to the house. Stacy was so startled by his presence that for a moment she said nothing.

Tanner, who had been watching her through the glass doors for over an hour as she danced and talked with half the people in the room, smiled at the surprise he knew must be feigned. It was an old game, often played in social circles. Not that he cared. He intended to know this woman very well before she left in the fall.

"I didn't know anyone was out here," Stacy finally spoke when her breathing returned to normal.

Again Tanner smiled. Most of the debutantes he knew believed that coyness was the way to attract a man. If Stacy preferred that method of sweet innocence, it was fine with him.

"Would you rather be alone?" Stacy asked kindly, not seeing Tanner's smile in the dark.

"Don't go in on my account," he told her. "I realize it's warm inside."

Stacy sighed with relief and moved away from the doors. She stepped to the railing a good ten feet from Tanner, thinking what a nice voice he had but wondering what he looked like. Stacy glanced out over the gardens, but the moon was very dim and beyond a shape or two, she could make out little.

"The Madisons have a lovely home," Stacy commented absently.

"It's nice," Tanner observed, his voice bored. "A little small perhaps."

Stacy stared at his silhouette and then up at the grand expanse of mansion before her. Clearly this man was accustomed to a home far larger than her grandfather's.

"You haven't told me your name," Stacy's companion suddenly said to her.

"Oh, I'm Stacy Daniels. Lucinda Warbrook's niece."

"Stacy would be short for—?"

"Anastasia."

"Hmm, Anastasia. That's a lovely name. I think it fits you." Tanner was well aware that he was doing some pretending of his own. Since he'd seen her in the park he had set about learning everything about her he wished to know. Unmarried, 21 years old, not spoken for, and of course what his eyes had told him the first time he'd seen her—tall and beautiful.

"I'm Tanner Richardson."

"Tanner," Stacy said with surprise. "I've always liked that name." Relieved that he had shared his name, Stacy chatted on about a young man from home with the same name.

Stacy would not have been quite so friendly had she been able to see the calculative look in Tanner's eyes as he studied her from the shadows. From where he was, the lights from the ballroom gave a perfect view of Stacy in her lovely green frock with its rounded neckline and short, puffed sleeves.

Stacy laughed suddenly. "I'm chattering on here, and you must be bored to death." Suddenly, her whole frame stiffened with embarrassment, but when she spoke her voice was as sweet and sincere as the woman herself.

"I'm sorry, Tanner. You must be waiting for someone, and now I've joined you and ruined it. I'll go inside and leave you alone."

"Come now, Stacy." Tanner kept his voice calm, but he wanted the game over. "We both knew you would come out here to join me."

A moment of silence met this remark. "I don't know what you mean," Stacy told him in genuine confusion.

"Of course you do." Tanner's voice lost some of its patience. He didn't care to keep up this pretense much longer. "Your eyes told me from across the room what I wanted to know."

Stacy tensed abruptly. It was *him!* Even though Tanner had not moved from the shadows, Stacy could now visualize this gorgeous man—very tall with dark brown hair and dark, compelling eyes. Lucinda's sudden hissing in her ear now made complete sense.

"I have to go in now." Stacy's voice was thick with shame and near desperation. Lucinda had warned her time and again to be careful with her eyes, but she'd never understood. Now by looking at a man and thinking him handsome, she had unwittingly given him a signal that she was interested. Lucinda would be livid.

Stacy moved back to the glass doors of the ballroom to the sound of Tanner's voice, but she didn't take in the words.

"I think Roddy is ready to leave now," Lucinda told Stacy. Stacy had come back to the dance an hour ago, and Lucinda had not seemed at all put out by her absence.

"You wait here by the cloakroom. We'll say our thanks and collect you in a moment."

Lucinda swept away before Stacy could frame a reply, which was just as well, since she was too tired to speak. She waved at a group of girls who were leaving and then slipped farther down the wall to lean against it and rest her feet. She knew it wasn't the least bit ladylike, but right now she didn't care.

"You left the balcony so abruptly that I didn't have a chance to tell you something."

Where he had come from Stacy didn't know, but suddenly there stood Tanner Richardson. He nonchalantly leaned one hand on the wall above her, and Stacy had to actually look up to see his face.

With a smile that was almost tender, Tanner turned on the full force of his charm. Stacy's heart pounded in her chest. She'd never reacted to anyone as she was doing now.

"I was going to tell you," Tanner went on quietly, his deep voice confidential, "that I *was* waiting for someone to join me. I was waiting for you."

Stacy could only stare up in stunned surprise. She couldn't

move or think, not even when his free hand reached for her and he gently touched the end of her adorable nose.

"I'll look forward to seeing you again, Anastasia," he whispered before straightening. A moment later he was gone.

Stacy didn't move or even breathe in the seconds that followed. Her heart felt as if it might pound through her chest.

"Why, Stacy." Lucinda's voice snapped her out of her trance. "Your face is rather flushed. Are you not feeling well?"

"Cinda," Roddy spoke with a laugh, "she's just danced for hours; what would you expect her to look like?"

Lucinda laughed with him, and Roddy helped her into her cloak. Stacy was thankful that no more was said on the subject as they loaded into the carriage and headed for home.

The next morning Roddy and Stacy enjoyed another ride in the park. When they returned, Stacy went directly to her room, but Roddy found Lucinda in a fury. Now he was in the parlor with his hostess and friend, making an attempt to calm her.

"Cinda," his voice was gentle, "wait to send for her. If she comes in now you'll terrify her."

"I don't care," Lucinda told him, although she did. "I've already sent Craig for her. I intend to have some answers *now!*"

Roddy sat down. When Lucinda was in high dudgeon there was simply no reasoning with her. If only she would settle down before Stacy arrived. But it was not to be. The moment she stepped into the room, Lucinda attacked.

"Where did you meet him?"

"Meet who?" Stacy asked. Her expression had gone from open friendliness to guarded fear upon seeing her aunt's ire.

"The Duke of Cambridge."

"I—" Stacy began to say that she hadn't met him, but Lucinda cut her off and began to pace.

"I warned you last night when I found you staring at him, but I can see my wishes mean little to you." She continued to rant and rave, but Stacy couldn't get beyond the fact that she didn't remember meeting a single duke the night before.

"I'm waiting for an answer, Stacy Daniels," Lucinda suddenly stopped and demanded. "When did you meet Lord Richardson?"

"Lord Richardson? You mean Tanner Richardson? He's the Duke of Cambridge?"

"Do not play games with me." Lucinda moved toward her, having completely lost her head.

"Lucinda!" Roddy's voice, sounding unlike Lucinda had ever heard it, checked her stride. She turned to find angry fire in his eyes, his face flushed. She was so startled by the change in him that she calmed slightly before turning back to Stacy. What she saw washed her in shame. All color had drained from Stacy's face, and she was staring at her aunt in stark fear.

"Sit down, Cinda." Roddy's voice had returned to normal, and Lucinda did as he commanded. She watched as Roddy approached Stacy and led her gently to a chair. Stacy kept her eyes on Roddy once he had seated himself, her eyes begging him to tell her what she had done. He did not disappoint her.

"The flowers on the table are for you," Roddy told her gently. He waited until Stacy noticed the huge bouquet of red roses before going on. "They are from Lord Richardson and came with a note telling you how much he enjoyed meeting you last night."

"Which is just ridiculous," Lucinda cut in angrily. "All you did was see him across the room. Isn't that right, Stacy? He's got more cheek than any ten men I know."

A short silence ensued before Roddy asked, "Did you see more of him, Stacy?"

Stacy nodded in misery, her eyes on her aunt, who suddenly looked crestfallen.

"I'm sorry, Aunt Lucinda. It was so warm in the ballroom, and I needed some air. I didn't know he was on the balcony. I didn't know he was the man from inside, and he never said he was a duke. I'm so sorry, Aunt Lucinda."

Stacy's face was so full of anguish that the last vestiges of anger drained completely out of Lucinda. The room *had* been like a furnace last night, and it was all so innocent on Stacy's part.

On the other hand, Lucinda was convinced that Tanner Richardson didn't have an innocent or honorable bone in his body. She was going to have to keep her head about this or lose control of the entire situation.

"Don't be upset anymore, my dear," Lucinda finally told her. "It wasn't your fault, and it's going to be fine. Did Tanner touch you in any way?"

"No," Stacy told her, and then her eyes grew huge. "I almost forgot. He did touch my nose with his finger."

Lucinda's eyes slid shut momentarily. When she regained control she asked, "Did he say anything improper?"

"No."

"You're certain?"

"Yes, ma'am."

Lucinda nodded. "Stacy, Tanner is not for you. He's young and titled, but he's also very cynical, and that is *not* the type of man for you." Lucinda looked at Roddy and gained his approving nod.

By unspoken agreement, however, neither Roddy nor Stacy's aunt went on to tell her that Lord Richardson's interest in her would not lead to marriage. Stacy was upset enough as it was, and they now knew how closely she would need chaperoning. Her trusting and innocent nature made her a possible prey to any and all disreputable men of title.

The three of them talked for a while longer before Lucinda suggested that Stacy check on preparations for lunch. Roddy and Lucinda continued to talk after she'd left.

"You can control Stacy's actions, Cinda, but you have little to say over Lord Richardson's."

"True," Lucinda said regretfully. "But if he tries anything with Stacy, he'll have to go through me."

"Well, you're certainly his match, Cinda, but have you considered the possibility of Stacy falling for him?"

The eyes Lucinda turned to him were dim with pain. Roddy moved close enough to slip an arm around her. Lucinda let her head fall against his shoulder, her heart silently contemplating how many years she'd begged Andrew to allow Stacy to come to London. Lucinda wondered that she could have been so unsuspecting of all that would entail.

TANNER SWEPT INTO THE BALLROOM, completely unconscious of the picture he presented. The black pants and coat hung on his muscular frame without wrinkle or gap, and the white cravat at his throat only heightened the deep tan of his face.

He nodded to several greetings of "Good evening, your Grace," but beyond that he was left alone. His eyes scanned the crowded dance floor for a sign of Stacy. This was the third dance he'd attended this week in order to speak with her, and she hadn't been present at the first two. Tanner told himself if she wasn't here tonight, he would go directly to Lucinda Warbrook's and demand to see her.

The incongruity of the situation began to dawn on Tanner. He hadn't been involved with a woman since Leslie died. So why now? Tanner had no answer. He had met Leslie the same way, spotted her at a ball and then sought her out. Of course at the time he didn't know how self-seeking she was or how desirable the title of duke was to her, the title that his brother had held at the time.

Suddenly Stacy came into view. Just the sight of her caused Tanner's doubts to fly. He didn't know much about her, didn't know if his being a duke would matter to her or not, but he knew this—he found her unforgettable. For the moment Tanner believed this to be enough.

In order to be more discreet, Tanner moved from the edge of the dance floor and began to patiently watch her and wait for his chance to approach.

"He's danced with you twice, Stacy," the younger girl said with wide eyes. "I hope you're ready for a proposal."

"Oh, Liz," Stacy shook her head at a friend she'd come to know through her weeks in London. "I think he's only being kind."

Liz exchanged a glance with the two other girls of the group, Barbara and Annemarie, and all three giggled. Stacy laughed at their teasing and shook her head again. They all wanted to be married so badly, and now a man at the ball, one who seemed to be two feet shorter than Stacy, had danced with her twice and given them all reason to think they would be bridesmaids.

"I need to go to the retiring room," Barbara said in a sudden whisper, and Stacy, with a swift glance at Lucinda who was standing nearby, moved off with the other three.

Lucinda held her place and watched them go, finally feeling at ease over letting Stacy out of her sight. The flowers had arrived over a week ago, and Lucinda had been ready for a battle that never materialized. She mentally shook her head over her own reaction. She should have known young Richardson would never follow through. He was the type of man who wouldn't commit himself to anything.

Lucinda frowned at her own uncharitable thoughts. Why was she so adamant against the man? She knew him to be a skeptic. She also knew he'd had a terrible childhood and first marriage, but that didn't make him a brute. It was just that his looks so reminded her of her husband, dead many years now. He had not been an easy man. Never faithful for more than a month, he had been two-faced about his infidelity to boot.

As unkind as it seemed, Aubrey Warbrook's death had come as a relief to Lucinda. He had killed the love she had for him while she was still a bride. Lucinda wanted so much more for Stacy.

❦ ❦ ❦

"I know I'll end up right back in here," Liz was saying as the four young ladies exited the retiring room, "but I must have something to drink."

"Good evening, Stacy." Tanner's low-pitched voice brought all four of them about, but his eyes were for Stacy alone.

"Hello," Stacy returned softly, forgetting for the moment who he was and thinking he was even more good-looking than she remembered. She glanced at her companions and found them staring at her with eyes like saucers. Their looks reminded her of Lucinda's reaction to her speaking with this man.

Stacy curtsied suddenly and turned to go back to the dance. The other girls had already done the same, so when Tanner moved to fall in step beside her, they ended up a little behind the rest. Not that the girls missed anything; they turned constantly to look at their companion and the duke.

As they neared the dance floor, Stacy began to panic. If Lucinda saw her with Lord Richardson, she would be very upset. With a move born of desperation, Stacy stopped, thinking she could bid this man goodbye and go back with the others. To her horror they did not stop, and she found herself alone with Tanner.

She glanced at the floor in misery, not wanting to offend him but knowing Lucinda would be outraged. When she looked up it was to find herself under Tanner's close scrutiny, a small smile playing around his firm mouth.

"You look lovely this evening, Stacy."

"Thank you, Lord Richardson," she answered, finally allowing herself to meet his eyes.

"So it's Lord Richardson now. On the balcony it was Tanner."

Stacy's hand came to her mouth in humiliation. "I'm so sorry, your Grace. I had no idea. It won't happen again."

His low chuckle sent a chill down Stacy's spine.

"On the contrary, Anastasia, I hope I hear it often." There it was again—the soft, warm sound of her name. Stacy felt lost and breathless. She stood looking at him as though she'd taken leave of her senses. Not until he repeated the action of touching her nose, ever so tenderly did she realize where she was and to whom she was speaking.

"My aunt," Stacy nearly stuttered and took a step back. "She will wonder where I've gone."

Tanner nodded wisely, knowing that now was not the time to try to talk with her.

"Go ahead, Stacy. I'll see you later."

Stacy didn't stay to question him about his words, but turned and nearly ran. Her heart, pounding from her encounter with the duke, slowed with relief when she spotted Roddy as soon as she returned to the floor. She stepped to his side, and he turned to her with a smile which died when he saw her flushed face.

"Is he here?" he asked after just a moment.

Stacy nodded.

"And you spoke to him?"

"Yes. I'm sorry, Roddy. He just appeared, and I didn't know what to do."

Roddy took her hand in his and led her onto the dance floor. As they danced he spoke softly—words to calm her, words to let her know she hadn't erred.

"I don't know how to tell Aunt Lucinda," Stacy admitted.

"Let me handle it, dear." His voice was paternal. "You just enjoy the remainder of the evening, and I'll be close by."

Stacy nodded gratefully and went from Roddy's arms to those of an older gentleman whom she'd met earlier. He and his wife had been friends of her aunt's for years, and Stacy looked forward to a relaxed dance and visit. Tanner, however, had other ideas.

The music had barely begun when he stepped forward and cut in. Stacy looked at her partner, but he didn't seem the least put out. He smiled in a grandfatherly fashion and turned her over without a backward glance.

Stacy held herself stiffly in Tanner's arms and for a long time never looked higher than his cravat.

"I'd like to see more of you, Stacy," Tanner said when they had danced for a time.

"You would?" Stacy asked, finally looking up at him.

"Yes. In fact, I'd like you to meet me tonight."

Stacy wasn't even aware of her feet as she stared into his eyes and listened to him. "Meet you where?"

"In your aunt's garden. I'll be there at 1:00."

"I'll have to ask Aunt Lucinda."

Tanner smiled, willing to go along with her innocent act just to be with her. "Oh, but I want it to be a secret, just between the two of us."

His voice and eyes made it seem special and wonderful, but as dreamy as Stacy felt she still answered immediately. "I couldn't do that. I couldn't leave the house at night without telling Aunt Lucinda."

The smile left Tanner's face abruptly. She was taking this too far.

Stacy had no idea what caused the change in him, but she saw it in his face and felt it in the arm that held her.

"I really hoped you would agree." Tanner's voice was clipped now. "Maybe one of the other women here would be interested in a moonlight stroll with me, since you are obviously not."

"I'm sorry I can't go with you," Stacy told him. Her bubble had abruptly burst, and hurt etched every word. "I hope you have a nice time with...with whoever accompanies you." Stacy's voice had grown softer with every syllable until the last word was little more than a whisper.

Tanner stared at her in amazement. He couldn't believe she was actually turning him down. They finished the dance in silence. Tanner was coldly angry, and Stacy had no idea what she'd done wrong. When the dance ended, it was a relief to be led off the floor.

"I can't believe you didn't go out there," Lucinda said to Roddy before Stacy returned to their side.

Roddy sighed. "I never dreamed he would go that far. The damage was done the moment he took her in his arms. It would have brought nothing but humiliation to stalk out there and demand her return."

Lucinda nodded unhappily and watched anxiously as Tanner returned Stacy to their side. She glared at Tanner upon seeing Stacy's pale features, but the young duke seemed totally unaware of anyone's presence.

Without a word, Stacy's confused face caused Roddy to suggest an early evening. Stacy looked so relieved at the suggestion that the three of them left immediately.

Stacy worked very hard over the next two days to put Tanner from her mind. She and Lucinda had talked, calmly this time, and Lucinda had told Stacy that considering all the circumstances, she had done well. Lucinda surprised her speechless by apologizing for underestimating Tanner's boldness and for taking her out and not staying with her.

"I've decided that we need to slow down a bit. It's always been more my desire than yours to attend a different ball every week, and now I think that for your sake, Stacy, we'll stay in for a time."

"I'm sorry, Aunt Lucinda."

"No, child, it is I who am sorry. You've gone along to please me and been hurt because of it...and after I told Andrew I would take such good care of you."

Lucinda did nothing this time to disguise the tears in her eyes. Stacy rose and went to put her arms around her aunt.

"I've had a wonderful time, Aunt Lucinda. Please don't think I'm disappointed or unhappy. It's too bad that I'm not more experienced in social settings or with men, but—"

"No, dear," Lucinda cut her off. "Never be sorry for your innocence. Your trusting nature is a precious gift. Someday someone very special will come along and treasure you and that gift for all of his life."

Tanner's face immediately popped into Stacy's mind, but she did her best to push it away, smile at her aunt, and give her one final hug.

❖ ❖ ❖

Three weeks later Roddy, Lucinda, and Stacy went shopping. Stacy thought Lucinda amazing as she careered her way through the day, never seeming to tire or grow too warm. At the last shop, Stacy had to beg off.

"If I'm going to have any energy left for the Royal Gardens, I'm going to have to rest."

"I quite agree. Cinda, you're on your own for this one."

Lucinda regarded her companions with a raised brow and condescending look before sweeping out of the open carriage and into the shop. Roddy chuckled at her departure and then looked up to see Stacy studying him.

"That's certainly a serious face," he said with a smile.

Stacy didn't smile. In fact she looked so hesitant that Roddy sobered.

"What is it, Stacy?"

"It's something that's none of my business."

"Concerning me?"

"Yes," Stacy answered and studied him some more. His look was so open that she felt emboldened. "Why have you and Lucinda never married?"

Roddy nodded and regarded her seriously. When he spoke, Stacy could tell he'd given the matter great thought.

"I value Lucinda's friendship above all else in the world. Were I to introduce romance between us when she did not share my feelings, I would ruin everything we have. I simply can't take that chance."

"But you must know she loves you," Stacy reasoned.

"Yes, she does love me, but she isn't *in* love with me. There is a difference, you know. I'm her best friend, just as she is mine. I can go on living with the knowledge that she will continue to be."

"She is in love with you, Roddy," Stacy told him softly.

Roddy didn't go so far as to shake his head, but his look was more than a little dubious.

"She's loved you for years. She told me herself."

Roddy stared at Stacy. The intensity in his eyes frightened her a little. She had started something here, and as much as she might regret it, she decided to see it through.

"When I first came to London, we talked of it. I asked her why she wasn't married to you, and she said it was because you'd never asked."

Stacy watched Roddy's eyes slide shut and felt as if her insides were being torn in two. She was not easily given to tears, but this was almost enough to make her sob.

Roddy's gaze turned beyond the carriage then, and Stacy left him to his thoughts. She knew Lucinda would be returning soon and wondered if she should apologize. As it was, Roddy quietly thanked her just before Lucinda emerged from the shop.

The Royal Botanic Gardens were riotous with color during midsummer. The day was a bit warm for a long stroll, but they walked leisurely along until Roddy proclaimed that he would die if they didn't stop for tea.

Stacy, feeling very much that Roddy and Lucinda needed a few moments alone, slowed her pace and let them move ahead. A lovely bloom caught her attention as the path wound its way back to the carriage, and Stacy stopped to take in its fragrance. When she looked up, Tanner stood some ten feet away.

His look was rather stern, but Stacy couldn't mask the softening of her eyes at just seeing him again. He scared her a little, and she knew he was not the man for her, but her heart turned over every time she thought of him.

"Stacy," Roddy's voice suddenly called to her from beyond the shrubs.

"I'm coming, Roddy," Stacy answered immediately before looking back at Tanner and a woman beyond him. Even at a distance and standing in profile, the woman looked lovely.

Stacy met Tanner's eyes as she spoke. "I'm glad you found someone to go on that stroll with you, Lord Richardson." Stacy dropped her eyes then and moved away. Tanner did not try to follow.

"I WILL NOT ALLOW YOU to see her." Lucinda's tone was calm, but her insides were trembling. "She doesn't want to see you."

"I would like to hear that from Stacy," Tanner challenged, much as he had been doing for the last half hour.

"There is no need," Lucinda insisted. "As I've said before, she cannot see you."

"Why?" Growing perilously close to the end of his patience, Tanner fired the single word at her.

"I'll tell you why, because I know you're not here to ask for her hand in marriage, and I will not allow you to play games with my niece's life.

"If in fact I have misread your intent, please correct me, but unless your intentions toward Stacy are honorable, you will not socialize with her."

Tanner stood silent, his anger at a boiling point just beneath the surface. After a moment, Lucinda's brows raised and her shoulders lifted in a shrug. Her voice was void of accusation when she spoke.

"Your silence has answered my question, your Grace."

Tanner continued to stand quiet. He grudgingly admired Lady Warbrook for the way she stood up to him, but he did not care to be thwarted. He wanted Anastasia Daniels, and Lucinda had made it very clear that the only way he could have her was in marriage. He'd been married once, and he was not going to fall into that trap again.

If he and Stacy were to form a relationship that was mutually beneficial to both of them, fine. They didn't need the confines of marriage to do it. Lucinda had said his intentions were not honorable, but to him they were. Tanner had never had a mistress before, but he knew when he finally made Stacy his own, he would treat her like a queen. He would be faithful to her, and she would know no humiliation at his hands. He was one of the wealthiest men in England and well able to care for her in any style she desired.

And when it was time to end their relationship, not that he believed there would be a need for many years, there would be no messy scenes. He would tell her goodbye and give her enough money to do anything she pleased for the rest of her life. There was simply no need to marry.

Lucinda watched as Tanner leaned down and picked up the riding gloves he'd dropped on the table. He turned toward the door without a word, and Lucinda did not try to speak to him. His pride had obviously been wounded, and she had no desire to rub salt in the wound. It was relief enough to see him go. He must realize now that she meant business concerning Stacy. Stacy, she reminded herself, must not know that he'd even been to call.

Across the foyer in the library Stacy chose the book she desired and moved back toward the door. She hadn't even bothered to close it, since she'd known just what she was looking for. Halfway across the carpet, however, she was so startled that she dropped the book and simply stared.

Tanner stood in the doorway, his eyes hooded and almost angry. Unlike the day before in the park, Stacy's gaze didn't soften; this time his look was too foreboding, and she was too surprised to find him in Aunt Lucinda's home.

Stacy watched as his eyes traveled over her dress. It was the red velvet she'd brought from home. Without moving from the doorway, he spoke.

"That color is dreadful on you."

Stacy shrugged apologetically and glanced down at the skirt. "Aunt Lucinda doesn't care for it either."

At the sound of her voice Tanner had to draw nearer; it was as though he had no choice. He stopped a foot away from her and, feeling mesmerized, just stared into her wide, blue eyes.

Every woman who's ever meant anything to me has been full of lies and deceit, he thought. *Can this sweetness in her be real, or does it only last as long as she gets her way?*

"I'm not the marrying kind, Stacy," Tanner told her without preamble.

He spoke the words as though they'd been discussing the matter, but as abrupt as they seemed, Stacy wasn't surprised to hear them. She nodded, her eyes regretful but understanding.

It was almost more than Tanner could take. He wanted her to show her true self, to yell at him or lash out, but instead she continued to offer him only sweet sensitivity.

Suddenly his hands grasped her upper arms in a grip that was firm but not bruising. It was as if he needed to be touching her to make his point.

"I'm *not* the marrying kind, Stacy, and your aunt is completely unreasonable."

His grasp had brought her so close that Stacy could feel his breath. She should have felt frightened, but instead her heart turned over with love for him. Her voice told him as much.

"I'm not sure what you want of me, but I must do as Lucinda asks. It's what my grandfather would wish." Stacy paused before going on, almost talking to herself. "July is already here. Just a few weeks now, and it will be time for me to go home. It will be easier then."

Defeat washed over Tanner. He hadn't really expected her to leave with him on the spot, but he had halfway hoped she would at least be open to some discussion. It never once occurred to him that she didn't even realize he wanted her for a mistress.

Tanner didn't speak again. He felt he had said it all. As his hands slowly released her, his eyes moved slowly over her face, as if to memorize every detail of her lovely features. When his inspection was complete, he brushed a soft kiss across her lips, moved to the door without looking back, and walked away.

Stacy found a chair and sat down hard. Her eyes focused unseeingly on the book she'd dropped on the floor. She sat for the next hour and stared at it, wondering how she was ever going to get over Lord Tanner Richardson.

Just four days before Stacy was to leave for Middlesbrough, she and Roddy took a long ride in the park. As they rode, Stacy would fall into moments of quiet contemplation. Roddy knew she was thinking of Tanner. He alone knew that she'd seen him in Lucinda's library. What Stacy didn't know was that Tanner had not given up that day. He'd been to see Lucinda twice more in an attempt to reason with her, explaining what a wonderful life he could offer Stacy.

Amazingly, Lucinda had not been offended. She had confided in Roddy that she'd seen a certain vulnerability in Tanner, one that touched her heart and caused her to put aside her reservations. It was as though she understood him, when in fact, she should have been insulted that the man wanted Stacy for a mistress and not a wife. Roddy knew that she struggled with how closely he resembled Aubrey, but she had also admitted that although Aubrey was a rake, Tanner had shown no such signs.

Roddy knew her heart was softening, and he was rather fascinated by her handling of the whole affair. However, he also knew Lucinda would never settle for less than a proposal of marriage.

Roddy's musings were cut off suddenly when a stray dog rushed from the bushes and snapped at the heels of Stacy's mount. Roddy called for her to watch herself, but Stacy was obviously too preoccupied.

Taken unawares, her horse pranced suddenly. Stacy lost the reins. She was groping frantically for control when the dog dashed forward again and the horse reared.

Roddy watched in horror as Stacy was thrown. She landed hard on the grassy turf and lay still even as Roddy jumped from the back of his mount and rushed to her side. He heard the pounding of hooves, the rush of feet, and the sound of someone coming to subdue the dog and catch Stacy's horse, but Roddy's eyes never left her white face.

"Stacy," he called urgently and placed a hand on her pale cheek. Roddy's heart pounded in fear when she did not respond. The same heart leaped in relief when someone's hands joined his own. He watched as they probed gently about her head and neck.

"We'll take her to Lady Brent's."

Upon hearing that stern voice, Roddy's eyes snapped up. He shouldn't have been surprised. The Duke of Cambridge managed to appear wherever Stacy went. There was no thought of arguing with the younger man; all thoughts were for Stacy's welfare. And if Tanner's concerned face was any indication—it looked carved from stone—she would receive the best of care.

The next minutes passed in a flurry of activity as Tanner ordered a gawking youth to Featherstone to warn Andrea of their arrival. Roddy remounted and captured the reins of Stacy's horse while Tanner lifted Stacy in his arms and swung abroad his own horse. Featherstone was just moments away, but it felt like forever to Roddy.

Stacy was unconscious through the transport and the summoning of the doctor and Aunt Lucinda. In fact nearly 30 minutes passed before she opened painful eyes to find Tanner bending over her, Roddy hovering in the background.

Lady Andrea was also in attendance, but Stacy did not notice her.

"What's happened?" she whispered, her eyes on Tanner's face.

"You were thrown from your horse. How do you feel?"

She felt horrible but didn't answer. Her head was pounding and it hurt to blink, but Tanner was there and for the moment the pain didn't matter. He looked tired to her. Without thought of place or circumstances Stacy reached and tenderly brushed the dark hair from his brow.

Tanner caught her hand and held it as though he were drowning. Roddy's gentle clearing of his throat reminded him they were not alone. After returning Stacy's hand to the coverlet, he stood and moved from her side. All of this was accomplished just before Lucinda swept into the room.

Tanner had little choice in the next minutes but to stand back and watch as Lucinda talked with Roddy, Andrea, and then the doctor when he arrived. Stacy lay silent during the proceedings, and when the doctor said she could be moved, Tanner held his place as Roddy saw her to Lucinda's waiting coach. Lucinda was on her way out when she stopped and turned back to the room. Andrea was by the sofa Stacy had just vacated, and Tanner was by the mantel, his look guarded.

"Thank you for seeing to Stacy," she began to Tanner, but had to stop and clear her throat. "She means more to me than I can say, and I am grateful for your assistance.

"I am concerned, however, that she was seen on your horse. The gossip concerning your visits to the house has been swiftly escalating. As relieved as I am that she is going to be fine, I fear this latest incident will destroy what is left of Stacy's reputation.

"Given a choice I would want you to repeat your actions in order to ensure her safety, but I find myself rather thankful that she is scheduled to leave for home in four days' time. She will be free from the gossiping tongues of London and hopefully put this painful time behind her."

The room was utterly silent when Lucinda left. Andrea was uncertain what she should do or say, and Tanner's face, although impassive, had drained of color during Lucinda's speech.

Andrea knew all the signs—Tanner and Stacy were in love. Tanner, however, had worked at his reputation as a confirmed bachelor, and Stacy was as guileless a girl as Andrea had ever met. It wasn't very hard to see why Lucinda was worried about the relationship.

Andrea searched for some words to take the pain from the young duke's eyes. When none came, she prayed. She was still praying when he thanked her kindly for her assistance and made his way for the door.

Tanner pushed his mount until the horse was blown and lathered. He'd sought out one of London's largest parks in an effort to ride and think. It would have been an ideal time to return to his estate in the country, but putting that many miles between him and Stacy was more than he could take right now.

If he couldn't take the miles between London and Winslow, what would he do in four days' time when Stacy went home for good? Tanner's torturous thoughts plagued him. When had Stacy Daniels gotten so deeply under his skin? And why? What was it about the girl that was causing him to consider marriage, something he vowed would never happen again?

His faithless wife came to mind then, as did his brother, William, along with all the pain he had experienced in the first months after their deaths. The betrayal and anger and then the cold bitterness that ate at him for more than a year before he determined not to give them another moment of thought. Now, sitting alone on horseback in a remote section of London, he let down the wall for a brief look back and was stunned that the anguish of their affair could still cut so deeply.

But in the midst of this agony he was amazed to see someone else's pain. He saw Stacy as she thudded to the ground from atop her horse, and then her eyes when they opened as she lay so pale on the couch at Featherstone. He'd known that her head hurt. Yet she made no word of complaint, only looked at him in tenderness before brushing the hair from his brow.

Tanner's chest rose with a deep sigh. He was ready to return home, slowly now, but with a solid purpose in his heart. He wasn't certain he could live with his decision concerning Stacy, but the thought of her leaving London was simply not to be entertained.

LUCINDA REGARDED TANNER with serious eyes as he stood across the library from her the morning after the accident. He had quietly and with surprising humbleness asked for Stacy's hand in marriage. It was what Lucinda had been hoping for. With this commitment, she now believed he would make Stacy a fine husband, but it suddenly occurred to her that she didn't know Stacy's heart.

Roddy had assured her that Stacy loved Tanner, but Lucinda had never heard this from Stacy's lips or really seen anything to confirm it. Lucinda's guilt over all her niece had been through weighed heavily upon her. The last thing she would do was force Stacy into a union she did not desire.

"I find your offer quite satisfactory, but I will not accept until I've spoken with Stacy."

"Are you worried that she won't agree?" One of Tanner's brows rose in what Lucinda could only label a sinister fashion.

"Exactly," Lucinda told him. "I realize it's not the custom to consult the woman, but Stacy is not some bubble-headed girl who cannot be trusted to know her own mind. I will speak to her and let you know."

Tanner's look was full of amusement now. "You'll be wasting your breath, Lucinda." He called her by name for the first time. "I assure you, Stacy will accept."

"Nevertheless," the older woman stated firmly, "I will find out for myself."

"On three conditions," Tanner told her. Lucinda knew she was now seeing the man, the duke, who always had his own way. "You must find out within the hour how she feels, and you must do so without telling her of my offer."

"And the third condition?"

"You will allow me to ask her for her hand in marriage."

Lucinda looked perplexed. It was happening a little too swiftly for her comfort, but she didn't know how to slow the process.

"Yesterday I watched Stacy fall from a horse and lie unconscious in the park," Tanner said when Lucinda remained silent. "I want the right as her intended to visit her and see for myself that she is well. I want this settled *today*."

Lucinda felt she had no choice. She had managed to hold him off for many weeks now and knew it was not wise to push her advantage. She would never have given into Tanner's request for a mistress, but now that he'd made a legitimate offer of marriage, Lucinda felt she needed to go along with his desires as much as she was able.

"As you wish. I will send word to you as soon as I know. And," Lucinda paused, "you may plan on joining us for dinner. Come early, and I will see to it that you have a few minutes alone with Stacy. And I do mean a *few* minutes."

Tanner nodded and replaced his hat. "Until 7:30?"

"Seven-thirty," Lucinda confirmed and stood quietly as he left.

"Another pillow, Lady Stacy?"

"No, Rayna, I'm fine. You don't need to stay. I'm going to sit here very quietly. I promise to ring if I need something."

The maid looked uncertain, but Stacy put her head back against the settee and shut her eyes until she knew she was alone. She smiled and opened her eyes when the door closed. They were all like a bunch of mother hens.

Most of Lucinda's staff were beyond their fortieth year, and they had all adopted Stacy when she moved in. She was surprised she had put on only a few pounds since coming—they were forever sneaking things into her room. They showed Stacy repeatedly how much they cared.

Up to now all the pampering had been fun, but after Stacy had been brought home yesterday, they'd all been frantic. She did have a concussion, but she was not dying as Rayna and Craig both seemed to think. It would be wonderful to walk in the garden, but knowing it would stop the hearts of half the staff, Stacy resigned herself to staying in her room.

When Lucinda knocked on the door, Stacy nearly lay back and pretended to be sleeping. But she had never been good at deception and simply waited for the entrance of the next anxious servant. To her surprise it was Lucinda.

"How are you, dear?" Lucinda asked after placing a kiss on her cheek.

"I'm fine. A little tired perhaps, but I'm doing well."

Lucinda smiled, seeing that it was true. Stacy's color was good, and she had already learned from Rayna that she'd had a good night's sleep. They talked on for a time, and Lucinda asked to see Stacy's needlework. It was in a basket by the settee, and in a moment Stacy had retrieved it to proudly display her art.

"It's beautiful, dear. I especially love the use of the blues."

Stacy smiled her thanks and gazed on as Lucinda continued to study the intricate needlepoint. When Lucinda spoke, her voice was so casual that Stacy was taken unaware.

"It was very kind of Lord Richardson to take you to Lady Brent's yesterday."

Lucinda watched surreptitiously as the color crept into Stacy's cheeks and her eyes slid shut with remembrance. Lucinda's own eyes closed for a moment as well, and when she looked at Stacy again, the younger woman's gaze was distant and soft. Lucinda would have felt stunned had she known that Stacy's mind was reliving Tanner's gentle kiss in the library.

"You're looking a bit flushed, my dear," Lucinda said softly when she could. "Maybe you should sleep for a time."

"Maybe I will." Stacy grasped at the chance to be alone with her thoughts. "Thank you for coming up to see me, Aunt Lucinda."

Lucinda's hand gently patted Stacy's cheek. Once out in the hall, Lucinda found that her hands were shaking. She scolded herself and tried to calm down before she was forced to dictate her note to Tanner.

Ten minutes later, back in her room, she was able to write it herself. It said simply that they would discuss the terms of the betrothal immediately following dinner.

Had Tanner not insisted, Lucinda would have kept Stacy in her room for yet another night. It helped to remind herself that Stacy had looked very well that afternoon.

"You look lovely," Lucinda told Stacy as she met her outside her bedroom door.

"Thank you," Stacy said simply and stared down at the cream-colored gown that hung with lace. Rayna had brushed her hair out long and straight, and beyond a simple comb at the crown of her head which pulled the hair from her face, she was unadorned.

"I really wanted you to stay one more night in your room," Lucinda said as she hooked her arm through Stacy's. "But you have a visitor."

Stacy glanced with surprise at her aunt, but didn't question; she simply walked along as Lucinda led her to the upstairs salon. Lucinda stopped outside the door and turned to face Stacy.

"Tanner Richardson is waiting for you. I'll give you a few

minutes alone before Roddy and I come to collect you both for dinner."

Stacy's eyes had grown large on this announcement, but she had no time to reply. Lucinda turned on her heel and marched back down the hall. Stacy looked at the back of her aunt and then at the doorknob for only a moment before turning it and stepping quietly inside.

Nearly the entire expanse of carpet separated them as Stacy closed the door and stood just inside. Tanner was by the window, looking incredibly handsome and larger than ever in formal black evening clothes, with a white shirt and black tie. He stared at Stacy before stepping to the fireplace and speaking.

"Come over here, Stacy."

Stacy obeyed without question, moving with natural grace to stand some two feet away. The distance was too far for Tanner's taste, and with a gentle touch he reached for her hand and drew her closer.

Tanner looked into her wide, trusting eyes and knew frustration. Without a doubt Lucinda would hold to her word of coming back in a few minutes, and there was so much he wanted to say to this woman.

"I have asked Lucinda for your hand, and she has agreed to my proposal," Tanner began, hearing the tick of the clock so near his ear on the mantel. "Now I wish to ask you, Anastasia. Will you be my wife?"

Stacy's breath left her in a rush. Her face flushed and her mouth dropped open. "You wish to marry me?"

For some reason her reaction amused Tanner, and a huge smile broke across his face. "Yes, I do, and if you don't answer me quickly I won't even have time to kiss you before we gain an audience."

Suddenly Stacy's smile matched his own. "You kissed me in the library. Do you remember? I thought I would have to be content with that for the rest of my life."

"Oh, sweetheart," Tanner said softly before pulling her into his arms. She was a perfect fit.

Stacy didn't think she would ever breathe again. Tanner's hold felt like a walk through paradise. She wanted his kiss to go on and on.

Fortunately Tanner's head was more level. He broke the kiss and stepped away from her just before the door opened to admit Roddy and Lucinda.

Stacy spent the rest of the evening floating on a cloud. She couldn't have told anyone what was served for dinner or who talked at the table. She was so happy that she didn't even mind being sent upstairs early so the others could talk business.

Her cocoon of joy lasted until right before she fell asleep; right up to the moment when she realized she wouldn't be seeing her grandfather in a few days as planned, and she would probably never live in his home in Middlesbrough again.

Nine

THE NEXT MORNING, before the wedding agreement could be drawn up and signed or the banns posted for the coming wedding, Stacy went in to see Aunt Lucinda. Lucinda was at her writing desk in her bedroom, already making a list for Madame Angelica concerning Stacy's wedding trousseau. She had been half-expecting her niece, so as soon as Stacy appeared, Lucinda put her task aside.

"Aunt Lucinda, may I speak with you?"

"Of course, my dear."

Both women made themselves comfortable in chairs by the window.

"I'm trying to write to Papa, but I just can't find the words," Stacy began. "I love Tanner, but I feel as though I've betrayed the man who has loved and taken care of me since I was a child."

Lucinda rose and went back to her writing desk. She opened the top drawer and withdrew a letter. Returning to Stacy, she opened it and began to share.

"This arrived just a week after you did, my dear, but there has never been a reason, until now, for you to see it. I shall read it to you.

> Dear Lucinda,
>
> I know that Stacy must be well ensconced in your care by now, and I wish you both a wonderful

summer. As you may or may not realize, Stacy is the type of girl who would gladly lay down her life for someone she loves. There have been times over the years when this has not been an asset; now is just such a time.

I told Stacy that no one would push her into a marriage and I meant it, but I also fear that Stacy might deny her heart if she fears hurting me or missing Morgan. I want Stacy to follow her heart. I trust you to judge the type of man who might show interest, and if you find him worthy of my precious girl, then act in wisdom.

Stacy works hard to see that those around her are happy. Above all else, Lucy, see to Stacy's happiness, for there are times when she does not look after it herself. Give her my love and to you also.

Andrew

Stacy was not a woman given to tears, and in fact none filled her eyes, but her heart was so full she could not speak.

"I will ask you what your grandfather would at this moment." Lucinda gazed at her tenderly.

"Are you happy, my dear?"

Stacy could only nod.

"Then I will write Andrew and tell him all that has transpired. I will also say that you will be writing soon to give him the wedding date and details."

Stacy's answer to this was to throw her arms around her aunt. Lucinda laughed as she embraced her, thinking she would topple a smaller woman.

"You run along now, dear; I've got things to do."

Stacy was more than ready to comply now that her mind was set to rest. Returning to her room she sat down at the table by the window, now knowing that she could write that letter. It wasn't as easy as she believed, however. Before she'd written two words, her mind began to wander. The quill was set aside and soon forgotten. Stacy never even noticed the cool breeze coming in the window and moving her hair. Her mind was wholly taken up with Tanner and what he might be doing at the moment.

Stacy might have been pleased to know that Tanner was thinking of her, except that his thoughts were turning rather pensive. His breakfast sat growing cold as he let his mind dwell on the night before.

Dinner had been a delight, and Lucinda, with a few suggestions from Roddy, had been more than reasonable concerning the marriage contract. Not that Stacy's dowry mattered to Tanner in the least. She could come to him with nothing more than the clothes on her back, and he would still marry her.

The now-familiar tightening in his chest that happened every time he thought of her was coming on again. She was so precious. Tanner's eyes closed when he remembered the way she felt in his arms and the way she had shyly returned his kiss.

Without warning, the face of his first wife, Leslie, swam before his mind's eye, her expression very soft and open as it had been when they'd first met. She too had been sweet and seemingly innocent, promising to love and honor him for all of her days.

With an abrupt gesture Tanner rose from the table, his breakfast completely forgotten. *It isn't too late to back out,* he told himself. *The papers have not been signed or the newspapers notified.*

"I fear this latest incident will destroy what is left of Stacy's reputation."

Lucinda's words suddenly sounded in Tanner's ears, and he stopped dead on his way into his study. The way Stacy's eyes had looked last night, so full of trust, caused Tanner to shake his head as if to clear it. Still, the black cloud of his past still lingered. With a decisive turn he moved for the stairs.

"Price," Tanner bellowed. The servant appeared at the top of the stairs as if by magic.

"Yes, your Grace."

"Riding clothes. And order my horse saddled." His reply was curt, but he simply had no time to be civil. He had to see Stacy, and now. There was no other help for it.

"I wish you could have seen her face when I read that letter. She was so relieved, but I worry a little that Tanner likes to have his own way and will run right over the top of her if she stands in his way."

"I don't know," Roddy spoke contemplatively. "If you could have seen his face when he bent over her on the grass . . ." He let the thought hang.

They sat silently for a moment in Lucinda's small parlor until Roddy suddenly leaned forward and kissed Lucinda lingeringly on the lips. Her eyes were quite round when he pulled away.

Roddy had always been affectionate with her and a kiss from him was not all that unusual, but in the past few weeks he'd kissed her nearly every chance he had. The kisses were a good deal more personal than they'd ever been before. And when he wasn't kissing her, he was holding her hand or placing his arm about her waist.

"You're doing quite a lot of that lately." Lucinda couldn't resist commenting about the kiss. To her surprise, Roddy looked pleased that she'd noticed. His smile was almost smug.

"Any objections?" Roddy's voice was far warmer than she was used to hearing it.

"No," Lucinda said, and suddenly felt herself blushing like a girl.

"Did I cause that flush?" Roddy's grin nearly left his face.

Lucinda could only stare at him. "What has come over you, Roddy?"

She was more confused than ever when he only kissed her again and sat back in contentment. She watched him reach for the newspaper he'd been enjoying and settle down to read. He obviously wasn't going to answer her.

Lucinda might have run from the room if he had. Roddy Caruthers, who had been in love with Lucinda Warbrook for years, was now amid his plan of attack to win the lovely lady's hand.

It wasn't that he doubted Stacy's words about Lucinda's loving him; it was just that he wanted to take no chances of losing her. He was no longer afraid of rejection, but of not being taken seriously. They had been friends for so long that if he suddenly declared himself, she might not believe him sincere. Such an action would also cause her to question the change in him after so many years. He knew he would be honest with her, and in so doing might lead her to believe that Stacy had somehow betrayed her trust.

So with his usual level head, Roddy decided to bide his time. He'd waited many years; a few more months wouldn't matter. He'd be alongside Lucinda as she saw Stacy safely married; then it would be his turn.

He could still feel Lucinda's eyes on him at the moment, and indeed, was about to take pity on her and explain, but Craig entered quietly to tell Lucinda that Lord Richardson had arrived.

Lucinda's brows rose. She thought they would not see him until the next day when the papers announced the engagement, but perhaps he had come about something other than his engagement. Lucinda nearly laughed at her own thoughts when she saw Tanner's face. There was no doubt that he was here to see Stacy.

"Hello, Tanner," Lucinda greeted him as Roddy stood and the two shook hands. "Please, sit down."

"Thank you, Lucinda," Tanner responded but remained standing, "but I'd really like to see Stacy." Tanner had to bite back the word "alone."

He stood erect and waited for Lucinda's response. At the moment he was tense enough to force his way into Stacy's room, and Lucinda was obviously aware of this fact. Her voice was very gentle when she answered him.

"She's in the garden, Tanner. When you're done, maybe you'd both like to come in and join us in the large salon for tea?"

Tanner accepted with a nod of his head and moved toward the door. Lucinda and Roddy exchanged a glance after he left, but neither of them spoke.

Stacy pushed herself from the grassy turf and stood looking down at her progress. Aunt Lucinda had a gardener, but his skills among the English daisies were lacking. They were a small flower and took careful weeding. Stacy could understand why he didn't care to bother, but she loved the work.

She dusted her dirty hands together and had just wiped the moisture from her upper lip when she looked up to see Tanner approaching. With a quick glance at her filthy hands, she put them behind her back.

"Hello." Tanner's bass voice ran over Stacy's nerves as he stopped some five feet away and greeted her, his eyes serious.

"Hello." Stacy's own voice was breathless. She was thrilled to see him but knew she must look a mess.

Tanner's eyes moved over her, taking in the dirt smears on the front of her dress, her hair falling from its chignon, the hands held carefully behind her back, and finally the smear of mud above her upper lip.

"What are you hiding behind you?" he asked as he moved to a nearby bench and made himself comfortable. Stacy watched his legs, clad in knee-high black boots and gray riding trousers, stretch out seemingly for miles before she looked back to his face. His brows were raised in expectation, and Stacy remembered that he'd asked her a question.

"Just my hands," she answered honestly.

Tanner looked skeptical. "You're sure?"

"Yes," Stacy said, beginning to feel rather silly. With her hands still out of sight, she moved to the opposite bench, carefully tucking her hands under the folds of her skirt as she sat down.

As surreptitiously as she made the move, Tanner didn't miss a thing. He'd told himself if he could only see her, he would feel better, and in fact he was growing more relaxed with every passing second. She was the most restful woman he had ever known.

"How are you, Tanner?" Stacy's sweet voice broke into his musings.

"I'm doing fine."

"Are you really?" Stacy's voice seemed to lift with pleasure.

"Yes. Why do you ask?"

Color leapt into her cheeks as she admitted softly, "I thought you might have come to tell me you changed your mind."

Tanner found it very disconcerting to be read so easily. It caused him to realize just how little he really knew this woman. She was soft-spoken, graceful, and very trusting, but beyond those qualities, Tanner was at a loss.

It became suddenly clear to him that he was going to marry this woman. He knew that more doubts would surface as the days went on, but he *was* going to marry Stacy Daniels.

"I haven't changed my mind," Tanner told her seriously, and Stacy had to look away from the intensity in his eyes. She cast about for something to say and only looked at him when she was ready to speak.

"Did you see Lucinda and Roddy? They're inside." Stacy knew she sounded inane, but he was still watching her so intently that she began to feel very unsettled.

"Yes." Tanner's scrutiny eased some. "They're expecting us later for tea."

Stacy could only nod, glad she was alone with him but not certain what to say.

"When is your birthday, Stacy?" Tanner asked suddenly.

"Not until October."

"And you'll be—?"

"Twenty-two," Stacy supplied nervously. "That's rather old, isn't it?"

"Not in the least," Tanner told her emphatically, feeling quite glad that she wasn't a starry-eyed teen.

"When is your birthday?"

"Next May. I'll be 29." Tanner hesitated before a warm sparkle lit his eyes. "Rather old, isn't it?"

Stacy laughed, and Tanner found he liked the sound. Spotting a newspaper by her side then, he noticed at the same time that she was still hiding her hands.

"What have you been reading?" Tanner asked, gesturing toward the paper.

"*The London Times.* I just finished an article about Nanking."

"Nanking?" Tanner questioned her. He had read the same paper and not seen the feature.

"Well, yes," Stacy said hesitantly, wondering if he'd be bored if she shared. But he had that expectant, almost impatient look she was coming to recognize. She hurried to explain.

"Nanking, China, is a city that sits on the Yangtze River. The article says that an army of 500,000, composed entirely of *women*—" Stacy was now warming to her subject—"and led by *female* officers, was formed in Nanking during a rebellion."

Stacy stopped when she realized her hands had come out of hiding to gesture as she spoke. She quickly hid them and shrugged apologetically. "I just found it rather interesting."

Tanner did not reply but sat staring at her as if seeing her for the first time. Stacy felt like a fool. She stood awkwardly.

"If Aunt Lucinda is expecting us for tea, I'd best go freshen up."

With surprising agility for a man his size, Tanner stood, moving silently to block her path. He reached his long arms around her and gently brought forth the hands she'd hidden once again to hold them within his own.

He examined the dirt under her nails and on her palms and then looked to find her standing still with mortification. She was staring no higher than his shirtfront.

"You were weeding?"

Stacy nodded, utterly humiliated. She was engaged to a duke, and here she was digging in the dirt like a child at play. What must Tanner think?

"You did a nice job," Tanner told her as though she'd asked the question out loud. Still, she wouldn't look at him.

"Look at me, Anastasia," he commanded, and Stacy felt helpless to resist. Tanner spoke when her eyes met his.

"There is nothing to be embarrassed about, sweetheart. If you enjoy gardens, then you're going to love Winslow."

"Winslow?"

"My home in the country."

Stacy never thought of his living anywhere but London. She was still taking this in when she questioned him about the dirt.

"And you really don't mind my working in the garden?"

"Not in the least."

Stacy's sigh was of such relief that Tanner smiled.

"I even like you with dirt on your upper lip."

This time Stacy didn't sigh with relief. Her eyes widened in horror. Tanner only laughed as he gazed into those huge, blue orbs.

Ten

WHEN THE LETTER ARRIVED from Stacy's grandfather, it was nearly enough to put her in tears. He would not be at her wedding. Andrew explained very gently that he couldn't have been happier for her, but his eyesight was so unpredictable now that he feared embarrassing her by falling in the aisle or some equally foolish act.

If Stacy could have talked with him and heard this in person, she might have felt better, but reading of his decision made her feel helpless with grief. She debated going home to visit until the wedding day, but Lucinda talked her out of it, explaining that with fittings for her trousseau and dozens of other tasks, she was needed in London.

To top it off, a letter from Elena came the same day. She was expecting again, and Noel did not want her making the long trip in such warm weather. The double blow was devastating to Stacy.

She sat in the window seat of the upstairs salon, completely awash with heartache. Tanner had come to the door, not entering, but simply enjoying the way the sunlight played on her golden hair. Stacy didn't notice his presence.

When she finally heard his footsteps on the carpet, she turned. Hurting over the news from home, it was the first time she didn't feel delighted at seeing him. This was especially surprising since Tanner had just been away for a few days. He noticed the change in her immediately and tensed over what she might say. It didn't occur to him until he saw the letters in her lap that her reaction might not have anything to do with him.

With Stacy curled on the window seat there wasn't much room, but Tanner managed to sit down beside her. With a glance at the papers in her lap, he spoke.

"Bad news?"

"Yes," Stacy told him in a voice he'd never heard before—thick, almost husky. Tanner carefully studied her face, noticing not for the first time that Stacy was not prone to tears.

"My grandfather can't make the wedding."

"Not enough notice?"

"No, that's not it. His eyesight is failing so badly and—" Stacy cut off, swallowing hard. "Would you like to read the letter?"

Tanner took it from her outstretched fingers and read swiftly and silently. His look was very compassionate when he finished, but Stacy's gaze was directed out the window, her lovely profile etched in misery.

Tanner noticed the other note in her hand.

"Is there more?" he asked as he returned Andrew's letter.

"Yes. Elena can't come either. She's married to my grandfather's cousin, Noel, and although Noel is old enough to be my father, Elena is my age and we're very close."

"Yes, I remember your telling me."

Stacy looked into his wonderful dark brown eyes for just a moment before turning to the window once again. Tanner gave her the silence, his mind thoughtful.

"I'm sorry, Tanner," Stacy spoke abruptly, and Tanner watched her make almost a physical effort to cheer up. "You've come to visit me, and all I do is sit here and mope. How was your trip?" She smiled at him, but it didn't quite reach her eyes.

Tanner could have kissed her on the spot. Lucinda had mentioned to him one day that Stacy usually put the happiness of others ahead of herself, but this was the first time he'd actually witnessed it.

"Would you like to go for a walk or a ride?" Stacy asked when Tanner stayed quiet. She felt a headache coming on and wondered if the change of scene might do her good.

"I think a ride sounds delightful, but you should write your letter first."

"My letter?" Stacy asked, wondering what she had missed.

"Why to your grandfather, of course, telling him to expect us a few days after the wedding. We're going to honeymoon in the Cleveland Hills and spend some time in Middlesbrough."

"You told me you wanted to honeymoon in the south of France."

"France will still be there in a year. We'll go for our first anniversary."

Stacy's hands went to her mouth. Her eyes searched Tanner's face for signs of teasing but found only caring.

"Oh, Tanner," was all Stacy could say.

He felt her tremble as she laid her cheek against his shoulder. Never had he known someone for whom it was so satisfying to give of himself. She never took anything for granted or lightly. It had taken a gem the size of a bird's egg to gain that kind of expression from Leslie.

Tanner's heart clenched. Why did Leslie always come to mind? She and Stacy were not even remotely the same, and yet since becoming engaged, she haunted his times of peace with Stacy. He remembered the one who lied and cheated on him at times when he should have been enjoying the precious woman at his side.

"Thank you, Tanner." Stacy lifted her head so she could see his face. "I love you," she whispered, her heart so full she could hardly breathe.

"You're welcome," he spoke gently, his eyes holding her own. Stacy thought he might kiss her, but a moment later they were joined by Craig, who was there to tell Stacy that Edmond Black had come to call.

Tanner's uncle was as different from his nephew as any man could be. Tanner was very tall; Edmond very short. Tanner's hair was dark with just a touch of gray at the temples. Edmond's hair was the color of new straw, and even though he was years older than his nephew, there didn't seem to be a gray hair in sight. Tanner's frame was very muscular, from his broad shoulders to the heavy muscles in his legs. Edmond had a round look about him that could only be described as dough-like.

And this was not where the differences ended. Tanner was quiet, sometimes broodingly so. His uncle seemed to talk nonstop and loudly. He wasn't always very discreet about his subjects either, and several times Stacy noticed a look of near anger cross her intended's face as his uncle carried on raucously.

Stacy didn't really find him offensive, just boring. In fact, she had only been half-listening to him for the past hour, allowing her thoughts to wander to her honeymoon with Tanner. One sentence from Edmond's mouth, however, brought Stacy quickly back to earth.

"Been telling him for years that he needed another wife. Some say, 'The third time's a charm,' but I believe in number two myself." Edmond, who had never been married, carried on, completely oblivious to Tanner's black look or Stacy's shocked expression.

Lucinda, who had been silent through this exchange and not caring one wit about her breach of manners, rang for tea in the midst of Edmond's diatribe.

"Oh, tea," the older man stumbled. "Is it that late already? Sorry, Lucinda, must be off. Standing engagement, you know.

So nice to meet you, my dear," he offered to Stacy, never noticing how pale her face had become. "Are you coming, Tanner?"

"I'll be along." Tanner rose and watched as Edmond bid his hostess goodbye and hurried out the door to his usual Friday afternoon poker game.

Stacy still hadn't looked at him, and the paleness of her face only reminded him of Edmond's loose tongue, angering him all the more. Thinking to put the subject to rest for all time, he asked her to walk him to the door. Stacy complied.

"Edmond talks too much," Tanner's voice was tight when they stopped and were alone in the entryway.

"But you were married?"

"Yes, but we will not speak of it." Tanner's voice was livid now, and Stacy's stomach clenched. "She's dead and has nothing to do with us. Do you understand me, Anastasia?"

Stacy nodded. She realized that his anger was not directed at her, but still it terrified her. She'd rather cut off her own hand than disobey him.

"I'll come by and see you tomorrow. Maybe we'll go for the ride we missed today."

Again Stacy only nodded. Tanner had nothing more to say to her and turned toward the door without touching her. He usually ignored his uncle's indiscretion, but this time he was going to find him, and when he was through, Edmond Black was going to think twice before talking about his nephew's past again.

An hour later Tanner returned to his town house, feeling satisfied over his confrontation with Edmond.

They had not actually come to blows, but Tanner believed he'd made himself more than clear concerning Edmond's propensity to talk. He had no doubts that the older man would continue to gossip at will, but Tanner also believed that neither his, Stacy's, nor Leslie's names would be mentioned.

Back in the parlor, Lucinda waited for Stacy to return. When Stacy did not make an appearance, Lucinda sought her out in the foyer. She found her standing very still, staring at the far wall.

"Come back in for your tea," Lucinda spoke as she placed a gentle arm around the younger woman's waist.

Stacy obeyed mindlessly, sitting down and doing nothing with the cup Lucinda placed in her hands. Not until Lucinda sat beside her and touched her hand did she seem able to think.

"I had no idea."

"Of course you didn't, my dear, and I wasn't certain if I should tell you."

Stacy nodded with understanding. It really had been Tanner's place to tell her, but he didn't want the subject discussed.

Lucinda watched Stacy, her heart in pain. Aubrey had held many secrets while they'd been married, and Lucinda wanted desperately for Stacy's marriage to be different. If she didn't believe with all of her heart that Tanner really cared, she would have called the marriage off right then. There was so much Stacy didn't know, but again Lucinda was uncertain how much to share. She decided to be brief.

"Stacy," she began. "Tanner did not have a happy childhood, nor did he have a happy first marriage. In fact they were so painful that Tanner has had difficulty putting those times behind him. He's going to react harshly at times because of those memories. There will be areas that he's going to feel are better left alone. It's not very fair to you, but right now, that's the way it is. Maybe in time Tanner will feel he can share. If you have any doubts about the marriage, Stacy, you can tell me."

"No, Aunt Lucinda, no doubts," Stacy told her without hesitation. In truth, a huge weight had been lifted from Stacy's shoulders. Tanner barely knew her. In time, after they were married and had a chance to really know one another, Tanner would open his heart.

Stacy's mind went to the times, including today, that she had told Tanner she loved him. He always smiled tenderly or kissed her in response, but he never said those words to her.

Stacy knew he felt them; she knew it with all her heart. Hearing them had been important to her until now, but suddenly words didn't matter anymore. Just as Tanner would someday share his past with Stacy, he would also come to tell her about the love he carried in his heart.

Eleven

TWO DAYS BEFORE THE WEDDING, Stacy experienced a severe attack of nerves. The thought of becoming Tanner's wife, the Duchess of Cambridge, was suddenly overwhelming. Fortunately Roddy, a gentle presence in Stacy's tempestuous world, was on hand when the panic hit.

"I'm really just a country girl, Roddy. I don't know if Tanner realizes that. I've never been to court. I never even had a desire to go to court. I really am just a country girl," she repeated herself. "Have I ever told you that I love to go fishing?"

Roddy smiled at her lack of artifice. "You're going to be the loveliest bride of the year," he told her.

"But then I'll be married." Stacy stated the obvious, and Roddy had to hold his laughter at her look. "What if I'm not a good wife? What if Tanner needs me to organize a dinner party or a weekend with friends? I've never done anything on a large scale. I can't imagine what Tanner would say if he knew. I just can't imagine."

"Can't imagine what?" Tanner's voice asked from the edge of the room. Stacy turned to him, her color high, her voice sounding like that of a lost little girl.

"Middlesbrough is not London, Tanner," she told him.

"All right," Tanner answered carefully as he moved toward her.

"My grandfather is not a duke."

"I believe I knew that." Tanner's voice was extremely gentle. He'd come over because he had to see her, had to be near her calm and gentle presence. Finding her like this, eyes fever-bright with anxiety, caused him an even greater sense of satisfaction because he knew he was the one who could put her mind at rest.

"Sit down, Anastasia," he told her.

Stacy, not having heard him, shook her head in despair. "You don't understand."

"Yes, sweetheart, I do. Sit down, and I'll tell you."

Stacy sat then and stared in misery at Roddy and then at Tanner. "I don't know how to be a duchess."

"Sweetheart," he called her again and sat beside her.

"Tanner—"

"Shhhh. I am not marrying you so that you can entertain my guests or be a lovely feather in my cap, although I certainly appreciate your beauty. I'm also not marrying you to compete with some other duke or to be on the front page of the social papers." Thinking this settled it all, Tanner fell silent.

"Then why are you marrying me?" Stacy couldn't resist the question.

"Because I want you for my wife," he told her simply.

"All right," Stacy replied compliantly, wanting to please him. However, she didn't really feel much better. It would have been wonderful to hear that Tanner was marrying her because he loved her. Stacy pushed the thought away. She usually wasn't so emotional, but the largeness of what she was about to do—commit herself for life to Tanner—was beginning to weigh upon her.

Tanner, watching her so quietly, wondered what was troubling her. He only hoped Stacy would be able to calm down and enjoy the wedding and festivities. He wasn't entirely sure if she was aware of what the crowd would be like, but now was certainly not the time to tell her.

Roddy did a quick change of subject in the next moment, and Tanner was able to watch Stacy collect her wayward thoughts. By the time Lucinda joined them she seemed to be herself. In fact Stacy was calmer than Tanner by the time he took his leave. He knew that once he left, he wouldn't see her again until she walked down the aisle.

The streets of London were thronged with well-wishers for the wedding of the Duke of Cambridge. That he was marrying a virtual unknown made it all the more romantic, and the wedding coaches could barely move amid the good wishes of the gentry and common folk alike.

"How does it look?" Lucinda asked Roddy as he peeked out the window.

"Like a riot, but we'll get there." Roddy settled back and smiled at the wide-eyed Stacy, who did not return his grin.

No one spoke for a time and the young bride-to-be was relieved. How *unsheltered* her world had become in the last weeks. She would never have dreamed that a crowd of this size would gather for the wedding of a duke. She could understand if this was for the queen or a princess, but not a duke and his nearly common bride. It was inconceivable.

"Stacy, are you all right?"

"Yes," she answered her aunt immediately, but her voice was wooden.

"You don't sound all right."

The comment made Stacy sigh. "I'm just a little overwhelmed by all of this."

For once Lucinda did not lose patience with her. She smiled tenderly and spoke in a soothing voice.

"While the wedding and reception are going on, you'll be convinced that it's going to last forever, but before you know it, you and Tanner will be married and on your way."

Stacy actually managed a smile at the thought. The remainder of the ride was made in silence and not until they arrived at the church did Stacy see what her aunt's words meant.

It seemed that before she had a moment to think she was dressed in her wedding finery and standing with Tanner before the bishop. Stacy had to quell laughter over the way the poor man had to tip his head to see their faces; they literally towered over him. At one point, she risked a glance at Tanner, who had also turned his head to look down at her. Stacy watched as one lid dropped in a flirtatious wink. From that moment on the service and reception were a blur.

The coach lurched into motion and Stacy leaned back against the seat with a sigh. Her feet ached dreadfully, but she had done it—she'd married the man she loved. A glance to the side of her found Tanner leaning against his corner of the seat, just watching her. Stacy smiled with childish delight at him, and he grinned in return and reached for her hand.

She was about to speak, wanting to tell him she'd never experienced so many emotions in her life as she danced for hours and met what appeared to be half of London, but her stomach growled quite loudly. She turned away from Tanner, thankful that the dim interior of the coach hid her flaming face. In the semidarkness she heard her new husband chuckle.

"We'll eat when we get to the house," he told her.

"Winslow?" Stacy asked, curiosity overwhelming her embarrassment.

"No, Winslow is too far. Don't forget we have a train to catch tomorrow."

"I haven't forgotten," Stacy told him and looked with love into his eyes. She couldn't imagine a more caring act than Tanner's willingness to change their honeymoon plans. Just thinking of it made her want to throw her arms around him, but she didn't think the time was right for that.

Without warning, Stacy's thoughts moved to motherhood. She had never told Tanner that she desperately wanted to be a mother, but it was true. She loved Elena's girls and ached for children of her own. She wasn't good at many things, but Stacy somehow knew that she would be a fine mother.

She was contemplating the wonderful idea of presenting Tanner with a son in nine months' time when the carriage abruptly halted. The door opened immediately, and Tanner swung down and turned to give Stacy a hand. She smiled her thanks.

"I thought I'd lost you for a moment," he spoke as they moved up the steps to the front door.

"I was just thinking."

"Want to share?" Tanner asked and then chuckled. They had stepped inside the door of his London home, and he had lost her again. Most men with homes as large as Tanner's country home cared only to have a small town house in London, but Tanner was not most men. Although not as large as Winslow, his London residence was substantial. He watched Stacy's head move carefully as she saw this home for the first time. Lucinda had forbidden her from visiting while it was still a bachelor's domicile.

Tanner loved it when Stacy was awed, as she was now. He also loved it when she tried not to show it. He admired her self-control as the staff gathered. The introductions were performed by Campbell, who was head of housekeeping, and before Stacy knew it she was being shown to her room.

It was a relief to find Rayna there. Lucinda had sent her to assist Stacy for her entire honeymoon. The faithful maid had laid out one of the beautiful dresses from Stacy's trousseau and, after buttoning her into it, began to brush her hair. Tanner loved it long down her back, so after Rayna pulled it back from the sides, Stacy asked her to let it hang.

Just 20 minutes later, a very hungry Stacy entered the private dining room at the back of the house. There had been a lavish feast at the wedding, but no time to eat, what with well-wishers and every man in the room wanting to dance with the bride. Stacy frowned when she remembered that she had only danced with Tanner twice.

"That's quite a fierce look. You must be starved," Tanner commented, having arrived just ahead of her.

Stacy's face relaxed into a smile as she crossed the small room to stand before him. She loved the fact that she had to look up to see him. He was the most handsome man she had ever seen and as hungry as she was, she somehow wished they were going to be alone for the remainder of the evening.

This was an impossibility as Stacy soon learned. The thought had barely formed when the food arrived. The duke and duchess took their seats and were served a sumptuous feast of roast goose by the staff.

Tanner was well satisfied watching his wife eat. She didn't pick at her food, but ate what she was hungry for and until she had a sufficiency. Their talk over the table was equally satisfying as Stacy questioned him about the many different people she'd met at the wedding. Tanner was pleasantly surprised to learn that she knew the Duchess of Briscoe.

"Sunny Hawkesbury?"

"Yes. Aunt Lucinda and I had tea with Lady Andrea just weeks after I'd arrived. Sunny came as we were leaving. She knows Elena."

Tanner nodded. "Did you like her—Sunny, that is?"

"Very much."

"Then you'll be pleased to know she and her husband are our neighbors. They live at Bracken, less than an hour's ride from Winslow. I wouldn't be too surprised to arrive home and find an invitation to dinner or tea from them."

Stacy had never thought about their being invited as husband and wife to dine, but now that Tanner mentioned it, she found she liked the idea immensely. She decided she would have to learn who their neighbors were and have them in as well.

"Are you finished?"

Stacy came out of her musings to find Tanner watching her.

"Yes," Stacy told him, and sat still as he pushed his chair back and approached. He took her hand as she stood, and with a gentle squeeze said, "I'll see you upstairs."

Stacy smiled into his eyes before she moved away from the table and toward the door.

Twelve

RODDY TENDERLY LINKED HIS FINGERS with Lucinda's as he sat down beside her in the open carriage. It was just two days after the wedding, and Roddy had asked the woman he loved to go for a drive. He refused to say where they were headed, but Lucinda, feeling young and lighthearted with the wedding over, readily agreed.

The streets of London were rather quiet for midmorning, but Lucinda and Roddy barely noticed. They talked of the little things that only good friends share, and each time Lucinda tried to learn their destination, Roddy only smiled with mischievous delight. Twenty minutes after they had left Lucinda's, the carriage pulled onto a quiet street in a lovely part of the city and stopped before a grand mansion.

"Why, Roddy," Lucinda spoke with surprise. "This is the old Wood mansion."

"Come along, my dear" was his only reply as he stepped from the carriage and held out his hand for her. He led her to the front door. Lucinda paused in indecision when Roddy opened it without knocking and stepped inside.

"Come along," he turned back to say to her. "It's all right."

Lucinda followed him uncertainly and gaped at the interior. Not only was no one there to greet them, but Lucinda could not see a stick of furniture in any direction.

"Well, what do you think?" Roddy wished to know.

"Of what?" Lucinda asked, feeling more confused than ever.

"This home."

Lucinda looked around. "Roddy, it's beautiful, but I'm still not sure what—"

"Have I ever told you that I love you, Lucinda? I mean, really told you how I felt? I'm not sure that I have."

Lucinda was so dumbfounded by his words that she could only stare at him while he paced around and spoke.

"It's taken me forever to gain the courage to ask you about us, and I'm still nervous. It helped to buy this place, but I'm still uncertain."

"Uncertain over what?" Lucinda asked, wondering if she had heard him correctly about the purchase of the mansion.

"Uncertain if you'll take me seriously when I ask you . . . to be my wife. I'm sure you've noticed a change in me. That was to help you see where my intentions were headed. Then I found this house and thought it would be the clincher.

"Now, I still have time to back out of the deal, but if you like it, it will be ours after we're married."

Roddy stopped then. Lucinda's eyes were swimming with tears.

"I've loved you for so long, Roddy," she whispered.

"As I have you." His voice was just as soft. "Now, what's it to be, Cinda. You have two questions to answer—yes or no to my proposal, sloppy as it was, and yes or no to the house?"

Roddy paused then and took a deep breath. "Please let the first one be yes, Cinda."

"Oh, Roddy. I don't care where we live."

Roddy's chest heaved with relief for just an instant, and then he was there, standing before her, his arms reaching to hold her close. Lucinda's eyes closed when she felt his arms, and then his lips pressed against her cheek before they met her own. Lucinda's heart pounded. She was going to marry her best friend; she was going to be Roddy's wife.

Stacy's second train ride was vastly different from her first. Then she'd ridden in crowded conditions with the Binks and ate the food Hettie had sent with her. Now she was experiencing a whole new world with her husband. They ate in a private car, had a private sleeping compartment, and not once did she grow cold or have to clean up after herself. It was her first taste of life as a duchess, and although Stacy tried to take it in stride, she knew that she often looked like a child at a circus.

Tanner seemed greatly amused by her response, but also touched. He was as tender a husband as Stacy could have dreamed of, and it seemed that she loved him a little more with each passing hour. By the time they arrived at the train station in Middlesbrough, Stacy was floating on a cloud of adoration.

Price hired a coach as soon as they disembarked. Within minutes they were on their way to Morgan.

"Tanner," Stacy spoke when the coach was underway. "My grandfather is not a wealthy man."

Tanner looked at his wife's face and felt the familiar squeezing sensation around his heart. She was infinitely precious to him. He knew very well that Andrew Daniels was without substantial means and had already spoken with Price on the matter. All concerned were to see to it that Stacy was not made uncomfortable in any way.

"Tanner, did you hear me?" Stacy spoke again when he remained silent for so long.

"Yes. Does it bother you that your grandfather isn't a wealthy man?"

"It doesn't bother me; I grew up that way. I just don't want you to be, well, inconvenienced."

"Will we have a bed?"

"Of course." Stacy blinked at him in surprise.

"And food to eat?"

"Yes."

"Then I shall be quite comfortable."

Stacy nodded, tucked her arm within Tanner's, and laid her head on his shoulder with a sigh of contentment—a contentment that wavered as soon as Stacy and Tanner were alone in her bedroom. She watched him take in their modest surroundings, finishing with the small bed.

"I'm sorry, Tanner. I wish the bed were bigger."

"Oh, I don't know," Tanner said calmly. "It means I'll need to snuggle very close to my wife tonight."

"You mean you really don't mind?"

"Will you mind my snuggling close?" Tanner asked with a raised brow.

Stacy laughed. She darted around a chair and pointed at him.

"That was not a challenge."

"Challenge or not, this should be an interesting game," Tanner countered as he began to stalk her. Just as Tanner was about to catch Stacy, a knock sounded on the door.

Tanner looked rather perturbed over the disturbance, but Stacy claimed victory as she ran to answer it.

"Your grandfather is awake now and would like to see you," Peters told her as soon as she opened the door.

Stacy's heart swelled with pleasure. She had felt crushed an hour ago when they'd arrived and been told that her grandfather was sleeping. She had begged them not to disturb him, but her desire to see him now was so intense that she ached inside. Unfortunately, Tanner wanted her attention right now also. Hesitantly she answered, unaware of Tanner's approach from behind her.

"Peters, please tell my grandfather that I'll be down in a short while."

"Make that a few moments," Tanner cut in. Stacy swung around in surprise. "Lady Stacy and I will be down in a few minutes."

Peters nodded, and Tanner shut the door on his departure.

"Are you certain, Tanner?" Stacy immediately began. "I can tell Peters that—"

Tanner silenced her with a kiss.

"We'll go downstairs and see your grandfather. I'm looking forward to meeting him."

Stacy sighed, and her hand came up to stroke his cheek. "Thank you, Tanner."

Tanner sighed also, but for another reason. He was not used to putting his wants aside for others, but the look on Stacy's face when she'd found her grandfather asleep caused him to feel unusual compassion.

Tanner kissed Stacy again before taking her hand and holding it all the way downstairs, releasing her only when Stacy saw her grandfather and moved to hug him.

"Oh, Papa," was all Stacy could say as he held her. She always thought him a big man, and he was tall, but after Tanner's solid strength he seemed very thin, almost gaunt. Not that this mattered to Stacy. She was so content to be with her grandfather for the first time in months that for the moment nothing else really mattered.

"Good morning, your Grace," Peters greeted Tanner the next morning.

"Good morning. Have you seen my wife?" Tanner had wakened to an empty bed and no sign of Stacy or Rayna. Price had no information as he dressed, so as soon as he was decent, he'd made his way downstairs.

"Yes, my lord," Peters answered. "Lady Stacy and her grandfather have gone fishing. Would you like your breakfast now, my lord, or directions to the pond?"

Tanner, an expert at hiding his feelings, was struggling for the first time in years to keep his mouth closed. The man said his wife had gone fishing. *Fishing.* His statuesque, lovely bride was sitting on the banks of a pond, fishing. The idea was inconceivable.

These riotous thoughts invaded Tanner's mind for only seconds before he noticed Peters' patient stance, reminding him that he'd been offered breakfast. He was hungry, but his curiosity over his wife's fishing won the battle.

"I'll take those directions to the pond," Tanner said softly and listened intently as Peters spoke. Feeling like a vagabond, Tanner reached for several biscuits, eating as he walked toward the pond. He believed that his wife really was fishing, but the novelty of the idea forced a need in him to see for himself.

"Now that's five to my one," Stacy said with a sigh as Andrew brought in another fish. "I must have lost my touch."

"Indeed. It's the life of the idle rich that you now lead."

Stacy laughed in delight at the image his words portrayed, but then she grew very serious.

"It does take a little getting used to."

"I imagine it does. It must also make it hard to come here with all of our worn surroundings."

"Now that's where you're wrong," Stacy told him sweetly. "Morgan will always be in my heart, old furniture and all."

"I'm thinking of leaving it to Noel and Elena."

"I think that's very wise, but I hope you're not in any big hurry to leave us." Stacy's voice had been light, but Andrew did not reply.

"Is there something you're not telling me?" Stacy asked now, her voice fearful.

"It's nothing you don't already know. I just don't know what I'll have to live for if I lose my eyes completely."

"Oh, Papa," Stacy's voice was soft with pain. "I won't tell you I understand because I'm sure I don't, but please know how much I need you. If you can't keep going for yourself, then keep going for me. I can't stand the thought of your being gone."

Andrew took his gaze from the pond and stared intently at Stacy's tear-filled eyes. He was surprised to see those tears; he could hardly remember her ever crying. In fact the tears did not spill but sat pooled in her great blue eyes. Only one thought came to the old man. Was there a sweeter woman in all of England? Andrew was sure there was not. After a moment he reached and patted the hand she'd lain on his arm.

"Worry not, my dear. I shall keep on, if for no one else, then for you."

Stacy hugged his arm and brushed a quick hand across her eyes. They fished in silence until Stacy felt a mighty tug on her line. She stood with a shout, as did Andrew to watch as she worked the line and brought in the biggest catch of the day.

This was the scene upon which Tanner walked. He stood transfixed as he watched his wife laugh and unhook a good-sized trout from her line. Before he was noticed, he had time to take in the whole scene.

Andrew was bundled from head to foot, but Stacy was wearing only a dress, a dress that had been patched many times over and was too tight across her bosom. He wondered how many years she'd had it. Her hair was also coming down around her face, and there was a smear of mud under one eye.

"Oh, Tanner," Stacy suddenly spoke, and Andrew turned. "I didn't hear you come up."

Tanner hated the uncertainty he heard in her voice. His own voice was meant to soothe as he smiled and came forward.

"So when do we eat this catch, for breakfast or lunch?"

"Well..." Stacy began, still looking uncomfortable with a fish in her hand and a look of stark vulnerability on her face.

"We'll eat them for lunch," Andrew interjected, not noticing Stacy's hesitancy, or choosing to ignore it. "Why don't you run ahead to the kitchen, Stacy, and see that Mercy gets these."

"Yes, Papa," Stacy answered and moved to obey him, but Tanner caught her hand when she would have passed by him in silent embarrassment. He stood staring into her eyes. Stacy glanced over to see that her grandfather had begun to fish again, his back to them, so she spoke softly for Tanner's ears alone.

"You must be wondering what kind of woman you married."

"As a matter of fact I am."

Stacy looked crushed.

"I'm probably going to need the next 50 years to decide which woman I like better—the woman who has a wardrobe full of silks and satins and usually smells of flowers, or the adorable urchin before me, whose cotton dress looks like a rag and who smells of fish."

"You're really not angry or ashamed of me?"

"I'm furious and my reputation is shot." Tanner's tone was dry.

Stacy chuckled low in her throat and went on her way. Tanner sent her off with a smack to her backside and then joined the older man on the banks. Stacy's pole was nearby, but Tanner did not reach for it. Fishing held no interest for him.

"You don't fish?" It was the first time Andrew had talked with Tanner alone. Tanner genuinely liked his wife's grandfather and answered easily.

"No, sir, I don't."

"How about hunting?"

"Yes, I hunt. Do you?"

"Not with my eyes growing so unpredictable. My younger cousin, Noel, hunts. If you've a mind to be here awhile, you could go with him. He'd know all the best areas."

They were silent as Andrew pulled in another fish. Tanner watched him for a time, but then his gaze strayed across the pond to the beautiful area beyond. While Tanner studied the scape, Andrew, whose eyes were clear that day, studied Tanner.

There was plenty of temptation at a time like this to give speeches, but Andrew knew they would do no good. Either Tanner was going to take good care of Stacy or he wasn't, and Andrew sincerely doubted that anything he said would make a difference.

What he'd seen so far looked good, but Stacy had been raised in a different world, and her level of trust was very high, even when it ought not to be. As a duke, Tanner was certainly used to having his own way, and Stacy was a people pleaser. The old man shrugged mentally. It was out of his hands. As much as he'd like to wring a promise out of this young duke that his granddaughter would be well cared for, he knew better than to even try.

As it was, Tanner began to speak, cutting into Andrew's musings. He extended an invitation to Winslow, if ever Andrew wanted to make the trip, and then proceeded to tell him of the house and grounds. By the time they returned to Morgan for breakfast the older man was feeling much better about this young man.

In the next ten days that they visited, Andrew was given a measure of peace concerning Stacy's happiness. It wasn't anything specific, but Tanner proved repeatedly in the little things that he said and did that he cared deeply for his new wife.

Because Andrew didn't know when Stacy would come again, the goodbyes at the end of their visit were harder than the ones in the spring had been. But from what he could tell, he believed Tanner was going to do right by Stacy. Beyond that Andrew could only hope.

Thirteen

STANDING IN THE DOORWAY of the master bedroom, Stacy was pleased that Tanner had warned her before they arrived. This room, the suite actually, was as massive as everything else at Winslow.

On one end were Stacy's spacious sitting room and large dressing room. From Stacy's tour, she knew that Tanner's sitting and dressing rooms were of the same size. Centered between these four smaller rooms was the bedroom itself.

The master bedroom was a room in which all the furniture played court to the huge bed that stood against the main wall. The headboard was over six feet high with pillared columns on the two corners. It was ornately carved in a rich cherry wood and inlaid with mahogany and ash. Large windows with beautiful smokey-gray hangings looked out over the perfectly manicured acres of Winslow.

If she leaned very close to the glass she could see the other wings, which housed dozens of rooms: bedrooms, private sitting rooms, small dining areas, a multitiered library, a music room, studies, lovely galleries, servants' quarters, and more than Stacy could keep track of.

The kitchen was at the rear of Winslow, off the first floor. Although Stacy had only gained a peek, her impression of hundreds of square feet of floor space and gleaming pots hanging and tables spread out was permanently stamped in her mind.

Her thoughts spun as she remembered the large number of kitchen staff alone. How would she manage all of this?

Stacy shook her head as the direction of her thoughts threatened to overwhelm her, and was relieved to see Rayna come to the edge of the room.

"I have your correspondence here, my lady."

"Oh," Stacy spoke with surprise, not having expected this. "Thank you, Rayna." She took the letters and glanced through them.

"I believe your aunt has been in touch with you," Rayna spoke respectfully. "She wrote to me also. If after you read your letter, my lady, and like the idea—my answer is yes. If there is nothing else, I'll continue your unpacking."

Stacy nodded, feeling confused as Rayna walked away, but she swiftly turned her attention back to the small pile of letters in her hand. After walking into her sitting room, she made herself comfortable in a chair and began to read. The first letter was from Lucinda. Stacy's eyes widened on two occasions, first when she wrote that Rayna could stay with her if the situation was suitable, and then again when Lucinda told of her upcoming marriage to Roddy.

Stacy's eyes slid shut in rapture at the latter news. They were so perfect for each other, and Stacy knew they loved one another deeply. A small smile played around the corners of her mouth when she considered the fact that she had probably helped things along when she'd talked with Roddy in the carriage. Stacy chuckled softly over how much fun it was to be a matchmaker.

The next letter was from a woman named Chelsea Gallagher, a neighbor apparently, and one whom Stacy hadn't met. She wrote to welcome Stacy to the area and to offer her congratulations. Chelsea also expressed her wish to meet Stacy soon.

Stacy pondered for a time as to whether she had seen this woman at a social gathering or at the wedding and decided that she simply couldn't recall. With a resigned shrug she opened the last note—it was from Sunny Hawkesbury. Sunny wrote to ask if she and her sister-in-law, Chelsea Gallagher, could call on her the afternoon of the twentieth. Stacy was smiling with delight at the prospect when Tanner entered the room.

"That's quite a smile," Tanner chuckled as he pulled his wife from the settee and into his arms.

"I got a letter from Sunny Hawkesbury. She and Chelsea Gallagher want to come to see me on the twentieth."

"That's this Friday. You'd better reply right away."

"How do I get word to them?"

Tanner, who had been bending his head to kiss her, straightened in surprise.

"You send a servant."

"Oh," Stacy said inadequately, feeling very young and gauche under his raised brow.

Tanner saw the color rise in her face. He bent and pressed a kiss to her brow and then spoke with his arms wrapped securely around her.

"I came up to ask you to go riding with me. Write your note, and I'll give it Price. If ever you have a question, see Price; he'll take care of you. After you've finished with your reply, you can slip into a riding habit and we'll get a ride in before dinner."

Stacy smiled gratefully and did as he asked. Within 40 minutes, she'd sent word to Sunny and was riding across the meadows of Winslow with her husband. Only once did she think of Lucinda's news and took a moment to share it with Tanner, who didn't seem surprised at all. As Tanner stepped up the pace to a gallop, Stacy wondered where her aunt and Roddy were now.

"Something is wrong, Cinda."

"No, Roddy, it's not."

"You're not being straight with me. Have I done something?"

"Oh, no," Lucinda shook her head, but she refused to look at him. They were at the new house on Bates Street, Brentwood. The painters had been there that day, and Lucinda and Roddy had come to see the results. The wedding was set for one month's time, and Roddy wanted to be certain that everything was just right.

Roddy did not press Lucinda as they continued their tour, but when Lucinda would have bid him goodnight at her front door, he came in without asking. She started toward the stairs, but he captured her hand and led her into the library. The fire burned warmly, and after they were seated on the sofa, Roddy spoke. Lucinda still had not looked at him, but Roddy told himself he wasn't leaving until he was sure he understood her silence.

"What's frightening you, Cinda?"

Lucinda drew a quick breath. He had so easily guessed her problem was fear. She wanted to deny it but couldn't find the words. Her throat closed with tears. Roddy's next sentence was her undoing.

"I'm not Aubrey."

Lucinda put her face in her hands and sobbed. Roddy's arms surrounded her. Her frame shook with harsh weeping, and Roddy let her cry. When it seemed that she was calming, he produced a handkerchief and Lucinda took it gratefully.

"I'm sorry," she said shakily, "I don't know what's come over me."

"I think I do. I think for years you've convinced yourself that Aubrey was unfaithful because of some deficiency in you. That's a lie, Lucinda. Aubrey wasn't faithful to you or to anyone, including himself. His infidelity was *his* problem, not yours.

"I'm not going to be married to you for a month and then go looking for greener pastures. If I'd been that kind of man, I would have proved it a long time ago. You're all the woman I want, and will ever want."

Lucinda was staring into his face, now close to her own, as though she were seeing him for the first time. He was so wonderful, more wonderful than she deserved.

"Do you believe me?" Roddy asked.

"Yes, I do," Lucinda said with wonder and then knew she had to be completely honest. "However, I may be plagued by doubts again."

"If you are, come to me, Cinda, just as soon as the fears surface."

Lucinda leaned forward and kissed him then, but Roddy held himself in check. They lived in an age and time where intimacy was a casual thing. Not so with Roddy Caruthers. Lucinda was precious to him, and even knowing that she would be his wife in a month was not enough to press him into doing something he felt was wrong.

Just a few weeks now, Roddy told himself as he exited. *She'll be mine to have and hold in just a few weeks.*

Stacy sat on the huge bed their first night at Winslow and tested the softness. She didn't lie back, but bounced a little on her seat and then got comfortable against the headboard. With the ease that years of practice afforded her, she then reached for her hair.

Rayna had brushed it smooth for her, but for as long as she could remember she'd braided it down her back at bedtime and did so now. It made her hair much easier to manage in the morning. Even though Tanner liked it hanging free, Stacy's mind was on other things and she acted out of habit.

She had just reached for a book on the nightstand when Tanner joined her. She watched him make himself comfortable against the footboard and then stare at her.

"How do you like Winslow?" he asked.

"Oh, Tanner," Stacy said, setting the book aside, her eyes

bright with enchantment. "It's the loveliest home I've ever seen. I can't think of what your impression must have been when we were in Middlesbrough."

"I was quite comfortable at Morgan, and I enjoyed your grandfather tremendously. Hettie tends to step out of place quite regularly, but since she doesn't live *here,* I think I'll survive."

"She's rather protective of me," Stacy returned apologetically.

"So I noticed. I've gained the fiercest looks from her. I don't know if she really believes we're married." Tanner's voice was dry.

Stacy laughed. "She's been like a mother to me, and even though she's negative and scolds a lot, I can't think of what I'd have done without her."

"Your parents died when you were young, didn't they?"

"I was little more than a baby. I don't remember either of them. It's always been Papa and Hettie and of course Peters. He's been like a father also."

"I have an ancestor that reminds me of Peters. His portrait is in the north wing. I'll have to show it to you sometime."

"Is the north wing always so cold?"

"Actually it is. It gets very little sun and has always been drafty."

"It's more than the temperature, though," Stacy said, her eyes on some distant spot. "The colors used in the decorating are cold too. It's nothing like the rest of Winslow. When I walked through there it felt like a completely different place."

"My grandmother had dreary tastes in decorating. Everything else has been remodeled. The north wing has what's left of her furniture. Feel free to redecorate."

"Is it used very often?"

"Almost never," Tanner answered her.

"Then I don't see any point in spending the money. If you want me to, I'll do it, but it seems like a waste."

"It's up to you," Tanner told her softly, but his mind was not on the north wing. It was on discovering that his wife was not a spendthrift. He didn't know a woman alive who didn't like to spend money on everything she could get her hands on. Tanner wondered how many years they would be married before she stopped being a surprise.

Fourteen

STACY PEERED INTO THE MIRROR for the fifth time and then paced the room some more. Sunny and Chelsea were scheduled to arrive in an hour, and Stacy was a nervous wreck. She so wanted to make a good impression, but she was convinced that they would find her out of place in a home as lovely and grand as Winslow.

Stacy stopped suddenly and mentally scolded herself. Her mind was headed off into all kinds of whimsical nonsense, and that was ridiculous. After a final glance in the mirror, she made herself walk calmly down the wide staircase to see if the parlor was in readiness. She met Tanner as he came from his study.

"Ah, here you are. I was just headed to see how you were doing."

"I'm doing fine," Stacy told him much too brightly, her face pale.

Tanner's voice was meant to be reassuring as he continued, "When do your guests arrive?"

"In 48 minutes."

Tanner had to hide a smile at her precision. She had obviously worked herself into a fine state and was on the brink of panic.

"I've known Chelsea Gallagher and her husband, Rand, for

years. She's a fine woman, and of course you've already met Sunny."

"Of course," Stacy agreed, feeling worse than ever. "I don't like my dress," she added absently.

"Then why are you wearing it?"

"Because it's part of my trousseau, and I can't let it hang there."

"Change your dress, Stacy," Tanner told her calmly.

"I don't have time."

Tanner gently took his wife's hand and began to lead her back up the stairs.

"You think I'm acting like a child, don't you?"

"No, I don't," Tanner answered her. "I think you're understandably nervous because this is the first time you've entertained here. Hating your dress only adds to the problem. Rayna!" Tanner finished with a shout to Stacy's maid.

When Rayna appeared, Tanner gave her orders and Stacy was amazed at how much calmer she felt from just listening to him.

"Lady Richardson does not like this dress, and quite frankly it's not my favorite either. Please see her into something more comfortable." With that he turned to Stacy.

"Do not rush. If your guests arrive early, I will keep company with them until you come down."

Stacy's chest heaved with relief. "Thank you, Tanner."

Tanner's long-fingered hand tenderly captured her jaw. "You're welcome, sweetheart, and trust me, you're going to do just fine."

Chelsea Gallagher was nothing like Stacy expected. She was older than Sunny, even though they were sister-in-laws. In fact, she was old enough to be Sunny's or Stacy's mother. She had a youthful air, however, and was beautiful in her own right. Stacy, who was at times rather uncomfortable with her figure, was quite pleased to find Chelsea more heavily endowed than she was herself.

Chelsea was not as tall as Stacy, but her overall figure was more filled out. Sunny was also on the tall side, but her figure was willowy. Her tummy was becoming nicely rounded, giving evidence of the child to come.

Sunny hugged Stacy as soon as she arrived, and Chelsea shook her hand so warmly that Stacy's fears melted. There was no lack of conversation in the time that followed as Stacy described how she and Tanner met and her honeymoon trip. The next two hours flew by, and Stacy couldn't believe how much she was enjoying herself.

It took some time, but Stacy suddenly realized how closely these women were related to Lady Andrea, Aunt Lucinda's friend.

"You haven't met my brother, have you?" Chelsea asked at one point.

"No."

"Well, where was Brandon that day we met in London?" Sunny interjected with a frown.

"I think he came just as our carriage was leaving," Stacy told them and then frowned herself. "Brandon is your brother?"

"That's right," Chelsea told her.

"Then Lady Andrea is your mother."

Chelsea smiled as she made the connection.

"I completely missed that. Will you tell me about the rest of your family?"

"Certainly. My youngest brother is Dexter. He's married with children. Miles and Holly are my own children. They're both grown and married, and they've made Rand and me grandparents three times over."

"You can't be a grandmother," Stacy interrupted.

Chelsea and Sunny exchanged a look, and then both laughed. Chelsea heard this comment often, and it was always a source of great amusement to her. She told Stacy that some days she felt like a *great*-grandmother.

The women did not stay much longer. Stacy walked them out to their carriage when they took their leave. Tanner suddenly appeared at her side to assist both ladies inside the coach.

"We would love to have you over for dinner in a few weeks," Sunny told the newlyweds.

Tanner glanced at Stacy for approval before turning back to the Duchess of Briscoe.

"We'll plan on it," he told her.

"Goodbye until then," Sunny called out the window as the carriage pulled away. When she settled back inside, Chelsea spoke.

"He's in love with her, Sunny. I wouldn't have believed it if I hadn't seen it with my own eyes."

"They seem very happy," Sunny agreed.

"But you're concerned about something," Chelsea interjected, watching the younger woman carefully.

"Oh, you'll only say I'm full of doom and gloom if I say it, but they are still newlyweds, and I know that Tanner's had some deep hurts. Brandon didn't go into detail, but he intimated that things have been pretty rough. Stacy couldn't be sweeter, but I can't help wondering whether Stacy will be able to stand the blow if Tanner's hurts do surface."

"We'll keep praying," Chelsea told her, and in fact they took time right then to lift the young couple to the Lord.

Two days after Chelsea's and Sunny's visit, Tanner made a fast trip into London. He spent more time in the carriage than tending his business, but he had several important matters to care for. One was a visit to his Uncle Edmond; the other was made with Stacy in mind. Both were attended to as swiftly as possible, but the day was long and he missed Stacy terribly.

Not for one moment, not even when he met with his uncle, could he dispel her from his thoughts. He wondered briefly if he was becoming obsessed but dismissed the thought immediately. He had no more determined to put her from his mind when he found himself wondering what she was doing right then.

Tanner would have been pleased and surprised to find that Stacy was digging in the garden just as Tanner had told her she could do. Not all of Tanner's staff was as friendly as Stacy would have liked, and there were times when she preferred to be out-of-doors and away from their watchful eyes.

Even though Joffrey was head of housekeeping, things seemed to be a little more finely tuned when Price was in attendance. Stacy couldn't help but wonder if Joffrey was rather remiss in his duties. It didn't seem possible, since even when in good humor Tanner was a demanding lord. But as Stacy thought about her weeks at Winslow, she realized the staff was not lax when he was present but only with her.

The thought caused her to frown, and she sat back on her heels. She didn't know what to do about the situation. Stacy knew that if it came to an out-and-out battle, she would wash her own clothes and get her own meals before she would confront anyone. Just the thought of confrontation made her stomach ache.

Stacy went back to her weeding, but her stomachache did not go away. It was then that she realized the sun had dropped low in the sky. It was dinnertime, and she was famished. Pushing herself off the ground, she moved toward the house.

Rayna was there to meet her, and Stacy, hungry as she was, enjoyed a leisurely bath. She knew the evening was going to drag with Tanner away, and a long soak in a tub filled with scented salts was just what she needed.

Supper was delicious, but by the time Stacy finished, she missed Tanner so much she didn't know how she would pass the evening. She opted for a book from the library and was headed that way when he came in the front door. Not caring in the least if the servants were watching, Stacy flew into his arms.

"I missed you," she told him as he bent so she could put her arms around his neck, pressing her soft cheek to his. It took Stacy a moment to realize she was not being hugged in return. He dropped a kiss on her nose before she moved back in order to stare up at him. She stood back and looked at her husband, whose arms were behind his back.

"I missed you too," Tanner told her as he straightened, but Stacy's mind was now on his arms.

"You're hiding something."

"Indeed I am."

Stacy tried to move around him, but Tanner simply moved with her and kept his secret concealed. Stacy finally stood still again and faced him.

"Is it for me?" she asked with a smile.

"Quite possibly," Tanner answered and Stacy saw how much he was enjoying this. She put her own hands behind her back and simply stared at him.

"Did you stay busy today?" Tanner asked.

"Yes," Stacy said simply, but couldn't stand the suspense any longer. "Do I get to see what it is?"

"Are your hands clean?" Tanner asked, sounding much like a parent. He ruined the effect, however, when his eyes lit with suppressed laughter.

Stacy, like an obedient child, brought her hands forward for his inspection.

"You've been digging in the dirt, haven't you?"

"Guilty as charged," she told him and joined his inspection of her chipped nails.

Tanner gave a deep, mock sigh and brought a large box out from behind his back.

"I'm not sure this is fitting for an urchin like yourself, but here it is."

Stacy's eyes widened in a way that Tanner loved, and he held the bottom of the parcel while she removed the lid and drew forth an exquisite gown.

"Oh, Tanner," Stacy breathed. "It's lovely."

"This is to replace the one you don't like."

Stacy held the dress out in front of her and stared. The dress was a very pale pink silk with snow-white lace. The skirt had multiple gathers at the waist before falling straight to the floor without ruffle or layer. The bodice and sleeves were both of bertha styling, and Stacy did not have another dress like it in her wardrobe. It was the most wonderful gown she'd ever seen.

Gently hugging it to her, she spoke. "I'm going to save this for something very special."

"Anything you wish," Tanner told her, feeling inordinately pleased at her response. He really had thought about her way too much, but she was obviously worth every reflection.

The evening turned out to be a wonderful surprise for Stacy since Tanner was home early and wanted to eat in the privacy of his sitting room. Stacy sat with him through the meal, and they talked of their day apart. When Tanner finished his meal, he dismissed the servants early and they were left alone until morning.

Fifteen

SEPTEMBER WAS DRAWING TO A CLOSE when Tanner told Stacy he was going to have to be away for a few days. Stacy listened in silent dismay as he told her casually that he would have to leave on the second of October and would not return until late on the third.

"Edmond insists that we go and see some breeding stock. I don't know why he doesn't want to part with his own brass for such nonsense, but he assures me this is an investment I can't pass up."

"Did you want me to come with you?" Stacy offered, hoping her voice sounded normal.

"Thank you for offering, my sweet, but I can assure you this trip will be dry-as-dust—strictly business. It's also going to be rather rushed because I want to be back home as soon as I can."

"I'll ask cook to prepare something special," Stacy said, a sudden idea springing to mind, "and we'll dine together when you return."

Tanner stood from his place at the breakfast table and came toward her.

"I love the idea, sweetheart," he told her as he stood by her place, "but I'll be very late that night. Hopefully I can slip into bed without disturbing you, and then I can tell you all about the trip the next morning. In fact, we'll take the day off. We'll sleep late and be very lazy all day and do anything you want."

Tanner kissed her cheek and moved toward the door, telling her over his shoulder that he had some work to do in his study. Stacy lifted her coffee cup very slowly to her lips. She simply didn't know how to tell her husband that his business trip was going to keep him away for her birthday, October 3.

"He's planning a surprise party," Stacy spoke out loud, causing Rayna to come back into the dressing room.

"Did you call me, my lady?"

"No, Rayna," Stacy told her with a smile. "I was just talking to myself."

Rayna nodded and Stacy settled back in the tub, a huge smile of contentment covering her face.

Two slow days had passed since Tanner had announced his plans to be gone. He had been busy and didn't notice anything out of the usual in his wife, but Stacy had agonized over whether or not to tell him.

Now there was no need. It was all a ploy to throw her off guard. Tanner was simply pretending not to be aware of her birthday so he could come home early and surprise her. Stacy lay back in the tub until her water grew cold. All she could think about was the wonderful man she had married.

"If I didn't know better, I would think you're glad to see me go," Tanner commented the morning he was scheduled to leave.

Stacy chuckled softly. "Don't be silly," she told him, straightening his cravat. "I even offered to go with you, remember?"

Tanner studied her soft, mischievous eyes and felt fear spiral through him. Leslie had never been sorry to see him leave. It took years before he learned that it was because she had never been without other men. The last one was his brother.

"Tanner, is something wrong?"

Tanner shook his head to dispel the images that had leapt into his mind.

"No," he forced the word as he turned toward the door. "I'd best be on my way."

"All right." Stacy's voice was uncertain now. He hadn't even kissed her goodbye. She followed him all the way downstairs and out the door, finally coming to a standstill on the porch to watch him stride away. When Tanner stopped just short of boarding the coach and turned back to her, Stacy spoke, her voice not able to mask her confusion.

"Take care of yourself, Tanner. Tell Edmond I said hello."

Tanner said something too softly to be heard and was back in front of her in six strides. He pulled her almost fiercely into his arms. Stacy was breathless when he released her, but she managed a few more words.

"I love you, Tanner."

He didn't speak, but his gaze softened and the back of his hand came up to stroke her cheek before he turned, strode to the carriage, and was driven away.

Stacy didn't stand on the steps for very long. She was too excited about her coming birthday. With her own long-legged steps she mounted the stairs to make certain her dress was perfectly pressed for the following night.

It was close to midnight before Tanner made his way up the stairs on the night of the third. Price, who had not traveled with him this time, was in attendance, and without a word Tanner undressed and moved soft-footedly into the bedroom and toward the bed. He was nearly on top of it before he realized that the covers had been turned down but the bed was empty.

With a feeling of dread, one that had hung with him since he'd left, he walked toward Stacy's dressing room. Finding it empty, he moved to the sitting room.

Stacy, dressed in her new gown, was seated by the fire, and sitting very upright in a chair. As he approached, Tanner saw that she was awake and staring at him. Upon seeing the new dress, anger rose within him so swiftly he thought he would explode. She had known he would not be home until late. For *whom* had she dressed?

"Why are you up and dressed like that?" Tanner was amazed that in his anger his voice sounded so normal.

When Stacy answered she did not sound guilty, only unhappy. "I thought you were giving me a surprise party."

A stunned silence followed this announcement as the anger drained out of Tanner.

"I am giving you a surprise party," he admitted after several heartbeats. "On your birthday, the thirtieth."

Tanner heard her sigh.

"Whom did you ask about the date of my birthday?"

"Lucinda," Tanner answered, feeling more confused than ever.

Stacy actually managed a small laugh. "Lucinda has never been able to get dates straight. My grandfather's birthday is the thirtieth, not mine."

The room was silent for a full 30 seconds.

"Anastasia," Tanner finally said, his voice deep and intense, "are you trying to tell me that today is your birthday?"

The question was no more out of his mouth than the clock on the mantel chimed 12 times. When it ended, Stacy answered him.

"It was yesterday, actually. I thought you knew, Tanner, and that your trip was a cover for a surprise party. That's why I didn't tell you."

Tanner's relief over the fact that she'd not been with another man was short-lived. He'd *missed* his wife's birthday. In just a few strides he was before Stacy's chair, taking her hands and pulling her into his embrace. Tanner's heart pounded with dread as he held her tightly against him.

"You're crushing my new dress," Stacy told him, but her concern was half-hearted.

"I'll buy you a new one—I'll buy a closet full of new dresses." The words came from above her as Tanner rested his chin on her head and continued to hold her close.

"I'm all right, Tanner," Stacy told him. "I wasn't all right before you came home, but I am now."

Tanner's eyes slid shut with pain. He hated the thought that she must have urged Rayna to do her best, and then sat in her room, looking beautiful and waiting for a party that never materialized.

"I'll make this up to you." Tanner now held her by the arms and tried to study her face in the small glow of the fire.

"There is no need," Stacy assured him. "I understand, and it wasn't your fault."

He ignored her words. "Would you like your present now?"

"You have my present?" Stacy was indescribably pleased. She told herself that it wasn't the day itself that mattered, but the celebration. At the moment it suited her fine that her birthday "party" was going to be just her and Tanner, sitting together while she opened her gift.

"Wait here," Tanner urged, and Stacy stood still for the minutes he was gone. It took a little time, but when he returned he was carrying a jeweler's box and a lighted lantern. He lit the other two on the mantel before presenting the box to Stacy.

"Happy birthday, sweetheart."

Stacy opened the top and gasped. Inside lay a necklace.

There didn't seem to be any more to it than gold and diamonds, seemingly hundreds of them.

"Oh, Tanner. It's simply breathtaking."

"I take it you like it?"

"I love it, but—"

"But what?" Tanner prompted her when she stopped and looked at him in horror.

"What if I lose it?"

Tanner made a low sound in his throat, one of complete disregard.

"I'll buy you another." This said he lifted the priceless object from its bed of satin and hooked it around his wife's neck. Stacy was trembling as she looked in the mirror that hung over the mantel.

"Oh, Tanner." Stacy didn't seem capable of other words. Without warning she turned and threw her arms around his neck. She tried to thank him then, but was interrupted by a huge yawn that she simply couldn't suppress.

"We'd better get to bed." Tanner's voice was amused.

Stacy yawned again. "Would you mind if I didn't come right now, Tanner?"

The change in him was instantaneous. "No." His voice was cold, belying the word. "What is it you need to do?"

"It's nothing," Stacy assured him quickly, startled by the change in him and the note of intolerance in his tone. "If you'll unbutton me, I'll get ready for bed."

It was as if a bucket of ice had been thrown on their celebration. Tanner knew he'd caused it with the tone of his voice, but her reluctance to join him in bed disturbed him no end.

In silence he unbuttoned Stacy. She reached for the back of her neck and unhooked the necklace. Standing still, necklace grasped in her hand, she watched her husband stalk from the sitting room. By the time she gained the bedroom, Tanner was in bed. For the first time there seemed to be a wall between them. Tanner told her goodnight but did not touch her.

"Thank you for the necklace," Stacy said from her side of the bed.

"You're welcome," Tanner answered briefly, leaving Stacy in the dark as to what she had done or how she was supposed to fix it.

An hour later Stacy lay listening to Tanner's even breathing and knew she was going to have to get up. It had all been so innocent. If only she had told him right away that she needed something to eat, he might not have grown angry. Stacy silently sighed at her own lack of courage, her own inability to stand up for herself.

With very subtle and quiet movements, she slipped from the covers. She didn't light a lantern until she'd reached her sitting room and then carried it out into the hall. If Tanner had been hungry, he'd have rung for a meal, but Stacy couldn't bring herself to wake someone just to wait on her.

She had just entered the kitchen and set the lantern down when her husband's voice sounded behind her. He was coldly furious.

"What are you doing down here?"

"Oh, Tanner," Stacy's hand flew to her throat. "You startled me."

"Answer my question." He ignored her fear. "What are you doing down here?"

"I'm sorry I woke you. I tried to go to sleep, I really did, but I'm hungry and I thought if I ate something, I could sleep. I'll come back up now so you won't be disturbed."

Stacy picked up the lantern, but Tanner didn't move. Stacy, afraid of angering him more, simply held her place.

"Why didn't you tell me?" Tanner was calming.

"I wanted to, but you seemed so upset. I thought I could wait until morning."

"Why didn't you ring for something?"

Stacy shrugged, feeling miserably inadequate to be a duchess. But that was not all. Things had not been completely right between them since they said their goodbyes for the trip, and Stacy, not really understanding the problem but assuming she'd done something wrong, didn't know how to put the relationship back on firm footing.

"Do you really need something to eat?"

"I can wait until morning," Stacy hurried to tell him, but Tanner just stared at her until she felt compelled to apologize.

"I'm sorry for whatever I've done wrong, Tanner. I think it must have started a few days ago. I'm not really certain, but whatever I've done to make you upset, I'm sorry."

Tanner couldn't take the way her eyes stared at him beseechingly or the sound of her sweet voice in misery. Thoughts of Leslie had ridden him hard since he'd agreed to marry Stacy, but never as roughly as in the last 48 hours. His black mood was terrifying his wife, and he was going to have to get a grip on himself. He was just about to say something when there was a rustling on the far side of the room.

"Excuse me, my lord, but I thought I heard voices." Winslow's cook stood across the room. "Is there something I can get for you?"

"My wife is hungry."

"Very well, I'll fix you right up." The rather plump woman was cheerful for the middle of the night. "Would you care for something, your Grace?"

"No. Just see to my wife."

Tanner left then, and Stacy felt utterly wretched. She stared at the door long after he exited, asking herself what she'd done.

"Now, my lady, if you'll just make yourself comfortable in the dining room, I'll bring something right in."

"I'll be fine here," Stacy told the older woman absently, missing the servant's shocked expression.

Cook watched Stacy take a chair at the small, crude table

and worked at keeping her voice level. The lord and lady simply did not eat in the kitchen! The kitchen was for servants, not the duchess; she deserved the best. However she simply said, "I'll just be a moment with your food."

Stacy sat, staring at nothing in particular until cook put a dish of sliced fruit on the table.

"There now. Why don't you start with that? I worried about you, my lady, when you didn't want your supper," she spoke in a motherly tone. "I'll have something more for you in a jiffy."

Tanner came out of the shadows at that moment and placed a heavy quilt around Stacy's shoulders. His hands were gentle and Stacy was thankful for the warmth, but she was decidedly uncomfortable when he sat down across from her.

"Why didn't you eat your dinner?"

Stacy swallowed a slice of apple before answering. "It was foolish of me not to."

"But why didn't you?" Tanner pressed her.

"I thought the surprise party would be a dinner party," Stacy admitted quietly, her eyes down.

Tanner's hand went to the back of his neck. Stacy still did not look up, or she would have seen the pain in his eyes.

You're a fool, Tanner Richardson, he told himself. *And you don't deserve this dear girl. She was honest with you and you took her head off.*

Stacy finished her meal in silence. Her stomach felt better, but her heart felt as if a giant hand was trying to squeeze the very life from it.

Tanner held her chair out when she was done and waited as she thanked cook. He escorted her up the stairs. When they were once again in the bedroom, he took her jaw in his hand, forcing her gaze to meet his.

"I've been in a wretched humor these past days, but things will be different tomorrow. You have nothing to be sorry about, and in the morning we'll celebrate your birthday properly."

Stacy, clinging to the tender, calm sound of his voice,

nodded with relief. She was still rather emotionally drained, but when they climbed into bed, she fell asleep just moments after the covers were settled around her.

Sixteen

Stacy's back rested against the base of a large tree, her legs stretched out in front of her. Tanner's head was in her lap, and thus far the day had been idyllic.

Both duke and duchess had slept late, eaten a leisurely breakfast, and gone for a long ride into the bluffs beyond Winslow. They had ridden for miles, and Stacy was amazed that they were still on Richardson land. Everything about Winslow was beautiful. Stacy said as much to Tanner.

"Including the mistress of the manor," Tanner commented. Stacy smiled at the compliment.

"Did I tell you that I saw Hawk while I was away?" Tanner asked suddenly.

"Hawk?"

"Hawk is Brandon Hawkesbury's nickname."

"Oh," Stacy said with surprise and then, "Is Sunny feeling better?"

"Yes. She was terribly disappointed that she had to cancel the dinner plans, but she's going to have you to tea soon."

"She didn't lose the baby, did she?" Stacy's voice was pained at the very thought.

"No. It was a nasty virus according to Hawk. The doctor has ordered her to take it easy, but the pregnancy is still strong."

Stacy sighed with relief. She was already excited about the arrival of this new little one and knew she would have mourned the loss. She had even started the baby's gift; it was a beautiful blanket in multiple colors appropriate for either gender, but secretly Stacy hoped Sunny would have a girl.

"I think I've lost you," Tanner commented as he sat up beside her and leaned against the tree.

"I was thinking about Sunny's baby."

Her voice was so wistful that Tanner stared at her. She sounded like having a child was the most precious thing on earth. Tanner frowned slightly. He did not have the heart to tell her that it might not ever happen for them.

He'd suffered a raging fever as a child, and the doctor had told his father that one of the long-lasting side effects might be sterility. In all the years he and Leslie had been married, she had never conceived. The fact had never really bothered him before, but now he wanted to give his wife a baby. His heart felt weighted down over what he assumed was an impossibility.

"I think I've lost you." Stacy echoed his phrase a moment later, and Tanner smiled down into her eyes before they began to talk of the coming winter.

The day ran on in a quiet and peaceful vein. Both bride and groom felt renewed in their relationship, and Stacy, although she had no answers to her husband's quicksilver mood changes, still believed Tanner loved her. She would work at this marriage for as long as it took him to say the words.

"I'm so glad you're feeling better," Stacy told Sunny as she hugged her. It was early the next week, and the women were finally getting together at Bracken for tea.

"I don't know when I've been so sick. Brandon said there were moments when I didn't even recognize him. He also told me that Sterling was frantic at times, having not seen me for so many days."

"Poor little thing," Stacy sympathized. "He must have been so confused."

"He was. I'm still taking it slow, but it's good to be up and around and spending time with both Sterling and Brandon."

"Is everything really all right with the baby?" Stacy's voice was anxious, and Sunny was quick to reassure her.

"Everything is fine. I wasn't able to eat for a few days, and that was a concern, but I'm back on track now."

Stacy's sigh was so heartfelt that Sunny smiled.

"Do you like children, Stacy?"

"Ever so much," she admitted, her eyes alight with pleasure.

"And Tanner, how does he feel?"

"I don't know," Stacy told her honestly. "We've never really spoken of it."

Sunny hesitated only a moment before asking her guest a very personal question.

"Do you think you might be expecting?" Sunny was ready to apologize if she'd been out of line, but Stacy's face was as open as ever. She shrugged slightly before answering.

"I don't think so. But I do wonder what signs I need to look for. Oh, not the obvious of course, but my cousin Elena is never ill when she carries a baby, and I thought that was one of the first warnings."

"It's different for every woman," Sunny told her. "I know that's no help to you, but I've known women who were not sure they were pregnant for several months and others who knew within days. Chelsea told me that she wasn't sick for even a day. However, my niece Holly was ill the entire nine months."

"That sounds awful," Stacy grimaced.

"It wasn't much fun," Sunny agreed. "But God gave them a beautiful baby, and Holly said it was worth every moment."

"I imagine it was." Stacy's voice was a bit dreamy, and

Sunny couldn't stop herself from hoping that God would give this couple a baby.

Keeping Sunny's recent illness in mind, Stacy did not stay long. However, their time together was sweet. The Richardson coach was coming around for Stacy when Sunny remembered she had a wedding gift for Lucinda and Roddy. The Hawkesburys were not going to make the special event, but Sunny sent best wishes through Stacy.

As the coach started for Winslow, Stacy fingered the neatly wrapped gift, her mind going to her aunt and Roddy. A smile of pure enjoyment broke across her face knowing that Lucinda would be preparing right now for the wedding. She and Roddy would be man and wife in one week's time.

"Is everything ready at Brentwood?" Lucinda asked her man, Craig, for the tenth time that day.

"Yes, my lady. All is prepared."

"And the groom's gift?"

"He's very comfortable in the stables." Craig's voice was calm.

Lucinda nodded but didn't answer. Her mind, moving from the magnificent horse she'd bought for Roddy, was already thinking on the clothes she'd purchased for their wedding trip. She simply couldn't decide which suit she should travel in. Maybe she would ask Roddy. But the thought no more materialized when she thought of something else for Craig to do. He was on his way out of the room when she stopped him.

"And, Craig, please see that Stacy's room is ready for her."

"I will, my lady, but I assumed the duke and duchess would be staying in Lord Richardson's town house."

"You're probably right, but I want the room ready just in case."

Craig left with only a nod of his head, and for the first time in days her mind slowed to a stop. It stopped on Stacy. Lucinda smiled.

They would be coming tomorrow, or was it the next day? *Well, no matter,* Lucinda thought. *I'm going to marry the man I love, and Stacy is coming.* Lucinda was so overwhelmed with peace and happiness that she simply sat, doing nothing, until Craig came and asked if she was ready for tea.

Tanner lay back in bed, reading some papers and waiting for his wife to join him. Just moments later Stacy entered the room, and Tanner smiled to see her hair down. He opened his mouth to speak, but as she neared the bed, he noticed that her expression was a bit strained. Tanner wondered if he might have imagined it, but knew better when she climbed onto the bed and not beneath the covers. He watched her kneel gracefully on her side of the bed, not actually keeping her distance, but just out of reach. Her expression was clearly preoccupied.

"Tanner," Stacy began, her voice telling of her distraction, "are you going to Lucinda and Roddy's wedding? I'm not sure if you ever said."

"Yes, I'll be there. Has that been bothering you?"

"Not exactly; I just couldn't recall if you'd told me."

Stacy fell silent then, and Tanner watched her, wondering at her mood. He didn't have long to speculate.

"Tanner, may I talk with you?"

"Of course," Tanner answered automatically.

"I heard from Elena," Stacy began, not even looking at Tanner. "She says the girls are fine and her pregnancy is going well. She writes that she's very large but feels good anyway."

Stacy glanced at Tanner then. He was not hearing a word she said. His eyes were back on his papers. Stacy sighed inwardly and resigned herself to keeping her feelings inside. She was moving to the side of the bed to draw the covers back and climb in when Tanner realized what he'd done.

"Is that all Elena said?"

"No," Stacy told him, still standing. "But I don't have to talk about it right now."

The pain in her voice made Tanner ashamed. He forced himself to shift against the headboard with a pillow at his back for comfort. Once settled, he gave her his full attention.

"What else did she say?" His voice was gentle, and Stacy, desperately needing a lifeline, sat down on the side of the bed.

"She said that my grandfather has lost nearly all of his sight. Even on good days he can see next to nothing." Stacy's voice told of her agony. "I've known this was going to happen for a long time, Tanner, but it's so hard. It's bad enough when he has poor days, but to lose his sight completely is almost more than I can take." Stacy's voice caught, but she didn't cry.

"Does Elena say how he's taking it?"

"Actually, she does, and she says that he's doing very well. It's just so difficult when I'm not there. I know Elena is giving me a straight story, but she doesn't live with Grandfather, and he's such a private man. I wish Peters had written to me. I'm going to get a letter off to both him and Hettie before we leave for London."

Stacy was silent for a moment after that. Tanner waited for her to speak. It took a little time, and she kept her eyes on the wall as she shared.

"He's always been there for me, Tanner, a tower of endurance. He's the only father I've ever known. I hate to see him vulnerable like this."

Stacy looked at her husband then. His eyes were intent on her and tender with caring. Stacy drew in a shuddering breath.

"Will you hold me, Tanner?"

His arms came out without words, and Stacy sighed deeply as he cuddled her against his chest.

"With or without his sight, your grandfather is still the same man. The man who took you to him when your parents died, and the man who still loves you today."

"Oh, Tanner," Stacy sighed.

"It's true," Tanner continued, his voice gentle. "He'll always be Andrew Daniels, and he'd probably resent any intimation otherwise."

Stacy nodded. She'd nearly forgotten her grandfather's pride.

Seventeen

"THE HOUSE IS SET UP for the ceremony and reception now, but as soon as Roddy and I leave for our wedding trip, the staff will move everything from both homes."

Closeted in Lucinda's bedroom, Stacy and her aunt talked about the wedding that would take place in approximately 48 hours.

"Did you have to let some of the staff go?" Stacy's voice was resigned.

"Actually, no," Lucinda told her with satisfaction. "Roddy has always had a very small staff. A few of my own were a bit frantic over being made redundant, but I assured them we would need them all.

"Now," Lucinda did a quick change of subject, "Roddy is due anytime, and before he comes I want you to come with me so I can show you the wedding gift I bought."

Lucinda rose and began to lead the way from the room.

"Where is it?" Stacy asked once they were in the hall.

"In the stables."

"The stables?"

Lucinda only laughed at her niece's look and proceeded to take her outside.

Stacy had never seen her aunt as nervous as she was just one hour before the wedding. It was a small affair, less than 70 guests, but Lucinda seemed unaccountably nervous.

Stacy stood beside her in an upstairs bedroom at Brentwood. The younger woman did not speak but offered support with her presence.

Maids came and went, but at one point they found themselves alone. The room was quiet for only a moment, and then Lucinda began to speak, as though to herself.

"Aubrey was not a kind husband. I'm afraid he was very selfish and he's left me with a rather negative view over certain aspects of marriage."

Stacy, without having to be told, knew what those aspects were.

"He didn't visit me very often, but when he did, there was no tenderness or caring. We never even spent the night together; Aubrey always went back to his own bed."

Stacy knew that it was time to intervene. Lucinda's voice had grown steadily sadder until Stacy feared she might cry. Stacy went to her and gently put her hands on the older woman's shoulders. Lucinda looked up at her, and Stacy spoke with a tender type of boldness that was totally foreign for her.

"Roddy Caruthers is the kindest man in all of England. He's also the most gentle. I've never seen a man more in love than Roddy. I can imagine that it's very hard to dispel Aubrey from your memory, but he's gone and Roddy's here. Aubrey made your life miserable while he was alive. Don't let him do it to you again in his death."

Lucinda stared at Stacy with new eyes. She was so right. Lucinda took a few deep breaths and made an effort to calm herself.

"Thank you, my dear," she spoke kindly, and then began to wonder aloud about her intended.

"I wonder how Roddy is doing?"

"Would you like me to go and talk with him?" Stacy offered and saw a relief on Lucinda's face that didn't need words. After kissing her aunt and telling her she'd see her downstairs, Stacy made for the door.

Once out in the hall she was spotted almost immediately by Tanner, who came up behind her and startled a small squeak out of her.

"Oh, Tanner!" Stacy's voice was breathless.

Tanner's arms had come around her.

"You look luscious in this blue thing."

"Thank you," Stacy told him, smiling up into his eyes both with love and the fact that he called her dress the "blue thing."

"When do I get my wife back?"

"Well, I have to go see Roddy, and then I'll come downstairs."

"That's not what I meant. I mean when do you stop playing wedding so I can take you back to Winslow?"

"Well, I told Lucinda I would handle things through tomorrow, but we could leave the day after that. Unfortunately, we have a weekend party at the Cradwells' almost as soon as we get home."

Tanner's eyes closed in long-suffering. "I'd completely forgotten about that."

"It would be fine with me if we didn't go," Stacy admitted, wanting very much to be alone with Tanner.

Tanner kissed her nose. "It would be fine with me as well, but we've turned down every one of their invitations, and because Price has already accepted for us, we had better be there."

Stacy did nothing to hide her chagrin, and the adorable face she pulled gained her another kiss.

"I've got to go," Stacy told Tanner after that.

He released her reluctantly and watched as she went to Roddy's door. Stacy knocked and turned to see Tanner's long-legged strides taking him back toward the stairs. He threw a smiling look in her direction just before he disappeared from view, and Stacy's heart skipped ahead a little faster.

Stacy was swiftly brought back to the present when Roddy's

door opened. His man, Carlson, stood beyond the portal, his expression solicitous.

"Carlson," Stacy began. "May I see Lord Caruthers?"

"Certainly, my lady."

The servant disappeared into the room. A moment later Roddy was at the door.

"Why, Stacy!"

"Hello, Roddy," Stacy spoke from her place in the hall. "I was just in with Lucinda, and she wondered how you were doing. I told her I would check."

"I'm fine. How is she faring?"

Stacy sighed gently. "She's a bit nervous."

"Over the wedding?"

"No," Stacy answered, her face heating slightly.

Roddy took in Stacy's pink cheeks.

"Tonight?" Roddy was always so perceptive.

Stacy nodded, her face still warm. "It might have been presumptuous of me, but I reminded her that you are not Aubrey."

Roddy's smile threatened to stretch off his face. He leaned forward and kissed Stacy's cheek.

"It sounds as though I couldn't have handled it better myself."

Stacy's smile of pleasure was genuine.

"I'd better get downstairs," she said a moment later.

"All right. But before you go I want to thank you. I'm not sure if you remember our day in the carriage, but your words changed my life."

"I remember. I was horrified at first, thinking I'd been completely out of line."

Roddy kissed her cheek again. "Lucinda is going to be my very own, Stacy, and I have you to thank for that."

Stacy took her leave then, walking on a cloud as she moved toward the stairs. Once she gained the lower level, several people wanted to talk with her, but she finally managed to slip into the seat next to Tanner.

Just minutes later the assembly was standing for the bride. Lucinda was resplendent in cream-colored satin and lace. Three tiers made up the skirt that fell so full from the waist that it touched either side of the double doors as Lucinda entered. The boat neckline was very flattering to Lucinda's face, and Stacy felt a surge of pride over how lovely her aunt looked.

The ceremony was short and tender. No one in the room could have missed the love that radiated from both bride and groom, and in a very short time the bishop was pronouncing them husband and wife.

A marvelous array of food was presented then, all prepared and eaten in their new home. There was no wedding dance, but the bride, groom, and all guests spent hours talking and eating. Lucinda had warned Stacy that she and Roddy would be slipping away without warning, so when neither one of them could be found, Stacy smiled and knew they were headed off on their trip.

The day finished in a whirl, and Stacy, in a near state of exhaustion, fell into bed that night. Tanner was tired as well, but they had a drowsy conversation before sleep came.

"Roddy sure knows how to pick wine. The champagne was excellent."

"Was it?" Stacy asked over a yawn.

"Didn't you have any?"

"No. I don't like champagne."

"What did you drink at our wedding?"

"Water."

"Even when we toasted?"

"Um hmm. If there wasn't a servant nearby, I just pretended to have something in my glass."

Stacy fell asleep to the sound of her husband's laughter.

❦ ❦ ❦

Just three days after Stacy and Tanner returned to Winslow, they were on the road again, this time to the Cradwell estate. Stacy would have gladly remained at home, but Tanner had said they were going and she would never have argued.

They didn't have a long drive, no more than 90 minutes, but Tanner had chosen to ride for most of the way, so Stacy was in the carriage alone. It was not exactly a lonely time, but she didn't know the Cradwells well and wondered what type of weekend it would be. The very fact that it was a whole weekend and not just an evening or afternoon was taking some adjustment in and of itself.

Coupled to this was some very real anxiety as to how well she would fit in. She would have begged Tanner to turn the coach around if she'd had even the slightest inkling of how little she would have in common with her hosts and their other guests.

THE CRADWELL MANSION WAS BEAUTIFUL to Stacy's eyes, but she didn't care for the grounds. Tall hedges lined nearly every walk, blocking Stacy's view of the gently rolling hills she loved so well.

Tanner led the way up to the front door, which opened immediately. Stacy glanced around the grand foyer before their host arrived. The next few moments were a confusion to Stacy, but she remained silent.

"Tanner," Jeremy Cradwell spoke as he approached. "Welcome."

"Thank you, Jeremy." Tanner shook the younger man's hand, concealing his surprise over being greeted by Lord and Lady Cradwell's son and not the senior Cradwells themselves.

"I don't believe you've met my wife, Jeremy. Stacy, this is Jeremy Cradwell. Jeremy, this is my wife, Lady Stacy Richardson."

"It's a pleasure to meet you, Lady Stacy." Jeremy didn't care for the fact that she was taller than he was—it put him off terribly—but she was the duchess. Thus he did manage to make a suitable welcome and kiss the back of Stacy's hand. "You're sure to grace our weekend with your beauty."

"Where are your parents, Jeremy?" Tanner asked as soon as Stacy had reclaimed her hand.

The younger man did not meet Tanner's eyes. "They're not going to be here this weekend."

Tanner's own eyes narrowed, but still Jeremy would not look at him. He was certain the invitation had been from Lord and Lady Cradwell. Finally Jeremy shifted his gaze from beyond Tanner's shoulders to his eyes.

"You're not thinking of leaving, are you, Tanner? I've got a hunt planned, and I was counting on you."

Tanner was just a few years older than Jeremy, but at the moment he felt like a father figure. Jeremy had never been forced to grow up. This party in his parent's home, in their absence, was just a small example of a young man who had been pampered all his life and never told no.

Without even having to ask, Tanner knew that Jeremy's guests for the weekend would all be young and single. He made a quick decision, his manner gracious, but he was still very much in control of the situation.

"We'll stay, Jeremy, but I'll warn you, if there's any foolishness, we will leave without a word of explanation or apology."

Jeremy didn't care for the note of authority in his guest's voice, but still he nodded in acquiescence. What else could he do? He was counting on Tanner, with his knowledge of the land and excellent marksmanship abilities, to lead the hunting expedition.

Tanner also held a position of power that not even Jeremy's father, with all his wealth, could match. If Tanner wanted to leave, no one would gainsay him.

Moments later a servant led Lord and Lady Richardson to their rooms. A maid hovered nearby, hoping to unpack, but Tanner told her to come back later. Stacy spoke as soon as they were alone.

"Is there a problem, Tanner?"

"Not exactly," he told her as he began to peel off his dusty riding clothes. "It's just that I hadn't realized that Jeremy was hosting this party. He can be a little wild.

"I'm more than willing to join a hunt, but Jeremy and his

friends have been known to add drinking to their sport. I'm not about to hunt with a drunken bunch of kids and get myself shot."

Stacy couldn't stop wringing her hands. She was truly frightened by her husband's words. Tanner came to her, gently rubbing her arms with his hands.

"I didn't mean to alarm you. I won't let the situation grow out of control."

Stacy nodded but didn't look very happy.

"What are you thinking?"

"That we could be snuggled in at Winslow, just the two of us."

Tanner smiled and kissed her brow. "We won't be at Winslow, but we'll make our excuses as soon after dinner tonight as we can. I too would like to spend some time alone with you."

Nigel Stanley checked his appearance in the mirror for the fourth time. Perfect. She was actually here! Stacy Daniels Richardson, whom he had worshiped from afar for so long, was finally within reach. He had never had the nerve to approach her in London, but now he would wait no longer.

The fact that she was married made no difference to him. He knew that most London marriages were a farce—without love or caring, intended only to produce an heir. Nigel knew that if he could only gain an introduction to Lady Richardson, he could win her over. He hadn't lived in England very long, having grown up in France where his father was a diplomat, but he was certain, without ever having met the man, that her husband didn't care a wit for her. Nigel fully intended to take advantage of that. He was certain that as soon as Stacy saw the love and caring in his eyes, she would understand all he wanted to be to her.

With a final glance at his appearance, he moved toward the door, rubbing his hands together in anticipation.

❦ ❦ ❦

"Your aunt was recently married, wasn't she?" a young woman questioned Stacy that evening before dinner.

"Yes," Stacy answered. "She married Roddy Caruthers."

"It was rather a private affair, wasn't it?" another young woman approached and interjected. She sounded offended, and Stacy wasn't sure what to say.

"You make it sound like you expected to be invited, Beth," the first young woman accused. "You don't even know Lucinda Warbrook."

Beth tossed her curls. "How do you know if I know her? Why just recently I was invited to—"

"Hello, ladies."

Stacy watched the faces of her companions as a tall man stepped into their group. In an instant all angry looks were gone, replaced with brilliant smiles and fluttering lashes.

"Hello, Nigel."

"You're all looking lovely this evening," Nigel smiled at them, thinking how easy it was to converse with people you didn't care for in the least. He hadn't even looked at Stacy yet, but he could already feel his heart pounding. Fear that he would be a tongue-tied fool when the introductions were made was escalating.

Stacy stood quietly and only half-listened to their exchange. She was not really heeding their words, so when they turned to include her, she forced her mind to attend.

"This is Lady Stacy Richardson," the kinder of the two girls began. "And this is Lord Nigel Stanley."

"It's a pleasure to meet you, Lady Stacy." Nigel bowed over her hand and let his gaze search her face.

Stacy, always kind, smiled with genuine warmth. The other women, watching the exchange, shared a swift glance when they noticed Nigel's besotted look. Stacy, on the other hand, only took his attention for kindness.

"I'm going to get something to eat," Beth tossed out belligerently, miffed over Nigel's attention to Stacy. The other girl said she would go with Beth.

Stacy, having been starved for hours, asked to join them. Both girls looked at her strangely but included her. Stacy made a polite farewell to Nigel, smiling at this kind stranger who was almost as tall as her husband. She had noticed that his build was slighter, and that he was quite handsome with his dark hair and mustache, but beyond that he was of little interest to her.

Trying to decide if she'd not noticed his signals or was just being coy, Nigel stood still after she left. He kept his place at the corner of the room, watching her until he saw her husband appear at her side.

Stacy was appalled over how hungry she was. The dinner hour was scheduled for no later than usual, but she felt famished. It wasn't like her to snack between meals, but when the hors d'oeuvres table was laid out, Stacy felt she could have attacked every dish.

She was on her second plateful when she popped something into her mouth that was so salty it puckered her lips. Stacy searched for something to drink, but the only thing laid out was champagne. No one was attending the table at the moment, and Stacy wasn't sure she could have spoken if she tried. In a move of desperation, she lifted a glass and downed the contents in nearly one swallow.

It didn't help in the least; in fact, Stacy thought it made things worse. Her mouth felt so dry she couldn't even swallow her own saliva. She lifted another glass and then another. Stacy was on her fifth glass when Tanner noticed her and moved in her direction.

"I thought you didn't like champagne," he commented, taking in Stacy's flushed face.

Stacy took another sip before answering. "I don't, but I ate something so salty that I had to have a drink."

Tanner watched as she finished her glass and reached for one more.

"How much have you had?"

"Quite a bit, I think." Stacy stopped speaking suddenly and giggled. Tanner, telling himself not to think of Leslie, moved away from her without warning. His intent was to get her some real food. He had only been gone a moment when Nigel appeared at her side.

"Oh, hello, Nigel. Have you had something to eat?" Stacy's voice was too loud and cheerful, but Nigel, having missed the champagne exchange, thought it was all for him.

Before he could answer, Stacy turned to look for some more food. She wavered a bit but would not have fallen; however, Nigel used her unsteadiness for an excuse and reached for her. His hands were carefully holding her waist when Tanner reappeared.

"Oh, Tanner, there you are. Have you met Nigel?" Stacy had been barely aware of his presence or his hands on her as she searched the table, but she remembered him when Tanner returned, and did not want to appear rude.

Tanner did little more than coldly nod in Nigel's direction before taking his wife's hand to lead her away. A minute later he sat her down at a table, and a plate was placed in front of her.

"Oh, Tanner, is it dinnertime? I'm so hungry."

With that Stacy began to eat with relish. She never noticed that they were alone or that Tanner, who was sitting beside her, did not have a plate. Her food was almost gone when she couldn't restrain a jaw-popping yawn.

"I'm sorry," she apologized. "I'm a little sleepy."

"Let's head upstairs."

"All right," Stacy agreed and reached for her plate.

"Leave that here."

Stacy put it down but looked longingly at the remains. Tanner thought she'd had enough so he urged her away from the table. However, Stacy reached forward at the last minute and grabbed her half-eaten roll. It was all Tanner could do not to shout with laughter as he led his beautiful, graceful, and usually dignified wife away from the party munching on a biscuit.

Once upstairs Tanner debated turning Stacy over to Rayna, but Stacy had become very preoccupied with the doors that led off of their room, and before she put herself back out in the hall or landed in a closet, he decided to put Stacy to bed himself. All went well until Tanner got to her shift, whereupon there was a gentle tug-of-war. Stacy had decided she wanted to sleep in it.

Tanner eventually let her have her way, and the moment she lay down, she curled on her side, happy as a child, and went to sleep. Tanner stood watching her for quite some time. He was certain that she wasn't even aware of the other man at the table, and he knew with a certainty that the drunkenness was an accident, but it was all so reminiscent of Leslie.

Tanner stood silently, knowing he was going to have to deal with this or ruin the entire weekend. As he stood still he remembered the way she had thrown her arms around him and with a loud declaration of 'I love you, Tanner,' given him a long, loving kiss. The only problem was that she had missed his mouth by a good inch.

Tanner began to undress himself, finally deciding not to rejoin the party. Most of the guests had been on their way to getting far more drunk than Stacy, and Tanner had no desire to join them. He slipped beneath the bedcovers and pulled Stacy against him. As sleep crowded in, his thoughts turned to Leslie one last time. Tanner pushed them away with anticipation of the hunt on Sunday.

Nineteen

THE NEXT MORNING Stacy squinted up into Tanner's grinning face, groaned, and pulled the covers over her head. She heard the laughter in his voice as he spoke.

"Aren't you going to come out and kiss me good morning?"

"My mouth tastes terrible, Tanner; you don't want me kissing you."

He laughed out loud then, and Stacy burrowed a little deeper into the mattress. Tanner sat down beside her on the edge of the bed.

"I promise not to say a word about your breath."

Stacy remained silent.

"Or the fact that you're sleeping away a beautiful morning."

Again Tanner was met with silence.

"Rayna brought you a pot of tea and toast."

The covers were slowly lowered until Stacy's eyes were peeking out.

"Did you say tea?"

In answer Tanner poured a cup and held it for her. Stacy shifted herself up against the headboard and took the cup from his waiting hand. Her first taste was a sip, but when she found the temperature to be perfect, she took a long drink before setting the cup back in the saucer with a sigh.

"I needed that."

"And I still need that kiss."

Stacy smiled and they leaned toward each other simultaneously. After they'd kissed, Tanner invited Stacy to go riding.

"I thought you were going to hunt."

"The hunt is tomorrow morning."

Stacy hid her disappointment. She had hoped that the hunt would be today and after Tanner returned, he would be ready to head home. She knew she'd made a fool of herself in front of the other guests last night, eating everything in sight and then drinking champagne as though it were water. If Tanner had gone hunting this morning, Stacy could have stayed out of sight until they were ready to leave for home.

But Tanner was already in riding clothes. Stacy mentally shrugged. At least going riding would get her away for a time. Maybe they would be alone and Stacy would have some time away from this group of strangers with whom she had yet to find something in common.

An hour later, Stacy got her wish. She and Tanner rode out, Tanner on his own horse and Stacy on a bay. They stayed away until lunchtime. To hear Jeremy Cradwell talk, Cradwell horses were the finest in the country. Stacy was not sure she believed that, but the horse she'd been given to ride was a good mount. Stacy was more pleased over having Tanner to herself than anything else.

They were just coming out into some open land when two riders approached—a man and a woman. As they neared it became obvious that one of the guests was out riding with a groom.

Tanner greeted the woman politely but impersonally. Stacy smiled at her but looked to Tanner in confusion when he let her pass with so little exchange.

"Tanner, why didn't you speak to her?"

"I did speak to her," he told his wife. "I said good morning."

"But beyond that? Why didn't you ask how she was doing?"

"Why would I do that?"

Stacy bit her lip, having a hard time believing that Tanner could be so cold to a friend.

"Stacy," Tanner went on patiently when he saw her face. "I don't even know that woman. She looks familiar, but I'm sure we've never met. Why would I speak to her?"

"Oh," Stacy said softly, wondering how she could have been so wrong. "I'm sorry. I thought she was the woman who was with you at the Royal Gardens."

It took a moment, but Tanner's eyes suddenly lit with amusement. "I'm sure you did see her at the Royal Gardens, but she wasn't with me."

"But I saw you," Stacy said softly, wanting desperately to understand.

"Yes you did, sweetheart. You saw both of us, but we were not together. I let you assume that we were, but I guarantee you we were *not*. I followed you to the Royal Gardens that day, and I can assure you I was quite alone."

Stacy's eyes rounded, but her mouth curled at the corners. "I wouldn't have thought you capable of such duplicity, my lord." Stacy's voice was dry.

"At least I don't jump to conclusions," Tanner reminded her just as dryly, and Stacy was suddenly very glad. She had thought of the woman from the garden on several occasions, hoping that she had not been painfully in love with Tanner but unable to feel sorry that she, Stacy Daniels, had been the one to marry him.

"What does that smile mean?"

"I'm not sure I should tell."

"Of course you should."

"I don't know, I read somewhere that a woman should always keep a few secrets."

Stacy heeled her mount forward on those words, so she missed the frown that momentarily covered Tanner's face before he kicked his own horse forward to join her.

After lunch, Tanner joined an afternoon round of cards while Stacy took herself off to the Cradwell gardens. Some of them were designed as mazes, and though they were interesting, Stacy soon tired of the high shrubbery walls. On her way back toward the house, she spotted what appeared to be a conservatory. Stacy walked to it with a sense of anticipation. She opened the door and called a greeting, but no one stirred or answered. Stacy went inside and closed the door, not at all unhappy to have the building to herself.

The conservatory was lavishly filled with plants and flowers. The day was cool, and the warm temperature inside felt lovely. Stacy had wandered around for the better part of 20 minutes when she heard someone enter.

"Hello," a voice called, and Stacy came out from behind a huge fern to find Lord Nigel Stanley. She couldn't remember his name but smiled kindly anyway.

"Hello."

"Having a look around?"

"Yes. Lady Cradwell has a wonderful array of plants. She even has them labeled. It's a help to me; I've never seen some of these varieties before."

Stacy spoke with her eyes on the foliage, but Nigel Stanley had eyes only for Stacy. It had taken quite a bit of following her and bolstered courage to get this close, but now that he had, he saw that she was even lovelier in the daylight than she had been the night before.

"I'm sorry," Stacy said, finally looking at the man beside her. "I can't remember your name."

Nigel hid his disappointment. "That's quite all right. I'm Lord Nigel Stanley."

"Of course. I'm sorry, Lord Stanley. I'm Lady Stacy Richardson. Are you having a nice time?"

"Yes," he returned, smiling secretly and wanting to laugh over the fact that he might not know her name. With his eyes intent on her face, he continued.

"My weekend seems to be getting better all the time. I was hoping I'd see—"

A gong rang out just then and anything else Nigel might have added was cut off.

"What was that bell?" Stacy asked.

"Oh, that's just the gong for the forage Jeremy has planned." Nigel's voice was bored, dismissive even. "I'm sure you're not interested in—"

"The forage?" Stacy spoke with surprise and started for the door. "I had no idea it was so late. I hope you enjoy the plants, Lord Stanley." Stacy added this last thought from the doorway, only just remembering her manners, amid worry that Tanner would be looking for her. In her hasty exit she never saw the way Nigel's hands balled into fists as frustration turned to rage.

Tanner was in his third garden and had just about given up locating Stacy when he heard voices on the other side of the hedge. He didn't recognize Stacy's voice or the voices of the two speaking, and was about to move off when he heard his wife's name mentioned.

"Lady Richardson?"

"Yes. I tell you Lord Stanley is smitten with her."

"Nigel? Who told you?"

"No one had to tell me. I could see it with my own eyes. Nigel *is* nice looking, but Lady Richardson would be a fool to leave a man like Tanner."

"I wouldn't mind," the other voice giggled. "If she did, I might try to hook Tanner myself."

Tanner, telling himself not to overreact, moved away to the sound of their high-pitched laughter. He came out of the hedged-in garden just as Nigel was leaving the conservatory. Tanner stood and watched him, suddenly remembering the way he'd held Stacy's waist the night before. Tanner was in the mood for a confrontation, but Nigel, without having seen the angry duke, turned and walked the other way.

Just as well, Tanner thought to himself, logic returning. *I don't think I could talk to either one of them right now.*

With that Tanner headed back to the stable. He ordered his horse and less than ten minutes later, set out on a ride, hoping to clear his head of the black thoughts that persisted.

Stacy sat in her room long after she was dressed, not going down to dinner even when she knew everyone would be sitting down at the tables. She had not seen Tanner since he went to play cards and she had gone to the gardens and the conservatory.

In truth she was now starving, but her worry of Tanner overrode her physical needs. Stacy had dismissed Rayna and was pacing on her own when he walked in. Stacy couldn't disguise her delight.

"They told me at the stables that you'd gone for a ride. Did you have a good time?"

Had Tanner not been wearing dusty riding clothes, he'd have crushed her in his arms. It had taken many miles, but Tanner had finally seen himself for a fool. It was none of Stacy's doing if a besotted young pup gawked at her. And since Stacy was as lovely as she could be, Tanner told himself he better get used to it.

"Yes," Tanner finally answered, "I did have a good ride."

Stacy stood staring up at him, her heart in her eyes.

"I'm late. Why don't you go down for dinner?"

Hungry as she was, Stacy declined. "I've waited for you."

Tanner tenderly stroked her cheek with one long finger before calling for Price. Stacy talked with Tanner as he enjoyed a quick bath and questioned her about her day.

"I didn't really care for the gardens, but the conservatory was lovely."

Tanner tried to push down the alarm he felt rising within him. "The conservatory? You were in there?"

"Oh, yes," Stacy enthused, having missed Tanner's hesitancy. "It's wonderful. I've never seen such a variety of plants and flowers."

"Were you alone?"

"Yes. Oh," Stacy suddenly thought, "no, not all the time. Lord Stanley came in, but the hour had gotten away and I wasn't able to talk to him very long."

Tanner was dressed now and moved to stand before Stacy. He looked into her guileless eyes and again called himself a fool. His own eyes lit with caring as he bent and kissed Stacy's brow and then her lips.

"Shall we go to dinner?"

Stacy nodded, wondering at Tanner's tender look even as he took her arm and escorted her downstairs.

Twenty

IT WAS WITH A GREAT DEAL OF PRIDE that the Duchess of Cambridge saw her duke off on the hunt the next morning.

Talk around the dinner table the night before had been about the hunt. Not one man, not even those jealous of Tanner's position, could find a single fault in Tanner's expertise as a hunter. Stacy had had no idea. He was, from all accounts, one of the finest shots for miles around.

Tanner took all the comments in stride, but Stacy could tell that he was pleased, and when she took time to think about it, she wasn't surprised at his skill. Stacy was starting to see that Tanner excelled at each thing he did.

With her new knowledge of Tanner's ability, and knowing that he was going to lead the hunt, Stacy wondered if the buttons on her dress would hold as she watched him ride away at the front of the pack.

Stacy felt a little lonely when all the riders had gone and the dust had died down. She glanced around at some of the women talking among themselves, but felt no warmth or effort on their part to include her. She thought about the conservatory but was, in reality, in a mood to be alone with her thoughts. After a trip to the library, she made her way up to her room and settled in with a book until lunch.

Over lunch Stacy sat with four women she didn't know and Nigel Stanley. The women talked constantly of the things they read in the London social papers, and Stacy, being in complete ignorance, stayed quiet. She noticed Nigel's eyes on her from time to time, but he was across the table and quiet himself, so Stacy finished and left the dining room as soon as it was politely possible.

She had decided on a walk, but as soon as she was outside and spotted the conservatory, she changed her mind. With everyone else still at lunch, she knew she would find it empty. Her step quickened with anticipation, even as she hoped Tanner would be returning soon and they could leave for Winslow.

Nigel could barely hold his seat or his tongue once Stacy rose and left the table. The remaining women, vulgar cows in his estimation, began to talk of her in scathing tones. They started by declaring that she was a giant, was socially inept, and wouldn't hold the duke's attention for more than six months. Nigel secretly hoped they were right about the last item.

He knew that this was his last day to declare himself. Nigel sincerely doubted they could meet at length before the party was over, but if he could only tell her he was available, she would certainly jump at the chance to meet him later. He knew very well how busy most dukes were. It was just a matter of time before Tanner began to neglect his bride, and when Stacy began to look for attention elsewhere, Nigel determined that he would be in view.

With a move as casual as he could manage, Nigel rose from the table. He would go right now and find Stacy in order to tell her of his feelings. As Nigel made his way toward the door, he deliberately pushed away all he'd seen of Stacy and her husband over the weekend—every tender glance and every loving touch. He staunchly refused to believe that the duke and duchess might genuinely care for one another.

Stacy walked slowly through the glass building, amazed at how much she'd missed the day before. She thought she'd heard someone come in the door just a moment past, but no one called out and Stacy didn't even look. Whoever it was, she knew the structure was big enough so that they could stay out of each other's way. It only took a moment before Stacy had completely forgotten that anyone had come in, making it all the more startling when Nigel suddenly appeared at her side.

"I was hoping I'd find you here."

"Oh!" Stacy gasped, her hand flying to her throat. "You startled me."

"I'm sorry," Nigel's voice was tender. "I wanted to talk with you."

"Oh." Stacy smiled now. "What did you need?"

Now that he had her full attention, Nigel found himself tongue-tied. She was so lovely and tall. He could just imagine how well she would fit in his arms.

Nigel stood mute for so long, his eyes glazed over with passion, that Stacy's smile turned into a confused frown. Seeing that frown, Nigel thought she might be thinking of leaving. He acted in haste and grabbed her hand. When Stacy gave her hand a tug, Nigel would not release her.

"Lord Stanley," Stacy began, "please let go of me."

"No."

Stacy's breath caught. "I'm a married woman," she said on a gasp.

"That's all right," he declared fervently. "I need to touch you, and now that I have I know nothing matters except the two of us."

Stacy's eyes grew round at this announcement, and she tried in earnest to regain her hand. Nigel only transferred his hold to her wrist. Stacy began to panic.

"Please, Lord Stanley—"

"Call me Nigel. I'll call you Stacy, and you can call me Nigel."

Stacy shook her head and tried to move away, but with Nigel holding her wrist, it was impossible.

"Please," Stacy tried again, fear now pounding in her chest. "You're hurting me."

Nigel dropped her wrist immediately. Stacy reached for and rubbed the offended member, and then turned to run for the door.

"Please don't go!" Nigel's voice, now strangely high-pitched, stopped her. Stacy turned to him and began to back away, suddenly afraid to take her eyes from him.

"Stay away from me," she spoke with more calm then she felt, glancing behind her to see that the door was in sight. "I'm sorry if I gave you an impression to the contrary, but I am happy in my marriage."

"I love you," Nigel told her, "and I know that you love me too."

"*No,* Lord Stanley." Stacy's calm was deserting her, and she knew she was going to make a run for the door any moment. Nigel knew it too. The next time Stacy glanced to the exit, he grabbed for her.

Stunned to be grasped and pulled against this stranger's chest, Stacy did not immediately react. But only seconds passed before she put her hands against his chest in order to push him away. Stacy, no weak thing, did manage to put some space between them, but when she threw her head back in order to gain more leverage, Nigel put his lips against her neck.

Stacy begged him to release her and struggled in earnest, but he was too strong. The blood was just beginning to pound in her ears when she heard Tanner's voice. At least she thought it was Tanner's voice—she'd never heard him so angry.

"Get your hands off my wife!"

Nigel released her, and Stacy half-fell against one of the shelves. She righted herself and looked up to see a Tanner so furious, he terrified her. He had come at Nigel and was now holding him by the lapels. As upset as Stacy was over the attack, she suddenly feared Tanner's actions more, feared he would kill this man in anger.

"Tanner, please, don't."

He spun on her, still gripping the other man and pinning Stacy to the floor with his gaze.

"Protecting your lover?" he snarled.

"No!" Stacy denied breathlessly, aghast that Tanner could ask such a thing.

"Your wife and I are in love."

Both Tanner and Stacy turned to look at Nigel. Stacy couldn't believe her ears. Tanner had dropped Nigel's coat-front, but he truly looked capable of homicide.

Stacy opened her mouth to say something, but Tanner cut her off.

"Get out of my sight, Stanley. If I ever see you again, I'll kill you."

For the first time since he entered the conservatory, Nigel pulled himself out of his dreamlike haze. He looked at the fury in the duke's eyes and actually feared for his life. He ran for the door without a backward glance.

Wanting desperately to be taken into Tanner's arms, Stacy was jolted to the core when he turned his icy gaze on her.

"Get to the house and have Rayna pack your things. You have 15 minutes to be in the coach, or I'll leave without you."

Stacy could only stare at him. She saw the clenching of his jaw, a sign of pure fury, but seemed unable to move or speak.

"Did you hear me, Anastasia?"

His voice was calm now, deadly calm. Fear spiraled through Stacy as she ran for the door herself.

Twenty-One

THE 90-MINUTE RIDE HOME TO WINSLOW was the longest of Stacy's young life. Tanner was on his horse and she was alone in the carriage with her own torturous thoughts. Shudders ran over her frame repeatedly as she thought of the way Nigel had grabbed her in the conservatory.

At one moment Stacy glanced down to see a ring of dark bruises around her wrist. It was almost more than she could take. She had been bruised and manhandled, and Tanner obviously thought she'd welcomed Lord Stanley's attention. Stacy finally curled into a ball on the seat and tried not to think about anything the rest of the way home.

Two hours after they'd arrived at Winslow, Stacy lay in a steaming tub. She had searched for Tanner for over an hour, but he was not to be found. There was no doubt in Stacy's mind that this was deliberate.

The servants, never very congenial to Stacy, were extremely remote, and after an hour of their cold treatment, Stacy had sought out Rayna and a hot bath. She was not the least bit hungry for the food Rayna brought on a tray, so Stacy soon climbed into bed. It was early, but she was feeling so weak she was not even certain she could sit up in a chair.

Sleep did not come swiftly, but even as the time stretched into hours of restless tossing and turning, Tanner did not appear. It was well after midnight before exhaustion claimed Stacy, and even then it was not a relaxing night.

Stacy did not know until morning that Tanner had not been to bed all night. Feeling more tired than she'd ever been in her life, she dragged herself from beneath the covers and moved to her dressing room. Once over the threshold, Stacy saw something that stopped her in her tracks.

"Rayna?"

"I'm sorry, my lady." There were tears in the servant's voice. "Lord Richardson said I was to pack all of your things."

Stacy's hand came to her mouth. The action was almost too much for Rayna.

"Would you like some tea, my lady?" The servant's voice broke.

"No, Rayna, thank you. Please just help me dress."

This task was accomplished in some haste, and without a word to her maid, Stacy went in search of her husband. Her legs felt weighted, as did her heart, but she had to find out what was going on.

Stacy found Tanner in his study. There had been no answer when she knocked so she was surprised to find him at his desk when she opened the door and peeked inside.

"Tanner?" Stacy spoke softly, but he did not raise his head from the papers he was studying.

Stacy was trembling, but she entered the room anyway. After closing the door she stayed by the portal, hoping he would speak or at least look up. He did neither.

"Tanner, may I speak with you?"

"Has Rayna finished with your packing?" Tanner finally looked up, but his voice was so detached that Stacy found herself preferring his anger.

"I'm not sure. Where are we going?"

"*We* are not going anywhere. You are leaving."

"Where am I going?" Stacy's voice shook, but she somehow managed the words.

"I don't care where you go."

Stacy could not believe her ears. She knew that Tanner was upset with her, but nothing could have prepared her for this.

"Tanner," Stacy's voice spoke of her hurt and bewilderment. "Can we talk?"

"There's nothing to talk about," he stated. Some anger had entered his tone now, but his voice was controlled as he went on.

"I've been a fool to actually believe you were different, but you're not. You're as faithless as other women. You're better than most with your innocent eyes and sweet smile, but you couldn't keep the pretense up forever—the very reason I never wanted another wife."

"You didn't want a wife?"

"No." Tanner had finally stood, but his voice was still calm and cold. "Lucinda would never listen to reason. I never wanted you for a wife, only for a mistress. I was a fool to have agreed. Were you only my mistress, your little meeting with Stanley wouldn't have made a bit of difference."

"Tanner, I didn't meet Lord Stanley in the conservatory. I didn't ask him to kiss me or touch me."

It was the worst thing she could have said. Mentioning what Nigel Stanley had done turned Tanner's face a dull red. He was so furious that Stacy would have fled the room, but she couldn't make her feet move.

"Get out," his voice was low with fury.

Stacy managed to turn then. Her hands were trembling on the knob, attempting to open the door, when Joffrey pushed it toward her from the other side. Stacy stepped back and stood in surprise, but Joffrey barely glanced at her as he entered the room and spoke.

"Lady Richardson's bags are ready, my lord."

"Load them in the coach." This said, Tanner returned to his desk.

Stacy stared again at Tanner's bent head.

"Please, Tanner," she whispered, knowing he heard her. "Please let me stay so we can talk about this."

He never looked in her direction. Knowing that she could not take his disapproval any longer, Stacy waited only a moment. With her stomach churning so that she feared she might be sick, Stacy walked out of the study, leaving the door open behind her. The front door was open as well, and Price stood near. Rayna appeared out of nowhere with Stacy's cloak and ushered her outside; Price followed.

"The coachman will take you wherever you wish, my lady," Price informed Stacy.

"But I can't stay here." It was more of a statement than a question.

She sounded so much like a pitiful child being driven away from home that Price had to clear his throat before answering.

"No, my lady."

"The London town house?" Stacy asked, not thinking where else to go.

"No, my lady. I'm sorry."

"I don't know where to go." Stacy knew it was not normal to discuss this with a servant, but she had no one else.

"If I might make a suggestion," Price hesitated, but Stacy only looked at him. He went on gently, "I'm sure your Aunt Lucinda would welcome you."

"Aunt Lucinda? I don't think she and Roddy are back yet."

"I'm sure their staff would make you comfortable."

Stacy looked to Rayna, who nodded, certain of their welcome. "Come into the coach, my lady. We'll go to London and see your aunt."

Stacy had no idea how she looked. There was no color in her face, and the servants had watched her sway on her feet several times. If they didn't act quickly, they'd be forced to lift her unconscious body into the coach. Price knew that even if she did faint, it would not soften the master's heart.

Stacy finally nodded. She walked down the steps and turned to look back at the home she loved. She'd never seen anything to match its beauty and grandeur. Now with only a brief look, and hoping against hope that she would see it again some day, Stacy turned back, allowing Price to assist her into the coach. Moments later they were on their way to London.

"Stacy," Lucinda called to her great-niece from the edge of the bed, waiting for her to awaken. Stacy did stir, but very slowly. Lucinda's heart broke as she watched her smile, eyes still closed, clearly having forgotten the events of the last three weeks. Lucinda wanted to break down when the smile abruptly died and her eyes opened.

"I'm sorry to wake you, dear," she spoke quickly to cover her emotions. "I thought you would want to know that Tanner is in London." Lucinda knew this was abrupt, but believed it to be best.

Stacy pushed herself into a sitting position, her eyes intent on her aunt's face.

"Did he come here?" Stacy tried to keep her voice neutral, but Lucinda caught the note of hope.

"No, dear. Roddy was out last night and saw him at their club. You were asleep when he came in, and we thought it best not to wake you."

Stacy nodded, her gaze going to a distant point across the room. Prior to the last three weeks Stacy had never known the true meaning of pain. The coach ride from Winslow to Brentwood was made in a fog of disillusionment and hurt. The honeymooners had not arrived, but just as Price had predicted, the staff welcomed Stacy and made her comfortable.

A week had passed before Roddy and Lucinda made an appearance, and although they were upset over the fact that Tanner had sent her away, they were not at all upset that she had come to them.

The entire story emerged from both sides in the days that

followed. Stacy told Lucinda and Roddy everything that transpired and then asked Lucinda point-blank what Tanner had meant when he said he'd never wanted to marry her. The telling had been hard, but Lucinda started with all she knew of Tanner's first wife, including her infidelity and death. She then told of Tanner's offer for Stacy.

It had been the hardest thing Stacy had ever faced. For months, even before she and Tanner married, Stacy had convinced herself that this man loved her but just couldn't say the words. Now she knew that the words would never come because he didn't feel them.

"What are you going to do?" Lucinda broke into her reverie.

Stacy took a deep breath. "I've decided to return to Middlesbrough. I was going to tell you today. I'd planned to write Tanner about my decision, but now that he's in town, I'll try to see him."

"Are you sure you want to go all the way to Middlesbrough, dear?" Lucinda couldn't hide the pain in her voice. "What if you had a place of your own? I haven't done anything with my house, and Roddy still has his town house."

Lucinda would have gone on, but Stacy's sweet voice stopped her. "I can't take London, Aunt Lucinda. The gossip kills me. I don't feel I can even show my face. And there is something else."

Stacy hesitated, and Lucinda stared at her.

"I think I might be pregnant."

The older woman's heart sank in her chest. "Will you tell Tanner?"

"No" was Stacy's soft but immediate reply. "I have found that I don't really know Tanner at all, but I do know that even though we've been apart, he still won't want anything to do with me. There is a remote chance that by telling him I'm pregnant I might change his mind, but knowing that he wanted me back only for the baby would put me in agony for the rest of our marriage. I'm not even positive that I am expecting, but if there is a baby and Tanner ever wants me, I want it to be for me and not because of our child." This was all said calmly, but with conviction.

Lucinda nodded throughout Stacy's explanation and when she finished, urged her to follow her heart. Stacy had grown up so much in the last months, Lucinda couldn't have been prouder. When Lucinda left the room so Stacy could dress, the feeling of pride still lingered, but so did a feeling of loss, the loss of Stacy's innocence.

Two hours later Stacy stood in front of Tanner's town house and tried to breathe normally. She was so fearful of his anger that she wanted to climb back into the coach and return to Brentwood. One thing was stopping her. Almost everything had changed in the last weeks, but there was one fact in this whole ugly mixup that had been unfailing. Stacy was still head over heels in love with Tanner Richardson.

She wished it wasn't so, but wishing was not going to change her heart. So with a feeling of doom hanging over her head, Stacy went to the door and knocked. She nearly sagged with relief when Price answered the door.

"Hello, Price." Stacy's voice was hesitant. "Is he here?" Stacy's heart had leaped into her eyes, and even knowing how Tanner was going to react, Price could not turn her away.

"He's here," Price told her and drew her inside.

"May I see him?" Stacy asked as soon as the door closed.

"He doesn't really care to be disturbed." Price attempted to soften what Tanner had actually said.

"Oh, Price, I'm sorry to put you in this position, but will you please ask him to see me?"

Price nodded reluctantly, and Stacy stood still as he moved to a door off the entryway, leaving it open as he let himself inside.

"I told you I wanted quiet." Tanner's voice was little better than a growl.

"I'm sorry, sir, but Lady Richardson is here and would like to see you."

"Well, I *don't* care to see her. Tell her to get out."

Stacy had expected nothing more, but she still felt as if she'd been slapped. She remained still until Price reappeared, again leaving the door open. The loyal servant said nothing, only looked at Stacy and felt an urge to kick his long-time master.

"Maybe I could leave a message for Lord Richardson," Stacy suggested, trying to keep her voice from shaking. Price nodded and did nothing to stop Stacy when she moved toward the open portal. Stacy halted just outside where she could see Tanner at his desk. He never looked up, but she knew he heard every word. She spoke to Price without ever taking her eyes off her husband.

"Please tell Lord Richardson that I'm taking the train to Middlesbrough to my grandfather's. Tell him that if he wants to talk with me, he only needs to send word and I'll return immediately. I don't plan to come back unless he contacts me, but, please," Stacy's voice wavered and she hesitated before going on, "please also tell him that I love him."

Stacy stood for just a moment longer, but Tanner never looked up. Price, seeing that she had gone deathly pale again, gently took her arm and led her to the door and down to the waiting coach. He saw her on her way, silently holding his own anger in check over the way Tanner had treated her. How Lord Richardson could think that Stacy was anything like Leslie was beyond him.

Price hovered nearby for most of the day, hoping that Tanner would come to his senses and go after her, but the young duke never left the house. It was with great pain that Price received word the next morning that Stacy had taken a northbound train out of London.

Twenty-Two

Middlesbrough
Six Months Later

Stacy carefully lowered herself into a chair and smiled at Elena's laughter.

"You can laugh, Elena, but I'm not sure I'm going to live through this," Stacy said good-naturedly.

"Trust me, you will. And you'll be so thrilled with the little person God gives you, you'll actually forget all of this discomfort."

"I hope you're right. I can't believe I've two weeks to go."

"You might not go that long," Elena said as she studied Stacy's huge abdomen. "You certainly *look* like the baby could come anytime."

"Tanner is a large man; maybe the baby is just big." Stacy gently rubbed her stomach as she spoke.

Watching her, Elena felt an ache beyond words for the pain Stacy had known these last months. But at the same time, she rejoiced, for it was because of that pain that she'd come to Christ. Stacy came home from London ill with grief and exhaustion. She'd been welcomed with open arms by her grandfather, and they were as close as they'd ever been, but it was to Elena that Stacy turned for comfort.

It was during some of the first days, when Stacy was beside herself with anguish, that Elena gently introduced her to the One who could fill the void in her heart and soothe the pain. In a quiet moment with both Noel and Elena present, Stacy surrendered her life and heart to Jesus Christ. She'd always heard of the death, burial, and resurrection of Jesus Christ, but she had never applied any of the facts to herself in a personal way.

Elena had pointed out in a tender way that the Bible, God's Word, says that all have sinned and need a Savior. Stacy read the Bible verses herself and realized for the first time what a supreme act of love God had displayed by sending His Son to die in her place. With a heart aching to be comforted, Stacy reached out in belief to accept Christ's gift of salvation.

"Any word from Tanner?" Elena asked gently, as she often did—not to pry, but so Stacy would know how much she cared.

"No, no word."

"Do you still write?"

"Every week."

"What do you usually say?" Elena voiced a question she'd never broached before.

"I tell him about village events and how grandfather is doing. Sometimes I talk about you and Noel and the children. I even tell him how I fill my days."

"But you never mention the baby."

"No. I've been tempted, Elena, I really have. But whenever I feel that I just *have* to tell him, I remember that he thinks I've been unfaithful. He probably wouldn't even believe that the baby is his."

"How about your newfound faith? Do you ever talk about Christ?"

"Not in so many words. Tanner can be so hard, and I'm afraid of his scorn. I'm sure he'll think I've turned into some kind of religious fanatic. I tell him I'm praying for him, but I never come right out and say I'm a new creature in Christ."

Elena nodded, thinking Stacy was the most amazing woman on earth. Elena had met Tanner Richardson only once, and now found herself having to fight the feeling that the man did not deserve a wife like Stacy. She knew that Stacy, a wonderful example to Elena, continued to show love to him even after he'd sent her away with a coldness that was frightening. Stacy's explanation of Tanner's first marriage was a great help, and although Elena didn't understand, neither did she hate Tanner. She continued to pray for him even as she was completely confused by his actions.

A sharp, indrawn breath from Stacy suddenly snapped Elena out of her musings. Elena looked over to see Stacy breathing hard, her face a mask of shock. As the contraction abated, she spoke.

"That hurt," she gasped.

Elena's voice was tender. "Yes, it does, but you really will be all right."

"I want to go home, Elena." Stacy's voice was just short of panic. "I want to see Papa."

Elena didn't answer because she was already ringing for a servant. Within five minutes Stacy was headed to Morgan, Elena by her side. Stacy had another contraction in the coach and another as she walked in the front door. Hettie was there to assist her, and her grandfather, who was almost completely blind now, hovered nearby. Elena spoke words of encouragement as they made their way upstairs, and all of them wondered if it was going to be a long day and possibly a longer night.

"She's lost a lot of blood."

The physician's voice came to Stacy as if through a fog. She wanted to open her eyes and ask whom they were talking about, but her body wouldn't obey. At least the pain was gone. Her brow furrowed when she realized she hadn't heard a baby cry. Wasn't all the pain supposed to give her a baby? Again she wanted to ask questions but couldn't seem to make herself speak. She floated on the brink of sleep for some moments before she drifted out completely.

It was a day and a half later, when Hettie was forcing water down her throat, that Stacy woke to coherency. It took a moment to find her bearings, but after just a second of awkwardness she lifted her head and drank with thirst. Hettie's eyes were suspiciously moist by the time Stacy lay back down with a sigh.

"Thank you." The younger woman's voice was little better than a croak.

Hettie had to clear her throat before she could speak in her matter-of-fact tone. "I thought we were going to lose you, love."

"My baby, Hettie." Stacy's senses were quickly returning to her, and she gave no thought to her own life. "Where is my baby?"

"He's in the cradle yonder."

"He?"

"Um hmm. A boy—the biggest I've ever seen."

"A boy." Stacy said out loud, but in her heart she prayed as a strange mixture of delight and sadness filled her.

I've given Tanner an heir, Lord. Will he ever know? Will he ever want us back? My little boy is the future Duke of Cambridge. Will the present duke ever acknowledge him?

Please give me peace. Please help me to see Your hand in all of this so I can go on and be the mother I need to be. Please cause Tanner to miss me and send for me.

A verse came to Stacy then, one from Philippians 4, exhorting believers to give up anxiety and put everything in God's care. She meditated on the words until she felt drowsy again. She would have dropped off, but the sound of a small cry brought her fully awake.

The little person in the cradle was at full volume by the time Hettie got to the cradle, lifted him into her arms, and brought him to his mother's side. Hettie jostled him gently as she spoke.

"Do you feel up to nursing, love? I've a girl here from the village, a nice clean girl named Felicity whose baby is a month old. She's let him nurse since she's plenty to spare, but I thought you might want to do it yourself."

Stacy could only stare at the longtime servant. What was she talking about? Had she really been asleep that long?

"What day is it, Hettie?"

Hettie saw the confusion in her mistress' face and kindly explained.

"The baby was born late Wednesday night and this is Friday morning. We had to get him some nourishment."

Stacy nodded, her face clearing. She wouldn't have believed she could sleep that long, but then she realized how achy her body felt. Suddenly the doctor's comment about the loss of blood made sense. The thought of another woman feeding her baby was a bit disconcerting, but she was glad someone had been found.

"Well, love," Hettie went on, "do you want to give it a go? I've no doubt you'll have plenty of milk, but it's a full commitment once you start."

Every inch of Stacy's body ached, but at the moment all that mattered was the howling infant just out of her reach. With the rise of Stacy's arm, Hettie moved. She gently laid the little lord in the crook of his mother's arm and fought tears once again.

Stacy took one look at the screaming infant and laughed. He was red with fury, his face balled up in anger, and Stacy didn't know when anything was so precious or so funny.

"Shhh," she spoke softly, laughter still filling her voice. "Don't cry, my darling. Mummy's here."

To Stacy's delight and amazement, the baby stopped crying and turned yet unfocused eyes toward her voice.

"There now," she continued tenderly. "Everything is going to be fine. Hettie and I are going to take very good care of you." Stacy spoke for a few minutes longer, but the infant's fascination with the voice was quickly overridden by hunger. Once again he began to howl.

With a bit of maneuvering Hettie helped Stacy into a position on her side so she could nurse her baby. Her body screamed at her to lie still, but she ignored its demands and stared in fascination at the child who finally lay quiet at her breast. He was beautiful, with a head full of blond hair and skin like the petal of a rose. In fact he was pretty enough to be a girl. Stacy said as much to Hettie.

"It might be better if he had been" was Hettie's negative comment.

"Why do you say that?"

"If his father gets wind of his arrival, he'll probably come and take the boy."

Hettie did not stick around after she spoke these depressing thoughts, and Stacy, who suddenly had much on her mind, was glad for some moments alone.

"What are you going to call him?"

The question came from Andrew Daniels as he sat at Stacy's bedside. After feeding the baby she had slept for a time, but now she'd had some lunch. Even though she was as yet unable to sit up, she felt much refreshed and was thrilled with her grandfather's presence.

"I was thinking on that just before I fell asleep. He's going to be Andrew." Stacy watched as a look of delight came over the old man's face. "Andrew Tanner Richardson, and I'll call him Drew for short."

Andrew cleared his throat a few times. "It's a fine name. He's a fine boy."

"He is, isn't he?" Stacy's voice held the tone of a child desperately needing approval. Again Andrew cleared his throat.

"We almost sacrificed you to have him, and I wouldn't have cared for that, but I'm glad he's here."

"Are you really glad he's here? I mean, I made such an awful mess of my marriage. I wasn't really sure you'd be pleased about my having Tanner's child."

The viscount's face tightened in anger. "The breakup of your marriage was not your fault, and I don't want to hear you say such a thing again. It's your husband who's the loser. He's got a beautiful wife and now a son, and it's *his* loss for not claiming either of you."

Stacy had grown very quiet in the midst of his anger. When the old man was done, he turned fading eyes to her face. He could barely see her, but the serenity in her gaze was unmistakable. She had changed so much since coming home and spending time with Elena. At first it had been hard for Andrew to see her turn to Elena so often, but then he watched her go from despair to hope and he could no longer find it in his heart to begrudge her the help.

And if the truth be stated, Stacy's relationship with Elena had caused no distance between her and the man who raised her. Grandfather and granddaughter were as close as they had ever been.

"Are you going to write Tanner and tell him he has an heir?" The question came after just a moment of silence, but Stacy answered immediately.

"No. I seriously doubt that his knowing would change anything, and it would only feel like one more rejection."

"But you will continue to write to him?"

"Yes. As soon as I'm on my feet again. I tried to get Hettie to take down a letter for me, but when she found out it was to Tanner, she refused."

Andrew nodded. Hettie had muttered to herself for an hour after Stacy's request, and it wasn't at all hard to figure out what had set her off. The older woman had never taken to Stacy's marrying someone from London, no matter who he was. Then when she'd met him, she thought him too good-looking and smooth to be real. Once Stacy returned to Middlesbrough, and Hettie had heard the entire story of the way she'd been sent away, dislike had turned to loathing.

Andrew's reflections were interrupted when Stacy yawned. "I'd better let you get some rest," he commented.

Stacy smiled sleepily. "I could use some sleep. Hettie said that Felicity has been wonderful, but Drew can be rather demanding and I want to continue feeding him myself." This was punctuated with yet another yawn as Stacy's eyes slid shut.

She was almost asleep when her grandfather rose to leave and was uncertain later if he tenderly touched her hair and cheek or if she only dreamed it.

Twenty-Three

MORE THAN
TWO YEARS LATER

"WOULD YOU LIKE SOMETHING, Lady Stacy?"

"No thank you, Mercy. Grandfather should be here any minute, and I'm really not hungry."

Stacy fell silent then and continued to watch her son eat. He was working on bread with jam. A cup of milk sat at his elbow, and he already sported a milk mustache. Completely unconscious of the adorable picture he presented, Drew sat staring out the kitchen window at the half-dozen ducks that waddled complacently across the grass.

"You look miles away," Mercy commented as she sat down beside Stacy and studied the younger woman's face. Stacy knew that this type of familiarity with servants was unheard of at Winslow or even at Roddy and Lucinda's, but this was all Stacy had ever known.

"I just can't believe he's two," she told Mercy with a voice of wonder. "I don't wish the months back, but I do wonder where the time has gone."

"It flies, it certainly does. Did you say Lord Andrew is going with you today?"

"Yes. Drew misses him terribly when he doesn't come to the pond, and that was all Grandfather had to hear to be convinced. Anyway, Papa claims that you don't need eyes to catch fish, only the feel of them tugging on your line."

Mercy chuckled. Having Stacy and the child with them had been like a tonic for the old viscount and his entire household. Mercy had no trouble believing that the old man would do anything the boy wished. Andrew's sight had been completely gone for months now, but his face was constantly wreathed in smiles since his great-grandson was always at his side.

"Are we ready to go then?"

Peters had led Lord Andrew into the kitchen just then, and before anyone could answer the viscount, Drew was out of his chair and running to embrace those long legs.

"Drew, you're getting jam on Grandpapa," Stacy said to her young son as she stood readying to leave.

Mercy moved toward Drew with a damp cloth. The little boy obediently removed his arms from Andrew and held his hands out for Mercy's attention. Andrew nearly protested, but he, as well as the rest of the household, had found out during Drew's first year what it had finally taken to make Stacy a fighter. She would brook no interference with the discipline of her son.

This did not make her impossible to live with; in fact, quite the opposite. Everyone concerned was thrilled with the outcome. Lord Andrew Tanner Richardson, whose status as the future Duke of Cambridge outranked everyone's at Morgan, was the sweetest, most obedient child any of them had ever encountered. He was not perfect, but Stacy dealt with all willfulness swiftly and effectively, thus showing Drew his boundaries and his mother's love.

"Well, are we ready?" Andrew asked again, peering down as though he could actually see the small child at his feet.

"Ready," Drew said and reached for Andrew's weathered hand.

Stacy led the way with the poles and then came Peters, walking a step ahead for Andrew, the older man's arm tucked in his. Drew skipped along with childish ease, chattering all the while. It was a bit of a jaunt to the pond, but he didn't seem to notice.

"I saw the ducks," Drew said to Andrew, catching his hand again.

"Did you now? How many were there?"

"I think 200."

Everyone walking to the pond smiled. It was Drew's standard number. Stacy was in the habit of saying, "I have at least 200 things to do today." So the little boy was only mimicking his mother.

Just ten minutes later the three fishermen were seated on the banks of the pond, their lines in the water. Drew's string did not have a hook on the end, which was for everyone's safety, but he was quite serious about fishing nevertheless. He had appointed himself as guardian to his grandfather and the older man's hook and line. His own pole was poised over the water, but he spent all of his time watching for a tug on Andrew's line.

"I think I've got one," Stacy called just a few minutes after her pole went into the water.

"Oh, Mumma," Drew jumped with excitement, dropping his own pole. "Can I help? Can I?"

"May I," Stacy corrected automatically, "and, yes, you may. Here you go." She passed him her pole and kept her hands ready to assist. She laughed out loud when Drew couldn't lift the heavy catch from the water and ended up backing up the bank and dragging the poor dying fish from the pond.

"Drew." The little boy had no more finished with Stacy's fish when Andrew needed him. Drew was swift to attend. So that her grandfather could enjoy the moment, Stacy, out of habit, quietly described everything she was seeing.

They fished on in such a fashion for more than an hour, until Peters came to retrieve Drew. It was the boy's naptime and indeed he was beginning to flag. They had talked that morning about the fact that Drew would go to nap with Peters that day, but still there was some protest.

"No, Mumma, not yet."

"Drew." Stacy's voice was stern without being loud. "You will go with Peters immediately, and you will not fuss about it!"

Drew stood for just a moment, and Stacy watched a look of acceptance come over his face. She spoke again. "Kiss Grandpapa and then come and kiss me."

Drew did as he was told, and just moments later he was skipping off with Peters, chattering fifteen to a dozen. The two remaining fishermen were quiet for a time, but Stacy was fairly certain she knew what her grandfather was thinking. She was correct of course, and when he spoke, it was confirmed.

"You should have let the boy stay."

"I appreciate your not saying that in front of Drew, but you're wrong. He needs his nap."

Andrew chuckled. "I wouldn't have believed anything could change you so much, but becoming a mother certainly has."

"I will admit that becoming a mother alters everything, but the greatest changes in me have little to do with motherhood."

"You mean this thing between you and God?" Andrew's skeptical voice spoke volumes.

Stacy sighed very quietly. Her grandfather refused to believe that a person could have a personal relationship with God or his Son, but at least he was talking. This was the first time he'd brought the subject up. Stacy was usually the initiator, and when she did talk of her beliefs Andrew changed the subject very quickly. Seeing an open door for the first time, Stacy chose her words carefully.

"I believe the Bible, God's Word, to be true. And in His Word, I've read how much I mean to God and how much He wants to mean to me. My belief is a choice, Papa, one that I'm more than satisfied with."

"What about the church?" It was a sore subject between them.

"The bishop never has answers to my questions," Stacy explained as she had before. "I don't think he studies the Bible at all. I haven't given up on the bishop, but it concerns me that he only stares at me in dismay when I ask questions and tells me that I must not take the Bible too literally. Well, that's absolute rubbish." Stacy's voice was very earnest, but not accusing or angry. "Noel and Elena have spent enough time in God's Word to help me. If they don't have an answer to my questions, they at least know where to look.

"The Bible is our standard and if we shift our foundation, we're going to fall. It was in the Bible that I read that because I was a sinner without a Savior, I was headed to a lost eternity. But I've now met that Savior, and I know where I'm headed.

"I love you, Papa, but I think the very reason you argue with me is that you're afraid. You have no peace about your eternity, and that terrifies you; it would me also. I have peace, and if you would let me read the verses to you, I could show you how to have it too."

"Does your Bible also teach you how to speak disrespectfully to your elders?"

Stacy wanted to cry, but now was not the time. She hadn't been disrespectful, and they both knew it. Her voice was gentle when she went on, and unbeknownst to her, somewhat defeated.

"I'm sorry if you find me disrespectful, but if that's all you got out of what I just said, I'm even more sorry for what the future holds for you."

A heavy silence fell between them, and Stacy prayed. She asked God to give her patience and not to say things that would antagonize her Papa or drive him further from the truth. She loved him so much, and it was at times like this that she had to remind herself that God loved him more.

You are not the one who saves, Stacy, she said to herself.

"I'm ready to go in now," Andrew said then.

"All right," Stacy answered simply and rose to help him. In the past she would have apologized for what she said, but just in the last few days she had realized that was a mistake. She needed to be bold for Christ. She had spoken the truth, and she couldn't possibly be sorry for that.

That her grandfather expected an apology was more than obvious by the time they arrived at the house. He stood just inside the kitchen, his face turned toward her, a look of confused anticipation in his eyes. Stacy did not satisfy him.

"Would you like me to get Peters or ask Mercy to fix you something?"

Andrew was silent for a moment, and Stacy knew he would opt to go to his room.

"Peters, please." His voice was low, and Stacy had all she could do not to throw her arms around him and beg his forgiveness. It was so hard to admit that the man you have always loved and respected was wrong. She swiftly moved from the room before she could change her mind.

"Does Grandpapa love Jesus?"

Stacy smiled. It was bedtime, and Stacy had just read Drew a Bible story about Jesus and His disciples. What a question to come from her son the very day she'd laid things on the line to her grandfather!

"I'm not certain how he feels right now, Drew, but we can pray that he'll understand how much God loves him."

"God loves me."

"Yes, He does," Stacy agreed and wrapped her arms around his sturdy little form.

He was the image of his father, and at times it pained Stacy to look at him. He was tall for his age, which was no surprise, and other than Stacy's straight, thick, honey-blonde hair, he was every inch Tanner Richardson's child.

Because Drew lived in a houseful of adults, his speech habits and vocabulary were rather advanced. She read to him from the Bible every night and was amazed at how much he retained, and how excited he became whenever Jesus was in the story. Stacy believed his understandng of the Scriptures was a gift from the Lord.

It had been a temptation to sugarcoat the truth of Christ's death and resurrection, but Stacy had not yielded. She knew well that this was the foundation of all she believed. The sooner Drew understood, the sooner he could make his own decision and commit himself to Christ. Stacy prayed for his belief every day as she did for her grandfather's and everyone else's at Morgan.

She also prayed for Tanner. She asked God to prepare his heart for acceptance. Stacy was beginning to believe that she would never see him again, but still she prayed. Each and every time she considered writing about Drew, she knew it would be a mistake. But at some point Stacy knew she needed to explain to Tanner about what had happened to her concerning Jesus Christ.

Tanner had always been cynical about things concerning the church, something that had never bothered Stacy before to any great degree, but now it made her fearful of how he would respond to her beliefs. "Religious fanatic" was sure to be the nicest thing he would have to say.

The thought gave Stacy no peace, and she wrestled inside of herself often as she tried to give her husband to the Lord. At times she would lie in bed and dream about their first weeks together, when he made her feel treasured and cherished. Stacy ached for her husband's love, but knowing how godless their life had been cast something of a damper on her memories.

Tonight as Drew fell asleep, Stacy remained by his bed and let herself remember. After a time she prayed.

"Please save Tanner, Father, and bring us back together. I know You love him, and I believe You would want us to raise Drew together. How long do I wait, Lord? He never acknowledges my letters. I know unless he sees him, Tanner will never believe Drew is his son, but You can work this out, Lord. You can move in hearts and lives so that Your will is done and You are glorified."

The day ended, but Stacy's faith and hope did not. Days and weeks passed. She continued to pray, committing her life and loved ones to God. But time moved on, and before Stacy's eyes she watched her son blossom toward his third year. At the same time, she watched her grandfather wither as he approached his last.

Twenty-Four

DREW GALLOPED ALONG BESIDE HIS MOTHER on the way to the pond, pausing now and then to inspect a stone or watch a bird. It took some time, but eventually he turned and noticed that Peters was not following with his grandfather.

"Where's Grandpapa?"

Andrew had not fished with them for several weeks, but Drew still asked after him every time they went.

"He wanted to rest today." Stacy's line was becoming standard. "We can go to his room as soon as we're done, however, and show him our catch."

Drew seemed content enough with this, and Stacy was glad when he did not chatter on. Her grandfather's ill health was a source of great concern for her these days, and some quiet hours at the pond were just what she needed. However, Drew had other ideas. He was quiet only until he remembered the special event of the next day.

"Are we going to have cake?"

Stacy smiled. He knew they were because Mercy had talked of nothing else for days, but she answered him anyway.

"Yes, we're having cake."

"And surprises?"

"Surprises too."

"When?"

"Oh, maybe a little bit all day."

"I'll be two."

"No, you're two now. Tomorrow you'll be three."

"Please show me the fingers."

Stacy placed her pole on the ground and used both of her hands to carefully position Drew's tiny fingers until three stood in the air.

"This is three," he stated.

"That's right. Tomorrow you'll be three."

"How old are you?" the small boy suddenly asked.

"Very old," Stacy told him with a twinkle in her eye.

"Two hundred?"

Stacy laughed and grabbed for him. She tickled him and laughed at his small giggles until they both lay spent on the ground. After just a moment Drew heaved a great sigh and sat up in order to peer down into his mother's face.

"I love you, Mumma."

"I love you, Andrew."

"I'm Drew."

"I love you, Drew."

The little boy smiled, and Stacy smiled in return. They didn't fish again for a time because Drew wanted to hear a story. Stacy told him all about Noah and the ark God told him to build. Before Stacy could finish naming the animals that came two by two, her almost three-year-old had fallen asleep in her arms.

"It's a train, Grandpapa! Look at it, look at it."

Drew shoved his favorite birthday present into his great-grandfather's hands and waited for him to respond. They were sitting around the fire in the main salon, for Morgan was cold until midsummer.

"Well, now," Andrew spoke with proper seriousness. "An engine. Who's going to drive this fine train?"

"Me," Drew nearly shouted and proceeded to make the sound of a train so his great-grandfather would be convinced.

"And who will you take on your train?"

"Mumma and Mercy and Hettie and Peters."

"What about Grandpapa?" his mother wanted to know.

"Oh, yes!" Drew shouted as he climbed into the old man's lap, never seeing his grimace of pain. "Grandpapa will be up in the engine with me, won't you, Grandpapa?"

"Of course I will." Andrew's voice sounded strong, the only thing that kept Stacy from removing her son from his lap. Drew was not a tiny child any longer, and Stacy knew how frail her grandfather's legs had become. His color was better today, however, and Stacy took that as a sign of hope. Just four nights past he'd labored for breath for several hours. They had thought it the end.

"What else did you receive?" Andrew asked of Drew.

The child named a few items, but his concentration was on his train and he didn't really answer. Believing that respect was important, Stacy would have said something, but her grandfather looked so content to have Drew now leaning against him and playing with his train that she went ahead and told him herself.

"He received a pair of long britches from Hettie. They're dark brown and fit him perfectly. A red flannel shirt came from Mercy. It's trimmed with brown cord and looks wonderful with the trousers. Peters gave him a wooden whistle, and Noel, Elena, and the children gave him the train. The train is red with black wheels and trim and printed on the side are the words 'London and Birmingham.' I bought him a new comb, and I knitted him an afghan for his bed. It's every shade of green and quite large—wide enough to cover his entire bed."

This said, Stacy placed the edge of the blanket in her grandfather's lap so he could feel the weave. Drew had moved to the floor, so Andrew took a moment to handle the blanket.

"Very soft," he approved. "You always do nice work."

"I'm glad you think so, because I'm working on one for you."

"Do I have to wait for my birthday?"

"No. I'm over half done; you should have it sooner than that."

Andrew nodded. "Drew?" he spoke softly.

"Yes, Grandpapa?"

"Come up here a minute. I want to give you my present."

The word present was enough to shift Drew in a hurry. He put his train aside, and by the time he stood before Andrew he was squirming with excitement.

"This gift belonged to me when I was just your age. I'm going to give it to you, and I want you to take very good care of it. Do you promise?"

"Yes, Grandpapa."

Stacy had no idea what the gift would be, and both she and Drew grinned in delight when Peters suddenly appeared with a child's wooden rocking chair.

"Oh, Mumma," Drew exclaimed. "It's for me!" With that he plopped his small bottom into the seat and began to rock. His mother's voice came to him very softly, but with warning.

"Andrew."

"Oh," he jumped from the chair and moved to Andrew. "Thank you, Grandpapa. Thank you for the rocking chair."

"You're welcome. Does it fit you?"

"I fit," he told him and sat back down to prove it, even though the old man couldn't see.

Watching her grandfather, Stacy felt something tug inside of her. He suddenly looked older and more tired than Stacy had ever seen him, but there was also a contentment about him. Stacy wondered if maybe the rocking chair had been quite special to him and giving it to Drew, his only great-grandchild, was more significant than any of them realized.

"I believe I'll rest now," Andrew told them and stood to go. Drew hugged his legs before he got away, and Peters began to lead him from the room.

"I'll bring you a tray later," Stacy called to him.

"All right," he said and kept walking. Stacy watched, unable to decide if he was moving more stiffly or not. She prayed then as she always did that he would understand his need for Christ while there was still time. Her prayers had been increasing lately and held a special urgency. It seemed clear that Andrew's time with them was coming to an end.

Two days later, in the middle of the night, Peters wakened Stacy from sleep. She had been dreaming about Tanner and Drew, and her first thought was for her small son.

"Is it Drew?"

"No, Stacy. Your grandfather is asking for you. He's having trouble breathing again."

Stacy's wrapper went around her as she ran, and within seconds she was at her grandfather's bedside.

"I'm here, Papa," Stacy said and watched his eyes open. She knew the lamplight made no difference to him, so she turned the wick higher in order to see him.

"Stacy" was all he said before staring sightlessly in her direction.

"I'm here, Papa. Don't try to talk."

The old man's eyes closed, his breathing labored on. Stacy's own breath came in gasps as she realized he might be slipping away before her eyes. Suddenly his eyes opened.

"I need to tell you something."

"Please don't try to talk," Stacy begged him, thinking he needed to conserve his strength.

"I talked to God, Stacy. For the first time, I really talked to God. I've lived my life for myself, but when I almost died last week, I knew I wasn't ready to meet Him. I think I took care of it, but tell me again, Stacy. Tell me how you come to God."

Stacy's voice shook with emotion and she didn't know how she would speak, but the words came. "The Bible says believe on the Lord Jesus Christ and you will be saved, Papa. I simply told God that I need to be saved from my sins and that I believed His Son could save me. I asked Him to be the Lord of my life."

Andrew's eyes closed again. "It's taken care of then. I was certain that it was, but I needed some reassurance from you. I'm not afraid to die now. I wish I could be here with you and Drew for years to come, but my body is tired and I'm not afraid to go. God will take care of both of you. I'm sure of that for the first time."

"It might not be time, Papa." Stacy was so overcome with emotion she could barely talk. "Just rest now. I'll be here."

The old man nodded and slept for nearly an hour. Stacy sat in a chair right by his side, her heart so full she could hardly move. Her grandfather had come to Christ! Her heart was overflowing with thanksgiving. She wanted to shout and dance.

He's Yours now, Lord. I would love to have more time with him, but even if tonight is the night, he's Your child and You've given us both your peace. Stacy, whose throat was clogged with tears, couldn't pray anymore. She sat trembling, half with fatigue and half with joy, her heart too full to form thoughts.

Stacy had just began to doze when Andrew woke. He asked Stacy to read to him. She chose the Twenty-third Psalm, a psalm she'd read all her life, but one that had taken on new meaning in the last three and a half years. She was now certain it would be new to her grandfather as well.

She read and then prayed, and Andrew listened as best he could. The night moved on in such a manner—Andrew and Stacy dozing for a time and then waking to share the Scriptures again and again. Andrew said little through this, speaking only once to thank her for showing him the way, to tell her of his love and to ask her to tell Drew of his love also.

In her exhausted, emotional state, his words were almost more than Stacy could bear, but she praised God for hearing them since this was in fact Andrew's last night with her. He fell asleep just before dawn, and this time he did not waken.

❦ ❦ ❦

Stacy had no more than let Drew finish his breakfast before she scooped him up and headed to the pond. She sidestepped all of his questions concerning his grandfather and didn't really start to talk to him until they were seated by the big willow that sat at the edge of the water.

"Where are the poles?"

"We're not going to fish today, Drew. I need to talk with you."

"We can't show Grandpapa our catch."

"No, we can't, but our having a talk is more important right now." Stacy stopped then. Where to start? He was so little, but she knew he had to be told. He was much too aware of Andrew's movements to hope that he wouldn't notice or miss him.

"I talked with Grandpapa last night, and he told me something wonderful," Stacy began as Drew sat in her lap and looked trustingly into her eyes. Her voice wobbled only slightly, but she continued. "Grandpapa told me he loves Jesus. Isn't that wonderful?"

"We love Jesus too. And God," Drew told her with big eyes.

"Yes, we do," Stacy said with a smile, knowing he did not yet understand that God and Christ were one.

Stacy glanced up at the tree, wondering how she should continue. She had to tell Drew that his Grandpapa was gone, and she simply didn't know how.

"I think that fish is dead."

Stacy's head snapped down in surprise. She thought he'd been watching her, but she now saw that his attention had begun to wander. Stacy's own eyes drifted to the dead fish that floated on the water, and suddenly she had the words.

"How do you suppose that fish died?"

"I don't know," Drew answered, his eyes intent on the already decomposing fish.

"Things do die, don't they, Drew?"

"Um hmm. Mercy and I saw a dead mouse in the kitchen."

"I remember that. Drew," Stacy called his name and waited for him to turn to her, "people die too. Did you know that?"

The small boy didn't answer, but only stared at her. The subject was new to him.

"Everything dies—mice, fish, and even people, but when that happens we know that it's all a part of God's plan. He gives life, and He says when it's time for someone or something to die."

Stacy hesitated. Drew still watched her. Tears filled her eyes when she said the next words. Drew had never seen his mother cry.

"Grandpapa died this morning, Drew. His body was old and tired, and God said it was time for Grandpapa to leave this earth. Before he died though, he told me he loved Jesus, and that's why I'm certain God took him to heaven to be with Him.

"He also told me that he loves you, but that he knows and trusts that God is going to take care of you and me. We won't have Grandpapa here with us anymore, Drew, but God is going to take care of us."

It was not surprising that Drew had no questions. She knew that much of what she said had been too old for him, but she would just keep telling him and reassuring him until he understood.

Stacy had already thought out the aspect of Drew seeing Grandpapa's body and decided she would not subject him to that. The man he knew—the loving, alive, vibrant man—was gone. She saw little or no point in showing Drew his cold, white, earthly shell.

They took a long walk before going back to Morgan. In that time Drew did not mention his great-grandfather. Not until he was going down for a nap did he say he wanted to see him. Stacy had to remind him that the old man was gone, and Drew cried because he wanted his grandfather and didn't understand why his mother would keep him away.

Stacy allowed him his tears and lay next to him long after he slept. Stacy's own tears finally came. Not a torrent, because her wonder and joy over Andrew's salvation was too wonderful for it to be a time of complete sadness. She joined Drew in his nap while she was still praising God for His saving love.

Twenty-Five

THE MOURNERS AROUND THE GRAVE were few. Andrew Daniels was an old man, and many of his friends had passed on before him. The bishop was present, but Stacy had asked Noel to officiate the ceremony. He did a wonderful job, and Stacy nearly broke down several times as Noel honored and praised God for His love and mercy. That, as well as the way Drew's little hand clung to her own, made her aware of just how vulnerable Drew was right now. She felt him tremble at times.

She knew that this had little to do with the actual death, because he did not fully understand the word, but his world had been turned upside down with the "disappearance" of his great-grandfather, as well as the appearance of strangers in the forms of Roddy and Lucinda.

They were positively taken with the child, but he was still feeling a bit overwhelmed with the events of the last days to get overly close to them. They wisely did not push their attention on him, but Lucinda broke down on several occasions over what she exclaimed was the most precious child in all the world. Such actions were unusual for her, but Stacy believed it had much to do with the passing of her brother.

Everyone gathered back at Morgan when the funeral service was over. The staff was visibly upset, but all rallied and prepared a large meal for the mourners. Stacy acted as hostess, seeing to it that all were comfortable. It never occurred to her to have someone else take over. Lucinda would have been the logical choice, but she was too distraught to do much of anything.

At one point, when there was a lull in the activities, Stacy and Elena found themselves alone. They embraced warmly.

"Did Noel tell you about Papa's decision?" Stacy asked.

"Yes." Elena's eyes were glowing.

"Oh, Elena." Stacy's voice was awed, her own eyes wide with wonder and joy. "I've been selling my Lord short. I never dreamed He would save Papa so near the end, but He did. I already miss him so much, but God has given me such a peace that I can hardly—"

Stacy had to stop. Sometimes words weren't necessary between close friends; this was such a time. Elena hugged Stacy again before they finally made themselves comfortable and really began to talk.

"Roddy and Lucinda have already talked to me about coming back to London with them."

Elena nodded. "Roddy spoke with Noel. What are you going to do?"

"I'm not sure yet. The thought of leaving you is dreadful, but what if this is God's way of repairing my marriage? I know that Tanner is never going to come here; he's had over three years to prove that. Maybe if I was back in London, he'd want to see me."

"And that's what you want?" There was no censure in Elena's tone, only caring.

"As frightened as I am of Tanner, I would like my marriage back. I would desperately love for Drew to know his own papa. When Lucinda mentioned our coming to live with them, she also offered to get us a place of our own if we preferred that, so I know we'll be taken care of. I just don't want to do anything that's going to be harmful to Drew. Tanner can be so hard, and the London gossips can be ruthless."

"You could always give it a try," Elena told her.

"What do you mean?"

"I mean that Noel, the children, and I are going to move here to Morgan just as we all decided, but Noel would never get rid of our place. It's not very big, so if things don't work out for you and Drew in London, you can move back here, either to Morgan or our house."

"Oh, Elena" was all Stacy said. Such a thought had never occurred to her. For weeks now she'd prayed about some way to open a door between her and Tanner, and now this might be it. She knew she was going to have to be the one to reach out, and although her faith was small concerning the outcome, she was willing to try.

The image of Tanner's angry face, as he'd been in the conservatory and then at Winslow the day he'd sent her away, flashed through her mind. The fear she felt took her breath away.

"Stacy, what is it?" Elena had watched her pale.

"I was thinking of Tanner. He still has the power to terrify me, but I've got to do this, Elena. I don't know how I'll be when we're finally face-to-face, but I've got to try to save my marriage."

"It's going to be all right, Stacy." Elena's voice was soothing. "I've already gotten a letter off to Sunny about Andrew's death, knowing you would be too upset to write. You've had lots of contact with her in the last few years, and I know she'll be there for you if you return.

"I certainly can't predict what Tanner will say, but knowing that Sunny will be there, a sister in Christ, comforts me over your leaving."

"In all the uproar, I'd forgotten about Sunny and Brandon," Stacy admitted. "It does make it easier to go, knowing how close they live."

"So you think you'll be back at Winslow?"

Stacy nodded. "I don't know why, and I don't think it will be easy, but, yes, I think I will end up back at Winslow. The only thing that would stop me is if Tanner refuses to let Drew come with me. If that happens I'll return here."

"Drew is the image of his father. How could he turn him away?"

Stacy's smile was sad. "By not seeing him at all. You don't know Tanner, Elena. He can be very hard. He thinks I've deceived him, so I dare not hope that he will even want to see Drew."

Elena could only stare at her. This had never occurred to her. Stacy didn't notice her look. Her mind was running from one person to the next. First she saw Drew, and then she saw Tanner.

If it comes down to proving Drew's parentage, Stacy thought, *I won't need to say a word. Tanner need only see his son's face.*

"I won't let her tell me no, do you hear me, Roddy? I tell you I won't leave here without them."

Roddy did not answer from his place in the bed, but continued to lean against the headboard and watch his wife's agitated movements. Her voice wobbled with unshed tears.

"I had no idea they had so little. Did you see the furniture in the salon? It's a mess. All this time they've been living like paupers, and I've had so much." Lucinda broke down then just as she'd been doing for days.

"Come on, Cinda," Roddy called to her and pulled the covers back on her side of the bed. Lucinda moved with leaden steps and climbed in, sobbing all the while.

"Did you see Stacy's dress?" Lucinda wailed as Roddy pulled the covers around her. "It's one from her wedding trousseau. She hasn't had anything new in all this time. I just can't stand it." The tears increased for a time before subsiding into huge shuddering breaths. Roddy waited for just such a time to speak.

"I think Stacy will come with us."

"You do?" Lucinda's voice held hope.

"Yes, especially if you let me handle it. Now, don't be hurt," Roddy added when he felt her stiffen in his arms. "Stacy and I have always been able to talk, and I think she will be honest with me. If you really want her and Drew to come home with us, you'll let me handle it."

"I do, Roddy. I desperately want them to come." All anger had drained from Lucinda in the light of wanting Stacy and Drew with them. Lucinda was willing to try anything.

"I do also, but there are some things we need to talk about." Roddy paused before going on firmly. "Lucinda, you must let Stacy mourn as she wishes."

"What do you mean?"

"I mean, no balls, no teas, and no shopping unless she wishes to do so. This will be nothing whatsoever like her first visit. She's been married and now has a child. The growing up she's done in the last three and a half years is remarkable.

"Since we've arrived, I've watched how she handles Drew. A more devoted mother I've yet to see. Carlson has talked to the servants here at Morgan and tells me that motherhood is what it took to make Stacy bold. She will brook no interference with the way she raises her son, and from what I can see she needs no outside help.

"Cinda, you must examine why you want them to come with us. If it's to play mother to that boy, then it won't work; he's already got a mother. If it's to mother Stacy or run her life, then it still won't work. She doesn't need a mother or anyone to tell her what to do. She needs a friend with a listening ear, even if you don't agree with all her decisions."

Lucinda stared up into her husband's face. He knew her so well. She did like to run other people's lives and took it for granted that they wanted her to, but Roddy was right about Stacy. She was a different person now. She'd even gone to calling them by their Christian names without using aunt or uncle. It was yet another sign of her maturity.

Lucinda suddenly realized that it had been Stacy who had been the pillar of strength for everyone at the funeral and then downstairs in the large salon. This young woman, whose only parent-figure had just died, was the one to see that all were taken care of and comforted in this time of loss. She had become an independent and capable woman in her own right. Lucinda wasn't certain that she was even needed, but she still wanted Stacy and Drew with them more than she could say.

"What if Tanner wants her back?" Lucinda voiced the thought as soon as it surfaced.

"Then that will be her decision." Roddy returned logically. "It doesn't seem likely. They've had no contact and he hasn't even asked about her in all these years, but nevertheless, Stacy will make her own choice and we will support her no matter what."

Lucinda sighed. Again he was right.

"Will you speak with her in the morning?"

"Yes, as soon as I'm able."

Lucinda was quiet for a time. "Is my face all puffy?"

"It's just terrible. I can barely stand to look at you."

Lucinda tried not to smile, but it didn't work. "I love you, Roddy."

"I know," he said with a wide, cheeky grin. "And you know the feeling is quite mutual."

Hearing those words, Lucinda sighed again, this time with pure contentment.

"Uncle Roddy and I would like to talk. Can you find Mercy and see if she needs some help?"

"I want to stay here," Drew told his mother.

Stacy glanced over his head at Roddy, who was sitting patiently across from her in the library. She didn't want to send Drew away because he wouldn't understand and he'd been rather clingy that morning. Stacy understood completely; still, she did want to speak with Roddy.

"Why don't you see what Aunty Lucinda is doing?"

"Aunty Lucinda cried."

"Yes, she did. But she's not crying now. She would be very happy to see you."

"You can ask to see her jewelry. It's very pretty," Roddy put in. Even though Drew was considering the idea, he was clearly not convinced. To Stacy's relief, Mercy chose that moment to ask Drew to test some cookies in the kitchen.

"Can I bring some in here?" Drew wanted to know before he left.

"In a while," Mercy told him while Stacy was still trying to frame a reply.

"All right," he said, but he didn't look very happy. Stacy gave him a silly smile on his way out the door that wrung a small laugh from him just before he disappeared from view.

"He's a fine boy, Stacy."

"Yes, he is," she agreed, her eyes still on the closed portal. "He's more precious to me than I can say."

"You've done a good job with him."

"It's a lot of work, but he's a delight to be with."

They fell silent for just a moment, Stacy wanting to tell Roddy that she and Drew would come to London but waiting in case he and Lucinda had changed their minds about the offer.

"I think you know what I want to ask you, since we've already talked of it," Roddy began, "but before you give an answer, I want to tell you a few things. I've reminded Lucinda that this will not be like your first visit. We are not going to take over your life or Drew's life. We want you to come and stay as long as you like, but we aren't going to parent you; we realize you don't need that."

Stacy smiled so widely that Roddy stopped.

"What are you thinking?" Roddy's eyes widened comically in mock anticipation.

"I was going to tell you, yes, I would like to come, but then I was going to ask you if Lucinda realized that it would be different this time." Stacy's voice was so relieved that Roddy laughed.

"She'll be thrilled with your answer, Stacy, as I am."

"I appreciate the offer, Roddy. It feels as though we've been thrown a lifeline." Stacy paused then and went on slowly. "But there is something you should know. I'm hoping above all hope that if I return to London, Tanner will be willing to see me. He certainly hasn't been an exemplary husband, but if there is hope for my marriage, I'm willing to try. I would also like Drew to know his papa."

"Have you ever told Tanner about him?"

"No. I'm sure you understand why."

"Indeed, I do. It doesn't matter to us why you're coming; we just want you there." Roddy stopped for a moment and looked unsure. Stacy understood his expression when he continued.

"I see Tanner now and then, and I'm sorry to say that he's never asked about you. Please don't get your hopes too high, my dear."

Stacy sighed deeply, but it was no more than she expected. "Thank you, Roddy. If the truth be known, I'm feeling rather pessimistic about the whole thing. If at any time I feel there is any threat to Drew, I'll leave immediately, but I must try. For the sake of Drew and my marriage, I must try."

"Lucinda won't be thrilled, but I know she'll stand by you."

Stacy thanked Roddy, but beyond that she didn't reply. She knew that should they disagree on some issue, she was finally ready to face her aunt without fear, but she wasn't so confident about her husband. The thought of his anger was still enough to make her physically ill.

Twenty-Six

LONDON

"I'VE GOT NO BUSINESS running halfway across the country at my age."

Stacy ignored Hettie's grumbling just as she'd done for the last hour. They were all exhausted from the train ride and even though Stacy had told Hettie to leave the unpacking for the next day, she refused. Stacy was going to give the other woman just a few minutes more, and then she would shoo her out so Drew could sleep.

The train ride had seemed endless. Saying goodbye to Elena and the staff at Morgan had been a draining experience. Stacy half-believed that she would be with them again soon, but leaving the security of their love and heading into a future that was all a mystery had hurt.

At least Stacy had Hettie along. Hettie was not the easiest person to live with, but she loved Stacy and Drew to distraction, and she never said a critical word concerning Stacy's faith in Christ. This had not been the case with Peters or Mercy. Both of them had struggled with the change in her. It had taken Stacy quite some time to finger the reason, but she eventually deduced that her conversion was threatening to them. Things eased after a time, but neither one was open to the gospel.

Now she was in London. No real doors, not even on the train, had opened up for Stacy to talk with Roddy or Lucinda, but Stacy hoped that even if they disagreed, they would take on Hettie's attitude and not Mercy's.

Thinking of Mercy right then made Stacy want to weep, a sure sign that she was too tired. Drew had eaten and was now playing with his train, but she could see that he was drooping. Fighting the urge to bathe him, she decided to put him to bed immediately. With surprisingly little fuss she convinced Hettie to abandon her unpacking, and within minutes Drew was tucked up for the night, with Hettie going to bed as well.

Stacy bathed herself, pleased to have Rayna assisting her after three and a half years apart. In a reasonably short time, Stacy was ready for her own bed. She'd made one final check on Drew and wasn't at all surprised to find Hettie on the sofa in his room. She had a room of her own, but old habits die hard, and Hettie was used to guarding over Drew like a mother bear with a cub.

It was with a smile that Stacy finally placed her head on her own pillow, able to hear the old woman snoring all the way from Drew's room. Just before sleep came, however, Stacy's thoughts turned to Tanner. She tried to push them away, but didn't succeed. In her dreams she was almost certain that she could feel his arms surrounding her.

"Andrew Tanner Richardson, *what* are you doing?" Stacy asked her son two mornings later.

"Sliding. Aunty Lucinda said I could."

Stacy turned unbelieving eyes to her aunt, who was standing nearby. "Did you really give him permission to slide down the banister?"

"Yes," Lucinda answered meekly and then hurried on excitedly. "It really is all right. There aren't many things for Drew to play with here, and I really don't mind."

"Lucinda." Stacy's voice had turned patient. "The buttons on some of his trousers will scratch the handrail."

Lucinda shrugged helplessly, looking much like a child caught in the act. "I want\him to have fun, Stacy, and that's difficult in a houseful of adults."

"He has never known anything but a houseful of adults," Stacy reminded her aunt, and stared at her until she nodded. She then turned to Drew.

"You may slide down the banister. But," Stacy added when his face lit and he started toward the stairs, "an adult must be with you, and you must be wearing the right pants."

"Are these?" Drew shoved his stomach out until it seemed he would topple. Stacy hid a smile.

"Yes."

The word was no more out of Stacy's mouth when Drew went charging for the top of the stairs. Both she and Lucinda watched as he slid down the banister, giggling all the while. He was allowed to slide four more times, and then it was time for breakfast.

Roddy, Lucinda, Stacy, and Drew all ate together in the small dining room. The day before, their first real day at Brentwood, had been very low-key with meals taken in their rooms. This was the first meal where Drew had eaten with his elders. Roddy and Lucinda were so fascinated by Drew's manners and eating habits that they barely talked to Stacy.

It was at this time that Stacy realized they would never have grandchildren; Drew was as close as they would ever come. She suddenly saw her son through their eyes. He was immeasurably precious to her, but in the eyes of a "grandmother," he was a treasure without equal. A treasure who could slide down the banister and even scratch it, play in her expensive jewels, or eat chocolates for breakfast. A treasure who never really did anything wrong, at least not intentionally.

"Aunty Lucinda."

"Yes, my darling."

"I don't like red grapes."

Stacy was proud of the way Lucinda opened her mouth, closed it, and looked to her without answering.

"I want you to eat your grapes, Drew," his mother intervened.

"I like green grapes," he told her.

The table was silent as Stacy reached for Drew's plate and swiftly cut some of his grapes in half.

"See. They're a little green inside. Now try one and if you still don't like them, you only need to eat the grapes I've cut in half."

Drew did as he was told and ended up eating them all. Lucinda was finishing her coffee when the little boy wanted to get down, so she gently washed his hands, making a great game of it, and took him away to see the garden.

More coffee was poured for both Roddy and Stacy, and they began to talk with the ease of old friends. Roddy shared some London events, what the Queen and Prince Albert had been doing and the latest battle in Parliament, but for some reason Stacy's mind strayed to the last time she was in this home.

Lucinda and Roddy were just married, and she had just been sent away from Winslow. Suddenly Stacy pictured Nigel Stanley's face and asked a question that had long been on her mind.

"Has anyone heard from Nigel Stanley in all of this time, Roddy?"

"No, actually. There were various rumors after you left. Some said he sailed for America, wanting only to escape with his life. Some say that Tanner tracked him down and had it out with the man, and that's why he's not been seen again."

Roddy's last statement so alarmed Stacy that she paled.

"Stacy," Roddy admonished her softly. "The gossip mongers love a sensational story. You don't really believe Tanner capable of murder, do you?"

Tanner's livid, almost unrecognizable face swam before Stacy's eyes. He'd told Nigel that if he ever saw him again, he would kill him.

"Stacy?"

"I don't know," she admitted. "He was so angry, and he did threaten Nigel before we left the Cradwells'."

"Oh, I heard about all that, but that hardly makes him a murderer. Men say strange things when they're enraged."

Still Stacy did not look comforted. She didn't want to even consider that Tanner could do such a thing, but that was exactly the way she was thinking. She said as much to Roddy.

"I understand why you might feel that way, Stacy, but try to put it from your mind. I really don't think there is any validity to it. And if you do plan to see Tanner, suspicion is the last thing you need clouding your judgment."

Stacy's shoulders sagged with relief. Roddy was right. The whole idea was nonsense. Her hand covered his where it lay on the table.

"Thank you, Roddy. I need your level-headed logic."

"No thanks necessary, my dear. It just shows what a wonderfully compassionate person you are that you would be concerned about the man whose actions caused you such pain."

"I have prayed for Nigel from time to time, and I'll continue to do so when he comes to mind."

Roddy stared at her, simply amazed. He wouldn't have believed that Stacy could be any more tranquil or compassionate than she had been the summer of 1853, but she was. There was a peace and tenderness about her that was nearly irresistible. Roddy was very drawn to her, not romantically, but as a loving father who delighted in her company. He also had the feeling that if Tanner ever got within close proximity, he would be as overpoweringly drawn to her as Roddy was himself.

"Have you thought about contacting Tanner yet?" With thoughts of Stacy's husband, Roddy asked the first question that came to mind.

"I've thought about it but not decided on anything definite. Do you have any ideas?"

"Would you rather be in London or go to Winslow?" Roddy needed to know.

Stacy thought. "I don't want to see Winslow again unless I can stay. I loved our home, and going out there only to be sent away might be more than I could take. I guess I'll bide my time and hope he comes to London."

"I think that's wise. I don't believe I would try to surprise him; men don't like that. If he comes to town, I would send a note asking if you could call or if he would like to meet you somewhere. Who knows, he may even be willing to come here."

"Do you think so, Roddy?"

Roddy patted her hand and shocked Stacy speechless with the next words out of his mouth. "Even if he doesn't, my dear, you just keep praying. God will take care of you."

"God made flowers," Drew told Lucinda as they sat on a bench in the garden and ate the cookies that someone had delivered to them from the kitchen. "He made the whole world, even the animals and birds."

"Did He now?" Lucinda murmured absently, not really hearing Drew's words, just feeling delight that he was becoming more comfortable with her. He was such a gift, a balm of sorts, applied directly to the ache inside of her over her brother's death.

"May I have another cookie?"

"How many have you had?" Lucinda was making a genuine effort not to spoil him.

"I think 200," he told her with a great smile.

Lucinda laughed and hugged Drew. This was the scene Roddy came upon.

"Well, it looks like you two are having fun."

"Indeed, we are," Lucinda told him, her arm still around Drew.

"Where is Mumma?" Drew was looking beyond his Uncle Roddy, his brow lowered in concern.

"Your mother is inside. Did you want to go and find her?"

Drew nodded with relief and jumped down from the seat. He ran along the path to the house. Roddy and Lucinda followed more slowly.

"Oh, Roddy," Lucinda spoke when he was out of earshot. "He's so dear."

"That he is, just like his mother."

"What is Stacy doing?"

"I'm not certain. We were discussing Tanner. She might be writing to him."

"If he comes," Lucinda said after a rather pregnant pause, "he'll take them away, and we won't have Drew."

"We can always go see them."

"What if Tanner doesn't allow that?" Lucinda felt panicked over the thought.

"Tanner has never had any argument with us, and too, Stacy is different. She's stronger now. I don't know how she'll be with Tanner, but I just can't believe that she wouldn't allow us to see her or Drew."

"I hope you're right, Roddy." Now Lucinda's voice was wistful. "I truly hope you're right."

Twenty-Seven

"HOW DOES A TRIP to the Royal Gardens sound?" Stacy posed the question just two days later and stunned nearly everyone at the breakfast table. Not knowing what she was talking about, Drew went on eating his toast. Lucinda was clearly uncertain, and Roddy put his newspaper down to look at her.

"We wouldn't need to make a great show of it," she explained. "But I would like to get out, and I know Drew would enjoy the paths and flowers. If you'd rather not join us, I'll understand. Hettie will be with us. I'd like to go right there and come back. We wouldn't stay overly long, but mourning or not, I *need* to get out."

A silence that lasted an entire minute fell over the table.

"I think it's a good idea," Lucinda finally said, her voice serene. "I'm going to stay in for now, but I do think you should go. Roddy, will you be joining them?"

"Unless you'd like me to stay."

Lucinda smiled at him, and Stacy saw a glimmer of the aunt she remembered. Since she'd arrived in Middlesbrough, she had not been the same.

"Thank you for offering, but I shall be quite fine alone. Now, Drew," she added, "you're going to be visiting the Royal Gardens, one of my favorite places. You must come back and tell Aunty Lucinda everything."

Drew nodded. "Mumma, what is Roll Gardens?"

"Royal Gardens," Stacy corrected him with a smile. "They are much like Aunty Lucinda's gardens, only larger and with more flowers."

And so they were off. Roddy wisely ordered a closed carriage for the ride, and Hettie joined them inside. Drew was allowed to look out the window, and his questions were nonstop from beginning to end of the journey.

The gardens were all that Stacy hoped they would be—a riot of springtime color that was so glorious to see and smell that she wished they could stay all day. Drew had inherited his mother's love of the outdoors, and just as she knew he would he ran and skipped until his face was flushed with exertion and pleasure. At one point he spotted a fountain and nearly turned inside out with excitement.

"Oh, Mumma! We can fish! We can fish!"

"No, my darling, we can't. This is a fountain, not a pond."

Drew looked crestfallen for just a moment, but then he spotted a bird and once again they were off. Hettie trailed after him, this time with Roddy and Stacy coming in their wake. The paths had not been crowded in the section they traveled, but whenever they did pass someone, Stacy averted her face. Roddy was sensitive to this and did what he could to aid her privacy.

Stacy was not ashamed, just desiring as little publicity as possible. The desire for solitude and the beauty of the day reminded her of Morgan, naturally turning Stacy's thoughts to her grandfather. She couldn't help but think how much he would have enjoyed this stroll with them.

Then Stacy remembered her last hours with her grandfather as well as the last time she was here. The last time she'd been to the Royal Gardens she had not yet understood her need for a Savior, but God had reached down and rescued her, just as He had her grandfather. She continued her walk with a heart filled with joy and prayers that her life would be a testimony of God's saving grace.

Roddy, Stacy, Drew, and Hettie had only been home from the gardens for two hours when Craig came to Stacy's bedroom door. As usual, his manner was formal, but Stacy knew he genuinely cared for her.

"You have a visitor, Lady Stacy."

Stacy had written a letter to Tanner but had not sent it. Still she wondered if it might be him. Her heart pounded in her chest before Lucinda's head servant continued.

"The Duke and Duchess of Briscoe are waiting for you in the large salon."

Sunny and Brandon.

"Thank you, Craig." Stacy beamed at him and nearly ran down the stairs when he held the door for her. She didn't stop to school her features or fix her hair, but burst into the room like a small child at Christmas.

Sunny rose as soon as she saw her, and the women met in the middle of the room in a huge hug. They separated long enough to laugh and stumble over each other's words before hugging again. When Sunny released Stacy at last, Brandon was there to take her place. Tears stung at the back of Stacy's eyes at the feel of his solid arms. He was so like Tanner in height and build.

"How are you?" Sunny asked when she'd finally claimed Stacy's hand and pulled her over to sit beside her on the settee. "I'm all right," Stacy smiled at both of them. "Did Elena tell you in the letter?"

"About your grandfather? Yes!"

The women hugged again.

"Tell us about it," Brandon urged, and Stacy did. There were tears swimming in Sunny's eyes when she was done.

"I miss him so much," Stacy admitted. "But knowing where he is gives me such a peace. I keep seeking out verses that talk about heaven, so I can try to imagine how wonderful it must be."

"Study verses about God too, Stacy." Brandon spoke now. "Heaven is God's home, and when we know Him, I think heaven and our time with Him becomes clearer. There is even a verse in Revelation, chapter 21, that says there is no sun or moon in the new Jerusalem, which is heaven, for God's glory illuminates that holy city."

"Thank you, Brandon." Stacy's voice was awed and humble. "There is so much I don't know. Thank you for telling me that."

He smiled at her, and Stacy's heart turned over. *Oh Father,* she prayed silently. *Please save my Tanner. Please give us a marriage like this one—one that's built in You.*

"Have you seen Tanner?" Sunny's question cut through Stacy's thoughts.

"No. I don't think he's in London right now. I've written him a letter asking him to see me, but I haven't posted it. I'm afraid I don't have high hopes. He hasn't wanted me in over three years, and I doubt if that has changed."

Sunny reached for and squeezed Stacy's hand. "We're still praying."

"Thank you. Brandon, do you ever see him?"

"From time to time."

Stacy couldn't disguise the love in her face or her voice. "How is he?"

"I think he's fair," Brandon answered honestly. "He was quite thin for a time after you left, but he's filled out again. He doesn't smile much, but he always wants to talk. I think he gets lonely."

Stacy drew in a shuddering breath as pain squeezed around her heart. She was silent for a moment, praying again about what she should do. She decided suddenly not to do anything. God might have something special planned, and if she went rushing ahead on her own she could ruin everything. With this decision came such a peace that Stacy knew she was doing the right thing.

"Are you all right?" This came from Brandon, who along with his wife had been carefully watching Stacy's face.

"As a matter of fact, I am." She told them simply that she was not going to mail her letter but would keep praying.

"Well, there's one thing you won't need to pray about any

longer," Sunny said. "You are going to join my Bible study with Andrea."

"Oh, Sunny," Stacy breathed. "Are you certain? I mean, won't Lady Andrea mind?"

"It was her idea. That way when I can't be there, the two of you can meet."

Stacy's eyes closed in relief. She had felt rather adrift with her separation from Elena and Noel.

"I don't know what to say."

"Say yes," Brandon told her, making it sound so simple.

"Yes," Stacy said and was still beaming at both of them when the door opened.

"Mumma?" a small voice called, sounding on the edge of tears. Stacy turned in surprise.

"Come here, Drew," she called to him. He'd been down for over an hour, and Stacy had planned to be there when he awoke. She wondered what woke him early. Brentwood was larger than Morgan, and he was still a little confused by all the doors and hallways. In fact, Stacy was surprised that he'd found her at all. Hettie must have fallen asleep, or he'd have never gotten downstairs.

Both Sunny and Brandon watched the small boy approach, his hair on end, his face flushed from sleep. Stacy pulled him into her lap. After he laid his head against her chest, he closed his eyes again. Stacy glanced over to find her guests' eyes glued to his small face.

"I know what you're thinking," Stacy spoke softly, referring to Drew's resemblance to Tanner. "Since you're going to be praying, the first thing you might ask of God is that He would move in Tanner's heart so that he'll see this child."

The Hawkesburys nodded, but no one said anything for a time.

"Would you like me to pray right now?" Brandon suddenly asked, his voice hushed.

Stacy glanced down to see that Drew was sound asleep before motioning with her head.

They didn't join hands, but Brandon's soft, deep voice surrounded them as he committed Tanner, Stacy, and Drew to God. He asked for wisdom on Stacy's part as well as their own, and then believing it to be God's will, he prayed for Tanner Richardson's salvation.

Twenty-Eight

NOT UNTIL THE FOLLOWING DAY did Stacy learn that her trip to the gardens had been a mistake. Brentwood sat on a quiet street and until she went out, her presence in the city had been undetected. Well, such privacy was over; she and Drew had been spotted and were now public news.

Roddy had been to his club that morning so he was able to report that the Duchess of Cambridge was on everyone's lips. She had even made the papers. Stacy found herself staying close to Drew all that day as if he somehow needed protection. Drew wanted to go out into the yard, but although the garden was surrounded with a high stone wall, she kept him inside.

Stacy wasn't sure if she was overreacting or not, but she didn't know what else to do. The temptation to mail her letter to Tanner was nearly overpowering. She wanted to know where she stood. If she mailed the letter and Tanner still wanted nothing to do with her, she could return to Middlesbrough.

If there had been any dread in returning to London, it had been for this reason. Knowing that Noel and Elena's house was available to her and that her grandfather had left her a small legacy made her want to walk away from all the gossip and scandal, but she knew such an action would be hard on Lucinda and Roddy.

When Stacy took a moment to consider the idea she realized she'd been giving in to impulse and emotion. Maybe the gossip would die down and she could live a normal life. She tried not to let it bother her, but even the servants who weren't as familiar with her began to watch her with speculative eyes.

"How are you, my dear?" Lucinda had found Stacy in Drew's room. She wasn't hiding exactly, but neither did she feel like wandering the house.

"A little shy of the windows and yard, but doing well."

Lucinda sighed. "The gossip mongers of the town can be such a trial. I'm glad he's too young to take much notice," Lucinda said, nodding her head in Drew's direction. He was sitting on the floor with his train and a small stuffed bear.

"The only problem is his complaint that I won't let him out in the yard."

"I think you're wise. We really are quite protected and secluded here, but you're big news." Lucinda's voice was dry, and this wrung a smile from Stacy.

"I came up because I wanted to remind you that Roddy and I will be away for part of the day tomorrow. Roddy has some property he must check on, and I said I would go with him."

"We'll be fine. Roddy found a trunk of old toys. Hettie is cleaning them, and by tomorrow Drew will have more treasures than he'll know what to do with."

"Good. I've asked cook for a special meal tonight to shake off your feeling of captivity. We won't be around until late afternoon tomorrow, so this will be your official welcome-to-London feast."

Lucinda's voice was so dramatic that Stacy had to laugh. Drew, not to be left from the festivities, wanted to be in his aunt's lap. Lucinda cuddled him close and sang a silly rhyme in his ear. The three of them passed a fun hour before Craig came to say that lunch was served.

Tanner had been in London for two days, and everywhere he went, people gawked in his direction and whispered. He was not one who paid the slightest attention to gossip, even when it concerned him, but this was affecting his purpose for being in town and that was getting on his nerves.

He had come to London on business just the day before, and within the hour had learned that his wife was in town as well. The gossip mill also said she was accompanied by a small boy.

Planning to stay about a week, he was swiftly changing his mind. He had nearly decided he would tell Edmond to finish the business and take himself back to the solitude of Winslow when the questions began.

Could he really leave London knowing she was here? Could he have Stacy this close and not see her? What did she look like now? How could she come back to London with another man's child? Tanner felt such a mix of emotions that it staggered him. One minute he was livid with remembered pain, and the next moment he thought he must talk to her before he could possibly go on.

It was early afternoon when he made his decision. After all she was his wife; he would see her if it pleased him to do so. Her presence in London was disrupting his whole life, and he had rights. Maybe he would send her out to Winslow until life could right itself again. His mansion was huge; he never had to see her if he didn't want to.

Tanner suddenly remembered the boy. Rumor had it that he looked like a Richardson, but that was ridiculous. No doubt the boy would prove to be nothing but trouble. But if he knew Stacy, and he believed he did, she would never consent to giving the child up.

Tanner ordered his carriage and found himself consumed with thoughts of Stacy all the way to Brentwood. He finally admitted to himself that he had missed her. He hated himself for the weakness, but it was true. To fight the feeling, he grew angry.

By the time he arrived at Brentwood he knew exactly what he would do. He would send Stacy to Winslow, but this time he would be in control. If he wished to see her, he would send for her, but outside of that she was only his wife. She would do as she was told and live where he told her to live. Right now he wanted her at Winslow. The boy came to mind one last time, but Tanner pushed him away. He would deal with the brat when the time came.

Drew's attitude had been poor at naptime. He had been nearly delirious with the toys Hettie had produced, and by the time he needed to eat lunch and nap he was totally spent. He had been quite cross with his mother when she wouldn't allow him to sleep with every toy Hettie had cleaned. When he spoke back to her repeatedly, Stacy had been forced to paddle him—something she hated to do. Drew had been quite repentant afterward, and they'd prayed before he'd fallen asleep.

Now Stacy was in her own room, much in need of rest herself. She didn't lie down but made herself comfortable in a chair that sat by the window. She gazed out the window at an area that was nearly like a forest. It was one of Stacy's favorite views, so unlike many parts of London with its sewer-lined streets and filthy houses.

She pondered the view for a time, but she was tired. Her eyes were sliding shut when her doorknob turned. She looked up in surprise. No one had knocked. Thinking it was Drew, she began to rise. Stacy was standing in front of the chair when Tanner pushed the door open and walked in. She froze in place when he pinned her to the spot with his dark, compelling eyes.

Before either of them could speak, Craig appeared and

hovered anxiously in the background. Stacy glanced toward him in an effort to tell him she would be all right. She wasn't certain herself, but she knew that Tanner would only send him away, and none too gently.

"My lady?"

"It's all right, Craig." Stacy found her voice and watched as the elderly servant exited reluctantly. He closed the door soundlessly behind him.

Stacy looked back at her husband and forced herself to breathe.

"Hello, Tanner."

"Stacy." His disinterested voice belied the way his heart leapt at the sight of her. "What brings you to London?"

"My grandfather died."

This gave Tanner pause. This particular bit of information had not reached him.

"I'm sorry for your loss."

"Thank you."

"But that still doesn't answer my question."

Stacy, unable to take her eyes from him, finally shrugged rather helplessly and then stared at the floor.

"Lucinda and Roddy wanted me to come, and I felt it was best at the time."

Stacy heard footsteps, and her eyes flew up to find him approaching. If he was trying to intimidate her, it was working. He stopped just scant inches in front of her and stared down into her face. Stacy was amazed at what she saw. Tanner still cared. He tried to show her otherwise, but Stacy had caught the slightest glimpse of caring.

"What are you thinking, Anastasia? Afraid I'll kiss you?" Tanner's deep voice questioned softly.

Stacy couldn't answer.

"You are my wife," Tanner told her as if she was the one who'd forgotten. "I will kiss you whenever I feel like it. Do you understand?"

Stacy could only nod.

"Tell a maid to pack your things; you're coming to Winslow." Tanner's voice had turned curt as he abruptly turned away.

"You want me at Winslow?" Stacy found her voice.

"Did I not say as much?" His impatience was evident. "A carriage will be here for you in two hours."

Two hours! Stacy nearly panicked. She said the first words that came to mind.

"I have a son."

Tanner, who had been heading toward the door, stopped in his tracks. He turned with maddening slowness and stared at Stacy.

"I'd heard as much," he said in a voice that was stone cold. "I suppose you may bring the child, if he causes me no trouble."

Stacy was horrified at his words and tone. She was on the verge of refusing him as it was, but he went on and Stacy completely lost control.

"Who knows," Tanner said with a negligent shrug as he again turned to the door, "maybe I'll grow to like the boy and get rid of you."

"No." The word was spat out, and Tanner turned in amazement. No longer was Stacy standing frightened before him. Her hands were balled so tightly in front of her that they were white. She was trembling from head to foot, her face flushed with rage.

"You'll not take my son. He needs me, and I won't let you take him. I won't go with you. You can't make me. You'll not take my son from me." Her voice was furious and desperate, and in just a few strides Tanner covered the distance between them, his own anger completely gone, replaced by something he could not define.

"Stacy," he spoke with more calm than he felt, his hands grasping her upper arms. "I won't take the boy."

"No, you won't!" Stacy was still beside herself.

"I won't separate you from your son."

"I won't let you. I won't let you hurt him."

"I won't hurt the boy or take him from you."

Stacy stopped long enough to listen to him and study his eyes. She went on, still boldly, but her tone was calming.

"Promise me, Tanner. Promise you'll not take him from me."

"I promise, Stacy." He gave her a little shake to make sure she was listening. "He can come with you to Winslow, and I'll not hurt him."

Stacy took a deep breath and tried to relax and believe him. Tanner felt her nearly violent trembling under his hands and grew angry at himself for wanting to enfold her in his arms. He had thought it would be such a pleasure to hurt her as she'd hurt him, but it was not turning out that way at all.

With another abrupt movement, he dropped his hands and turned away. "You and the boy will be ready to leave in two hours."

Stacy's hand flew to her mouth.

"Tanner." Her voice was now fearful and subdued.

"What?" He turned back with his hand on the door, his brow lowered menacingly.

"I'm not certain I can leave just now."

"Are you telling me no, Anastasia?" His voice was so low and angry that Stacy could barely force the words from her throat.

"No, it's just that I need to tell Roddy and Lucinda goodbye and explain where I'm going. They're not here right now."

Tanner seemed to consider the idea. "When will they return?"

"Not for several hours."

Again Tanner paused. "A coach will be here at 8:00 tomorrow morning. Be ready, Stacy. I don't want to have to tell you again."

He didn't wait for an answer this time, and since Stacy's legs gave out as soon the door closed, she was glad the chair was directly behind her.

"He terrifies me just as he always has," Stacy said out loud to the Lord. "I haven't changed at all. I was going to be so strong, Lord, and I was terrified."

Defeat washed over Stacy as she prayed and tried to calm herself. She had asked God to open a door, but she never dreamed it would be like this. This door had brought the north wind. As Stacy quieted, God reminded her of His sovereignty. Tanner's arrival was no mistake. This was the door God intended, cold wind and all. Believing that, Stacy would meet the challenges beyond that door with hope.

She sat for only a moment longer until she realized how much work needed to be done. She gathered both Hettie and Rayna in order to explain the situation. Hettie was to travel with her, but not knowing what Tanner would want, Stacy did not feel at liberty to ask Rayna to accompany them. Both women were clearly disapproving of the move to Winslow, but Stacy, needing both of them to pack for her and Drew, ignored their looks. Her husband wanted her back. She had no illusions of paradise, but at least Tanner wanted her at Winslow.

Tanner suddenly found himself with nothing to do. For over an hour he paced the study floor at his town house. He would not leave London until he was certain that Stacy was on her way to Winslow. He now wished he'd forced her to leave on the spot so he could get on with his life. He was a fool for letting her change his mind.

The smell of her skin and bath oil suddenly assailed his senses, and Tanner looked down at his hands. She had felt as wonderful as ever. Her eyes, so huge and blue, had been just as he remembered—with a mixture of wonder and innocence. Not wanting to dwell on this, he forced his mind to move on.

Her reaction to a comment he hadn't meant scared him. He'd never seen her that way. He'd heard that motherhood could do that to a woman the way nothing else could, but he had not been prepared for her response.

"She must have loved the boy's father," Tanner heard himself say out loud and stood still as rage and agony ripped through him. He knew then that he would have to be very careful. The last thing he wanted was another's man child beneath his roof, but if that's what he had to put up with to have Stacy, he would do it. He had seen her, and that was all it had taken to make him admit to the truth, infuriating as it was. He wanted Stacy. Right now nothing else mattered.

Twenty-Nine

THE NEXT MORNING LUCINDA STOOD STILL and forced her hands to her sides. The sight of Drew coming down the stairs with his train and bear was enough to make her wring her hands.

She had come home the day before from a marvelous but tiring day with Roddy, only to be met with Stacy's news. Lucinda cried herself dry before falling into an exhausted sleep. She woke early, before 6:00, knowing that Stacy would be up and readying herself to go. And now, even though it was just a little before 8:00, she felt utterly drained.

Stacy had shared about her faith in God, but Lucinda was too angry to trust. What kind of God took a person's family away? She had been planning to visit her brother that very summer, but God had taken him in the spring. Lucinda would never have admitted to herself that her own selfish lifestyle had kept her from visiting Andrew more regularly.

Now Drew and Stacy were leaving, and after just a few days too, making Lucinda more bitter than ever. They needed her, she was certain of that. And she needed them.

Roddy stood beside her while all of this ran through Lucinda's mind. He shared Lucinda's grief, but he would not say anything that would stand in the way of Stacy's happiness. Lucinda was quite certain that Tanner would not do right by his son, but Roddy believed differently. Just as he'd known that Tanner would once again be taken with his wife—after all, he'd ordered her to Winslow just moments after he arrived—Roddy also believed that one look at his son and Tanner's heart would be lost.

"Well, we're ready," Stacy said as she finally gained the foyer. "Thank you for everything, Roddy and Lucinda. I don't know when we'll be back to London, but I hope you'll come and see us."

"No one can keep us away," Lucinda stated as she put her arms around Stacy. Each knew that her *no one* referred to Tanner.

"Goodbye, my precious." Lucinda's voice wavered as she hugged Drew, and she didn't tarry long with her embrace.

Lucinda stood at the door with her sodden handkerchief, but Roddy scooped Drew up in his arms and walked them down to the carriage. Hettie climbed aboard with a sour comment about her old bones, and Stacy turned to her dear friend.

"Will Lucinda be all right?"

"I think so. It might take some time, and we will need to visit or she'll be miserable."

"Please do, Roddy. I don't want to fight with my husband, but if Tanner isn't going to let me see my family, I won't stay." Stacy paused and then looked chagrined. "Of course, I say that now, but the minute he looks at me I'll shake."

Roddy smiled at her words. "You'll do fine, and we will come to visit even if we have to charge the castle gate."

"What castle?"

Stacy looked stunned. At times it was so easy to forget that Drew was present and taking in every word.

Roddy kissed the little boy's cheek and handed him over to his mother. Stacy passed him in to Hettie and then turned to embrace Roddy. They didn't say another word to each other, but Stacy waved from the window as soon as she was inside. She couldn't be certain, but it looked as if Roddy's eyes were wet. Stacy smiled into his eyes as the carriage moved away to Lucinda's cries of goodbye and I love you.

Stacy had completely forgotten how long the ride to Winslow could be. The carriage stuck in the mud on two occasions, and each time it took considerable maneuvering to get them moving again. These interludes were a delight to Drew, who was rather bored with the bumpy ride and had nothing to play with save his train and bear.

Stacy wouldn't have minded the ride so much, except that she'd been under the impression that Tanner would be with them. When he hadn't been with the coach that morning at 8:00, Stacy thought they would be meeting him. Now they were only about 45 minutes from Winslow, and there had been no sign. Stacy decided to sit back and not worry about it.

Just short of an hour later, Winslow came into view. Not even Hettie could find a negative word for its grandiose beauty. Stacy's chest heaved with pleasure at the sight of it. She had truly loved their home.

Let this be a beginning, Father. I don't know why Tanner came ahead of us, but let this be a time of repair for this damaged marriage. Help Tanner put his pride away and accept Drew so we can be a real family.

"Mumma."

"Yes, dear."

"I'm hungry."

"All right, darling. We'll be inside in just a moment."

And indeed they were, but it was not the warm welcome Stacy had expected. It was Joffrey and not Tanner who was at the door to meet them, and his manner was even more frigid than Stacy had remembered.

"Hello, Joffrey. Is Lord Richardson here?"

"No, he is not."

"Oh." Stacy was starting to feel alarmed. "Is he out riding?"

"No." Joffrey's voice clearly said it was none of her business, but he still explained. "Lord Richardson is still in London. When he plans to return I do not know. I did receive word that you were coming, but since his lordship is not here, maybe you should return to London."

"My orders were to bring her ladyship here," a gruff voice spoke up from behind Stacy. It was the grouchy old carriage driver. Stacy smiled at him gratefully, but he didn't return the smile.

He had not come inside for Lady Stacy, but for himself. He was tired and nothing could make him drive all the way back to London right now. Knowing Joffrey as he did, he'd come inside just to make certain that the self-seeking head of staff didn't talk the duchess into returning.

"Very well," Joffrey stated with a sigh, as though Winslow were his own and he alone was put out by their presence. "I'll show you to your rooms."

Ignoring Hettie's dark looks, Stacy followed, thankful to be going to her room and getting a chance to be alone. She glanced over her shoulder and sighed with relief to see a footman handling their trunks. For a time she felt certain she would have to lug her own.

Her pleasure over the trunks was short-lived. Stacy's heart sank when she saw that Joffrey was leading them toward the north wing. Her heart begged God to give her strength and to calm the resentment rising within her that Tanner would be so thoughtless.

"Will two rooms be enough?"

Stacy stared at Joffrey, amazed at his daring. He clearly hated her and was doing nothing to hide it. She knew Hettie wanted her to take the servant down a peg, but surprisingly enough she felt too much compassion for that. They were all taking their cue from the duke, and he despised her. Stacy told herself not to be a quitter, but she knew if the coachman was willing she would leave immediately.

"Two rooms will be fine," Stacy answered finally and entered the room with Drew. She nearly balked when she felt how cold the air was once she passed over the threshold.

The three of them stood still as the trunks were placed on the floor and the servants left. Joffrey started to leave but turned back. His manner said that it caused him great pains to do so.

"Dinner will be served at 6:30 in the main dining room." This said, he left, closing the door behind him.

Stacy looked over at Hettie to see that the old woman's jaw had actually swung open. Had Stacy not felt so miserable, she would have laughed.

"Mumma, I'm hungry."

Stacy quickly knelt in front of him. She hugged him before answering, more for her own need of comfort than his.

"Joffrey left before I could tell him that we haven't eaten. I'll get you something, all right?"

"I'm cold."

"Well, Hettie can warm you up—"

"I'll see about the food," the old servant cut in, her voice odd. Stacy stared at her, thinking she must be very tired, and then nodded.

As soon as Hettie left, Stacy changed Drew into warmer clothing and played a game with him, intended to warm them both. She was hungry herself, and the feeling that no one outside of London cared for them was pressing down on her with every passing second. Stacy would have been greatly cheered if she could have seen Hettie downstairs in the kitchen right then. At least she would have been certain that someone at Winslow cared for her.

"I told you earlier," Joffrey said with his nose in the air, "dinner will be served at 6:30. As a servant, you may eat when the duchess is through."

"Don't you try your uppity ways with me," Hettie nearly hissed at him. "Now you've got ten minutes to have a tray up to Lady Stacy—a nice full tray for all three of us."

"I do *not* take orders from elderly servants who do not know their place."

Hettie's thin chest heaved, and her eyes narrowed. "I mean what I say. You've got ten minutes to have that tray ready. If you don't, I'll tell Lord Richardson everything. He can't stay away forever, and when he comes I'll tell him every word you said." Hettie turned and started away, but paused and looked back.

"And you'd best remember one more thing. That's the duchess you're serving up there, and that boy is the future Duke of Cambridge."

Joffrey looked uncertain for the first time. Hettie left, and cook erased the smug expression from her face just before Joffrey turned to look at her. She began putting a tray together without being asked, determining then and there that she would be the one to deliver it.

Four days passed before Tanner returned to Winslow. Stacy found out quite by accident that he was back when she ran into Price in the hallway.

"Hello, Price." Her voice told of her genuine pleasure at seeing him, but Price read the strain in her face.

"Good morning, my lady."

"Are you just back from London?"

"Last night," he told her gently.

"Is..." Stacy began and hesitated. "Is Tanner with you?"

"Yes, my lady, he's here."

Stacy did not want to keep him, so she thanked him and moved back to her rooms. It was like living as a prisoner. She was afraid to let Drew make any noise for fear of disturbing someone. The notion was ridiculous since they were so far away from the rest of the house, but Stacy was not coping very well. In fact, the strain was beginning to tell on both of them. Stacy knew she was losing weight, and Drew's tan little face was growing pale and drawn.

Stacy hoped all of that might change with Tanner's arrival, but this was not the case. Two more days passed, and in that time he never sought them out or even saw them. Stacy was totally confused as to why she'd been brought here. He wanted nothing to do with her. She reminded herself how much she was hated. He was trying to humiliate her, and unfortunately it was working. Stacy felt more downtrodden then she ever had in her life. Thankfully, Drew's sneezes changed all of that.

He and Stacy were playing on the floor where they spent much of their time. They had tried going out of doors, but both the gardener and the stablemaster had made it quite clear with their looks and actions that their presence was not wanted. Stacy could not rest under their frowning looks and shaking heads.

Now this morning Drew began to sneeze as he played. Stacy felt his forehead and found it cool, but his little hands were so cold she felt frightened. She gathered him into her arms and held him almost fiercely. Drew let out one more sneeze, and Stacy realized this was the very thing she had feared—but she was doing nothing about it. She could handle the fact that Tanner didn't care about her, but Drew was another matter.

"Hettie," Stacy announced as she put Drew back on the floor and rose. "I need to see Lord Richardson. Will you please see that Drew stays warm?"

Stacy's color was high as she said this, and Hettie nearly cackled with glee. The old woman had wondered how much more Stacy was going to take.

"Bye-bye, Mumma."

"I'll be back soon."

"Hettie?" Drew spoke when his mother had left.

"Um hmm?"

"Why are you smiling, Hettie?"

She didn't answer his question. "Come over here, Drew, close to the fire. Sit in my lap, and I'll tell you a story."

Tanner Richardson, a man of tremendous willpower, had been struggling for days to forget that his wife and her son were in the house. He hadn't gotten a thing done in all that time, but this morning was different. He had finally forced his mind to the task at hand and had put in several productive hours of work on business matters. He was not happy to have someone knock on the study door.

He opened his mouth to say that he did not want to be disturbed, but hesitated. Stacy, never far from his mind, might be seeking him out. He sincerely doubted it, but on the chance she was he wanted to hear what she had to say.

"Come in," he called and watched with satisfaction as his wife came tentatively through the door.

"I'm sorry to disturb you, Tanner, but I need to ask you something."

"What is it?" His voice sounded more impatient than he felt, but it had its usual effect. Stacy's hands came together in a nervous gesture, and her voice turned hesitant.

"Would it be possible for us to move out of the north wing?"

Tanner frowned. "I was under the impression that you chose the rooms yourself."

Stacy didn't know how to reply to this. It wasn't true, but she couldn't bring herself to tell of Joffrey's actions, reprehensible as they were.

"What seems to be the problem?"

Stacy nearly sighed with relief that he cared enough to ask.

"The rooms are rather cold."

"Well you can certainly ask Joffrey to supply you with extra blankets." His voice was that of a parent addressing a simple child.

"We're not cold at night, just during the day."

Tanner's mouth twisted cynically. "Now, that's the problem, isn't it. You have no business keeping that boy in all day. You've probably coddled him until he's a monster. Get out during the day, Stacy, and you won't be cold in your rooms."

This said, Tanner bent his head back over his papers. She had been dismissed with his tone and gesture. She stared at the top of his head for a moment, but the fight had gone out of her. She turned and let herself back out the door. Once outside, she stood for a moment in misery.

"That was telling him, Stacy. You really set things straight."

"Were you speaking to me, my lady?"

Stacy hadn't even noticed the faithful servant.

"No, Price," she told him softly.

The servant watched for long moments as she moved up the stairs with a heavy tread. When Stacy was out of sight, Price moved into the study.

Thirty

PRICE MOVED ABOUT THE STUDY VERY QUIETLY, not wanting to disturb his lordship but sensing he might be needed. He delivered the coffee he'd been carrying and prepared it just as Lord Richardson liked, but the cup was not touched. Tanner sat with his eyes on some distant spot, his papers in front of him, forgotten.

"Did you pass my wife when you came in?"

"Yes, sir."

"How did she seem?"

Price hesitated, and Tanner finally looked at him.

"She seemed," Price hesitated over the words, "she seemed somewhat defeated, my lord."

Tanner wondered why this brought him no pleasure. Again he had believed it would be good to see her humbled and miserable, but he hated this.

"It isn't like Stacy to complain." Tanner said this more to himself than anyone else, but Price still answered.

"I believe that her concern might be for the child's well-being."

Alarm slammed through Tanner. It didn't matter that he wanted nothing to do with the boy; the thought of his becoming ill was not to be tolerated. And then there was Stacy. She had not been happy with the way he'd treated her, but there was something more.

"Did Lady Stacy look all right to you?"

"She seemed thin, my lord, but I have not seen her of late and am probably not the one to judge."

But Tanner was one to judge. She did seem thinner, even since he'd seen her at Roddy and Lucinda's.

And why wouldn't she? Tanner asked himself in disgust. *You treat your animals with more kindness than you've shown your wife.*

"Have Lady Stacy, her maid, the boy, and the boy's nurse, moved down the hall from my room."

"Her maid, sir?"

"Yes, her maid." Tanner's voice was testy.

"Oh, Hettie," Price clarified. "Of course, sir." Price would have moved to the door then, but Tanner's face was that of a thundercloud.

"Are you saying my wife has no maid?"

"No, sir, but she does have Hettie."

"That's all? Just Hettie?"

"I believe so, sir. There is no other staff of which I am aware."

"Who takes care of the boy?"

"I believe Lady Richardson and Hettie do it themselves, my lord."

Tanner wasn't sure what to do with this. He had sent Stacy away, too angry to care if she had anything to live on. And by the time he had wondered about it, she had moved back to Middlesbrough where he knew her grandfather would take care of her. But now the old man was dead. He'd seen Morgan. Andrew Daniels had not died a wealthy man. What was Stacy living on?

"Would you still like Lady Richardson moved, my lord?" Price asked. Tanner was glad of the interruption.

"Yes. Have Joffrey arrange it. Have him see that they're made very comfortable. On second thought, see to it yourself. Do you know the rooms I want?"

"Yes, sir. Down the hall from yours. I was going to put the

child and Hettie in the two adjoining, and Lady Stacy directly across the hall."

"Good. And Price," Tanner began when the servant began to move away, "tell Lady Richardson that I will expect her to join me for dinner tonight. Seven o'clock."

"Yes, sir."

Price left, and Tanner finally reached for his coffee. He brooded for a long time on the situation in his home, a situation of his own creating. He asked himself many questions, ending with whether or not he should have left Stacy in London. He didn't have answers for each question that came to mind, but to his last, it was an unqualified no.

Stacy moved toward the north wing but did not return immediately to her room. She stood in the massive hall down from the door and looked out the window. It was a cloudy day, and Stacy thought it fit her mood.

"I thought I could do this, Lord, but I'm failing miserably," she whispered out loud. "What is my responsibility here as a wife? Do I stay no matter what? Do I honor Tanner's wishes, no matter what he expects of me? I wish Elena were here to talk with. It's not as if we have no place else to go. This is not a fit place with us tucked away all the time and the servants glaring at us when we make work for them.

"Tanner has done everything in his power to kill my love, Lord, but it's not working. My heart still turns over every time I see him. I need some help, Father. I need something to tell me if I should keep on here. I can't do this on my own."

Drew began to cry from inside the room. It was the best thing Stacy could have heard. As she moved to see to the trouble, she realized she was not more restful over the situation, but Drew needed his mother and that was all that mattered at the moment. She felt that she'd utterly failed him by coming here and keeping him shut away like so much excess baggage. He trusted her to see to his best, and up until now Stacy had been too afraid of Tanner to do that. Well, no more.

As she opened the door to the bedroom, she determined that as soon as she could figure a way to return to London and then Middlesbrough, she would do so. Tanner hadn't wanted her for three and a half years, and even though it looked for a time like things had changed, he didn't want her now. As much as it pained her to admit it, there was no reason to stay.

"You're moving us?" Stacy questioned Price just 30 minutes after she'd made her resolution.

"Yes, my lady. Lord Tanner has selected rooms for you in the other wing. If you'll come with me—"

Price cut off when Drew came from behind his mother to see whom she was talking with. He had been behind her skirts, thinking this all a game, when he popped his little face out and then moved his whole person to stare up at the unfamiliar servant in their room.

Price cleared his throat and opened his mouth to speak, but nothing came. He couldn't seem to take his eyes from the child. When he finally looked up, it was to find Stacy smiling at him, her heart in her eyes.

"Thank you, Price."

"For what, my lady?" The man's voice was hoarse.

"For reacting as you did."

Price's expression told her he understood, but he still looked as if he couldn't believe his eyes. He had never doubted Lady Richardson's faithfulness to her husband, but the face of this child was enough to stop him in his tracks.

Price had been employed by Tanner's father to serve as Tanner's valet; he had been 12 years old at the time. Tanner had been four and a mirror image of the child before him. Price found himself wanting to let out an emotional shout for the first time in years. His lord had an heir, a beautiful male heir.

Price cleared his throat and slowly said, "If you'll come with me, Lady Richardson, I will see that you, young Lord Richardson, and Hettie are settled comfortably."

"Maybe I should have Hettie pack our things."

"Lord Richardson's orders were clear—a maid will take care of that. He also wanted me to tell you that he'd like you to join him for dinner this evening at 7:00."

"Thank you, Price."

And so it was that the small band of neglected visitors followed Price out of the north wing to their new rooms. Stacy ignored Hettie's comment about it being long overdue; she was just glad that Tanner had not been as indifferent as he'd acted.

Drew skipped along, holding Hettie's hand and trying to take in parts of Winslow he'd never seen. Hettie kept him moving fairly fast, but Price noticed the child's interest and asked Stacy to contact him if she wanted young Lord Richardson to have a tour.

"I appreciate the offer, Price, but since Tanner hasn't met Drew, I think we should wait."

"As you wish, my lady. This will be your room."

Price opened a door, and Stacy entered with relief. They had been heading in the direction of the master bedroom, and her mind was put to rest to be given another just now.

It was a bedroom she remembered, and in fact was one of her favorites. Done completely in navy and a deep shade of rust, it was one of the warmest bedrooms in all of Winslow. There was a sitting room off the bedroom and a huge dressing room. Everything was spotless, and a maid stood in attendance, preparing to pour tea.

"Please wait for Lady Richardson's return," Price told the maid before leading them across the way to Hettie and Drew's rooms. They were as marvelous as her own, but other than having Drew wash his hands in the basin they did not linger. They quickly moved back across the hall to enjoy tea in Stacy's sitting room.

An hour later, Tanner, on the way to his own room, was stopped in the hall when he heard a child laugh. For long moments he stood. Another giggle sounded, and with it all doubts about moving them closer evaporated. He knew he was going to have to meet the child eventually, but not just yet. Hearing that laugh and knowing he'd done right by Stacy and the boy was enough for now.

Thirty-One

FOR THE SECOND TIME IN JUST WEEKS, Stacy found herself rushing down the stairs to see Sunny Hawkesbury. Joffrey had put her guest in the main salon. Stacy would have chosen a smaller, cozier room for their meeting, but she was glad to see her anywhere. The friends embraced warmly and then sat close together on the settee to talk in quiet tones.

Sunny wasted no time in asking questions, telling Stacy to tell her if she was out of line.

"First of all, are you all right?"

"I think so. The events of the past week have been rather hard, but I think things might be turning."

"Can you tell me about them?"

"When we arrived Tanner wasn't here. I wasn't prepared for that, but the worst thing that happened was that we were given rooms in the north wing."

"What were the problems?"

"It's oppressive, cold, and dreadfully dreary. I thought Drew might be catching something so I went to Tanner about moving, but he said no. However, he must have had second thoughts because he did move us. We're in lovely rooms just down the hall from the master bedroom."

"What did he say about Drew?"

"He hasn't seen him yet."

Sunny glanced around the cavernous room. "That's not hard to believe. Winslow is larger than Bracken. I take it Tanner doesn't see much of you, either."

"No, but he has asked me to join him for dinner tonight."

"Will you go?"

Stacy's smile was self-mocking. "You don't tell Tanner no—at least I don't."

"Stacy," Sunny's voice turned urgent. "Is he hurting you?"

"No, not the way you're thinking. My heart feels rather battered, but he doesn't touch me."

"Should you be staying here?"

"I believe so, yes. I was ready to leave, although I don't know how I would, when he moved us to more comfortable rooms. I rather took that as an indication that I should keep on here."

"Stacy, what did you mean, you don't know how you would leave? Surely you can order a carriage for yourself."

"I'm not sure. You see, the servants don't really care for me. Some of it's my fault because I'm not very assertive, but I feel as if—"

Joffrey chose that moment to enter with the tea tray. He had not knocked but simply entered of his own accord.

"I assumed my lady and her guest would care for tea?" Joffrey's voice told them how much he knew he was appreciated.

Stacy glanced at Sunny, who indicated no with a slight shake of her head.

"No, thank you, Joffrey, not just now." This came from Stacy.

Joffrey's face and body movements communicated his deep affront, and Sunny could only stare at him. Stacy, being used to such things, did nothing. Collecting the service, Joffrey caught the shocked look in the Duchess of Briscoe's eyes. He swiftly schooled his features into humble servitude before leaving the women alone.

"Is that normal?"

"I'm afraid so."

"I can't believe Tanner puts up with it."

"They don't do it to Tanner."

Sunny stared at her friend and thought furiously how she could help her. This was awful, but what should she say? She was still thinking when Stacy asked, "Should I stay here, Sunny?"

"Are you afraid to stay?"

"I am afraid, but not for the reasons you might think. I'm afraid of being swallowed up by Tanner because I won't stand up to him. I'm afraid he'll take Drew from me. Oh, not actually remove him from Winslow, but take his affections until he won't remember that he has a mother. I think I can stand many things, Sunny, but not that."

Sunny was about to reply, but the door opened again. Sunny was ready herself to tell the servants to leave them alone, but it was Tanner. He crossed the room in long-legged strides so like Brandon's that she smiled to herself.

"I'm sorry to bother you, ladies, but Price told me Sunny was here. Would you mind giving these to Hawk? Tell him I'll be over in the next few days to discuss them."

"I'll make sure he receives them."

"Thank you, Sunny." Tanner's tone was congenial, his eyes kind, but as he transferred this gaze to his wife, his look became intense.

"Did you need something, Stacy? Shall I send Joffrey in?"

"No, thank you, Tanner. We're fine."

"All right." The words sounded like he was through, but he continued to stand and study his wife's face.

"Did you get my message from Price?" Tanner's voice had changed and become intimate and low.

"Yes, thank you. This evening, seven o'clock."

"Good." Tanner spent another few seconds studying her as though to memorize her features, then bowed to both ladies and went on his way. It had appeared as though he was searching for something in her expression. Both women wondered if he found what he'd been looking for.

"I didn't know what to tell you before he came in here, Stacy, but right now I think you should try to stay."

Stacy was beginning to agree, but she still asked, "What changed your mind?"

"His face, more specifically, his eyes. He still believes you've duped him in some way, but he's so drawn to you he can't stand it. I believe he would have joined you on this settee had I not been here."

They continued to talk for another 20 minutes and then Sunny said she had to be leaving. Stacy hated to see her go, but she praised God for the visit. Sunny left her with some words of encouragement.

"Read the third chapter of First Peter, Stacy. Please don't mistake it for saying that you should stay here no matter what happens to you or Drew, but it might help you to know how to pray.

"If you need to talk and you can't come to me, send word with a servant. I'll come to you. Outside of that, pray, and I hope God will lay it on my heart to come to you."

"Thanks, Sunny. I hope I can come to Bracken soon. Drew would love to play with your boys."

"Oh, Stacy," Sunny sparked. "I didn't even think of it! Please come sometime soon. I know my boys will love Drew."

The women hugged, and Stacy stood in the front yard even after the Hawkesbury carriage was out of sight. Wishing she could go for a walk, she gazed out over the landscape and then realized there was no reason she couldn't. Drew was somewhere with Hettie, and a stroll, even a short one, in the springtime sun would do her good.

Watching her from the study window, Tanner wondered at her thoughts as she walked slowly toward the garden. He was still studying her when a small boy darted out from the side of the mansion. That Stacy was surprised and thrilled to see him was obvious with the way she scooped him into her arms and began to swing around. Another woman, presumably Hettie, had come behind the boy, and Tanner saw the three of them heading off into the gardens and out of sight.

How did a man tell his wife that he was willing to forgive her past indiscretion, but that he wanted nothing to do with her illegitimate child? He wanted her back in his life, but not the boy. He would have to tread carefully for a time. Tonight probably would be too soon, but in time he would find a way to have Stacy again and on his own terms.

Stacy's dinner with Tanner was on her mind as she put her son to bed, and even though she read him a story, she was terribly preoccupied; preoccupied until Drew decided to pull one of his question-and-answer sessions.

"How tall will I be?"

"I'm not sure."

"Taller than Hettie?"

"Probably."

"As tall as you?"

"You might be."

"Will my hair get long?"

"Well, we'll have to keep it cut. Do you want it to get long?"

"No, I don't like it on my neck. Do you like it on your neck?"

"I don't mind too much, unless it gets very hot. You need to go to sleep now."

"Where is Grandpapa?"

"In heaven. Remember we talked about that just yesterday. When we believe in Jesus Christ, we die and go to heaven and live with God."

"Tell me about heaven, Mumma."

"You are stalling, Andrew. Now go to sleep."

"What's stalling?"

Stacy shook her head. "Sleep." She couldn't stop the smile that threatened, however, and Drew grinned back at her when it burst into full bloom on her mouth. She cuddled him close for a time, kissing his soft, warm cheek and telling him he was her little love. He was nearly asleep when she rose.

Hettie went to the door with her, and Stacy paused, knowing that something was on the woman's mind.

"Drew asked me about dying just the other day. Do you want me to tell him what you just said?"

"I tell Drew that, Hettie, because it's what God's Word says, so he can believe it's true. So to answer your question, yes, I would. Would you like me to show you the verses in the Bible that tell us that?"

Hettie nodded. "Sometime, yes, but I'm tired tonight."

"All right. Goodnight, Hettie."

"Will you be in your room in the morning?"

"What do you mean?"

"I mean, should Drew come and find you if you're not in your own room tomorrow morning?"

Stacy didn't know how to answer her. Suddenly the way Tanner looked at her earlier that day gave her pause. Why hadn't it occurred to her before? Not until Stacy had gained her room did she remember she hadn't answered Hettie's question.

"If you're not in your own room."

The words kept sounding in Stacy's head as her hands fluttered nervously over her hair. She checked her dress, a peach silk creation covered in thin black stripes that she had saved for special occasions, repeatedly before going down the stairs. Even though she looked wonderful, her stomach was in knots. She adjusted the lace at her wrist and neckline at least six times, acting as if this was her coming out and not merely dinner with her spouse.

Stacy had almost convinced herself to calm down when she spotted Tanner waiting for her at the bottom of the stairs. He looked gorgeous and larger than life in black evening dress. Stacy was so busy gawking at him that she missed the last step.

Her eyes were the size of saucers when she found herself falling and then caught up tight against Tanner's chest. Stacy looked up into his passion-filled eyes and couldn't speak. She felt panic coming on. She was not ready for this.

"I'm hungry," she suddenly blurted, her eyes still huge in her face.

Stacy's vulnerability touched that spot in Tanner's heart that was so often affected when Stacy was near.

"Shall we go into dinner?" Tanner asked softly as he set her gently away from him.

"Yes, please." Stacy's voice was quiet with gratitude, and Tanner offered her his arm and led her to the dining room. Stacy had no idea what the evening would bring.

Thirty-Two

HOURS LATER STACY LAY ALONE IN HER BED and recounted her dinner conversation with Tanner. It had been a disaster.

"I saw you walking toward the garden today."

"I couldn't resist. After Sunny left I was drawn almost against my will." Tanner was being his most charming, and Stacy was fairly relaxed. "Your gardeners do a wonderful job."

"They would probably appreciate your praise."

Stacy was thinking that they wouldn't want her anywhere near them when Tanner asked, "How is your meal?"

"Everything is delicious, thank you."

"Are you settled in your room?"

"Yes. It's a beautiful room."

"Well, I hope you don't get too comfortable."

Stacy's eyes flew to her husband at the other end of the table, but he was bent over his plate and didn't notice. Stacy took a deep breath and forced herself to speak.

"If you don't plan on my staying at Winslow very long, maybe it would be best if I left right away."

Tanner frowned at her for just an instant. When his face cleared, he explained.

"I wasn't referring to your moving from Winslow, only from your bedroom."

Suddenly Stacy wasn't hungry anymore. It didn't matter that half of her meal was still on the plate, she knew she was through. Stacy still loved her husband, but she was having a hard time forgetting that he thought she'd had another man's child. With this in mind, she found it hard to believe that he desired her at all. Even if he did, would it last? Or would he grow angry again and push her away at a moment's notice.

"Doesn't the idea appeal to you?" Tanner asked, having carefully watched Stacy's face.

"It's not that."

"What is it?"

Tanner's tone had become slightly impatient, and Stacy wished she'd kept her mouth closed.

"I asked you a question, Anastasia."

"You've made it quite clear that you desire me, Tanner, but I doubt if desire is enough to build a marriage on."

"Meaning?" He was angry now, and Stacy's stomach churned.

"Meaning that as soon as you think I've betrayed you again, I'll be sent away once more."

It was the worst thing she could have said. Tanner was so furious his face flushed.

"You make it sound as though I imagined the events at the Cradwells'."

Stacy couldn't answer.

"I was there, Stacy." Tanner now stood, his voice tight with rage. "I saw Lord Stanley's hands on you." He stopped and tried to control himself before going on in a cold voice. "I think you might be right. Whatever is left between us is probably not enough to work with."

He had left the room then, and after a moment Stacy herself had gotten slowly to her feet.

Now Stacy lay and tried to think of how she could have handled the evening differently. After just moments she realized that it would have happened no matter what. Maybe her comments had brought it on a few weeks early, but there was no way that this arrangement was going to last. Tanner still carried too much bitterness over something he wasn't even willing to discuss.

Knowing she was not going to sleep, Stacy rose and decided she would start her packing. She lit a lantern and moved around the room collecting things, not bothering to put on her wrapper. The maid Price had sent to do her unpacking had done a wonderful job of laying her things out and making everything feel "homey," but now Stacy was forced to search every drawer and surface for her belongings.

She had worked along steadily for close to an hour when her bedroom door opened. Stacy was startled by the intrusion and then alarmed when Tanner came through the portal. He was still wearing his dinner slacks. His white shirt, now without the tie, was open at the throat.

Without a word, he moved to Stacy. She wanted to step away from him and the intensity in his eyes, but she was too stunned to move. For all Tanner's severity, his touch, when he finally stopped before her, was extremely gentle. He reached for and grasped her upper arms, pulled her close and then bent to kiss her.

Stacy was so unprepared that she didn't at first react. Tanner's kisses were a homage to her loveliness, and within just seconds he'd made her feel like the cherished wife of old. Stacy was so confused she couldn't think. At last he raised his head and spoke. His voice was gentle.

"You're not leaving Winslow, Stacy. You're my wife, and I want you here. If I said something that intimated otherwise, disregard it."

Tanner glanced around the room, already having summed up the situation.

"Do not put all of these things away tonight. Go back to bed; someone will see to them in the morning."

Stacy opened her mouth to speak, but Tanner went on.

"Do as I tell you. You look too tired and thin for my liking. Now into bed and sleep."

Stacy could hardly believe it when he turned her and gave her a small push toward the bed. She climbed beneath the covers. As she lay on her back, Tanner bent over her.

"Go to sleep," he said one last time and kissed Stacy again. He turned the lantern down, and in the remaining glow Stacy watched him leave. She fell asleep as she was asking God what she was going to do with this man who so confounded her.

Tanner finally sought his bed. He'd been in the study earlier when Price came in. It was quite late, and Tanner, surprised to see him still up, had told him to go to bed. But Price had not come to serve his lord.

"There is a light burning in Lady Richardson's room, my lord. Would you like me to send a maid to her or check on her myself?"

Tanner had not immediately told Price that he would check on Lady Richardson himself; there was suddenly too much on his mind. The very fact that Price would ask him such a thing spoke volumes. No one it seemed, least of all the staff, knew Stacy's status at Winslow. Oh, she was the duchess; that was clear. But he saw for the first time that they didn't know what to do with her.

It suddenly became apparent that this had to do with the boy. He had told Stacy, in so many words, to keep the child out of his way. She had taken him a little too literally. He'd been half hoping to see the child up close at some point, but Stacy, fearing it would cause a disturbance, wasn't going to let that happen. He saw then that he was going to have to go to them in order to prove to her that he would not harm the boy.

Their conversation over dinner came back to him at that point. He hadn't meant to mention their separate bedrooms, nor had he anticipated Stacy's fearful response when he did. When he'd calmed down, her reaction made perfect sense.

As Tanner settled the bed covers around him he reached for the empty side of the bed and simply let his arm lie. She had actually intimated that she'd been innocent at the Cradwell party. Tanner didn't believe that for a moment, but maybe he had overreacted three years ago. She had seemed sorry for her actions, and Leslie never had been. Stacy had acted as if she wanted to stay; Leslie had been happier when he was miles away.

Tanner didn't sleep for many hours that night. He was too busy plotting how he would romance and woo his wife. He told himself that she didn't deserve it, but if that was the way it had to be, he would at least give it a try. His only regret at this point was that he was probably going to have to befriend the boy to do it.

"Now, this shoe is an island, so you must sail your ship far around it, Drew."

Stacy and her young son were on the floor of her sitting room two nights later. Drew's face was still flushed from his bath, and he was all ready for bed. Since it was still a bit early, he and his mother were playing "boats" with several of Stacy's shoes.

"This is the pirate boat, Mumma. It's coming to get you."

"I'm going to sail away, Captain Drew. You can't catch me."

Drew let out a shriek of laughter and jumped up to move one of the other shoes.

"This is a pirate too," he cried. "I've got you. You have no cannon and I—" Drew abruptly halted, and Stacy looked at him. He was staring at something behind her. He then moved quite close to where she was half-lying on the floor. Stacy's heart began to pound even before she sat up and turned to see Tanner.

What she saw nearly broke her heart. All color had drained from Tanner's face, and his eyes were locked on Drew. He moved to sit in the nearest chair, one by the door, without even looking at it.

"Mumma?" Drew whispered softly to his mother. It was just what Stacy needed to open her mouth.

"Drew, this is Lord Richardson."

"Richardson?" He was too bright not to recognize the name.

"Yes. He's letting us stay here at Winslow. Please go and introduce yourself."

Drew scrambled immediately to his feet and went to stand before Tanner.

"Hello, sir," he bowed from the waist. "I'm Drew—"

"Andrew," his mother started him again."

"Andrew Tanner Richardson."

With that, Drew put his small hand out, and Tanner, in a near state of shock, shook it.

"You're tall," Drew said when he regained his hand.

"Yes." Tanner's gaze had softened, and Drew's fascination with this tall stranger bubbled to the surface.

"Mumma is tall."

"Yes, she is."

"Are you taller than Mumma?"

"Yes, I am."

"I might be tall."

"Yes, I think you might be."

"Grandpapa was tall. He's in heaven."

Tanner had no reply to this, but he was content just to sit and stare into Drew's captivating little face.

"Drew," his mother called to him after just a moment. "It's bedtime now."

As if on cue, Hettie came to the door.

"Go with Hettie, and I'll come and kiss you later."

Drew threw his arms around his mother and kissed her exuberantly. Stacy cuddled him close for as long as she dared before releasing him to go with Hettie. He was nearly to the door when she called his name.

"Andrew."

"Oh," the little boy stopped, facing the large man in the chair. "Thank you for meeting me, sir. Goodnight, sir."

Stacy was so proud of him she could have sung. When the

door closed, however, and she found herself alone with Tanner, she couldn't remain on the floor. She rose and gathered the shoes they'd been playing with, returning them to her dressing room. When she came back into the sitting room, Tanner was just as she'd left him.

Stacy couldn't quite bring herself to look at his face, so she took a seat on the sofa, taking some time to adjust her skirt before she looked into his eyes. To her utter relief he was not angry.

"Why didn't you tell me?"

Stacy took a breath. "After all that has passed between us, I wasn't sure you would believe me." She paused and then went on with her eyes in her lap. "And in truth, I wanted you to want me back for *me*."

Nothing had ever rocked Tanner's world the way events of the last ten minutes had, and for Tanner Richardson, that was saying quite a bit. He had a son. *A son!* He was a man who had believed he could never help create a child, and here he had a beautiful boy who sported his high cheekbones and dark brown eyes. Except for Stacy's straight, thick, honey-blonde hair that fell so perfectly across his forehead, Drew looked just like his own childhood portraits.

"He's a fine boy," Tanner managed at last. "You've done a good job with him."

"He is a good boy," Stacy agreed, now able to look up at her husband.

"How old is he?"

"He was three last month, the tenth of April."

"And you call him Drew?"

"Yes. It was easier since we were living with my grandfather, and now he prefers that to Andrew."

"You should get him out more," Tanner said, but it was not a criticism.

"I didn't want to do that until you'd met him and seen what a well-behaved boy he was. He can be rather rambunctious at times, and I didn't want him to disturb you."

"Winslow is his home; he can go where he likes."

Stacy nodded, trying to hide how crushed she felt inside with the way he'd said "his home." She tried to push it away before she read to much into it and put herself into agony.

Tanner stood, seeming almost anxious to be away. "I'll leave you now. I have some things to do in my study. Goodnight, Stacy."

"Goodnight, Tanner." Stacy said the words automatically, uncertain that it was going to be a good night at all.

Tanner locked the door of his study before turning the lamps high and moving to the safe. He spun the dial effortlessly and in moments the door swung open. However, his hand shook when he looked inside and reached for a thick bundle of papers. A moment later he sat at his desk, every letter Stacy had written placed in front of him.

When the letters first arrived he had never read them; not for months did he even open them. Price would always announce that one had arrived, but Tanner would tell him he didn't want to see it.

Then about six months after Stacy left, the letters stopped. Tanner didn't know what to think. He questioned Price. To his relief the faithful servant had saved every bit of her correspondence. Tanner had read through them all in an evening and then sat in agony when it seemed that she would write no more.

What if she's dead? he'd asked himself. He had said he didn't care, but he was lying to himself. This and many more questions had tormented his confused mind for two weeks. Then a letter arrived. She hadn't missed a single week after that, and Tanner read each one as it arrived.

Now he carefully looked at the date of each letter. It only took a few minutes to see how the dates matched. Stacy had not written those two weeks in April because she was having his baby. Again questions swarmed his mind. Had it been hard? Had she been sick? Even though she'd been in bed, couldn't she have written? Had Drew been a difficult or sickly baby? It wouldn't seem so now, but three years was a long time.

And what would the next three years bring? This was the last question Tanner allowed himself to ask, because he couldn't stand not having answers.

Thirty-Three

AFTER DRESSING THE NEXT MORNING, Stacy went in search of Drew. He usually came to her while she was still in bed. Stacy wondered this morning if he wasn't sleeping in. She was met by a disapproving and worried Hettie, who said that the duke had come for her son just moments earlier.

"Didn't even ask—just told him to come and of course Drew followed like he'd known him all his life."

Stacy told herself not to be alarmed, and in truth she wasn't, but she did feel curious as to where they might have gone. She was on her way down the stairs when she saw Drew ahead of her, still in his nightclothes, sliding down the banister and giggling with all his might.

"Andrew Tanner Richardson." Stacy's voice was firm but not harsh. "You asked me when we arrived if you could slide on this banister, and I said no."

"Come now, Stacy," Tanner said before the boy could say a word. Stacy had gained the foyer but hadn't even seen him as he lounged against one wall watching his son's antics. "What's the harm?" he went on critically. "You're acting like a silly old woman."

"Silly old woman," Drew echoed, and Stacy turned to her son in outrage.

"*Andrew Richardson!* You will not speak to me in such a way or ever call me names. Do you understand?"

The little boy was crushed. "Yes, Mumma."

"Go right now and find Hettie so you can get dressed."

Drew, very subdued, moved to do as he was told. Stacy waited until he'd met Hettie at the top of the stairs before turning to Tanner. He had pushed away from the wall and now stood alert. The betrayal he saw in Stacy's eyes was almost his undoing. Her pain-filled voice made it worse.

"Obedient children do not just happen. They are the result of months of hard work. As you can see, Tanner, you can undo all of that work in a fraction of that time." Stacy's voice caught, but she went on. "You promised not to take him."

She turned then to run up the stairs, but Tanner caught her on the third step. His hands held her waist, but Stacy would not turn around.

"My promise still stands. I won't take him."

"I wish I could believe you," Stacy admitted. It was easier to be honest when he wasn't looking at her.

"I grew up without a mother, Stacy. I would never separate the two of you, not even emotionally, especially now that I'm aware."

Stacy turned then. The difference in their heights was removed because Stacy was on a higher step. She looked directly into his face as she said, "I didn't know your mother died when you were young."

"She didn't. She just didn't want me."

Stacy looked into his wonderful, dark eyes and slowly shook her head. "How could she not want you?"

Tanner shrugged. The pain in his eyes was only slight. The years had dulled the ache. "She never wanted any of us, not my father, my brother, or me. Sometimes I can still hear her telling my father she was a fool for having married him and an even greater fool for giving him sons."

"Oh, Tanner" was all Stacy could say.

"It's not going to be that way for Drew. This is your home now, our home. I don't know if I can ever forgive you for what you did, but Drew's going to have his mother and father with him."

Stacy sighed. "You still believe the worst, Tanner, even after seeing Drew?"

"Drew is obviously my son, Stacy, but we won't speak of the other." His voice said there would be no argument and, as usual, Stacy acquiesced.

When Stacy looked defeated, Tanner's hands gently stroked her waist. "Come have breakfast with me. Bring Drew if you'd like."

Stacy saw it for the olive branch that it was. She hated living under this false accusation, but for now she was going to have to let it drop. It wasn't ideal, but maybe in time he would come to see that there had never been anyone but him.

"What is it?"

"It's an egg dish. Now I want you to try some."

The three-year-old's face was so comical that Tanner had to raise his napkin to his mouth to hide his smile. If he wanted to provoke his wife at that moment and probably earn himself a tongue-lashing, all he had to do was laugh. He certainly admired her way with Drew, especially when she must have been tempted to laugh herself. Tanner knew he would never have made it.

The duke was correct about his wife's desire to laugh. When Drew started to eat, Stacy sent a warning glance in Tanner's direction, but not even she could hide the twinkle in her eye before turning to her own plate.

Tanner was just starting on his third cup of coffee when he realized that a nanny or nurse should have been doing Stacy's job. He pondered on the different women who had been in charge of him and his brother over the years, and then knew it would be years before Drew appreciated having his mother there instead.

While most women were sewing or visiting with friends, Drew's mother was teaching him to eat correctly and to respect his elders. It suddenly occurred to him why. There would not have been money in the viscount's household for a luxury such as a nurse. Tanner determined to ask Stacy if she wanted to hire a nanny, but he knew what the answer would be.

"Tanner," Stacy cut into his thoughts, "would it be a problem if I visited Bracken today?"

Tanner's brows rose to his hairline. "You certainly don't need to ask permission to go calling, Stacy. Just order the carriage and go."

"Thank you, Tanner," she said softly. He almost told her that wasn't necessary either.

"Am I going to Racken?"

"It's Bracken," his mother corrected him, "and, yes, you are. You can play with Lady Sunny's little boys."

"Do they have toys?"

"I'm sure they do," Stacy answered absently and reached for her cup of tea. She wouldn't have been quite so calm if she'd seen Tanner's shocked look.

He had a sudden image of his son playing with shoes on the floor of his mother's sitting room. Something painful tore inside of him at the way his wife and son had been living for the past three years. This was his family home; all of his childhood toys must be here somewhere.

Tanner excused himself a very short time later. Stacy was surprised to see him go so suddenly, but she was thankful for their brief time. She would have been even more thankful if she'd known that he was ordering the house servants at Winslow to ready the nursery for Drew while he and Stacy were at Bracken.

"Oh, Sunny, you should have seen his face when he saw Drew. I thought my heart would break."

"He didn't question his parentage at all?"

"No," Stacy answered and went ahead to tell her the entire story. "God is so good," Stacy said as she finished.

"How about the verses; were they an encouragement?" Sunny's voice said she hoped they had been.

"'Likewise, ye wives, be in subjection to your own husbands that, if any obey not the word, they also may without the word be won by the conversation of the wives, while they behold your chaste conversation coupled with fear; whose adorning, let it not be that outward adorning of plaiting the hair, and of wearing of gold, or of putting on of apparel, but let it be the hidden man of the heart in that which is not corruptible, even the ornament of a meek and quiet spirit, which is in the sight of God of great price. First Peter 3:1-4.'"

"I can't believe you memorized those verses," Sunny said in amazement.

"I cling to them," Stacy told her, "and it's been such a comfort. But my favorite verse isn't with those. It's at the middle of chapter three. 'For the eyes of the Lord are over the righteous, and his ears are open unto their prayers; but the face of the Lord is against them that do evil.'"

"You challenge me, Stacy. I haven't memorized a verse in several weeks."

"Oh, Sunny, I think God understands. You said that Preston had a cold and then you and then Sterling. I think at times like that you have to concentrate on the verses you already know."

Sunny's brow drew down in a mock frown. "I thought when we studied that I would be teaching you. I really needed to hear that, Stacy. Thank you."

Stacy smiled. "There is so much I don't know, Sunny, and I'm still too timid. I haven't even told Tanner about my conversion. I need boldness."

"Has there been an opportunity to tell him?"

This gave Stacy pause. "Now that you mention it, I'm not sure if there has. Maybe I need to give it more time."

"It sounds like you'll have the time. And don't forget your verses so fast. Your life will show him better than words."

"Yes, it should. My pride rears its head, and I want to shout at Tanner and defend myself. His words about not forgiving me were hard to take, so I concentrated on his wanting a real family. I've prayed about that for so long."

"Speaking of families, did you want to check on the boys?"

"Yes. Drew will be growing hungry soon."

"As will Sterling and Preston. We can have tea when they're settled with lunch."

❧ ❧ ❧

"Oh, Mumma," Drew cried when his mother appeared at the nursery room door.

"Hello, my darling. Having fun?"

Drew ran to hug Stacy. "They have real boats!" His voice was breathless with excitement. "Lots of boats!"

Stacy's grin was as large as her son's eyes.

"How about some lunch?" Sunny asked the gang, and they responded loudly.

Stacy studied them as they moved out of the room and down the hall. Sterling was a most handsome young lad, sporting his father's dark hair and eyes. He was just short of his sixth birthday. Preston was less than a year older than Drew, and his hair was as dark as Drew's was fair. They were of the same build, Preston being an inch or so taller, and both were the picture of young health.

Since he was a little older, Sterling was inclined to be more serious, whereas both Drew and Preston were in some ways little more than babies. Sterling was wonderfully patient with all of their antics, and Stacy had not as yet heard a cross word between them.

After seeing that they were nicely settled, the Hawkesbury nanny in attendance, Stacy and Sunny went to the small salon for their tea.

They made themselves comfortable and talked as if Stacy had been back for years instead of weeks. The Duchess of Cambridge had a small sandwich halfway to her mouth when her husband and Brandon walked into the room. Stacy, suspecting she might choke if she took a bite, replaced the sandwich and sat still while Tanner approached.

He bent as soon as he was near, grasped her jaw, and kissed her. Stacy stared up into his face a moment, her own face still cupped in his hand, before speaking.

"You could have ridden over with us." Stacy prayed that he was not checking up on her.

"In truth I was in need of a ride. My horse has been getting fat of late. If you don't mind my company, however, I'll go back with you."

"All right," Stacy smiled sweetly, the first real smile since her husband had come for her. It was so reminiscent of their first months as husband and wife that Tanner had a hard time taking his eyes away. Only Brandon, coming to greet Stacy, moved him on.

In the next few minutes, the men took seats and were served tea. The conversation ran from one subject to the next until Parks, head of housekeeping at Bracken, came to the door.

"I'm sorry to disturb you, my lord," he said to Brandon.

"That's all right, Parks. What is it?"

"Nanny reports that young Lord Richardson bumped his head while playing and is quite inconsolable."

Stacy began to rise.

"I'll go," Tanner told her. He moved to the door, Brandon behind him.

"You look thunderstruck," Sunny commented when the men left.

"I'm just surprised that he wanted to go."

"I guess I'm not. Whenever he visits here and the boys are present, he always speaks to them with genuine interest. I think he really loves children."

Sunny talked on, cutting off only when the men reappeared, Drew in his father's arms. He was not crying, but his fair head lay on Tanner's shoulder and the evidence of tears was on his cheek. Tanner deliberately took the settee next to Stacy and as soon as Drew saw his mother, he reached for her.

Stacy took him on her lap but looked down to see that he was smiling back at Tanner.

"You certainly don't look any worse for wear," Stacy commented and looked for the bump. Some tears filled Drew's eyes, but they did not spill.

"I believe it was quite minor." Tanner's voice was dry. His son might have overreacted, but he was adorable while doing it.

"I think what you really need is a nap," Stacy said.

Drew's lip quivered, but Stacy's voice was firm.

"You will not fuss about it, Drew. Now let's say goodbye to Lord and Lady Hawkesbury."

Tanner came behind his wife and son to say his own goodbyes, but he was rather preoccupied. Why hadn't it occurred to him that Drew cried harder because he was tired? He decided he could learn a lot about parenting from Stacy.

Tanner would have laughed at his own seriousness if he could have seen Brandon's and Sunny's amused expressions after he left. Of course, they would have been the first to admit that they had no idea what it was like not to meet your son until he was three.

Thirty-Four

As USUAL, STACY WAS STARVING. She had eaten a large dinner and even enjoyed Tanner's presence in the process, but that felt like hours ago. She tried to sleep, but it just wasn't going to work. After fighting the urge for just a few minutes, she decided to go to the kitchen. She knew the feeling and was certain it would not go away.

With a decisive move, she threw the covers back and reached for her wrapper. It came to her as she was leaving her room that Tanner would simply ring for something, but Stacy's relationship with the staff was only just slightly warmer now than it had been when they first arrived.

Cook, Price, and of course, Hettie were the only servants who did not act as if they were doing Stacy a favor every time she called on them. It was only when Drew needed something that she was bold enough to speak up, which of course was the very reason Stacy was walking toward the kitchen this late at night, feeling rather clandestine about fixing herself a snack while the rest of the mansion slept.

Tanner climbed the stairs rather late that night. He'd had some figures to go over concerning a land deal he and Brandon were involved in, and he'd not been satisfied with the outcome. They had already talked of it several times and were going to talk of it again in another few weeks. Tanner had wanted the paperwork out of his head so that he could once again concentrate on Drew and Stacy.

As was swiftly becoming his habit of the last few weeks, Tanner moved to Stacy's door. Each night before he went to bed he would check on both her and Drew. He'd have much preferred Stacy to join him in his own room, but that had not yet happened. She was growing less wary of him each day, and he felt that given time they would once again live as man and wife.

This didn't immediately erase all the past, but Stacy had a good memory; she would not forget his reaction last time and play him for a fool again. Tanner wondered briefly if she'd had other men while in Middlesbrough and then realized that such thoughts were dangerous. He shifted his mind away from such visions as he soundlessly opened Stacy's door.

Tanner did not like finding her bed empty, but he remained calm as he moved across to Drew's room. His heart was silently telling Stacy that she had better be there. When she was not, he decided to wake the entire house to look for her but refrained from doing so until he checked the upstairs and then made his way down the stairway.

She was not in the library or the gallery. He wondered if he'd missed her somewhere on the second floor and was actually halfway up the stairs when he thought of the kitchen. He almost laughed. If Stacy were hungry she would never ring for a servant. With a smile on his face he moved toward the kitchen.

Lady Richardson had just finished an apple and was starting on a piece of pie when Tanner came in the door. She froze, a crumb of food at the corner of her mouth, and watched him approach.

"It seems we have mice—tall, blonde mice."

"I was hungry," Stacy told him unnecessarily, still trying to decide if she was in trouble.

"I can see that." Tanner used his handkerchief to wipe her mouth and then stood staring at her.

"Don't stop on my account," he told her. "Go ahead and eat."

Stacy did so, but it was not easy with Tanner staring at her. His gaze was warm as he watched her. He even pulled a chair up, so his eyes were level with hers.

"Would you like something?" Stacy asked.

"To eat? No, thank you."

Stacy finished her pie. "You're making me nervous," she admitted, a small quiver in her voice.

"You're not afraid of me, are you?"

"I'm not sure what to say to that."

"You are afraid," he stated.

"Of our being together, no, but of my having you for a time and then your pushing me away again, that terrifies me."

Surprisingly this did not anger Tanner. He looked as though he understood. Unfortunately he felt no guilt over the way he'd sent her away. In his mind he had been wronged. If Stacy would only comport herself faithfully, he would care for her all the days of her life. He felt whether or not she stayed was all up to her.

Suddenly Tanner held out his hand. "Come here, Stacy" was all he said. It was hardly an explanation, but Stacy went to him when he reached for her. They kissed in the kitchen, and she had no protest when Tanner lifted her and carried her upstairs.

She had prayed long and hard about this time, wanting with all of her heart to do what God would have her to do. *Maybe,* Stacy reasoned, *this will be one more way to show Tanner that my love has always been constant.*

The next morning Tanner eased quietly out of bed, careful not to wake Stacy. He stared down at her, thinking there wasn't a lovelier, more giving woman in all of England. At this moment he could almost believe her when she claimed that he had misunderstood the scene at the Cradwells'.

With feather-soft movements he reached for his robe and left the room. Stacy had come in with just a light wrapper on the night before, so Tanner was headed to her room to find her a robe. He didn't want her feeling at all uncomfortable when she awakened.

Stacy's bed was as he'd seen it, covers thrown back and left. There was no sign of her robe, so he lit the lantern and went into her dressing room. He paid little attention to her dresses but quickly spotted a thick, white robe and took hold of it. He was on his way out when he spotted an envelope. He would normally have given little notice to such a thing, but it was addressed to him.

Tanner set the lantern down and looked at the front of the letter. "Lord Tanner Richardson" was written out in Stacy's hand. Tanner removed the folded letter without a moment's hesitation.

"Dear Tanner," it began. "I'm not sure if you knew I was back in London, but I arrived just this week. I am staying at Brentwood with Roddy and Lucinda. I would like to see you. I know I told you I would not return unless you sent for me, but my grandfather has died and I've come at Lucinda's bidding.

"I would like to see you, Tanner. I would like to talk about the Cradwell party and explain about Nigel Stanley. I made a terrible mistake, and if we could only talk, I feel we might resolve this painful thing between us."

There was more, but Tanner stopped reading. He had been ready to believe it had all been a mistake—that he had misunderstood. This was harder to take than Leslie's betrayal. Stacy's sweetness wove its way into his heart until he felt like a snared bird. He had loved that snare when they had first married, but after Stacy's betrayal, he'd felt like it was strangling him.

Tanner threw both the letter and Stacy's robe to the floor and exited the wardrobe and bedroom with long, angry strides. He dressed with Price's help, giving terse orders all the while.

"Pack my bag; I'm leaving. See to it that my *wife*"—it cost him just to say the word—"does not get too comfortable in my bed."

"You do not want me to accompany you, my lord?"

"No. I shall be gone at least a week, but that's no one's business. Handle my correspondence as best you can. No social engagements at all."

"Yes, my lord."

Just 20 minutes later Tanner was in the coach and headed to London. He was not entirely certain what he needed to do there, but he had to put some space between himself and his adulterous wife. He thought he could put it behind him, but right now that didn't seem possible—the letter had finally told him that what he'd believed all along was true.

The night they had spent together ran through his mind, and Tanner knew he would always desire his wife. His next thoughts were of his son, the precious little boy he was just getting to know. Tanner's head fell back against the squabs. He would never break his promise, but agony ripped through him that he could not live in peace with the boy's mother.

* * *

Stacy woke slowly and smiled. Surprisingly, she didn't feel any disorientation waking up in the master bedroom. She knew exactly where she was and, with the smile still on her face, rolled toward Tanner's side of the bed. A lopsided frown replaced the smile when she found the bed empty.

"Tanner," Stacy called softly, hoping he was in his dressing room.

"Tanner," she tried again and sat up when the door opened. She lay down swiftly however, quickly covering herself with the bedclothes when Price appeared instead. She grinned at him from the pillow, even though she was somewhat embarrassed, but her smile slowly faded at Price's serious face.

"Is Lord Richardson dressing, Price?"

"I'm sorry, my lady, but Lord Richardson is not here."

"By not here, do you mean not upstairs?" Her tone was almost too much for the man.

"No, my lady."

"He's left Winslow?"

"Yes, my lady. Would you like me to send Hettie to you?"

"No, Price, that's all right. I'll get up as soon as you go."

Price bowed his way out, and Stacy lay still for a moment. If he had left money on the pillow beside her, she couldn't have felt any cheaper.

Five minutes later Stacy was standing in her dressing room. She bent slowly and picked up the robe and crumpled letter. It didn't take long to figure what had happened. Stacy's eyes closed in agony.

"Oh, Tanner," she whispered. "What have you done?"

Thirty-Five

STACY WAS SORRY SHE CONFIDED in her aunt. Lucinda was so angry she could hardly see straight. Tanner had been gone three days now, and her aunt and uncle had arrived that morning. They were in the large salon at Winslow. Drew was on the huge Persian carpet that covered the floor, but Roddy had brought him a toy and he was not listening to the adults.

"First he takes you from us," she raved, her voice soft but venomous. "And then leaves you here like so much excess baggage. He's an absolute beast. I want you to pack your things immediately. You and Drew are returning with us."

Stacy only shook her head, calm in the face of her aunt's ire.

"How can you stay here?" Lucinda was incredulous.

"Because I want my marriage to work. Running away will accomplish nothing."

Lucinda sat back in utter defeat. Roddy studied his wife and then commented.

"Unless you fear for your safety, I think you're wise, Stacy. What you've told us is heartbreaking, but I think Tanner is confused."

"Confused!" Lucinda snorted scornfully, but a look from Roddy silenced her.

"If he is confused," Roddy continued, "then maybe you can work it out when he returns."

"I thank you for the vote of confidence, Roddy, but he'll probably be angry when he returns. And as you know, Tanner's anger has a way of intimidating me."

"But you don't fear he'll harm you?"

"At times I feel emotionally spent, but no, I don't fear Tanner that way. I think Tanner is wrong to react as he does, but part of the problem is mine because I'm not bolder when I know I'm supposed to be. I decided a few days ago that leaving cannot be an option, or every time I'm upset I'll want to run."

"So you'll stay here no matter what?" Stacy could hear tears in Lucinda's voice.

"I won't go so far as to say that, but I will stay on just as long as I can and hope that means I'll be here for the next 60 years."

It was not what Lucinda wanted to hear, but Stacy believed she was making the right choice. The first time Tanner growled at her she knew she'd be tempted to hide, but for now, for her sake as well as Drew's, she must stay.

The subject was dropped when Drew wanted to go upstairs. Stacy rose to accompany him, but Lucinda, her eyes alight with adoration for Drew, offered to go instead. Stacy was happy to agree. Not until after they'd gone did Stacy take her seat and notice a very thoughtful look on Roddy's face.

"My, but you look serious," Stacy commented lightly. To her surprise Roddy did not laugh at his own somber demeanor.

"How did you come to this decision, Stacy? I mean, to stay here with Tanner?" Roddy asked.

"I believe it's what God wants me to do," she answered simply.

"But how do you *know?*" Roddy's face was filled with yearning. "Has God spoken to you in some way?"

"Through His Word, yes. I believe God speaks to His children through the Bible. I've matured through my study; in fact, I'm a different person now, Roddy, and that's because of the time I've spent in God's Word."

"And you really believe that the Bible is the inspired Word of God?"

"Yes, I do, Roddy."

"But what if you simply can't find the answer you're looking for? Then what do you do?"

Stacy smiled. "God has never let me down, Roddy. If I truly need to know something, He shows me. I don't mean going off on some tangent in order to disprove whether or not Jonah really was swallowed by a fish and lived to tell about it. I'm talking about real-life issues that apply directly to my heart and change me forever."

Roddy nodded slowly and admitted softly, "I'm still working through the cross."

Stacy's smile was tender. She wasn't exactly sure what he meant, but she could hear Drew and Lucinda coming back to join them. "I'll be praying for you, Roddy, and if there is anything I can help you with, please don't hesitate to ask."

Roddy thanked her and then spoke softly before they were interrupted. "*Do* you believe that Jonah was literally swallowed by a huge fish?"

Again Stacy smiled. "With all my heart."

Stacy was ready to change her resolve over staying almost as soon as Tanner came back a week later. She knew he would not seek her out, and she had no intention of mentioning the letter, but Stacy forced herself to see him in order to know where she stood.

"Welcome back, Tanner," Stacy ventured hesitantly from her place just inside the study door, glad to have even gained entrance. "Did your trip go well?"

"Sufferably," Tanner answered without ever looking up from his desk.

"How was your birthday?"

This got the duke's attention. His head came up, and he looked at her in surprise. Stacy began thinking she'd mistaken the date all these years.

"It was your birthday two days ago, wasn't it?"

"Yes." Tanner's voice was cold. He seemed to be angry that she remembered when he had not.

"It doesn't sound like you celebrated." Stacy tried to be cheerful. "Shall I ask cook for something special for lunch?"

"I'll be busy."

"Dinner then?"

"No. I have work to do, Stacy."

She watched his head go back down and knew she had to ask the next question if it killed her.

"Tanner, would you rather we leave?"

Brown eyes burned into blue, and Stacy held her breath.

"Do as you like." Again the head went back down.

"So we can stay?"

"I don't—" Tanner stood and began to shout, but cut off when he saw his wife blanch.

He was still angry enough to throw her out, but thinking about it and actually doing it while looking into Stacy's vulnerable, strained features were far different.

"You're welcome to stay." Tanner's was calmer now. "But I am a busy man, so I would appreciate being left alone."

Stacy nodded and turned to the door. Her hand shook as she tried to open it, forcing her to try again. She exited the room without once glancing back to see her husband watching her, an unreadable expression on his face.

"Here we go." Stacy swung Drew back up onto the bank and they started their trek home.

Two weeks had passed since she'd talked to Tanner in the study. He rarely spoke to her, although there were times when he sought Drew out and talked with him.

Just when she didn't think she could bear up under the strain, the Lord used Drew to rescue her.

"Mumma, can we fish?"

It was on Stacy's lips to say no because there was no water, but she suddenly remembered a creek that she and Tanner had passed years ago while out riding. It would take some legwork, but Stacy was sure they could walk it.

Today was their sixth trip. Stacy did not say yes every day, but in truth she needed the outings as much as Drew did. The servants, with the exception of Price, were more unpleasant than ever, and Winslow had become an oppressive place for Stacy. Hettie had come down with a summer cold that went straight into her chest, so Stacy and Drew were on their own much of the time.

"I'll carry the fish," Drew now said, and Stacy gave him the string. She knew he wouldn't last long with the heavy line, but she let him try. They were both tiring as they neared the rear of the Winslow stables, but Drew still had energy to chatter. He made Stacy laugh on several occasions, and she was still laughing when Drew cried out.

"Oh, look, Mumma, it's Lord Richardson. We can show him our catch."

This was the last thing Stacy wanted to do, but Tanner was standing ahead of them in the path, watching their approach. The twosome had no choice but to walk right past him.

"We fished," Drew said as soon as he was in close proximity. "See our catch, Lord Richardson!"

Stacy had stopped, and Drew now took the fish and ran from his mother's side to hold up the string of trophies. Tanner moved toward his son and hunkered down to Drew's level.

"It looks as if you've been busy."

"Mumma caught them, and I helped. Someday I can fish with a hook too."

"I'm sure you'll do very well."

Drew chattered on, and Tanner paid close attention. Stacy would have been surprised to know that he was watching her as much as listening to Drew.

She was dressed in a worn day-dress, looking more like a scullery maid than a duchess. Not that it mattered; Tanner found her lovely whatever her attire. Her face was flushed and her hair a mess, and Tanner suddenly realized they had come from behind the stables and not through them.

"Where did you fish?" He stood in one easy movement, his voice nonchalant.

"At the creek."

"Did you walk?"

"Yes," Stacy answered slowly, sensing for the first time that he might not be too happy about that. "It really isn't far, and we needed to get out."

"I don't want—" Tanner began, his tone severe.

"Mumma?"

"Andrew," Stacy turned to her son when he cut in, "Lord Richardson is talking. Do not interrupt." Stacy turned back to Tanner, but he was staring down at Drew. Stacy followed his gaze to find her son standing with his legs close together and a look of near panic on his face.

Oh my, Stacy thought, thinking that if she took care of Drew's needs, Tanner would be angry. To her surprise, Tanner stepped in. He swiftly scooped Drew into his arms and headed into the bush off the path.

Stacy heard low voices beyond the shrubs and shook her head in wonder. One moment her husband was completely unapproachable and then next he was taking his son into the bushes. Although, if Stacy thought about it, Tanner was always kind to Drew. It was to her that he was unapproachable. He didn't seek Drew out very often, but his face and voice were very gentle when they were together.

Drew marched out of the bushes then, Tanner on his heels.

"Mumma, can Lord Richardson eat our fish too?"

"Of course, darling; we have plenty."

"I'll tell cook," Drew stated and started toward the mansion once again. Stacy thanked Tanner for seeing to Drew's needs and moved along the path. She wasn't certain if Tanner followed or not, but right then she couldn't make herself stay and be scolded over the fishing trip. Feeling every inch a coward, she rushed along behind Drew to the kitchen.

Three hours later Tanner came from his study in time to see a maid taking a tray upstairs. The unmistakable smell of fish wafted through the air. Tanner frowned at the woman's back. Hadn't Drew wanted to eat with him, and hadn't Stacy agreed?

"Did you need something, my lord?"

Tanner turned to find Price in attendance.

"When is dinner?"

"Seven o'clock, unless of course you wish to change the time?"

Tanner knew it was just now six.

"And what is cook serving?"

"I believe Lord Drew requested that you enjoy some of his fish."

Tanner nodded. He'd assumed that they would be eating together and realized then that he should assume nothing. His disappointment was keen. He had looked forward to eating with his son and seeing Stacy. His anger was wearing off, and even though he was in no mood to allow her any foothold in his life, she was still a delight to the eyes, and because she didn't chatter constantly, a very restful person to be with.

"Please tell cook that I wish my dinner now, and served with my wife and son."

Price bowed and left to change the arrangements. Tanner, not bothering with a coat, took the stairs two at a time to find Stacy and Drew.

Stacy had just seated Drew at the table in her sitting room and was about to serve him when Tanner knocked on the door. Stacy stared up at him, uncertain about his presence until Tanner's brows rose almost mockingly.

"Come in," Stacy quickly invited, feeling flustered.

Tanner spoke once he was inside.

"I thought I'd been invited to eat fish with you."

"Oh!" Stacy said. "I'm sorry, Tanner, I didn't realize. Please sit down."

She rushed to pull up another chair to the small table and serve him. Tanner frowned at her actions, looking around for the kitchen maid. He would have questioned Stacy about this, but there was another knock at the door.

Each evening at 6:00, a tray was delivered by a kitchen maid to Drew and Stacy. The maid never stayed to serve them in any way, but now that Tanner was present, not only one maid came to attend him, but three. The plates uncovered from Tanner's tray were filled with sumptuous foods and added to Drew and Stacy's meager fare. Stacy and Drew never received any more than one piece of bread each—Tanner had an entire loaf. He had butter—they never saw the stuff. They felt blessed if they received one vegetable—Tanner's tray had four.

Stacy, fighting resentment over the way she and Drew were treated, busied herself with her son's plate, filling it with the best food they'd eaten since arriving. Then she cut his fish and got the spoon into his hand. He bumped his water at one point, but Stacy caught it. It wasn't until that moment that she glanced up to find Tanner's gaze on her.

He'd been talking with Drew, and Stacy, who was still in turmoil inside and had not said a word, only listened. She thought she'd been hiding her feelings but realized now that her color must be high with her agitation. She was more angry at herself than anyone else for not telling Tanner on the spot that this was the best they'd eaten.

As soon as Drew was well ensconced with his food, Stacy lowered her eyes and dug into her own plate. She didn't care if she was being watched or not, she was suddenly so hungry she was shaking.

"Mumma," Drew suddenly said. "We didn't pray."

Stacy took a deep breath and praised God for this gentle reminder. "You're right, my darling. Shall we pray now?" Where Stacy found the courage to suggest this without even looking at her spouse, she didn't know, but pray she did.

"Father in heaven, we thank You for this food and all Your blessings. Please keep us this night that we might wake tomorrow to know You and serve You better. In Your name we pray. Amen."

"Amen," Drew echoed and picked up his spoon once again. Stacy retrieved her own utensil and only then did she look up to see Tanner staring, but this time he was looking at Drew, contentment etching his handsome face.

"It's good that children pray," Tanner finally commented. Stacy nearly dropped her fork. She recovered swiftly, however, and put in her own gentle oar.

"I find that prayer is also good for adults. That, along with time spent reading God's Word."

Tanner's attention turned to her, his eyes thoughtful. "I wondered at your having a Bible near your bed."

"I read it every day." Stacy spoke calmly but was amazed that he'd even noticed.

"Why?" he asked bluntly, as if doing such a thing was only for the weak.

"I have a yearning to know more. I have a relationship with God through His Son, Jesus Christ, and I want to know Him better."

Tanner clearly did not know what to do with this answer. He didn't believe that God involved Himself in people's daily lives. That type of thing was reserved for the Old Testament times, when God spoke through a burning bush or met Moses on the mountain to give him the law. And yet Stacy was so sincere. She was not the type to go off on some emotional religious experience, and the serenity in her eyes as she'd answered him was unmistakable.

Tanner went back to his plate, and Stacy knew the discussion was over. It hadn't been much, but he'd at least listened to her without ridicule. Stacy continued to eat as well. Drew started to chatter right after that, but Stacy's mind was praying and she did not attend.

Thirty-Six

THE STUDY DOOR BURST OPEN, and Tanner, having been disturbed, came out in a dreadful humor. Stacy and Drew had been on their way to the front door, and Stacy, thinking Tanner was away again, was chasing Drew and making him giggle loudly. They both shrank back when he stood before them in a towering rage. Stacy, fearing he would shout at Drew, called to Hettie.

"Drew," she told him when the old woman appeared, "go on to the coach with Hettie; there's a good boy. I'll be out shortly."

"I'm sorry, Tanner," Stacy said when Hettie and the boy were gone. "We didn't realize you were here."

Tanner's mood was not improved by her apology. Stacy, thinking it best that she just leave, took a step away.

"Do they not have dressmakers in Middlesbrough?"

The question was not lost on Stacy. She was wearing a dress of dark blue satin with matching bows and white lace on the bodice and neckline. It was one from her wedding trousseau—in fact all of her dresses were from her wedding trousseau.

"Well, actually I gained quite a bit of weight when I was carrying Drew, and I wasn't able to wear many of my gowns. Some of them are virtually new." Stacy stopped, thinking this explanation enough, but Tanner still scowled.

"You're leaving?"

"Yes. We're going to Bracken. I hope it will be quiet for you then."

Tanner didn't even bother to acknowledge her statement. Without so much as a by-your-leave, he turned on his heel and walked back to the study.

"So you think things might be a little better?" Sunny asked.

"Well," Stacy tried to explain, "Tanner's moods are usually pretty black, but he's been very attentive to Drew and sometimes he's very kind to me. One night—" Stacy began and went on to tell Sunny what had happened over the dinner table with Drew, the prayer, and their discussion afterward.

"It was very brief, but then a few nights later Tanner showed up at Drew's bedtime. I always read Drew a Bible passage, and Tanner actually stayed to listen. It was the parable of the prodigal son from Luke 15. Tanner seemed fascinated. Now he looks at me as if he doesn't know me, but it's not in a negative way. Does that make sense?"

"Yes. You think he might be warming up?"

Stacy shrugged ruefully. "He wasn't too happy when I left this morning. I always seem to underestimate Tanner. I've been so relieved on several occasions that he hasn't seemed to notice my clothing, and then this morning I discovered he hasn't missed a thing."

"Upset, was he?"

"Yes. I know my clothes are all out of date; Lucinda made that quiet clear, but it just hasn't been important, Sunny. When you think of all that's gone on in my world in the last few years, you can probably see why having the latest outfits was not a priority."

"It's a matter of pride."

"You think I'm being prideful?" It was hard for Stacy to hear this, but she needed to be made aware.

"Not you, Stacy. Tanner. He's a duke, a wealthy one. He wants you dressed in the finest attire money can buy."

Stacy's look was comical. "I've never thought of it that way."

"It might be best if you did, because I wouldn't be too surprised if he suddenly decided to do something about your wardrobe."

Stacy nodded in understanding. They both knew that "something" meant a shopping trip to London.

"Thank you, Sunny," Stacy said softly, and for the moment the subject was dropped. It was time to go upstairs. Earlier, the boys had asked their mothers to have tea with them in the nursery.

For the second time since Stacy returned to Winslow, Tanner "followed" her to Bracken. She had been other times on her own, so she knew he was not checking on her, but the emotions she felt when he appeared were riotous. Actually they were the same emotions that occurred nearly every time he sought her out—some fear, but also some hope that maybe he had come because he'd missed her.

The women were still in the nursery when Tanner and Brandon came in. Tanner did not immediately speak to her beyond a short greeting but talked with Brandon, Sunny, and the boys. Stacy noticed the way he studied the children, and something in his expression made her wary. She didn't have long to wait. Tanner refused tea and just ten minutes after he arrived, he turned to Stacy.

"I want us to leave for London."

"Right now?"

"Yes."

"All right," Stacy stood. "Would you like me to go home and pack?"

"You and Drew are already packed. Hettie is waiting with the carriages." His voice was not harsh, but Stacy could tell that he was not feeling overly patient.

"Oh." Stacy was not certain how to reply to this, but she knew she needed a moment of privacy. "Drew and I will just take a minute to prepare, and we'll be right down."

Tanner's nod was almost curt as he told them he'd be waiting downstairs and abruptly left the room. Stacy made swift thank-you's, and Sunny took her and Drew to a retiring room. Stacy's heart sank when Drew decided he needed to sit down on the commode. Stacy knew it would do no good to rush him, but she could almost feel Tanner's impatience from downstairs.

When they finally started to rush down the stairs, Drew got it into his head to examine everything they passed. Tanner was in sight when he stopped the last time to look at a bronze statue.

"Andrew!" Stacy's voice was sharp with panic. "Lord Richardson is waiting for us. Come now."

Afraid of his fury, Stacy kept her head lowered as they passed. Sunny walked Stacy and Drew to the carriage, and Tanner and Brandon followed more slowly.

"Come again when you can stay," Brandon told the other duke.

"I'll do that, Hawk. Thank you."

"I might be out of line," Brandon continued as they walked, "but Stacy gave Sunny the impression that you've accepted Drew as your own."

"Of course I have." Tanner frowned darkly at him, but Brandon was not so easily intimidated.

"Then why the Lord Richardson?"

"I don't know what you're talking about."

"Your son calls you Lord Richardson, and Stacy calls you by your title when she's speaking of you to Drew."

Tanner's air left him in a rush. He hadn't even noticed. He'd had a formal relationship with his father, never calling him anything but "sir," but not even he and his brother had been expected to call him by his title.

"It's your choice, Tanner," Brandon said softly. "And the last thing I want to do is interfere. It's just that Drew obviously thinks quite a lot of you, and I think he's a fine boy."

"Yes, he is," Tanner admitted, looking his friend in the eye. "I'll see you later, Hawk."

"Goodbye, Tanner."

The two men shook hands, and Tanner covered the remaining distance to the carriage and pulled himself inside. Stacy and Drew waved briefly from the window before settling back for the long trip to London.

Tanner could not get Sterling and Preston from his mind. He'd come to Bracken determined to take Stacy away and dress her in London's finest, and then he saw his son with the Hawkesbury boys. Tanner had not even thought about Drew's clothes. In all fairness, Stacy had done an admirable job with their son's wardrobe, but next to the smart outfits and fine fabrics of the other boys' clothes, he looked dressed in homespun cloth. It didn't take more than a second to know that he wanted better for his son, a son who chattered nonstop for the first 15 minutes of the ride before falling into an exhausted sleep in his mother's lap.

Stacy settled him on the seat beside her and gambled a look at Tanner. He'd been in no mood for chitchat when he'd come into the carriage, and other than an occasional comment to Drew or an answer to the boy's questions, he had been quiet. Stacy knew she would find out sooner or later what was on his mind, but not having been privy to his conversation with Brandon, it came as a complete surprise when he finally told her.

"I don't want Drew to call me Lord Richardson. I want him to know who I am."

Stacy blinked at him. "All right," she replied slowly. "Would you like to tell him?"

"What do you think?" Stacy had never seen Tanner humble; it was a little hard to grasp.

"I think he'll be thrilled."

"That isn't what I meant. I meant should I tell him, or would he take it better from you?"

Stacy thought. "Why don't we tell him together? He's awfully little, but I think I can make it clear for him. If you were there also, you would know firsthand if he understood."

"At bedtime then," Tanner said, but Stacy feared it would only excite him and cause an hour of work to get him to sleep.

"I think dinnertime would be better."

Tanner stared at her. It was such a surprise to have her contradict him in any way. There had been no heat, but he could see that she was adamant. Not for any other reason did Stacy stand up to him. He suddenly remembered how much trouble he'd been in over the banister, and for the first time in weeks knew a desperate urge to please his wife.

"Dinner it is. What time would you say is best?"

"Drew usually eats at six."

"Six o'clock then."

Drew began to stir, so the adults fell silent. Stacy kept her eyes on her son until he settled again, but the conversation did not resume.

"Lord Richardson asked me to give you this, my lady."

Stacy took the paper from Price's hand. It was an itinerary laid out for the next few days. According to the schedule she had an appointment with Madame Angelica for the following day. She was to be fitted for summer, fall, and winter wardrobe.

Drew had an appointment with the tailor two days after

that, but Stacy thankfully saw that the tailor would be coming to the town house.

"If you have any questions, my lady, just ring for me. I would be happy to explain."

"How long will we be here, Price?"

"Probably not as long as you might think," he took the liberty of telling her. "Your clothing can be picked up by one of the coachmen and delivered to Winslow."

Stacy breathed a sigh of relief and thanked Price. He had read her concern so accurately. London was always a trial for her, and if she had needed to wait for three wardrobes, they could have been there for weeks.

Price went on his way after that, and Stacy settled down to write Lucinda. If she'd read the schedule correctly, she had a day between her own fitting and Drew's. With a bit of maneuvering she could get a visit in with her aunt and uncle.

The meal that evening was very relaxing. Tanner was most charming, and he made Stacy and Drew laugh on more than one occasion. When it seemed that Drew was finished with his dinner, Stacy petitioned God for help one last time and plunged in.

"I have something special to tell you tonight, Drew," Stacy began, knowing she had to do this in her own way. Only her fear that Drew would be hurt in some way by the news gave her the boldness to handle it as she saw fit.

"Do you remember my telling you about baby Moses?"

"He went in the water."

"That's right. Did Moses have a mother and a father?"

"I think so."

"Yes, he did, because that's God's way. How about Adam and Eve in the garden? They had children, didn't they? A mother, a father, and children make a family.

Stacy paused when Drew needed a drink, and then asked, "Who is your mother, Drew?"

"You, Mumma." He smiled as though she were making a game.

"That's right. Who is your father?"

Stacy didn't know which was more heartbreaking, the confusion in her son's eyes or the yearning in her husband's.

"Lord Richardson has the same name as you, doesn't he, Drew?" The little boy looked at Tanner and then back at Stacy. "His name is Tanner Richardson and your name is Andrew Tanner Richardson. That's because Lord Richardson is your papa."

"What about mumma?"

"I'm still your mumma," Stacy swiftly assured him. "I always will be, but now you have a papa too."

When Drew looked back at Tanner, the duke smiled at him. Drew smiled in return, and Tanner reached forward and brushed the hair over his forehead. Drew's grin broadened, although Stacy wasn't certain he actually understood. Stacy doubted that Tanner was as calm outside as he appeared, but she was thrilled with the way it had gone.

Conversation started up again among the three of them, and whenever Drew started to call Tanner sir or lord, someone would gently correct him. Stacy wasn't certain as to how much he was beginning to understand until it was bedtime.

"Would you like Papa to carry you to bed?" she asked.

Drew's eyes flew to Tanner's, and Stacy's smile was huge as he swung his small son up into his arms.

"Off we go, son." It was as if it happened all the time.

Stacy nearly floated into Drew's bedroom. They were going to be a family! Tanner was not what you'd call warm to her, but he didn't seem quite so angry.

Thank You, Lord, Stacy silently prayed. *Thank You for giving us another chance. Please help us to make the best of it.*

Thirty-Seven

MADAME ANGELICA, LONDON'S PREMIER DRESSMAKER, rattled off a string of sentences in rapid French to Tanner. Stacy had to hold her mouth shut as Tanner replied back in French. When pleasure and something akin to greed lit the woman's eyes, it wasn't hard to figure out that Tanner had told her what he sought.

"Come in, my lady," Angelica nearly cooed. She had dozens of seamstresses and assistants, but this was a duchess, and for this reason Angelica would see to the fittings herself.

"Thank you."

Stacy and Tanner followed her, Stacy noticing as they walked that she had the disconcerting habit of muttering to herself in French. Stacy wondered what the dressmaker was saying as they were led into the private dressing room.

"I need my tape," Madame Angelica explained briskly and rushed off still muttering to herself. Stacy looked to Tanner.

"She's quite taken with your figure, but she says your dress, one of her own magnificent creations, is sadly out of date." Tanner's voice was so bored as he recited this that Stacy blushed.

She found herself wishing that Sunny had never mentioned Tanner's pride. He was only doing this for himself, because it was shaming his reputation to have his wife seen in outdated clothes. Stacy felt resentment rising within her.

"Now then." The dressmaker was back. "I will help you out of this gown," she began, and then the rest was in French. Just moments passed before Stacy found herself in her underclothes, being measured from head to foot.

"Now, I have a dress, the latest style and almost complete, but the fabric, you see, is flawed. I would like you to try it just for fit."

Stacy agreed with a nod of her head, and the older woman was gone and back in record time, carrying a gold creation over her arm. The dress was slipped over Stacy's shoulders, settled around her hips, and buttoned up the back. Madame Angelica had forgotten yet one more thing, and as she rushed off, Stacy was given her first full look in the mirror. She was horrified by what she saw... why not even her shift was that low!

Stacy told herself not to overreact; maybe there had been a mistake. But as she studied herself in the mirror, she knew there had been no error. Her hand came slowly to her mouth as her stomach churned.

Oh please, Stacy silently begged her husband. *Please don't make me go into public this way.*

Stacy was so shaken that tears filled her eyes. Knowing that Tanner was somewhere behind and to the side of her, Stacy carefully moved her face away from him as well as her own image in the mirror. She racked her brain for a solution, but she was too much in a panic and none came. Tanner would be furious if she made a scene in the dress shop.

A chance glance in the mirror told her that Tanner had moved until he could study her face in the reflection. Stacy swiftly turned her tear-filled eyes away, but the hand she'd placed over the missing material told Tanner all he needed to know.

"Now then." Angelica was back.

"The dress is too low," Tanner interrupted before she could say another word.

"But Lord Richardson," Madame Angelica replied, clearly

shocked, "it is the latest style, and your wife's figure, ooh la la—it is perfection. How can—"

"It's too low," Tanner stated again, and this time his voice did not invite Angelica to argue.

With a heartfelt sigh, she asked, "What is it you wish?"

"Lady Richardson will show you."

Stacy was still shaking, but she managed to show Angelica what she had in mind. The plump dressmaker was not at all happy, but she gave no further argument.

Just a short time later Stacy was back in her own dress, and the process of choosing patterns and fabrics began. She learned that Tanner had magnificent taste, and Stacy had to do little more than nod while he, Angelica, and all her helpers sorted their way through patterns and bolts of cloth.

It wasn't until they were back in the carriage that Stacy was given a chance to thank Tanner. He frowned at her as though the words were not necessary, so Stacy let the subject drop as well as her eyes.

"I've never been tempted toward criminal actions before," Lucinda told her husband. "But I want to steal this child."

Roddy laughed. He certainly knew how she felt. Drew had been spending the day with them, and even though they had known he should have a nap, the time had just flown. Now he was asleep in Roddy's lap, and the two adults present could not keep their eyes off of him.

"I love the way his face flushes when he sleeps," Roddy murmured.

"I've missed him so much. I was even hoping things wouldn't work out between Stacy and Tanner so he could come back here."

"Cinda." Roddy's voice was a soft rebuke. "That's a horrible way to think, and besides, Winslow is closer to us than

Middlesbrough, which is where I suspect Stacy will go if Tanner ever sends her away again."

Lucinda's brow furrowed. She had thought of this, but it was not something of which she approved. Roddy saw the stubborn look on her face and frowned in concern. Lucinda had been running people's lives for years, and even though she said little to Stacy, Roddy knew she still wanted to run hers as well.

From time to time Roddy had worried over his wife's busyness, but never like he did now. When it came to Stacy, and most especially Drew, she was like a woman possessed. Roddy had tried to talk with her on a number of occasions, but she always grew very agitated and he would let the matter drop.

He contemplated bringing it up now but hesitated, feeling a coward. Another hour passed. Just as he was finally ready to say something, Tanner and Stacy arrived. Even though he was grateful, he felt cowardly for his relief.

The day after the dress fitting, a Richardson carriage pulled up in front of Featherstone. Stacy glanced out the carriage window to see Lady Andrea waiting for her. The first day in town, after Price had given Stacy the itinerary, she had been on the verge of sending her note to Lucinda and Roddy suggesting they have tea. However, a note arrived from Brandon's mother before Stacy could do anything.

How she had known that Stacy was in London, Stacy could not imagine, but she was thrilled to be able to accept. The note she had finally sent to Lucinda and Roddy asked them if they would like to have Drew while she was at the dressmaker's and with Lady Andrea. Stacy felt a twinge of guilt at not spending the following day with them, but wanted very much to see Lady Andrea and felt her family would understand.

"My dear," Andrea said warmly as she came forward and embraced Stacy. "I'm so glad you came. Come inside. I've a splendid tea laid out. Is Drew with you?"

"He came to London with us, yes, but right now he's at Brentwood."

Andrea smiled. "Lucinda must be thrilled."

Stacy moved inside with her hostess and when she'd laid off her things, she asked Lady Andrea how she'd known of her presence.

"I was in need of some papers from Bracken," the older woman told her. "Brandon sent them by coach yesterday, and when they arrived I found that Sunny had added a letter telling of your visit."

"I'm so glad she did. I don't care for London all that much, and it's nice to come here where I can forget the gossips and even the dressmaker."

"Was it so bad?"

Stacy pulled a face. "I hadn't realized the necklines had gone so low."

Andrea nodded understandingly. "I'm afraid they become barer every year. Is that what Tanner wanted for you?"

Stacy sighed gently, still feeling very thankful. "No, he didn't. I was quite nearly in tears in the dressing room, and he didn't push me. I know Madame Angelica thought we were mad, but at least my dresses will be modest."

"It's amazing isn't it? I mean, the little ways God takes care of us?"

"Oh, my," Stacy agreed fervently, "I certainly found that out this last year."

Andrea poured the tea then, and Stacy shared some of the ways God had worked in her heart and at Winslow. Andrea's eyes filled with tears as Stacy shared how thankful she was for the little things, like being moved from the north wing. Then she told of the great things, such as Tanner's wanting Drew to know of his parentage.

Andrea's handkerchief was in her hand when she told Stacy she would be praying that Tanner would continue to grow closer to her and Drew. They fell silent for a time, and then Stacy spoke thoughtfully.

"I could have a better attitude about the fittings. Lucinda adores shopping and fittings, and when I lived with her she finally despaired of ever changing me."

"Sunny positively hates shopping, so do you know what she does?"

"No."

"She sends her measurements to Madame Angelica. She's been doing it for years. When the wardrobe is completed, it's all sent to Bracken. When the gowns arrive she needs an occasional tuck here and there, but she has a marvelous maid who can do that for her. She dresses in the latest with none of the pains of fittings."

"What a marvelous idea! I might ask her about that when I return. Of course I won't need anything for a time, but it's certainly a handy idea."

The next two hours flew by as the two women shared about everything under the sun. Stacy had a few questions about the passage of Scripture she was studying in Romans 12. Lady Andrea proved a great help. Stacy's own words to Roddy came to mind as the coach moved toward Tanner's town house.

God has never let me down. When I truly need to know something, He always shows me.

Thirty-Eight

BY THE TIME TANNER, STACY, HETTIE, AND DREW arrived back at Winslow, Stacy was so tired she could hardly move. The ride seemed to lengthen every time she made it. She let Hettie feed Drew while she bathed, and as soon as she'd read to him and tucked him in, she took herself off to bed. She slept dreamlessly all through the night but woke earlier than she would have liked.

Stacy rolled to her stomach, determined to go back to sleep, but a sudden tenderness in her breasts caused her to open her eyes. She lay for some time thinking on the fact that this tenderness wasn't so sudden; she just hadn't given it any heed. It had been this way with Drew also. Long after Stacy should have given attention to the other signs, she would not let her heart face the evidence before her. Stacy sat up slowly. She and Tanner had only shared one night. Was it possible?

"Of course it's possible."

Stacy reached for her Bible. She read about Sarah, Abraham's wife, and how she had a child when she was 90. Sarah wasn't perfect, but she had faith in God. Stacy turned to Hebrews 11:11 and read that Sarah found God faithful to the promise He made to give her a child.

"You've given me no such promise, Lord, but You have said that You will never leave me or forsake me. If there is to be another child, help me to see Your sovereignty in its conception.

Tanner is so difficult to live with, but I don't have to answer for his actions, only for my own response.

"I'm afraid to tell Tanner, Lord. Please be with me. Please give me boldness. Please use this to soften his heart, and if it doesn't, give me the right words."

Stacy waited three more days before approaching Tanner, carefully monitoring the condition of her body. He was in his study as usual, and Stacy could see that he was not happy to be disturbed. She'd prayed long and hard about this conversation, however, so she stepped forward with more boldness than she ever had before to take a chair in front of his desk.

"I'm sorry to disturb you, Tanner, but I need to speak with you."

Tanner placed his papers back on the desk and sat back in his chair; his face a study in indifference. Stacy cleared her throat.

"I'm pregnant, Tanner. I must be some weeks along, but I just now realized it."

Nothing. She was met with absolute silence; his face never changed expression.

"Tanner, did you hear me?"

"Yes, I heard you."

Stacy sat nonplussed.

"Are you worried the child isn't yours?" she asked, desperately trying to gauge his true feelings.

"Is it mine?" Tanner's voice was still unresponsive.

"Yes."

The duke shrugged, and Stacy realized she had been prepared for anything but his indifference. She stood slowly, thinking that if she stayed in the room she might break down, but something stopped her from exiting. At the door, Stacy turned and faced her husband again. He had not gone back to his papers, so Stacy was able to speak with her eyes holding his.

"When you came for me at Lucinda and Roddy's, I came back to you because I was afraid to say no, but there was more, Tanner. I also came because I believed it might be God's way of repairing my marriage.

"I've never stopped loving you. When you wanted me back, even before you knew that Drew was yours, I took that as a good sign. But it hasn't been good. You despise me, and the staff takes their cue from you. I would love to stay right now and work on our marriage, but I must think of our unborn baby. Drew and I will be leaving for Lucinda and Roddy's as soon as we're packed." Stacy paused, seemingly out of energy, but an unprecedented boldness came over her.

"I never really stood a chance, did I, Tanner? Leslie saw to that. Well, I'm not Leslie. I'm Stacy. The letter is still in my dressing room, Tanner. You're welcome to go and get it. This time I hope you read the whole thing."

Tanner never moved from his chair as the door closed. He knew Stacy would actually leave, and because he thought the distance might do them some good, he did not try to stop her He was surprised, however, when she left without seeking him out again. Two hours later the carriage pulled away, and she hadn't even brought Drew in to say goodbye.

You just want her because she's not here. All this time she was right beneath your roof, and you ignored her. Now that she's gone you want to talk to her. The feeling will pass.

Tanner knew he was lying to himself. He had said all of this to himself and more, but Stacy had only been gone one week and he had never known such loneliness. Tanner had held himself in check most of the time Stacy had been there, watching her from down the hall or from a window when she wasn't aware. To let her know that he thought of her and Drew constantly would not do. If he became vulnerable to her, she would only hurt him again. Or would she? Tanner was beginning to doubt his own sanity.

Almost of their own volition, Tanner's feet moved toward Stacy's bedroom. Her dressing room was nearly empty, but just as she'd said, the letter was there. Tanner started at the beginning again.

> Dear Tanner,
>
> I'm not sure if you knew I was back in London, but I arrived just this week. I am staying at Brentwood with Roddy and Lucinda. I would like to see you. I know I told you I would not return unless you sent for me, but my grandfather has died and I've come at Lucinda's bidding.
>
> I would like to see you, Tanner. I would like to talk about the Cradwell party and explain about Nigel Stanley. I made a terrible mistake, and if we could only talk, I feel we might resolve this painful thing between us.
>
> There has never been anyone but you, Tanner. I was very naive concerning Lord Stanley, and I didn't understand his intentions quickly enough to allow me to escape him, so when you came in, it looked as though we'd met. I don't know what possessed him to tell you we loved each other because I'd never seen him before the party, and, aside from that, I was already in love with you. Please send for me, Tanner, and give me a chance to explain.
>
> Always yours,
> Stacy

He balled the letter in his hand, but not out of anger. For weeks now he'd kept Stacy at arm's length, never letting her close to his heart. He had been ready to believe her innocence, but when he'd read the first part of the letter where he thought she'd all but confessed, he'd gone back to keeping her as far from him as possible.

Leslie's face swam through his mind. For the first time he pushed it away with barely a thought. Stacy herself reminded him that she was not Leslie. That fact was never more evident to Tanner than it was right now.

His anger had been putting distance between him and Stacy even before they were married. If he was going to get his wife back, Tanner knew he was going to have to get a grip on himself. He'd ask her first. If that didn't work, he'd *tell* her she was coming back so he could prove he was ready to be the husband and father he needed to be.

Tanner knew he couldn't take one more day without her at Winslow. Even though the shadows were long, Tanner ordered his carriage. Price packed and accompanied him, and the next morning he was at Brentwood, ready to see his wife.

"What do you mean she's not here?"

"Just what I said," Lucinda told him unsympathetically. "She's not here, nor is Drew. They've gone to stay with friends in the country."

Tanner frowned. The only friends Stacy had in the country were their neighbors around Winslow, and outside of Brandon and Sunny, he knew she wouldn't visit them. Even without asking, Tanner knew she was not at Bracken.

"When do you expect them back?" Tanner was keeping a tight grip on his temper.

"Oh," Lucinda said airily, covering the fact that they'd only just left, "Stacy desperately needs a rest. She'll probably stay until the baby is born."

Tanner would tolerate no such thing. It was the second week in October and he'd already missed her birthday. There was no way he'd let anyone keep him from his wife and son until sometime the next year.

"Tell me where she is, Lucinda."

"No."

"Did Stacy ask you to hide her?"

Lucinda hesitated just long enough for Tanner to realize she was lying. "Yes, she did. She's tired of the way she's treated at Winslow and tired of you. You're despicable and cruel, and you don't deserve her! She never wants to see you again!"

It was quite obvious that Lucinda was verbalizing her own feelings and those she wished were Stacy's.

"You have no right to play with people's lives, Lucinda." Tanner's voice was calm, and Lucinda looked uncertain for the first time. "Now tell me where she is."

The older woman looked as if she might be considering it, but then her chin came out and she slowly shook her head. Tanner's eyes bored into hers, but still she did not flinch. Without a word, Tanner turned on his heel and walked out.

"You deliberately waited until I was gone, and then you sent them away," Roddy railed at his wife. "How could you, Lucinda? You cannot run other people's lives."

"Now you sound like Tanner." She spat the words.

"Tanner was here?" Roddy was incredulous, but Lucinda, having regretted telling him, would not look in his direction. He'd returned an hour earlier with flowers for both Stacy and his wife and a hat for Drew, only to be told they been sent away, and no one except Lucinda knew where. All of their own coachmen and coaches were present, telling Roddy that Lucinda had hired someone else. Roddy had no one to question.

"Lucinda, did you tell Tanner where she is?"

"No, and I won't tell you. You're too soft, and I know you would tell him. I'll not give Tanner Richardson another chance to hurt my girl."

Roddy sat down in absolute defeat. He'd never seen Lucinda quite this consumed. When Stacy arrived he'd been troubled about the relationship. But when Tanner came looking for his wife—in Roddy Caruthers' book that meant he cared.

Oh, Cinda, he thought as he watched her try to ignore him. *What have you done?*

They didn't speak of it again, and after a few days Lucinda began to believe that Roddy had come around to her way of thinking. There was a strain between them, but Lucinda refused to acknowledge it, smiling a little too brightly when Roddy was in the room and suggesting one party or tea after another. She would have been livid if she'd known that Roddy was investigating Stacy's whereabouts each morning when he left the house.

Tanner stayed in London for a week but came up with nothing. He considered calling in the police, but Lucinda was Stacy's aunt, and he wanted to avoid that at all costs. He was on the verge of hiring an investigator when he thought maybe he should check with Brandon and Sunny. He knew Stacy wouldn't be there, but he hoped that with all the time Stacy spent with Sunny, the duchess would know something.

He arrived unannounced at Bracken near dinnertime, but the Hawkesburys made him feel welcome. Soon he was sitting down to eat with them. Tanner had no idea how drained he appeared.

"Did you know that Stacy left Winslow?" he asked partway through the meal.

"Yes," Sunny answered. "I just received a letter."

"A letter? Does it say where she is?" Tanner nearly rose from his chair.

"Why, she's in London with Roddy and Lucinda. Didn't you know?"

Tanner sighed deeply and explained. Sunny's emotions were wrung out once again by this unsettled couple. Just when it seemed that Tanner was finally ready to be a husband to Stacy, Lucinda had to pull this.

"Did she ever say anything to you, Sunny, that might tell me where she is?"

"I don't think so. I mean, Lucinda has friends everywhere, in the country and all over London. Maybe someone on her staff would know something."

"Or you might try questioning your own staff, Tanner. They might be of some help."

"I doubt that," Sunny said softly, but Tanner had heard.

"What did you mean, Sunny?"

"Your staff is not very close to Stacy, so I doubt if she would confide in any of them."

Tanner studied her and knew there was more. "Is there anything else you'd like to tell me?"

Looking uncomfortable, the duchess suddenly knew what Stacy was at times afraid of. There was an intensity about Tanner that could be unnerving, but she knew she had to be honest.

"Some of the staff at Winslow make things pretty hard for Stacy."

"In what way?"

Sunny explained what she'd seen and the little Stacy had shared with her. "Stacy isn't the type to complain. In fact, if it wasn't for Drew, she probably wouldn't have said a word, but Drew naturally brings out the mother in her. She talked to me out of concern for him."

Tanner was quiet, but a hardness entered his eye. He remembered his fish dinner with Stacy and Drew and how little food they'd had on the table before his trays arrived.

Just looking at him, Brandon could see that his friend was developing a plan. After a moment he asked, "What will you do?"

Tanner answered immediately. "I'll go back to Winslow

and dismiss the staff. Then I'll have Price start interviewing for replacements, people who understand that their sole duty is to make my wife and son comfortable. After that I'll go to London and hire an investigator to find Stacy."

Thirty-Nine

STACY WANDERED THROUGH THE GALLERY, her round tummy preceding her, and studied the portraits of generations of Blackwells. Some looked stuffy and old before their time, and some looked like they had lived life to the fullest.

Of course it wasn't fair to judge a person by his portrait, but Stacy felt as if she had to examine them all before seeking out the one she came to see, the one who reminded her of Tanner.

Lord and Lady Blackwell were no relation to her husband whatsoever, but one of their ancestors bore a striking resemblance to Tanner. It certainly wasn't the same as being with him, but it was nice to look into brown eyes so like his and to study that firm chin that even Drew was beginning to sport.

Stacy now stood before the portrait. It was as she remembered it, but today she didn't enjoy it as much because she missed Tanner terribly and ached over the fact that he hadn't sought her out. It seemed that things really were over between them. Stacy thought maybe she should return to Middlesbrough. Lord and Lady Blackwell couldn't have been kinder, but Stacy was starting to lose hope.

With Stacy's feelings about London, Lucinda had had no trouble coaxing her out into the country. However, she had been here for weeks with almost no contact from Lucinda and none at all from Roddy. The letters that had come from her aunt were so bland, never addressing Stacy's questions, that she felt completely out of touch. Stacy missed everyone so much she was considering returning to Brentwood for a visit before leaving on her way north, but the first time she had mentioned a possible trip, Lady Blackwell had acted oddly.

Stacy had thought little of this and decided to stay put for the time. But then the previous night, when once again Stacy mentioned going to see her aunt and uncle, Lady Blackwell stumbled all over her words until Lord Blackwell gently explained that they were rather busy right now and maybe another time would be best.

Stacy couldn't believe her ears. Surely they understood that she could go without them. Not to mention the fact that this was the first time they'd denied her anything. Up until now they couldn't do enough for her. She and Drew had been lavished with gifts to meet every possible want or need. Meals were centered around them and so sumptuous that Stacy thought she might be putting on more weight than necessary.

She mentioned it to Hettie at one point, but Hettie only shook her head.

"You're swollen with child. How did you expect to look?"

"I guess you're right," Stacy sighed. "But if Tanner ever does come for me, he won't be able to get his arms around me."

"Are you still hoping for that?"

"You know I am."

The older woman snorted.

"Now what does that mean?" Stacy wanted to know. In all of the weeks that Stacy had been waiting for Tanner to come Hettie had never said a word against him.

"It means that even if he is looking for you, I wonder if he'll be able to find you."

"What are you saying, Hettie?" The duchess' voice became firm.

"I'm saying I don't like the way we left London. Your aunt was so nervous she jumped at the slightest noise. And it seemed strange to me that a hired coach and driver brought us here."

Stacy stared at her, and understanding dawned. *You knew, Stacy,* she said to herself. *You've known for days that all was not right here, and you've wondered for weeks why Lucinda and Roddy never visited. Tanner didn't come, and that's all you've cared about. Instead of drowning in self-pity, you should have been more aware.*

"What are you going to do?" Hettie asked.

"Nothing right now. I'm going to sleep on it and then confront the Blackwells in the morning."

"You make it sound as if it were bedtime."

"I know it's just past lunch, but I think better in the morning. If the Blackwells won't help me, I'll have the day to decide how to get us back to London."

Hettie finally agreed that it was a good plan. Both women would have been filled with joy had they realized that even as they spoke, help was on the way.

If Roddy had ever thought there was anything dimwitted about his wife, he now knew better. He would never have believed that she could so completely cover her tracks. It seemed as if Stacy and Drew had vanished off the face of the earth.

Not a single coach company would admit to having done business with her, nor would any of the coachmen. He racked his brain for every family they knew, even the slightest of acquaintances, and had them all checked out, but to no avail. Weeks later, he'd finally written to Noel and Elena, not wanting to upset them but desperate to find Stacy.

Elena had written back, stating that they had heard from Stacy. She had misplaced the letter, but remembered that she and Drew were doing fine and staying with someone named Blackmore or something similar.

It had been all Roddy needed. Little wonder he'd never considered the Blackwells. Decades before, Lady Blackwell and Lucinda had quarreled. Lucinda hadn't spoken to her in 30 years.

Now as Roddy's carriage took him deep into the country, he let his heart feel all the ache he'd tried to squelch. Never had he been so disappointed in anyone as he was with Lucinda or himself, for he knew he was partially to blame.

Lucinda had been running the lives of others for years, and Roddy had allowed it with nary a word. He realized now that he should have been bolder on countless occasions. He could have and should have told her to mind her own business.

Roddy wondered if perhaps this was why Stacy was so special to him. They both feared confronting the people they loved the most. Stacy had been so heavy on his mind in the last weeks that the thought of getting this close and being wrong made him a bundle of nerves. He also began to know panic at the thought that Stacy would be there, but the Blackwells would forbid him entrance.

"Please help me, God," Roddy prayed, not for the first time. He knew it was a selfish prayer and that finding her was partly selfish also. He had questions he needed to ask, and he believed with all of his heart that the only person who could answer them was Stacy.

Stacy heard voices from her place in the library. They were not raised in anger, but something was not right. She was able to come to the door without being spotted and did so to eavesdrop shamelessly.

"I tell you she's not here." This came from Lady Blackwell.

"And I believe that she is." Stacy heard Roddy's voice but kept still.

"I don't know where you've gotten this ridiculous notion, but I must ask you to leave."

"I will not leave until I'm certain Lady Stacy and her son are not here."

"Please—"

"No." Roddy's voice was firm. "Now tell me the truth; tell me where—"

Roddy cut off when Stacy suddenly stepped into view. The sigh that escaped his chest was heartfelt. Stacy came forward, but Lady Blackwell wouldn't look at her, even when she spoke.

"Lucinda asked me to keep you and hold all of your letters to Brentwood. It had been so long since she and I had—" The older woman stopped and looked helplessly at Stacy. "I'm sorry."

Both Stacy and Roddy watched her walk away, head down, steps laden. It was a posture that Stacy would have normally pitied, but the import of Lady Blackwell's words were pressing in upon her. All these weeks, months actually, she'd waited to hear from someone or dreamed of looking up and seeing Tanner approaching, but no one had even known where she was. No one but Lucinda.

"Roddy, what has Lucinda done?"

Roddy took in her flushed features and doubted his wisdom in coming.

"Where can we talk?"

Stacy took a breath. "The morning room."

She led the way. Once inside Roddy saw her comfortable on the settee. Her color still worried him, but he knew he had to take this all the way.

"Did Lucinda really hide us?"

"I'm afraid she did."

"And she didn't tell you?"

"No. It's taken me this long to learn of your whereabouts."

"Has Tanner been to Brentwood, asking for me?"

"A week after you left Winslow." Roddy's tone was regretful.

Stacy eyes slid shut in agony. The fingers of one hand came to her mouth, and Roddy watched in amazement as tears slid out from beneath her closed lids. She was trembling all over, and the earl was becoming frightened.

"Please, Stacy, please don't get so upset. I know what a shock it must be, but I'm thinking of the baby as well as you."

"How could she, Roddy?" Stacy whispered. "All this time I thought he didn't care. I was going to the Blackwells in the morning to tell them I would be returning to London and then Middlesbrough. How could she, Roddy?"

"I don't know." Roddy's voice was sad. "Tanner has always reminded her of Aubrey, and she's still very bitter over his memory."

"I can't begin to tell you how I've longed for my husband," Stacy went on. "I left because of his indifference. The servants were very hard to take, but I could have stood almost anything if only he would have shown me he cared. Did he just come to see if I was there, or to take me back to Winslow?"

"I wasn't there, but he told Lucinda he *would* find you."

"Maybe he didn't actually look."

"Yes, he's looking. He even hired a private investigator to locate you."

"Oh, Roddy! How do I get word to him? How do I tell him where I am?"

"I'll get word to him, Stacy, but I wish—" Roddy paused.

"What is it, Roddy?"

"I wish you would pray for me."

Stacy was dumbfounded.

"Not about Tanner; he'll be very pleased to hear from me," Roddy explained. "But I've got to go home and face Lucinda with this. Things have been pretty strained between us, but she's never shown remorse. When she finds out that I've learned of your whereabouts, she'll be livid."

"Of course I'll pray for you, Roddy," Stacy told him, but

then she paused. "There is something more, isn't there, Roddy? You have something on your mind."

Roddy opened his mouth once and then closed it. Stacy waited.

"I want what you have," Roddy admitted softly, his eyes searching hers. "I'm trying to pray and be like you, but something is missing."

Stacy smiled so tenderly that Roddy's heart began to pound. He knew she would have the answers; he knew she would not turn him away.

"Tell me, Stacy. Tell me about Jesus Christ."

So Stacy began. She assumed Roddy knew nothing and started at Christ's birth. She explained that His birth had been prophesied for years, and that it had been the fulfillment of a promise.

She told Roddy about God's promise to Simeon that he would see the Savior before he died, and how Joseph and Mary took Jesus to the temple in Jerusalem where Simeon saw him. Stacy explained about the second trip when Jesus was 12, and how his parents had found him in the temple amazing the elders with his knowledge.

"He began his public ministry when He was 30, and He called 12 men to work alongside of Him. One of those men, Judas, would betray Him, but even this was used of God so that Christ could be our Savior.

"After three years of public ministry Christ was arrested, beaten horribly and then died on the cross, but He didn't stay dead, Roddy." Stacy was growing very animated, and Roddy hung on her every word. "They buried him in a tomb and covered the entrance with a huge stone, but an angel came and the stone was rolled away. The grave was empty, and burial clothes lay discarded.

"Every church I've ever been in sports a crucifix; not an empty cross, but one with Christ hanging there. But Christ isn't dead. The Scriptures say he rose again the third day and now sits at the right hand of God the Father. He has bridged the gap between a holy God and sinful man."

"I can't begin to tell you how you've helped me," Roddy replied. "I thought you would say it's too late, that I've lived too much of my life without God."

Stacy shook her head and smiled. "My grandfather was nearly on his deathbed when he confessed Christ, and I know he's in heaven because God is faithful to His promises. You can have that same assurance, Roddy."

Roddy took Stacy's hand and held it gently. He was so anxious he was trembling, and Stacy was reminded of the way she felt when Elena and Noel sat with her and led her to Christ. It was much the same now.

Stacy sat quietly as Roddy prayed. His voice faltered on several occasions, but she just held his hand and prayed for him as he spoke in his heart to God.

Roddy raised his head, and Stacy saw peace in his eyes.

"It's taken care of now."

Stacy threw her arms around Roddy and tried to squeeze the life out of him. He hugged her in return and then spoke, his voice fervent.

"I meant what I said to God, Stacy. I truly want to live for Him."

"Oh Roddy, I can see that you do."

"I'm just worried about sin. I told God I want to put Him first, but what if I do sin?"

"I'm afraid it's not if, Roddy, but when. But there is hope. First John 1:9 says, 'If we confess our sins he is faithful and just to forgive us our sins, and to cleanse us from all unrighteousness.'

"Sin never pleases God, but it's going to happen. What we do with that sin makes all the difference in our relationship with God."

"So there is a chance I won't go to heaven when I die?"

Stacy shook her head vehemently. "No, Roddy. Nothing could be further from the truth. Read Romans 8. That whole passage is to believers in Christ. It says that nothing can separate us from the love of God. That's not a promise to the whole world, Roddy—just to believers like you and me.

"When I said it's what we do with that sin that makes all the difference, I was talking about confessing that sin and turning away from it, thus restoring a right relationship with God through his Son."

Roddy took a deep breath. He was not discouraged, just overwhelmed with joy. They talked until Hettie sought Stacy out, telling her that Drew was looking for her. Drew was thrilled to see Uncle Roddy, but on this particular day, Stacy did not allow him to stay. She and Roddy talked through dinner until they were both spent. They also talked again in the morning before Roddy left.

"Does Lucinda even known you were looking for me?"

Roddy shook his head regretfully. They were standing outside Roddy's carriage, and he was headed to see Tanner at Winslow.

"I was afraid she would do something to try to move you. Are you sure you won't come with me?"

Stacy shook her head. "No, I'll stay here in case he doesn't want me back."

"I know he does."

Stacy tried to believe that.

"You will come for me if he doesn't want me, won't you, Roddy?"

"You don't even need to ask."

With that Roddy kissed her cheek and climbed into the carriage. Stacy promised to pray for him and he for her, and then she waved until he was out of sight.

Forty

THE EVENING OF THE THIRD DAY was upon Stacy, and still she had had no word from Tanner or Roddy. It occurred to her that she didn't really know where the Blackwells lived. It had taken a day's carriage ride to come from London; maybe it took longer than that to come from Winslow. She had no sense of direction as they'd come from London and not fearing anything underhanded, she had not bothered to pay attention.

"I'm too tired to think about this right now."

Stacy spoke this to no one, having dismissed her maid and sent Hettie to bed. The older woman had not felt at all well lately, and Stacy knew that the job of trailing an active three-year-old was starting to tell.

After sitting on the side of the bed, she bent over her swollen stomach to strip off her stockings and then let her hair down. It felt good to shake it free. Wearing nothing but her nightgown, she stood to scratch first her head, where the pins had sat, and then her tummy, which seemed to itch constantly.

She drew the covers back, too tired to even read. She sat down on the edge of her bed and was in the process of turning the lamp low when the door opened.

"Hettie?" Stacy called as she squinted toward the dim doorway.

"No, it's not Hettie."

The air rushed out of Stacy at the sound of her husband's

soft voice; she was thankful to be sitting down. Stacy's eyes, now growing accustomed to the darkness, watched as he entered, shut the door, and approached. Tanner stopped just a few feet in front of her and simply stared down.

Stacy swallowed. "Did Roddy talk to you?"

"Yes. I would have been here yesterday, but he had trouble tracking me down."

Stacy didn't know quite what to say to that. Tanner looked wonderful to her, but the expression on his face was unlike anything she'd ever seen before. She couldn't gauge what he might be thinking.

"How is Drew?" he asked, his voice still rather hushed.

"He's doing well."

"Good. Here," Tanner continued as he bent low and adjusted her pillow. "Lie down. You need your rest; we're leaving for Winslow in the morning."

Stacy did as she was told, never taking her eyes from his face. His look was serious now, and after he'd adjusted the covers around her he placed his hand against her cheek and just left it there for a moment. Stacy's lids were growing heavy, and as much as she wanted to stay awake and talk with him, sleep was crowding in. She felt his hand stroke her hair, but she was deeply asleep when he pulled a chair close, turned the lamp a little higher, and just stared at her.

"We're not going to be separated again, Stacy," Tanner whispered. "I promise this was the last time."

It didn't matter to him that she didn't hear. He felt better having just voiced his thoughts. He let his eyes move over her and felt something squeeze around his heart at the extent of her pregnancy. Had she missed him? Was she able to travel to Winslow?

Tanner could have questioned these things for hours, but he made himself stop. He was here now, and if appearance could be trusted, Stacy was doing very well. Outside of that, little else mattered.

Stacy did not awaken early as was so often the case. This morning, light was streaming through the windows when her eyes opened. She woke up facing away from her side of the bed, and one of the first things she noticed was the indentation in the other pillow. Tanner! Stacy sat nearly upright. Tanner had come last night; she hadn't just dreamed it. He'd really been here, *and* in bed with her. Stacy wouldn't have believed that she could sleep that deeply, but now that she thought back, a vague impression of a warm presence came to her.

Stacy lay back, tempted to stay in bed for the next hour and just think about her husband. However, Tanner and Drew had other ideas. They burst through the door with barely a knock.

"Mumma! Look who's here."

Stacy's mouth dropped open as she saw her son so elevated. She never imagined where Drew's head would be if he sat on his father's shoulders, but he was high. Tanner swung him easily to the floor, and Stacy hugged him close when he scrambled onto her bed.

"How did you sleep?" Tanner had come near to the edge of the bed and stood staring down at Stacy.

"Well. Thank you."

"Are you up to traveling today?"

"I think so. Is it far?"

Tanner nodded. "With your condition we'll have to make a stop tonight and won't arrive at Winslow until late afternoon tomorrow."

Stacy noticed that his face and voice gave nothing away. She wished she could tell if he found this an inconvenience or possibly a duty. Stacy felt so perplexed with her thoughts that she transferred her attention to Drew.

"Where did you leave Hettie this morning?"

"She's in bed," Drew told her. Stacy felt alarmed. It was much too late for Hettie to still be abed. Stacy shifted Drew to the side and eased from the bed.

"I need to check on Hettie," Stacy spoke as Tanner stepped back and allowed her to reach for her robe. She glanced up to find his eyes on her stomach and self-consciously pulled at the fabric over her swollen waist. Tanner's eyes came to hers, and Stacy wished once again that she knew his thoughts. Stacy tried not to believe that he found her repulsive, but the thought did enter her mind.

Tanner would have continued to watch Stacy, but Drew captured his attention. Stacy was in her robe and out the door before he knew it.

"Where is Hettie's room?" Tanner asked his boy as he swung him back onto his shoulders.

It had taken quite a bit of tactful negotiating, but Tanner had finally convinced Stacy that she should leave and Hettie should stay put. He had followed his wife to the older woman's room and found her very ill indeed. Naturally, Stacy had wanted to stay and nurse her, but Tanner had put his foot down.

The next suggestion had been that they all simply stay until Hettie could go with them. Tanner was gentle, but adamantly against this also. With much talk between Stacy and Lady Blackwell, it was finally decided that Tanner would take his family home and send a carriage back for Hettie in two weeks' time.

When Stacy and Drew were finally ready to go, Tanner made one last trip to the sickroom. He could tell that Stacy was still apprehensive, and he wanted to be able to reassure her that he'd checked on Hettie again. To his surprise, Hettie had gained enough strength to take him on.

"You will have excellent care. In two weeks," Tanner was speaking from where he stood by the bed, "a Richardson carriage will be here for you." Tanner did not go on to say that he'd greased a few palms to see that she would be treated like a queen while at the Blackwells'.

"Who will see to Stacy and Drew?"

It irked Tanner that the old woman used their Christian names, but he held his tongue.

"They'll be well taken care of."

"Like they were before—with not enough food and living like prisoners? They couldn't even walk in the garden without the gardeners coming out to glare."

This was the first Tanner had heard of the gardeners being rude as well, but he continued to assure Hettie.

"All of that is changed now. My wife and son will have the best of care."

"What if the baby comes?"

"The baby's not due for weeks."

"Drew was early. Stacy nearly died; did you know that?"

Tanner's heart slammed in his chest, and he could only stare at the sick old woman.

"I've never liked you," Hettie went on, her voice growing weak. "And I know that you think I'm out of line to be saying this, but there's no one to care for Stacy without me."

The words completely taxed her. She lay, chest heaving, her eyes angry, but also pleading with the duke. Tanner wanted to go to Stacy on the spot, but something in Hettie's face compelled him to console her one last time.

"It is as I've said." This time Tanner's voice did not allow her to argue. "All that is changed now."

Tanner's intense gaze held Hettie's for just an instant, and then he was gone.

Stacy squirmed in the seat and told herself to go to sleep, pray, or do anything that would take her mind off of how badly she needed to relieve herself. They had been traveling for over two hours without a stop, and Stacy thought she might burst. Had he been in the coach with them, Tanner might have noticed her discomfort, but he'd opted to start the journey on horseback.

Drew had fallen asleep almost as soon as they had left, and even though Stacy had shifted his head from her abdomen for some relief, she was now growing desperate. Suddenly Drew stirred.

"Mumma," he said in a sleepy voice. "Mumma, I need to be excused."

Stacy's fist flew to the top of the carriage, and seconds later the coach slowed to a stop. When the door opened, Tanner stood there.

"Drew needs to be excused."

"All right." Tanner's voice was calm. "I'll see to him."

"I'll take care of him!" Stacy nearly shouted in his face. Tanner blinked at her tone before stepping back quickly when she barged her way from the carriage. Understanding was only seconds in coming, and he was calling himself every kind of fool as he followed her into the privacy of the woods.

"Here, Stacy, I'll see to Drew."

Tanner didn't give Stacy time to argue as he lifted Drew in his arms and went in the opposite direction. Stacy wasted no time but shot behind some bushes to see to her own needs. Some minutes later she made her way comfortably back to the carriage. Tanner and Drew were already there, and Stacy saw instantly that Tanner's horse was tied to the rear of the carriage.

"Lady Blackwell sent a large hamper along. Would you like to stop now?"

"I'm really not hungry," Stacy told him. "Would you like to stop?"

"No, we can wait." Tanner's voice was cordial as he ushered her and Drew into the carriage. Drew sat in his father's lap then and entertained the older lord for the next two hours. Stacy lasted only 20 minutes before she let her head fall against the side of the coach and went to sleep.

"The White Stag" was the sign above the inn door as Tanner saw his family into the public room that evening. The great room was clean and sparsely occupied, making the duke and his party all the more conspicuous.

Stacy stood holding Drew's hand as Tanner had a few words with Price. Every head in the place was turned in their direction, but Stacy kept her eyes on Tanner. Some minutes passed before the innkeeper led the way upstairs.

The room the man opened for them was clean, but small. It sported one full bed, and Stacy wondered about the sleeping arrangement. She didn't wonder long, however. As soon as the innkeeper left them, Tanner explained in a soft voice while Drew stared at his reflection in the glass of the window.

"We'll have our dinner up here, probably delivered in a few minutes. Price is going to be across the hall, and Drew will sleep with him."

"I thought Drew would be in here with us."

"There really isn't room. And," Tanner went on when Stacy opened her mouth, "do not even suggest that the two of you stay alone because I won't allow it. Price has one of my pistols, and I have the other. This is the safest arrangement."

"If the inn is not safe, why are we staying here?"

Stacy's voice was as low as Tanner's, but he could read the panic in her eyes. His hand came up to touch her cheek as he answered.

"The White Stag is one of the more reputable roadside inns, but since our clothing and coaches spell money, they all carry a measure of risk. I assure you, no harm will come to Drew when he's with Price, and any man coming to this door will have to go through me."

Stacy had little choice but to agree. She wondered if they should have stayed on the road. When she said as much to Tanner, he adamantly shook his head.

"You are nearly out on your feet, and we all need to eat."

"I need to eat." Drew had left the window and now stood looking a bit anxious at his father's side; it had been a long day. Tanner lifted him into his arms.

"Our food will be here at any time, and then you're going to spend the night with Price."

Drew's eyes rounded. "Price?"

"That's right, and then in the morning you'll come back in here for breakfast and we'll head home."

"To Roddy's?"

"No, my darling," Stacy interjected, her heart turning over for him. "We're going to Winslow."

Drew looked uncertain.

"You know Winslow," his father said. "Your room is brown and gold and you have a huge nursery to play in."

Now it was time for Stacy to share Drew's confusion. Mother and son stared at Tanner until he frowned fiercely.

"You were never shown the nursery, were you?" Tanner's voice was tight, but Stacy could see that he was trying to control his anger and that it was not directed at her.

In answer to his question, she only shook her head and tried not to think about going back to Tanner's difficult staff. More might have been said on the subject, because Stacy truly believed it needed to be discussed, but there was no more opportunity. Someone knocked then, and their food was delivered.

Because they left the inn early and the roads were fairly dry, they made good time going home. The coaches pulled up just after noon, and Tanner held Stacy's elbow as they went inside. Standing ready to greet them was a man Stacy had never seen before.

"This is Reece," Tanner explained. "He is the new head of housekeeping. He will introduce you to the rest of the staff as needed."

"Hello, Reece," Stacy, in a state of shock, spoke to the kind-looking man.

Reece bowed low, his posture and very expression begging to serve her. "Welcome home, my lady. I hope we can serve you well. This is Juliet." Reece brought forth a young maid. "She will be your personal maid until you wish to choose another. Would you like Juliet to go with you now?"

"No," Tanner answered for her. "I'll see my wife upstairs and will send for you later."

"Yes, my lord." Reece bowed again and backed away so they could pass. Several other staff members were present, all complete strangers to Stacy. Their faces were all wreathed in smiles, however, and the young duchess had the impression that any one of them would hand her the shirt off his back.

Once Tanner and Stacy gained the upper floor, Stacy questioned her husband.

"I take it you've replaced some of the staff?"

"Not some of them, but the whole."

Stacy stopped in the hall. "Even cook?"

Tanner gently shook his head. "Let me amend that, I've dismissed everyone but Price and cook."

Stacy just stood and stared at him. She would have continued to do so, but he reached for her hand and led her through a door. Not until that moment did Stacy realize it was the master bedroom suite. With a heart pounding with unidentified emotion, Stacy allowed herself to be led through her old sitting room, past the dressing room, and into Winslow's spectacular master bedroom. Tanner brought them to a halt but didn't turn to Stacy or even look at her. Stacy hated to question him and break the sweet communion that had existed between them since he came for her, but she had to know.

"Tanner, if you're going to change your mind about my being in here with you, I'd rather start down the hall."

"We've slept in the same bed for the last two nights." Tanner's voice betrayed none of his feelings.

"I realize that," Stacy spoke evenly. "But you didn't really have much choice."

This time Tanner didn't answer. He reached for the small satchel in Stacy's other hand and tossed it onto the bed. Stacy knew that would have to be answer enough.

Forty-One

THE FORK IN STACY'S HAND felt weighted as she tried to eat the lunch set before her. She had been quite weary for several days before Tanner came for her, and frankly she was tired of being tired. But what could she do? It must be the pregnancy.

A glance at Drew told her he was equally exhausted, and Stacy knew it was also the carriage ride home. She was looking forward to putting him to bed and climbing in herself. However, it wasn't that simple.

At Roddy and Lucinda's or at the Blackwells', she would have taken Drew right into bed with her, but she didn't feel as free to do that here. Her bed now was also Tanner's, and she didn't know if he approved of such a thing.

At the moment, Stacy missed Hettie terribly. Irrepressible Hettie, with her sharp tongue and stubborn ways, would have taken Drew off to his bed, put herself in the fireside chair in his room to sleep, and allowed Stacy to find her own rest. Stacy had just about decided to go to Drew's room with him when Tanner came to her rescue. He entered the small dining room and bent to speak closely into her ear.

"I've asked Price to put Drew down for his nap so you can rest."

"Oh." Stacy was surprised and uncertain. "I don't mind putting him down."

"I know you don't, but he and Price are getting along well, and Drew will do well with him until other arrangements can be made."

This statement sounded somewhat cryptic to Stacy, but she was too tired to argue. She watched her son carefully as Tanner broke the news to him, waiting for him to cry for her or complain. Once his face and hands were clean, however, he kissed his mother and skipped off with Tanner's man as if it were an everyday occurrence.

Juliet was waiting for her in her sitting room, and although Stacy felt a bit awkward in her presence, Juliet's manner was kind and matter-of-fact. Within minutes Stacy was down to her shift and tucked into bed. The sheets were cold at first and caused her to become quite wide awake for a moment, but it didn't last. Very soon, while praising God for bringing her home and for Tanner's efforts to take care of her, Stacy fell sound asleep.

Two hours later, she was just beginning to stir. She rolled to her back, feeling fully refreshed and contemplating rising when Tanner came in from his dressing room. He sat down on the edge of the bed and leaned over her. Stacy stared up into his face, wishing again that she knew his thoughts.

"I'm glad to see you looking so rested. When I came into the dining room I thought I might need to carry you upstairs."

"I doubt if you could lift me at this point."

One of Tanner's brows flew upward. "Your face is just starting to fill out so you look like the girl I married, Stacy."

Stacy's eyes widened, and Tanner shook his head.

"I suppose you've got some silly notion that I find you repulsive while in your present state."

Stacy blushed at his perception. "The thought did cross my mind."

"Oh, Anastasia." Tanner's voice was low. "Nothing could be further from the truth."

Stacy watched his eyes move warmly over her, his scrutiny ending with her stomach and the way it rounded the blankets. For the first time, he touched her. Stacy lay still as he placed his hand gently on her distended abdomen and splayed his long fingers wide.

"You might get kicked," Stacy whispered, as if a louder voice might break the spell.

The baby moved as though on cue. Stacy watched her husband's face as he moved his other hand to his wife's stomach and stared in wonder.

"Will you be cold if I draw the covers back?"

"No."

Tanner did so, anxious to feel the baby through just the light fabric of her shift, but it seemed that the little person inside had settled once again.

"Does he move often?"

"All day."

"Does it bother you?"

"Only when I'm trying to sleep."

"Your stomach is hard." Tanner's hands were still spanning her middle.

"Harder sometimes than others."

"Am I hurting you?"

"No," Stacy chuckled. "Drew climbs all over me. Speaking of Drew, I should get up and check on him."

"He's been up a few minutes, and he's still with Price. Before you go to him, I want to talk to you about something."

Tanner's hands came away from her now, and after he replaced the covers, Stacy lay watching him.

"I've hired a nanny."

Stacy's entire frame stiffened. Alarm covered her face as she half sat up.

"Tanner, I—"

"Just a minute," he cut her off, but there was nothing dictatorial in his tone. "Let me explain."

"Hettie—" Stacy started again.

"Will come back as ornery as ever, I have no doubts about that." Tanner's voice was dry. "But her recovery will not erase the years. She's getting too old to be shadowing a boy as active as Drew."

The words so echoed Stacy's thoughts of late that she lay back to hear him out.

"The nanny's name is Mrs. Maxwell, and she was recommended to me by Sunny." Tanner let that sink in a moment before going on. "She is not here to take yours or Hettie's job, but to give you both a hand. She will have no other responsibilities here at Winslow other than to see to Drew. She will be free to help at a moment's notice."

"Is Drew with her now?" Stacy's voice was accusing, but Tanner did not take offense.

"No, as I said, he's with Price. I honestly think he will fall for her as soon as they meet, but I didn't want that to happen without talking to you."

"How old a woman is she?"

"Mid-fifties."

"Where is her husband?"

"She's a widow. Her children are all grown. She has two grandchildren, who, I have assured her, would be welcome to visit here if you approve her staying."

Stacy took a deep breath. She was a little surprised that Tanner had done this after he'd gone to so much trouble to fire and rehire the staff for her. Stacy hated to admit it to herself, but Tanner's hiring a nanny without first talking to her felt just a little sneaky. Such thoughts flew out of Stacy's mind, however, on Tanner's next sentence.

"She shares your beliefs."

"She what?" Stacy could hardly believe her ears.

"Mrs. Maxwell believes as you do, that you can have a personal relationship with God. I think if you meet her, you'll find her most suitable for Drew's needs."

Stacy momentarily found herself without words. With the exception of Price, Tanner was not in the habit of becoming well acquainted with any of his servants. Stacy couldn't help wonder how he'd come by this knowledge.

"Will you meet her?" Tanner pressed, his expression giving nothing away as he watched Stacy's face.

"Yes, I will. I've been concerned about Hettie for some time. She's been with me for so long she seems more like a mother than a servant. I know you balk at our familiarity, but I can't cast her aside."

"I think I understand. I have a feeling that Hettie will do some balking herself over any changes we make, but on the inside she's bound to be relieved."

Stacy could hardly argue with that. *And who knows,* Stacy thought to herself. *If Mrs. Maxwell is a sister in Christ, maybe she'll have some positive impact on Hettie.*

Mrs. Maxwell was all Stacy could have prayed for. She was gentle-mannered and soft-spoken, and her humble willingness to please put Stacy immediately at ease with her. Stacy was present when she met Drew, and just as Tanner had predicted, he took to her right away.

It took a number of days for Stacy to recover from the long carriage ride, and during that time Mrs. Maxwell was invaluable. She seemed highly sensitive to Stacy's fatigue and would, with the most gentle of urgings, distract Drew from talking overly much or making unreasonable demands.

Stacy couldn't have been more grateful, as word came to them just a few weeks after they'd arrived home that Hettie would need to stay where she was. Lady Blackwell assured Stacy that Hettie was not on her deathbed, but that she was still very ill. Stacy wanted to go to her, but in her condition Tanner had to refuse.

To relieve Stacy's mind, however, Tanner sent a servant to check on Hettie and return with a report. It was just as Lady Blackwell had said. She was not dying, but neither was she ready for the long journey home to Winslow.

Drew cried when he learned that she would not be home for Christmas, and in fact Stacy felt close to tears herself. It was the first time they'd been apart during the holidays.

Forty-Two

STACY FOUND SOUTHERN ENGLAND in January to be warmer than usual as far as the temperature went, but the "weather" inside Winslow was still on the cooler side. Stacy, thinking her relationship with Tanner was finally on solid footing, found herself confused. After spending much time in prayer concerning the matter, however, Stacy was reminded just how intense Tanner's personality could be.

He was throwing himself into a business deal at the moment, and other than at the dinner table, Stacy wasn't seeing much of him. He came to bed long after she slept and was up before she woke. He wasn't even taking time out for Drew. Stacy found herself keeping her son quiet once again for fear of disturbing Tanner and incurring his wrath. He had been a bit on edge lately, and Stacy knew his temper was close to the surface. It seemed too that he was distancing himself again, but Stacy prayed that she was only imagining it.

However, Stacy was not imagining Drew's despondency. The little boy had quickly come to love Mrs. Maxwell, just as Tanner had predicted, but he was missing Hettie's and his father's attention terribly. His little face was solemn most of the time, and he simply wasn't his old chattery self. It was this melancholy, the quiet his mother was imposing on him while in the house, and the overall upheaval of their life in the past months that caused Stacy's heart to melt. For several days

Drew had been asking to go fishing, and Stacy had simply not had the energy. He never fussed or made a sound when she said no, and in some ways this made it all the harder.

"Can we go fishing today, Mum?" Drew would ask. He'd taken to calling her Mum most of the time now, and his sweetness when he said it made her want to give him the world on a silver platter.

"Oh, Drew," Stacy would reply, "I don't know if I can manage it today."

"All right, Mum." He would smile at her just a little. "After the baby has come, could we then?"

So when Drew sweetly asked Stacy again if they could fish, she agreed. The baby was due in a month, and she was feeling tired and huge, but she said yes anyway.

Stacy informed Mrs. Maxwell in the middle of the afternoon, when she would have normally taken Drew for a few hours. "Mrs. Maxwell, if anyone is looking for us, Lord Drew and I have gone fishing. We will be back in a few hours."

The nanny never blinked or commented beyond a respectful "Yes, my lady," but Stacy could feel her surprise. At the moment, however, she didn't care. She walked out to the stable with her son to collect the poles, all the while asking herself if she could drive a pony trap over her enormous stomach. One look at their small size, however, and she changed her mind. She couldn't bear the thought of a pony pulling her or of having to control one of the larger animals.

Drew had actually had a nap that day. Often these days he did not fall asleep, but after nearly two hours of sleep he was in rare form. Stacy had to call him back several times. He was so excited to be out and making noise that he simply forgot himself.

They both worked up something of a sweat on the way, but because the air near the creek seemed cooler to Stacy, she was thankful they had both dressed warmly as they settled down to fish. In no time at all they caught several. The smell, which usually never bothered Stacy, was a bit strong to her today, but

Drew was so helpful and entertaining that she determined not to let it spoil their time.

The beginning of the walk home wasn't much fun for Stacy. Drew carried the fish himself, but Stacy's legs felt like lead as they trudged through the fields toward Winslow. However, Drew, who was still feeling like he'd been set free, managed for at least part of the time to pull Stacy's mind from her painful body and legs.

"I'm going to eat a whole fish by myself."

"Are you now?"

"Yes, and then I'm going to share with Papa and Mrs. Maxwell."

"I'm sure they'll enjoy that. Will I get some fish?"

"Oh, Mum!" Drew's huge eyes were comical. "You'll get the first one because you caught the most. Remember that big one?"

Stacy laughed when Drew stopped on the path and made fish lips. She roared when he moved his lips and crossed his eyes. She was still laughing when Winslow came into view. Drew was beginning to stagger under the weight of the fish, which only added to his hilarity. Stacy was so glad they'd gone that she swooped suddenly and caught Drew in her arms, fish and all.

"I love you, Drew."

"Oh, Mum, I love you too. Papa!" Drew, while still in his mother's embrace, spotted his father. He was coming toward them on the path, his face expressionless but his stride purposeful.

He bent and lifted Drew as soon as he was beside them. He then reached for the string of fish without looking at Stacy and led them back to Winslow. Stacy sighed gently to herself. He was coldly furious. As tired as she felt, she knew she would be in tears if he shouted at her.

Drew talked to his father nonstop on the short walk inside, and Stacy realized how much she missed his joyful, happy moods. He was so rarely solemn that it had been like watching a different child.

Mrs. Maxwell was waiting for them, as was Reece. The fish were handed off to Reece, who immediately retired them to the kitchen. Drew was still in his father's arms, but Stacy didn't wait for Tanner to give the orders.

"Drew, please go with Mrs. Maxwell now. She will give you your bath. I'm going to eat in my room tonight, Mrs. Maxwell. Will you please bring Drew to me when he's ready for bed?"

"Certainly, my lady. Come along, Lord Drew. We'll have you cleaned up in no time."

"I caught fish, Mrs. Maxwell. I used a hook."

"Did you now?"

Stacy watched them for a moment and then without even glancing at her husband took the stairs herself.

You're a coward, Stacy, she rebuked herself as she walked away, knowing that Tanner was still standing at the bottom of the stairs. But try as she might she could not make herself go back down or even find the energy to turn around and face him.

Thankfully, Juliet was waiting for her in her sitting room. For a young woman she was certainly competent, and in a very short time, Stacy was luxuriating in her bath. The aches in her body and even the coldness in her husband's eyes gradually receded. She soaked for nearly an hour before Juliet brought her a lovely peignoir. It was voluminous, something Stacy's shape welcomed.

"Would you like a dressing gown, my lady?"

"Yes."

When she was warmly covered, Stacy sat at her dressing table and let Juliet brush her hair. Since it was wet, the maid left it down so Stacy could sit before the fire to eat and let her hair dry.

Dinner was quite the feast, but Stacy was not overly hungry. She felt thoughtful, meditative even, over her outing with Drew. Tanner would not seek her out, she was certain of that. And even if he did bring the subject up, Stacy realized she was not sorry for her actions. In fact, the joy she saw in her little boy's face was enough to convince her that she would do it again should he ask.

A knock at the door interrupted Stacy's musings, and a moment later Drew and Mrs. Maxwell came through. Drew sat in what was left of his mother's lap, and Mrs. Maxwell took a chair out of the way.

"Are you going to read to me tonight, Mum?"

"Well, now," Stacy spoke softly, her eyes on his precious face. "I'm rather tired. How would you like to tell me a story?"

Drew's eyes rounded with delight.

"All right. How about the story of Ruth? Would you like to hear that one?"

Stacy was telling him yes when Tanner came soft-footedly into the room. Drew did not notice his presence, and Stacy, although surprised to see him, did not give him away.

"Ruth was married, but her husband died," Drew began. "She lived in Moab with her mother, I think." Drew didn't understand about in-laws, so Stacy let it pass. "Anyway, they went back to where Naomi lived, and then Ruth went to work in the fields. Bozus—"

"Boaz," Stacy corrected him.

"Boaz," Drew started again, "owned the field, and when he saw Ruth he told his servants to be kind to her. They were, and then Naomi sent Ruth to Boaz, so Boaz would know he could marry her. They were married and had a baby named Jesse."

"Obed," Stacy corrected gently.

"Oh, that's right, Obed. And then Obed had Jesse and Jesse had David and then," Drew's voice grew as triumphant as Stacy's whenever she told the story, "a long time later, Joseph was born, and he was married to Mary, and Mary had *Jesus*. Jesus was not Joseph's son, because He was the Son of *God*."

"Oh, Drew." Stacy's voice was soft with wonder. She had talked to him about these things almost from the time he was born, but Stacy had not realized just how much he had taken in. She could feel Tanner's eyes on them in the dim light of the fire, but she kept her own gaze averted. A jaw-popping yawn from Drew reminded Stacy of how late it was getting.

"You best head off now, my darling."

"All right, Mumma. Good night."

They kissed sweetly, and then he crawled from her lap and moved toward Mrs. Maxwell. Tanner chose that moment to come out of the shadows.

"Come along, old man," he said as he swung Drew up onto his shoulders and moved to the door. "I'll cart you off to bed."

"Good night, Mum," Drew managed one last time. Mrs. Maxwell followed her young charge, and Stacy found herself alone. She was growing more weary by the second, so she took herself toward the bedroom before she fell asleep in the chair.

Knowing it would be disastrous at this point to lie down, Stacy sat on the edge of the bed to read her Bible. She read from Jeremiah 9, verses 23 and 24.

"Thus saith the Lord, Let not the wise man glory in his wisdom, neither let the mighty man glory in his might, let not the rich man glory in his riches, but let him that glorieth glory in this, that he understandeth and knoweth me, that I am the Lord who exerciseth lovingkindness, judgment, and righteousness in the earth; for in these things I delight, saith the Lord."

These were the verses Lady Andrea had shared with Stacy concerning Romans 12. Stacy had been worried about her attitude. She feared that she might be thinking of herself more highly than she ought to by telling people how God was working in her life and heart. The verses in Jeremiah gave her peace, as long as she gave God the glory, she was moving with a right attitude and heart. The verses also gave her a direction for prayer, something she would have spent some time doing right then, but she was growing very weary.

She stood and removed her robe, absently wondering when Tanner would come to bed. She had just turned the lantern down low when he entered. Stacy turned from the bed where she'd been ready to climb in and watched him. He stood for a moment, his eyes seeming to assess her before moving to turn the lantern higher. Stacy said nothing to the cold anger in his eyes, and Tanner, obviously expecting something, began to pace. Stacy watched him in silence. Finally he stopped and pinned her to the floor with furious eyes.

"It is beyond me, Anastasia, how you could go fishing in your condition."

He began to pace again, and quite suddenly Stacy was overcome with anger, rage actually. Her hands fisted in front of her. When Tanner stopped and pointed a finger at her, ready to go again, Stacy cut him off.

"Don't you say a word to me, Tanner Richardson! Don't you even so much as scowl in my direction!"

Tanner was so taken aback by this outburst that the anger was surprised right out of him.

"Drew's entire life has been turned upside down in the last year. His grandpapa, the only father he'd ever known, suddenly leaves, and he can't talk to him or play with him anymore. Then we move to London where everything smells and he sees water but he can't fish. You come on the scene when he's finally beginning to adjust to Brentwood, and we're whisked out here to Winslow where we're treated like so much baggage—and unwanted baggage to boot!

"He no more finds out that you're his father, then we go away again. Now his mother is starting to rival his pony for size, and his father is so busy with work that he doesn't have a moment to give him.

"I *will* take Drew fishing if he asks me, and *no one* will gainsay me! I will take him until my pains begin, if that's what it takes for him to know that he's loved and cared for."

Stacy was trembling from head to foot. She turned and walked on shaking legs to the window and simply stared at the glass. Never had she felt so angry and alone. She heard Tanner come up behind her but didn't move or speak, not even when his arms came around her and he rested his chin on top of her head.

"You're trembling." His voice was a whisper.

Stacy didn't reply.

"I must admit to you that I've never looked at it from Drew's standpoint. Suddenly your actions make complete sense."

"I meant what I said, Tanner."

"I know you did."

"Drew needs me to be as normal as possible."

"I understand."

They fell silent then, and Stacy felt bone weary without being sleepy. She thought her body could melt with exhaustion, but her mind was still moving like a team out of control.

"I need to lie down, Tanner."

He didn't reply, but immediately lifted her and moved to the bed. She landed softly against the mattress where his hands gently tucked her in and made her comfortable.

"Can you go to sleep now?" he asked.

"I'm not sleepy, just weary."

Reaching to turn down the light, Tanner suddenly stopped. He sat on the edge of the bed and stared at Stacy.

"You've been busy lately," Stacy commented, not able to read his thoughts through his eyes.

"Yes" was all he said.

"Tanner," Stacy spoke, feeling suddenly brave. "Should we talk about the Cradwell party now?"

"No." Tanner's answer was immediate, but not angry.

Stacy looked disappointed, so he explained.

"I realize now that Stanley was out of his head, and that you were innocent of all he claimed, but I'm not ready to hear what happened."

Stacy nodded, and a weight that she had become accustomed to suddenly lifted from her shoulders. He believed her. After all this time he knew she had been faithful. *Thank You, Father; thank You, Holy God.*

"How was your delivery with Drew?"

The question was so far from Stacy's own thoughts that she didn't immediately answer him.

"Was it hard?" Tanner became more specific, thinking she'd misunderstood him.

"I think most deliveries are hard, but when you see the baby, you tend to forget all about the pain."

Stacy saw that he was not satisfied with her answer. She tossed around in her mind for what he needed, and suddenly Hettie's face came into view. This was why Tanner had put distance between them, why he had been working so hard. Hettie had talked and scared him about the birth. Stacy was as certain of this as if she herself had heard the conversation. With a voice tender with compassion, she asked, "Are you worried about something, Tanner?"

He didn't answer. Stacy knew she had to be honest.

"They tell me I nearly bled to death after Drew was born. I was rather out of it, so I don't recall everything. Drew was over 24 hours old before I was even coherent enough to learn that I'd had a baby boy."

Tanner licked his suddenly dry lips. "And do you not dread the coming birth?"

"No, I guess I don't. I was down for two weeks—"

"I know," Tanner cut her off. "You didn't write."

Stacy stared at him, confounded by the fact that he would know this.

"I interrupted you; go on."

After just an instant, Stacy did. "I did lose a good deal of blood and was down for two weeks, but after that I never looked back. I have a peace, Tanner. I certainly have no guarantees concerning life, but if I had to make some type of guess concerning the future, I would say that I'll be here to be your wife and a mother to the children.

"If in fact God's plan is quite different from that, I still have peace. I know where I'm going, and I trust that He will take care of the three of you in my absence."

Tanner refused to believe in something he couldn't feel or see. Her peace and trust were a mystery to him, but he admired her tremendously. At one time he'd thought of her as weak, but now he saw that Stacy's faith made her stronger. However, he had no desire to discuss any of this with his wife. He knew she would gladly talk of it at any time, but the subject made him uncomfortable, and so he turned his attention to the baby. Stacy saw his eyes go to her stomach.

When Stacy first arrived back at Winslow, and Tanner seemed so fascinated with her shape, Stacy thought he would be taking a more consistent interest, but this was not to be. She finally understood the reason he had put space between them; he'd been afraid of losing her.

Without asking this time, Tanner lowered the covers just enough. The fabric of Stacy's gown was sheer, but even this was too much. With tender movements and eyes centered wholly on Stacy's extended abdomen, he moved the garment aside, baring her stomach for his touch.

The baby had been quiet for quite some time, but Tanner's gentle touch roused a response. Soon the baby was kicking and making Tanner's face light with wonder. Tanner thought he could stay in such a position all night, feeling Stacy's soft skin and the child within her, but a glance at her face stopped all movement. She was sound asleep.

Tanner stared at her a moment and then bent and quietly kissed the skin of her stomach before softly restoring her gown and the bedclothes. He quickly readied himself for bed and climbed in beside her. Stacy moved only slightly when he shifted close and put his arm around her. He didn't know when anything had felt so good as to lie beside her and hold her close.

Oh, Tanner, he said to himself as sleep crowded in. *How much you've missed.*

Forty-Three

"MAY WE GO FISHING TODAY, MUM?"

Stacy's attention was elsewhere, so she did not answer her son. Tanner, who was breakfasting with his wife, heard Drew's question and simply waited to see how she would respond.

"Mum?"

"Yes, darling," she now acknowledged him.

"May we go fishing today?"

"Oh, I think that would be fine. This morning?"

Drew nodded anxiously, and Stacy smiled at him before glancing at her husband. Tanner's look was a bit stern, but Stacy met his gaze, her chin rising in the air ever so slightly. Tanner quickly lowered his gaze to his own plate before she could detect the gleam of amusement.

He'd wondered from time to time what it would take to make a tigress out of his wife, and now he certainly had his answer.

"When exactly will you be going?" This came from Tanner. Even though Stacy's heart was pounding, she answered calmly.

"In about an hour."

Stacy sounded like she was addressing a servant. Tanner felt like laughing, but kept it well hidden. He simply nodded and went back to his breakfast.

Stacy contemplated his bent head for a moment and then speared a slice of tomato from her plate. The last three days together had been incredible. Tanner couldn't have been more attentive. He ate every meal with Stacy and Drew and even lay down with Stacy when she took her nap. She knew he never slept, but he was there when she drifted off and there when she woke.

One such afternoon, before Stacy fell asleep, she questioned him as to his recent business deal. His answer surprised her.

"I've turned the entire thing over to Edmond."

"I didn't think you trusted Edmond with business details."

Tanner shrugged. "It's his money as well as mine. If he wants to mess it up, he'll be out as well."

"But what about your money?"

Again Tanner had only shrugged, causing Stacy to stare at him until he kissed her and told her to go to sleep. She had given way to slumber, but the memory came back so strongly now that she paused in her eating.

"Is your food all right?"

"What?" Stacy gave him a blank look.

Tanner stared at her and stated the question again.

"I said, is your food all right?"

"Oh, yes. I was just wool gathering."

"Are you in pain, Stacy?" Tanner's voice was low.

"No," Stacy answered in surprise and wondered what her expression had been. A glance at Drew told her he was attending every word, so she smiled to reassure him.

"If you're done eating, Drew, please go with Mrs. Maxwell. I'll come for you when I'm ready to go."

"Should I change into fishing clothes?"

"Yes, Mrs. Maxwell will know the ones."

Tanner spoke as soon as Drew had left the room.

"I'll meet you in the foyer when you're ready."

"You're going with us?" It had crossed Stacy's mind that he might, but she had immediately dismissed the idea.

"Yes. I'll drive you out and bring you back."

"Thank you, Tanner," Stacy said with a smile. Tanner's gaze warmed noticeably in the light of her pleasure.

Tanner went back to eating, but Stacy was thoughtful. What a strange marriage they'd had thus far, but it seemed to be coming around. Stacy thought of how many other times she had expected her marriage to improve only to be disappointed, but swiftly pushed the thought away. This was here and now, and this was what she would work on and pray for, not dwelling on the aches and mistakes of the past.

Husband and wife parted soon after with plans to meet and go fishing. Stacy took herself back to her room, and Tanner, after ordering a small, enclosed buggy, told Price he needed warm hunting gear. Less than an hour later, Tanner stood wearing knee-high suede moccasins and buckskin pants and shirt as he stared out the window at the pouring rain.

He wasn't completely convinced that the sudden rain would deter Stacy and Drew's plans. They were, he realized, a hearty pair, and Stacy was most determined to please her son. With a sudden, brilliant idea that he hoped wouldn't land him in trouble, he moved toward the door.

Stacy moved toward the nursery, ready to find Drew and start on their way. She knew it was pouring but told herself it could stop anytime. If Tanner had ordered a covered coach, they could just wait out the rain. The thought of being outside in the rain at all gave her a sudden chill, but she pushed it away and told herself to buck up.

Knowing that Tanner would be waiting, she walked on to the nursery, a long, narrow room done in all shades of green and filled with every conceivable type of toy. When she arrived, however, she found that Tanner was not downstairs but had reached the room ahead of her. He and Drew were in deep conversation on the rug. Tanner was stretched out on his side by the fire, seemingly miles of him, and Stacy for once was able to sit down and listen.

"What is it called?" Drew asked again, as he ran a hand over his father's shirtfront. He was sitting cross-legged near the older man's chest and speaking directly into Tanner's face.

"Buckskin. Made from the hide of a deer."

"It's soft. Do I have buckhide clothes?"

"Buckskin," Tanner corrected him. "I'm not sure that you do. Would you like some?"

"Yes." Drew's eyes stared into Tanner's. "Then I could wear them fishing."

"Do you and your mother fish in the rain?" Tanner's voice was a study in casualness.

"Oh, yes," he answered simply. "Sometimes you catch more fish."

Tanner nodded. "I think that sounds like good fun, but you know your mother needs a little extra care these days."

Drew nodded. "She has a baby in her tummy." He held out small hands, about ten inches apart, to show his father the baby's size.

"Yes, she does," he said with a smile. "And until the baby is born, which will be very soon now, she needs to take extra rest. Most of the time fishing is fine, but in the rain she could catch a chill."

"And then the baby would catch a chill. The baby feels what Mum feels and eats what she eats."

"That's right, so maybe for today we had better not fish."

"All right." Drew sounded neither happy nor sad, but accepting.

Stacy watched Tanner scrutinize Drew, knowing that he was trying to read his son's thoughts.

"So what shall we play instead?"

Drew's mouth dropped open in a way that shamed Tanner. "You're going to play with me?"

"Anything you'd like," Tanner stated softly.

Delighted with his father's offer, Drew made a lunge for Tanner's neck, and a moment later they were wrestling on the nursery room rug, something Tanner had never done with his own father.

The morning passed in great fun that went from wrestling to trains, boats, pretend fishing, and back to trains again. They included Lady Richardson in their play, and although she didn't wrestle, both of Stacy's "men" laughed when Tanner helped her to the floor and she groaned all the way down. The three were not disturbed until just an hour before lunch.

"I'm sorry, my lord." This came from Reece as he soundlessly opened the door. "Lord and Lady Hawkesbury and their sons are here to see you."

"Sterling and Preston?" Drew had come to his feet.

"Yes, Lord Drew."

"Go ahead with Reece, Drew," Tanner told his ecstatic son when he looked to his father. "And tell them your mother and I will be right down."

Tanner helped Stacy to her feet and then to their room so she could freshen up.

"You can go ahead, Tanner. I'll be right down."

"I'll wait for you," he told her simply and sprawled in a chair while she sat before the mirror and repaired her hair. After just a moment, Stacy caught Tanner's eye in the glass.

"That was quick work on your part when the rain began."

Tanner grinned. "I'll admit it was impulsive, but after your outburst a few days ago, I thought I stood a better chance with Drew."

"You make me sound like a shrew." Stacy's voice was dry.

"Maybe it would be easier if you were."

This comment made Stacy take her hands from her hair and turn to her husband. She watched him for a moment but didn't know what to say. Tanner finally shrugged.

"Don't mind me. It certainly isn't your fault that at times I forget I have a wife and son."

"Are you trying to tell me you *want* me to nag you?"

"Maybe just a gentle reminder now and then."

Stacy knew this needed no reply, so she turned back to the mirror and just moments later stood.

"You could have called your maid to do that," Tanner commented as they moved out the door.

"True. But I didn't mind doing it myself."

"Are you really up to seeing anyone today?"

"Certainly. I feel fine."

They were at the top of the stairs when Stacy looked up to find Tanner studying her.

"What is it that you expect to see, Tanner?"

"If only I knew," he admitted. "You will tell me when your pains begin?"

"I think you'll know."

Tanner slowly shook his head. "You rarely ask for help, and you never complain. I'm afraid you're going to excuse yourself from the dinner table some evening, and by the time I get upstairs it will be all over."

Stacy put a hand on her husband's cheek and stroked softly. "You probably won't want to be anywhere near me when I'm giving birth, but I will tell you when things begin. If you're not here, I'll send word if I know where you are."

"I'll be here," Tanner assured her in a voice that only a fool would argue with before he captured the hand on his face to lead his wife downstairs.

"How can you believe the Bible to be God's Word? What in your opinion gives it merit?" Tanner asked Brandon after lunch, when both men had settled in the study. The children were with Mrs. Maxwell, and the women were in one of the small upstairs salons.

Brandon could not say how they'd come onto this discussion of God and the Bible, but because it was a first, he wanted to remain amicable and keep the door of inquiry open.

"I'm rather glad you asked that Tanner," Brandon complimented him.

Tanner stared at him in surprise. Knowing Brandon's stand on the Bible, he'd been expecting some sort of attack or rebuke for questioning the Bible's validity. Brandon's openness caused him to wait almost anxiously for a reply.

"If the Bible is not entirely from God, then the basis of authority for most of what I believe is cracked and unreliable." Tanner was clearly listening to every word, so Brandon went on.

"You asked what gives it merit; I'll tell you. Some 3000 times the Bible specifically, directly, claims to be from God—not man's word about God, but God's word about man.

"I'm also amazed how so many prophecies made hundreds of years before their intended fulfillment actually came to pass."

"What does that prove?"

"Have you read the Bible, Tanner?" Brandon challenged him quietly. "Written by many men, each author agrees about problems and themes that are very controversial. For instance, the world culture in Old Testament days overwhelmingly believed in many gods; yet the Old Testament authors unanimously affirm the existence of one God and creator of all.

"They also affirm the universality of man's sinfulness and the need for the blood of an unblemished sacrifice to remove the guilt of sin. One author's theology never contradicts another's—all contribute to one single system of belief."

This was new to Tanner, and he took time to think about what Brandon was saying, but he was still not persuaded. After a minute he asked a question that had long disturbed him.

"What about the inconsistencies?"

"What inconsistencies?" Brandon pressed him.

"Stacy told me once that she takes the Bible literally when it talks of the whole earth being flooded or Jonah being swallowed by a huge fish, but the Bible also says God has feathers. Am I to believe He's a bird?"

Brandon smiled and answered gently. "The charge that the Bible is strewn with inconsistencies is hardly a new one, Tanner. But I have found it necessary to distinguish between inconsistencies and problems. There are many problems, to be sure, but I've found that with objective bias and careful research, the apparent inconsistencies dissolve in the face of honest study."

Tanner could not argue with this because he had never put in any time of "honest study." He was deeply impressed by Brandon's knowledge, but the real impact came from his deep conviction and the way he'd spoken of it. However, Tanner was not convinced. He believed himself more than capable of handling his own affairs and taking care of his own. Why would he need God? It was a question he wouldn't have been so comfortable with if eternity had come to mind.

Had Brandon been able to read his thoughts he would have questioned him on that very subject. But as it was he could not read his friend's thoughts, and when Tanner changed the subject, Brandon felt he had little choice but to let the matter drop.

"You look wonderful," Sunny commented as she took in Stacy's healthy glow and round figure.

"I look huge," Stacy corrected her. "Sometimes I find Drew staring at me, and I know he's trying to decide which is larger, his mother or his pony."

Sunny chuckled, well able to remember how Stacy felt. At this point in any woman's pregnancy, it felt as if her condition was going to last forever.

"I'm so glad you felt free to come by," Stacy told her friend. "As you can imagine, I'm not getting out these days."

"We knew you were back, but I wasn't certain if we should call. Suddenly I couldn't stand it any longer. Was it pretty awful?"

"Yes and no. I never really expected Tanner to be in touch, so I wasn't surprised when I didn't hear from him. And then after I'd learned that he didn't even know we were staying at the Blackwells', it was torture. Roddy told me he came to Brentwood a week after I'd left."

Sunny nodded. "He came to Bracken, looking beside himself. We talked for quite some time. I don't know if you'll be upset, but I told him about how badly the servants treated you."

"I'm not at all upset, but do you know what he did?" Stacy asked.

"He told us what he had planned. Did he do it?"

"Yes. Price is still here, and so is cook. That's it. Not even the stable hands stayed. Sometimes I feel wretched about it, but then I remind myself that they all made their choices."

"That they did," Sunny agreed, not at all afraid of sounding harsh. She'd been waited on her entire life and honestly believed that both lord and servant could make the best or worst of it. Knowing what an undemanding person Stacy was, Sunny knew that the original servants at Winslow had been completely out of line.

"What do you hear from Roddy and Lucinda?" Sunny asked.

"From Lucinda, nothing, but Roddy came to Christ when he came to see me at the Blackwells', and we've had quite a bit of communication."

"Oh, Stacy," Sunny exclaimed and hugged her friend. "You must be thrilled."

"I am that. God had certainly prepared his heart for our time together. Roddy was so eager to let God fill the void he felt inside. Now he's like dry ground in the rain with the way he's reading the Word and growing."

Stacy had no desire to gossip, so she did not go on to say that he was also doing amazingly well considering that he and Lucinda were not living together at the moment.

"But you say that Lucinda has not been in touch?" Sunny inquired.

"I've written her twice," Stacy explained, "asking her to write to me so we can talk this out, but I've not heard a word. I love Lucinda and I've already forgiven her, but I did tell her I want some answers. She's obviously not ready to give them to me."

"Another thing to pray about."

"Yes," Stacy agreed.

Much to everyone's delight, Sunny and Brandon ended up staying for the greater part of the day. However, Stacy found it taxing. In fact she was so tired that Tanner had to hold a surprise he had been keeping over until the following day. The look of delight on Stacy and Drew's faces when he brought Hettie into the breakfast room the next morning was worth the putting aside of his own feelings about the old servant.

Forty-Four

LUCINDA KNEW THAT ALL OF LONDON was talking about her and Roddy. It was not the gentle variety of gossip as when they'd been married or what a handsome couple they made, but it was the vicious type, the type Lucinda herself had often engaged in. Minds and tongues were speculating everywhere as to why the Earl of Glyn's wife had chosen to move from their home.

Some said it was because they'd ruined a beautiful relationship by getting married in the first place. Others said that nothing could last forever, and some even said that the affections of both parties had drifted and each decided to seek out greener pastures.

Lucinda knew better than anyone how far the rumors were from the truth. The fact that the Blackwells lived so far distant from London was the only reason the duplicity of Lucinda's actions toward Tanner and Stacy were not on every tabloid in the city.

Lucinda kept telling herself she didn't care. She staunchly put aside all emotions and went shopping and to the theater whenever she desired. She did not see other men, but she had determined to be as worldly as ever, a facade she couldn't quite manage in the lonely confines of her own room.

This morning she was feeling every one of her years and so

lonely for Roddy that she wanted to weep. Their last conversation, the one she managed to submerge so deeply within her mind that she hadn't thought about it in all these weeks, came back to her now so sharply that Roddy could have been standing in the room with her.

"How could you?" Lucinda spat in anger.

"How could I what? Go after Stacy? Return her to her husband?"

"How could you go behind my back?"

Roddy stared at her in disbelief. He'd returned from his search for Tanner to find that Lucinda had received word of his actions and had moved from Brentwood to one of London's finest hotels. She was beside herself when he sought her out at the hotel, but her worry had nothing to do with Roddy's well-being in the last four days, only the exposure of her subterfuge.

"How can you possibly accuse *me* of going behind *your* back?"

"You don't understand," Lucinda railed. "He's going to hurt her again, just like he always has. She thinks she wants him, but she doesn't really. She was probably completely over him by the time you got there, but you've sent Tanner to her and now he'll give her no choice but to return."

"You couldn't be more wrong." Roddy's voice told his wife he was growing furious. "She was miserable and lonely without him. You can ask her yourself."

"How could you?" was all Lucinda would say.

"Your line of reasoning frightens me. In fact, *you* frighten me," Roddy told Lucinda coldly. Lucinda's eyes widened with shock. However, Roddy went on without mercy. "You wait until I leave, and then you sneak Stacy and Drew away, and now you stand there and ask me how I could go behind your back. Like I said, you frighten me." Roddy turned to the door but paused just before leaving. "When you're ready to come to your senses and talk about this, Lucinda, you know where to find me." With that Roddy had walked out. They hadn't spoken since.

Now the words, the entire scene, unfolded so clearly in Lucinda's mind that she felt a stab of pain around her heart. He had been so right. At the time she had refused to see her own wrong. She had accused him so she didn't have to face her own actions. But now...

Lucinda could not finish the thought. It had been weeks since she'd seen him. What if it was too late? What if Roddy had given up on her and begun to look for another?

Lucinda found this thought so unbearable that without care for how she looked, she snatched her cloak and ordered her carriage. She was at Brentwood before she really had time to think about what she would say, but she needed to see Roddy so badly that she didn't care. It felt strange to come to the door as a guest, but Roddy's man, Carlson, greeted her warmly and, thankfully, told her that his lord was in.

Carlson tried to show her to the parlor, but Lucinda declined. She was still standing in the entryway, taking in the sights and smells of her beloved home, when she heard Roddy's footsteps. He stopped just two feet away from her and drank in the sight of her flushed face and messy hair. She was wearing a simple day-dress, with no jewelry or special fixings, and Roddy thought her beautiful.

Lucinda was feeling quite the same way. Roddy had never looked more wonderful. He was jacketless, but his shirt was very white and crisp and his necktie was the same color as his eyes. He stood tall, with his back straight and every hair in place. Lucinda's eyes ate up the sight of him.

"Hello, Cinda," he said gently and in the next instant she quite nearly threw herself into his arms. She sobbed without disgrace and was still sobbing when Roddy led her into his office, gently helping her get comfortable on the sofa. When Lucinda's sobbing had subsided, he began to question her gently, his arms still tightly around her.

"Why have you come?"

"I missed you so."

"I missed you too. Are you back to stay?"

"If you'll still have me," Lucinda hiccuped.

"There was never any question of that, Cinda. My love for you is constant, but if you haven't apologized to Stacy then you need to do that."

"She wrote me twice, but I was too angry to write back."

"And how do you feel now?"

Lucinda sniffed. "I still think Tanner will hurt her, but I feel just wretched for hiding her. It was so foolish of me. Do you think she'll forgive me?"

"I'm sure she will."

"And you, Roddy? Can you find it in your heart to forgive me?"

"I already have."

Lucinda let herself be cuddled against his chest for a long moment. She was no longer crying, but she felt weak and shaky all over. Some minutes passed in silence, and then Lucinda sat up suddenly.

"I'll go to her, Roddy. I won't write. I'll go to Winslow and make things right."

"I think that's a wonderful idea, my darling, but the baby is due very soon now, and I wonder if maybe you should wait."

Lucinda's face was a mask of horror. "The baby! I'd almost forgotten about the baby. Oh, Roddy, what have I done?"

Roddy thought that her tears were spent, but he was wrong. She was off again on a flood of weeping that took some time to calm. When Roddy was certain that Lucinda was ready to listen, he told her she could write to Stacy, but that they would not visit until sometime after the baby was born. Lucinda agreed without argument.

There was something different about Roddy. He was taking charge of things in a very soothing way, and Lucinda, only too happy to be back in his care, was for the first time in her life thrilled to let him lead.

❦ ❦ ❦

Tanner thought that if Stacy shifted one more time in her chair, he was going to come undone. It was obvious she was uncomfortable, but she was not at the moment going to say anything.

Tanner's eyes kept straying to Hettie, who was knitting in a chair but whose eyes constantly drifted to her mistress. He was trying to read in Hettie's face what Stacy would not admit to. All at once, Tanner could stand no more. He stood and nearly accused his wife.

"You're in pain, aren't you? I wish you would just tell me."

"But I'm not, Tanner." Stacy's voice was reasonable. "I'm not feeling the best, sort of achy, but I'm not in labor."

Tanner's seat hit the chair very hard. He really thought this was it.

"I think I would like to go to bed, however," Stacy continued. "I know it's early, but I'm tired."

Tanner nodded and rose, trying hard not to dread the next days or weeks. He was certain the baby was coming tonight, but he was not excited, only anxious. This was all new for him, and he simply wanted to get it started and over with. He knew that Stacy wouldn't appreciate his feelings, so he kept them to himself.

Five hours later, he wished he'd voiced his thoughts, if for no other reason than to have them off his chest. Stacy had fallen asleep immediately, but not Tanner. He had still been awake at midnight and at one. At any other time he'd have gone off and done some work, read, or even taken a walk, but his need to be near Stacy right now put him in bed at nine o'clock and kept him there even when all he did was stare at the ceiling.

Tanner finally drifted off somewhere around two in the morning, which was the cause for all sorts of confusion when Stacy woke him at three.

"Tanner," Stacy called softly, but her husband did little more than stir.

"Tanner, can you wake up?"

"Um."

The response was slightly more than the first time, but not enough.

"Tanner, I need you to get Hettie."

Her voice was louder this time, and Tanner finally stirred.

"What did you say?"

"I need Hettie."

"What do we need Hettie in here for?" His voice sounded very crabby, and Stacy had all she could do not to laugh.

"Things are starting, and I want Hettie."

"Things? What things?"

Stacy did laugh this time, but another contraction hit and her breath was cut off in a sharp gasp. Understanding finally dawned, and Tanner flew out of the bed. He didn't bother with his robe. If Stacy had been able to speak, she would have told him to cover up for poor Hettie's sake.

The sun had been up for hours when Stacy, feeling utterly spent, lay back against her pillows. She knew she had less than a minute before she would need to push again, but right at the moment, she didn't know where she would find the store.

"Is this one worse, Hettie?"

"Than Drew?"

"Yes."

"I can see you're not going to bleed as badly this time, but the pains are all 'bout the same, I 'spect."

Stacy would have replied, but another pain was on top of her. Tanner had been with her for most of the time, but when he'd become shaky, Stacy had finally sent him away to eat something. He was just coming in as the pain subsided.

"I feel like I can't keep this up," she admitted softly, and Tanner looked into her exhausted eyes with tenderness. He thought she was the most amazing woman on earth.

"I'll be here for you."

"What if I can't do it, Tanner? What if I can't push again?"

Tanner did not need to answer because another pain racked Stacy's body. He supported her back as she pushed.

"I see the head," Hettie cried, and new strength seemed to pour over Stacy. She waited anxiously for the next contraction, ready to do whatever was asked of her in order to meet this baby.

"Here it comes, Hettie," Stacy gasped, and the old woman stood ready.

A long minute passed.

"One more and we'll have it," Hettie crooned, and she was right. The next contraction hit, and the old woman cackled with delight.

"A girl! A big, healthy girl with a head full of black hair!"

Stacy lay back and laughed weakly with relief. She wanted to reach for the baby, but her arms felt weighted. A glance at Tanner made her chuckle again. He was staring at the squalling red infant in Hettie's hands as if he were in a trance.

Tanner Richardson had never seen anything so miraculous as the birth of his daughter. She was a mess, all red and curled up and howling at the top of her voice, but he thought she was the most precious thing he'd ever seen.

I love her, he thought to himself. *She's my daughter, and I love her. I love her the way I loved Drew the first time I set eyes on him.*

The magnitude of his thoughts was overwhelming. He glanced down at Stacy, her own eyes now back on their daughter, and thought about what she'd just given of herself. She'd been in agony to accomplish this wonder, and now she was smiling and talking to their baby.

"Don't cry, my darling. Mumma's here. Don't cry. May I have her, Hettie?"

"Just another minute, and she's all yours."

Hettie finished the cleanup, and after wrapping the baby in a soft warm wrap, she handed her to her mother. Stacy crooned softly into the baby's face and after a moment, the tears stopped. She couldn't rock her very well, but she moved her arms just enough. Within moments, the baby was asleep.

"Would you like to hold her?"

Tanner's eyes flew to Stacy's. He'd been so intent on the baby that he hadn't immediately realized she was speaking to him. He shook his head.

"Another time" was all he said.

"All right." Stacy watched him for a moment. "Are you disappointed that it's not another boy?"

"Not in the least," Tanner told her. There was so much more that he wanted to say, but none of it would come. Had they been alone he might have tried, but Hettie's presence along with that of three housemaids caused him to keep still.

He was suddenly very tired. Tanner opened his mouth to tell Stacy that he was headed off to get some rest, but her eyes were already closed, the sleeping baby still tucked in the crook of her arm. Seeing this, Tanner made his way from the room to find his own rest.

Three hours later Tanner returned to the bedroom to find Stacy awake and partially sitting up. He strode confidently into the room, but slowed somewhat when he saw the baby at her breast. That Stacy planned to nurse the baby herself had never occurred to him. He wasn't certain how he felt about this. He loved his daughter, but he'd had the distinct impression that when she was born, he could have his wife back. Selfishness was beginning to rear its ugly head.

"Hello," Stacy greeted him and watched as Tanner came to the bed, sat down, and leaned against the footboard.

"How are you feeling?"

"I'm fine. Did you get some sleep?"

"Yes. I was just in with Drew. He wants to see you."

Stacy nodded. "I asked Hettie to wait until I'd fed the baby."

"Did you nurse Drew?"

"Yes," Stacy answered, and for the first time understood the odd expression on Tanner's face. It was on the tip of Stacy's tongue to ask Tanner if he objected, but she knew she couldn't do that. She had already made up her mind.

"I'm sorry you don't care for the idea."

Tanner noticed that she did not offer to stop. "It's not that I don't care for the idea as much as it takes a little getting used to. I know I'm being selfish, but I thought I would be getting my wife back."

"I think you will be getting me back, but I won't tell you that she'll never interfere. We've created this child together, and I think my care of her is important. It would be easier if we'd been living together all these years, but in truth it isn't all that much time to sacrifice. Drew stopped nursing before he was nine months old. In fact, he tapered way off around six months."

Tanner nodded. He was not overly upset and, in truth, the idea was becoming easier all the time. He stared down at the baby and then shifted to his stomach so he could watch her.

"I think she's done."

Stacy gently bounced her a few times, and she began to suck again.

"She keeps falling asleep, so I have to give her little wake-up calls."

"Does it hurt?"

"Not hurt exactly, but it will take some time for my skin to toughen up and grow accustomed to the sucking."

Tanner was silent as he watched for the next few seconds. When the baby seemed to be sleeping again, he asked, "What are we going to call her?"

"I don't know. Have you any ideas?"

"Was your mother's name Alexa?"

"Yes. How did you know that?"

"While we were at Morgan I was studying her portrait Your grandfather's man—"

"Peters?"

"Yes, Peters. He came by and said it was your mother and that her name had been Alexa Catherine."

"Alexa." Stacy tried the name on her tongue. "I don't think I would have thought of it, but I like it."

"Alexa it is then. Alexa Anastasia Richardson."

Stacy grinned in delight and felt amazed over how painless it had been. She'd heard that people could go for weeks with great struggles and quarrels over names, but this one was so perfect.

Alexa was done eating, so Stacy shifted her to her shoulder, covered herself, and gently rubbed the baby's back. Tanner continued to watch her, and after a moment Stacy asked if he wanted to hold Alexa.

Tanner sat against the headboard this time and carefully took the baby. She was sound asleep and even though he jostled her slightly, she never stirred. She was so tiny in his hands. Her head was slightly pointed at the top, but Stacy had assured Tanner this was from the birth and would change with time. Alexa's lashes were long and dark and lay like tiny fans against her cheeks. She was round and soft, and Tanner couldn't decide which he enjoyed more, the feel of her soft skin or her fragrance, which reminded him of a forest after the rain.

After a few minutes he shifted Alexa around until she lay in the crook of his arm. Stacy was silent as he stared down into the baby's face. Suddenly Tanner turned to her, his voice low, but almost fierce.

"If a man offered to make her his mistress, I'd call him out—but that's exactly what I did to you."

Stacy said nothing, but the pain of those days when she thought Tanner would never be hers and when he admitted that he'd never wanted her for a wife, came flooding back.

"I should have been pilloried for such a thing."

"It's over now, Tanner." Stacy's voice was gentle.

"It might be over, but I've never told you how much I regret my actions and words. I'm sorry, Stacy."

Stacy could hardly believe her ears as her husband apologized for the first time in their relationship. She stared at him, unable to frame any type of reply.

As it was she didn't have to. Tanner, still holding the baby, leaned toward her. It was the most tender of kisses, and when they parted Tanner looked into her eyes for a long time.

She didn't know what he was thinking and wasn't sure if she should speak. For the moment they were content to be silent in each other's company, a silence that lasted only briefly as Drew was finally allowed to come and meet his baby sister.

Forty-Five

"THREE MONTHS OLD TODAY," Stacy whispered quietly to her baby daughter. "What a big girl you are."

Just the sound of Stacy's voice was enough to send Alexa's body into a tempest of leg kicks and arm swings. Her small, round face was wreathed in smiles. She was a most delightful baby, and Stacy grinned down at her as they sat before the fire in the nursery. The warmer winter had made their cool spring feel all the colder, but Stacy didn't mind being forced indoors when the company was so delightful.

"Aunt Lucinda and Uncle Roddy will be here any time. Did you know that?"

Alexa, who didn't understand a word of it, smiled and kicked some more. Watching her, Stacy knew how amazed Roddy and Lucinda would be. She had only been a month old, still sleeping most of the time, when they'd last visited. Now her world was expanding, and she was turning into a real person. At the moment, however, her world was her mother's face. Alexa's eyes followed Stacy's every move.

"Mum," Drew called from the doorway. "Is Alexa awake?"

"Yes, she is. Come in."

"Alexa," Drew said to her in a voice that sounded like a growl as he bent over her and rubbed noses. Stacy watched. The baby grinned as if on cue. This was Drew's latest voice with his sister. The first month he always said her name in a very high pitch. The next month he drew the name out in a singsong way—Aaaalexaaa. Now he sounded like a bear. His sister loved it.

Drew had turned four just a month back, and he was a wonderful older brother. Already showing signs of being quite responsible, Stacy even allowed him to carry the baby at times. He took this job very seriously, even though Hettie nearly fainted whenever she watched him.

"When will Uncle Roddy be here?"

"Oh, soon, I expect. Which reminds me, I'd better feed your sister now so we can go for a time without being interrupted."

Stacy came off the floor in an easy movement, and after lifting Alexa into her arms, she took the rocking chair. Drew stayed to visit with her, and when Alexa was more than halfway through, Tanner also came into the baby's room. He bent low to kiss Alexa's head, scooped Drew into his arms, and then took a chair.

"I have to go to London at the beginning of next week." Tanner's tone was regretful.

Stacy frowned slightly. They had only just begun to enjoy married life again, and right now they felt like honeymooners.

"How long will you be away?"

"Four or five days. A week at the most."

Stacy was not thrilled, but she was accepting. Tanner watched her face and smiled inwardly. He would have said something very intimate to his wife just then, but his children were present. He hadn't wanted to be away from her for a moment in the last few weeks, and her frown over his news told him she felt the same way.

"May I go with you?" This came from Drew, and Tanner looked down in surprise at the little person in his lap. His first response was to say no, but when he took a moment to think on it, he wondered if it might be a good idea.

"Let me talk it over with your mother," Tanner told him, having already decided to take Drew along.

"All right." Drew naturally took this as a good sign, and his look became very hopeful. He was going to ask where they were going to stay, but Reece came to the door at that moment to announce Roddy and Lucinda's presence.

Having gained permission, Drew joined Reece when he went back downstairs. Stacy rang for Hettie. After the baby had been taken to her room, Tanner stood up. Stacy did also and caught his hand before he could move away.

"I really wish you would see her."

Tanner's eyes grew hard. Stacy was forgiving; Tanner was not. When they had come a month after the baby was born, Tanner refused to see Lucinda. He'd spent some time with Roddy, but if Lucinda was in the room, Tanner was not.

"She is really sorry."

"You can't give Lucinda an inch, Stacy. Give her half a chance, and she'll try to control your life again."

"I'm not going to let that happen."

"I don't see how you'll stop it."

"I take it you're planning to send me away again."

Tanner's arms were around her in an instant, and he brought her hard up against him. His face was so close when he spoke, she felt his breath on her cheek.

"You know I'm not."

"Then what are you worried about?"

Tanner had no answer, but as he stared into Stacy's eyes, remembering the way Lucinda had kept them apart, he knew he couldn't take it ever again.

"I think you like holding onto your anger," Stacy spoke solemnly. "I know she was wrong, and Lucinda knows it too, but I think you've made up your mind not to forgive her. You're holding onto that bitterness for no good reason."

"Do not," Tanner's voice had grown very cold, "talk to me as if I were Drew."

"Then stop acting Drew's age!" Stacy shot back at him and stepped from his embrace. Her voice shook when she spoke, but she did not look at him as she headed toward the door.

"You're angry and since your anger always scares me, I'm leaving now."

She got no more than three feet away before Tanner was pulling her back into his arms. He didn't kiss her but held her tightly against his chest. Stacy lay agreeably in his arms, telling herself not to apologize for speaking the truth. Tanner said after some minutes, "I'll try to come down, but I make no promises."

Stacy lifted her head to look at him. "Thank you, Tanner."

"You look marvelous," Lucinda exclaimed the moment she saw Stacy. "I thought you would have the baby with you."

"Hettie is changing her, and then she'll bring her down."

"Oh, good. I brought her a little something, and I want to see what she thinks."

"Something tells me she'll love it." Stacy's voice was dry, and Lucinda laughed when she realized what she'd just said.

"Hello, Roddy."

Stacy finally turned to hug this man who was so dear to her. After embracing, they stood for just an instant and stared at each other. Things were so special now that he'd come to a saving knowledge of Christ. He had always been a kind, gentle man, but there was a warmth and peace about him now that Stacy could not even begin to describe.

"How are you?" she asked.

"I'm fine. How about you?"

"I'm well."

"Is Tanner taking good care of you?"

Stacy's smile was tender, causing Roddy to reach out and gently squeeze her hand. No words were needed.

Lucinda had sat down to hold Drew on her lap and called to her husband.

"Come and sit beside me and see this little man."

Roddy complied. "You look more like your father every time I see you, Drew."

Drew smiled at Roddy, who was one of his favorite people, but an odd expression came over Lucinda's face. When Drew climbed from Lucinda's lap onto Roddy's, she said softly, "Will he see me this time, Stacy?"

"I honestly don't know, Lucinda. I asked him if he would, but I'm not sure what he will do."

"I've been telling Lucinda she must keep quiet, even if he does make an appearance."

"Is he right, Stacy? Should I really not bring the subject up?"

"Well," Stacy answered slowly, wanting to say the right thing. "You did write him?"

Lucinda nodded.

"And in the letter you already apologized?"

Another nod.

"Then I think I would stay quiet about the Blackwells unless the subject comes up. Tanner might be ready to put it behind him, and if he is it will only irritate him to belabor the point."

Lucinda was more than ready to comply with any suggestion. The three of them spoke of it for a few minutes more, and then Hettie appeared with Alexa. Lucinda and Roddy were both captivated with her. Alexa sat on her mother's arm and stared at the strangers with huge, dark eyes.

"She's adorable," Lucinda breathed.

"Would you look at those eyes," Roddy added.

"Alexa," Drew growled, and a huge smile broke across the baby's face.

If Roddy and Lucinda had found her cute before she smiled, they now thought her enchanting. They watched as she kicked her legs and smiled at her brother's antics. Lucinda came near and Stacy passed Alexa to her. Alexa smiled engagingly through the transition, even when she realized that she was no longer in her mother's arms.

She then proceeded to charm the stockings off of her Aunty Lucinda. She smiled and drooled with charm, before sticking a finger in her eye and causing great tears of self-pity to roll down her round, flushed cheeks. She was passed to Stacy, who had only just calmed her down when Tanner walked in and made her forget all about her eye.

Unless Alexa Richardson was eating, her father was her favorite toy. She smiled as he neared, and the legs that had been calm began to kick with delight. Tanner, his eyes alight with amused pleasure, made straight for his wife and daughter. He took Alexa into his arms, bussed her once on the cheek, and then turned to his guests.

"Hello, Lucinda, Roddy. How was the trip out?"

"Not bad," Roddy answered. "The roads are a bit wet."

Tanner nodded, and Stacy prayed.

"I'm headed out for a ride," Tanner continued. "Would you care to join me, Roddy?"

Roddy answered with a smile in his voice, "Your daughter is stiff competition, but I could use some exercise."

Tanner chuckled and spoke to the baby in his arms. "Are you working your wiles on your Uncle Roddy?"

He received a toothless grin for the attention, and Tanner couldn't resist kissing her again.

"Papa?" Drew spoke. Tanner looked down to find him standing at his feet and asking to hold the baby. He waited until Drew was settled in a chair and placed Alexa in his small arms.

Tanner seemed anxious to be on his way, so he and Roddy left just after Drew took the baby. Lucinda brought out her gifts for the children in the next few minutes, and as much as Drew enjoyed his new sweater and hat, and Stacy, holding Alexa, exclaimed over the new dress and shoes for her, the younger woman could tell something was wrong.

Lucinda's features were oddly strained, but not until Hettie had taken Alexa away and Drew had gone off with Mrs. Maxwell did Stacy ask. Lucinda's reply was so surprising that all Stacy could do was listen.

"She would never have reacted that way if Tanner was a stranger. Alexa's whole face lit up at the sight of him. All this time I thought he had forced you back here, that you were being treated like before.

"Tanner cares for you; he truly does! I thought he was just like Aubrey, but he loves his children—I can see it in his face. He was so tender with both Alexa and Drew.

"Oh, Stacy, all this time... What have I done?"

"It's over, Lucinda," Stacy knew it was time to cut in. "I won't say that Tanner hasn't hurt me, but, God willing, the worst is over. I'm not exactly a saint myself, I hope you realize, but I believe we're both committed to making this marriage work."

Lucinda drew in a shuddering breath. "Thank you for being so understanding. Roddy said that you were, and I know you've forgiven me, but I don't feel I deserve it. It's all a little hard to take in."

Stacy nodded understandingly, thinking this had been a long time in the coming, but well worth the wait.

"Stacy," Lucinda said after a moment, her voice a bit reluctant, "Roddy has been talking to me about his," she hesitated over the words, "experience with God."

Stacy hid a smile. "What did he tell you?"

"Quite a bit, actually. He's very excited. He says that you helped him."

"Yes, we discussed it at the Blackwells'. Roddy was really feeling rather empty inside and—"

"But we've patched everything up now," Lucinda cut her off, thinking she understood.

"I know you have, Lucinda, and I'm thrilled that you're back together, but the emptiness Roddy was experiencing was not physical or emotional. It was spiritual."

Lucinda stared at her niece. Never had she felt so left out as she did when Roddy and Stacy talked about God. At the same time she was interested. Lucinda had gone to church all her life, but she also had too many bad things happen to her to believe that God really cared about her. However, the change in Roddy was remarkable.

Stacy would have commented on Roddy's conversion then, but Lucinda began to look very uncomfortable.

Lucinda changed the subject by asking about Brandon and Sunny. Stacy let it go, but her heart was deep in prayer for Lucinda's salvation. However, the subject did not come up again, but God's care was evident in the marvelous evening they all shared.

Tanner finally seemed willing to put the past behind him and was a wonderful host. After the children were put down for the night, the four adults dined and talked. It was very late when the duke and duchess climbed the stairs for bed, but knowing Roddy and Lucinda would be with them for only a few days made it worth the loss of sleep.

STACY WATCHED TANNER, whose expression was serious, and debated whether or not she should intrude into his thoughts. Drew was not with them now, but just minutes before he had been in Stacy's lap. The two of them had been discussing the upcoming weekend at Bracken.

At the mention of the event, Tanner had become pensive. Stacy wanted to respect his moods, but she knew she would be miserable if they went when he didn't really care to.

"Tanner?"

"Yes?" He looked at her, his expression now open.

"Would you rather we didn't go to Bracken?"

Tanner almost smiled. Unless he worked at it, Stacy could usually read his thoughts just by looking at his face.

"I have no objections to our going to the party."

"But given your choice, you'd rather stay here?"

Tanner reached for her hand. "It seems that I am often having to share you. Roddy and Lucinda were here, and now we're headed off to a weekend of being separated by friends and activities." Tanner stopped when he saw amusement in his wife's face.

"Roddy and Lucinda left a month ago." Stacy's voice was dry.

"True." Tanner's voice had turned just as wry. "But then there's your time with Alexa. You knew from the beginning that I was going to be jealous of that."

"She does like to eat," Stacy admitted. The duke and duchess smiled at each other as they both visualized their butterball daughter.

"Seriously, Tanner—" Stacy had to go back to the subject at hand. "If you don't want to go, I know that Brandon and Sunny will understand."

Tanner kissed the back of her hand. "We'll go. I'm just being selfish."

"Drew certainly will be pleased," Stacy told him, feeling well pleased at the way Tanner was putting his own wants aside. "He's talked of nothing else for days."

"Well, he doesn't have long to wait now," Tanner commented as he went back to his book. "We leave tomorrow."

"When do Stacy and Tanner arrive?" Chelsea asked Sunny.

"Tomorrow. They live so close that it seemed silly to stay over, but it's more fun that way, so I talked Tanner into it."

"I haven't seen Tanner Richardson in years," Miles Gallagher commented.

"Well," Sunny told him, "he's doing fine, and you're going to love his wife and children. Oh, Miles," Sunny spoke suddenly. "I've written up a family tree. Will you look at it for me?"

"Sure."

Sunny moved to the small writing desk in the corner and returned with a small roll of paper.

"I haven't added the dates, but will you check and see if I have all the names down?"

Miles took the roll and his mother, Chelsea, leaned over his shoulder as they read.

Gallagher Family Tree

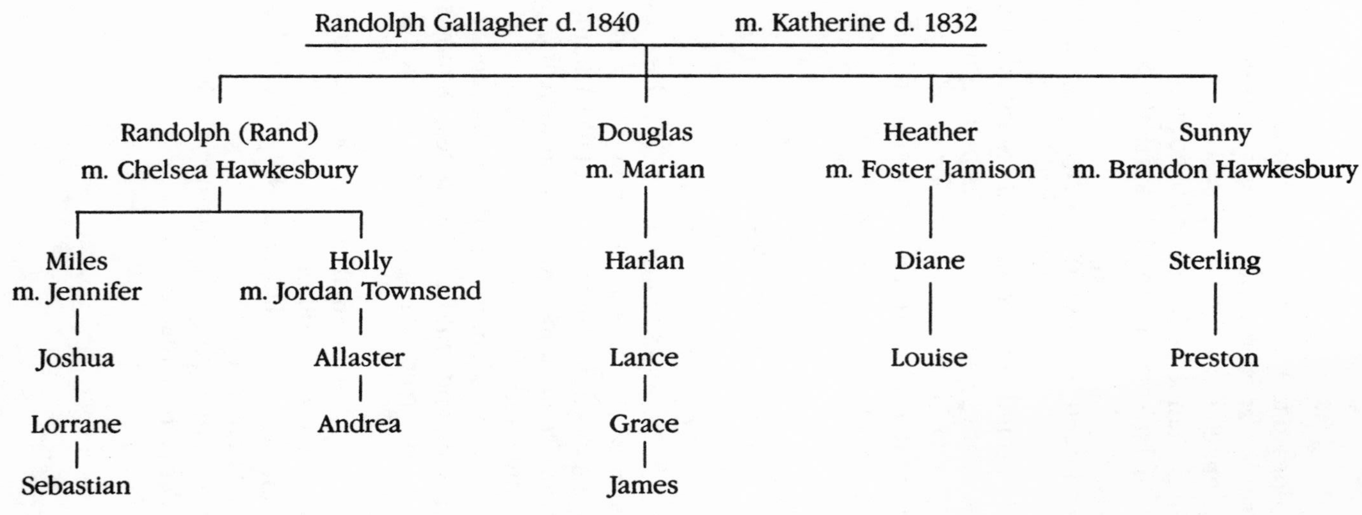

Randolph Gallagher d. 1840
m. Katherine d. 1832
Randolph (Rand)
m. Chelsea Hawkesbury
Douglas
m. Marian
Heather
m. Foster Jamison
Sunny
m. Brandon Hawkesbury
Miles
m. Jennifer
Holly
m. Jordan Townsend
Harlan
Diane
Sterling
Joshua
Allaster
Lance
Louise
Preston
Lorrane
Andrea
Grace
Sebastian
James

Hawkesbury Family Tree

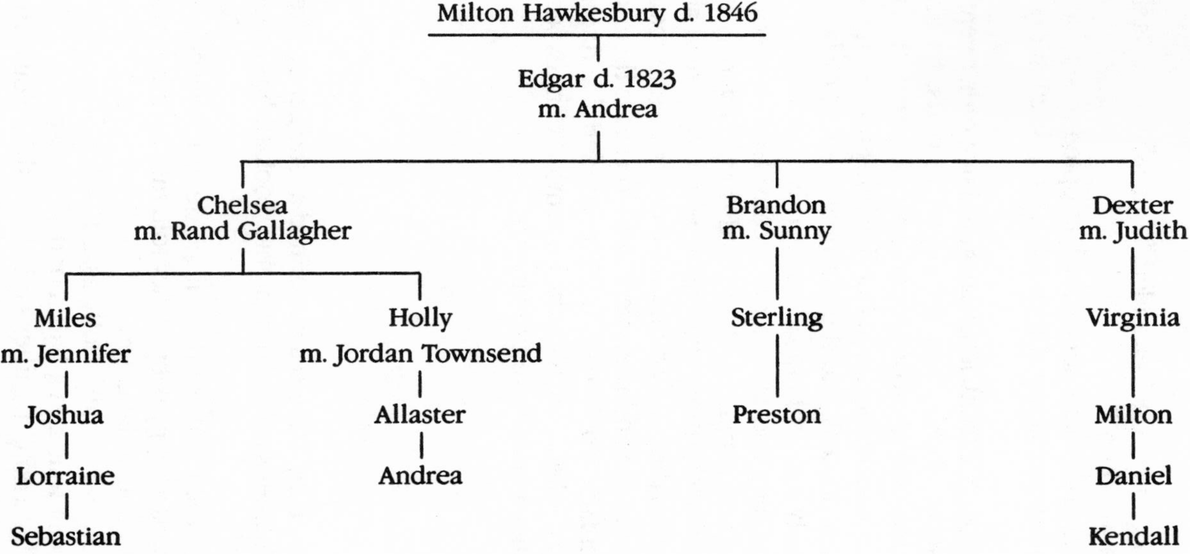

Milton Hawkesbury d. 1846
Edgar d. 1823
m. Andrea
Chelsea
m. Rand Gallagher
Brandon
m. Sunny
Dexter
m. Judith
Miles
m. Jennifer
Holly
m. Jordan Townsend
Sterling
Virginia
Joshua
Allaster
Preston
Milton
Lorraine
Andrea
Daniel
Sebastian
Kendall

"This looks good," Miles told her, "but you left out Aunt Lucy."

"Oh, Sunny," Chelsea added, "I guess you did. Is she coming this weekend?"

Sunny told them Aunt Lucy had opted to stay at Ravenscroft, her home set in the countryside just 20 minutes from Bracken.

Brandon's eccentric Great Aunt Lucy didn't venture out much anymore. She was getting on in years, but the main reason she stayed close to home was because she was still occupied with her writing. Her first book had been published with great success, and she was now working on her second. The family was still amazed over this.

Aunt Lucy had always been considered something of a beloved scatterbrain, but she had traveled widely over the years and seen things that most people only read about. In fact, most of the family didn't know of her adventures until her book came out and they were able to read it themselves.

Aunt Lucy would have made a wonderful addition to the hunting weekend, but with the huge mob Sunny expected, she knew they would have fun anyway.

"This baby," Chelsea exclaimed as she gently lifted Alexa from Heather's arms, "is adorable. Look at those round, rosy cheeks!"

"Does she ever stop smiling?" Jennifer wished to know.

"She is a happy baby," Stacy told them, smiling with pride at her precious daughter.

"How old is she?" Holly asked.

"About four and a half months."

"What a doll," Heather said. "Don't think you can keep her for long, Chels. I want her back."

The women had been visiting nonstop for what seemed like days. Stacy was having the time of her life. She had never been around so many believers at once, and found it to be the most encouraging time she had experienced in many months. Tanner seemed to be enjoying himself too.

The men were all out hunting and had been gone for hours, but Stacy was so involved with the children and the other women that she hadn't had time to miss Tanner. Both Brandon and Rand had a way of making Tanner feel at home, and even though all the men were believers who made no secret of their faith, Tanner had not put his guard up as usual.

When it was time for lunch and the men were not back, Stacy began to wonder. She tried to take her cue from the other women, however. When none of them seemed concerned, Stacy relaxed somewhat. She tried to remember how long Tanner had been out with the hunting party at the Cradwells', but it had been so many years ago that she simply couldn't recall.

"I wonder what's keeping the men?" Chelsea ventured out loud when lunch was over and the women retired to the upstairs salon.

"Did they say how far they were headed?" Sunny asked.

"I didn't hear anyone say," Holly replied.

"Well, Foster has closeted himself downstairs in the library. Shall I ask him?" This came from Heather, who was more than willing to check things out. But almost as soon as she offered, Brandon walked in.

Sunny's face lit for just an instant before she saw that his face was as pale as death. All the women watched as he walked straight to Stacy.

"There's been an accident, Stacy," he said without preamble, his voice breathless. "Tanner has been shot."

Stacy stood. "Is he alive?" she barely managed.

"Yes. We were closer to Winslow, so we took him there."

Stacy started moving for the door, but stopped abruptly and faced the room. "What about Drew and Alexa?"

"The children will be fine, Stacy," Sunny told her. "Just go," she urged. "We'll get them home to you as soon as possible."

Stacy nodded, still in shock. Sunny gave her a swift hug, and Brandon ushered her to the door and downstairs.

The coach had been traveling at full speed for nearly ten minutes before Stacy spoke.

"Where was he hit?"

"His upper chest, the left side."

So near the heart, her mind cried. She swallowed hard to keep from sobbing.

"Has he lost much blood?" she asked next.

"Yes."

Stacy didn't want to know any more. It didn't matter how it happened or who was involved, only that she was there in time. Stacy prayed as the horses' hooves ate up the ground between the estates.

I don't know what I'll see when we arrive. Please help me to be prepared for the worst, Lord. I know he hasn't come to You, Father, and for this I would ask You to spare him. Your will is perfect; help me to believe this with all of my heart. Help me to trust You even in this time of hurt.

Maybe this will be the turning point, Father. Maybe Tanner will see his need for You because of this. Please give me some assurance. Please let me talk to him before You take him to You.

Stacy realized then that she was praying as if she knew he was going to die, which was ridiculous. She began to alter her prayer, asking God to help her fight the numbness that seemed to be pervading her limbs, knowing she would be needed as soon as they arrived.

By the time they had pulled into the courtyard of Winslow, Stacy felt more in control. The ride had seemed to take ages, but doors opened seemingly of their own accord as the duchess's presence was made known. Stacy hurried indoors. With no care for watching eyes, she picked up her skirt and took the stairs two at a time.

She entered the master bedroom on swift, silent feet and stared down into the pale features of her husband. Both Rand and Miles Gallagher were present. Tanner's shirt was off, and a wrapping of sort had been bound around his chest. The side directly over the wound was soaked with blood. Stacy stared down at him and felt an amazing calm come over her.

"Has someone sent for the doctor?" she asked, her voice soft and in control.

"Yes. Jordan and Dexter have ridden to find him."

"I need Hettie," Stacy began. "Oh, that's right, she's with the baby. Eden," she said to a maid standing nearby, "bring me some more dressings and hot water, and please be quick about it."

Brandon, whose gun had caused the damage, now stepped forward. He'd been in a state of shock up until then, but seeing Stacy in charge propelled him forward to assist her. In just a matter of minutes he was carefully lifting Tanner so Stacy could change the wraps.

"Do you think the bullet is still in there?" Her voice was hushed, as though afraid to wake her patient.

"No. It went clean through."

"Good. Let's pad the back here. Reece?" Stacy called quietly to the faithful servant who came immediately to her side.

"Yes, my lady."

"Check as to whether a coach is bringing Hettie and Price. If not, see to it. I need them both immediately."

"Yes, my lady."

"Tanner," Stacy now spoke to her unconscious mate. "I'm going to take care of you, but you need to wake up and tell me how you feel."

Stacy felt better having said the words, but Tanner lay mute, his eyes closed, his skin almost clammy with cold.

"Let's get this sheet up around his chest now, and then a light blanket," Stacy went on. Again Brandon's hands were there to assist her.

The men in the room watched in some fascination as she worked. Stacy herself could not have told them where she had learned to do such things, but her husband needed her, and at the moment that was all that mattered.

The doctor showed up some time after Stacy and Brandon had washed their hands. Stacy stayed very close as he checked the wound. She took no offense when the doctor assumed Brandon had done all the work or when he addressed all of his questions to Lord Hawkesbury. Stacy was content to silently observe until the doctor reached for his bag and spoke.

"I'm going to have to bleed him."

"What did you say?" she asked.

"I'm sorry, my lady. I'm going to have to ask you to leave so I can bleed your husband."

"But he's already lost blood, more than he can spare." Stacy's voice was reasonable, but she felt panicked inside. Andrew Daniels had always been against this practice, and some of his beliefs had carried on to his granddaughter.

"It's still necessary," the doctor said, his voice resigned.

"No," Stacy told him.

The doctor did not look overly surprised. His gaze swung to Brandon. "Will you please take Lady Richardson from the room?"

Whether or not Brandon would have done such a thing, Stacy would never know. She didn't give him a chance to move.

"Reece!" Stacy used a voice none of them had ever heard before. "Remove this man at once!"

The doctor's mouth opened in shock, but Reece, surprised as he was by her tone, promptly came forward to do as he was told.

"You'll kill him," the man sputtered as Reece lay hold of the doctor's arm.

"You will *not* bleed my husband," Stacy told him, her eyes shooting sparks.

"He'll die otherwise." The doctor had pulled himself from Reece's grasp and was coming back to the bed. Stacy stood between Tanner and the doctor like an enraged warrior. The fact that she stood many inches taller than the doctor caused the man to stop.

"I said you will not bleed him, and if that is all the treatment you can offer, then get out." Stacy's voice was deadly cold.

The man was so flustered he could only stare at her. Brandon, Rand, and Miles had moved in such a way that they seemed to flank Stacy. The doctor glanced into their eyes and knew he would find no help from any of them. With a deep sigh he said, "I think you're making a grave mistake, and I won't be held responsible."

"Then by all means go," Stacy told him reasonably, not at all fearful of the responsibility.

The doctor sighed again. "I do have a poultice," he said, knowing he could not leave without doing something. "I can apply that to the wound if you'd like."

Stacy nodded, her voice soft but not apologetic. "Thank you."

The doctor was watched like a hawk as he bent over Tanner and applied the poultice and wrap. He left another poultice with Stacy and gave her instructions as to how to apply it before taking his leave. He was not a heartless man, but he honestly believed that Lord Richardson would be dead by morning.

Forty-Seven

"I WANT TO TELL YOU WHAT HAPPENED, STACY," Brandon said softly when he, Stacy, Rand, and Miles were alone in the room. The doctor had been gone just minutes, and now Stacy stood next to the bed, staring down into Tanner's pale face.

"It doesn't matter, Brandon," Stacy looked up and told him. "I know whatever it was, it was an accident."

"You're right, it was," Brandon agreed with her, his voice tight with pain. "But it was my gun, and I want to tell you."

Stacy's heart turned over when she saw tears in this man's eyes. She was not shocked or angry to learn that it had been Brandon's gun. She preferred that over it being the gun of one of the boys who had gone on the hunt and who might never get over such a mishap. Still, his obvious pain made Stacy ache for him. He cared deeply for Tanner, and she could well imagine how he must feel. On Stacy's nod, Brandon began to speak.

"I've never done anything so foolish in all my life. I pointed my gun—that is, I gestured with it to a place behind me—and my finger was on the trigger. I knew that Tanner was behind and to the side of me, but I thought it was the other side.

"The gun seemed to go off of its own accord. I know that can happen to anyone. My deepest regret is that I used the gun to point at all. I have two good arms for that. I can't think what possessed me. I'm sorry, Stacy."

Brandon's voice broke then, and Stacy went to him. She hugged this man who was so like her husband in size and listened as a sob caught in his throat. It never even occurred to Stacy to be bitter or unforgiving, and after a few moments they broke apart and Stacy smiled gently at Brandon.

"God is only good to us, Brandon. I know that He is going to use this in a mighty way in Tanner's life."

Brandon drew in a deep breath. He didn't know where Stacy found the strength to do it, but she was actually ministering to him. Rand and Miles came close at that point, and the men hugged Brandon and Stacy also.

"Now," ever-practical Rand spoke when everyone had their emotions under control, "what can we do for you, Stacy?"

Stacy had just opened her mouth to answer when she heard Alexa's cry in the hall. Her milk came down in a rush, and when she did speak, it was with her arms tightly folded across her chest. She spoke as calmly as she could.

"Please ask Hettie to give Alexa to Juliet, and then I would like to speak to Hettie." This was all accomplished in competent haste, and just minutes later Hettie stood before her.

"Hettie, Rand is going to take you to the village. I want you to find a wet nurse. You know the kind of woman to look for. If you need to bring several women for me to meet, then do, but I want to speak to whomever you bring *before* she goes to Alexa. When you leave, tell Juliet to bring Alexa to me."

"Yes, my lady." Hettie's voice was humble. She had thought to come back and find Stacy a mess, but Stacy's control was a comfort to everyone near her. Mrs. Maxwell, who had Drew, was just as calm. Hettie knew that she and Stacy shared the same faith and wondered if there could be a connection.

Five minutes later Stacy had cleared the bedroom so she could feed her daughter. She did this while sitting next to the bed, her eyes more on Tanner than her daughter. She fed Alexa only long enough to bring herself some relief and temporarily satisfy her baby.

Not until she'd returned Alexa to Juliet and changed her

clothing did she have time to think about where everyone was. Miles had gone with Hettie and his father. Brandon had gone down to Tanner's study to write letters to the family. Brandon's first letter was to Roddy and Lucinda, and the second was to Uncle Edmond.

Now Price, who had come in when Alexa was given to Juliet, was the only one in the master bedroom with Stacy. Price was the consummate gentleman's gentleman. As he stood on the opposite side of the bed and stared into Tanner's pale features, however, his emotions were starting to win the battle. Thankfully Stacy glanced at Price just then and recognized his plight better than he did himself. Stacy compassionately dismissed him.

Stacy was glad for a few solitary moments with her husband. He was so still it was alarming, but the gentle rise and fall of his chest told Stacy that it was not yet God's time for Tanner to leave this earth. Tanner had been placed on her side of the bed, so it was easy for Stacy to reach her Bible from where she sat. She turned to Psalm 135 and read quietly to her spouse.

"Praise ye the Lord. Praise ye the name of the Lord; praise him, O ye servants of the Lord. Ye who stand in the house of the Lord, in the courts of the house of our God, praise the Lord; for the Lord is good. Sing praises unto his name; for it is pleasant. For the Lord hath chosen Jacob unto himself, and Israel for his peculiar treasure. For I know that the Lord is great and that our Lord is above all gods. Whatsoever the Lord pleased, that did he in heaven, and in earth, in the seas, and all deep places. He causeth the vapours to ascend from the ends of the earth; he maketh lightnings for the rain; he bringeth the wind out of his treasuries."

When Stacy finished, she set her Bible aside and began to pray with her eyes on Tanner's face.

"I want him to know You, Lord," Stacy whispered. "I want him to have time to come to Christ, but Your will is holy. Help me to trust." Stacy could not go on.

She was suddenly back at her grandfather's bedside, listening to him tell her that he had believed in Christ. Stacy's eyes slid shut with remembered joy. God had saved her grandfather when he had just days left on this earth, and she knew He could do the same for Tanner. As much as Stacy loved Tanner, she knew God loved him more. This did not give her a guarantee concerning his eternity, but as she'd said to Brandon, God is only good.

"Don't let me forget that, Father."

The young woman standing before Stacy looked shy and a little frightened as she stared up at the Duchess of Cambridge. She had a very tiny baby in her arms, whose color was a healthy pink. Stacy noted that both were clean, and even though their clothing was coarse, it was well pressed and had no stains.

"What is your name?"

"Felicity, my lady."

Stacy could not immediately speak. Felicity had been the name of the girl in Middlesbrough who had been Drew's wet nurse. Stacy had prayed for wisdom concerning this decision and now wondered if this might be God's way of giving her direction.

"Do you feel you have enough milk for both babies, Felicity? I would not want you to starve your own child."

"'e ain't never been able to drink all my milk, Lady Richardson. A've always got plenty to spare."

"Your baby is a boy?"

Felicity's face lit with pride and joy. "'is name's Robert, after 'is pa."

Stacy smiled, even as an ache filled her. She'd planned to feed Alexa for at least six more months.

"Robert is a fine name. Do you understand that I would need you to live here at Winslow, Felicity, and be on constant call?"

"Yes, ma'am."

Stacy nodded, feeling satisfied. "I have just fed Alexa, but I'm certain she is still hungry. Hettie will take you to Alexa's room, and she will be the one to tell you when you are needed. Is everything clear?"

"Yes, my lady."

They discussed a few more specifics before Hettie took mother and son away. Stacy was tempted to watch and see how she did with Alexa, but she didn't think she could deal with the sight of another woman feeding her baby right now.

With a determined move, Stacy returned to the bedroom and Tanner's side. Brandon was sitting with him and seemed to sense that Stacy did not care to talk.

In the next hours trusted servants came and went. The poultice was changed, the bleeding had stopped, and Tanner was made as comfortable as possible. Both Stacy and Brandon prayed that he would wake soon, but it was not to be. By morning Tanner was still unconscious. A fever had begun to rage within his body.

Forty-eight hours later, Stacy's hand shook with exhaustion as she laid a cold cloth on Tanner's brow. His skin was so hot it burned her to touch him, but at least the thrashing had stopped. There had been times when Brandon had all but lain on top of Tanner to keep him on the bed.

Neither Stacy nor Brandon had slept, but at the moment Stacy felt beyond sleep. Brandon had just left to get something to eat, and Stacy now sat alone in the room.

Tanner's hand lay outside the covers, and Stacy reached for it. He was so warm, but she held the hand gently for just a moment and then began to grip it harder.

"I don't want you to die, Tanner," she whispered in some desperation. "Do you hear me?" Again her grip tightened. "I don't want you to die." Stacy's voice was still low but growing almost fierce in intensity. She squeezed his hand. There was still no response.

"Don't you die, Tanner," she now hissed at him. "Don't you dare. You can drum up some of that orneriness that we both know you're so capable of and fight this. Do you hear me, Tanner Richardson?"

Stacy was nearly shouting now and shaking Tanner's arm for all it was worth. A small groan came from his lips. Stacy stopped, horrified over what she was doing.

"I'm sorry, Tanner," she began to sob. "I'm so sorry. I didn't mean that. Please forgive me, Tanner. I'm so sorry." Her sobs were uncontrollable now, so much so that she didn't even hear Brandon come into the room.

"Come on, Stacy," he spoke gently. "Come get some rest."

"Please don't make me leave him, Brandon," she begged, her crying still very harsh.

"All right," he crooned. "Just come over here to the extra bed. Price set this up for you, and you haven't used it. It's time now, come on."

Brandon was afraid that if he called someone to assist him, Stacy would rouse and want to return to Tanner's side. Right now she was nearly asleep on her feet. Wishing Sunny was with him, he urged her onto the bed and covered her with a blanket. He didn't bother with her shoes or anything else, but stood by as she cried into the pillow and finally drifted off to sleep. When he thought she wouldn't stir, he turned his back on her and returned to the bed.

He was tired enough to sleep himself, and would soon, but for right now he needed to make sure that Tanner remained quiet for Stacy. He had tremendous peace that Tanner was going to come out of this and be fine, but Stacy would be of no use to anyone if she continued as she was. An hour later Price came to relieve him, and with Stacy and Tanner still sleeping, Brandon left that room to find his own rest.

Another two days passed before Tanner's fever broke and he awakened. Brandon sat beside him, holding Stacy's Bible open to the book of Luke. It took a moment before he felt Tanner's eyes on him.

"Welcome back," Brandon spoke softly.

Tanner licked his lips. "How many days?"

"About six."

"Stacy." It wasn't stated as a question, but Brandon knew that it was.

"She just went down to get something to eat. I can send Price for her."

Tanner's head moved on the pillow. "I won't be able to stay awake that long."

"All right. Do you remember what happened?"

Tanner's eyes had slid shut, but he still answered. "Yes. It could happen to anyone, Hawk."

Brandon's relief was indescribable. "Be that as it may, I am sorry, Tanner."

Tanner didn't answer then, but Brandon watched his hand lift slightly on the cover and knew that he'd been understood and forgiven.

"Would you like some more?" Stacy asked, holding a cup of strong beef broth for Tanner. He'd sipped half of it, but Stacy could see that he was flagging.

"No." The duke lay back, feeling rather spent. "I'm going to sleep for a while. I hate this weakness," he commented. It was the evening of his first day awake, but Tanner evidently believed he should have been able to jump out of bed from the start.

Stacy smoothed the hair from his forehead and then leaned to kiss his brow. When she sat back, Tanner reached for her hand and searched her eyes with his own.

"Did you read to me while I was unconscious?"

"Yes, every day, from the Bible."

Tanner continued to watch her. "You said something about the wind."

Stacy thought a moment. "That was from Psalm 135. It's a psalm that praises God for His power and provision with the way He brings forth the wind, rain, and lightning."

Stacy waited for a cynical look to cross his face, but it didn't happen.

"Did you pray for me too?"

"Constantly," she told him.

"Thank you, sweetheart."

With that, Tanner's eyes closed, but Stacy didn't move. She sat holding his hand long after it went limp in her grasp.

STACY SAW BRANDON, SUNNY, RAND, AND CHELSEA to the door. They had come to see Tanner that morning and stayed for lunch.

Two more days had passed, but he was still feeling very weak. The entire situation made him testy and frustrated Stacy was thankful that the visit from friends had worked to take his mind off himself for a short time.

Stacy was finding that Tanner wasn't the easiest patient, but she didn't complain. She had been very pleased to see the Hawkesburys and the Gallaghers, as their presence offered something new to her convalescing charge. He'd tried to get out of bed twice but simply couldn't manage it. At those times the staff cleared out because he was nearly impossible to be around.

Nothing was right. The bed was too hard and then too soft. His food was too hot and then too cold. Stacy had never seen him this way, but she weathered it all without so much as a word of protest. She knew it was nothing personal; he was simply frustrated over being kept down.

Some of his ire had cooled during and after his visit with friends, but by the evening he was his old cantankerous self. He had complained to Stacy no less than five times about his dinner, but she still said nothing, only fixed things the way he wanted them and continued to eat her own meal.

"Will you stop treating me like a baby!" Tanner finally snapped at her. Stacy's fork stopped halfway to her mouth.

"I'm not treating you like a baby, Tanner," she said reasonably.

"Yes, you are!" he insisted in a foul humor. "You have this tolerant look on your face as though you were dealing with Drew and just waiting for him to get over his mood."

"Tanner." Stacy's voice was still calm. "I know you don't care to be in that bed, but I'm *not* treating you like a child."

"Yes, you are."

Stacy sighed gently. "If Drew acted as you are, I'd put him across my knee. So you can see that you're not being treated like a child or you'd be feeling the pain of it this instant."

Suddenly they both smiled. That small example of just how self-centered Tanner was acting snapped the tension that had built.

It was just what they both needed. The meal was finished on a lighter note, and Stacy felt for the first time in days that she might be getting her old Tanner back. She was well pleased with this, but the best was yet to come, and it would happen the very next afternoon.

"This letter is from Noel and Elena," Stacy told him. "They obviously haven't received my letter about your wound—they want us to come up for some hunting as soon as we're able. Elena goes on to say that little Noel is getting just huge, and Brittany still asks about Drew every day.

"Now, these two are business," Stacy continued as she sorted the post. "Do you want them here or on your desk?"

"Why don't you give them to Price."

"I'll do that. Oh, I almost forgot—"

"Excuse me, my lady," Reece interrupted them.

"Yes, Reece. What is it?"

"It's Felicity, my lady. She's says her baby has a slight cold and could she please leave and go to the doctor in the village or send for him to come here."

"Send for him, by all means," Stacy told him. "And tell Felicity not to worry. I'll be in to see her later."

"One of our maids has a baby?" Tanner didn't speak until after Reece had left. Stacy nearly laughed at his baffled expression.

"No. Felicity is Alexa's wet nurse. Her baby is just six weeks old. His name is Robert."

Tanner could only stare at her.

"What is it, Tanner?" Stacy asked, not recalling that she and Tanner had never discussed this.

"Alexa needed a wet nurse?"

"Well, yes. I sent for one after the accident because I couldn't be with her all the time."

"But why couldn't you?"

Now it was Stacy's turn to stare. Did he really not understand how many hours she'd spent in this room? Her voice was gentle, however, when she answered him in just a handful of words.

"Because you needed me more than Alexa did."

Tanner's world rocked. Feeding Alexa herself had been very important to Stacy. He knew there was not another woman in all the earth like his wife. She cared for him without complaint. She took his verbal abuse without comment. And now, when he needed her, she had even set her baby aside to be with him. He felt humbled beyond explanation, and for the first time in his life he realized his true feelings for his wife went far beyond respect and admiration.

When Tanner had remained quiet, Stacy assumed he didn't want to hear any more letters. Stacy had stood to bend over him and check his dressing. He spoke while she was poised above him, a study in concentration.

"I love you, Anastasia."

Stacy froze, certain she had heard wrong. Her eyes moved slowly to lock with his.

"Yes, you heard me correctly. I love you, Stacy."

Stacy straightened slowly, and Tanner watched as her hand came to her lips. Huge tears puddled in her eyes and spilled down her cheeks. Tanner had never actually seen her break down before, and all he could do was watch helplessly from the bed.

A door sounded then, and both knew they were going to be interrupted. Stacy turned swiftly from the bed and moved to the window in an effort to control herself. Her whole frame shook as she tried to suppress sobs, but it wasn't working.

Price, who had been the one at the door, sized up the situation immediately and excused himself. Pain ripped through Tanner's chest and shoulder as he shifted to see her. He listened for a long moment to her tears before calling to her.

"Sweetheart. Come back over here."

She did not come immediately. He called to her several more times before she returned and he was able to urge her into the chair near the bed. Tanner gasped his way into a sitting position and handed Stacy the edge of the sheet to dry her tears.

"I just can't...I didn't think you would ever...that is, I hoped, but I didn't know..."

Tanner didn't try to quiet her. Her reaction spoke volumes to him as to how much she'd hoped and waited for him to say the words. It occurred to him suddenly, however, that she had not returned the words. In fact she hadn't said them in many months. Tanner wondered if perhaps she didn't feel as strongly about him as she once had. It saddened him to think that he might have waited too long, but he vowed that as soon as he was able to get out of bed, he would not just tell Stacy, but show her in a thousand different ways that his love was real.

Stacy walked around in a cloud for the remainder of the day. Tanner was feeling remarkably better by dinnertime, and Stacy later found herself pulled in two directions. She wanted to hold her husband and be held in return, but fear for his wound was very real. Tanner, on the other hand, had no such qualms.

After dinner, while Stacy was still checking his dressing, she felt Tanner's free hand in the middle of her back. Before she could even guess what he might be up to, he pulled her down against him and kissed her.

Stacy struggled, thinking that her weight would start the bleeding again.

"Tanner," she gasped. "You can't do that."

Stacy escaped and stepped away from the bed to talk.

"Tanner," she tried to sound stern. "Behave yourself."

"I am behaving myself. I'm behaving like a man in love with his wife. Now come back over here."

"No." Stacy sounded more adamant than she felt.

"Do as I tell you, Anastasia."

There was that tone. The one that always made Stacy feel helpless. She returned, sitting carefully on the edge of the bed.

"I love you," he said again. "And I want the spare bed out of here tonight."

Stacy shook her head. There was no way she was going to jeopardize his recovery by sleeping in the same bed and possibly endangering his wound.

"Yes, Stacy." Tanner's voice was velvety smooth, but even when he ordered, Stacy stood her ground. Tanner was none too happy with her over it, but he saw that he'd pushed far enough.

Stacy was lulled into a false sense of security when Tanner suddenly gave up. She left him for a time to ready herself for bed, feeling distinctly triumphant. She'd have fainted with horror had she seen Tanner actually standing by the bed after she left.

The effort was almost more than he could take, but once up, he found it not too bad. His injury screamed at him, but he ignored the pain and the trembling in his lower limbs. Just a few minutes was all he could last, but it was enough to give him confidence for the morrow. Thankfully he was back in bed before Stacy or Price could make an appearance.

Forty-Nine

"DO YOU HAVE PLANS TO GROW TEETH any time soon?"

The question was good-naturedly posed to Alexa by her papa. As usual, she grinned and even drooled with delight on the good side of his chest.

Drew had been in for an hour that morning, and now it was Alexa's turn. Stacy was careful to watch Tanner for signs of fatigue, but he seemed a hundred percent better. She smiled to herself when she thought of how swiftly the change had come about. It came with his declaration of love. Stacy's heart was swelling with joy over yesterday's events.

My husband loves me, she told the Lord the night before while spending some quiet moments alone in her sitting room. *It's more than I ever hoped for, Father. You have brought a miracle in this marriage, and I thank You from deep in my heart.*

"Stacy, I think she's doing something." Tanner's voice was distressed, his face chagrined.

Stacy glanced down at Alexa's red, strained features and laughed. She pulled the bellpull, and when Price arrived she asked him to send for Hettie. Hettie was completely undisturbed over the task at hand and crooned softly to her charge as she took her from the room.

"You look like you could use some sleep."

Tanner yawned before answering. "I think you're right. You wouldn't like to climb in with me, would you?"

Stacy smiled. "I've got some things to do, and then I'll come up. Do you want anything before I go?"

"No."

They kissed then, and Stacy made her way around the bed to gather some papers from a small writing desk. She quietly straightened a few things in the room, and then, with a final glance at her sleeping husband, made for the door. She had not reached the threshold of Tanner's dressing room when Price came in. He stopped in front of her, and Stacy studied his anxious eyes.

"What is it, Price?"

Price glanced at Tanner, and Stacy's eyes followed his, but he was asleep.

"Lord Stanley is here."

Stacy stared at him.

"Nigel Stanley?"

"Yes, my lady. He wishes to see you."

Stacy took a deep breath. What in the world could he want?

"All right. Tell Lord Stanley I'll be down shortly."

Price nodded and left. Stacy looked one more time at Tanner. He was on his side, facing away from her; otherwise Stacy would have seen that his eyes were wide open and dark with a myriad of emotions.

Nigel Stanley looked older to Stacy, older than she had expected. It wasn't that his hair had turned gray or that he'd shrunken in frame, but his eyes and mouth had lost their youth. There was a sadness in the depths of his eyes, and there were deep grooves at the sides of his mouth.

"Hello, Lord Stanley. I understand you wanted to see me." Stacy congratulated herself over her calm. She wasn't afraid of this man, but she did not want him in her life or disturbing her marriage as he'd done before.

"Yes, thank you for seeing me. I wouldn't have blamed you if you'd had me thrown from your property."

"Won't you sit down?"

He did, but Stacy could see he was not at ease. Stacy sat also and waited. Nigel cleared his throat at least three times before he began.

"I know that much time has passed, and I'm sorry for that, but I wanted to see you today to express my deepest regrets over my past actions. My actions on that day bring me extreme shame, and I know they caused you great distress.

"I stalked you that weekend, totally thoughtless of your person. It's something for which I have no excuse. I came to tell you how sorry I am for the way I acted."

Nigel stood abruptly, and Stacy did the same. He'd clearly come to say that and no more.

"Thank you, Nigel. I appreciate your stopping. The rumors were evidently false."

A ghost of a smile lifted one side of his mouth. "I suppose you heard that your husband killed me in a duel."

"Murdered you actually," Stacy replied, feeling shame that she'd ever believed such a thing of Tanner. "You did rather disappear."

"Having been raised in Paris, I had not been in London all that long when I attended the party. So when I made such a fool of myself over you, I thought it the better part of valor to make myself scarce."

"But you're back in England now?"

"Only on business. I'm married myself now, just six months, and we make our home in France."

Stacy smiled a very genuine smile. "I'm pleased for you, Nigel, and I wish you all the best."

"Thank you, Lady Richardson. Your understanding and forgiveness confound me, but I am eternally grateful."

He left then, being shown to the door by Reece. Stacy stood in the parlor where he'd left her.

How odd, she mused, but then thought better of it. He needed to make things right, and she admired his doing so instead of pushing that whole incident into some corner of his mind to pretend it never happened.

For the first time, Stacy was able to think of the Cradwell party without pain. The nightmare had come to an end; the problem had been resolved. She understood now that a part of her had still been living in the shadows of that painful time. Stacy felt now a sort of freedom come over her with Nigel's apology. She would have to tell Tanner, in a gentle way, what had transpired.

"Stacy."

Stacy's calm reverie was shattered. Her head snapped to the door. That had been Tanner's voice; she was sure of it. She ran for the closed portal, wrenched it open, and ran for the stairs. He was at the bottom, wearing only a robe. His face was completely drained of color.

"Oh, Tanner. Please go back to bed. Whatever possessed you to get up?"

"Where is he?" Tanner gasped as he sank to the bottom step.

"Who?" Stacy really didn't know.

"Stanley." Tanner could barely talk. "I know he's come to offer for you. I've got to set the record straight—you're mine and we both know it. Unless I tell him, he'll not believe you won't go with him."

Tanner was completely spent then, and Stacy put her arms around him until he caught his breath. She laid her head against his shoulder, and when she looked at him after a moment, found his color improved.

"He came to tell me how much he regretted his actions of the past. Nigel is married now and not even living in England. He's already left."

"He didn't want you?"

"No, and it wouldn't have mattered if he had."

Tanner pulled her head back down to his shoulder. He

held her close for long minutes. Stacy heard him sigh deeply before speaking quietly.

"I'm ready, Stacy. I'm ready to hear what happened."

Stacy lifted her head, and their eyes met. She never looked away as she told her story.

"I was so naive in those days," she began. "I look back now on the way Lord Stanley acted and wonder how I could have been so innocent, but I was.

"He watched me constantly. I realize now that his behavior was obvious to everyone but me. Had I understood, I would have been a little cooler to him, but since I didn't, I was my usual friendly self. Because he was already smitten, he took every smile as an invitation.

"He approached me in the conservatory on Saturday, but I still didn't catch on. Then Sunday, he completely lost his head. When you came in I was trying to push him away, but for all his slim build he was fairly strong.

"I'm sorry I didn't know, Tanner. I'm sorry—"

"Shhh," Tanner cut her off, his eyes still holding hers. "There is nothing for you to apologize over. *I'm* sorry I didn't give you time to explain. The loss has been my own.

"In the last weeks," Tanner told her, "I've figured out much of what you just told me. You're certainly right about Stanley; his actions were peculiar. His eyes looked of blood lust, like a hound on the hunt. I let my emotions run over the top of me, or I would have come to more reasonable conclusions much sooner."

Stacy sighed then and put her head on his shoulder. She'd thought that it was over when Nigel apologized. Now she was certain of it. Content as Stacy was to sit there all day, she remembered just how ill Tanner had been. Stacy was on the verge of suggesting they go upstairs when he spoke.

"I haven't been easy to live with. I know that, and I might be a little late in coming to this, but I'm going to make it up to you, Stacy. When I'm finally on my feet again, I'm going to show you I'm worthy of your love."

"Tanner," Stacy said, lifting her head. "Whatever are you talking about?"

"You've stopped saying it, you know. Not even when I told you I loved you did you say it in return—not that I blame you. But just give me time; I'll win your love back."

"Oh, Tanner. I've never stopped loving you, but when we first came back I knew you didn't want to hear it. I guess I just got out of practice. I'm sorry."

"I love you, Stacy."

"And I love you, Tanner."

He kissed her and then held her close once again. They made quite a sight at the bottom of the stairs, Stacy in a beautiful day-dress and Tanner in his robe, but no one disturbed them and they didn't care.

"I only just thought of something. We never took that trip to France, the one we were going to take for our first anniversary."

"No, I guess we didn't."

"So how about it? I figure we could leave in about a month's time. What do you say?"

The chances of seeing Nigel Stanley were slim to none, but still Stacy could not find any enthusiasm about going.

"Not interested?" Tanner questioned her silence, trying not to read anything there.

"Not in France," she admitted. "But I understand Greece is beautiful in the fall."

"Ah, Stacy," Tanner said with a sigh. "You're so good for my heart."

"Am I?" she smiled.

"Yes. And we'll have no more of this nonsense about your hurting my chest. I'm not up to much, but I want to hold you, and no one is going to stop me."

"All right," Stacy agreed. "I'll ask Reece to have the extra bed removed."

Tanner grinned. "I already did that."

Stacy would have spoken, but Tanner kissed her surprised mouth, and suddenly Stacy didn't have anything to say at all.

Epilogue

TWENTY-THREE YEARS LATER

STACY STOOD IN THE SHADE of a huge willow tree and watched her family's antics. She shook her head at their energy and then turned and made her way toward the house. When she arrived at the back terrace she sat on the swing, from which she was still able to see her children and grandchildren.

Drew, married to a lovely girl for two years now, swung his little daughter, Penny, high in the air and caught her on a burst of giggles. It always took Stacy's breath away to watch, but Penny clearly loved it. Hettie, who was too old now to get around, was sure to be up in her room watching as well.

Next Stacy spotted Alexa as she threw a ball to her son, Joey. Alexa was a Hawkesbury now, having married Sterling, who was the image of Brandon, three years before. Both couples were as happy as they could be. They had found Christian mates and dedicated their lives to Him first and then to one another.

Stacy's mind moved to Chase. He'd come after Alexa by a few years and had been away at school for some time. He had only just finished his studies and was now living in London with Roddy. Lucinda had died five years earlier, and everyone was relieved that Chase would be there to keep company with him.

Lucinda had never been very comfortable with Roddy's talk of Christ and the Bible. On her deathbed, however, she had told Roddy she had made things right.

The girls who had come after Chase were on the lawn now. Kendra was 18 and Pippa 17. They both missed Chase terribly, but it helped to have Drew and Alexa, with their families, near.

The Duchess of Cambridge continued to study her brood, but after a moment she no longer saw them. Her mind's eye had turned to Tanner and his behavior of the past week. Never had she seen him in such a mood. Not that he was usually impossible, but something had definitely changed.

So many years before he had promised Stacy that he would be worthy of her love, and he had been. They had experienced their ups and downs, but Stacy could never fault Tanner's efforts as a husband and father. His children adored him and better yet *knew* him, because he had taken the time in their lives to be there. In fact, before coming home from London that day, he'd planned to check on Chase and see to his well-being.

God's grace amazed Stacy repeatedly when she thought about the way all her children had come to Him, even though their father had had little voice in the matter for all these years.

Tanner still enjoyed his debates with Brandon, and in fact the four of them had only grown closer as the years passed, but Tanner, to Stacy's knowledge, had never made Christ his Lord. Still she prayed, believing.

"Wool gathering?"

Stacy smiled at the sound of that deep voice and rose to embrace her husband.

"How was your trip?" she asked, their arms still tight around each other.

"Good."

"And Chase?"

"Looking well. I think he and Roddy are going to do splendidly."

Stacy gave a heartfelt sigh. "That's a relief." She stood in the circle of his arms just staring at him for a full minute.

Finally she spoke. "Tanner, what's come over you? I can't quite put my finger on it, but you seem quite different."

Tanner gently kissed her brow, his look very tranquil.

"I believe the Scriptures call it being 'a new creature in Christ.'"

Stacy stood in quiet shock for the space of several heartbeats.

"Oh, my darling Tanner," Stacy whispered when she could talk. Her hands came up to frame his face, and she looked at him through tear-filled eyes.

"When did this happen, Tanner?"

"About a week ago," he said, his voice more serene than Stacy had ever heard. "It's been an especially fine year for my investments, and I was sitting in my office congratulating myself as usual for my fine business acumen, when it suddenly occurred to me that without God I would have nothing.

"I felt as if I'd been struck. You, the children—everything is from God. He is the Provider and Savior. I couldn't go on after that. I wrestled for some minutes, but I knew I could never again pretend that I had been responsible."

"But how did you—?"

"I've been listening to you talk to the children for years, sweetheart. I prayed and told Him that I believe in Him and need a Savior for my sins. And you well know He never turns anyone away."

Stacy was overcome then. Tanner could count on one hand the times he'd seen her break down in all the years they'd been married, and now this was one more to add to the list. Tanner led her to a seat then and let her cry. He was thankful that no one disturbed them.

When Stacy could control herself, Tanner began to speak. He told her how empty he'd been feeling inside for the last year and how much he'd begun to think of eternity.

"I'm not a young man anymore, you know. I'm 56 this year and I've lived much of that time for myself. It was more than time for a change, a permanent change."

"Oh, Tanner. Wait until Brandon hears," Stacy sniffed. "You can't know how he's prayed for you."

Tanner smiled. "I'm looking forward to seeing him. There's so much I want to know. So much I *need* to know."

They talked on for some time, and then Tanner stood, eager to go and share with his family. Stacy opted to stay where she was and watch the scene unfold. She smiled, tears coming to her eyes again, as they thronged him, arms hugging amid cries of delight and praise to God.

"I never wanted anyone else, Father." Stacy spoke out loud. "From the moment I laid eyes on Tanner, I knew my heart was lost. Then You chose me, now You have chosen him. In Your love You have given me my deepest desire."

A breeze had come up, and Stacy's words were gently snatched away. Not that it mattered. God had heard them and as soon as her family, who was now coming to see her, arrived, she would gladly say them again.

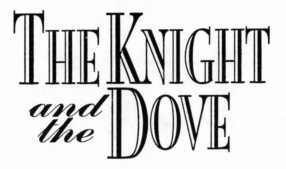

The Knight and the Dove

Lori Wick

HARVEST HOUSE PUBLISHERS
Eugene, Oregon 97402

All Scripture quotations in this book are taken from the King James Version of the Bible.

THE KNIGHT AND THE DOVE

Published by Harvest House Publishers
Eugene, Oregon 97402

Library of Congress Cataloging-in Publication Data

Wick, Lori
The knight and the dove / Lori Wick.
p. cm. — (Kensington chronicles)
ISBN 1-56507-289-8
1. Great Britain—History—Henry VIII, 1509-1547—Fiction. 2. Man -woman relationships—England—Fiction. I. Title. II. Series: Wick, Lori. Kensington chronicles.
PS3573.I237K58 1995
813'.54—dc20 94-29332
CIP

Printed in the United States of America.

95 96 97 98 99 00 01 — 10 9 8 7 6 5 4 3 2 1

To my pastor and his wife,
Phil and Denise Caminiti.
I praise God for your faithfulness,
encouragement, and willingness to be
used by Him. This dedication
comes with my love.

The Author

Lori Wick, known for her warm pioneer fiction, now takes readers to fascinating lands across the sea in the Kensington Chronicles. Lori is the bestselling author of twelve novels, including *The Hawk and the Jewel*, *A Place Called Home*, *Whatever Tomorrow Brings*, and *Sean Donovan*. She and her family live in Wisconsin.

Other Books by Lori Wick

A Place Called Home Series
- A Place Called Home
- A Song for Silas
- The Long Road Home
- A Gathering of Memories

The Californians
- Whatever Tomorrow Brings
- As Time Goes By
- Sean Donovan
- Donovan's Daughter

The Kensington Chronicles
- The Hawk and the Jewel
- Wings of the Morning
- Who Brings Forth the Wind
- The Knight and the Dove

The Kensington Chronicles

DURING THE NINETEENTH CENTURY, the palace at Kensington represented the noble heritage of Britain's young queen and the simple elegance of a never-to-be-forgotten era. The Victorian Age was the pinnacle of England's dreams, a time of sweeping adventure and gentle love. It is during this time, when hope was bright with promise, that this series began.

But now travel back 300 years, to an enchanting time when knights and chivalry and heraldry reigned, and King Henry's Tudor England set the stage for all that was to come.

Windsor Castle
1531

"What of Vincent of Stone Lake? He's a loyal lord."

"Yes, my liege, he is," James Nayland, chief adviser to King Henry VIII, spoke in agreement. "Vincent is most devoted. He's one of your dukes."

"I know my own lords, Nayland!" Henry's voice turned with irritation. "Does Vincent have sons?"

"Only daughters. Two."

Henry scowled at Nayland as though it were the other man's fault and then frowned at nothing in particular, his gaze on some distant spot. He was silent for just moments, however, his powerful mind moving in consideration.

"Tell me of Bracken, Nayland. Bracken of Hawkings Crest."

"Word has come to me that young Bracken has just returned from a trip to see his mother. She lives in the north country."

"He hasn't taken a wife, has he?" Henry's scowl was back in place.

"No, your grace. He's hardworking, engrossed in the running of his keep. I do not believe that such a thing has crossed his mind."

"A viscount, is he?" Henry's mind moved swiftly again, and

Nayland knew better than to even smile over Henry's earlier comment that he knew his own lords.

"No, my lord," he said stoically. "He's an earl."

"Vincent's daughter..." Henry speared his aide with another glance. "Marigold has been to court, but what of the other? Is she older or younger?"

"Younger. Megan must be 17 by now."

"Vincent would lay down his life for me," Henry said without boast. "I'm sure of this."

"As would Bracken, I believe," Nayland inserted gently.

"Yes," the king agreed. "He has proven himself loyal, but as you said, he is young. I think a union is in order."

Nayland smiled. If Henry felt it would be advantageous to the throne, he would marry an infant to a man gray with age.

"Send word, first to Vincent and then to Bracken," Henry commanded. "The choice of the bride is to be Vincent's, but we won't rush things. I want Bracken content as well. Tell both Vincent and the young earl they have a year. No, make it six months."

"As you wish," Nayland spoke humbly while making notes.

They did not discuss the marriage or Vincent of Stone Lake again. But Bracken of Hawkings Crest was the subject for long minutes to follow.

"WHO WAS THAT, Vincent?"

The lord of Stone Lake Castle turned slowly to see his wife enter the room but did not immediately answer her. Studying her a moment, he thought her beauty timeless; she was as lovely today as she'd been as a bride. But he also knew that her beauty sank no deeper than her skin. His eyes narrowed when he thought of the storm the king's news would induce.

"Vincent!" Annora's voice was no longer softly curious but harsh with irritation. "Is something the matter? Who was that man?"

"A messenger from Henry," Vincent told her.

Annora's eyes widened. "Is the news bad?"

"I fear you will think so."

Annora's eyes narrowed with anger. She had not bothered with a wimple, so she now swung her head, causing her mane of thick, blonde hair to fall from one shoulder.

"What nonsense do you speak?"

"Only that Henry wishes our family to unite with that of Hawkings Crest. He has ordered that our neighbor should marry one of our daughters."

Annora was well and truly horrified. "Surely not Marigold?"

Vincent shrugged. "She is the eldest."

"I don't care!" Annora's voice was turning shrill. "I will never allow her to settle for an earl. We'll keep Marigold hidden. If he never sees her, he can't choose—"

"I am to choose," Vincent cut in.

"Well, it's settled then," Annora said with a laugh that turned from relief to cruelty. "You'll have to send for Megan."

Vincent took a breath. "I will speak to Marigold first."

This time Annora laughed in true amusement. "She'll never agree. I'll fetch her myself, and you can ask her."

"You mean she's here?" Vincent's brow lowered. "I thought she'd gone to London."

"No, she's not leaving until tomorrow. I'll go now and send her to you."

"No."

Annora halted in her walk from the great hall and turned slowly back to her spouse. Vincent had to keep from flinching over the hatred he saw in her eyes, but his mind was resolute. He knew that all chance of convincing Marigold to marry would be lost if her mother spoke to her first.

"You will remain here, and we will speak to her together."

Annora took a seat, but Vincent could see that she was furious. He knew she might not speak to him for days or possibly weeks, but he was determined to have his own way this time.

Minutes later a servant was sent to fetch the elder of Vincent's daughters. Her parents settled down to wait in frigid silence.

Marigold never hurried unless it pleased her to do so, and Vincent hated to be kept waiting. Having taken lessons from her mother for the past 19 years, Marigold was an expert at irritating her father. More than 20 minutes passed before she made an appearance, but Vincent was still calm—in truth, he was filled with an amused anticipation. He knew his daughter to be deceitful above all women, and for the first time he rather looked forward to the creative excuse she was sure to give for not coming on time.

Sure enough, Marigold's look when she entered the great

hall was one of regret. Her eyes were wide with remorse, her lovely face apologetic, sweet even.

"I was told just this moment that you wanted me," she said softly. Her humbleness was so real that Vincent could only shake his head. To those who did not really know Marigold, she seemed so sweet. Vincent did know her, however, and wasted no time informing her of the situation.

"King Henry has ordered that our household be joined to that of Hawkings Crest," he spoke without preamble. "You will be married to Bracken."

All humility fell away. Marigold's face became a mask of hatred and disgust, turning her normally lovely features into a repulsive sneer.

"Never," she nearly hissed. "I am *not* ready to wed, and when I am, I will *never* settle for an earl."

Her words so echoed those of her mother that Vincent mentally gave up. However, Marigold was not through.

"You may wish to play lackey to the king, but not I. I'd rather die than be married to that oaf at Hawkings Crest, and if you don't have the spine to tell Henry, then I will!"

"It's just as I told you, Vincent," Annora cut in, her voice so like Marigold's. "You'll have to send for Megan."

"Yes!" Marigold caught onto the idea. "Send for Meg. She'll do anything for you, even sacrifice herself for the king."

Marigold suddenly turned to her mother. "I've changed my mind. I'm leaving for London today." She turned back to her father. "You must think me a fool to even suggest such an arrangement. Well, I'm not. I'm leaving now. I can't stand the thought of one more day in the same castle with you!"

Vincent stood still as both his wife and daughter, so similar in temperament and looks, swept from the room. He should have known that it was useless. Annora had done an admirable job on Marigold's mind all these years, but at least he'd tried.

Send for Meg.

The words still rang in his ears. He could see that he had little choice. At least Henry had given him six months. With a plan forming in his mind, he rang for his scribe. He would reply to his king, as well as send for Megan, but by the time she arrived he would have the situation firmly back in his control.

Sister Agatha, one of the older nuns at the Stone Lake abbey, made her way sedately down the corridor lined with small, sparsely furnished bedrooms. When she was less than halfway along, she stopped outside one wooden door and knocked softly. The door was opened immediately by a short, plump redhead whose wimple was askew and whose face and hands were dusty.

"Yes, Sister Agatha?" The voice was husky and breathless.

"The Reverend Mother wishes to see you, Megan."

"Now? I've only just returned from the village." Megan did nothing to hide the horror she felt, and the older sister had to fight a smile.

"She said 'immediately'."

Megan sighed, but not even the dirt could dim the brightness of her green eyes or hide any part of her adorable, expressive face.

"All right. I have to see to a particular need, and then I'll go."

Again Sister Agatha wanted to laugh. No one else in all the abbey would have dared refer to the need to relieve herself, but then no one else in the abbey was anything like Megan.

"I'll tell the Reverend Mother you'll be along directly."

Megan thanked her, and in her haste nearly slammed the door in the older woman's face. Agatha made her way back to her Superior's office to report on her conversation, which the Reverend Mother accepted calmly.

"I thought Megan was due back from the village just after lunch."

Agatha had taken a seat by the window and answered from there.

"I believe you are right, but Megan hasn't been on time in eight years; I can't think why she would begin now."

The Reverend Mother smiled, but only slightly. Sister Agatha was dying to ask about the message she knew had arrived, but she remained silent, praying for acceptance of whatever was to pass. Her eyes had been on the window, but they now shifted to see the Reverend Mother watching her.

"We're going to lose her," the older nun told her softly.

Sister Agatha's habit lifted with a huge sigh as she tried to deal with this news. They had all known it would happen someday. After all, Megan was the daughter of a duke, something all of them had constantly lost sight of, and it had never been her father's intention that she join the order.

"When?" Agatha now felt free to ask.

"The end of the week."

She nodded and when she spoke again, her voice wobbled only slightly. "Would you mind my not staying, Reverend Mother?"

"No, Sister Agatha. I quite understand."

Such permission was granted not a moment too soon, as Megan knocked on the door just seconds later. Sister Agatha answered it, but exited soundlessly once Megan was inside. The young redhead noticed the older sister's departure, but she was so self-conscious about her appearance that she had eyes only for the Reverend Mother, a woman whom she held in the highest esteem.

"Come and sit down, Megan."

"I'm sorry about my clothes, Reverend Mother. I didn't have time to change."

"You have just come from the village?"

Megan hesitated, knowing that her answer would evoke many more questions.

"Yes. I know I was supposed to return earlier..." Megan's rather low-pitched voice was earnest. "But one of the village women had her baby, and, Reverend Mother," Megan's voice turned dreamy, "she's the loveliest thing I've ever seen. She has so much hair, and she's so pink and soft. I just couldn't tear myself away."

Studying Megan's lovely young face, the abbess fought for control of her emotions, thinking things would never be the same after she was gone. She forced herself to remain calm.

"I was under the impression that it was your turn to go to the village and teach the children to read."

"Oh, I did that," Megan told her, her large eyes widening. "But you see, they were doing so well that I let them go early."

"But still you didn't return?"

"No, Reverend Mother. Old Mrs. Murch was working in her garden, and you know how bent her back is. I simply had to help her."

This explained the dirt, but all the Reverend Mother said was, "Then the baby was born?"

"Well, yes, but I didn't see her until after I'd talked with William. He still has it in his head to marry me. I told him how unsuitable I would be, but he won't listen."

Megan's distressed face was comical, but the word *marry* brought the Reverend Mother firmly back to the task at hand.

"It sounds as if you've had a busy day. As much as I appreciate your telling me honestly where you have been, that is not the reason I sent for you."

Megan nodded, having surmised as much.

"Your father wants you home, Meg." The older woman had used her nickname, a rare thing and one that warned her of the Reverend Mother's emotions.

"He has written to me, and you're to gather your belongings and return to Stone Lake Castle by the end of the week." The older woman, by Lord Vincent's request, omitted the news about marriage.

Megan said nothing. She rose and went to the window, her eyes far away. Not one of the nuns would have risen and turned from the Reverend Mother without permission, but Megan was not a nun. She was the daughter of a titled lord, a girl who had lived with them since the day after her ninth birthday. She was now 17, and the Reverend Mother knew that the abbey had truly become her home.

Annora, Lord Vincent's wife, had never wanted Megan. She was happy with her beautiful first daughter and never desired another child. If rumor could be believed, she had tried several purges to rid herself of her unwanted second pregnancy, but all attempts had failed.

Annora might have forgiven Megan had she been a male heir, but the fact that she was a girl, and redheaded as well, was enough to cause her to shun the child. However, much to Lady Annora's horror, Megan proved to be more than stalwart. The stouthearted little girl did everything in her power to gain her mother's attention, until it became obvious to Vincent that the two must be separated lest Megan come to physical harm at Annora's hand.

When Megan arrived at the abbey, she was insolent beyond description and so active that the nuns thought they would lose their minds. She ran away no less than twice a week and swiftly became a master at hiding and wearing disguises. The Reverend Mother thought they would never survive the first years, but much of that changed as Megan matured. Then near the time of Megan's fourteenth birthday, her heart became sensitive to spiritual matters.

On one occasion, when Father Brent was making his regular visit, Megan sought him out. The kind priest, who had come under the influence of Luther and other reformers, spoke to her about her eternal soul, and she humbly gave herself to Christ. The change from that point was remarkable.

Megan was still a hard worker and compassionate to a fault, but the peace that surrounded her was extraordinary. Her temper was still a struggle, and when it came to defending someone less fortunate than herself, no one would put it past her to take on a giant. Her conversion, however, had been very real.

She had learned to label her sins for what they were and also learned the sweet fellowship of obedience to God that comes from a wholehearted desire to walk with Him.

"Does my father say why I am needed?" Megan finally spoke from her place by the window. "I mean, he's not ill, is he?"

"No, Megan, your father is fine, but as for the reason, I will leave that explanation to him."

Megan nodded. She had a feeling this was something serious, but she could hardly expect the Reverend Mother to be the bearer of the bad news.

"Does he say how I'm to arrive home?"

The Reverend Mother smiled, her first genuine smile since Megan entered the room.

"Transportation has never been a problem for you before, Meg."

The young woman smiled in return. It was true. In her days of escape, she had hidden in hay wagons and cattle carts, dressed as a gypsy and walked with a traveling band, and even gone so far as to dress as a lad and go on horseback. Her generous curves had prevented that disguise in the last few years, but it was true, Megan always knew how to get where she was going.

The Reverend Mother told her that guardsmen from the castle would be arriving on horseback that Friday, just six days away. Megan accepted this news graciously, and when she was ready to leave the Reverend Mother walked her to the door. No words were spoken, but Megan hugged the older woman fiercely before leaving, thinking it felt as though she were already gone.

Two

LONDON WAS HOT AND NOISY as Bracken turned his horse over to a waiting groom, gave orders to a few of his knights, and made his way to the massive front door of his aunt's home. His long legs, clad in dark hose, ate up the distance with ease. He had not enjoyed the trip from his country estate, but a missive from the king, as well as one from his neighbor, forced him onward.

Bracken found his widowed aunt in an upstairs salon. With barely a word of greeting, he told her what he was about.

"I need you to return to Hawkings Crest."

"Why, Bracken," the older woman spoke in surprise. "I've only just arrived back in London."

"I realize that, Aunt Louisa, but I've just received word that I am to marry, and I need you back at the estate."

Louisa's eyes became huge on this announcement, but she remained silent, waiting for Bracken to explain. He did not disappoint her.

"The king has ordered me to take a bride from Stone Lake, from the household of Vincent Stone to be exact. I have also received word from Vincent himself telling me he has chosen his youngest daughter, Megan, and wishes her to live at Hawkings Crest for a period before we are wed. He wrote to me obviously believing that you were still living with me.

"I think his request a trifle odd, but since I can't refuse the king or my future father-in-law," Bracken's voice hardened slightly, "I feel I have little choice but to ask you to return and act as guardian."

Louisa studied her sister's oldest child in silence. Bracken was usually an amiable man. He was dark in both skin and hair coloring, and the full beard that covered the lower part of his handsome face gave him an almost sinister look. Louisa now studied his mouth and eyes. He was easily given to smiling and typically ready to laugh, but the man before her now was quite serious and clearly disturbed. For Louisa, who knew Bracken well, it wasn't hard to understand why.

Louisa had never known anyone happier in a marriage than her sister, Joyce, widowed now for six years. Louisa knew that Bracken wanted that same happiness. He was only 24 years old, and his aunt knew well that he was in no hurry to wed. In fact, she believed as much as he desired male heirs, he would stay single all the days of his life rather than live with a woman he didn't love.

"Will you come?" Bracken's voice cut into her musings.

"Certainly, Bracken, but may I ask a few questions?"

The young knight answered her with a slight inclination of his head.

"Is the girl willing?"

Bracken shook his head. "Vincent's letter did not say. He did write that she is just 17 and has been raised at the Stone Lake abbey."

A shudder ran over Louisa's frame. She could think of nothing worse. The girl would either be so austere that she would never warm up to Bracken, or, once released from the confines of the convent, so wild that she would never be faithful to her vows. However, Louisa kept all of these thoughts to herself. She decided then that she would brace up for Bracken, certain it was what her sister would want.

"Well, now," Louisa began. "She could have been much younger, so her age is an asset. And don't forget, Bracken, no matter where she was raised, she is Vincent's daughter. Without a doubt she will be graceful and a true asset to your keep."

Louisa secretly wondered if a girl raised in a convent would have a clue as to how to run a castle, but such thoughts remained unspoken as she watched Bracken visibly relax. Louisa relaxed herself, knowing she'd said the right thing.

"Have you ever met Megan?"

Bracken's eyes narrowed on a spot across the room. "I think I have. It was some years ago, and I must admit that it didn't go well. I made a fool of myself."

"What happened?"

Bracken smiled now, his first since arriving. "It was at court, before Father died. She was just a girl of course, talking with a group of other girls. I remember thinking I had never seen anyone with eyes so blue and hair so light. I gawked at her until she said something quite rude and the others laughed. I was humiliated, of course, but I haven't thought of it in years."

"So she's beautiful?"

"Yes." Bracken's smile became huge. "She is at that."

Louisa's smile matched his own. Her voice was gentle as she commented, "Beauty is not enough to build a marriage on, Bracken, but it certainly helps when a husband and wife find each other attractive."

Bracken's hand came to his bearded chin, and Louisa chuckled.

"You're asking yourself if she'll find you attractive, Bracken?"

Bracken now laughed at himself. "I am at that."

Louisa's voice became dry. "No such thought should plague you. I feel quite confident that she will think you handsome."

Bracken shook his head in true modesty before the two fell to discussing the dates. Megan was not due to arrive at Hawkings Crest for another two weeks, and the lord of the castle saw no reason for his aunt to have to make the trip sooner.

Bracken stayed on in London until the next morning, and by the time he left he felt somewhat resigned if not thrilled with the idea of marriage to Vincent's beautiful blonde daughter. He would do all that was asked of him.

Bracken did not go directly back to Hawkings Crest, but he and his men rode north on business. With Megan not arriving for two weeks, there was no need for him to hurry home.

The ride on horseback to the castle on Stone Lake was not a lengthy one, but Megan, having to fight anxiety with every mile, would have sworn that she had crossed the country. Her father had been to visit her just six weeks before, but Megan hadn't seen her home or her mother for more than two years. When she had visited that Christmas, she knew she would be returning to the abbey. This time she had no such security. This time it seemed she would be going home for good. But why?

This was the question that had plagued Megan from the moment she had left the Reverend Mother's office. Was her sister going to be wed? Was her mother ill? Had her father given her own hand away? Meg didn't think he would do this without talking to her, but she wasn't sure. Maybe her mother had decided it was time her youngest daughter marry.

"Oh, Father God," Megan prayed. "Help me to trust You and accept this reason Father has sent for me. I am troubled. Please help me to trust."

Megan's mind went to her last nights at the abbey. She had walked in her sleep each night, something she hadn't done for years. Typically Megan walked in her sleep only when some event of the day upset her.

The first night she had woken alone, shivering in the chapel with no idea how she'd come to be there. The other nights Sister Agatha had found her in the hallway and reported to her in the morning that she'd been on the move.

Megan never did anything dangerous or outrageous when she walked in her sleep, but there was always a very real fear that she would hurt herself. On one occasion she had fallen headfirst down a full length of stone steps. Another time she had wandered outside the abbey and slipped down an embankment into a deep ditch filled with water. Had the water been just inches deeper, Megan might have drowned.

After the first night, Megan had prayed for calm as sleep crowded in, but she had been up anyway. She also knew that she was prone to talk in her sleep if someone spoke. Megan had forgotten to ask Sister Agatha if she'd said anything profound or heinous; she knew she was capable of both.

Vincent paced the confines of his room for more than an hour before Megan arrived. His entire frame shook with emotion when he thought of his youngest daughter marrying against her will, but he saw no other way around the king's edict.

Vincent knew Bracken to be a fine warrior, a man of honor as well as might, and since Marigold would never agree to this match, he only hoped this trial period at Hawkings Crest would help Megan to find herself in a marriage that she at least found tolerable. Vincent had no illusions concerning love, but Megan was tenacious to a fault. Her father believed she would make the best of the situation. She always did.

"My lord?" one of Vincent's vassals said from just inside the door.

"Yes, Giles?"

"Lady Megan has arrived, sir. She awaits you in the great hall."

"Thank you, Giles," Vincent said, but did not move to the door. Once again he visualized himself telling Megan of Henry's letter, and remembered his wife's cruel pleasure in the whole event. Well, at least Annora was away for the day. Still, Vincent couldn't stop the shudder that ran over his frame as he at last moved toward the door.

Megan's eyes ran lovingly over the long tables and benches, the clean rushes on the floor, and the huge stone fireplace that graced the north wall. Megan thought about the rocky relationship she'd always shared with her mother, but she could never fault Annora Stone's ability to run her father's castle.

"Megan."

The young woman turned at the sound of her father's voice and nearly ran into his arms. It had been only weeks, but Megan was always so pleased to see him and now let herself be hugged like a child.

"How was your journey?"

"A bit long. I'd have done better on my own." Megan smiled teasingly at her father, causing him to chuckle, but then her eyes grew serious as did his.

"Are you all right?" she asked.

"Yes, but I have serious news. You are to marry."

Glad that he had told her outright, Megan took a deep breath and followed Vincent as he led the way to the fireplace. The great hall was strangely empty, and both were glad for the privacy.

"Can you tell me all?" Megan asked as soon as they were seated.

"Yes. Henry wants a union between Stone Lake and Hawkings Crest. I told Marigold that she was to marry, but you can well imagine how she responded to the idea of marrying an earl. She left just an hour after I told her, and I haven't seen her since."

"So the duty falls to me?"

Vincent nodded with regret. "Bracken has been the lord at Hawkings Crest for five years now, maybe six, and I know him to be a man of honor. He is young, but I believe he will make you a fine husband."

"So I am to marry soon."

"No. You'll be going to live at Hawkings Crest for a time—a trial period of sorts. It won't stop the marriage, but at least Bracken will not be a stranger to you on your wedding day."

Megan's eyes shifted to the fireplace. When she spoke again her voice was soft, her eyes still studying the cold hearth.

"I have never met Bracken of Hawkings Crest. I am surprised he chose me."

"Henry gave me leave to decide," Vincent admitted, not seeing a need to remind Megan that her sister would have nothing to do with the arrangement.

"And what will Bracken say when he learns he is to have me and not Marigold?" Megan asked, believing that all of England knew of Marigold's beauty.

Vincent caught his daughter's jaw and gently turned her face to him. "So many years away from your mother and yet you still believe her lies. Your beauty is deep within you, Meg, as well as on the surface. Bracken might find Marigold a beauty, but only until she showed her true self.

"Bracken may well be as dubious of the marriage as you are, but when he gets to know you he will thank me for the wife I have sent."

Megan smiled gently at her father. She loved her father and knowing that he regretted this for her somehow made the act easier. Megan believed that men spent the whole of their lives facing tasks they didn't care for; her father had done so without complaint. Megan told herself she would do no less.

"How long before I go?"

Vincent smiled in the face of her acceptance. "Two weeks. I know things might be a bit strained for you when your mother returns, but I want some time with you. I'll see you to Hawkings Crest myself."

"I assume Bracken's mother lives within the castle walls."

Vincent shook his head. "His aunt. I have not met her, but I trust the two of you will fare well."

Megan nodded, but neither one had much more to say. They

went for a ride a few hours later but did not discuss the trip or wedding.

The day turned out to be so full that Megan took herself off to bed at an early hour, still not having seen her mother.

Having talked with her father and gained awareness of the situation, she slept deeply that night. She would not have slept so soundly had she known he was to be called away early the next morning.

Three

"I HAVE SERVANTS FOR THAT, MEGAN." Annora's voice was cold, but Megan stood her ground. They were in the kitchen, and Vincent had been gone all of three days. To Megan it felt like a lifetime.

"Be that as it may, Mother, not one of them knew of this poultice for tooth pain." Megan's voice was respectful but unyielding.

"The servants take care of themselves. Do not disgrace your father's name by acting as a commoner."

Megan's eyes narrowed in anger. "The disgrace is on you, Mother, that you would allow one of your servants to writhe in agony with a sore tooth. Where is your compassion?"

"You will not speak to me in such a way!" Lady Stone nearly spat. "Your return has disrupted my entire life." Annora stopped to let this barb sink in but saw that Megan's face was calm. The older woman was so furious that for a moment she couldn't speak. When she did, it was with the full intention of wounding her daughter the only way she knew how.

"I have decided that you will leave for Hawkings Crest this day."

Megan's eyes widened, giving her mother great pleasure.

"But Father isn't here. He was to take me."

Annora's laugh was heartless. "Your father is more than capable of mounting a horse if he wishes to see you."

"But my clothing, Mother—" Megan tried to reason with her, seeing that she'd pushed too far. "My wardrobe is not complete."

Annora's lip curled with cruel enjoyment. "You seem to be more at home dressed in homespun cloth—look at you! Besides, you have one dress that will suffice, and you won't want to travel in that anyway. I'll send your clothing when it's ready."

Megan stood in mute horror, her whole body trembling with fear over the way she was being sent away. Her heart cried out to God to send her father home early, but it was not to be.

"Now ready yourself," her mother drove home her final thrust. "I will order a guard to escort you. You leave within the hour."

Annora swept away then, but it took a moment for Megan to realize the occupants of the entire room were watching her. Not one of the servants at Stone Lake loved their mistress, so Megan was met with genuine stares of compassion. The young servant girl whose tooth Megan had treated had tears in her eyes.

"I'm sorry, my lady."

Megan gently touched the dark hair on her head. "Don't fret, Merry, all will be well. You take care of that tooth, and I'll see you when I come again."

Megan left with all the dignity she could muster, hoping that no one could see how her legs trembled in shock and terror.

True to her word, her mother sent for her an hour later. Four horses stood in the courtyard of Stone Lake, and Megan fought down every emotion within her to keep her face calm. Hawkings Crest was miles away, and her mother was sending her on horseback with no caravan, which meant no maid, no ladies in waiting, and no entourage of any kind. Just four horses, and three male guards—none of whom she even knew.

One of them helped her mount. Megan kept her face impassive, not wishing to give her mother the satisfaction of knowing how fearful she was of going away to a strange man's castle. She thought of trying to reason with Annora once more, but just a glance allowed her to see the hatred in her eyes, and Megan knew she would be wasting her time.

Megan glanced at the men assigned to accompany her. She did not recognize any of them, but they caused her no fear. Her father would kill them if she came to harm in their hands. Megan thought how sad it was that they had more of a care for her than her mother did. Once on horseback, Megan spoke to her mother.

"Please tell Father that I said goodbye and that I look forward to seeing him when he visits."

Megan gained a small measure of satisfaction in seeing the flicker of uncertainty in her mother's look, but it didn't last. The older woman's chin came up before she bade her daughter goodbye in a cold tone.

Megan, whose throat was suddenly very tight, said nothing. She turned her mount and heeled her forward, tears clogging her throat as she rode.

The sun was dropping low in the sky when one of the men said they would make camp soon. Megan questioned how far they had to go and was told they would arrive at Hawkings Crest before noon the following day.

They came into a copse of trees that would be their shelter for the night. As glad as Megan was to stop, she ached all over as she forced her body to slide from the horse's back.

Not for the first time, Megan was impressed with her escort. There had been little conversation as they traveled, but their care of her could not be criticized. Now they made camp with amazing ease. Just an hour later, Megan was sitting comfortably on a log, eating rabbit that had been cooked over a spit. Within minutes she was feeling greatly refreshed, but when the man in charge, Hubert by name, recommended sleep, Megan was more than happy to comply.

Megan found herself near the fire, the men nearby to protect her, but as she lay down she wondered what her father would say of her situation. She knew that he had planned to leave Stone Lake early in the day with a full band of men and provisions, and have her to Hawkings Crest before nightfall. Megan also realized he would be furious if he could see her now. She debated the wisdom of giving him too many details. Praying that she wouldn't walk in her sleep this night, she drifted off, her blanket literally covering her from head to foot.

The attack on their camp came sometime after midnight. One second Megan was sleeping in her blanket, the next she was being rolled under some nearby bushes where she sat up and looked out in horror at the unfolding scene.

Men, seemingly dozens of them, were in vicious attack against her guard. Megan kept her hand pressed tightly to her mouth to keep from crying out as she watched one, then two, and finally all three of her guards fall dead to the ground. Some of the attackers were dead as well, but at least six men were still standing.

Megan continued to watch as one of them broke open her small trunk and howled in frustration. She watched her belongings fly everywhere.

"*Clothing!* I thought they had gold."

"Let me see," said another.

"Fool!" Raged yet a third, obviously in charge. "We lost men tonight over a trunk full of homespun rags."

Megan watched the first man lift the trunk and throw it toward her. She closed her eyes in anticipation of the blow, but the trunk landed beyond the bush.

"What now?" one asked.

"We move on," the third man said. "There's nothing here but some good horse flesh. Let's ride."

There was a flurry of movement as the men departed, taking all four of her father's horses with them.

When the battle had commenced, Megan thought it was going to last forever. Now that it was over, she wondered if only seconds had passed. She was trembling from head to foot, but the night was long spent before she could bring herself to crawl from the bushes to check on the men.

"Oh, Father God," Megan cried pitifully as she knelt beside Hubert and then the others. She asked God to give her strength and wisdom, but she didn't know when anything had so horrified her. They had died protecting her. The thought so overwhelmed her that after just a few minutes she crawled back into the bushes and rewrapped herself in the blanket, still shivering so violently that she had to clamp her jaw shut to keep her teeth from chattering.

Megan didn't know when she slept, but when slumber claimed her at last she dreamed that her mother was forced to bury these men and explain to their families why they were gone.

Megan heard the voices, but thinking she was still dreaming did not move. Not until a hand grasped her ankle, which protruded from the bush, did she let out a muffled scream and scramble further into the shrubs, twigs, and leaves scratching her face and hands.

"Well, one of 'ems alive, no mistake."

"A man?"

"Don't rightly think it is."

Megan heard more movement. The bushes parted, and a large, bearded face regarded her from without. It was fully light, but Megan held herself stiffly inside the foliage, hoping somehow they wouldn't see her and would leave.

"You can come out, miss. Not a one of us will harm you."

Megan licked her lips, undecided. It was hard to see past the branches and leaves, but she thought she detected a gleam of compassion in the man's eyes. He backed away a moment later, and Megan came slowly out the side, figuring it would put her in a position to run if there were danger.

"Coo," one of the men breathed as soon as she emerged. "Would you look at that 'air."

Megan's eyes searched their faces and immediately recognized them as a group of peddlers. She also saw that there was not a female among them. The men were all staring at her as if they'd never seen a woman before. Even through the dirt on her dress and brambles in her hair, the fact that she was a lady came shouting through.

"Are you hurt?" the bearded man asked, his soft voice seeming loud in the hushed circle.

Megan shook her head with unconscious elegance. She spoke then, and any doubts they might have had concerning her lineage dissolved with the cultured sound of her voice.

"We were attacked. My men fought hard, but they died protecting me." Megan's voice caught. Tears came to her eyes but did not fall.

"We've some bread and cheese here, miss. Would you care to eat?" This came from the bearded man, and although Megan was thankful for his kindness, she couldn't eat a bite.

"Can you tell us where you was headed?" asked a man so taken with the russet red of her hair that he wanted to touch it. Yet his voice and manners were respectful.

"Hawkings Crest," Megan told them. "I don't know how close I am, so I'm not sure if I should try to go home or head on."

"Home?" Again, the bearded man spoke.

"Stone Lake."

He nodded, smiling slightly. "It's a piece back to Stone Lake, and we're going directly to the Crest if you'd care to ride."

Megan was so relieved she could have wept. The men might have been surprised to know she had ridden in many a peddler's cart, but never before had she felt that one had been sent by God.

An hour later they were well down the road, Megan atop the cart sitting comfortably on a pile of rugs. They had pressed food upon her and she had finally eaten, but now the night was catching up with her. Megan couldn't stop the tears that poured down her cheeks. They were partly from exhaustion and partly from the loss of her father's brave men. Within another hundred yards, she was asleep.

Four

Hawkings Crest

"Now get back to work!"

The young woman who had been shouted at did as she was told, but not before she flipped her hair over her shoulder in contempt and glared at her uncle. The older man stood watching her a moment, his head moving in disgust.

"Pen giving you trouble again, Eddie?"

Eddie nearly growled. "My sister has never been able to control her. Has it in her head to work up in the kitchen, she does." His voice was filled with offense. "She's even working on her voice, trying to talk like a lady, no less. I tell you, Mic, that girl's in for trouble if she don't start to recognize 'er betters."

Mic clapped him on the shoulder. "You'll handle her, Eddie." The younger man started to walk away but stopped. "The peddlers are in."

"So I see. At least it's old Elias," Eddie observed, referring to the man with the dark beard. "He's fair."

Mic moved in the direction of the wagon, but Eddie went back toward the creamery. With Pen acting up, he was behind schedule. He decided to brook no more of her high-minded airs or her talk of the kitchens. With a disgruntled frown, he moved inside.

❦ ❦ ❦

"Thank you, Elias," Megan told him sincerely. She had awakened a half mile outside the walls of the keep and walked in behind the peddler's cart with the men, but now she took the time to thank her rescuers before moving toward the castle. Megan had found them all kind to a fault, and since she didn't know what kind of reception she would receive from the inhabitants at Hawkings Crest, it was a little hard to leave them.

But as usual Megan was made of stern stuff, and with a smile that encompassed them all, she moved rather stiffly toward the main entrance. It was a waste of time. The guards questioned her without listening to her answer, and Megan, knowing she looked even worse than when the peddlers found her, was not in the mood to argue her way inside.

She moved around the keep for a good 20 minutes, impressed with its cleanliness and order before spotting what appeared to be an entrance to the kitchens. A man, looking less austere than the front entrance guards, stood close by. Megan gathered her courage to approach.

"Will you please take me to Lord Bracken?" Megan asked calmly, but felt a fool at the man's look.

"Be away, woman. Return to your work."

He gave Megan the cold shoulder, and in disgust she stomped off around the corner of the building. She hadn't gone ten steps when she collided into something huge, or was it some*one*?

Megan's eyes slowly rose, and she looked up into the face of the largest man she had ever seen. She stumbled back in fear against a stone wall, her mouth opening and closing in panic.

"Lord, B-B-Bracken?" She managed to stutter, but the giant only stared at her, an unreadable expression on his craggy face.

Megan inched her way along, the giant turning with her, his eyes spearing her. When she had a clear shot, she ran. She never looked back to see if she was being followed, but ran behind the creamery and stood asking herself what to do next.

Megan stayed still for a long time, gaining her breath. It was tempting at this moment to join the peddlers. She was willing to do almost anything to escape this foreign keep and the antagonistic stares of its inhabitants, but she wasn't welcome at Stone Lake, so where would she go?

Megan decided to circle the building, thinking to inquire of Bracken with someone inside. Before she could open the door, a person came charging out. He was a good-sized man with a harried look, one that didn't improve upon spotting Megan.

"Why aren't you inside?"

Megan blinked but managed to say, "I need you to take me to Lord Bracken."

"Oh, heaven help me!" the man burst out, startling Megan into speechlessness. "Why must *I* be saddled with uppity female servants?"

Before Megan could draw a breath, she was grasped firmly by the forearm and taken inside.

"You must be new, so I'll give you some time to familiarize yourself. Have you worked the creamery before?"

Rage boiled up inside of Megan, who thought she would not be able to stand one more second of this. She was tempted to stomp on the man's foot and *then* inform him that she had designed the creamery at the Stone Lake abbey. All she said, however, was yes, she had. Megan figured if she worked for a time, she might better determine a way to get inside the castle. So just minutes later, Megan found herself working over a churn. She worked silently and efficiently, not speaking or looking at anyone, but feeling eyes on her. She also listened. If the gossip around her could be believed, the lord of the castle was not even there.

Megan could have howled with frustration, but refraining, simply worked silently until she thought her arms would give way. It was a tremendous relief to have the man who had grabbed her, the one the other women called Eddie, dismiss them for the day. Megan breathed deeply of the fresh air once she was outside.

She noticed the servants queuing up behind a cauldron of food and suddenly realized she was starving. Without a shred of pride left, Megan joined them. Heads turned to stare at her, but she ignored them. At the moment she would have given up her dowry for a bath, but food in her stomach was the next best thing.

The line moved steadily along, but Megan seemed to be the last, for no one stood behind her. She glanced up at one point to find the giant some ten feet away. He appeared to be staring right at Megan, and for a moment she could not look away from his steady gaze. Just then, the man in front of her sneezed loudly, and Megan dropped her eyes.

That the big man was of some importance was obvious, but he terrified Megan. She heard someone call "Arik" and looked up to see the huge man turn. He towered over the person who spoke to him, as he did everyone. Megan dropped her eyes just before the other man left and the giant turned his attention to her once again. It never occurred to her to ask him for help; he was too intimidating for that.

At last it was Megan's turn to eat. She took one of the few remaining bowls, which were carved roughly from wood and a bit greasy, and held it out to the man behind the cauldron. Megan ignored his odd look, so she didn't see the exchange with the giant behind her. Her bowl was suddenly filled to the top, and where the bread pan had been empty, it now held a full loaf. The man broke a huge chunk off for Megan, who thanked him humbly.

She then moved to a place against the wall and sank down to eat. There were no utensils, so Megan soaked her bread with broth for the first time. She ate like a man starved. Her bowl was over half empty and some of the shakes had left her body when she once again looked and found the giant's eyes on her.

Megan's face flamed with the way she'd been eating, and she set her bowl aside. To her surprise, the giant averted his gaze.

Megan's eyes dropped to her bowl, but when she looked up he was still looking away. Still hungry, she reached for the food again, and this time she finished every bite. The giant was still there, but he was not staring directly at her.

The sun was falling fast by the time Megan was through, and since it was midsummer, she watched many of the castle's inhabitants make their beds along the castle walls. Megan didn't care for the idea of sleeping on the ground without a blanket, so she rose slowly and surreptitiously made her way in the gathering dusk across the inner courtyard to the blacksmith's. The building was empty.

Wishing she could see a little better, Megan entered on nearly silent feet and soon found what appeared to be an empty stall. The hay smelled fresh, and she gingerly stretched out on her side. She was asleep inside of five minutes, and even when the giant of the castle, holding a lantern and ducking his head to enter, came to check on her, she didn't stir. She also didn't stir when he settled down for the night against the wall just outside the door.

By Megan's fifth day at Hawkings Crest, her life had developed something of a pattern. Every night she slept in the smithy's shop and ate with the other servants, but she was no closer to getting inside the castle than she had been the first day. Each day she worked in the creamery, but was never chosen to deliver the butter, cheese, or cream to the kitchens within.

Not that it would have done much good. It seemed that Bracken was still away. Megan struggled with her anger nearly every day over the way her mother had dismissed her. Her intended had obviously been expecting her on a certain day, a day her father surely must have known about. Megan's head told her that her mother, too, had known this all along, but her heart refused to believe it.

The work was just beginning. Eddie came out of the creamery then and found Megan just staring up at the castle. On the first day and even the second, Eddie would have ordered her back to work, but no longer. No servant had missed the way Arik kept his eye on this woman. The lack of comb for her hair and the simple homespun cloth of her dress made it clear that she was just a servant, but there was certainly no harm in this knight losing his heart to a servant girl.

In truth, they were all rather pleased for their castle giant, whose odd ways had caused many of them to wonder at times if he was even human. Arik seemed unaffected by the cold and heat, and few had ever seen him eat. He spoke so few words to anyone that the castle folk were not entirely sure what he saw in this red-haired maid, but they were happy for him nonetheless.

Megan finished her inspection of the castle and would have turned to go back to the creamery, but a shout came up from the wall. Although she was in no danger, she stepped back as the gates were opened and a large group of riders came inside. There was quite a stir, and it didn't take long, with the way the castle folk responded, to see that Bracken was among them. He stood out in coloring, height, and breadth, and Megan studied the proud tilt of his head from a distance.

Megan suddenly drew a deep breath. There was now a very real reason to gain entrance to the castle, but how would she do it? With a bit more thought, the inner bailey still in upheaval, Megan returned to the interior of the creamery. The day was early yet; she would find a way.

Bracken scanned the inner courtyard of Hawkings Crest with pleasure. It was good to be home. He spotted Arik at a distance, but something in the man's stance told him not to approach. He would like to have questioned him as to the keep's operations in his absence, but Arik could be mule stubborn.

Bracken could see, even from across the courtyard, that he didn't care to converse, and he knew from experience that nothing would provoke him to do so against his will. With a shrug, Bracken moved to the castle. In the meantime, he would question Barton, his steward, and deal with Arik later.

Bracken gained the great hall. As always his heart swelled with fulfillment. This had been his childhood home. His parents had run the castle well, and now that it was his, he took great pride in the way he had continued to work at its beauty and efficiency.

Many elaborate tapestries hung from the walls, and Hawkings Crest shields graced the stones over both of the massive fireplaces. The trestle tables and benches were of the finest wood, and Bracken knew that his staff could have a feast on those tables with an hour's notice.

Many knights and servants alike spoke to Bracken, nodding their heads in respect as he made for the wide, main staircase. By the time Bracken entered his bedchamber, a hot bath waited before a freshly laid fire in the hearth. Steam rose from the copper tub, and Bracken spoke to his vassal, Kent, as he undressed.

"Have you been on the field much?"

"Yes, sir," the ten-year-old replied proudly. "Every afternoon you were gone."

Bracken smiled. "Your father will be proud to hear it. I saw your parents while I was in London, and they asked after you."

Kent was bent over, scrubbing Bracken's back with a hard-bristled brush, and did not immediately answer.

"How is my mother?" he said with a slight pant.

"She is well. I would say the baby is due soon."

Kent nodded, his small face serious. "She promised to send word when the time came."

"Would you rather be with her? I'm sure I could arrange it."

The boy thought. He didn't know any man, not even his father, whom he admired more than Bracken. Bracken was huge and black as a bear, but when Kent had overcome his initial fear of Bracken's size, he had found a man with a heart of gold. He then realized his great fortune in his father's sending him to Hawkings Crest to serve as vassal. He cared more deeply about his mother than he could express in words, but even though he had only been there a few months, he couldn't stand the thought of leaving Hawkings Crest and its lord.

"I'll stay here."

"Very well."

The subject was dropped then, but Bracken made a mental note to keep Kent just busy enough to leave him no time to think. Kent was one of many young vassals Bracken had had in the years he had been lord, and as with many of the other boys, he'd come to care deeply for him. He was certain that as soon as the infant was born, all would be well.

Back in the creamery the first churns were ready to be delivered, and for the first time all week, Megan stepped forward and spoke.

"I'll take this for you," she said softly, gesturing to the churn she had been working.

Eddie had not heard her speak since the first day and had forgotten the husky quality of her voice. The quiet authority he heard gave him pause, but he was still going to refuse her. Megan, however, had other ideas. She lifted the churn and held his eyes with her own.

"Thank you, Eddie," she said softly, and before he could utter a word, she moved out the door.

Eddie glanced around, but no one else had heard the exchange, so he lost no face. He went after her then, but only to watch. He was not at all surprised to see Arik following her at some distance.

Bracken, bathed and now well-breakfasted, sat surrounded by his men in what was known as the war room of the castle. They had ridden for days, accomplishing a small job for King Henry without thought of personal comforts, and now that all were clean and well fed, they spoke of all they had seen. Arik was not among them. Bracken had sent for him, but he had not as yet made an appearance.

Hunting trophies of every size and type, as well as archaic weapons of war, lined this large room. It was a place where Bracken felt most comfortable. The men had been talking for the better part of 20 minutes when Megan opened the door, left it open, and took several steps inside the huge room.

Bracken did not recognize this servant and sighed gently. All too often new female servants sought him out, out of sheer curiosity. He was large and dark, and the sooner they saw him, the sooner they could put their minds to rest that he was not half bear as so many claimed.

"We do not need anything at this time," he said kindly to this scruffy-looking maid. "We'll send someone if we do."

"I need to speak with you, Lord Bracken."

Bracken's brow lowered. It was to be one of these; a servant girl who worked on her voice and mannerisms and who had visions of attracting the attention of the lord of the keep.

"Please leave us." Bracken's voice was hard this time, enough to put anyone off. To his amazement, this impertinent chit moved further into the room. Each one of his men had turned now, and Bracken felt anger kindle within him.

"I'm sorry to disturb you, Lord Bracken," Megan began, her voice humble and soft, her stance respectful. "I have wanted to see you for several days. I am Megan of Stone Lake. My father is Vincent. I did not know that you would be away, and I was uncertain what to do, so I stayed on here in your keep.

"While coming to you, my father's men were attacked some miles back. They were killed while protecting me. I came here with a group of peddlers, but I fear that no one was expecting me. I would seek your counsel, my lord, as to what to do next. I will stay on here if that is what you wish. If not, then may it please my lord to provide an escort for me to return to my father's castle."

Bracken sat in stunned silence for a full minute. His men, including Arik, who had suddenly appeared in the doorway behind this girl, had been watching the maid in their midst. Now they turned their gaze to their lord and waited his reaction. It wasn't long in coming.

He stood, his face a stony mask, and pointed a finger at Megan.

"Remove this creature from my presence." Bracken's voice was coldly furious, telling of his insult that she would attempt such duplicity. Bracken refused to believe that this scullery maid could be his future bride.

Unfortunately for Bracken, Megan's anger matched his own. All humility fell away like a cloak, and her eyes shot daggers at the men approaching.

"Do *not* touch me," she commanded with enough authority to stop the men in their tracks. Her eyes raked them before turning like hot coals onto Bracken.

"I am treated like a servant in your keep for five days, and if that isn't bad enough you now treat me like a dog! There is no need for your men to see me out; I shall leave on my own." Megan paused then, but even in her present filthy state she was magnificent. "*You*, Lord Bracken, can explain to King Henry why we will not be wed."

With that Megan swept from a room that was so silent Bracken could hear his men breathing. He had judged her a fake, but now he doubted his own eyes and ears. He glanced up to see Arik still in attendance.

"Has she been here for five days?"

Arik's head barely dipped one time in affirmation.

Bracken drew breath between clenched teeth. "I will check this story myself. We ride in five minutes."

NO ONE AT HAWKINGS CREST could have missed Bracken's departure with his men, but Megan gave it little heed. Not knowing how she would get there, or even if she would be welcome, Megan was going home. For the moment that was all she could think of.

Deep in thought, Megan was standing near the smithery, her mind preoccupied, when she suddenly spotted Arik coming from the castle. Megan started. She had assumed he'd gone with Bracken. She darted around the side of the building, knowing somehow that he must not see her. The area inside the walls of Hawkings Crest was like a small village or Megan would never have gotten away with what she did next.

At the rear of the smithery an old cloak of substantial size had been discarded, and Megan bent to pick it up. Her own stench had been most offensive to her senses for days now, but the oversized cloak made her dress smell like a blossom.

Nevertheless, she was determined. Having to choke down a small gag, she placed the cloak around her, covering her head and letting the garment dangle on the ground. She then moved like an old woman from around the side of the building, walking an irregular path toward the main gate. She had been praying all the while and now sent up a word of thanks when the gate opened for a small group of merchants that included a shoemaker and several women. Megan didn't know what the women did, but she hung behind them and as the door opened, adopted a gait that looked almost painful, and moved forward.

Arik had been standing stock still for many minutes and still hadn't spotted Bracken's lady. He knew well that Bracken didn't see her as his own, but she was. He had known from the moment he laid eyes on her. Now she had managed to disappear. Arik had learned over the years that one found something much faster by thoughtful looking rather than mad dashing-about. On this occasion, however, it was getting him nowhere.

He was turning for the smithery and the creamery when he saw the gate open. No one stood out, in fact he'd have sworn Bracken's lady was not among those leaving, but she had said she was going and something compelled him to follow this assorted group. He reasoned that if she was in the keep, he would lose nothing. If she was a part of this band, she was heading out into unprotected territory where no lady belonged.

With tremendous ground-covering strides, Arik started after the group. It wasn't long before he had to shorten his steps in an effort not to overtake them. A woman in an ancient cloak stood out to him, but he made sure to watch each one. With an occasional glance to the rear, Arik walked on. If Megan was in this group, he would not let her from his sight.

Bracken found that animals had already been at the dead bodies of Vincent's men. He eyed the scene with a combination of remorse and anger. He was sorry for such a brutal loss of life, but his anger stemmed from the fact that Vincent had sent only three men to escort his daughter to Hawkings Crest. From the letter, Bracken had been expecting a most cherished young woman, but this act on Vincent's part would speak otherwise.

At least he knew she had been telling the truth about the attack. Bracken began to wonder whom he'd seen at court so many years ago. Surely the blonde was not now a redhead. Bracken shook his head. Not even with the dirt removed would Megan match the beauty of the other girl. His own eyes told him that.

Bracken suddenly ground his teeth. A redhead! Since talking to his aunt he had been picturing a beautiful blonde, but the woman who had stood before him was most definitely a redhead. Bracken was not pleased. He had not liked red hair since a young vassal had come to Hawkings Crest many years earlier to serve under his father. The boy had had a shock of red hair, almost orange in color, and by the time he'd returned to his family, Bracken was more than relieved to see him go.

Bracken realized that Megan's hair was not orange, but he had never found redheaded women attractive. And why had she been dressed like a beggar and working in his keep like a serf? Bracken's frown was so fierce that one of his men, approaching with Megan's trunk, hesitated in his stride.

"What is it?" Bracken asked calmly, having accurately read the other man's thoughts and quickly schooled his features.

"A small trunk. It's almost empty, but the trunk itself is not damaged."

Bracken lifted the lid and pulled out a garment. It appeared to be much like the one Megan had been wearing when she had come to the war room. Bracken suddenly understood. These were clothes from the abbey. One more dig into the trunk and Bracken found another dress. This was cut from fine cloth, but it was not overly fancy. Again Bracken frowned. He would have thought Vincent could have done better for the girl. Maybe he expected Bracken to dress her. The thought did not please him. Bracken was not a miserly man, but he did not know this girl and seriously doubted at the moment if she truly was Vincent's daughter. That being the case, there would be no wedding, at least not before he had some answers.

Bracken shook his head to dispel his tempestuous thoughts. Right now he needed to return to Hawkings Crest. Men needed to be sent to bury these guards, as well as the dead thieves, and someone must be sent to London for Aunt Louisa. Megan may not be who she claimed to be, but if she *was* the daughter of a duke, things were looking bad, very bad indeed.

From his place behind the travelers, Arik watched the "old woman" drop farther and farther back. She still hobbled along, but when the last of the group turned at a small bend in the road, she suddenly darted into the trees. Arik came to a swift halt before taking his own place in the foliage.

He stood patiently and was not disappointed. That red head poked out after just a few minutes, and with a glance in all directions, Bracken's lady started back down the path, this time with the cloak thrown over her arm, her back straight and feet swift.

Arik moved out to follow her, but it was many yards before she noticed him. She came to such a sudden halt when she did that she nearly fell over.

Megan's heart plummeted at the sight of the giant man, but she was determined to go home and *no one*, not even this Goliath, was going to stop her.

"There is no need to follow me," she spoke from a distance, her voice uncompromising. "I don't know why you pursue me, but I wish to be left alone."

Megan, used to having her orders followed, turned on her heel and walked away. It didn't take long before she realized she had not been heeded. This time she decided to ignore him. It was only minutes after she'd made this resolve that she heard the riders.

There was no place to hide on this section of road, or Megan would have made herself scarce. She was quite sure it would be Bracken and his men, but she continued on her course, refusing to even glance at the horses when they came into view.

She would have learned something of Bracken's men had she looked. The men did not take her presence as calmly as she took theirs. They stared in horror at how far out on the road this young noblewoman had come without an escort. That she did not desire Arik's protection was obvious, and this concerned them as well.

Megan glanced back to see that the men had come abreast of the giant and were speaking to him. Seeing the giant idle, she picked up her pace but still heard Lord Bracken's words.

"Bring her."

Megan waited only a moment before she began to run. Even with the sound of her own feet pounding in her ears and the horses' hooves receding behind her, it became obvious to her that she was not being pursued by a rider, only an enormous man. He caught her in ten yards.

Arik took care not to harm her, but with the ease of snaring a hare he captured her wrist and turned her back to Hawkings Crest.

"Let me go," Megan ordered and found herself ignored. "My father will have your head for this, do you hear me?"

Arik continued to walk.

Megan tried digging her heels in, but it was of no use. Arik only walked on, and Megan was forced to follow or be dragged. She did follow but began to work on the hand holding her wrist. She tried prying his fingers up and, when she couldn't manage that, tried biting him. Nothing worked.

"You're hurting me," Megan said, changing tactics. It didn't work. Arik walked on. Megan was feeling positively violent just then, but thought better of kicking the man or lashing out with her small fists. She opened her mouth to offer the threat of violence, but Arik came to an abrupt halt. Thinking she had gone too far, Megan's heart slammed against her ribs as he turned and looked at her, but a glance behind him showed that they were already back at the castle.

Megan's heart calmed when she understood his intent. He was giving her the option of walking into the inner courtyard on her own. Something in her face must have indicated her willingness, because Arik dropped her wrist and stood back for her to precede him. Megan did just that, Arik falling into a respectful pace behind.

It never occurred to Megan to enter the castle through anything but the main door, but the guards had other ideas. She was stopped like a common serf, humiliation covering her until Arik evidently signaled from his lofty position. Megan wasn't sure what he did, and she was too upset to look, but the eyes watching her changed from aversion to speculation and the way was made clear.

Once inside the great hall, Megan held her head high with an effort. The room seemed to be teeming with people, and in the midst of them was Bracken, his size and look as ferocious as a great beast.

Why, Megan asked herself, *did I not notice how dark and menacing he is?*

"Come here," Bracken ordered before Megan could form an answer. Megan, as much as she wanted to run, felt her feet propel her forward.

Megan of Stone Lake was afraid of no one. At least this had been true up to now, but this man caused her to tremble with dread. She wanted to run home, throw herself into her father's arms, and cry her heart out, something she hadn't wanted to do in years.

Fortunately for Megan, none of her thoughts showed on her face. She stood before her betrothed, back straight and head high, and told Bracken in that instant that she was no commoner. However, this revelation did not soften Bracken's heart. There were too many unanswered questions for him to be at ease.

"I wish to have some answers from you." Bracken turned

away then and spoke over his shoulder. "Come here and sit down."

"No."

The word was not spoken loudly or with much force, but it stopped the young lord in his tracks. Megan's trembling increased when he turned slowly and pierced her with his eyes, but she kept her head high when she spoke.

"I have not eaten since last evening, and I wish to bathe."

"And I wish to question you." Bracken's voice told Megan that this was the end of the argument.

"Is this the hospitality I am to expect from Hawkings Crest? You give no thought to my well-being in your desire for an inquisition."

Megan had unwittingly hit the mark. Hawkings Crest was known for its hospitality, something in which Bracken took great pride. Megan couldn't have chosen more appropriate words.

"Lyndon," Bracken spoke without ever taking his eyes from the scruffy woman in his midst.

"Yes, my lord?"

"Bring one of the women to assist Lady Megan to a bedchamber and see to her needs.

"You have one hour," Bracken said, turning to Megan, "to be back down here for my *inquisition.*"

Bracken said the last word threateningly and a shiver raced up Megan's spine. She positively hated to be ordered about in this fashion, but when a woman old enough to be her mother appeared at her side, she left with only a glare in the earl's direction.

Nearly one hour later Megan finally rose from her bath. Helga, the servant assigned to her, was there with a piece of toweling, and she had finally stopped goggling. Megan was compassionate. She could almost hear the woman's thoughts.

This is the servant who works in the creamery! The one who came this morning bearing a churn!

Sometime during Megan's meal or bath, Helga must have realized that a mistake had been made. She had addressed Megan as "my lady" at least 15 times.

"I'm sorry, my lady," Helga spoke now. "I have no clothing for you."

"'Tis all right, Helga. Just fetch me the furs from the bed and then you can do my hair."

"Yes, my lady." The servant was swift to obey, and in just minutes Megan sat wrapped from neck to ankle as Helga stood behind her to brush out the mass of red curls.

The action caused Megan to relax completely. She had always been a survivor, but the last week had been more than even she was accustomed to. The fight with her mother still weighed heavily on her mind, and a quick counting of the days told her that it still wasn't time for her to have left Stone Lake, which meant that her father was probably still away.

Megan let out a deep sigh; she was growing very sleepy. Her stomach was full for the first time in days, and she was finally clean and warm. Her head began to nod. She noticed that Helga had stopped brushing, but she couldn't find the words to tell her to continue. A moment later something soft was laid next to her cheek and Megan stopped trying to think so her body could sleep.

"DID YOU NOT HEAR MY WORDS?"

Megan woke to the sound of an angry male voice, but she had no idea where she was.

"I told you to be in the great room in one hour. Is there something wrong with your ears?"

Megan's senses returned to her in a rush, and she looked up to find Bracken towering over her in a conspicuous rage.

"There is nothing wrong with my ears," Megan told him coldly when he continued to glare.

"Then why aren't you downstairs?"

"I have nothing to wear."

"I don't care—" Bracken began, thinking that women could be very tiresome over their wardrobes, but Megan cut him off.

"Yes, I can see that you don't care." She stood now, the furs still wrapped around her, feeling angry as well. "I have known a week of humiliation in your keep, and now you ask me to parade myself in your great hall without a stitch of clothing on. Well, I won't!"

They were toe-to-toe now, but hardly nose to nose. Bracken eventually noticed what she was wearing, and for the first time his normal good humor was restored to him. Here she was, wrapped in furs, hair all around her face, the top of her head stopping somewhere around the middle of his chest, and *she* was giving the orders. Bracken's eyes lit with amusement, and Megan's narrowed with indignation.

"Do you find this amusing, Lord Bracken?" Her voice was low, and he noticed for the first time how husky it was.

"Indeed, I do, Lady Megan," he admitted. "But," he spoke when she opened her mouth to berate him, "I *will* see that clothing is provided for you, and I *will* expect you to join me as soon as you are able. Does this meet with my lady's approval?"

Megan caught the sarcasm in his question, but she nodded just the same. The sooner they could talk, the sooner she might be able to leave.

She stood still while he exited the chamber and was still standing when Helga returned, surprising Megan by bringing both of the dresses that had been left in her trunk.

"What say you, Arik?"

"Concerning your lady?"

"Yes. When did you find her?"

"She arrived with Elias, the peddler. She tried to gain entrance to the castle but was denied." The huge man's voice was rusty from lack of use.

"And she ended up working in the creamery?" Bracken had been pacing the floor of the war room but now stopped for Arik's reply. He answered with a nod.

"Where did she sleep?"

"The smithy's."

Bracken's eyes slid shut. What on earth had possessed the girl to come early?

Watching him, Arik decided that now was not the time to say that the Lady Megan had arisen each night and tried to leave the smithery while still sleeping.

"While here in the keep, did she come to harm in any way?"

Arik didn't bother to answer or so much as lift a brow. It was a foolish question with him as her protector, and Bracken knew it the moment the words left his mouth.

"Bracken."

The young lord turned at the sound of his name. Lyndon, the knight as close to Bracken as his own brothers, stood just inside the door.

"Lady Megan is in the great hall."

Bracken nodded and shot a glance at Arik. The larger man was studying him, but as usual Bracken could not discern his thoughts. Without another word, he walked from the room, both Arik and Lyndon at his heels.

Megan could feel several eyes on her as she swept down the main stairway and into the great hall, but the hall itself was such a pleasant surprise that she gave the scrutiny little heed.

It was very spacious and could rival her mother's for cleanliness. It sported not one, but two mammoth fireplaces, and Megan thought how practical this was for chasing away the cold on winter days.

Megan stopped before the fireplace on the north wall and studied the family crest above the mantel. Twin hawks, wings up for landing, flew talons-first toward the center, where a shield which sported a huge male lion, his noble head proud, seemed to stare out over the hall. Megan was very impressed with the symmetry and grandeur of the entire crest. She was still looking at it when Bracken approached. Megan heard his footsteps and turned.

She watched him hesitate, and for some reason flushed with embarrassment. She knew she did not look her best. Her dress was not pressed, and she had no combs for her hair. She would have been stunned to know that Bracken's hesitation was over her looks, but not because he found them lacking.

He recalled the other times he had seen her: in the war

room, on the road, briefly here in the great room, and then up in a bedchamber. The first three times she had been covered with dirt, her dress a rag, but why when he'd seen her upstairs hadn't he recognized her loveliness?

His eyes now took in skin that looked like fresh cream, lips full and red, and eyes so enormous and green that they seemed to swallow her face. Added to all of this was the most glorious mass of hair he had ever seen. Suddenly it didn't make a bit of difference that it was red. In fact, he rather liked it. Maybe this woman had been to court after all.

It's wonderful when a husband and wife find each other attractive.

Aunt Louisa's words came back to him, and he could testify at the moment that at least part of that statement was true—he found Megan very attractive. But one look also told him that she did not share the sentiment. The eyes regarding him were trying to disguise their fear, but Bracken was not fooled. He knew it was time for business.

"Please, sit down."

Megan complied and watched as Bracken sat across from her. He was a large man, probably taller than her father and definitely broader. She had never seen anyone with such dark skin and so much dark hair. It covered his head in tight curls and even curled down the back of his neck. His forearms were covered and so was the vee of skin at the top of his tunic. The dark color of his full beard made his teeth look very white.

"How is it that you are here ahead of schedule, Megan?"

"My father is away, and my mother sent me. I don't believe she knew of the date."

"Your father was going to accompany you?"

"Yes." Megan was thankful that he didn't seem ready to question her mother's actions. She would have been ashamed to explain her mother's ruthlessness.

"And you lived in the keep?"

"Yes. I arrived Monday, and as no one expected me I stayed on."

"As a servant?" Bracken's voice was harsh, but he was not angry with her, just concerned.

"Yes." Megan's chin went in the air. "I saw no other way. The road home was long, and I'd already watched my men die under attack. I am not afraid of hard work and staying seemed most rational."

"Arik tells me you slept at the smithy's."

Megan's eyes flew to that giant who was standing against one wall across the room. He was looking back at her, and Megan couldn't suppress a shudder. He was so huge and silent.

"There is no reason to fear him. 'Tis true that he's a huge man, nearly seven feet tall, but he would die protecting you." Bracken's voice was soft now, and Megan's eyes went back to his.

"He can talk?"

Bracken smiled. "Yes, but he chooses to do so very rarely."

Megan nodded.

"Because you are early, Megan, there is no attendant here for you."

"I thought your aunt lived with you." Megan's eyes had grown even larger.

"Most often she does. She was coming early next week to stay until we are wed, but right now she is in London. I have sent a man for her. She will arrive sometime tomorrow."

"Oh." Megan looked flustered, and Bracken went on smoothly.

"It is certainly not ideal that you stay here tonight without my aunt in attendance, but as you slept unaccompanied in my keep for five nights, one more will hardly make a difference. And," Bracken added dryly, "we are scheduled to wed."

"Oh," Megan said again.

The single word caught Bracken's attention. His dark eyes studied her. "What did that mean?" he asked softly.

Megan swallowed. "Only that I wasn't sure if we still would."

Bracken did not want to tell her that he'd had the same doubts, and replied only, "I can't see that we have much choice."

Megan nodded and fell silent. Her father's intent was that she would know this man before they wed, but at this moment that seemed an impossibility. There was something too powerful and dark about him.

"Were you ever a blonde?"

The question, so innocently put, caused Megan's entire frame to stiffen and her face to grow rigid. Bracken was amazed at the change in her.

"You mistake me with my sister, Marigold."

"Is she older or younger?" Bracken asked, causing Megan to believe he was truly interested.

"She is older." Megan turned her gaze from him now, and her voice became flat. "Marigold's aspirations go far beyond the title of earl, so I fear you are stuck with me."

Megan never did turn her head, or she would have seen the amusement in Bracken's eyes. He didn't want Marigold, not after meeting Megan, but he found a bit of jealousy between sisters to be an entertaining thing. It would be some time before he learned that for Megan, Marigold was no laughing matter.

Bracken lay in bed for nearly an hour that night thinking on the day's events. He knew that Megan had returned to the bedchamber she'd bathed in and wondered if she was comfortable. He mentally shrugged. As soon as Aunt Louisa arrived, she would live in the tower apartments with her. After living in an abbey, Megan would certainly forgive him one night in a stark chamber. Bracken fell asleep then, but it seemed only moments instead of hours before Lyndon spoke his name in the dark.

"Bracken."

"What is it?" A trained warrior, Bracken was instantly awake.

"I think you should come to the hall."

Bracken rose without question, and after he had joined Lyndon on the stairs, both men stood in awe of the scene below.

Megan sat in a chair by the fire looking into the flames. She wore a borrowed night garment, coarse and many sizes too large for her. Beyond her chair, standing and still fully dressed, was Arik. As Bracken and Lyndon watched, Megan stood and started for the door, but Arik was there ahead of her, preventing her from reaching for the handle.

"No, my lady," his deep, gravely voice could be heard.

Megan tried to come around him, but he moved to block her. After a moment she returned to the chair, and Bracken walked down the stairs. He stared at Megan as he passed, but went directly to Arik. Before he could question him, Megan was on her feet again. She came to the door. This time Bracken heard her speak.

"I have to go home."

"No, my lady," Arik said, holding his body between her and the door. Megan's hands came out as if to push Arik off, but no one had moved to touch her.

"Mother sent me away before my clothes were ready. I have to see Father. I have no brush for my hair."

Megan tried to get to the door again, but Arik sidestepped and prevented it. At the same time, Bracken reached gently for her hand, enfolding it in his large one. Megan woke with a start. She stared up at Bracken and then at Arik before reclaiming her hand and tightly folding her arms across her chest.

"Did I say anything?" she asked, her voice so vulnerable that Bracken's heart constricted.

"No," he lied to her without conscience, knowing that if he told her she would feel shamed.

"Let me see you to your room, Megan," Bracken offered. The small redhead nodded and preceded him across the hall and up the stairs. They didn't speak, and Bracken was glad that Lyndon had made himself scarce. At the same time, another thought occurred to him: The tower apartments were not an option. His intended walked in her sleep. He had never known anyone who did, but a fall down the tower steps could mean her death. Bracken would never take that risk.

Seven

MEGAN HAD NOT YET MADE an appearance downstairs when Bracken cornered Arik in the great room the next morning.

"Whether or not you're in the mood to speak, my great friend, I need to know more about Lady Megan's actions last night. Did she walk while sleeping in the smithy's shop?"

"Every night."

Bracken had not been prepared for that answer. It gave him pause, and he stared at the giant knight without really seeing him. He'd been thinking Megan might walk in her sleep on a rare occasion, but evidently she had done it every night she'd been at Hawkings Crest.

"How did you stop her?"

"I didn't. I blocked her path."

"You never woke her?"

Arik's head moved in denial.

Megan chose that moment to come downstairs, and Bracken moved off after just a few words of instruction to Arik. He met Megan at the bottom of the stairs and noticed immediately that she looked rested but slightly wary.

"Good morning to you, Megan. Come, break the fast with me."

Megan allowed herself to be led to the head table and took a seat at the top of the long bench. Bracken took the large wooden chair that sat at the head of the table and studied Megan for a few silent moments.

"How did you sleep?"

Megan blushed, her eyes on her hands. "I never remember anything if I walk in my sleep, so until you woke me, I knew nothing."

"And when you returned to your chambers?"

She now looked at him. "I slept again right away."

Food was placed before them. For some time they ate in silence. Megan found the fare very appetizing and ate her fill. Bracken was done ahead of her, however, and while she finished, he told her he was working on a change in plans.

"When my Aunt Louisa lives with me, she always occupies the apartments in the tower. I had originally planned for you to live with her. With the long, narrow stairs, that is out of the question. I will have to make other arrangements."

"Do you mean to suggest that you will send me home?" Megan's voice was so hopeful that Bracken had to hide a smile.

"I believe your father wished for us to become better acquainted."

Megan shrugged. "I thought that since we've at least met, it might suffice to see one another a few times before we wed. Would that not serve the same purpose?"

They both knew it would not, but Bracken was amazed over the emotions her words evoked. For a man who would have gladly refused the king's orders, he was certainly working hard to think of ways to keep Megan with him. His pride, however, would not let him admit this to her.

"I'm sorry you do not wish to remain here, Megan, but if you recall, it was not my idea but your father's and the king's."

Megan blushed to the roots of her hair. He must not want this marriage any more than she did. She had no words. She had been adjusting to new situations all of her life, but this was by far the most difficult.

She did not want to be married yet, and having to live with this man who would soon be her husband was the most awkward experience thus far. Every time he looked at her or touched her in any way, Megan felt utterly defenseless. It was not something she enjoyed. For the most part, Megan was used to being in charge of her own wants. Now she had to answer to this man. He did not strike her as being cruel, but she could tell that he liked to have his own way as often as she did herself.

Megan had not come down early that morning. She had been praying—confessing, actually. She had grown angry many times the day before and had not confessed each occurrence to God on the spot. Her sins hung over her when she had wakened, and she knew she could not start the day with such a heart.

Bracken and Megan were still sitting silently in one another's company when Lyndon joined them. He didn't sit until Bracken gave him leave, but when he did it was on the end of the other bench, directly opposite Megan.

"Megan, this is Lyndon, a loyal knight of Hawkings Crest. Lyndon, this is my intended, Lady Megan of Stone Lake."

"Hello, Sir Lyndon."

"Hello, my lady. May I say that you grace our hall with your beauty."

Megan smiled at the handsome, blond knight, her first real smile, and Bracken stared at her until Lyndon spoke.

"I'm sorry to disturb you, Bracken, but I think you should know of the gossip in the keep."

"All right."

"Lady Megan was not disturbed in any way while working with the servants. I know you will be pleased over this fact, but you will not care for the reason. They did not recognize her as a lady in their midst but believe that Arik had claimed her."

Megan's face paled, and her eyes slid shut. She thought she might actually hate her mother at that moment. She was to live here and become the mistress of this castle, yet they all thought she had some sort of relationship with Arik. For a moment Megan felt beyond despair, but a sudden resolve stiffened her spine. She had risen to countless occasions in her life; would she now allow this one to rule her?

Both men had been watching her. Bracken was on the verge of speaking when Megan opened her eyes and said, "If you'll excuse me, gentlemen." She rose gracefully. "I feel a need for some air."

"Where are you going?" Bracken asked but was roundly ignored.

Both men watched Megan walk toward the main entrance, her head high, her face serene. At the door she spoke to a guard. Bracken watched the way the man bowed his head in respect as she walked away. She looked in control, but Bracken was not comfortable. With an easy pace that he didn't feel within, he followed, Lyndon by his side. He knew no physical harm would come to her, but at the moment he wasn't certain if she would be attacked verbally or not. Bracken would stand for no such thing.

Megan, no longer in convent dress, her hair shining with cleanliness, drew every eye in the inner bailey. She spoke to several folks as she moved along, to people she recognized and some she didn't. They all seemed to know her, but she didn't linger; her goal was the creamery.

Bracken had also come into the courtyard, Lyndon still with him, and in an effort to keep an eye on her and not be too conspicuous, wandered about much as Megan was doing. Things seemed to be going well for the first several minutes, but then he watched as she moved toward the creamery. Bracken's heart plummeted. Surely she was not going back to work!

"She's headed for the creamery," he commented to the man at his side.

"So I see" was all Lyndon said.

They watched her disappear within, and Bracken debated

his next move. A moment later the problem was temporarily taken from his hands. Kent appeared at his side to tell him that his men had need of him on the practice field. He walked away with long-legged strides, leaving Lyndon in the courtyard. As much as he trusted Lyndon, Bracken could not stop himself from looking back at the creamery until it was out of view.

"Hello, Eddie," Megan greeted the man easily as she crossed the threshold. She watched as he removed his cap.

"Hello, my lady."

Megan let her eyes roam the large, clean room and then began to walk slowly around. The women working within slowed some to watch her but continued with their tasks.

"You run this creamery with excellence, Eddie," Megan told him sincerely when she stopped at one point.

"Thank you, my lady. I'm glad you approve."

"Hello, Pen," Megan said as she continued her stroll. "Watch that edge when you pour."

"Yes, my lady." Pen reverently breathed the words. She did tend to be rather clumsy, but right now all she could see and hear was Megan—her dress, hair, her lovely skin, and the husky sound of her cultured voice.

"I'd like to make a suggestion, Eddie."

"Yes, my lady," the man said. They were back at the entrance now, and Eddie's heart sank with dread. Would she now take revenge for the way he had treated her? Eddie saw himself grabbing her arm the first day and had to stifle a groan. However, he was in for a pleasant surprise.

Megan began to make a most logical suggestion concerning the storage of cheese. Her voice was gracious, and her manner unassuming. Eddie felt as if she'd actually left the final choice up to him. She had also waited until the others couldn't hear. Eddie had not lost face and had gained helpful information in the process. When Megan left the creamery, he wished her a pleasant day with a most sincere heart, his cap still in his beefy hand.

"Oh, Lyndon!" Megan spoke the moment she was outside and spotted the knight; he'd been practically haunting the creamery, listening for raised voices.

"Yes, my lady?"

"Lyndon, where are the cows?"

"The cows, my lady?" Lyndon questioned her with little enthusiasm, thinking he would never forgive Bracken for leaving him there alone.

"Yes. The cows they milk for the creamery," Megan explained kindly.

"In the stables, my lady."

"And the stables are...?"

Lyndon stared into her face. How in the world did one deal with such a woman? She had the face of an angelic five-year-old and a backbone like an iron rod.

"The stables, Lyndon, where are they?" Megan questioned again, her voice not quite so cordial this time.

"Along the north wall of the keep, my lady."

"Thank you," Megan beamed at him and promptly turned and started in the wrong direction.

"Lady Megan," Lyndon called to her. "This way," he said when she turned. "I'll show you."

"Oh, thank you, Lyndon."

And off they set, Megan as pleased as a lass at play, and Lyndon feeling that he'd rather be forced to wrestle with Arik than have the charge of Bracken's intended.

"And she insisted on seeing my books!" Barton, Hawkings Crest's steward, nearly shouted.

"She told me that it's my fault that two of me birds have sores on their claws. Wants to reconstruct the whole cage, she does!" the falconer added.

"She actually accused me of stealing!" The steward spouted again. "Said she'd finish reading my accounts later."

Bracken stared at his falconer and steward in disbelief. His stableman and smithy were there also, but they had already had their say. He'd only been gone a few hours, but in that time Megan had evidently turned his castle and keep upside down. He glanced up to see her coming sedately into the hall and dismissed the men around him with a curt nod of his head.

"Megan," he raised his voice only slightly. "I wish to speak with you."

Megan stopped but did not draw close. "I'm busy right now, Bracken."

This was too much.

"Megan!" he bellowed, and she redirected her course to stand before him. She did an admirable job of hiding her fear of his anger. Bracken thought she looked utterly serene.

"My steward and smith have both been to see me, as have others. What have you to say for yourself?"

Megan shrugged innocently. "There are several areas that are in need of change, Bracken. I think your steward might be robbing you blind."

"He's been with me for years," Bracken, now red in the face, retorted.

Again Megan shrugged. "Be that as it may..." she let the sentence drop before plunging on, "your birds are not in the best of health. I have a poultice for their feet, but the bars will have to be sanded or the sores will return."

Bracken barely heard her as he began to shout. "I will not have you upsetting every servant in Hawkings Crest! I forbid you to visit the stables, and as for the other areas—"

"That won't work at all, Bracken," she replied, cutting him off in a calm voice. "If I am to be the mistress of this keep, I must stay abreast of its workings. Now, I really must be off, Bracken. I have yet to see the looms."

With that Megan swung away from him in a cloud of long skirts and red hair. Chest heaving, Bracken stood and stared after her until he realized he was being watched. His head moved toward the man who dared, ready to give him the rough edge of his tongue, until he met the amused gaze of his Aunt Louisa.

"She doesn't have blonde hair after all." His aunt's voice was mild.

"How do you know that's Megan?" Bracken shot at her, his mood still dangerous.

"Because you wouldn't let anyone else speak to you in such a manner."

Bracken's shoulders slumped with defeat. It was true.

"Come, my nephew." Louisa became all at once brisk. "Let's go into the war room, and you can tell me all that has transpired."

Eight

TWENTY MINUTES LATER LOUISA asked her first question, her expression one of stark disbelief.

"She actually worked in the creamery?"

"Don't look at me that way, Aunt Lou." Her nephew's look was helpless.

"Bracken," Louisa said patiently, truly wanting to understand, "I heard the girl. There is no way a woman with that voice could be mistaken for a serf."

Bracken shook his head. "Evidently she spoke to no one. She did her work, ate in the courtyard with the other servants, and slept each night at the smithy's."

Louisa just stared at him, and Bracken knew he had to tell all.

"There is more."

Louisa waited.

"She walks in her sleep."

The woman blinked. "You're certain of this?"

"I witnessed it myself. I was going to have her live in the tower apartments with you, but now that is out of the question."

"Yes, I can see that it would be." Louisa replied thoughtfully, and they both fell silent for a time.

"You say she actually slept in your blacksmith's shop?" Louisa seemed unable to let the matter drop.

"I'm afraid so."

"What will her father say?"

Bracken shook his head. "I can't think that he'll be overly pleased, but it was hardly my fault; her mother sent her early."

"Why would she do such a thing?"

"I have not been able to gain more answers. Megan talks in her sleep as well, and mentioned that she'd been sent without her full wardrobe. I would like to know more, but if she knows she spoke to me in her sleep, she will feel shamed."

Louisa's eyes softened. "You care for her, don't you, Bracken."

"Heaven help me, I do!" the young earl burst out. He came to his feet and began to pace. "I've known her 24 hours, and she has interrupted my entire life, but I can't get her from my mind!"

"What of the blonde woman you met at court?"

"Her older sister, Marigold. I spoke of her with Megan, but I do not think them very close."

"But you do find Megan attractive."

A sudden smile parted Bracken's dark beard, and his voice softened. "Ah, yes. She is as lovely a maid as I've ever seen. I do find her most comely."

Louisa was well pleased, but her practical side came to the fore. "Do you think her capable of managing a fortress as large as Hawkings Crest?"

"Yes," Bracken admitted grudgingly, thinking about the way she stood up to him. However, the face of his steward flashed into his mind as well.

"Nevertheless, you heard the men. It's not going to be easy." Bracken had begun to growl, but he worked at calming himself. Knowing his aunt would grasp his meaning beyond the words, he made one last comment.

"I am beginning to think that marriage to Megan might be more trouble than it is worth."

"But as you have reminded me, we have little choice in the matter." Megan's voice came from the doorway, and Bracken spun in surprise. "I will honor my father's wishes and those of my king and become your wife," Megan went on, her tone wooden. "But it is a relief to know, Lord Bracken, just exactly how you feel."

Megan left as quietly as she'd entered, and Bracken stood as though made of granite. Louisa's heart ached at the pain she saw in his face.

"I didn't mean it the way it sounded." Bracken's voice was hushed in the still room, and his eyes never left the closed portal.

"I know you didn't, Bracken. Maybe if you try to explain..."

But Bracken was shaking his head. "I think her pride is as great as my own. I will have to give her time."

Even with the little she had seen of Megan, Louisa was forced to agree. They spoke of sleeping arrangements for the next few moments and then went their separate ways, Louisa to settle herself in a suite of rooms down the corridor from Megan, and Bracken to the keep, hoping to get a glimpse of his bride-to-be without actually searching her out.

STONE LAKE CASTLE

"What do you mean she's not here?" Vincent eyed his wife in disbelief, but Annora did not flinch.

"It wasn't going well, so I sent Megan ahead."

"To Hawkings Crest?" Vincent's tone was incredulous.

"Of course to Hawkings Crest!" Annora snapped. "Where did you think?"

"But she wasn't expected."

Annora shrugged. "Surely someone was there. Honestly, Vincent, she was being most impossible. You know what she's like."

"You fool!" Vincent retorted scathingly, widening his wife's eyes with shock and then anger. "Anything could have happened. Has the caravan arrived back?"

"I sent no caravan." Annora kept up a brave front, but in truth she had regretted this action almost immediately.

"What say you?" Vincent's face had flushed with emotion as he tried telling himself that he had heard her wrong.

Annora raised her chin. "I sent Megan on horseback with three guards. I'm certain she fared well."

"So the men have returned?"

"No, but—"

Annora was cut off when Vincent grabbed her forearm with a strength she didn't know he possessed.

"Vincent." Her tone was wounded. For the first time she was a bit afraid. "You are hurting me."

"I'll do more than hurt you if even so much as Megan's reputation is harmed! Now, sit down, woman, and tell me all!"

Annora now knew real fear. Megan had always been such a headstrong survivor. It had truly never occurred to her that her daughter might fall into harm. Annora's voice shook, but she did as Vincent bid and relayed every detail, down to the minute, of Megan's departure. No small thing this, as she had never seen her husband so coldly furious.

Less than 15 minutes later, Vincent and a band of men rode out on horseback for Hawkings Crest. Just behind them rode more men and a large wagon laden with Megan's new clothing and all of her belongings. When they had all left, Annora made her way to the chapel. She didn't pray often, but if Megan was actually lost, she now feared for her daughter's life as well as her own.

Megan stood at the window of her bedchamber, looking into the distance and feeling thoroughly spent with her effort to quell her emotions. Walking into the keep that morning knowing that the servants actually believed her part of a liaison with Arik had been almost unbearable. She had made herself move among them, careful to keep her eyes from lingering too long on any one face, but it had been torture.

Then in the midst of the hurt, Megan had found herself more and more interested in the castle workings. Hawkings Crest was a fine stronghold, but every fortress had areas that needed improvement and Megan could see many at Hawkings Crest. Yet, Bracken had only thought her interfering. His shouting at her had affected her more deeply than she had let on. She hadn't even enjoyed seeing the looms, even though they were run with tremendous efficiency.

Megan suddenly found herself back in the bushes, hiding out of fear for life, listening and looking on in the dim firelight as her three guards were slain. Tears poured down her cheeks, and a sob sounded in her throat. She turned and lay across the bed, burying her face in the thick furs as harsh weeping overcame her. Megan prayed for strength, but at the moment she felt faithless. In the midst of asking God to bring her father soon, she fell into a restless sleep.

"Have you seen Megan?" The question came softly to Louisa's and Lyndon's ears just moments before Bracken spotted her coming down the stairs. She had not taken the midday meal with them, and it was now evening. He had no desire to treat her as a child, but he would not allow her to go hungry. Bracken left Lyndon and his aunt without comment and met Megan at the bottom of the stairs.

Megan came to a stop on the last step and simply stared at Bracken. He returned the gaze, taking in the lovely blush in her cheeks and her bright, serious eyes. Their height difference was lessened in this stance, and for just a moment no one spoke. Bracken turned in profile to her and offered his arm. Megan took it.

"Did you have a pleasant afternoon, Megan?" Bracken asked as they crossed to the tables.

"Yes, Lord Bracken, thank you."

"My aunt has arrived. I would like you to meet her."

"Very well." Megan sounded disinterested, but inside she was tense. She soon learned there was no need.

As soon as they neared, Louisa turned, a warm smile lighting her handsome features. Megan saw in an instant where Bracken inherited his dark coloring. Louisa's hair was as dark as her nephew's, with just a hint of gray at the temples. Her lashes and brows were equally as dark, and the eyes regarding her were a deep brown. The older woman now reached for both of Megan's hands.

"Megan, this is my Aunt Louisa," Bracken spoke. "Aunt Louisa, this is my betrothed, Megan, daughter to Vincent of Stone Lake."

"Hello, Megan," she said still holding Megan's work-rough hands in her own soft ones. "I'm so pleased to meet you."

"Bracken told me you were called away from London ahead of time. I hope my presence has not interfered in any way with your plans."

"Not in the least, my dear. I'm glad to be of service."

"Come," Bracken broke in. "Our food is served."

They all retired to the tables then, Bracken at the head, Megan to his right, and Aunt Louisa to his left. Lyndon sat by Louisa, and another knight, Kendrick by name, took a place on the bench next to Megan.

Bracken and Megan shared a trencher. Bracken was the consummate gentleman, seeing that all the best cuts of meat went to Megan's side of the wooden platter. Conversation flowed freely among Bracken and the others, but Megan had little to say. Bracken's eyes lingered on her for most of the meal, and by the time they finished, he felt he would do anything to see her smile.

As it was, he was about to get his wish. They had just stood when Clive, another of Bracken's vassals, announced Vincent's presence. Megan excused herself and moved with a calm face to the main doors of the castle, Bracken at her heels. She continued to walk sedately until she spotted him coming up the path, whereupon she ran the last six yards and quite literally threw herself into her father's arms.

Vincent hugged her close. When he released her to put one arm around her shoulders, Bracken, who was now upon them, was able to see her smiling face. It took his breath away.

"More wine," Bracken instructed a serving woman and then sat quietly as Vincent and his men ate their fill. In order to give them privacy, Megan and Louisa had retired to the south hearth, but there had been little talk until now. Bracken felt the time had come for him to explain. Vincent had not seemed at all upset, but Bracken knew by the way he greeted his daughter that there must be much on his mind.

"I want to tell you of your men, my lord."

Vincent forestalled him with a hand. "We saw their graves. I thank you for seeing to the burial. Can you tell me what happened?"

Bracken shook his head. "I know little. Megan said they died saving her."

"She was unharmed?" Vincent's gaze grew intense.

"It would seem so."

"And once she arrived here?"

Bracken drew a deep breath. "She was not harmed, but neither was she well taken care of."

Vincent began to scowl as Bracken filled him in about Megan's work in the creamery, and eating and sleeping in the keep.

"I'm sorry, Lord Vincent, I was not here, but I still take full blame since I did not make provisions for the possibility of an early arrival."

To Bracken's amazement, Vincent did not seem distressed. Instead his eyes suddenly lit with good humor.

"You say she slept in a stall?"

"Yes, Lord Vincent."

Vincent chuckled softly. "I think I want you to call me Vincent, and if I told you some of the situations Megan has gotten herself into over the years, you would understand my pleasure. Hear me now," Vincent's voice grew serious, "when I tell you that I would never countenance abuse toward the girl, but Megan is a survivor—always has been. If she had wanted into this castle before you arrived, she would have come."

Bracken's dark brows winged upward. It was true. Megan had been standing before him in the war room little more than an hour after he arrived.

"I'm only glad she was unharmed," Vincent said with quiet conviction.

"Can you tell me why she arrived early?"

Vincent's brow lowered, and all pleasure left his face. "Me gan and her mother do not get on. They quarreled, and my wife took it upon herself to send Megan here. Had I been present, I would have stopped her. Unfortunately, I arrived back late last night and knew nothing of this until this morning."

"And now that she is here, Vincent, do you wish her to stay?"

Vincent glanced up at Bracken and then down at his trencher to hide the gleam in his eye. This young lord was trying to conceal his interest, but it was there.

Good! Vincent's heart declared. *He is not a man to be bullied. With his mettle, he will make a fine spouse, worthy of my Megan.*

"Since your aunt is now in attendance," Vincent spoke aloud, "I see no reason for Megan to leave. I had planned on spending some days with her before she left Stone Lake, but I was called away."

"Stay now," Bracken inserted. "Stay at Hawkings Crest for as long as you wish."

"I may do that," Vincent replied slowly, not having thought of it. "I just may, but right now I wish to join Megan. I wish, for the sake of my men, to know what happened the night they were attacked."

Nine

"I'm glad your father arrived, Megan. I think he must have been worried about you."

Megan smiled and nodded. She had not yet seen how well Lady Louisa could read and understand people, but she was comfortable with her. She had experienced little comfort at Hawkings Crest, and she found this a relief.

"I think you must be right. It's so good to see him. We were to have some time together before I left, but then he was called away."

Louisa nodded, accurately guessing more than she was told.

"Do you have many siblings, Megan?" Louisa asked with just the right amount of interest.

"Just one sister, Marigold. I haven't seen her for some years."

"She is older?"

"Yes, by more than two years. We have little in common. Lady Louisa, are you sister to Bracken's father or mother?"

"I hope you will call me Aunt Louisa, and I am sister to Bracken's mother, Joyce. After Bracken's father died, our own father became ill. Taking all of Bracken's siblings, Joyce moved many miles north to our own family's keep, White Hall. Our father is dead now, too, but Joyce and the children have made their home there and are most content. You will meet her at the wedding."

Megan nodded, looking thoughtful. "Has Bracken a large family?"

"Yes. He is the oldest, but after him are Stephen, Danella, Brice, Giles, and Kristine. Danella is married and expecting her first child, but no one else has wed. They live for the most part with my sister. I think you will meet them all at the wedding."

Megan's eyes had grown during this recitation, but she managed one more question.

"And Bracken's father. Has he been long dead?"

"About six years. Greville died in battle, a great warrior he was. He made the king proud. Bracken is very much like him." Louisa added this last bit with gentle pride, while giving Megan a sweet smile.

Megan smiled in return and asked, "And what about you Aunt Louisa, do you have children of your own?"

Louisa did have children, two grown sons whom she adored, but she was not given time to answer before the men strode into their midst.

"I have no want to upset you, Meg," her father began, "but the men who escorted you have families. For their sakes, I wish to know how they died."

Meg nodded, her eyes briefly skimming over Bracken and Louisa before returning to her father. She told her story quietly, her eyes on her father or on the fire in the hearth. She didn't notice how Bracken's jaw became rigid upon hearing the way she sat in the bushes and watched the men die. Nor did she see the pain in his eyes when he heard fear in her voice as she asked her father if he thought she would ever see the attackers again.

"No, Meg," he assured her, taking her hand in his own. "You'll be safe at Hawkings Crest."

"So you're leaving me?" The anxious words were out before she could stop them, and Megan blushed as she dropped her eyes to her lap. An awkward moment passed before Megan spoke, her eyes still downcast.

"I'm rather tired. I think I'll go to my room."

Both Vincent and Bracken stood.

"Will I see you tomorrow?" she asked of her father.

"I'll be here."

With that, Megan briefly met his eyes, wished them all a good night, and walked from the hall. Bracken's eyes stayed on her until she was out of sight. A moment later he was relieved that Lyndon had need of him. He also bid his guests goodnight, leaving Vincent and Louisa alone.

"Would you like to be shown to your chambers, Lord Vincent?" Louisa asked solicitously.

"I believe I'll stay a while longer by the fire."

"May I join you?"

"You do me honor, Lady Louisa."

The two sat again. After a moment Louisa commented, "Megan is a lovely girl."

Vincent smiled. "I know she is not certain about staying, not that I blame her after such a rough initiation, but I truly think it is best."

"Bracken told me that she suggested her going home and his visiting from time to time before they wed." Louisa suddenly thought that such a statement might seem impertinent, but Lord Vincent answered readily enough.

"That's not possible," he said quietly. "Megan and her mother do not get on well. It would be a difficult time for both of them. It would also defeat the purpose of Megan becoming better acquainted with Bracken before they unite their lives."

"This is true," Louisa commented and then fell silent.

"They have not known a good start."

"This is true also."

Vincent speared her with a glance. She was choosing her words very carefully, and there was no need. He told her as much.

"In that case," Louisa said, "I'll tell you that Bracken seems very willing for this trial period. Megan, on the other hand, is not."

Much the way Vincent had surprised Bracken at the table, he now took Louisa unaware by smiling.

"You are pleased, Lord Vincent."

"Yes, I am. If I believed Bracken would shun and hurt Megan I would take her with me, but this situation has promise. Bracken will have to work hard to find Megan's harmonious side, but I know it will be worth his effort."

"She does seem to have a will of her own."

Vincent chuckled. "She's no man's plaything, and if Bracken can get beyond her lovely face and engaging curves, he'll find himself a wife whose worth cannot be measured."

It was one of the most wonderful things Louisa had ever heard anyone say. She stared at Vincent for a long moment, but his eyes were on the flames, a small smile playing around his mouth.

Louisa suddenly remembered the sleepwalking and felt concern. Maybe she should go upstairs. Did Megan's father know of the problem?

"Lord Vincent?"

"I'm sorry, my lady, I was not attending." Indeed, his thoughts had drifted far.

"Bracken tells me that Megan walks in her sleep. Should I check on her now?"

Vincent's frame stiffened. "Megan only walks in her sleep when something is upsetting her."

Louisa did not know what to say to this.

"Bracken asked me to stay on if I so chose. Maybe I shall do so." Again Louisa could not frame a suitable reply.

"I hope you will not find me rude, my lady, but I feel a sudden need to check on Megan myself."

"Of course, Lord Vincent. I shall escort you to her room."

The problem in the keep concerning the evening guard was swiftly handled by Bracken and Lyndon, so it wasn't long before the lord of Hawkings Crest stood alone atop the wall. The night was swiftly closing in around him; it was one of his favorite times of the day.

Bracken was not a religious man, nor one given to praying, but he did believe in God and that He was in control. He would have given much right then to say that he knew God better, in hopes that he would then know what plans God had for the future. Bracken found himself wanting a life with Megan in a way that he hadn't wanted anything in a long time.

He could easily envision the fine sons they would have and just as easily put Megan's fear of him at the back of his mind so that he could also envision a good marriage between them. It really made no sense. Megan clearly wished to be elsewhere, and he didn't even know the girl. But Bracken felt a sureness deep within him that Megan of Stone Lake was the woman God had planned for him.

Bracken shrugged. He was growing maudlin. It was impossible to know what the future held, and being the logical man he was, Bracken started toward the castle. There was no point in losing sleep over the matter.

Vincent was out of the castle early the next morning, but many of the castle folk were already astir. He walked through the keep and around the grounds and was pleasantly surprised to find Bracken and Lyndon returning from the practice field. Both men were gleaming with sweat, and Vincent saw that directly behind them was the jousting field.

"Good morning to you, Vincent," Bracken greeted him.

"And to you, Bracken. This is one of your knights?"

"Yes. Lord Vincent, meet Lyndon."

"It's a pleasure, sir," Lyndon said with respect and then took himself off to the castle.

"You're up early," Bracken commented as they walked easily in Lyndon's wake.

"Yes. I will accept your offer to stay for a few days, but with so little time, I did not care to lounge in bed."

"Good," Bracken returned sincerely. "I think Megan will be very pleased."

"And mayhap a little more willing to remain here and get to know you better."

Bracken smiled at his perception. "I do not wish to see her pine for you."

"Nor do I. Keep in mind, Bracken," the older man continued, coming to a stop, "Megan lived at the abbey for years. During her time there she learned a great deal, the most important of which is that her life there kept her unspoiled. Always remember that Megan will never yearn for a life of creature comforts. She does not put great stock in her surroundings as much as she does in the people surrounding her."

Bracken nodded. It was a good thing to know. Still, he knew that Hawkings Crest could offer her better.

"I don't know if you've been to see Megan's room, but that chamber is just temporary."

Vincent waved a dismissive hand. "You will find she is most settled. I would ask you, though, to take care with Megan herself. I speak without bias when I say she has many fine qualities, but that is not to say she has no faults. Pray, deal gently with her."

Bracken was impressed with the older man's honesty. "You are telling me she likes to have her own way."

Vincent smiled. "What woman does not?"

Bracken only smiled in reply, but he knew that if he pressed Lord Vincent, the older man would have to admit that Megan was in a class alone.

"I do not wish to stay here, Father God, but I will do as I am asked. Please help me to know control of my actions and emotions. Please help me to deal kindly with all here."

Megan stopped when Bracken came to mind. Did she mean him, too? In truth, she wasn't sure. She had no wish to be mean, but knowing that he felt her troublesome, along with his interest in her sister, made Megan want nothing to do with him.

Megan immediately warned herself not to grow overly emotional. She had no real proof that Bracken was interested in Marigold. After all, he had only asked a few questions, and Megan recognized her own sensitivity where Marigold was concerned.

A knock on her chamber door brought Megan to her feet. She found her father waiting without.

"Come and break the fast with me, Megan."

"Do you leave today?"

"No. I will be here for you."

Megan beamed up at him and took his proffered arm for the journey down the wide stone stairs.

"This flour has been sifted?" Megan asked the baker and let a handful run through her fingers.

"Yes, my lady."

"Please repeat the process."

"Yes, my lady," the man spoke, but Louisa, standing at Megan's side, could see that he was not happy.

The older woman had to keep from shaking her head. Vincent had been gone for two days, and Louisa had steeled herself for Megan's resentment or depression. She got neither. Megan was throwing herself into the workings of the castle with a vengeance.

Megan was the most fascinating woman Louisa had ever encountered. One moment she was tending to a slight wound on the finger of a small child and the next she was telling the milkers, in no uncertain terms, that they would do a better job of rinsing their pottery jars. Louisa knew there were a few who wanted to toss her into the moat, but most of the castle folk were beginning to adore her.

And Bracken was no exception. Louisa could see it in his eyes. Unfortunately, Megan did not return his sentiment. She might be talking with Lyndon, smiling at him in true affection, or even laughing at some outrageous remark from Kendrick, but the moment Megan became aware of Bracken's presence she became stiff as a poker. She was even warming up to Arik, but to Bracken she was chillingly civil.

"Aunt Louisa?"

"Yes, dear." The women had made their way from the kitchen and baking quarters and were almost to the great hall.

"Who is Black Francesca?"

Louisa came to such an abrupt halt that Megan started. The older woman took a moment to ask, "Where did you hear her name, Megan?"

"I heard Helga mention her to Lela, but I have met no one at Hawkings Crest with that name."

Louisa licked her lips. "She lives in the village."

Megan nodded serenely, but because she was very curious over Louisa's reaction, she pressed her.

"But who is she?"

Louisa hesitated for only a moment this time; surely Megan was mature enough to understand.

"She is the village prostitute."

Louisa was not prepared for Megan's reaction. Her eyes filled with compassionate tears.

"Is she very young?"

"I'm not sure," Louisa admitted and felt shame for the uncharitable thoughts she'd had toward Black Francesca in the past. On top of these thoughts, however, was one of horror. She couldn't stop herself from voicing it.

"You're not thinking of going to see her, are you, Megan?"

"Well, not right away."

"Megan." Louisa felt panic coming on. "I do not think Bracken would approve." *Disapproval* was too mild a word, but Louisa could think of none better.

Megan stiffened with outrage. "Why? Does Bracken visit her?"

"No!" Louisa's voice squeaked. "No, Megan, never."

Some of Megan's strain left her, but she still looked offended. Louisa sighed. It would seem that Bracken could do no right, not even when he was innocent.

"You judge Bracken too harshly, my dear." Louisa's words were spoken gently, but they had a powerful effect. Megan stared at the older woman and then dropped her eyes. Her fingers came to her lips, and she looked very contrite.

Louisa would have questioned her some, but Clive approached then, announcing, "Lady Louisa, Lord Bracken asked me to tell you that Lord Stephen and Lord Brice have arrived."

"Thank you, Clive."

"Bracken's family?" Megan questioned when Clive moved away.

"Yes, the two brothers closest to him in age. Will you come with me to meet them?"

"They will be hungry. I will join you when I've seen that something is prepared."

Louisa saw it for the excuse that it was and let it go, but she knew that Megan's fears were ungrounded. She was going to love Bracken's brothers.

Ten

"HOW IS MY MOTHER?" Bracken asked.

"Well," Stephen told him. "She sends her love, as do Giles and Kris."

"Has Danella's child come?"

"No, but she feels well."

Brice had remained silent during this exchange, and Bracken now transferred his gaze to him.

"What say you, Brice?" Bracken said with a teasing light in his eyes.

"Where is she?"

Bracken smiled. At 18, Brice was preoccupied with the fairer sex. He had been impressed, not dismayed, that the king had taken enough notice of Bracken to order him to marry. He'd thought that was something saved for lords with loftier titles. Now he wanted to know if his brother was to be saddled with an angel or a harridan.

"I believe she's inside. Yonder comes Aunt Lou. She'll know."

Louisa received warm embraces from some of her favorite nephews before she stood back and lovingly studied them.

"You're taller, Brice."

He smiled boyishly before she turned to Stephen and eyed him a moment. His looks so closely resembled Bracken's that it was startling.

"I was certain that Megan would like both you and Brice, but you look enough like Bracken that I can see she may have trouble." Louisa then turned a devilish smile on her oldest nephew, who tried to scowl at her but couldn't quite bring it off.

"What's this, Bracken?" Stephen teased. "Trouble in paradise?"

Bracken chuckled, but Brice cut in seriously.

"Aunt Lou is teasing," he said, believing with all of his heart that no woman in her right mind could find fault with Bracken.

He was soon to learn differently. Not ten minutes later they were inside and meeting Lady Megan, who stared hard at Stephen before transferring her gaze to Bracken. The lord of the keep was clearly amused by her reaction and smiled when he saw her chin go up in the air.

"My brothers are hungry," he said, his tone still light but his eyes watchful.

Megan's raised brows mocked him. "The food awaits, my lord." Megan started to swing away, but Bracken's voice halted her.

"Megan."

She turned back with reluctance.

"I wish you to join us."

It was not what she wanted to hear.

"Very well, my lord." Although clearly not happy, Megan allowed Bracken to take her arm and escort her to her place.

The meal progressed with much talk between Louisa and her younger nephews, but Megan and Bracken were distinctly quiet. The meal was coming to an end when Bracken leaned close and spoke for Megan's ears alone.

"What is it I have done, Megan, to vex you so?"

Megan looked at him for the first time. His face was close, and for an instant she studied his serious, dark eyes. This marriage had not been his idea, nor had it been his plan that she stay at Hawkings Crest. He may not really care for her, but she realized then that he couldn't force feelings onto his heart.

"I'm sorry, Lord Bracken, that my mood has been so poor. I will try my utmost not to brandish it upon you in the future."

"I appreciate your effort, Megan, but I'm sorry you're so unhappy."

Megan sighed. She hated being so obvious.

"I left my home abruptly; I would have wished for a little more time."

It was true, Bracken thought. She had left all that was familiar and had been given little time to adjust.

"Would it help to move you to a more comfortable bedchamber?" he suggested.

Megan shook her head; she was sincerely content. "I shall be fine where I am."

"Playing the martyr, Megan?" Why Bracken quietly baited the girl he didn't know, but it had its effect.

"No." Megan's chin was up, her voice cold. "If there is nothing else," her voice could now be heard by those at the table, "I have duties that need my attention."

Megan stood, nodded to those around her, and walked from the room, her bearing resembling that of a queen. It wasn't long before some of the others left as well, but Stephen found Brice standing alone, a fierce frown on his young face.

"Are you ill, my brother?" Stephen asked.

"What is wrong with her?"

"Her?" Stephen replied, although he knew exactly to whom Brice referred.

"Megan." Brice's voice held strong aversion. "How dare she treat Bracken in such a manner."

"Do not be too hard on her, Brice; she reacts out of fear."

"Fear!" Brice scoffed and finally faced his older sibling. "What has she to fear? Certainly not Bracken."

Stephen wisely held his tongue, but he did believe that Bracken was at the core of Megan's fears and thus her animosity toward him was clearly explained. The brothers did not discuss it again, but Stephen wondered when Brice would find that all men had feet of clay, even their beloved Bracken.

Megan had little contact with Bracken or his brothers in the days to follow, and as much as she tried to fight the emotion, despondency was stealing over her. It seemed to Megan that the castle and keep crawled with people and she could find no solitude of any kind. The only place where she found quiet was her room, but after too many hours within those walls, she had begun to feel vaguely suffocated, a feeling which didn't prove to be very restful.

Megan had not been sleeping well. Several times she had awakened in the chair by the fireplace but not remembered getting there. If she was walking in her sleep, what was keeping her from leaving the room? Not having an answer to her question made Megan even more restless. Feeling almost desperate, she made for the fortress gate and freedom. The guards did nothing to block her path, and to her amazement not even Arik seemed to notice.

Once outside the walls Megan walked on and on, some of the tall grasses coming over her knees. The scape surrounding Hawkings Crest was lovely, and Megan felt her heart calming as she took in the trees and lush landscape.

It really is lovely here, Father God, she prayed in her heart. *I thought nothing could match Stone Lake, but Hawkings Crest is like a rich paradise.*

Megan stopped and watched several squirrels at play, knowing they must have been young with the way they gamboled and chased up the trees. Megan's face broke into a brief smile before she continued to pray.

Please help me to find the same peace in my heart as I see in your creation. Father Brent taught me that contentment is my choice, Father God, and I have not been doing a good job. Please fill my heart and life with You so that my situation or circumstances do not matter.

She hiked on for over an hour, praying and praising God,

before sinking down under a tree. The sun sprinkled brightly over her in little patches through the leaves, and it wasn't long before its warmth lulled Megan to sleep.

"Have you seen Lady Megan?"

It was the question on Louisa's lips and then on everyone else's as Megan's absence became apparent. Bracken's face, that of a warrior with a mission, was void of emotional expression, but those who knew him well could detect the concern, the ache to know where she was.

When it became evident that she was not within the castle walls, some of Bracken's knights rode out on horseback, but the rest of the castle folk, including Bracken and his brothers, set off on foot. Megan heard their cries before she regained full consciousness, and when she did waken, she listened in horror to the call of her name.

With a head still muddled with sleep, Megan came to her feet and nearly stumbled out from beneath the trees. She was rushing along the edge of the forest when Bracken, Stephen, and Kendrick suddenly appeared. The towering rage on Bracken's face stopped her in her tracks. She watched as he spoke to Kendrick and then as he and Stephen covered the distance between them.

"Why are you out here?" Bracken's voice was curt.

"I wanted to be alone."

"So you left the safekeeping of the walls?" Bracken's voice betrayed his astonishment, telling Megan that he would never understand.

"Yes. I felt a need for solitude. I never meant to fall asleep."

"You foolish woman!" The words were spat at her. "I have the entire keep looking for you, thinking you abducted or harmed, and here you sleep! Indeed, you are a fool!"

Bracken seemed to be out of words then, or too angry to say

more. He turned on his booted heel and swung away from Megan and his brother. He was ten steps away when Stephen spoke softly.

"You disappoint me, Megan."

She turned hurting eyes to him, wondering from how many she would know rebuke.

"I'd never have guessed you for a woman who would stand mute while someone called you a fool."

Megan stared at him and then at Bracken, who was swiftly moving away. Her brow lowered menacingly before she raised her voice to be heard.

"I am *not* a fool."

Bracken stopped, turned, and stared back at her.

"Were you speaking to me?" he asked as if she had no right.

"Yes. You will not speak to me in such a fashion."

Bracken began to walk back to her so abruptly that Megan started. As he neared, she was reminded of his ire and began to back away. Bracken came right ahead, backing her into a tree and speaking in an angry growl after she bumped her head on the bark.

"What did you say to me?"

Megan swallowed.

"I'm not a fool." The words were whispered this time as green eyes, wide with fear and pleading, stared up at him.

Seeing that fear, Bracken's heart softened within him. When Megan had disappeared, he had been more frightened than ever in his life. He had handled her and the situation poorly, but flowery words were not in him. When he spoke, his voice was slightly less harsh but it was far from congenial.

"It is as you say, you are not a fool. I would ask, however, that in the future you do not leave the keep without informing someone. It is most troublesome to lay out a search."

Megan didn't sense her own trembling until she was alone once again. She stood against the tree for several moments, fighting down the despair she felt rising within. Would she ever find her place here? Would she ever do that which was expected?

Megan left the tree without any answers and was surprised to find Stephen awaiting her. He did not comment on the scene he had witnessed, but offered to escort her back.

"Thank you," Megan told him softly and began to walk slowly, thoughtfully, toward Hawkings Crest. After several yards, she commented.

"I fear I am nothing but an annoyance to Bracken." Megan didn't normally confide in strangers, but although Stephen looked like Bracken, he was a good deal kinder in Megan's eyes, and she felt desperate for someone to talk with.

"That isn't true," Stephen told her. He'd seen with his own eyes what was happening to his brother's heart.

"I fear that it is. I am a stranger here, and I am troubled that it will always be so."

"You have not given yourself sufficient time, Megan," he spoke familiarly to her, truly seeking to help. "Bracken was stern just now, but he does care. He would not have reacted so, had he not been fearful of your harm."

Megan had not looked at it in such a way. His words made her pause and think. The one time her father had spanked her sprang to mind. She had deserved his hand of punishment far more often, but not until she nearly frightened him to death did he strike her.

"Have I lost you?" Stephen's voice was kind.

"I was thinking of what you said and remembering a time when my father punished me severely. I deserved the punishment, but then I often did. This particular time, however, he did so out of fear."

"Were you very bad?" Stephen found himself captivated.

"I was," Megan admitted. "I bribed his young vassal into letting me dress in his clothing during a tournament. I found myself on the jousting field. I was quite nearly killed by a runaway horse." Megan glanced at her companion then and wanted to laugh at his look of horror.

"It's quite true."

"You say your father beat you?"

Megan nodded. "I couldn't sit down for several days."

"What would possess you to do such a thing?" Stephen was still trying to take it in.

"The usual," Megan said softly. "I was trying to gain my mother's attention."

Neither one felt like talking as they passed through the castle gates. Stephen was still amazed at this new insight, and Megan was completely wrapped up with dread over having to face Bracken at the tables that night.

Eleven

THE EVENING MEAL WAS NOT as bad as Megan had anticipated. Brice and Bracken were very quiet, but Stephen was charming, and Megan, feeling as if someone had rescued her, allowed herself to be coaxed into talking.

"So you lived most of your years at the abbey?" he wanted to know.

"Yes. In truth, the abbey feels more like home than Stone Lake."

"What did you do all day?" This came from Aunt Louisa.

"Well," Megan admitted, "when I first arrived I spent all my time running away or planning to run away, but as I began to grow more settled, I was given responsibilities."

"Doing what?" Stephen asked.

"The abbey is run very much like a keep," Megan explained, "only the nuns give everything away. The abbey has a creamery and small byre. The nuns weave, sew, bake, and cook, but nearly all goods are given to charity. I am proficient in all of these things because I worked right along with them. Then when I turned 15 I was allowed to go into the village several times a week to teach some of the children."

"Your father approved of this?" Bracken, who couldn't help himself, wondered aloud. The abbey did not alarm him but time alone in the village was another matter. Thinking he may have angered her, Bracken held his breath as Megan turned, but for once she was not offended by his line of questioning.

"My father had very definite ideas about my upbringing. He believed I would be a more compassionate mistress to my servants if I spent time in the village. I was never in any danger, you understand. Most of the townspeople knew of my parentage. Since it was common knowledge, they never believed we were trying to deceive them, and in truth, after just a short time, it was not something many even thought of."

Bracken couldn't imagine allowing his own daughter to work in the village, but without asking he somehow knew that Vincent's ideas stemmed from his reaction to his wife's personality. Megan was stern with the servants at Hawkings Crest, but she was never cruel. Bracken now saw that Megan was the woman she was because she had been separated from her mother's influence. From what little he'd seen and heard, it would at least appear so.

Had they been alone, Bracken might have questioned Megan further. But now was not the time, and he was left to ruminate on what she had said.

Megan was also left with a certain amount of speculation after Bracken made no comment to her story. Through the evening she pondered whether he agreed with her father or thought him a fool.

Two afternoons later Megan was feeling suffocated again. She knew better than to leave on her own, but she could not find Louisa or Bracken. The day had started well, and she did not want to do anything to spoil it, but she *had* to get out. A basket on her arm, she gained the courtyard and with relief spotted Arik.

"Arik," Megan spoke when she stood before him, having lost all fear of his size and stony face. "Bracken bids me to tell someone when I leave the castle walls." She paused and stared at his expressionless countenance, knowing full well that he had heard her. "I'm going into the fields to pick herbs."

Arik didn't blink, nod his head, or acknowledge her in any way, but after Megan held his eyes for just a moment, she turned away, the basket now swinging from her hand, her bright head shining in the sun.

She wasn't 15 steps outside the castle gate when she sensed with certainty that Arik had followed her. She didn't mind. His presence made her feel secure. Megan found the field she sought and happily sank down into the grasses, the morning sun warm on her back. Within minutes she'd forgotten everything around her. Intent on her task, she neither heard nor saw Bracken's brother approaching.

Returning from a hunting party in the woods, Brice had just sent his game ahead to the castle when he spotted Megan in the field. Her hair was a halo of red, a delight to any eye, but Brice frowned. Just days ago the entire castle had searched for her, and now here she sat alone outside the walls. Brice had covered half the distance when he spotted Arik.

He drew up short and felt shamed for his angry thoughts. He knew he was too hard on the girl. They were of the same age and would probably get along well, but Brice loved his brother and Megan's lack of effort in the relationship infuriated him.

He walked on again, but slower, all anger draining from him. He and Stephen would be going home in a few days, and his mother would wish to know how he and Megan got along. Brice was prideful enough to want to report to his mother that he'd done everything within his power to befriend her, not that he believed it would do much good.

"Good morning, Megan," Brice spoke when he was just five yards away.

"Oh," Megan's hand came up. "I didn't hear you, Brice."

He was in front of her now and sank to his knees some six feet away. "I didn't mean to startle you."

Megan shook her head and smiled slightly, her eyes on Brice for just an instant before she turned them back to her hands. She was most aware of his feelings toward her.

"'Twas not your fault," she said graciously. "I was so focused on my work, I didn't hear a thing."

Brice watched her work a moment. "What is that?"

"Sorrel. It's wonderful in soup."

Brice watched her a moment more.

"Did you not care to send one of the kitchen maids for this work?" It was meant to be a dig, but Megan didn't take it as such. Brice watched her look off into the distance and smile.

"This isn't work, Brice. I love it out here. I love the way the air is perfumed with the aroma of pine and wildflowers, and I love the way the wind moves the trees." Megan let her gaze roam until it landed back on Brice. His look embarrassed her though, and she swiftly dropped her eyes.

"I don't know why I prattle on so, Brice. I'm sorry."

Brice was overcome with shame. She had openly shared with him and he had made her feel a fool. His mind raced for a safe subject.

"My mother uses herbs for healing." Brice blurted the words, but Megan did not seem to notice.

"Oh, how I would love to speak with her. I know of only a few. Most of these are for the kitchen."

"She'll be here for the wedding."

Stark fear covered Megan's face for just an instant, but she quickly schooled her features.

"Yes, the wedding. I look forward to meeting her." Megan's voice told Brice that he had shaken her. Why? What could she possibly fear? Brice was actually on the verge of asking her when he spotted Bracken approaching.

"Bracken comes," Brice casually announced, and then watched in amazement at the change that came over Megan.

"Oh, I'm a mess," she mumbled as she swiftly dusted her

hands and came so awkwardly to her feet that she stumbled and fell back down. Brice was reaching to help her, but she regained her balance on her own and managed to put her chin in the air just before Bracken stopped in front of her.

"Aunt Louisa is looking everywhere for you," he said without preamble.

"I could not find her," Megan answered with quiet dignity.

"You could have told me."

"I could not locate you, either."

"So you just came anyway?"

"No. I told Arik."

"But he came with you!"

Megan's hands moved at her side in defeat. All fight was draining from her. Would she ever do what was right? This was as bad as living with her mother; worse, because there was no convent to return to. The thought made Megan tremble all over.

"I did as you asked, Bracken. I did not tell Arik to join me. I never thought—"

"That seems to be your problem," he cut her off. "You don't think of anyone but yourself."

Megan's eyes flashed with fury. That statement had been completely unfair. Megan turned from Bracken and lifted her basket. She left the men without word, her back straight, the basket handle over one arm. Megan had not gone ten yards when Arik moved to follow her. Bracken watched their progress for just an instant before transferring his gaze to the distance.

He was barely aware of his brother, so when he did look at Brice it made the younger man's stunned face even harder to bear.

"She's afraid of you," Brice accused, and the pain in his voice surprised Bracken. "Stephen said as much, but I didn't believe him. 'Tis true. She's terrified of you. She trembled all over."

Bracken had seen the trembling as well, but opened his mouth anyway to try to justify himself. Brice would allow no such thing; he cut him off with a downward slash of his hand.

"Don't speak to me right now, Bracken. I can't bear it. Mother is going to wish to know of your happiness and that of Megan, and I hate," Brice spat the word, "to tell her what I've observed."

Brice swung away, not toward the keep but back toward the woods. He still had his crossbow with him, and Bracken let him go, knowing he would be safe enough. Bracken took himself back to the keep. The noon meal would be served soon, and when they had eaten he would speak with Megan. He wasn't entirely certain what he would say, but Brice had been correct—he did frighten her.

Bracken contemplated the reason he teased and antagonized her and could only come up with one lame answer. He desired to see some emotion on her face, even a scowl, rather than the cold, expressionless eyes she often turned to him.

Knowing this did not excuse his behavior; nevertheless, it helped him to know what he should do, and that was apologize. If the opportunity presented itself, he would do so over the meal; if not, he would ask Megan to join him in the war room. He was not experienced in court manners or taken to gently wooing ladies, but he *could* tell Megan he was sorry for his actions because he sincerely was.

Bracken, so ready with his plan, fought disappointment when Megan failed to join him at the table. Indeed she did not make an appearance downstairs at all.

Megan, you can't hide in here all day, the small redhead said to herself. But even though her stomach growled, she made no move toward the door. If only she didn't have to face Bracken. She felt as if she must slip into armor every time she met the man, and right now she was too weary to fight.

Megan scowled when her stomach sounded again. She had just decided then and there to head down to the great hall when someone knocked on her door. Thinking it to be Louisa, Megan walked calmly toward the closed portal. She stood in stunned silence when she saw Bracken on the other side.

"May I speak with you, Megan?"

"Yes," she answered, and was about to move into the hall when Bracken's attention suddenly moved beyond her.

Without a word he stepped toward her. Megan was forced to retreat, but Bracken took little notice. He came fully into her bedchamber and just stared. The small room had been transformed. Tapestries and hangings were draped all over the walls. Carpets, thick and richly colored, covered the floor. The counterpane on her bed was a myriad of colors as well.

"You spoke the truth to me. You truly did not wish to leave this room."

"I am more than content in here." Megan's voice was soft.

Bracken came and stood before her now. He looked down into her face and thought her skin looked like that of a child's.

"I regret the way I treated you outside the wall today."

Megan was so surprised and relieved she hardly knew what to say, but she did manage a small "Thank you, Bracken."

He loved it when she left the "Lord" off his name, and for the first time he wished to hold her. She was often so stiff and prickly, but standing before him as she was now, her eyes soft and somehow vulnerable, he longed to take her into his arms.

Of their own volition, his eyes dropped to her lips. He was always amazed at their color. He knew that some women used tint to redden their lips, but looking at Megan's he knew that the dark, dusky red he was seeing was all her own.

Megan noticed his look, but did not understand it. She was even more naive about men than Bracken was about women. And the fact that she did not find herself comely always played a part. After just a few seconds under Bracken's scrutiny, Megan began to assume something was wrong with her appearance. Her mouth would have swung open in surprise had she understood that Bracken found her so lovely he wanted to kiss her.

Fortunately for both of them, Megan's stomach growled and broke the spell. Her manner became all at once brisk as Bracken's presence in her room reminded her of something that had been on her mind. She turned away from him, slightly embarrassed and asked, "Bracken, are you barring my door at night?"

"No," Bracken answered cautiously. "Why do you ask?"

"I think I must be walking in my sleep, because I have awakened occasionally in the chair by the fire. If that is true, I can't think what is keeping me inside—unless the door has been barred from without."

"Arik sleeps outside your door at night," Bracken told her softly.

Megan turned to face him. "Arik knows that I walk in my sleep?"

Bracken nodded, his eyes studying her face, and Megan suddenly remembered the night she woke in the great room.

"How long?" Megan asked, referring to Arik's sleeping arrangement.

"Since the first night after your father left."

Megan took a deep breath. "And what of the time after we are wed? Will Arik continue to lie outside the door and give the castle folk even more reason for gossip?" Megan was not angry, just chagrined.

"I have given great thought to that," Bracken told her. "I think we will bar your door. That way you'll be forced to exit through my room."

"And what good will that do?" Megan genuinely wished to know.

"I am a very light sleeper, Megan, and even if you did get past me, Lyndon would inform me."

Megan nodded. It put a woman in a very vulnerable position to be wandering through a strange castle in her sleep, but try as she might to calm herself before slumber, she was still up and about. Maybe with time her heart would settle in this new place.

"We have no wish to make sport of you, Megan." Bracken

thought he needed to explain, and indeed, Megan was comforted by his words, enough to let the matter drop with a simple thank you.

"Have you eaten?" Bracken asked then, and Megan was again warmed by his sudden show of concern. She shook her head.

"Then come, Megan. Come below and eat."

He offered his arm, and Megan took it. She did so praying that this new, kinder relationship would swiftly become the standard.

BRICE WAS STANDING ON THE WALL of the keep, his eyes taking in the countryside, when he realized Bracken's presence beside him. A glance to his side told him Bracken's own eyes were also on the scape, but after a moment, he spoke.

"Stephen and I may look alike, Brice, but make no mistake, it is Stephen who is well practiced with the words ladies love."

Brice nodded, his gaze now back over the land as he answered boldly. "You inherited Hawkings Crest and father's title when you were still a young man. Your responsibility has been heavy; Stephen's not near as much at White Hall. But that is still no excuse.

"Chivalry is dying all over England, but every time I see evidence of this fact, I think with pride, 'Never Bracken. Bracken is a knight of highest honor, never him.'

"But yesterday I was shamed. I have seen with my own eyes that Megan's fear is not of all men, but of you, and for this there is no excuse. As I watched her tremble I thought of how I would feel if a man treated Danella or Kristine in such a way. I would want to run him through with my sword."

Brice finally looked at Bracken and found the older man watching him. Bracken's pride was taking a beating, but Brice was correct. Bracken was supposed to be an example to his brother, and instead he'd incurred his rancor.

There weren't many men from whom Bracken would take such words, but his brothers were beyond value to him, and for this, Bracken took heed.

"You are right, Brice," he told him sincerely. "I have now committed myself to dealing more gently with Megan in the future, but there are times when I know not what to do with the woman."

Bracken's chagrined voice brought a smile to Brice's face. He thumped his older brother on the chest.

"She does have a mind of her own."

"Is that what you call it?" Bracken's tone was now dry.

"She'll surely match you wit for wit." Brice's voice was almost proud, a startling turn about from just days previous, but Bracken's brows rose as though Brice's own words proved his case. Brice accurately read his thoughts.

"Come now, Bracken. You surely want more than a pretty face. Even when you are tempted to lock Megan in her room, you'll have to admit that you do not want it any other way."

Bracken stared at his younger sibling. It was true. He didn't want a decoration for his castle, but a woman who could think and do for herself. Bracken felt a new sort of peace with this realization, a peace that would have been destroyed had he been able to see Megan right then.

"What is this entry?"

Bracken's steward, Barton, whose face was starting to resemble a radish, stared at Megan, whose own countenance was a study in tranquillity.

"It's for wheat."

"Wheat? For what purpose?"

Barton had to bite his tongue to keep from telling Megan to mind her own business. Instead, he said with false humility,

"Why, food for the castle folk, my lady."

"It costs this much?"

"Yes, my lady."

Megan studied the small man's face. He wasn't much taller than Megan and very thin, and from Megan's few encounters with him, she had also tagged him a liar. Indeed, Megan would have wagered her life on the fact.

"And how about this?" Megan pointed to another entry, and Barton silently cursed this woman who had been raised in a convent and taught to read.

"Miscellaneous."

Megan's eyes narrowed, but her voice was still serene. "Twenty pounds of miscellaneous?"

Barton's look was that of a child's, but Megan was not taken in.

"Before the sun sets, I wish to see an itemized listing of what you consider to be miscellaneous."

"Yes, my lady," Barton spoke from behind gritted teeth.

Megan turned away from him then, the record book still in her hand.

"But, my lady," Barton called to her, his voice in a panic. "I need the records book."

Megan stopped and stared at the man. "If the items I seek are recorded in the book, then why did you list them under miscellaneous?"

Barton was so angry that he prayed for Megan's death. Megan held his gaze before giving final orders and leaving.

"I am not through with the book, so I will keep it, and I will expect that list today."

"Bracken, may I speak with you?"

Bracken, so delighted that she had sought him out, rose from his chair in the war room with a smile. The smile faltered when she drew close enough for him to see the records book.

"Bracken," Megan began immediately, "I do not think your steward is being honest with you."

"Megan," Bracken replied, remembering what he'd told Brice and working to keep his voice patient, "you really don't need to disturb yourself with such details. Barton is more than capable—"

"Of stealing you blind," Megan cut him off. "Look at this entry for yard and cloth. My mother couldn't spend that amount in five years."

Bracken sighed, but did not reply. He was always made very comfortable within the walls of his castle and gave little regard as to how that came to be. His greater interest was his training fields and archery range, but he did not think it wise to say this to Megan.

"Can't you see it?" She persisted.

"In truth, Megan, the account books have never been that important to me. Show me the exact place."

Megan pointed with one small digit and Bracken bent low to inspect the entry. He turned his head after a moment to find Megan staring, their faces very close together.

"Don't you check these books periodically, Bracken?"

"No," he told her, feeling preoccupied with her nearness and the smell of her hair. He was a knight, trained in self-control, so none of his emotions showed on his face.

"What about Aunt Louisa?" Megan brought him back to the matter at hand.

"She can't read."

Megan gazed absentmindedly into his dark eyes and then off into the distance, totally preoccupied with the castle accounts.

"There are too many inconsistencies," Megan muttered, her mind still going over the pages of the book.

"Barton's been with Hawkings Crest for years. He was my father's steward."

"Could your father read?"

"No," Bracken admitted, and Megan's brows rose. She obviously believed she'd made her point.

Bracken held onto his control with an effort. He knew that she needed to have a hand in the running of this castle, but why must she turn things into utter chaos? Bracken had no desire to fight with her, and so chose to distract himself by studying the loveliness of her face.

Megan saw instantly that she had lost him, but it was beyond her as to what he might be thinking. She found him studying her mouth once again and wondered if she had food on her lips from lunch. A swift lick with her tongue told her nothing was there, and she felt even more confusion when Bracken's eyes narrowed. Megan thought he might be growing angry, but when he spoke his voice was soft.

"Just handle it, Megan," Bracken told her, thinking he had to get away. Megan watched in puzzlement as he turned abruptly and moved toward the door.

"So I may dismiss Barton?"

Bracken turned back at the door and told her simply, "No, you may not."

"Then how am I to—"

Bracken's raised hand forestalled her. He truly did not wish to fight, but neither could he remain.

"Just do your best, Megan."

The small redhead stood still long after the portal closed. What in the world was she to do with the man? He was kinder this time than ever before, but he clearly couldn't wait to be away from her. Megan was still standing in confusion when Aunt Louisa sought her out.

"Megan, there you are. Is everything all right?"

"I don't know," Megan admitted, her eyes now on the older woman.

"You spoke with Bracken?"

"Yes, and he was kind, but he looked at me so oddly."

"Oh?" Louisa's interest was piqued. "How so?"

"He stared at my mouth as though something were amiss. It's not the first time, either. And then he seemed in a great hurry to be away."

Louisa could hardly believe such innocence, but she knew it to be all too real. She debated telling Megan what Bracken's actions meant but changed her mind. He was going to have to win this woman on his own. Louisa had enjoyed a long talk with Brice and quite agreed with him. It was true that court manners came easier to Stephen, but Brice was right in saying Bracken had no excuse; it was his duty to do all he could to win Megan's heart.

"What am I to do?"

"Do not let it worry you, dear. Men can, at times, be complex creatures. I'm sure there was nothing wrong."

Megan nodded. She might have questioned Louisa, but in truth she didn't even know what to ask. Would it be easier when Bracken and she were husband and wife? Megan could only hope so. The reality of their wedding seemed to press in on her with more insistence every day.

Megan walked into the great hall three days later and knew instantly that something was amiss. There had been two groups of servants speaking quietly among themselves as they worked, but after spotting Megan, all seven women closed their mouths and transferred their gazes to the floor.

Megan would normally have given this little thought, but it had been happening all day. By evening she was fed up.

"Helga," she spoke to her personal maid, the first woman to have helped her at Hawkings Crest. "What is going on?"

"Going on, my lady?" Helga's eyes were wide with apprehension, and Megan knew she had come to the right woman.

"Yes," she replied, her voice changing to that of gentle persuasion. "It seems that there is news afoot—news that concerns me. I would only wish to hear of it."

Helga relaxed. She should have known her lady would just desire to understand. *After all,* Helga reminded herself, *it is just gossip. Lady Megan would surely not take heed.*

"Helga?" Megan brought her back to the matter.

"There are rumors, my lady, that Lord Bracken has gone to see Black Francesca." Helga barely kept herself from smiling. She knew her lady would laugh any minute at the joke of it all, and then she would be free to join her.

"Black Francesca?" Megan had gone utterly still.

"Yes, my lady." Helga became concerned for the first time. "All servants gossip, and those at Hawkings Crest are no different."

Megan nodded, her face still serene but her eyes cold. "I won't be turning in just now, Helga. I'll send for you later."

Helga stood and wrung her hands after Megan left. If the look in her eyes had been any indication, Lord Bracken would be gaining a visit, and soon.

"Did you see her?" Megan asked the moment she stepped into the war room, completely ignoring the men surrounding Bracken.

"See who, Megan?" Bracken asked, but he knew the answer.

"Have you been to visit Black Francesca?"

Bracken was very aware of his men. He knew they would have exited, but Megan stood between the group and the door, arms akimbo, her eyes flashing with rage.

Bracken wanted a wife and a lady to keep his home, but he was not going to let anyone monitor his every move. As much as he cared for Megan and truly thought he was coming to love her, he would not let her rule his life.

"Am I to check with you, Megan, before going to the village?" Bracken's voice said that her answer was only of mild interest to him.

"You do not answer my question, so I must assume you are guilty."

"Guilty?" Bracken's chuckle was sincere. "Nay, Megan. I have been to see Francesca, but no guilt rests on my head."

Megan's face flushed with temper. She walked until she stood before Bracken, her eyes so angry and hurt that Bracken had to harden his heart to bear it. When she moved, the men filed out so that when she spoke again they were alone.

"I will not marry you."

Bracken didn't so much as lift a brow. "We will wed, Megan," he spoke with surety.

"Never," she hissed. "I have saved myself for this time, but to you it is no worthy thing. I will not marry a man who would take our vows so lightly."

Bracken shook his head, thinking that if Megan didn't find her place she would be miserable.

"We will wed, Megan," was all he said.

Megan shook her head vehemently, causing red curls to swirl around her shoulders. "I will not stay here, and I will certainly not be joined to you." There was such loathing in her voice that Bracken grew angry.

"Stop this childishness, Megan. I tell you we will be wed."

Megan's laughter was harsh. "I am no child, Bracken, but a woman capable beyond your imagination. It is too bad that you will never understand all that you have lost."

On this cryptic statement Megan spun and headed to the door. Bracken didn't move, but his fist clenched in frustration. It had seemed for a few days that things were softening between them, but right now those days seemed weeks past. As hard as that was to bear, Bracken greatest hurt was that Megan would think him capable of such an act in the first place.

Thirteen

BY MIDMORNING OF THE FOLLOWING DAY, Megan was miles away from Hawkings Crest. She had learned through her escapes from the abbey that there was no time like the present, and so she had left less than an hour after her confrontation with Bracken. She had left Helga with the strictest of orders for the night, and even the next few days, but Megan sincerely doubted that anyone would truly miss her, at least not for a time.

It had not been all that difficult to escape the castle walls, but that would not have been the case if she had waited until after dark or until the following morning to leave.

Her night had been a long one. Megan was feeling the effects now, but she trudged on just the same. Sometime before dawn she had lain down and slept, but it was nothing whatsoever like a full night in her own bed. She stopped now and tried to gauge her whereabouts but found she was a bit disoriented.

The night her men were attacked suddenly flashed through her mind, but oddly enough she did not feel fearful. In many ways Megan felt safer on her own than she had with her guard; she was free to hide in caves or climb trees for protection. Over the years she had encountered the occasional boar or other fierce creature, but nothing that ever gave her more trouble than she could handle.

As the sun rose high in the sky, Megan's stomach roared. She found shade at that point and pulled some bread and cheese from the sack on her back. She ate ravenously and then searched for a stream. It took longer than she would have liked and put her somewhat out of the way, but the opportunity to slacken her thirst was worth every step.

Megan was just returning to the road when she spotted the peddlers. It took less than a heartbeat's time to see that it was Elias and his band—the same men who had rescued her weeks before. Megan debated stepping out into the road and asking for help, but before she could decide, they stopped. Megan froze in order to listen and watch from her place in the trees.

"What is it, Elias?" one man asked.

The bearded peddler didn't answer. His gaze swept the trees opposite Megan before he turned and seemed to stare right at her.

"Who's there?" Elias called.

Megan didn't answer.

"Come out," he continued kindly. "We won't harm you."

Megan debated only a moment more before going into action. She drew her ragged cape up over her head, made sure the bag of food on her back was in the proper "hump" position, bent over her walking stick, and moved slowly from the trees.

"It's an old humpback woman," Megan heard one say as she squinted up at them. Her mouth turned back into a snarl that beautifully portrayed the dark beans she'd pushed over two teeth. They gave the impression of teeth missing as well as darkening her saliva, making it look as if her whole mouth were rotted.

"I ain't an old woman," Megan spat, putting on her best cockney tone and glaring at the men. "Whatcha sellin'?"

"Are you hoping to buy?" This came from Elias, and Megan could hear the amusement in his tone.

"I ain't got no coin," she snorted.

"Where are you headed?" another man questioned.

"The abbey at Stone Lake, you nosy scoundrel. Can't a lady

have no privacy?" Megan gave a loud cackle at her own joke, and the men joined in.

"We're not going as far as Stone Lake, but we're going to The Crossings. Come," Elias spoke, "ride awhile."

Megan scowled at them. Her feet did hurt.

"I don't care to be badgered with talk for miles," she growled at them, but she was already moving in a painful gait to the wagon. Most of the men made no effort to hide their amusement, but Megan only limped her way to the back and allowed one of them to take her upper arm and help her aboard.

"Well, you're not starved, are ya?" he said, and Megan pulled her arm away.

"Don't be given me none o' your cheek. I'll take myself right back down, and you'll be a missin' the pleasure o' my company."

This brought a round of laughter from the men, but the horse was prodded into motion and they proceeded down the road. Megan told herself to say alert, but it wasn't possible. The ride was hot, dusty, and bumpy, and after very little sleep the night before, she couldn't stay awake. Within the hour her head was draped over a bag of rags while sleep wandered in and out.

They didn't make The Crossings by nightfall, but that was just as well for Megan. She had never intended to go that far. The Crossings was on the way to Stone Lake, but it was faster to go through the woods in order to gain the abbey.

The peddlers had paid her little heed throughout the journey, but when they camped that night, she was made welcome at their fire and to their food. No one was the wiser as to her identity until Megan shuffled off into the woods for privacy. Elias, whose hearing was as keen as that of a fox, heard her shuffling gait turn to easy steps when she found the darkness of the trees.

He waited until she returned and they both had food before he approached. It was the first time he had come close to her. His suspicions were confirmed immediately, but that didn't stop the amazement at his findings.

Megan didn't really mind his sitting near her but simply

turned her face into the shadows, the hood still hiding her face, and tried to chew with her back teeth only.

"I must say, my lady," Elias began, his voice almost too soft to hear. "You're one of the best I've ever seen."

Megan froze and then turned to look at him.

"How did you know?" The accent was gone; her voice was hushed.

"Your walk in the woods alerted me, and then if I may say so, my lady, there is no disguising the smell of your hair."

Megan transferred her gaze to the woods, and Elias stared at her profile. It was incredible. He couldn't see it now, but he remembered the gray cast to her skin when she'd come from the woods. That, along with the rotted teeth, rat's nest hair and hump on her back, caused Elias not to give her a second thought, but now, since he knew how she normally looked, this transformation was astonishing to the man.

"Do the others know?" Megan asked suddenly.

"I don't think so."

"And what," Megan went on, her voice still hushed, "will you tell the riders who overtake you? Have you seen the red-haired maid, whose father is lord of Stone Lake Castle and whose betrothed lives within the wall of Hawkings Crest?"

"I have seen no such woman," Elias told her as he transferred his gaze to the fire. "We gave an old humpback woman a ride, nothing more."

He heard Megan's sigh of relief and would have given up half his cart to know why she ran. But this was not his place. A peddler did not ask a lady, no matter how she was dressed, where she was going and why.

"Thank you, Elias," Megan whispered just before one of the men joined them.

Megan turned away, thinking she would have liked to tell him that she hoped he would trade at Hawkings Crest often, but then she reminded herself that she would not be there and wondered over the sadness that filled her on such a thought.

The night was uneventful, and early in the morning Megan

thanked the men, made them laugh, and parted from the group. She had a friend in the forest who took her the rest of the way on horseback, and she was at the abbey just hours later.

The food on Bracken's trencher was a delight to the senses, but he gave little notice. His eyes were on the staircase as he anticipated Megan's arrival with every breath, but she did not appear. It had been 48 hours since their quarrel, and he had not seen her once. He felt this pouting was ridiculous, but he was not going to search her out and say so. It was apparent to him that Megan needed to do a little growing up, and he refused to coddle her in this situation.

"Will you go to her, Bracken?"

"No." He turned then to look at his aunt. He picked up a piece of meat and chewed silently.

"What if she really isn't feeling well?"

Bracken snorted. "Is that what she is telling you?"

"Well, Helga is."

Bracken stared at her. "You mean you haven't seen Megan?"

"No," Louisa admitted. "Helga's been taking her food, and when I've gone to the door she says that Megan has asked not to be disturbed."

Bracken shook his head in disgust. It was worse than he feared. This was not brooding, but an out-and-out sulk, and Bracken could think of nothing more aggravating. She was clearly taking her childish tantrum out on the whole castle.

Bracken suddenly dug into his food. Watching him, Louisa knew the reason. She would have put money on the fact that he was going to confront Megan as soon as he'd had his fill.

Not five minutes after Bracken was done with the meal, he nodded to the family members at the table and made for the stairs. Helga, sitting inside Megan's bedchamber and trying not to be nervous, jumped at his knock.

"Lord Bracken," she said respectfully, opening the door just enough to peek out.

"I wish to see Lady Megan," Bracken stated.

Helga nervously cleared her throat. It was one thing to tell Lady Louisa that Lady Megan was ill and wished to see no one, but Lord Bracken was another matter.

"Is there some problem?" Bracken's voice was not loud or even overly stern, but Helga couldn't take it.

"I'm sorry, my lord," she cried. "I was just doing as I was told."

It took a moment for Bracken to comprehend the full import of her words, and Helga scrambled away just in time as he reached to push the door open wide. Angry, disbelieving eyes took in the perfectly made-up bed, the wallhangings and the cold fireplace. All was intact, telling him Megan had traveled light. The room felt as lifeless as a tomb.

Bracken turned to Helga then, who was white-faced with fright, and he saw in an instant that he could not place Megan's foolhardiness on this servant. As she said, she was doing as commanded. Bracken came to this resolve in a split second and now spoke like a calm warrior going into battle.

"How long has she been gone?"

"Two days, my lord."

Bracken nodded, looking preoccupied.

"The morning after we quarreled no doubt." The words were said more to himself than anyone, but Helga answered anyhow.

"No, my lord. She left right away."

Bracken frowned. "You mean that very night?"

"Yes, my lord."

"She's been gone 48 hours then." Bracken was utterly aghast, and fearful for the first time.

"Yes, my lord," Helga said unnecessarily.

"Did she say where she was headed?"

"No, my lord, I swear, she didn't say."

Bracken stayed within the chamber only a moment more before turning and striding out the door and down the main stairs. He was not a man to lose his head, but he was halfway to the stables before he realized it was much too dark to search that night.

"What is it, Bracken?" Brice had followed him without.

Bracken sighed. "Megan has left."

"The castle?"

"Yes."

"Alone?"

"Yes, and it's too dark to search tonight."

"You mean she's left no word of her whereabouts?" Brice was feeling more amazed and frightened by the second.

"No, but I'm certain she headed home. I don't think she ever wanted to leave there—she implied as much—so I'm sure she's made for Stone Lake."

"I'll go with you, Bracken." This came from Louisa, who had just joined the men.

"You knew she was gone?" Bracken frowned.

"No, but when you gained the great hall in such a hurry, I went to Helga myself. I take it we leave in the morning?"

"That is my plan, Aunt Lou, but I must have you remain here."

"But Bracken," the older woman's face was distressed, "when you return she will need an escort."

Bracken couldn't stop his snort of disgust. "She has no doubt traveled all the way to Stone Lake without a single thought for propriety; an escort won't matter now."

Bracken finally looked at Louisa in the gathering dusk. Her hurt face reminded him of his tone. With hands gently on her upper arms, he spoke again.

"In truth, Aunt Lou, we will be riding hard. I would like you to come along, but I do not wish to put you through that."

"But you will bring her back?"

"Have no doubt of it. Megan has not resigned herself to this marriage, but King Henry ordered it and her father did the choosing. Megan is mine, and I will return her to Hawkings Crest."

Nearly an hour later Bracken stood in the war room waiting for his knights to arrive. He had hardly moved from his place by the fire, his thoughts deep on the mistakes he'd made as well as the anger he felt that Megan would pull such a senseless escapade.

If she were in the room at that moment he would be strongly tempted to upend her over his knee. The sight of her, hair ablaze and eyes flashing, standing in that very room while she confronted him over Black Francesca suddenly swam before his mind's eye. What would a group of men do if they found a maid so lovely alone in the forest? Bracken's heart clenched at the thought, even as anger told him she should have known better.

The door opened suddenly, and Bracken turned. It was Stephen and he was alone. He spoke as he came forward, his look serious but his tone light.

"I understand that your dove has flown."

Bracken snorted in offense and turned from the fire, his gaze fierce.

"Do not be deceived, Stephen. Megan is no dove, but a red hawk with talons to gouge a man!"

"Be that as it may, Bracken," Stephen went on smoothly, "you'll not win the girl's heart with such words."

"I'm not the least bit interested in her heart," Bracken stated untruthfully, his voice still harsh.

"Of course you're not," Stephen said patronizingly. "That is why you've already gone to bed without a single worry. You'll sleep late in the morning and ride out when you feel like it to fetch her back."

Bracken let out a great sigh, his anger deserting him in a rush. His hand went to the back of his neck, and he stared at Stephen in torment.

"Why did you not explain to her about Black Francesca, Bracken?" Stephen's voice was gentle.

"It was a mistake," Bracken admitted. "I never dreamed she would flee. When I think of where she could be, I—" Bracken couldn't go on.

"We'll find her." Stephen soothed.

"You'll ride with me?"

"Of course."

"I'll bring her back, Stephen." Bracken repeated himself for the second time that evening, needing to convince himself more than anyone.

"I know you will, but you mustn't plan on dragging her by the hair. Court her, Bracken. Woo her until it would never occur to her to live any other place than Hawkings Crest."

Bracken would have loved to ask Stephen just how he should go about doing that, but they were joined by the other men. As Bracken's men gathered around him, all talk turned to plans for leaving in the morning. He wouldn't think of Stephen's words again for many hours, and when he did, Stephen would not be there to aid him.

Fourteen

THE REVEREND MOTHER SMOOTHED Megan's hair from her forehead and wrestled with her own feelings. She could never tell this dear girl that she must not come to them at the abbey, but neither could she sanction Megan's running from circumstances she didn't like or agree with. Bracken's actions were sorrowful, but Megan, from what the Reverend Mother could see, had little choice but to stay and make the best of things.

Megan was such a mixture of woman and little girl. At the moment she sat on the floor, her head resting on the older woman's knee, much the way she'd done as a child. One moment she was a woman capable and strong; the next she was a child, needing to be embraced and comforted. The Reverend Mother knew Bracken to be a man of few years, 20-odd, she was sure. Would he ever understand that at times Megan needed a tender father figure, since so many of her childhood years she'd been without one?

"Reverend Mother," a nun spoke as she came in the door then. She stopped upon seeing Megan. "I'm sorry, Reverend Mother, I forgot to knock."

"It's all right, Sister Blanche. What did you need?"

"Sister Mary Margaret is supposed to go to the village today, but she is not feeling well. Whom would you like me to send?"

"Please, send me." Megan's voice came softly from the Reverend Mother's lap. They had already talked for hours, and although there was more to be said the older woman wondered if maybe it wasn't best to let things lie for the present.

"Please," Megan begged again, seeing the Reverend Mother's indecision. The abbess sighed and looked down into Megan's face.

"All right." The older woman found the words easy to say after seeing the yearning in Megan's eyes.

Megan rose and kissed her. So pleased was she that she could return to the village that she nearly skipped from the room, her heart lighter than it had been in days. Just 20 minutes later she was in comfortable abbey clothes and walking down the main street of Stone Lake village.

She was early for lessons with the children, so she sauntered along until a familiar voice called to her from among the village smiths.

"Well, now, if it isn't little Meggie."

"Hello, Mr. Black," Megan said with a wide smile.

"Where 'o ya been keepin' yourself?"

"Oh, here and there," Megan told him with a grin.

"Going to teach the children today?"

"Yes. Tell Evan and Nigel to be there."

"A'll send 'em on."

Megan continued on her way, stopping to inspect Mrs. Murch's yard and even going so far as to tug a few weeds from her vegetables.

The work was light, and she could hear Mrs. Murch through the window. The old woman was snoring in a chair by the fire. Megan worked as soundlessly as she could, making her way to the rear of the small hut. She straightened when she heard footsteps behind her and turned to find William approaching. His look was one of a man in a trance, and Megan sighed very gently.

"Megan," William breathed, his eyes drinking in the sight of her. "You've come back to me."

"Oh, William," Megan said with a small shake of her head.

It was enough to draw William from his dreamy state, and he smiled in a way that Megan loved, wide-mouthed and boyish. A few years older, he was the closest thing she'd ever had to a friend. It had never occurred to her to fall in love with him, and even though she never made any bones about the fact that they could never marry, he still persisted.

"Are you married?"

"No."

"Good. Did you run from him?"

"Yes."

"Good," he said again, nodding with satisfaction and not caring for the reason as long as she wasn't hurt.

"Are you well?" he asked now.

"Yes, and you can end this inquisition."

"Ah, Meg, I love those big words you like to use on a simple farmboy like myself."

"Well, don't get too comfortable with them. I'm sure I won't be staying long."

"Oh, Meg." He was genuinely distressed now. "Why must you go away again? I've pined for you till I thought I would die."

"William, William, what am I going to do with you?"

"I'd take a kiss," he replied before he thought and watched Megan's eyes flash with temper.

"Do not speak to me in such a way, William Clayborne, or I'll slap your handsome face until your ears ring in your head!"

His look was very contrite, and Megan softened.

"How is Rose?"

William hung his head. "She's well. She misses you, although she can't think why. Says she has me for the first time ever."

"And well she should," Megan returned tenderly.

William's head came up.

"I care for her, Meg, you know I do," was all he could say before he simply stood still and gazed at her.

It had long been a thorn between them: Rose loving William

and William loving Megan and Megan wishing she never had to marry at all. Amazingly enough, there had never been any hard feelings between Rose and Megan. Rose adored Megan, and it didn't matter in the least that William was in love with her. Rose believed that William would love her someday and make her his wife.

Indeed, Megan had secretly hoped that such a thing would happen after she'd gone. Of course, she hadn't been away all that long, and now here she was again, making William's heart yearn for her. Megan wished she'd thought of that before asking to come and teach.

"I must go, William," she told him now.

"When will I see you?" He asked as he fell into step beside her.

"You won't. I'm sure my father will come for me any day, and I don't know where I'll be after that. I'm almost certain, that I won't be at the abbey."

"Ah, Meg—" he began.

"Give Rose my love," Megan interrupted, cutting him off.

"You could give me your love." It was said so softly that Megan almost missed it. She stopped and turned, tears of helplessness pooling in her eyes.

"No, William, I couldn't. I'm sure to be in enough trouble with Father as it is. You have always known how I feel. You would make any maid the finest of mates, but I can't be that girl. I'm not for you, William."

William stared at her with regret. She was the most wonderful woman he'd ever known, full of fun and caring and willing to give of herself without complaint or thought of payback. She was so lovely that he wanted nothing more than to cherish her for the rest of his days. In truth Rose, was just as lovely, probably more so in a technical sense with her blue-black hair and tall, shapely body, but it was to Megan that he had lost his heart.

"Will I truly not see you again?" William pushed the words past his tight throat.

"I should think not. I'm glad we had a few minutes, though. Go with God, William."

With that she was gone. William stood, frustration filling him. He had never been able to touch her, not even so much as to hold her hand. It wasn't fair; by all that was righteous, it wasn't fair.

"Bracken!" Vincent spoke with obvious pleasure as he gained the great hall and saw his guests. "Come in; rest yourselves. I'll see that refreshment is brought."

Vincent spoke to a servant, giving Bracken a chance to adjust to this exuberant welcome.

"This must be your brother," Vincent went on, referring to Stephen after he returned his attention to his guests.

"Yes, this is Stephen, and this is my other brother, Brice. You also know my knights, Lyndon and Kendrick."

"Yes, of course. You're all looking well. What brings you to Stone Lake?"

All the men froze, and Bracken frowned. "Why, to see Megan," he said hesitantly.

"Megan?" Vincent's brows rose with curiosity, but he did not seem alarmed.

"Yes. She is here, isn't she?"

"No." Vincent replied calmly.

"You mean you haven't seen her at all?" Bracken's heart now pounded with fear.

"No, I haven't. Maybe if you tell me why she left Hawkings Crest, I'll be able to tell you where she's gone."

"We argued," Bracken said briefly.

Vincent nodded, not at all surprised. "Then she'll be at the abbey," he said easily.

Bracken stood immediately, and his men followed suit. "Thank you, sir. We'll ride—"

"Sit down, Bracken, sit down," Vincent cut him off. "It's late enough in the day that your appearance at the abbey will not be welcome."

"But what if she's not there? We must leave here at daybreak to continue the search."

Vincent put his hand up. "I'm sure she is there."

Bracken sat back down, as did the others. His voice belied the way his heart still raced.

"She's been gone from Hawkings Crest for three days. How can you be sure of her whereabouts?"

"Because I know Megan. If you've quarreled, then she will seek the solace of the abbey."

Vincent frowned at Bracken's confused face. "Have you forgotten so soon, Bracken, that Megan and her mother do not get on?"

Bracken's face cleared, but his voice was somewhat harsh. "No, sir, I had not forgotten. Megan does not seem to get on with most people." It was an unfair statement and both knew it, but the older man did not comment.

It was still something that Bracken did not understand. Why would anyone choose to be away from home? Why not live in harmony with others? Was it really so difficult? Bracken felt that this was clearly one more example of Megan's desperate need to grow up.

"I'll send a servant to the abbey now who can report as to whether or not Megan is there. Sup with us now, and you and your men can go to the abbey in the morning."

Bracken looked hesitant.

"I feel it is best, Bracken," Vincent told him, his tone not dictatorial but confident and kind.

"All right," Bracken agreed after a moment. "If we learn that she is safely there, we'll wait."

He'd been so certain that he would see her that very night that his disappointment was keen. Thankfully, Vincent didn't give him long to think about it. Posthaste he dispatched a servant to the abbey, and moments later the men were shown to chambers in order to wash and join the castle folk for dinner.

❦ ❦ ❦

"Your father sent a messenger, Megan," the Reverend Mother said to the small redhead after supper.

"He has heard of my presence then."

"Yes."

"Am I to leave?"

"No. He only sought information as to your whereabouts. He told Sister Agatha that your betrothed is at the castle."

Megan nodded but did not speak.

"I'm sure Lord Bracken will be here in the morning, Meg."

Megan's face turned to panic. "Oh, please don't make me see him, please, Reverend Mother. Please tell him I've left."

"You know I would never lie for you, Meg." The older woman's voice was stern, and Megan felt shamed because she had asked Helga to do just that.

Her shame didn't last, however. With a note of desperation she said, "Then I'll really leave here. I can go and live with Japheth and Elvina in the forest. She's to have her baby soon and I know they would welcome me."

"What has frightened you, Megan?" the abbess spoke with compassion. "Is it Lord Bracken himself or something else altogether?"

The panic left Megan, and she looked utterly defeated. "I do not know." Her voice was hushed. "Everything began so badly between us, and lately I am not in control of my anger. It's all my mother's fault for sending me on as she did."

"We heard all about it, Meg, and indeed her actions have been wrong, but you must forgive her. You'll never know true peace within yourself or with Lord Bracken unless you do."

The evening was not far spent, and so they talked on for some time, but Megan did not deal with her heart as she should have. She was too busy worrying about the morrow's confrontation.

❦ ❦ ❦

"It's a pleasure to meet you, Lady Annora."

"We're pleased to have you," Megan's beautiful mother returned, smiling. "How is Megan?"

Bracken flicked a glance at Vincent, who cleared his throat before speaking.

"Megan is at the abbey. Bracken has come thinking she might be here."

It took only a moment for the full meaning to sink in and Annora's face to flush with temper.

"She has run from Hawkings Crest?"

"Yes," Vincent admitted.

Annora threw her hands in the air, unmindful of the way Vincent, Bracken, and all Bracken's men looked on.

"When will that spoiled child ever mature? I tell you, Vincent, she has no care for anyone outside of herself. If she were here right now, I'd slap some sense into her."

The tirade continued for a few moments longer, with Vincent looking uncomfortable and Annora not noticing anyone as she carried on.

Bracken was only half listening. He had not been able to get beyond Annora's statement that Megan thought of no one but herself. He had shared the very same thought, but it now struck him strongly that it simply wasn't so. She was foolhardy, but nearly everyone at Hawkings Crest had commented at one time or another about the little caring acts she did for others.

"Annora," Vincent spoke and finally got through. "I am hungry, as I'm sure are our guests."

Annora looked affronted at his words, but after tossing her head in the air she invited Bracken and the other men to come to the tables. The meal of quail was excellent and plentiful, and when Annora calmed down, she proved to be a gracious hostess. Bracken studied her from across the table and wondered how Megan could be so different in appearance and temperament.

Even when Megan was most upset, she did not rant as this woman had done.

He was still pondering this when he heard Megan's voice behind him. His heart vaulted in his chest as his head snapped back to find her, but instead he encountered a younger version of Annora. He knew in an instant that this was Marigold. He saw that she'd grown older since that day at court, but it was her nonetheless.

"I'm sorry to be so late," Marigold spoke humbly, soaking in the hungry, male eyes that stared at her. "I was sewing by the fire, and the time just got away from me," Marigold, who hated needlework of any kind, lied sweetly and stood still to let each man look his fill.

Vincent, who was not taken in in the slightest, opened his mouth to tell Marigold that she would have to find room at another table, but Annora jumped in.

"No matter, Marigold. Whenever you grace our hall with your beauty, we will gladly welcome you. Come, sit by me."

She too had seen the desirous looks in the men's eyes and felt more than pleased. Not because any of them could have her, but because Annora simply loved having what she considered the most beautiful daughter in all of England.

Vincent was nowhere near as happy to see her. He knew Marigold was home, but she rarely joined them for any meal. Vincent knew that a servant must have told her of the men's presence. Marigold seemed to grow more devious with each passing day, and her presence shamed him. It seemed he could exert no control whatsoever where she was concerned.

The only pleasure Vincent derived from the whole evening was the way Bracken looked at Marigold. The other men at the table were making near fools of themselves, but Bracken's gaze was hooded and cool. It did Vincent's heart good to see it, and it helped remind him to tell Bracken privately not to bring Megan back to the castle with both Marigold and Annora there. He felt it best that Megan be taken directly back to Hawkings Crest.

Fifteen

BRACKEN HAD BEEN WAITING for over an hour to see Megan when William entered the sunny courtyard of the abbey. He paid the man little heed as he thought about the morning. As anxious as he was to get away, Lord Vincent had been equally anxious to detain him.

He'd toured Bracken and the men around the Stone Lake castle much like a child showing off a toy. And then there had been the journey to the abbey. Bracken saw now that they had come way out of their way by going to the castle first. Megan certainly would have known this and gained the abbey in less time because of it. Still, this did not answer his question of how she had traveled. That, along with a dozen more queries, convinced him that he'd be talking to Megan for the next two days.

Of course, their talk would probably have to wait. If he knew his betrothed like he thought he did, he would have to command her to leave the abbey, and it would be days before she would speak to him about anything.

Bracken mentally shook his head as he pictured himself tossing her over his shoulder, mounting his horse, and riding away with her kicking and screaming all the while. Vincent had sent a mount for her, but Bracken knew this was no guarantee that Megan would use it. As comical as the scene would be to his men, Bracken was serious. If he had to take Megan on his own horse to get her home, he would do it.

"What is it, William? Why have you come?" Bracken heard the sister called Agatha say.

"I must see her, Sister Agatha. Where is Megan?"

Suddenly Bracken was all ears.

"She cannot see you, William." Sister Agatha's voice was compassionate but firm.

"But I must," the young man's voice pleaded desperately. "I just know that if I could see her one more time I could convince her that it's me she needs to marry."

Bracken was like a statue, sitting on a stone bench in the shadows outside the Reverend Mother's office. He watched the earnest face of the younger man and felt something stir within him. How did Megan feel?

"William," Sister Agatha went on gently. "What of Rose?"

"I care for Rose," William told her, "but it's Megan whom I love."

"She is not for you, William. Give your heart to Rose. I have known Rose since she was but a child. She is the woman for you, William."

The younger man's shoulders slumped with defeat. He knew her words were true. He was thankful that it had been Sister Agatha who had confronted him. He'd known her all his life, and she was always the soul of kindness. He could never feel shame with her.

"I can see Rose waiting for you, William," she went on. "Go to her. She will understand and comfort you."

William's sigh was audible, but he did as he was told. Bracken watched with even more questions as the other man turned and walked away.

"He has been here for some time, Megan. You must not keep him any longer."

Megan nodded. She had not deliberately avoided him, but it was almost certain she would be leaving here today, and she had been desperate to see Japheth and Elvina one last time. It had simply taken more of the day than she had anticipated.

"You'll stay with me?"

"Yes," the Reverend Mother said, "for a time."

Megan could do nothing more than agree, and in what seemed like only a second later, Bracken entered the room. The Reverend Mother was seated at her desk, and Megan remained behind the desk as well. She learned nothing from Bracken's expression; in fact, he barely spared her a glance, but his dress surprised her. She had never seen him so formally attired.

His hose and trunks were a rich black, and his tunic was dark gray, but the sleeves had been slashed, laced, and lined with black satin. Beneath this lay an off-white shirt, richly embroidered in black, gray, and pink. Bracken's hair and beard were brushed smooth, but as elegant as he looked, Megan still found his presence too authoritative for her comfort.

"Thank you for seeing me, Reverend Mother," Bracken began as he took a seat.

"It is my pleasure, Lord Bracken. As you can see, Megan is doing well."

Bracken's gaze flicked to her with a feigned lack of interest and then back to the sister. "I have come some distance, Reverend Mother, and I hope we will be able to come to terms."

"I understand your meaning, Lord Bracken, but I do not stand in the way of Megan's joining you. However, I am not her father and cannot and will not force her to go where she does not wish."

"It is to Megan that I must speak then?"

"Yes."

Bracken still did not look at Megan. She wasn't offended by this treatment; she knew she'd brought it upon herself. Bracken thought she had acted like a child and was treating her as such.

However, she was *not* going to return with him. She seriously doubted if even her father could make her do so. She knew it was not right to disobey her father, but she was so desperate right then that she wasn't thinking as she should.

"May I have a private audience with Megan?"

The wise Reverend Mother was not surprised by the question, but neither did she think she should give in too easily. If her guess was right, and it normally was, Bracken had been taking Megan for granted, assuming she would always be there and do as she was told. She would never have said such a thing to Megan, but the older woman thought this running away incident might open Lord Bracken's eyes to a few truths.

"Yes, you may see Megan alone," she stated after a long pause.

Bracken did not miss the way Megan's alarmed eyes swung to the Reverend Mother, but he still did not look at her.

"I will leave you now and return shortly. Megan will be safe in your care?"

Bracken nodded. Under the elderly nun's gaze he felt much like a young vassal rather than a knight of many years. He stood as the nun made her stately way to the door. He waited until the portal closed before turning back to Megan. Again she could read nothing from his face as he took in her attire. She'd had little choice but to don a habit, wimple and all. Bracken thought it made her look like an angel, but he knew better.

"Your clothing does not fool me, Megan," he said calmly. "I know what manner of woman stands beneath."

Her chin rose. "You do not know me at all."

"I know that you are willful and foolish." Angry emotion was now evident in Bracken's voice; indeed, in his very being.

"You know nothing but your anger," she told him. "And since I am no better with my own ire, I think we would do nothing more than make each other miserable. That, along with your lack of conscience, and I fear to say I want nothing to do with you." The last word was spat. There was such loathing in her voice that Bracken immediately calmed and said what he should have said days ago.

"Since the day I stood over your father's men in the forest and looked upon that useless waste of life, my men have been inquiring."

Megan blinked at this change in subject but did not speak.

"It was reported to me that men, strangers to the area and traveling with extra horses, had visited Black Francesca. In an effort to vindicate the lives lost while making a noble attempt to bring you to Hawkings Crest, I went to her myself to ask whether she had seen such men."

Megan was so crushed she could have cried. All this time she had thought the worst of him.

"Why did you not tell me?" she whispered, pain written all over her face.

Bracken sighed. "It was wrong of me, Megan, but you were just as wrong to accuse me without knowing the facts. I *do* take this arrangement seriously, and it angered me to think that you see me in such a light."

"I am sorry, Bracken," Megan told him in sincere repentance.

"As am I," he answered.

"But it changes nothing," Megan went on, her voice so reconciled that it caused Bracken's heart to sink with dread, since he was most determined to take her back.

"What do you mean?"

"I mean that my father wanted me at Hawkings Crest to give us time to know each other. I think you would be forced to agree that it was sufficient time to see it would never work between us."

"And what of the king's order?" Whenever he wanted to put all arguments aside, he always fell back on this.

"I will ask my father to speak with Henry and hope that he can be reasoned with. I'm sure you'll agree, Bracken, that both of us would be miserable."

But I wouldn't be miserable, Bracken reasoned to himself, *if only we could continue to talk as we are now.*

Unfortunately, it did not occur to Bracken to share his thoughts. As usual he resorted to force.

"You may ask your father to speak with Henry, but I will ask him not to."

Megan's anger immediately rose to the surface. He hadn't heard a word she said. "He'll never listen to you."

Bracken shook his head, mocking her slightly. "We will be married, Megan. When will you come to accept the inevitable?"

"Never," she nearly hissed. "You can force me to return, but I will fly from you again, make no mistake."

I hear your dove has flown. The conversation with Stephen came so swiftly to Bracken's mind that the air left him in a rush.

She is a red hawk, with talons to gouge a man.

But, Bracken, you won't win her heart with those words.

Bracken suddenly moved around the desk. He approached Megan so abruptly that she jumped and backed into the wall. Bracken would have given much to have Stephen's help right then, but he would have to try this on his own.

"I am most determined to have you as my wife, Megan," the big man admitted, his voice resolute but also very soft.

In her surprise, Megan could only stare at him.

"I am even willing to take you by force, and my men are aware of this. An army of 1000 nuns could not stop me, let alone the few dozen from this abbey."

Anger over his temerity covered Megan's face, but Bracken totally disarmed her with his next words.

"Come back to me, my dove. Come back to Hawkings Crest where you belong."

Bracken found the change in her miraculous. Her eyes softened, and her lovely mouth opened with surprise and pleasure just before her eyes slid shut with the weight of her decision.

Megan's eyes had no more closed when they flew open at the pressure of Bracken's lips on her own. It was a fleeting kiss, but gently given, and it stunned Megan beyond words.

"Come, my little Megan, come back to me," Bracken whispered. Her heart turned over.

"We will quarrel," she tried one last time, but her voice held no conviction.

"Then we will work it out." Bracken's heart pounded as he silently begged her to say yes. When still she hesitated, he was once again tempted to order her but somehow held his tongue. When he thought he could stand it no more and was indeed on the verge of commanding her, she spoke.

"All right. I'll return with you."

Bracken only nodded, afraid to say anything or to let emotion show on his face for fear of destroying her rather hesitant consent. Thankfully, the Reverend Mother arrived just after that.

"Megan will return with me," Bracken told her without preamble, and his opinion of her lifted when she did not look to Megan for confirmation.

"Very well. It is late in the day now. Will you please consider letting Megan stay with us until morning?"

It was clearly not what Bracken wanted to hear. "The ride is long; I would wish to begin now."

"I understand, but you will have Megan for years. We would beg her company for only one more day."

Bracken hesitated, and Megan chimed in.

"I will stay."

Bracken's eyes swung to her and found an angry frown on her face for his even daring to hesitate in agreeing to the nun's request. He knew he was going to have to acquiesce on this, but he was not happy about it. As Megan went off with the Reverend Mother, it occurred to him that he had literally talked Megan into returning with him. His only hope at this point was that she would not make him pay for it for the rest of his life.

"I did not explain myself, Megan," the Reverend Mother spoke as soon as they were in the corridor, "for fear that you would not stay and later be disappointed, but Father Brent is here. I knew you would wish to see him."

Tears sprang to Megan's eyes, and she hugged the elderly nun.

"Thank you, Reverend Mother. In truth, I do not think Bracken would have understood."

The Reverend Mother stopped abruptly on the path to the chapel, her look serious as she eyed this young woman who was like a daughter to her.

"You must not bait him, Megan. It is a mistake to constantly bludgeon a man's pride."

Megan was surprised at the vehemency in the nun's voice. It gave her pause for more reasons than her tone; her words rang true. Megan did pummel Bracken's pride on a regular basis. Not until that very instant did she think how he might feel to have everyone at Hawkings Crest know she had run from him.

And now today, before the Reverend Mother could even reason with him, Megan had spoken up and said she was staying until the morrow no matter what. Megan's conscience pricked her, but only for an instant. Father Brent was here, and she was going to see him.

"What of Megan? You saw her?" Stephen wished to know as he sat across the table from Bracken in the common room of the pub.

"Yes. She is well, but the Reverend Mother has asked that she stay until tomorrow. We will leave at first light."

Stephen nodded. "So it is to be a willing departure."

Bracken shrugged. "In truth, I can answer that only when the time comes. I do not feel the Reverend Mother would deal falsely with me, but I wouldn't put it past Megan to try something."

"So she was not pleased to see you?"

"No," Bracken admitted, and Stephen knew the first stirrings of anger toward Megan. Did she not realize how much

Bracken cared? Didn't she care that he had better things to do than chase her across the countryside, sick with fear for her safety?

When he thought about the way she'd been plunged into this affair, the anger dissolved. It was typical of Henry to use his subjects as political pawns, but it was most unfortunate that Megan had not lost her heart as swiftly as Bracken had. However, Stephen was not pessimistic. He knew that if Megan would only give Bracken a chance, she would find him a man who, although he didn't know flowery words, would indeed cherish her for all his life.

Sixteen

"HOW ARE YOU, MY CHILD?"

"Oh, Father Brent," Megan spoke with tears in her eyes, "I've missed you."

The old man gently touched the top of her head, his heart turning over with love for this girl. He remembered her so clearly at 10, angry and rebellious, and then at 14, kneeling to pray for the first time.

"I've missed you too."

"Have you been well?" Megan asked.

"I am as well as an old man can expect to be," he told her with a smile. Megan smiled in return.

"I am only here until the morning."

Father Brent knew all about this and only nodded. "Then I'm glad the Lord saw fit to put us together before you depart."

"Are you ever near Hawkings Crest, Father Brent?" Megan asked anxiously.

"It is far for these old legs, child, but please believe that if ever I am in the area I will stop there."

"I hope to see you."

"The Reverend Mother tells me you are to marry."

"Yes." Megan's eyes clouded.

"What is it, child? What is wrong?"

"It is not what I wish."

Father Brent had figured as much by her reaction. "Through the centuries many have married for love, Megan, but probably just as many married for political gain. How does your betrothed feel?"

Megan's face now flushed with anger, remembering the way he tried to rush her away. "He seems content enough with the arrangement. If only he would protest, Father might try to reason with King Henry on our behalf."

"But you say he seems pleased with the order?"

"Yes." Megan nearly choked on the word.

"If that is the case, can you not give him a chance, child?" Father Brent asked gently, but Megan's face was still set with outrage.

"It's not that easy," she burst out, already sorry she had agreed to return and at the same time confused about the pleasure of Bracken's kiss. In the next few minutes she told the old priest everything. She did not spare herself or Bracken but told all she could recall of that which had transpired in the last weeks.

"And now you're going to tell me," Megan concluded, her voice resigned, "that if I don't make peace with Bracken I'm going to be miserable."

"No," Father Brent said. "I'm not going to say that. This anger you feel—this anger that rides so close beneath the surface that it comes out at a moment's notice, this anger that you say is directed at your mother and Lord Bracken—is not toward them at all."

"Of course it is," Megan argued, but Father Brent would not let her continue.

"Is God sovereign, Megan?"

"Sovereign?" she stumbled over the word.

"The supreme ruler, in absolute, unlimited control of everything at all times," he explained.

"Certainly," Megan answered as soon as she understood. "He is God."

"So whose will is it that King Henry has sent this decree?"

Megan looked at him but didn't answer.

"And whose will was it, hard as it was, that your mother sent you ahead of schedule? God is in control, Megan, and has been all along. The anger that you feel toward all of these people and circumstances is actually directed at your heavenly Father."

Megan's lungs emptied on these words. Her hand came to her lips. What had she done? For weeks now she'd boiled with rage at Bracken, King Henry, her mother, and even her father, but they were not at the source. It was God and God alone. He was in control, and when all the rubble was cleared away Megan could see that she had been lashing out in fury toward *Him*.

"I can see that I've made you think," Father Brent went on compassionately. "And I would be glad to pray with you. But if I remember correctly, you would probably prefer to have some time alone."

"Yes, I would." Megan rose slowly.

"Then before you go, I would like to give you something."

Megan watched the priest bring out a square, thick volume from a bag at his side. It was not overly large, but when he handed it to Megan she found it quite heavy.

"It's the Psalms and Proverbs, Megan, and it's for you."

"The *Bible*?" she whispered incredulously. "In *English*?"

"Just two books, child, but I know God will use them to bless and teach you. I must warn you, Megan, there are some people who would burn such a volume; you must take care with it lest you lose it."

"I will," she said, tears standing in her eyes. "Thank you, Father Brent. Thank you so much."

The elderly man smiled as Megan clasped the book to her and moved toward the door, confident that she would take care of the Scriptures as well as the sin of which she was now aware. He knew that some of the sisters were waiting to see him, but he took time then and there to pray for Megan's heart.

⚜ ⚜ ⚜

"Delight thyself also in the Lord, and he shall give thee the desires of thine heart. Commit thy way unto the Lord; trust also in him, and he shall bring it to pass. And he shall bring forth thy righteousness as the light, and thy judgment as the noonday. Rest in the Lord, and wait patiently for him; fret not thyself because of him who prospereth in his way, because of the man who bringeth wicked devices to pass. Cease from anger, and forsake wrath; fret not thyself in any way to do evil."

Megan finished reading out of Psalm 37 and then wept into her pillow.

"I have sinned against you, Father God. I have been enraged against Your holy plan," Megan cried out quietly. "I do feel like a pawn in the king's game, but You are in control, and I now confess my anger. Please cleanse me, Lord, so that I may know Your peace. I have wanted my way more than Yours, and I confess that as well.

"I know that I'll stumble in this again, Father God, but help me through each trial. I have been so hard on Bracken. I have been so impossible to live with. Help me to care for him and to be the wife I need to be. Help him to deal gently with me and with kindness. Help me to forgive King Henry and my mother and to really see this as Your hand.

"My desire is to do your will, Father God. Please help me to be strong in this pledge. Thank You for sending Father Brent to me. Thank You for his words of rebuke. Help me to heed them from this point on. In Your holy name I pray, Amen."

Megan lay spent now, her body heavy with fatigue but her heart light with her confession. The way she had been acting, the defensive way in which she'd lived, was all so clear. Bracken still intimidated her in many ways, but she could see now that he had been trying.

Megan was not at all hungry, but she wanted to speak with the sisters whom she would not see again. She was weary as she made her way from her room, but the look on Megan's face made it very evident to both the Reverend Mother and Sister Agatha that something had changed.

❦ ❦ ❦

In the morning Megan made her goodbyes swiftly. Leaving the sisters this time was nearly as painful as the first. However, there was a marked difference about her, a serenity, and she caught Bracken staring at her as he helped her onto the back of the horse.

"I'll be leading as we begin," he told her. "You will ride about halfway back. If you have need of me, just send Stephen."

Megan nodded. "Thank you, Bracken."

She watched him stride away, and it wasn't two minutes before they moved out in a double line of about 25 men. Kendrick was beside her, and Stephen was to the front. She didn't know the other men, but they talked as they rode. She soon learned that the man behind her was Owen and the man in front and to the side of Stephen was Stafford. Stafford, along with some of the other men, was not a knight of the realm, but rode in fealty to Bracken's keep.

"What is in your sack, Stafford?" Owen called, a teasing note in his voice.

"You're a busy thing, Owen," Stafford told him in no uncertain terms.

"I'd rather like to know as well," Stephen cut in. Megan could see the smile on his face.

"Stafford is in love with Pen, Lady Megan," Kendrick told her. Megan nodded and smiled as well.

"I know Pen," she stated and watched Stafford's neck go red. "I met her at the creamery."

Stafford couldn't help himself; he turned to look at Megan. Indeed, Pen had told him all about Lady Megan's work out there, and he was still amazed.

While he was still staring at her, Megan said, "She's very pretty."

"I think so," Stafford admitted.

"So what did you buy?" Owen persisted.

"Come now, Owen," Kendrick chided, "do not force the lad to tell."

"Have you asked her to marry you?" Megan asked, feeling a bit nosy herself.

"Of course, Lady Megan," Stafford told her.

"And what did she say?"

The other men laughed because they had seen the adoring look on Pen's face whenever Stafford was near, but the young knight still only smiled and answered her.

"She said yes."

"So when are you to marry?"

"We're not. I mean, not until I've gained Lord Bracken's permission."

"Why don't you ask him?" It all seemed so elementary to Megan, but Stafford did not answer.

"Bracken takes his job as lord very seriously, Lady Megan," Kendrick gently told her. "Pen is a part of Hawkings Crest and so her well-being, as well as that of the other servants, is of interest to Bracken. He is not a moody lord, but if he says no to Stafford's suit of Pen, the subject is closed. Stafford would rather wait for the correct time."

Megan nodded, her mind busy. "Would you like me to ask him?"

"No!" The word was shouted in unison by all four men, and when Megan got over her surprise, her laughter floated high into the air. A moment later Stephen deliberately dropped back to ride beside Megan so he could see her face.

"Stay out of it, Megan," he warned with a playful smile, yet with a significant light in his eyes.

"But Stephen," Megan said with great exaggeration that all the men could hear, "I'm sure I could get him to see reason. Bracken does everything I ask."

Now it was time for the men to laugh. Stephen, having seen that she would not pursue the matter, moved back into position.

Megan had never ridden so far in one morning. By the time they stopped for the noonday meal, she feared that her legs were completely asleep. But another need was pressing in with far more insistency, and the moment Stephen helped her alight from her horse, she made for the woods.

"Megan," he called to her and followed. "You mustn't run off."

Megan turned and stared at him, her voice reasonable. "I assure you, Stephen, I must indeed."

He knew exactly of what she spoke, but he didn't believe the forest was safe for her.

"Just let me check for wild game, Megan, and then you can go."

The redhead's laughter met his ears, and she put a comforting hand on his arm.

"I just walked these woods, Stephen, in an effort to gain the abbey. I assure you, I will be fine."

Stephen was so surprised by this reminder that he stood still as she walked away and disappeared within the trees.

"She seems in a fine mood," Bracken commented, having come upon them and heard the laughter.

"She does at that," Stephen commented. "And she was certainly determined to get into the woods. I think we came too far without a break."

Bracken grimaced and reminded himself to be more mindful of her needs. "You checked the woods before you let her go?"

"She wouldn't let me," the younger man admitted, knowing what would follow.

"Stephen!" Bracken's voice rose to scold before he began to follow Megan. Stephen grabbed his arm.

"You can't go in there."

Bracken stared at him and then at the forest and sighed heavily. "I tell you, Stephen, I truly do look forward to the day when this betrothal is over and she is mine in earnest."

The men were still standing together when Megan reappeared. Her step was casual until she spotted them. She came to a slow halt a few yards from them.

"Am I interrupting something?"

"No," Bracken assured her swiftly, thinking she looked a bit tired. He came forward and took her arm. "Come, eat and rest awhile. We have many miles yet to go."

Megan learned the real meaning of those words hours later. They had rested for a time after the noonday meal, but with only the exception of a short stop a few hours after that, they had ridden on. Bracken had come back on several occasions to ride with her. Megan had enjoyed his company and explanations of their location. He'd been very solicitous as he'd shown her several points of interest, and Megan had actually been sorry to see him go.

The sun was dropping in the sky and twilight was settling over the land when Megan's eyes grew heavy. She caught herself drifting several times, and twice she nearly fell asleep. When her head eventually nodded and her body went completely limp, she fell to the outside of the line, making it impossible for Kendrick to catch her. One moment she was secure in the saddle, the next she was tumbling toward the ground.

Seventeen

MEGAN NEVER ACTUALLY LOST consciousness, but the world felt as if it had tipped, righted itself, and then all at once come alive. Horses and dust were all around her. Men were shouting. She shook herself quickly and scrambled to her feet just before Kendrick and Owen reached her.

"Are you all right, my lady?"

"Yes," Megan told them, but she wasn't sure it was true. Her shoulder hurt, and so did the side of her head. Megan shook her head slightly to dispel the image of hurtling through the air, but it didn't work. An involuntary shudder ran over her.

"Are you all right, Megan?" Stephen, who now stood with the other men, asked.

"Yes. Maybe I could just walk for a time."

"There is no need for that. You'll come on Warrior with me," Bracken said reassuringly. He had suddenly appeared and was moving toward her. However, Megan was not so comforted. She retreated, her hands outstretched as if to hold him off.

"Oh, please, Bracken, don't make me. Your destrier is so huge, and if I fall—"

"I'm not going to let you fall, Megan." Bracken's voice was warm, and meant to comfort, but Megan did not attend.

"Please let me walk, Bracken, please. Just for a time."

Bracken heard the tremor in her voice, looked at her for a moment, and then turned and walked back among his men. After a moment they dispersed. It looked as though they were setting up camp.

Megan could not stop the trembling that ran all over her frame, and as fast as the darkness was closing in, Bracken saw it clearly.

"Come rest here, Megan; the men are preparing some food."

"We're camping here?"

"No. Just taking a rest."

A blanket had been laid almost at her feet, and it was a relief for Megan to sink down onto it. Food was brought, and it swiftly became clear that they had stopped for her alone. For this reason she did not allow herself to relax. It would have been heavenly to stretch out and sleep, but Megan made herself sit upright and eat swiftly.

She thanked the men who had served her and stood up just as soon as she finished. Megan would have stayed on the ground for hours if she'd known what Bracken had in mind to do next.

"Are you feeling better?" He had been close by the whole time. He saw now that the journey had been too much for her and was angry at himself for not sensing it earlier. Nevertheless, all he could do now was try to make the best of it.

"Yes, thank you."

Bracken signaled, and Megan watched as his horse, a huge beast of war named Warrior, was brought forward.

"Where is my horse?" Megan asked as she tried to calm the alarm rising within her.

"One of my men will bring him along," Bracken said as he swung himself astride. Before Megan had time to react, she found herself lifted in Stephen's arms. Their intent was immediately clear to her, and she stiffened with fear.

"Put me down, Stephen."

The fear in her voice wrung his heart, but he knew that Bracken would have it no other way.

Seconds later, Bracken was reaching for her, and Megan found herself sitting across the front of his saddle. Her hands fisted in the fabric of his tunic and her eyes were huge as she pleaded with him.

"Please, put me down."

"No, Megan." Bracken's voice was gentle and as soft as hers had been. "The day has been long, and you are tired. I won't let you fall."

Megan shook her head, and for an instant she buried her face against his chest. She was trembling so violently that her teeth chattered. Bracken's heart turned over, but he knew this was best. Megan's head came back up, and her eyes as well as her voice pleaded with him.

"I'm sorry I ran from you, Bracken," she sobbed. "Please don't punish me this way."

"'Tis no punishment, Megan," he told her gently, "but a way to keep you safe."

Megan chose that moment to notice they hadn't even moved.

"Why don't we just camp here?" she asked hopefully.

"Because we are only two hours' ride from Hawkings Crest. It is safest to carry on. We shall all be tired, but our beds await us, and that outweighs the risk of sleeping in the forest and going in at dawn."

Megan took a deep breath and made herself loosen her hold on his clothing. She then noticed the large arm at her back. It was like she was leaning against a fallen tree. Bracken's face was disappearing in the darkness, but Megan looked up and saw him watching her.

"I won't let you fall," his deep voice rumbled out from under her shoulder that was against his chest. Megan sat still as Bracken gently plucked a leaf from her hair.

Megan would have spoken, but Brice suddenly appeared.

"All are in readiness, Bracken."

"Good."

"How are you, Megan?" Brice then asked.

"I'm all right," she told him, but her voice said otherwise.

"You didn't hurt yourself in the fall?"

Megan shrugged. "A little on my head and shoulder."

"Which shoulder?" Bracken inquired.

Megan motioned to the one against him, and a moment later she was being lifted like a child and turned. When she was settled once again, Bracken spoke to Brice.

"Let's move."

Brice gave the order, and within minutes they were surrounded by men and moving down the road. Bracken felt Megan tense against him, but knowing that she would soon understand he would never let her fall, he stayed quiet. Megan did eventually relax. Her head fell against his chest, and he could see that her hands now lay limply in her lap.

Megan roused after just 45 minutes of sleep, but she did so easily. All the tension had left her. For an instant she lay still and listened to the thud of Bracken's heart. It was a comforting sound, and the arm and chest around her were warm and safe. After a time she raised her head, rotated her shoulders, and then tried to look up into his face. It was very dark.

"I didn't mean to fall asleep."

"I'm glad you did," he told her easily. "I'm sorry it's been such a long ride."

Megan sighed. "I really have no one to blame but myself."

Bracken didn't comment, but he had smiled slightly in the dark. For a time they rode in silence.

"Can you tell me of William?" Bracken's question had come out of nowhere for Megan, and she took a moment to answer.

"William Clayborne?"

"I am not sure. A man came to the abbey. His name was William, and he was seeking you."

Again Bracken heard her sigh.

"Have you ever been in love, Bracken?"

He could have told her that he was in love right then, but said instead, "Why do you ask?"

"William is enamored with me. There is a wonderful girl—her name is Rose—and she loves William deeply. But he thinks he wants me."

"You do not think him capable of knowing his own mind?"

"I don't know."

"And you, Megan, do you love him?"

"No," she answered softly, but without hesitation. "I care for William. He has been a good friend, but I do not love him. He believes with time that I would have a change of heart. I do not think we could be happy."

"And what of us, Megan?" Bracken questioned while betraying none of the vulnerability he felt within. "Will we ever find happiness together?"

Megan turned to him in the dark but could not make out his features.

"I do not know, Bracken, but I pray so."

He didn't say anything, but after a moment he gently pressed Megan's head back onto his chest. She stiffened for a instant, but it wasn't long before she picked up the beat of Bracken's heart once again. Just seconds later she relaxed. Something was happening within her where this man was concerned, and the swiftness of it astonished her. Megan could only conclude that because she'd surrendered the anger in her heart, God was finally able to work.

Comfortable as she was, Megan began to grow sleepy again, but even in her fuzzy state she was cognizant enough to thank God that Bracken had insisted she ride on his horse.

Megan had apologized sincerely to Helga for asking her to lie, and the faithful servant had been gone from Megan's presence for only five minutes before Louisa came through her door. The moment the older woman saw her, she pulled Megan into a fierce embrace. Then Megan was forced to stand helplessly before Louisa and watch her cry.

Megan did put her arms back around Bracken's aunt, but she was overcome with shame when she realized how little thought she had given her in the last days. In all her selfish running away, it never once occurred to her that she had scared Louisa sick. She confessed this to God as she released Louisa, and then apologized to the woman herself.

"I am so sorry, Aunt Louisa."

"It's all right, Megan," she cried. "As long as you are safe."

Megan hugged the older woman yet again, and Louisa tried to contain herself. Having arrived back late the night before, most of the castle had been quiet and Megan had gone directly to her room. She had not seen Louisa until daybreak, when she nearly burst into Megan's room. The prodigal bride-to-be was up, already reading the Psalms, and so glad to see Louisa that she almost cried herself.

"I am famished," Megan admitted suddenly.

"As am I," Louisa said. "Let us go below and break the fast. How are your mother and father?" she inquired as they started down the stairs.

"I don't know," Megan told her. "I didn't see them."

"Megan," Louisa said in a surprised voice, "why ever not?"

"I did not go home. I went to the abbey."

They had gained the great room now, and Louisa abruptly stopped. "But surely they came to see you."

"No," Megan told her with a shake of the head.

Louisa could only stare at her. Megan had thought nothing of this up to now, but suddenly she felt ashamed. She wasn't sure if the shame was for herself or for her parents, who didn't appear to care for her.

Bracken had spotted the women's descent and now approached. He studied Louisa's face and then Megan's flushed cheeks and frowned. He would have thought that Louisa would be thrilled to see his betrothed.

"Is there some problem?" Bracken asked.

"No, no," Louisa spoke swiftly, glancing first at Bracken and then back at Megan.

"I'm sorry I acted so, Megan."

Megan smiled in understanding, but her heart was still troubled. Bracken, reading this, wanted to know more.

"Megan?"

She looked at him. "Aunt Louisa was just surprised that I didn't see Father and Mother."

"I thought they would at least come to the abbey, Bracken," Louisa put in softly.

Bracken read and understood the compassion in his aunt's eyes.

"I saw them," he said.

"You did?" Megan had forgotten this.

"Yes. I did not know you had gone to the abbey until I'd talked with your father. He seemed to think it best to leave things in my hands, so we didn't stop back at the castle on the way here."

Megan nodded, now recalling the messenger who had come to the abbey.

"You did see my mother?" Megan, picturing Bracken at Stone Lake, asked, a sudden thought striking her.

"Yes."

"How was she?"

Bracken glanced at the floor and then at Megan. She saw instantly that he was amused, and for the first time she felt like laughing herself.

"I would say that she was not very happy to learn you had gone to the abbey." Bracken's voice was dry.

He put it so delicately, that for the first time, Megan smiled at Bracken. It quite nearly took his breath away.

"She didn't wish to see me?" Megan asked with huge, innocent eyes that sparkled with impish glee. She knew well what her mother thought of her and ofttimes chose to laugh rather than cry.

Bracken's smile went into full bloom as he offered his arm to Megan. He sent a speaking glance toward Louisa. The older woman took his cue, as well as his other arm, and the three went silently on to the tables to eat.

Eighteen

"'TIS TRULY THE ODDEST THING I've ever known," Bracken admitted to Louisa. "Lord Vincent came as swiftly as he could when Megan first came here, but in truth it's as if they don't even care. He never even mentioned seeing Megan at the abbey. He seemed more intent on our touring his keep than anything else."

Louisa looked troubled. It was the end of Megan's first day back, and Bracken had finally sought out his aunt in her chambers.

"And you say that Lady Annora was only angry, not concerned?"

Bracken's look turned fierce. "She was livid, and then when that creature, Marigold, appeared, her manner was so sweet I felt ill."

"It's taken some time, Bracken, but I finally realized I've met Marigold. We, too, were at court at the same time, and I hate to say it, but a more avaricious woman I've yet to encounter."

"She's certainly self-seeking," Bracken put in. "We never even exchanged words, but I could see from across the room that she thinks of little beyond herself."

"And do Megan and Marigold get on?"

Bracken was suddenly struck by a vivid memory. It was right

after Megan arrived. They'd been talking by the hearth, and Marigold's name had been mentioned. Bracken recalled being amused by what he thought to be sibling rivalry.

"I think not," he said now. "We have never actually spoken of it, but I sense that Megan and Marigold have much the same relationship as Megan and her mother."

"And what is that exactly?"

Bracken's face was covered with pain. "Nothing but animosity. Annora does not seem able to stand the thought of Megan, let alone the sight of her. I tell you, Aunt Lou, when I think of my own relationship with my mother, I can hardly reckon with what I see in Megan's family."

Louisa nodded in full understanding.

"You love her, don't you, Bracken?"

"I do, Louisa," he admitted softly. "I will admit that at first it was strictly carnal. I was captivated with her hair and face, but now I've seen things in her that have nothing to do with her looks.

"She fights me, but I so admire her mettle. She is unendingly kind to the servants, but she brooks no lying from those who would seek to cheat me."

Louisa suddenly chuckled. "She certainly doesn't like Barton."

"Indeed." Bracken now chuckled as well. "I wonder when the next battle will be fought."

"Could she be right, Bracken?"

Something in Louisa's tone made Bracken take his eyes from the fire and look at her. In truth, what proof did he have that Barton would never steal from him? Barton had worked under his parents since before Bracken could remember, but neither his mother nor his father could read. Bracken could read some, but he never bothered to question the man's doings. He was more interested in his training fields and the external functions of the keep.

"I think maybe it would be wise to listen to her," Louisa suggested softly, and for the first time Bracken was open to the idea and not threatened by it.

"I quite agree with you. I'll not seek the matter out, but if she comes again, I'll do my best."

Louisa felt very pleased. She had nothing against Barton, but never had she met a woman of Megan's integrity. Louisa was very certain Megan would never have accused someone whom she did not believe with all her heart was in the wrong.

Bracken did not stay much longer. When he left, his thoughts were on Megan. Louisa too was thinking of Megan, but also of her sister, Joyce, and what she might think of Megan when they at last could meet.

"It's time for us to go," Stephen told Megan, Brice by his side.

"Go where?"

"Home," Brice said, smiling at her look of surprise.

"But I thought—"

"That we lived here?"

Megan hesitated. "No, not that; it's just that I've only been back a week, and I thought you would just be here indefinitely." Megan shrugged helplessly, and Stephen hugged her.

"Does Bracken know?"

"Yes, and Aunt Lou. We don't leave today, but if the weather holds, by the end of the week."

Megan's hands came to her waist now, and she took on a look of teasing. "I was just coming to the point of being able to stand the sight of you, but if you're going to be that way about it, then off with you!"

"You could come with us," Stephen suggested, his voice teasing as well.

"Now why would I do that?"

"To meet Mother." Brice told her simply, jesting also, but not sounding like it.

Megan's face took on such an expression of interest that the two men exchanged a glance of panic.

"Now, Megan—" Stephen began, knowing what Bracken would say, but the little redhead was not listening.

"It's not a poor idea at all, is it? I'm sure Bracken wouldn't mind. I'm always underfoot as it is."

"What is it Bracken wouldn't mind?" the one being talked about wished to know as he came and stood before the group. His hearted skipped a beat when he saw his brothers' looks of guilt and Megan's triumphant countenance.

"I'm thinking of seeing your mother."

Bracken frowned. "Well, of course you'll see her...when we are wed."

"No, now. Stephen suggested it."

Bracken's eyes swung to that fellow, who was smiling painfully, before returning and pinning Megan to the ground. "You mean go to White Halls with Brice and Stephen now?"

"Yes." Megan's face was filled with delight, but Bracken was scowling.

"I don't care for this idea," Bracken said in a voice he thought would end the subject. He was wrong.

"Why ever not?" Megan wished to know, still congenial.

"Your father wanted you here so we could know each other better."

As usual Bracken had resorted to this excuse, and Megan was sick of hearing it. With a tremendous scowl of her own, she replied, "Well, what else is there to know?" Megan was angry for the first time in many days. "You insist that you want this marriage and that I am to run your castle and keep, but only as long as I don't interfere with your plans and wishes. You are in a good mood until I cross you, and then you're frightening. I am to stay out from underfoot, and the only real place I have any say is in my own bedchamber."

"That isn't true," Bracken told her firmly. Under attack, he had completely forgotten about his plan to listen to her.

"Of course it is. You won't even discuss that thief who keeps your books, and now two of your falcons have died. The others will die also unless you allow me to do something with the falconry. The creamery needs work as well, and so does the byre."

"I have men to see to that." Bracken was angry now himself.

"But they are not following through, and you're too busy with your men to notice," Megan shot back. "If I'm to be nothing more than a figurehead, I might as well go on a journey with your brothers and meet the rest of your family."

"I will hear no more on the subject, Megan," Bracken now said in a voice that left no doubt as to his black mood; indeed, it was as dark as his looks. "You are staying here, and that is the end of it."

Megan's chin came into the air. She glared at Bracken for an instant and then turned and walked toward the castle. She was out of earshot when Brice said, "We're sorry, Bracken. We were but jesting."

Bracken grunted with irritation. "She's obviously quite anxious to be away. One moment I think I know her, and the next I am a man lost."

"What exactly do you mean?" Stephen asked.

"She has seemed so content," Bracken burst out. "We have not had one harsh word since the journey."

"But the more time she spends here, the more discontented she is with the way you run things," Stephen spoke up.

"She told you this?" Bracken's eyes swiftly turned to him.

"No, Bracken." Stephen's voice was matter-of-fact. "She didn't have to. You are right, she has been doing better. But by her own admission she's been looking around the castle, and she's not happy with what she sees. She's even less happy when she knows she can't come to you."

"Of course she can come to me," Bracken argued.

"And hear what?" Stephen shot at him. "That she is to stay in her own place? Or that no matter what she suggests, you will make no changes?"

Bracken opened his mouth and shut it, so Stephen went on, this time very quietly, but with deep fervor.

"Aunt Lou is wonderful, Bracken, we all know that, but she is not true mistress here. She is more than happy to leave the account books to Barton and the running of the keep to you. We eat like kings when Aunt Lou is at work, and our bedding, as well as the rushes on the floor, are always fresh. But Megan clearly wants more.

"You're going to have to ask yourself if you want to be married to an Aunt Louisa or to a Megan of Stone Lake. If it's Megan, as I strongly expect it will be, you're going to have to free her, Bracken."

"What do you mean?"

"I mean, let her be who and what she is. You're so afraid of losing her that you're holding on too tight. Even her wish to ride with us was innocent. I can imagine her curiosity about Mother and the rest. She understands the workings of a castle— she's already proven that—but if you don't start trusting her, she'll build a wall so high between you that you will never find a way to scale it.

"In the end she'll be your wife, but only because she's been forced. Let the dove go, Bracken, and I truly believe she will fly right back into your arms."

Even Brice was staring at Stephen by the time he finished. The brothers teased Stephen often about his sweet way with women, but neither one of them had ever heard him quite so passionate.

"What say you, Brice? Do you think Stephen right?"

Brice shook his head slightly. "I do not know, Bracken, but even I can see that as things stand it's not working. What harm is there in trying things Stephen's way? You may find Megan more than willing to meet you in the middle."

Bracken nodded and thanked his brothers, and when he turned away, both thought he might seek out Megan immediately. This was not the case. Bracken turned toward the creamery. From there he would go to the falconry and then to the byre. It rubbed him sorely to be doing so, but maybe it was time to make some changes.

The three brothers were very surprised to see Megan at the table for dinner that night, and even more surprised when she was cordial to all, including Bracken. Some of the light of the past week had gone out of her eyes, but it was clear to all that she was trying. Her effort wrung Bracken's heart, but it wasn't until the next day that they had any time together.

"Lady Megan," Noleen, one of the maids, began when she found Megan bending over a loom. "Lord Bracken would like to speak with you."

Megan straightened, glanced at her, and then looked back. "I think it should work now, Elva," she said to the girl at the loom and then turned to Noleen once again.

"He's in the war room, my lady."

"Thank you, Noleen," Megan replied, moving to the door. She was not dreading this confrontation, but neither was she pleased. She knew she'd been out of line the day before, but sometimes it was so hard to apologize. In truth, Megan was sorry only for her tone. She had been meaning to say everything else for weeks, and in many ways it was a relief to have it out. Megan could only wonder why he would wish to see her.

She gained the door of the war room at an easy pace, her composure serene. Inside, however, she was in a royal turmoil. Megan opened the door herself and found Bracken within. He had been sitting, but now rose and held a chair.

"Please be seated, Megan."

Megan did as she was asked and sat uncomfortably for an instant while Bracken stayed behind her chair. Certain her hair must be a mess, she had to force her hands to stay in her lap. When it seemed that an eternity had passed, Bracken came around the chair.

"Your father has sent word to me," he began as soon as he was seated opposite.

"Is he well?"

"Yes, but Henry has been in touch and wishes to know if we have chosen a date."

Megan stared at him. "For the wedding?"

"Yes."

Megan stood abruptly and walked to a window. She took a deep breath and fought down feelings of panic. She lived every day, certain that at any moment Bracken would tell her he had changed his mind about the wedding, but it never happened.

"Is there some problem, Megan?" She could tell from his voice that he had stayed in his seat. She was thankful for this.

"I don't know. I guess I've not truly accepted the fact that you actually wish to wed me."

"What is so difficult to believe?"

Megan turned her head to see him. "Is it really so hard to understand, Bracken?"

"No," he admitted. "But even with our differences, I think we will suit."

Megan stared at him in exasperation and then turned back to the window and muttered, more to herself than Bracken, "You should marry Marigold."

"I do not wish to marry your sister."

Megan didn't even turn to him. "You might feel differently if you could see her."

"On the contrary; I have seen her."

Megan spun so swiftly Bracken thought she might have injured her neck. "You've met Marigold?"

"Yes."

"When?"

"Well, many years ago at court, and then just last week at Stone Lake Castle."

Megan stared at him.

"What is it, Megan? Did you think I would be struck dumb by her beauty and fall in a heap at her feet?"

At any other time Megan would have laughed at his words, as well as his dry tone, but not now, not about Marigold.

"I don't know what I thought; it's just that—" She stopped

and shrugged, her eyes telling Bracken that she was beside herself with pain and confusion. She turned back to the window, and after a moment heard Bracken approach. He did not touch her or say a word, but Megan was very aware of his presence behind her. When she could stand it no longer, she spoke.

"Why do you stand there, Bracken, and not speak?"

He did not immediately reply. Megan turned to confront him, her eyes begging him to answer.

"I am enjoying the smell of your hair."

His answer worked on her just as his words had at the abbey.

"Oh, Bracken," she said softly. "What am I going to do?"

Her question was not lost on him. "You're going to marry me," he spoke gently. "And the two of us are going to do our best to make a life together."

Megan sighed. "Are you certain about Marigold?"

Bracken's eyes suddenly became very amused. "Yes. My brothers and knights were quite smitten, but she is not the woman for me."

"And you think I am?"

"I do not think; I know."

His words warmed Megan considerably, and Bracken studied her complexion, which always reminded him of the bloom on a peach. Megan saw the answering warmth in his own gaze, but she was unprepared for the way his head lowered. She drew in a sharp breath and stood still in anticipation.

A servant chose that moment to knock on the door. Bracken froze, his lips just a scant inch from Megan's, and stared into her eyes. Megan stared back, unable to identify the emotions surging through her.

"We must set a date, my dove," he said softly when the knock sounded again. He preferred kissing her to discussing the wedding, but she seemed pliant all of a sudden.

"All right."

"September," Bracken said softly, pushing for all he was worth.

Megan nodded, not certain at the moment what year it was, let alone the month.

Whoever was at the door had given up, but Bracken, even though he still wanted to kiss her, now stood to full height, much pleased at how easy it had been. Megan continued to watch him, and Bracken knew it would only be a matter of minutes before the charm dissipated and Megan understood what she had just agreed to.

Indeed it was only seconds. Bracken was at the door when Megan found her voice.

"Did you say September?"

Bracken looked back from the door. "Indeed, I did."

"But this is mid-July."

Bracken's mouth turned up in a very satisfied way.

"Yes, Megan, I know."

When the door had closed in his wake, Megan let her back fall against the window casing. Only one thought came to mind, and she voiced it to the empty room.

"What in the world have I done?"

Nineteen

Two days later Bracken and Megan stood together as Stephen and Brice rode out of Hawkings Crest. Megan was already so lonely for them that she wanted to weep.

"Will you miss them?" Bracken asked her.

"Yes. I miss them now."

"Before you know it the wedding will be upon us, and they will return, bringing with them my whole family."

Megan turned to look at him and saw that he was very pleased with the prospect of seeing his family. His smile increased her wonder over what they must be like, but she didn't question Bracken concerning them. With plans to go back to the castle, Megan was on the verge of excusing herself, but Bracken suddenly said, "What would you do differently in the falconry?"

Megan was surprised, but recovered swiftly and answered in a humble voice, "My father has had several birds for more than 15 years. Your falconer told me that his oldest bird is four years old. I think the main problem is that he is taking too many birds from the wilds. He needs to raise the birds from eggs and keep his pens cleaner and more comfortable."

Bracken believed his birds were important but thought the job sounded huge. And as with his steward, his falconer had been with Hawkings Crest since Bracken was a child. Bracken's hand went to the back of his neck. Did she think that he or any of his servants could do anything well?

"I have upset you," Megan said when he did not reply or look at her.

"No, Megan, but I do wonder if you think I am of any use at all."

Megan didn't know what to say. She had come to love Hawkings Crest and felt he'd done an excellent job of its upkeep.

"Forgive me, Bracken." Megan's voice was now a bit pained. "I have given you the wrong impression. It is true that I feel some things should change, but they are not many at all. Indeed, there is much more that I admire. I have never seen finer horses, and your training fields are beyond compare."

She paused as a look of complete surprise crossed his face, but then kept on.

"But as with most keeps, the lord is more interested in one area than another. The same goes for the mistress of the castle. I want to see things improve in the account books, the byre, and the creamery because these areas affect my management of the castle and castle folk."

"And what of the falconry?"

Megan's cheeks heated slightly, but she did not drop her eyes. "It has long been an interest to me, and over the years my father has taught me much. I do not wish to interfere, but I can see there are things you can do to improve your falconry. You won't see an immediate benefit, but in time your birds could be very strong."

Bracken nodded. "Tell me what you have in mind."

In just seconds she had laid out a plan of such logic that Bracken was mentally kicking himself for not listening to her earlier.

"So you feel the birds need more air?"

"They need more of everything. Air, sunlight, and whatever else it takes to mimic their natural environment. They are only to be kept in the mews when they are molting. Not only will they be healthier, they will hunt better."

Bracken nodded. "And what plans had you for the byre?"

Megan did not need to be asked twice. The castle was forgotten as the lord and his lady walked in the direction of the cow barn. Megan was not pushy or demanding in her suggestions, and Bracken was once again amazed at her intelligence and instinctive ideas.

It was a godsend that Bracken was able to see Megan at her most competent. It only caused him to love her more. But a new side was soon to reveal itself, one that would cause Bracken's heart to completely melt where Megan was concerned.

"Your mother has sent a messenger, Megan," Louisa told the younger woman the following week.

Megan was not surprised. She knew that Bracken had sent word to Vincent concerning the September 20 wedding date, just ten weeks away. She also knew that her mother would want to come and start working on her wedding dress.

"What did she say?" Megan asked before she remembered that Louisa could not read. The older woman only smiled and handed her the piece of parchment.

Megan saw instantly that she had been only half right. Annora did want to work on Megan's clothes, but not at Hawkings Crest. The letter said in no uncertain terms that Megan should return to Stone Lake immediately. Megan knew there was no real hurry, but Annora liked to have things done very quickly, and where Megan was concerned she was never long on patience.

"Is she coming?"

"No. She wants me at Stone Lake."

"Oh." Louisa thought this sounded fine. She did not notice Megan's lack of enthusiasm. "Shall I go with you?"

"Oh, Aunt Louisa, that would be wonderful," Megan responded, loving the idea. "But I have to go right away." Megan nearly apologized.

"I shouldn't think that would be any problem. Let's find Bracken right now and ask him to arrange a guard." This proved to be easier said than done. No one in the castle knew of his lordship's whereabouts, and not until they tracked down Arik did they learn he was on the practice field.

They found him dripping with sweat. Kendrick had just trounced him soundly on the jousting field, and he was not happy with his own performance. He was a knight, he reminded himself, not some smooth-faced boy, and yet he had fought like young Clive on his first assignment. Thus, he was in a foul mood and not at all happy to see the women. Unfortunately, he didn't bother to mention that his black disposition had nothing to do with them.

"Why have you come?" he asked bluntly.

Megan was instantly put off by his tone, but Louisa, looking forward to going to Megan's home, barged right in and explained.

"She wants you at Stone Lake Castle?" Bracken questioned just minutes later.

"Yes," Louisa meekly answered for Megan, now seeing that they had chosen an inappropriate time.

"Why?"

Megan's chin rose. "It's not my idea, Bracken, so you need not scowl at me so. It would suit me fine to stay right here, but I have no real reason to refuse my mother. If you do not wish me to leave, then *you* may contact Annora and explain why I don't need a wedding dress."

As often happened, her anger amused him. She was so little and feisty, and unless he was angry himself, when her eyes flashed green fire he found her adorable. Megan would have groaned had he shared his thoughts. She did make such a diligent effort when it came to the sin of anger, but right now all she saw was the sparkle in Bracken's eyes, and being laughed at was unbearable to her.

"I am so pleased that I can serve as jester for your keep, my lord, and now that you've had your fun, I will take my leave."

She turned on her heel, but Bracken's arm shot out, and he caught the back of her skirt in one large fist. Megan stiffened with rage and insult but would not turn to look at him.

"Release me!" she commanded, her arms now stiff at her side, her hands balled into fists.

Bracken ignored her and spoke to Louisa.

"When did you wish to leave?"

"As soon as possible."

Bracken nodded before transferring his gaze to Megan. Louisa saw him smile at the back of her. She also watched as he pulled gently on the fabric in his hand until Megan was forced to back up or fall. Not until she was nearly touching him did she suddenly spin and whip the fabric from his grasp. Louisa took her exit on that move.

Megan now stood, her magnificent bosom heaving, and glared at her betrothed. She was ready to give him the sharp side of her tongue, but he disarmed her with one gently put sentence.

"I do not wish you to run from me when you are angry."

Megan stared at him.

"It does no good," he went on. "It only puts walls between us that must be painfully torn down at another time."

Megan's shoulders slumped in defeat. It's so true, she thought, *and once again I have sinned with anger.*

"I'm sorry, Bracken."

"As am I." His voice was sincere. "I was not making sport of you."

"But you did laugh," Megan said, trying to understand.

"Not because I see you as a buffoon, but out of delight."

This made no sense to Megan at all, but Bracken was so new at expressing himself he didn't know how to carry on. Instead he said, "I'll order a guard right now. We'll be ready to leave in less than an hour."

"We?"

"Yes. I'll be going with you."

Megan frowned. "Because you do not trust me to return?"

"No," Bracken answered honestly. Such a thing had never occurred to him. "I would know that you have arrived safely at your father's castle and will return in good health as well. I can't see to this if I'm not with you. That is all."

Megan could only nod. She thanked him quietly and turned away from the field.

How long, Lord, she prayed silently. *How long will I forget myself and sin against Your name? I confess my anger and ask Your strength to resist this sin.*

Megan finished her prayer by asking for forbearance when seeing her mother. It seemed she could never please Annora, but as she could think of little else but seeing her, Megan was feeling very faithless by the time they left for Stone Lake.

The ride was long, and because they hadn't left Hawkings Crest until after the noon meal, they even spent a night camped in the forest. But to Megan's mind, she was standing before her mother before she felt prepared.

Her mother surveyed her with censorious eyes, and for the first time Megan found something over which to be thankful. Her mother was never a hypocrite. It wasn't easy that she never spared Megan's feelings in front of others or put up a false front, but she was honest. She believed that everyone was able to see the deficiencies in her youngest child.

"Go and bathe. I have fabric here, but you can't possibly get near anything when you reek of horses."

Megan began to move away.

"Don't slouch!" Annora barked at her. Megan, whose shoulders were already straight as a line, put them back unnaturally. She kept on toward the stairs and did not look back, even when she heard her mother say, "Well, at least you seemed to have dropped some weight. I'm sure Lord Bracken does not want a fat bride."

"Annora!" Vincent reprimanded her in a whisper of great heat.

"Do *not* defend her, Vincent," Annora came right back at him, not bothering to lower her own voice. "You know I'm right. Now, please introduce me to Lady Louisa."

The introductions were made, but poor Louisa heard little of them. At one point during the confrontation with Megan and her mother, Louisa had had to put a restraining hand on Bracken's arm, and she was still so shaken by what she had seen and heard that she didn't know if she'd replied well to Lady Annora or not.

A gracious hostess when she chose to be, Annora commented kindly, "You must be weary. Would you like to see your chambers?"

"Yes, please." Louisa's voice was wooden, but Annora did not seem to notice.

"And you, Bracken, would you like to go up also?"

Bracken answered with little more than a nod of his head, but Annora paid little attention. She knew how moody men could be. She saw them both to their rooms, unaware of the way Bracken kept an eye on his hostess. He went to Louisa's room just as soon as the hallway was clear.

"I wish to be alone," Louisa spoke on his knock.

"It's me, Aunt Lou," Bracken said, and the door was opened immediately. He hugged her the moment the door closed.

"Oh, Bracken," she whispered, barely holding tears as she stepped from his embrace. "I had no idea, not a clue."

"I know," he said. "I was certain the situation had to be difficult, but I wasn't aware of the full extent myself. I must admit that I've judged Megan too harshly where the relationship with her mother is concerned."

Louisa went to a chair. She was trembling so badly that she had to sit down.

"I'm angry at Annora," she admitted. "But I'm furious with Vincent. When he was at Hawkings Crest, he made me think his love for Megan was indescribably deep, but as soon as Annora fought with him, he backed down like a man defeated. If he truly loved Megan, how could he do such a thing?"

"I do not know, but I don't think I can take much more."

"What will you do?"

"I am not certain. Were she already my wife, I would not have remained silent, but when the situation is like this, I hesitate to act."

As soon as he had seen that Louisa was going to be all right, Bracken returned to his room and paced for a time. He was most anxious to see Megan, but it had taken more contemplation on what he'd seen to strengthen his resolve in another man's castle and with that man's daughter. In the end he reasoned that although Megan was not yet his wife, he didn't have to stand back and see her abused in any way.

With that thought firmly planted in his mind, he left his bedchamber. A servant was passing, and with the authority that came naturally to him, he said, "I wish to see Lady Megan."

"Yes, my lord," the servant responded, swiftly changing direction. "I'll show you the way."

Once at the door, Bracken knocked. The door was opened by another servant after just a moment.

"I wish to see Lady Megan," Bracken repeated.

"Of course, my lord. Just one moment."

The door was closed in his face, but the woman was back directly.

"Lady Megan asks if she can meet with you in a few minutes."

"That would be fine."

The servant came out into the hall. "I'll show you to the salon."

Bracken followed without a word and was inside the spacious upstairs salon for less than five minutes before Megan joined him. He could see at a glance that she had bathed, and this reminded him of his own unwashed state. At any rate, the loveliness of her face and form did not distract Bracken from what he considered to be a more important matter—Megan's heart. And Bracken planned to know the state of that vital member before either one of them left the room.

"How are you, Megan?" Bracken wasted no time.

"I'm well," she told him, having understood exactly why he wished to see her. "Bracken, don't mind Mother. She is often like that." Megan smiled to reassure him, but Bracken was not convinced. The young earl refused to believe that Annora's words had no effect. Bracken wanted to know more but wasn't sure how to question her. While he was still weighing his next words, Annora herself interrupted them.

"Megan, I am ready for you."

Does her voice always sound so harsh and impatient when she speaks to Megan? Bracken wondered.

"I trust that I'm not disturbing anything," Annora said belatedly, and in a voice that said it wouldn't have mattered.

"No," Megan answered with a swift look at Bracken. "I'll see you later, Bracken."

"Yes," was all the young knight could manage before both women swept out of the room.

Much to Bracken's surprise, the remainder of day was not a disaster. He even managed to find some time with Megan in the late afternoon. They were not alone exactly, since the great hall was always occupied, but they had taken two chairs by the hearth and actually talked for an hour without being disturbed.

"How did the dress fitting go?" Bracken had searched his mind for several minutes for something to talk about and was feeling quite proud of his opening.

"Well, there isn't a dress yet, only fabric. I liked one in particular, but Mother wanted another."

Bracken couldn't stop the stiffening in his body. "Which one did you choose?"

Megan's smile was genuine. "Which do you think?"

Bracken reluctantly smiled back. "Do you ever grow weary of her way with you?"

"Oh, yes," Megan admitted, her eyes now far off. "It's easier not to be here, but God has taught me many things through my relationship with my mother."

Bracken frowned. "You make it sound as if it is God's will that she treat you so."

Megan's head tipped to one side. "In a way, it is. It is not a mistake that she is my mother."

"I don't understand."

"I believe God is sovereign, which means He rules over all and has a purpose in each circumstance. If that's the case, Bracken, then He is in control of *everything*—even when it doesn't please Him."

Bracken had never thought of it that way. He believed in God, but he also believed in himself. He never hesitated to mentally give God the honor for his strong body and wealth, but Bracken believed that if he wanted something, he would have to fight for it. Before this conversation, Bracken would have said that God controlled all, but he wasn't sure what to do with Megan's belief concerning her mother. God had put the heavens and earth into motion—Bracken was certain of this—but right now he was not convinced that God's hand still moved.

"I know that doesn't excuse Mother, but as I said, God has taught me things." Bracken had stayed silent for so long that Megan felt she had to go on. He now nodded in acknowledgement but changed the subject.

"Do you know how long your mother needs you here?"

"No, she doesn't say. Is there a reason we need to be away?"

"No, but I enjoy my own home."

"You could leave me," Megan suggested, although she hated the idea.

Bracken didn't answer verbally, but slowly shook his head. He would never leave her here at Annora's mercy. The subject changed, so Bracken was unaware of what a relief his staying was for Megan.

Not long afterward, the young couple was joined by Louisa

and Lyndon. The four visited until it was time for the evening meal. On a whole, the evening ended on a fairly high note, but Bracken was still concerned over Annora's treatment of Megan. Her manner toward her that evening was subtle enough that he felt it would have been inappropriate to comment, but he took himself off to bed hoping they could leave soon and feeling very thankful that Marigold was not present.

Twenty

BRACKEN WOKE IN THE NIGHT and knew instantly that someone was in his bedchamber. His breathing never changed, so as not to alert the intruder, but he was fully cognizant and ready to spring into action at the slightest provocation. He was startled upright when he suddenly heard Megan's soft voice.

"I must see if he understands."

"Megan?" Bracken spoke and reached for his robe before moving from the bed.

"I'm sure he'll change his mind."

Bracken heard the words but did not understand. He lit a torch and placed it in a sconce on the wall before turning and finding Megan in a chair by the cold hearth. Bracken could hardly believe his eyes as she sat dressed in a long, heavy night garment. Not looking at him, she still continued to speak. Bracken caught the words as he came nearer.

"I will do my best to make him understand."

"Megan," Bracken said gently. "You may not be in my room."

"I must find Bracken," she said.

"I'm right here."

Megan shook her head, and it was then that he realized she was asleep. With Arik on guard, the situation at home was so well in hand that Bracken had completely forgotten about the problem.

"Megan, wake up and go back to your room."

"Not until I find Bracken and make him understand."

"Understand what?"

"That I have always looked this way. I have at times been a glutton, but not now, not for many years. I have always looked heavy."

"You look fine."

"My mother is sure to be right; she always is. Bracken will not want a fat wife."

"Bracken does not think you're fat."

It was spoken with such authority that Megan paused. Bracken knew that if he touched her she would awaken, but maybe now was the time to clear this up.

Of course, Bracken now reminded himself. *She never remembers anything in the morning.*

For some reason the thought of waking her bothered Bracken. He remembered so clearly the night he'd touched her and woken her in the great hall at Hawkings Crest. She had seemed vulnerable and shaken, and Bracken hoped it would never happen again. There must be another way. In just a moment, Bracken had a plan.

Megan was talking again, but Bracken ignored her and went to open the door. Lyndon, who had been sleeping in a small chamber to the side of Bracken's room, now heard the noise and joined him. He watched in fascination at what Bracken did next.

The young earl went behind Megan's chair and carefully lifted the back legs from the floor. Why Megan was sitting down, he wasn't certain, but as he expected, the action unsettled her, and she stood. Bracken then moved the chair against her and she took a step forward. It took only a minute for her to notice the open door. Bracken followed her far enough down the hall to see that a maid, having only just discovered her absence, had now come out of Megan's room.

"Come, my lady," Bracken heard the girl say. He stood still until they disappeared behind the closed portal and then turned back to his room. Lyndon stared at him in the dark, thinking how well he'd handled the situation.

"Would you like me to stand guard at her door?"

"Thank you, Lyndon, but I think the maid will take care of things now."

The men stood silently for a moment.

"It is amazing that she can sleep like that," Lyndon commented with wonder in his voice.

"Do you think I should have woken her?" Bracken was suddenly not sure.

"No, you did exactly right. I have never known a woman with such courage and pluck who also needed to be handled so delicately."

"Nor have I," Bracken added.

A moment later they parted, each to try to finish the night's rest in his own bed.

Megan and Louisa broke the fast together, both having slept a little late.

"I haven't stayed in bed that long in years," Louisa admitted.

"Did you not sleep well?"

"Not really," Louisa told her and then fell silent. Megan became alert.

"What is it, Aunt Louisa? Is your chamber uncomfortable?"

"My chamber is fine," she assured the younger woman.

"Then something is bothering you," Megan stated.

Louisa only looked at her, and after a moment Megan dropped her eyes. "I think I would have walked here from Hawkings Crest, as I did before, rather than cause you and Bracken such pain over this household."

"I had no idea, Megan." Louisa's voice was just over a whisper.

Megan smiled ruefully. "It's funny sometimes."

"What is?"

"Me," Megan admitted. "I will stand toe-to-toe with Bracken, even if I'm terrified, but it's not often that I will confront Mother."

"Why do you suppose that is?" Louisa asked. Until that very moment Megan did not know; suddenly it was so clear.

"Because Mother will never back down." Megan's voice showed surprise at her discovery. "She would rather fight around the clock than admit defeat. Bracken does not treat me so. He is in many ways a more mature person than my mother."

It seemed an odd thing for a daughter to say, but Louisa could see it was true.

"You seem to have accepted the situation, Megan."

"I guess I have. I've never lived here for very long; indeed, I have not considered this place to be my own for many years, so I see no reason in trying to alter things.

"And of course now I'm going to wed Bracken, so truly, any home I've known here will be a thing of the past. Aside from all of that, God has shown me that He will never leave me, no matter where I dwell."

Louisa reached for Megan's hand. "I so admire your faith, Megan."

"It is nothing unusual, Aunt Louisa. I would be glad to tell you of it."

"I would like to hear."

Megan smiled, her heart speeding up with anticipation and delight as she tried to think of a place where they would be certain to have privacy. She thought the chapel might be best, but before she could suggest such a thing, Annora entered the room. That she was upset was obvious from across the floor.

"Megan." Annora's voice was penetrating.

Thinking her mother would come closer, Megan stood, but she stayed at a far range.

"I would have an audience with you."

Megan apologized to Louisa with one glance and received a sympathetic look in reply. Megan had no more reached her mother when Annora turned abruptly and led her daughter down a passage and to the room her father used for a den. As with most of the Stone Lake castle, it was immaculate and beautifully furnished, but the coldness of the woman who ruled over it made the room seem chilled.

"You will tell me immediately what you did last night."

"Last night?" Megan asked, her brow drawn in puzzlement. "Before I went to bed?"

"No." Annora's voice was frigid. "I mean when the castle lay sleeping and your father and I *thought* you were asleep as well."

"I don't know what you mean," Megan tried to explain, but her mother's face became so red that she left off what she was saying.

"I know you were in his room, Megan—I know you visited Bracken's room last night."

"Mother, I didn't," Megan began, but got no further.

Annora's open hand seemed to come out of nowhere. She slapped Megan's cheek with such force that her head snapped back.

"Do not lie to me!" Annora was screeching now. "You're sure to be with child; we must move the wedding date."

"No, Mother, I swear to you."

Annora struck her again, and while her ears were still ringing, Megan moved, her hands feeling for the furniture as her eyes flooded with tears. The side of her face felt on fire, and for the first time Megan actually feared her mother. Her voice quivering, she spoke from behind a chair.

"I have done nothing wrong, Mother," Megan began, but Annora came after her.

"You lying little strumpet. My maid saw you. Do you think me a fool? And after all your father and I have done for you, you come home and disgrace us while we sleep."

Annora continued to pursue Megan, her intent very clear, but Megan's back was finally at the door. She could see that it was no use trying to reason with her enraged parent, so she dashed the back of her hand across her wet eyes and ran.

"Megan! Come back this instant!"

The small redhead ignored the outburst and continued to flee. Louisa was still in the great hall and took in every detail of Megan's pitiful face, but Megan didn't see her. All she could think of was escaping her mother, and she ran as if her life depended on it.

"Lyndon?" Louisa called to the young knight from across the inner bailey, just ten minutes later.

The handsome young man approached her with a smile on his face that abruptly disappeared when he neared. Louisa's eyes were red and puffy, and the strength in the hand that grasped his arm felt desperate.

"I must find Bracken," she whispered.

"This way," Lyndon said shortly.

A moment later Louisa stood before Bracken, who had been inside one of the turrets mending a halter. The moment she saw him, she began to tremble.

"Bracken, please find Megan. Something awful has happened. Annora was angry, and then Megan ran from the great hall. Oh, please." She could say no more, but nothing more was needed.

Bracken left her in Lyndon's care and began to step away.

"The chapel, Bracken," Lyndon spoke before his lord was out of earshot. "I saw her going toward the chapel. Try there."

The tears had finally stopped, but the trembling remained. Megan knew her mother would never seek her out in the chapel, but the shock and hurt were slow in receding.

"Please help me, Father God," she whispered in the quiet of the chapel. "Please help me to be calm, and please don't let her find me. I have to find a way to explain. If Bracken had been there he could have told her, but if I go and look for him, she's sure to find me."

The tears were starting again, so Megan stopped and tried to calm herself. She wasn't very successful but stayed on her knees until she heard the door open. She bolted into the shadows, but she knew that whoever had entered had heard her gasping sobs.

The footsteps on the cobbled floor halfway up the center aisle were unnerving, but Megan tried not to breathe. She nearly collapsed with relief when Bracken said, "Megan, are you here?"

Megan took a huge breath but stayed in the shadows.

"Is my mother with you?"

"No, it's just I."

Still wary, she emerged from the shadows but did not approach. Bracken came forward as soon as he spotted her and stopped just a foot before her. It was on his lips to make light of the tears, even chide her for overreacting to whatever had occurred, but just enough light from the window streamed onto Megan's face to stop the words in his throat.

With her hands clenched together in front of her, Megan stood still, her eyes on Bracken's face. She remained utterly silent as two of his long fingers came out to rest ever so gently on the underside of her jaw. Very carefully he turned her bruised cheek full into the light from the stained-glass window. The entire cheek was very red and puffy except for a raised cut and a bruise that was forming on the cheekbone.

Megan could not see his face then, or she would have witnessed the movement of his beard, his own jaw bunching, as he regarded Annora's handiwork. He tried to control his emotions before he spoke, but he couldn't quite manage.

"Who did this to you?" he said, knowing already.

Bracken had dropped his hand, but Megan saw it clench at his side. Even if she'd been blind, there was no mistaking the anger in his voice.

"My mother," Megan said, and more tears came. "Please talk to her Bracken, please tell her I didn't visit your room last night."

Bracken's eyes slid momentarily shut. Agony ripped through him. He should have awakened her. When he spoke, his voice was deep with regret.

"You were in my room last night, Megan," he began, and watched her eyes go wide with shock. "But you were sound asleep."

"Oh, no," Megan sobbed. "I never even thought. I mean, it's usually disruptive to me when I visit here, but I just didn't think. And the maid is new. I never thought to warn her."

The tears that had been trickling now came in a torrent as Bracken wrapped his arms around her. Megan sobbed into his shirt for several minutes.

Bracken's hand was gentle beyond description as it smoothed her hair, but his heart was a mass of enraged determination. When Megan calmed some, Bracken's hands went to her upper arms and he held her out in front of him.

"I'm taking you away from here."

Megan blinked at him. Her eyes felt gritty, as though someone had rubbed sand into them.

"Where are we going?"

"Back to Hawkings Crest."

"What will my parents say?"

"It doesn't matter. I won't allow you to stay here a day longer."

Megan opened her mouth to speak but realized she had no words. No one had ever shown her the kind of caring Bracken was now demonstrating. Her mother's word was law, and everyone, including her father, accepted her mother's actions, reprehensible as they were.

Suddenly lighthearted with emotion, she agreed to Bracken's plan with just the smallest nod of her head. A moment later they were moving back outside and toward the castle, where Bracken would leave Megan in Louisa's room and in her keeping until they could be away.

Twenty-One

BRACKEN FOUND LORD VINCENT in his bedchamber. At any other time Bracken would not have disturbed him in such a place, but at the moment the older man could have been bathing and Bracken would have demanded a hearing.

"We are leaving," he said without preamble.

Vincent nodded. "I have just been informed of Annora's behavior. She did not handle things well; I understand how you must feel."

"Megan will not be back."

It wasn't until that very moment that something in Bracken's tone arrested Vincent's attention. He rose from his place by the window and approached his houseguest. He gazed at the younger man for long moments before deciding he did not like what he saw—repugnance and fury.

"What do you mean she will not be back?" Vincent finally demanded.

"I mean that I'm taking Megan from Stone Lake within the hour, and she will not return here again."

"Her dress is—"

Bracken cut the older man off with a downward slash of his hand.

"I care not for her dress. It is her safety I am thinking of—something she can not find in this castle."

"That is ridiculous! What of the wedding?"

"The wedding will be at Hawkings Crest."

Vincent was now angry himself. "This is my daughter you speak of. You will not tell me—" He stopped on Bracken's short bark of mirthless laughter.

"I will tell you *many* things," Bracken told him ruthlessly. "We speak of Megan not as your daughter but as my betrothed by Henry's order. At one time you told me you would never countenance abuse toward Megan, but the shrew to whom you are married has become violent, and you do nothing. I will remove Megan from her claws before I become violent myself. Dress fittings or meetings of any kind will take place at Hawkings Crest, where I can keep an eye on the woman you seem incapable of controlling."

As far as Bracken was concerned, the meeting was finished, but Vincent's anger now spilled over. His face boiling with rage, Vincent let Bracken get as far as the door before he threw what he believed would be a lethal barb.

"And what of the fact that Megan was spotted coming from your room last night?"

"Aye," Bracken said from the door, his voice still angry but now controlled. "She was there as you say. Asleep on her feet."

Bracken had been the one to throw the final barb, and when the door slammed, Vincent sank into a chair. His dear Megan, so innocent of Annora's charge, haunted his mind. Annora would never see reason. Bracken had been correct, he was incapable of controlling his wife. Vincent suddenly felt old beyond his years.

As when they had journeyed from Hawkings Crest, Bracken's party once again camped in the woods. Stopping well before dark, Bracken was able to take a careful assessment of how his aunt and betrothed were faring.

Louisa looked tired, but her spirits were high. He knew for a fact that she was tremendously relieved to be leaving Annora and the situation at Stone Lake. As they ate, Bracken studied Megan's face, her eyes specifically. He found that she did not seem overly tired, but neither did she appear to be at peace. Louisa ate with them, causing Bracken to hold his comments, but when the older woman rose to see to a private matter, Bracken spoke.

"How fare you, Megan?"

"I'm all right," she told him humbly.

Bracken was not convinced. "Has your mother long made it a habit of striking you?"

Megan nodded. "For as long as I can remember."

"And what would your father do?"

"Remove me, much as you have done."

"But there were no repercussions for your mother? He never tried to change her?"

"No," Megan said with some surprise. "I don't think such a thing ever occurred to him."

They fell silent for a moment, and then Megan asked the question that had been on her heart since they left the inner bailey at Stone Lake.

"My father did not come to bid us goodbye. Did you have words?"

"Yes. I told him I was taking you, and you would not be back."

Megan stared at him. "What of the wedding?"

"It will take place at Hawkings Crest."

Megan now stared into the gathered dusk. Bracken heard her sigh before she softly asked, "What if my parents do not come for the wedding?"

Bracken gently captured her jaw with his hand and spoke after he'd urged her eyes to meet his own.

"I will still make you my wife, and in so doing, I will have the authority to never again allow your mother, or anyone else, to harm you." He steeled himself to hear her protest, but she acquiesced with a small move of her head. Bracken let his hand drop and would have reached for Megan's small one as it lay in her lap, but Louisa was returning.

"I am glad you're still sitting here, Bracken," Louisa spoke with pleasure as she gracefully sank onto the rich counterpane that had been laid out on the forest floor. "I want to ask you a question. What is to be done about Megan's dress?"

"Her dress?" Bracken frowned at his aunt and then turned his attention to Megan's clothing. She looked fine to him in a gown of dark green with rust-colored trim. Indeed, he found her beautiful.

"Yes, Bracken," Louisa continued patiently. "Her wedding dress."

"Oh." It was clearly the last thing on Bracken's mind, and Louisa had to hide a smile. It was on her tongue to jump in with several suggestions, but she sat patiently and let Bracken think. He did not disappoint her.

"Let us give Lady Annora a few weeks to contact Megan and possibly make reparations. If that doesn't happen, then go to the village and do whatever it takes to see that she is properly outfitted."

"As you wish," Louisa stated, feeling well pleased.

Bracken stood then, his eyes sweeping back to Megan's enchanting face, framed by an abundance of dark red curls, before once again resting on Louisa. "Spare no expense," he told his aunt as he moved off toward his men.

Two weeks passed without word from Megan's mother or father. Megan was not surprised that her mother had not been in touch, but her father's lack of communication cut deeply. He had never been a man to lavish great attention upon her, but up until now, Megan had always felt that he cared. Now she was beginning to wonder. It was only just becoming clear to her that he had never once taken her side, at least not strongly enough to deal with Annora or suggest repercussions as Bracken had mentioned. The thought weighed on Megan's heart. She spent much time in prayer over it, but there were times when she would take her eyes from God's sovereignty and the situation would get her down.

It was at such a time that Bracken spoke with Louisa concerning Megan's dress. The older woman immediately approached Megan, who was a little shocked and very pleased that he had actually remembered. The women decided to leave for the village directly after the noon meal.

The day was warm but not miserable, and Arik, along with a few other men, went with the ladies. Protection was not really needed for the village, but the guard gave Bracken peace of mind as he stood in the inner bailey and watched them ride away.

The trip was fairly routine for Louisa, but Megan, so new to the area, considered it an adventure. She had never been into the town near Hawkings Crest and was more than a little curious. Megan found that it was not a long ride, 20 minutes or less, and the first thing she spotted was a church. It was a simple, squarely built structure, but since not every village sported a place of worship, it was a pleasure for Megan to see. She wondered if they would have time to visit and possibly speak with the local priest.

She was very aware of the attention she and Louisa produced as they rode in on Bracken's finest horses and in clothing of luxurious fabric rich with color. Her face, never haughty, was serene, and her smile melted the hearts of several children and a few old women. They dismounted before a pub, the men assisting them.

"We shall meet you back here in an hour," Louisa informed them, not wanting to be dogged by these men while she shopped.

"Very well, my lady," the shortest of the men answered, but Arik, as they soon learned, took no such notice. He walked slowly, some 20 odd paces behind Megan, but with the clear intention of not letting her out of his sight. Megan didn't really care. Indeed, the thought of shopping had so buoyed her mood that she didn't mind at all.

"I think in here, Meg," Louisa said just ten yards down the street.

The women entered a small shop full of various dry goods. It was clean and smelled of fresh leather, but Megan could see at a glance that it held nothing suitable. She was surprised when Louisa did not immediately turn to go but instead walked rather noisily through the store, talking loudly to Megan, touching fabrics and commenting on every one.

Megan was still staring at Louisa as if she'd taken leave of her senses when a woman appeared at the rear. Where she had come from Megan was not exactly sure, but when she saw Louisa she smiled a gape-toothed smile and motioned her over with one long, crooked finger.

Louisa followed, and Megan, out of sheer curiosity, was right behind her. They moved behind a high shelf and through a doorway, and Megan immediately saw that this was the woman's living quarters. The bed, washbasin, and kitchen table were all set very close together in the same room. There was also a door, short and not overly wide, and closed tightly. The old woman stopped before it and drew forth a key. When it was unlocked, she pushed the door wide. She stepped inside, Louisa at her heels and Megan just behind.

"New," she proclaimed as she fingered an especially fine bolt. "Just in, it is. Bought from Elias the peddler."

Stacked on shelves and hanging from pegs in every conceivable nook and cranny, rich accouterments of every type littered the room, but Megan saw none of them. She could not tear her eyes from the fabric in the woman's gnarled hands.

"Megan, what is it?" Louisa asked, having just seen her look.

"The fabric. My mother had chosen this and one other. She preferred the other and that was to be my dress, but this one," she paused, "this was my choice."

Louisa smiled, although Megan still did not notice.

"We'll take it," the older woman spoke softly. The proprietress chuckled softly as she named an exorbitant price.

"That," Louisa stated calmly, "is outrageous." Whereupon she started to dicker with the woman in a way that finally gained Megan's attention. She listened to Louisa in awe and began to wonder if she knew Bracken's aunt at all. She barely gave an inch, and when the bartering session was over, Louisa took the fabric in triumph. It had cost the moon, but she was well pleased. Other notions were purchased, although not haggled over, and within 30 minutes Megan and Louisa were back on the street. Arik was standing nearby, as Megan knew he would be, and fell into step behind them once again.

"Louisa, I've never seen you like that."

Louisa laughed at herself. "I can't begin to tell you how much I enjoy it." She lifted the plainly wrapped package. "And I think you'll agree that it was worth it."

Megan laughed in return, but a moment later Louisa said soberly, "Megan, I'm so sorry your mother sold your dress fabric."

"Thank you, Aunt Louisa, but she didn't want that one for me. I don't know why she bought two and gave me a choice; she had already made up her mind."

"And what of the other fabric? Will you end up with two wedding dresses?"

"No, I'm sure not." Megan shook her head in resignation. "If my mother comes to the wedding, she will no doubt be wearing a dress made from the other cloth."

"But wasn't the color fit for a wedding dress? Surely she will not shame the bride."

"No, there will be no shame. This fabric is most fitting. The other was a light blue velvet."

"Oh, Megan," Louisa said with pleasure. "This cream satin will be so much more beautiful on you. I hope you're pleased."

Megan hugged the other woman. The setting was not the best, but she felt so full of joy that she could think of no other way to express it.

Her joy might have been dimmed somewhat had she looked

up to a second-story window above the tavern and seen the woman standing above.

"What are you looking at?" The question came from the man who was lying on the large bed in the sparsely furnished room.

"My sister," the woman at the window answered.

This brought the man from the bed to look out. After a moment, he offered his estimation.

"She's not the beauty you are."

Marigold smiled, her eyes still on Megan. "Few women are."

Roland Kirkpatrick, third son of Lord Kirkpatrick, smiled in return. She was right, of course, but he would never tell her so. She was already so vain she believed herself too good for him. Marigold had never let him touch her, and she wouldn't today, but he didn't care. He told himself that just to be near her was enough.

Marigold had been blackmailing him for weeks. She had found out just days after the incident that he had been behind the killing of her father's men and the stealing of his horses. He had believed them to be carrying gold. Roland cared not one wit if Vincent knew of his actions, but the knowledge had given Marigold a certain form of power, and as long as she kept coming to him for favors—money and whatever small jobs her scheming mind could conjure up to keep her from soiling her own hands—he was content to let her believe she had him at her mercy.

He watched now as she let the curtain fall back over the glass. He knew she was about to leave, so he decided to beat her to the punch.

"I've got to be going," Roland said smoothly, and was well satisfied with the momentary look of surprise in her eyes. "I'll see you later."

"Yes." Just that swiftly, Marigold was back in control. "Who knows when we may need to do business again."

Roland smiled at her, his look amused, but he didn't answer. He would have been pleased to know that she stood thinking about him for a long time afterward.

❧ ❧ ❧

"Has it been terribly upsetting to you, Megan, that you left your home in such a way?" Louisa wondered that she hadn't asked before, but now the time seemed right. Tired but successful, they were riding home, and because the men were several paces off, Louisa felt free to ask.

"It is hard, Aunt Louisa, but not impossible. At least it hasn't been."

"What do you mean?"

"I mean that the kinder Bracken is to me, the more I see a lack in my family. I had no idea anyone could care like that. It's just another way the Lord is taking care of me."

Suddenly Megan's family was forgotten. "You refer to the Lord so often, Megan. Don't you think He cares for all?" Louisa asked.

"Yes," Megan answered carefully, "but not all embrace Him as I have chosen to do."

A glance told Megan that Louisa had no idea what she spoke of.

"I would venture a guess that most everyone in England believes in God. Would you say that's true?"

"Yes," Louisa agreed readily.

"But I would also guess that not even a fraction of that many believe in His Son, the Lord Jesus Christ. That's where the separation comes. I have confessed to God that I am a sinner and that I need a Savior. People need more than just a belief in God or a Sovereign Ruler. They also must believe in His Son and His lifechanging work on the cross."

"But I believe Jesus died on the cross," Louisa reasoned.

"Yes, Louisa, but do you believe He died to save you from your sins?"

Louisa had no answer to this, and Megan's voice became very tender.

"There is nothing magical here, Louisa. It is a simple act of faith, given by God, to trust in His Son's saving power. In such a state, life here on earth is abundant, and afterward there is the promise of life eternal with Him."

"So you do not believe that all people go to heaven?"

"No, I don't," Megan said, her voice still very kind.

She debated saying more, but the castle was now in view. Megan prayed for an opening, but Louisa was ready, at least for the time, to ponder their conversation on her own.

"I will think on all you've said, Megan."

"I'm glad, Louisa. And if at any point, even in the middle of the night, I can be of help to you, please come to me."

"I will, Megan. Thank you."

The remainder of the ride was made in silence as both women thought and prayed. However, Louisa's prayer was different. For the first time she wondered, since she didn't believe as Megan did, if God actually heard her.

Twenty-Two

"YOU ARE A THIEF AND A LIAR," Megan stated calmly.

"I have been steward here for over 40 years!"

Megan snorted with unladylike contempt. "Is that what you call what you do—acting as steward? As far as I can see, you rob your lord blind and grow fat at his expense."

The little man's face turned puce. Megan knew she had been merciless, but there was simply no getting through to this man.

"I will see Lord Bracken over this," he threatened when he could finally speak.

"Don't bother," Megan told him. "Just pack your things and get out."

Again the man looked as if he were on the verge of collapse.

"Lord Bracken will listen to me."

"He might," Megan's tone was maddeningly moderate, "but you will find I am patient. It may take time, but I will prove your true worth." Megan hesitated as her spirit of fair play came to the fore.

"It's not as if you haven't been warned, Barton. We have talked of this many times. My check on the books just this morning showed more entries which I cannot trace."

"You have been in the books again?" He was clearly outraged. "You had no right!"

"I have every right!" Megan shot back, having taken all she

was going to. "And I am also within my rights to repeat myself—pack your bags and leave Hawkings Crest."

Barton trembled with anger, but he was wise enough to see his own defeat. With a head held high in what he would have called righteous indignation, Barton swept from the room. Megan felt no sense of elation or satisfaction. With all of Barton's knowledge of the castle, it would have been wonderful to have him stay, but Megan would never countenance such deceit.

Believing she had done what was necessary, Megan tried to put the incident behind her and move on to another task. She was halfway up the stairs when she remembered Bracken. The thought of him caused her to tuck her lip beneath her teeth. What in the world was he going to say?

"She did *what*?"

"Now Bracken," Lyndon tried to sound reasonable.

"Yes, Bracken," Louisa put in. "You did say you would listen to her more."

"I can't believe this." Bracken spoke as if he hadn't heard either one. "All this time I think things are going smoothly, and now she does this. Why did she not talk to me?"

"I don't know, Bracken, but she has been unhappy about Barton for many weeks."

"In truth, Bracken," Lyndon added, "she did come to you, just last week, but you put her off."

Bracken opened his mouth and shut it. This was true. Megan had come to him at the archery butts when he was working with Kent. Bracken had sent her away without ever getting back to her. Nevertheless, he did not care for the way she'd handled this.

"She should have talked to me."

"Be that as it may, Bracken, it won't do any good searching

her out and blasting her with your temper." Louisa's voice was almost angry, and Bracken turned to look at her. He was slightly amused by her fierce frown and thought how often Louisa had championed Megan since she'd come to live at Hawkings Crest.

"Is that what I do? Blast her with my temper?" He was almost laughing now. Louisa was not.

"You know you do, and if it happens this time, I won't speak to you until the wedding."

All Bracken's amusement fled. "Lou, what is really bothering you?"

Tears welled in the woman's eyes. "She told me that no one has ever shown her the kindness you have. I know you're upset, but I can't stand the thought that you'll hurt her when she's coming to trust and need you so."

The words were very sobering to Bracken, and he tenderly laid a hand on his aunt's shoulder. At the moment he did want to search Megan out and make himself heard, but Louisa was right; he would only frighten and upset her. Yet, every time he thought of Megan going on her own and dismissing Barton, his anger threatened to consume him.

"I will do my best not to fight with Megan, Louisa, but I will talk with her about this."

Louisa could only nod.

"Have you seen her?" Bracken asked of Lyndon.

"Actually I have. I believe she was headed toward the tower."

Bracken nodded, thanked them, and moved toward the door of the war room. Louisa and Lyndon shared a glance. They both hoped that the harmony they had known in the past weeks was not about to be destroyed.

Megan had been on a mission of counting bedrooms, but had long since given up. She'd had no idea how vast Hawkings

Crest really was. *Why, all of England could come for the wedding,* Megan thought, *and we could make comfortable each and every one.*

She was in the tower salon now, checking on something Helga had told her about and feeling well satisfied that there would be room for all guests.

Megan walked the edge of the carpet until she spotted the trouble: It seemed that the hem was fraying. Kneeling at the edge of the rug that lay before the fireplace, Megan saw that Helga's observation was correct. She would have to order it trimmed. So intent was Megan on her task that she never even heard Bracken enter or noticed as he stood quietly against one wall watching her. She stood, ready to walk directly in front of him, when he spoke.

"Going somewhere, Megan?"

Megan started violently and then grew angry. Her arms akimbo, she faced him squarely.

"Bracken! Don't you ever do that again. I never heard a thing."

Bracken only looked at her and asked himself for the tenth time what he was going to do. He had told Brice many weeks ago that he did not want just a pretty face to decorate his castle, but how far was he willing to let her go?

"What brings you to the tower?" he asked at last.

Megan relaxed upon hearing his calm tone. "I was trying to ascertain whether or not we had enough bedrooms for the wedding guests." She now smiled in self-mockery. "I now see that I have wasted my time."

Bracken's own eyes took in the room. Large and airy, it was but one of many just like it, and that did not include the many bedrooms. Megan was right—the castle was a mammoth dwelling.

"I understand our keep is now short a steward."

Bracken was not looking at her or even turned in her direction. The statement had come out so abruptly that Megan was taken completely unaware. She tilted her head slightly to glance at his handsome, bearded profile, but he was still inspecting the room.

"Yes," Megan said.

Bracken then turned to look at her. "That is all? Yes? No explanation?"

"I felt I had no choice," Megan said shortly.

"You could have consulted me."

"You would not listen. I assumed you no longer cared."

"It was never my intent to make light of the situation, Megan; Barton has been with my family for years."

"I am heartily sick to death of hearing that!" Megan burst out so vehemently that it was Bracken's turn to be startled.

"It doesn't seem to make any difference to you that he was *stealing*. Do you hear me, Bracken, he was *stealing* from you! I spoke with him; I gave him a chance; but even knowing that I could read and monitor his actions changed nothing. I was still finding entries that could be nothing short of theft."

They stood, eyes locked, Megan now red in the face and Bracken's face looking as though like it was made of stone.

"I still say it wasn't your place."

"You're right!" Megan shot back at him. "It was yours."

She watched his eyes grow hard, and the fight drained out of her. When she continued, her voice was soft.

"If I've learned anything about you while living here, Bracken, it's that you're no fool. This is why I am confused. Only a fool would allow a man to stay in the name of sentiment when that man was stealing from him. I did this for you. I did this for Hawkings Crest. It would seem I've done wrong."

Megan turned for the door, but Bracken's voice stopped her.

"Don't go."

Megan stopped but did not turn.

"Look at me, Megan."

She shook her head no. Tears had come to her eyes, tears she hated herself for. She did not want him to see them, but she heard him move and knew that in a moment he would stand before her. When he did stop, Megan turned her face away in an attempt to hide her eyes.

Bracken did not turn her face to his, but he could clearly see the tear that slid down her cheek. He could also see that she was trying to hold others back.

"Mayhap I am thickheaded," Bracken said reflectively. "You might need to ask me more than once and not give up so easily. Just as you have learned about me, I have also done some learning of my own, and I would say you are not a quitter."

"No, I'm not," Megan agreed, and then realized that quit was exactly what she'd done.

"But you did not pursue the matter with me, and now I wish you had."

Megan nodded; he was quite correct. She chanced a look at him.

"Next time I'll be a shrew."

Bracken took on a look of mock horror. "You mean there's more?"

Megan tried not to smile, but failed. "I'm sure I'll think of something."

Bracken smiled in return, and his voice turned thoughtful. "Just three weeks now, and you will be mistress of this keep."

Megan nodded, feeling more at peace with the prospect than ever before. "Does that have you worried?"

"No," he told her. "I think you will do well."

There wasn't anything that could have given Megan as much pleasure. She smiled at him, and Bracken thought, not for the first time, that they should talk more. They were both so busy and ofttimes going in opposite directions, but whenever they had a chance to speak, he could tell that Megan became a little more comfortable with him.

At that point they walked down to the great hall together. As they moved it came to Bracken without warning: He was swiftly coming to prefer Megan's company over anyone else's. The thought so surprised him that when Megan said she had to see

Helga, he barely heard her. It was a thought he pondered on for the remainder of the day.

Stephen rode toward Hawkings Crest in easy companionship with his cousins, Derek and Richard. Brice would bring their mother to the wedding, as well as escort everyone but Danella, whose baby was very young. Stephen had found himself with a need to be in London and so arranged to ride to Hawkings Crest from there with Louisa's sons.

Having not seen each other for weeks, they talked of many things, but the subject of Bracken's betrothed was not raised until they were just a few miles from the castle.

"So, Stephen," Richard asked. "What can you tell us of Megan?"

"Did your mother not write to you?" he questioned evasively, while trying to keep the smile from his face.

"Yes," Derek told him. "She dictated a letter, but other than the red hair, she didn't really describe her at all. What is she like?"

"Maybe your mother was trying to be kind."

The other men were silent for a moment, looking first at each other and then at Stephen.

"Does she have red hair?" Richard, the younger of the two brothers, wished to know.

"Yes, but it's as bright as a fresh carrot and frizzy around her head like a bird's nest." Stephen's tone was cheerless.

Both of the other men now had looks of pity on their faces, and Bracken's brother had to bite the inside of his cheek to keep from shouting with laughter.

"But she's very sweet," Derek now volunteered. "Mother said as much."

"Yes, she is sweet, and as soon as you get past her face and figure you'll probably like her immensely."

"As bad as all that?"

"I'm afraid so," Stephen told them with a sigh that would have worked on any stage.

"What of Bracken? Is he angry over the arrangement?"

"No. I would say he's resigned himself."

Stephen had to change the subject then, or he would have given himself away. As they finally rode through the gates of Hawkings Crest, he had to restrain himself from rubbing his hands together with anticipation.

Twenty-Three

MEGAN STOOD OVER A LONG, LOW TABLE in the kitchen and bent her sharp mind as to why the sauce she was working on still tasted bitter. There were not many people in the room at the moment, and Megan's attention was on her work, so it was more of an irritant than anything else when she felt a slight tug on her hair. She glanced down to the side to see if one of the children had come in, but when that place was empty she went back to tasting.

When it happened again, Megan's head came up and her brow lowered. She had not imagined it. She turned slowly at first and then more swiftly when she spotted the man behind her.

"Stephen!" Megan tried to look stern.

"Hello, Meg." Stephen's grin was devilish. "You looked in need of a distraction, so I am here."

"A nuisance is more like it." Megan's eyes sparkled back at him for just an instant.

Her words did not dim his smile in the least, but it became very tender when Megan continued to watch him. Stephen witnessed the change in her.

"I take it your family is here?" Megan asked very softly and hesitantly.

"No." He shook his head gently.

Megan's eyes widened.

"I came in with Derek and Richard."

"Louisa's sons?"

"Yes."

"Does she know?"

"She's with them now. Come, I'm sure they want to meet you."

All hesitancy was gone as she was swiftly flooded with relief. Megan took the arm Stephen offered, and as they walked toward the great hall she began to question him about his recent travels. She noticed that he seemed inordinately pleased about something, but she shrugged it off, supposing he was glad to be back at Hawkings Crest.

"It's so good to see you both," Louisa beamed at her sons. They were in Louisa's bedchamber, and after she'd hugged them both twice, they settled themselves by the windows.

"How are things in London?"

"Fine," Derek answered her. "Are you missing it?"

"Yes," Louisa admitted. "Although I'm having a great time with Bracken and Megan."

A look suddenly passed over the faces of both men and Louisa became instantly alert. "That's an odd look I'm getting," she commented, attempting to keep her voice light.

Richard shrugged. "Stephen told us of Megan. He said that she was very sweet, just as you had mentioned in your letter, but as for the other," Richard hesitated uncomfortably, "I guess Bracken has rather resigned himself."

Louisa studied her son's face as her mind ran with every possibility. To what could he be referring? She was on the verge of asking when she remembered that they had ridden out with Stephen. Never one to stand in the way of a harmless prank, Louisa forced a giggle back down her throat, knowing a laugh right then would give the whole thing away. She then wondered just how bad Stephen had made Megan out to be.

"Where are my manners?" Louisa said suddenly and with the intent to distract. "You must be hungry. Come below."

They continued to speak companionably as they descended the large staircase, the men completely innocent of Stephen's scheme and Louisa nearly licking her lips in expectation.

"And who is going to order the wheat?"

"Barton did that as well?"

"Yes," Bracken told her shortly. Whereupon Megan bit her lip and stared at her intended.

Lord and lady were standing in the great hall. Bracken's hands were clasped behind his back, and he was slightly bent at the waist, so that he nearly leaned over Megan as he proceeded to quietly destroy her day.

"My mother's cook sees to that," Megan finally commented, and Bracken only continued to spear her with his eyes. She had been under the impression that the matter concerning Barton was settled, but she had been wrong. Clearly Bracken had not fully forgiven her.

"I'm sorry, Bracken," she said when he refused to speak.

"Sorry doesn't see to the feeding of this keep."

Megan looked away from him then. Stephen was standing nearby, but Megan couldn't meet his eyes.

"What would you like me to do?" Megan asked after a moment, her eyes on the floor.

"First of all, don't act so innocent; it doesn't work on me."

Megan's gaze shot upward, her mouth opening in surprise and hurt.

"Secondly," Bracken went on, "you can find us another steward. Until such a time, you will have to oversee the duties—*all* of them."

The young lord would have gone on then, but Arik entered

and approached. Upon Bracken's order he had been to the village, and Bracken, seeing that he was now ready to report, turned to him. Megan saw her chance for escape and took it.

Bracken had turned to Arik, and after just a minute he happened to glance back at Megan. He took a second look when he found her gone. He spun in a fast circle as his eyes took in the whole of the great room, but other than Louisa, Derek, and Richard coming down the stairs, nothing had changed. Helga was by the other hearth, women were working at the tables, someone was shooing one of the dogs outside, and in the midst of it Megan had quite literally vanished.

He looked to Stephen, but his brother would only grin at him without remorse. Bracken's scowl was fierce, but he eventually looked back to Arik who had waited patiently to finish the report on his findings in the village.

Moments later they were joined by Louisa and her sons. Arik took his leave, and Bracken, after tamping down his irritation with the small redhead who lived in his castle, greeted his cousins warmly.

"Come to the war room, and we'll talk there. I wish to hear of your journey."

"I'll go and order some food," Louisa put in as the men moved forward in a group. Had anyone been looking, they might have noticed the tense line around Stephen's mouth, but he came behind his brother and cousins, and all missed it.

The men were halfway across the floor of the war room when Bracken stopped dead in his tracks. Sitting under a window on the far wall, the account book opened in her lap, was Megan.

"I was not finished talking with you," Bracken spouted without preamble, his family forgotten.

"Well, I was done listening," Megan exclaimed before she thought.

"You," Bracken said, pointing a finger at her, "are the most infuriating woman on the face of the earth."

"And you, sir," Megan shot back, "are rude beyond compare."

"Rude?" Bracken was clearly confused. "What are you talking about?"

"I'm talking about letting me believe that the incident with Barton was behind us and then searching me out to throw it up in my face."

"His jobs are not being done." Bracken's voice told her that this reason excused his manners.

"Then you should have spoken to me."

"I did." Bracken's hands were now outstretched in frustration.

"You did not. You waited until you were snorting like a wounded bull and then sought me out to take me apart piece by piece." Tears were evident in Megan's voice now, and Bracken stood quietly. Neither was aware of his audience.

Stephen, standing nearest the door, chanced a look at his cousins and could almost read their minds.

This is the one both Stephen and Mother said was sweet, but to whose looks Bracken has had to resign himself?

Stephen wanted to chortle with glee, but the timing was all wrong. While he stared at them, Derek and Richard looked to him. Both men told him with one glance that they would get even. Stephen's only reply was to grin unrepentantly.

"I did not mean to attack you," Bracken admitted quietly and started toward her. The men took their cue and departed.

"I was not aware of all Barton's responsibilities. It is not the same for the steward at Stone Lake Castle."

Suddenly Bracken took Megan's hand and pulled her to her feet. He stared down into her eyes for a full minute and for the hundredth time asked himself what he was going to do with her. But this time was different; this time he knew the answer. With the words, *just love her*, ringing in his heart, he said, "We will keep at this, Megan, until we get it right."

Megan stared at him in confusion, so he explained gently.

"I come to you too harshly, and you run whenever you are upset. Eventually I will learn to speak to you with kindness, and you will learn to stay still."

Megan calmed in the face of his tender logic. She liked the way he stayed with something. Never before would she have considered herself a quitter, but compared to Bracken, who came back repeatedly in an attempt to do better, she was just that.

"Come and meet my cousins." Bracken, still holding her hand, turned for the door. Megan stood still and let their arms stretch to the limit.

"The men with Stephen...they are Louisa's sons?" She looked and sounded rather aghast.

"Yes," Bracken told her calmly. "I'm sure they wish to meet you."

"Not after what they just witnessed." Megan shook her head with shame. "They probably wish they could leave."

"No, Megan." Bracken was now amused, knowing how his young cousins would view her. "I assure you, they are waiting very close by."

Megan did not know how he could know such a thing, but with a gentle tug on her arm he urged her toward the door. She soon learned he was correct. Stephen, Louisa, and her sons were waiting not three yards away.

"Here they are," Louisa spoke with pleasure. "Come, Megan, and meet my sons."

Megan approached, her cheeks slightly pink, completely unaware of the charming picture she presented. The square-cut neckline of her gown, the nipped-in waist and full skirt, all trimmed in gold braid, only accentuated the loveliness of her figure. Her hair, pulled back in a length of the same braid, was like a mass of red fire around the creamy skin of her face and neck.

Bracken performed the introductions. "Megan, these are my cousins, Richard and Derek."

"Hello," Megan spoke softly and nodded to both men when they bowed politely before her. She had the impression that something was amiss, but didn't become sure of it until the men raised their heads and studied her with unusual intensity.

Megan's gaze flicked to Bracken, whose look was passive, and then to Stephen who looked a little too angelic for her taste. A glance at Louisa told her the older woman was fighting back laughter. Megan knew then that Stephen had been up to tricks.

She didn't mention the matter, but with one look told Stephen she was onto him. He grinned at her in the same unrepentant way, and a few moments of light conversation followed. Knowing they would meet again at the evening meal, all went their separate ways. Richard spoke when he was finally alone with his brother.

"I think some just retribution is due here."

"Toward Stephen? I quite agree. What do you have in mind?"

Richard was quiet for only an instant. "Today would be too soon, but definitely before the wedding. We'll need everyone's help, including Megan's."

Derek loved the look of mischief in his sibling's eye, and his smile widened as Richard mapped out a plan.

At the meal that evening Megan found that Louisa's sons were as kind and gentle as the woman herself, and there were stories and much laughter as they ate a meal of rich soup filled with onions, leeks, cabbage, beans, and pork. There was dark bread on the side and cheese as well. The sweet was cream with a combination of fruits from the trees at Hawkings Crest.

Megan noticed, however, in the midst of all the good food and fellowship, that Louisa did not seem to be having the best of times. This was a great surprise to the younger woman, for she had known how much Louisa was looking forward to Richard's and Derek's arrival. Megan didn't really know Bracken's cousins, but they seemed very kind. Maybe Louisa had quarreled with one of them.

Megan tried to put it from her mind, but at bedtime, when Louisa was still heavy on her heart, Megan decided to seek her out. Her knock on Louisa's door was answered by Louisa's maid, Kimay, and when the servant told her mistress it was Megan, she was bade to enter. Megan was slightly surprised to find Derek in the room as well. Louisa's features were strained. Megan debated whether or not she should remain, but with one glance at Derek's confused face she came more fully into the room.

"I have no wish to intrude, Aunt Louisa, but is there something I can do?"

Both young people watched as Louisa stood and moved restlessly around the room. She nearly paced before stopping by the bed and facing them.

"Before dinner Derek informed me of a decision he's made, but I am confused."

Megan, desperate to help without intruding, turned to Bracken's cousin. His face was not shuttered, so Megan spoke gently.

"Can you tell me, Derek?"

He nodded. "I have decided to give my life to God—Jesus Christ, actually."

Megan's heart leapt, but she knew that now was not the time to react with outward joy. She turned back to Louisa.

"What is the problem?"

"He says he's giving himself to God. Don't we all belong to God, Megan? What in the world could he mean?" Louisa was near to tears, and Megan did some fast thinking. After just a moment she began to understand. It was one thing for Louisa to have her future niece dedicated to Christ, but when it was her son and she did not understand or share the belief, it somehow said to her that she had failed as a parent.

"I believe Derek feels much as I do, Louisa. I knew a void within my heart, and I understood that Jesus Christ alone could fill that void. A surrendering of oneself to Christ doesn't lessen a person in any way or make it so they have less to give. Indeed, it gives one a greater life to offer.

"Derek's decision should pose no threat to you, Louisa,"

Megan went on very gently, "unless you feel God is calling you to do the same and you are trying to run."

Megan had shot the arrow straight into the heart of the matter. One moment Louisa was standing defensive and scared, and the next she was sobbing with grief and pain. Derek was the one to approach her, and he led her carefully to a chair by the fire.

"I feel as though I can't find Him," Louisa sobbed. "I have watched you, Meg, and I have tried, but I feel as though I will never have your God. And now Derek has come to know Him, and I am still lost."

Derek slipped his arms around his mother, and Louisa cried into his shoulder. Megan sat across from them and begged God to give her the words. She knew He was just waiting to show Louisa the way.

Megan thought that Derek might want to share, but when he remained quiet for several minutes and Louisa seemed more in control, Megan spoke softly.

"Louisa," Megan called to her and waited until she met her eyes. "In the sixteenth psalm, God says He will show us the path of life, in His presence is fullness of joy, and at His right hand are pleasures forevermore. God is not hiding from you, Louisa. He is waiting very patiently for you to reach out to Him."

"I don't know how."

"It sounds to me like you're well on your way," Megan told her with a smile.

"Really?" Louisa's tear-stained face grew hopeful.

Megan nodded. "The Proverbs say that every word of God is pure, and that He is a shield to those who put their trust in Him. Do you believe God's Word, Louisa?"

"Yes, but I have heard so little."

Megan nodded again, this time in understanding. It had been a true privilege to be raised at the Stone Lake abbey, and now that Megan had been given her copy of the Psalms and Proverbs, she had spent many hours studying what she could of God's Word.

"Then I shall tell you what God says, unless Derek would rather."

"Go ahead, Megan," he told her with an encouraging smile.

"Psalm 22 tells of Christ's death and suffering on the cross; His very thoughts are recorded. And then in Psalm 32 it says, "Blessed is he whose transgression is forgiven, whose sin is covered.... I acknowledged my sin unto thee, and mine iniquity have I not hidden. I said, I will confess my transgressions unto the Lord, and thou forgavest the iniquity of my sin.... For this shall every one that is godly pray unto thee in a time when thou mayest be found.... Thou art my hiding place; thou shalt preserve me from trouble; thou shalt compass me about with songs of deliverance... Many sorrows shall be to the wicked; but he that trusteth in the Lord, mercy shall compass him about."

"Oh, Megan," Louisa breathed. "I need only to pray and tell God that I trust Him to deliver me from my sins. He will be merciful to me if only I will ask."

Megan beamed at her and then at Derek, who spoke softly.

"It is just as Megan said, Mother. God is only waiting for you to call on Him."

"I can see that now," Louisa said. "It wasn't clear before."

"Did you want to be left alone, Aunt Louisa?"

"No, dear. I want you both here."

Megan and Derek fell quiet, and after a moment Louisa bowed her head. "I now confess my transgressions to You, dear God, and I trust in You, Lord, to forgive me. Please fill the void in me as you have done for Derek and Megan. Please cover me with Your mercy and let me find a hiding place in You forevermore. Amen."

Louisa's head came up, but Megan could barely see her for the tears. They began to talk all at once. Louisa had dozens of questions and so did Derek. It didn't take long for Megan to see just how new a believer Derek was. Megan did not know the answer to each question, and couldn't really promise to find out, but she told them what she did know. They spent over an hour rejoicing in Louisa's new life in Christ.

The hour was far past midnight before anyone even mentioned bed. Louisa was walking Derek and Megan to the door when she made a comment that brought the younger woman to a standstill.

"I can't wait for Joyce to arrive. I can't wait to tell her."

"Bracken's mother?"

"Yes," Louisa beamed at her. "She told me of her own decision more than two years ago. I can't wait to see her."

Louisa hugged Megan before she stepped out the door and moved on her way. Megan could hardly believe what she had just heard. Not even seeing Arik, outside her door (obviously under the impression that she was in for the night), could disrupt the prayer of her heart.

Bracken's mother believes, Lord; she belongs to You. Oh, Father God, it's such a gift. I don't know if I ever knew just how much You love me.

Twenty-Four

"BRACKEN?" MEGAN CALLED TO HIM from her place in the doorway of his bedchamber. She had never come anywhere near this room, but her need to see him had driven her upstairs to where Lyndon had directed.

"Yes, Megan," he spoke as he approached from within the shadowy chamber. Kent had opened the door and now stood back.

"May I speak with you?"

Bracken's eyes roamed her face. She looked tired and upset, and he found his heart burgeoning within him that she would come to him at all. At the moment he thought he would hand her the moon if she asked it of him.

"Why don't I meet you in the salon."

"I believe Louisa is sewing in there."

Bracken opened his mouth to say that he would ask her to leave but changed his mind.

"Give me a moment, and we'll walk to the tower."

Megan waited in the hallway. Just a minute later, Bracken joined her. They walked silently up the stairs to the tower and when they had gained the first large salon, Megan led the way inside. The room was empty, as Bracken knew it would be, and although he wanted to make himself comfortable in one of the chairs, Megan continued to stand.

She seemed nervous, and it wasn't long before he found out why. She faced him squarely, forced herself to look into his eyes, and said, "My attempts to hire a castle steward have failed miserably. I have let you down as well as all of Hawkings Crest."

Bracken hated her shame. He had never worked at anything the way he had worked at this relationship. He was very pleased at the way she'd come to him, but not at the shame he had caused her to feel.

"The task before you is not easy, but I feel you are doing a fine job. Do not rush yourself. Take your time in finding the right man."

His words were no help. Tears did not come to her eyes, but her voice wobbled horribly.

"But there is so much to do, and the wedding approaches. I do not think I can keep up the pace."

"Then you must delegate the jobs. You take too much on yourself."

Megan's eyes were huge. "You told me I was to see to Barton's duties personally."

Alarm washed over Bracken. That was exactly what he had said. How could he have forgotten? No wonder she retired so early these last nights and looked so tired by the middle of the afternoon.

Without speaking, Bracken took Megan's hand and led her to the double settee. He sat beside her after she'd sat down, but he could see instantly that she was not relaxed. Her back was stiff as a poker, and she did not lean into the upholstered support.

"Megan," Bracken began tenderly.

"I'm not going to cry."

"It's all right if you do," he said kindly.

"No, it isn't," Megan declared. "You are going to think you are marrying a child, not a woman grown and capable. I—"

Megan cut off when Bracken's arms went around her and he swept her over against his chest. Megan looked up into his face, and tears filled her eyes.

"I'm sorry, Bracken."

"Shhh," he hushed her, pressing her head down against his shoulder. "I have asked too much of you. We will find Lyndon, and he can take over some of your duties. The rest we will delegate as well. I will not have my wife sick with exhaustion on her wedding day."

Megan's look was so comical that Bracken chuckled.

"Now what goes through that fascinating head of yours?"

"The wedding. I have lived here as Megan of Stone Lake for so long that sometimes I find it hard to believe we are really going to wed." Megan looked up into Bracken's eyes. "Do you ever find it hard to believe?"

"Ahh, no," he drew the words out for several heartbeats and shook his head very slowly. The next moment his head lowered, and his lips touched down on Megan's. The kiss might have turned more intimate, but a voice spoke from the door.

"Have I missed the wedding, Bracken?"

Bracken's head came up, and a huge smile split his face.

Megan's response was not so pleasant. Her head spun, and she stared in panic at a small, plump woman with hair so black and curly that Megan couldn't help but wonder how she ever managed a brush through it.

In the wink of an eye, Bracken had them both off the settee and was turning Megan toward the door.

"Megan, I want you to meet my mother."

Megan's mouth opened in horror. "Your mother?" she squeaked.

Bracken was urging her forward, but Megan's mouth was still moving like that of a fish out of water. Joyce did not seem to notice, and enfolded Megan in her arms as soon as the younger woman was within arm's reach.

"I'm so pleased to meet you, my dear," she said when she was finally holding Megan in front of her. "Louisa said you were lovely, but I had no idea."

Megan had still not made a suitable reply, but again, Joyce did not seem to notice. She turned abruptly to Bracken.

"And what business have you taking advantage of this girl before the vows are spoken?"

Bracken only smiled, his eyes alight with pleasure.

"Now, come and hug me, and I'll think about forgiving you."

Bracken gave his mother a hug that lifted her free of the floor. He dropped a kiss onto her cheek just as he set her back down and spoke with one arm still around her.

"Hello, Mother."

"Hello, dear." Joyce's face was now wreathed in soft smiles. "How are you?"

"I'm doing well. How was your trip?"

"Long, but worth seeing you and Megan."

Joyce now transferred her gaze back to her future daughter-in-law. She reached out and touched the soft skin of Megan's cheek.

"Oh, Megan, Megan, how long I've prayed for you. You must come below right away. The rest of the family is dying to meet you." With that she swept away, and Bracken began to follow. He was out the door by several paces when he realized Megan had not accompanied them.

"Megan," Bracken spoke as he poked his head back in the door.

"I'm so ashamed."

Bracken came back in.

"There is no reason. Mother was but teasing. She does that quite often. I can assure you—we've done nothing to feel shame over."

"But she's right, the vows have not been spoken."

Bracken sighed gently. "It is as I say, Megan; we have done nothing wrong, and in little over a week, we will be free before God and man to touch each other at will."

Megan's face flamed, and Bracken knew he would have to let the matter drop. He gently took her hand and led the way toward the stairs, thinking as he went that marriage or no, they might not be as free as he hoped.

❦ ❦ ❦

Megan laughed until she had tears in her eyes. She was in the upstairs salon with both Joyce and Louisa, and the two older women were telling stories from their childhood. Megan didn't know when she'd been more entertained.

After having what Megan considered a poor beginning, she and her future mother-in-law had certainly made up for lost time. Lady Joyce was one of the most delightful women Megan had ever met. Her walk with God was so close that she found joy in nearly everything. In some ways she was a quiet rebuke to Megan, who tended to worry overly much and wanted her way in most matters. Joyce was a true example of the joy Megan read about in the Scriptures.

Megan had not been in attendance when Louisa told Joyce her news, but Louisa reported that it had been a very tearful scene. There were further tears when Joyce then came to Megan to thank her for the part she had played. Megan had been present when Joyce had shared the news with her family, and the look on Bracken's face was still in her mind. He appeared to be skeptical yet yearning at the same time. And Megan was struck by how little conversation they'd had concerning religious matters.

His sweet treatment of Megan had been growing as the days passed, but there was very little time for them to be alone. Nearly every barrier was down between them, and Megan had few reservations over the marriage.

"Now, Megan," Joyce suddenly said to her. "When will your parents arrive?"

"I'm not sure they will," Megan told her matter-of-factly.

Joyce's look became very intense then, and her voice changed as well.

"Can you tell me why?"

Leaving some of the details out, Megan simply reported that Bracken had taken her away from a difficult situation and she had not heard from her parents since.

Joyce nodded her wise head as she completely heard Megan out, and then asked, "Would you say that your mother is a prideful woman, dear?"

"Yes." Megan didn't even have to think.

"Then I should expect her if I were you. It's not every man and woman who draws Henry's attention as Bracken and you have. She would never wish the gossips to say that she showed a lack of interest in you."

Megan was extremely impressed with her logic. Such a thing had never occurred to her, but it was so true. Annora was not a hypocrite, but she did like to be seen making socially correct moves.

"I had resigned myself to not seeing them, something to which I'm rather accustomed," Megan admitted, "but I think you are correct. They will be here, possibly at the last moment and only until the ceremony is over, but they will come."

"Will you be glad if they come, Meg?" Louisa asked.

"Yes and no. You can see my quandary now more than ever, Louisa. It is easier to be away from them, but if I never see them, then I will have no opportunity to share Christ."

"Oh, Meg," Louisa said. "You have been such an example to me."

"I have also been a dreadful stumbling block as I struggled with some horrible sins. I'm only glad that God can save His chosen ones despite all I do to destroy His work."

"You are too hard on yourself, Megan," Joyce told her. "We all sin, but you show a clear pattern of trying to change, and those are the children God can work through no matter what."

Megan smiled at her, and they talked on. It was so wonderful to have the time. Bracken had been good at his word, and many of Megan's duties had been delegated until after the wedding. Her dress was done, and she was feeling more rested each day.

"I was hoping I'd find you together," a voice spoke from the doorway. All the ladies turned to see Richard and Derek enter and close the door.

"You're welcome to join us," their aunt told them, "but we

must warn you—it's women's talk."

Both men smiled at Joyce.

"In truth," Derek's voice was low, "we just need your momentary attention."

"Sounds intriguing," Louisa said in a false whisper and found out very soon that she had guessed correctly. The men were seated, and the women listened in rapt silence for several minutes. After a time Megan asked but one question.

"When do you want this done?"

Richard answered. "The wedding is in four days' time, so I think sometime tomorrow will be perfect."

Megan's smile was huge. They spoke of the plan for several more minutes, and then the men went on their way. Megan, no longer diverted by Richard's plan, also took her leave. She had become resigned to not seeing her parents; now she needed time to prepare her heart.

"Why, Marigold," Annora spoke with pleasure to her oldest daughter as she entered the younger woman's bedchamber, "I love that dress. Is that what you will wear to Megan's wedding?"

"No, Mother." Marigold's voice was bored. "I've decided to go to London."

Annora was taken off guard.

"But you can't, dear. Megan is to be wed."

"I realize that." Marigold sounded testy, which was unusual where her mother was concerned. "I just won't be able to make it."

"But of course you can. We leave tomorrow. The wedding is but four days off."

"That's enough, Mother," Marigold snapped at her. "I tell you, I *won't* be going."

Annora didn't know when she'd been so hurt. She believed that Marigold was acting completely out of character, when in fact the two of them had simply never been at cross purposes before. Never had Annora made plans for Marigold and really cared one way or the other if she fit herself into them. But Megan's wedding was quite another matter. She tried again.

"I think maybe you're not feeling well, dear. Why don't we sleep on it? You'll see reason in the morning."

Marigold glared at her mother. Annora was so taken aback that she didn't know what to say or do. Marigold saw the look on her mother's face and grew furious. She *hated* to have her plans thwarted.

"Honestly, Mother!" Marigold snapped. "Megan and I are not even close."

"But you haven't seen her in years."

"Yes, I have! I saw her in the village at Hawkings Crest just weeks ago." The words were out before she could stop them, and Marigold turned her back on her mother's look of absolute shock. Marigold was furious with herself for blurting out such news and worked desperately to control her voice and features.

"You saw Megan?" Annora asked when she recovered her voice.

"Yes," Marigold spoke slowly, still keeping her back to her mother. "We didn't have a chance to speak, but she looked fine."

"But why were you at the village there?"

Marigold's lip curled with hatred, but she actually maintained her voice.

"I was simply meeting Roland Kirkpatrick. You know, Lord Kirkpatrick's son." Marigold made it all sound so innocent that Annora immediately took the bait. After all, Lord Kirkpatrick was a duke. However, Annora momentarily forgot that Roland was not the oldest son.

"Is he interested in you?"

"I think so." Marigold was now able to turn with a smile that covered the lies in her heart.

"Oh, Marigold, my darling, that would be wonderful."

Marigold falsely agreed with her and was able to keep her

mother happy until Annora remembered a task that needed attention elsewhere.

Once outside the room, Annora realized that they had not finished speaking of the trip. She shrugged, however, sure that Marigold would make the proper choice and attend her sister's wedding.

She wouldn't have gone away with such confidence had she read Marigold's real thoughts. That selfish young woman planned to be far away from Stone Lake even before the sun set that night.

Twenty-Five

"BRACKEN?" LOUISA'S VOICE WOBBLED slightly as she approached Bracken in the hall the very next day.

"Louisa, what is it?" Bracken stood in concern.

"Megan is gone." Louisa bit her lip, and Bracken's face clouded.

"What do you mean? She can't be gone."

"She told Helga that you quarreled last night."

An audience of family members was gathering now, each one looking tense as he watched the thundercloud covering Bracken's face.

"It's true that we did have words, but I was certain she was beyond this."

"Beyond what?"

"This childish habit of running away." Bracken's angry eyes stared off into the distance until all watched his expression turn to cold acceptance.

"I am glad it happened now," he spoke with regret.

"What do you mean, Bracken?" This came from Stephen, whose strained features matched Bracken's.

"I can see it was too great to hope that she was ready for such a union. I see now that she is little more than a child."

"Oh, Bracken." His mother's voice held tears.

"I am sorry you have come all this way," Bracken turned to

face his family, his features a study in anguish. "It would seem the wedding is off."

"No, Bracken," Brice said. "I'm sure if you will but find her, you can work this out."

Bracken slowly shook his head. "I won't be looking. She clearly does not want me, and I can see now that's best. It is also best for me to let her go."

Bracken strode from the main hall. His family stood in desolation. Even Joyce looked like a statue, her youngest daughter, Kristine, clutching her mother's hand.

"I've got to make him see reason," Stephen spoke as he started after him. The others did not move. They had seen that look in Bracken's eyes before and knew that this time his mind was made up.

All of Hawkings Crest fell into a depression as the day moved on. Chores were done and some work was accomplished, but no one was even hungry. Stephen had gone to Bracken, but as the others in the family had predicted, it did no good. After growing angry with Stephen for again taking Megan's side, Bracken took himself off on a ride. He was gone for hours, and Stephen and Brice had never been so upset.

They tried to talk with their mother, but it seemed to pain her all the more, so they made their plans quietly. They would go after Megan themselves. They even enlisted Richard's and Derek's help, and the men geared up and sent for their horses.

They were in the courtyard, Stephen already mounted, when Bracken rode through the gates with Megan sitting comfortably across the front of his saddle. They drew up, just as precisely planned, and Bracken captured the back of Megan's head in one great hand and gave her a hard kiss on the mouth.

Stephen was still staring at them in utter stupefaction when Richard put a hand to his chest and said in a high, dramatic voice, "She's very sweet, but her hair is the color of fresh carrots and frizzy like a bird's nest. Bracken has resigned himself to her looks. He's doing this for the king."

Stephen's face was more than they could have hoped for.

"It was all planned," he said in wonder as he took in each expression. "You all knew," he went on, continuing to stare at each of them.

Brice, Richard, his mother—everyone had been involved. The full import was slow in coming, and when it hit, Stephen threw back his head with a shout of relief. He swung from his horse and nearly ran to Bracken's mount. In the blink of an eye he had taken Megan down and hugged her, laughing all the while.

Bracken now joined them, claimed Megan, and moved toward the laughing group.

"You should have seen your face."

"That will teach you, Stephen."

"It's not often we catch you out."

"I wish I could see it again."

"You certainly deserved it."

Stephen laughed in good humor, but his eyes finally narrowed on his cousins.

"I hope you know that I might not be done with you."

Richard, who was an inch taller, approached him, his manner playfully threatening.

"You had better be, Stephen. I stared like a fool at our lovely Megan, so hear me well, dear cousin, you had better be done."

Stephen's hands went in the air. "I concede, I concede."

"Come now," Louisa called to all. "We have all played our parts well to the point that some of us are starving. I have had Kimay sneaking food to me from the kitchen all day." The group laughed at this admission. "Let us all go in and eat."

Cheers went up for that good news, and as Bracken draped his arm around Megan once again, her heart swelled with joy. What a precious family she was marrying! Megan had never known such contentment among so many.

There was just one question that persisted. If Joyce had made a decision for Christ, what of her children? How was it that they did not seem to share her belief? Megan thought she could figure Bracken, since he would have already been lord of Hawkings Crest and away from the family, but what of the others? Megan could see that they all had strong convictions, but she doubted that each could claim to be a true follower of Jesus Christ.

Megan determined then and there to have some answers. She was to be wed in just two and a half days' time, but before then, she must strive to learn the background of her husband's relationship, or lack thereof, with God.

"Oh, Megan," Joyce spoke in pleasant surprise the next morning as the petite redhead came from the kitchens. "I have something for you, a wedding gift of sorts. Would you have time now to come to my room?"

"Of course." Wondering if this might not be her chance to speak privately before the wedding, Megan followed her.

"It's a gift that belonged to my husband's mother," Joyce continued as they walked. "She gave it to me just before I wed Greville, and now I want you to have it."

Megan was intrigued. Joyce's rooms were in the tower, and it was a few minutes before they entered.

"Sit here, Megan." Joyce indicated a chair. Megan took a seat and watched as Joyce moved to a small trunk at the foot of her bed. She returned with something dangling from her hands.

"It's a jeweled belt," Joyce explained. "It's been in Greville's family for years. I want you to have it."

Megan's hands came out in wonder. The ornamented belt was exquisite. Stones of every conceivable color were set in fine chain-style gold. Megan stood to slip it around her. It was a perfect fit. She beamed at Joyce and then gave her a tender hug.

"I will treasure it always."

"Mayhap," Joyce spoke when they were seated once again, "you will have the opportunity to give it to *your* future daughter-in-law."

"Mayhap," Megan agreed before they both fell silent.

"There is something on your mind, isn't there, Megan?"

Megan nodded. "My father wanted me to live here at Hawkings Crest before the wedding so that I would know Bracken when we wed. It has worked better than I ever expected, but there are some things of which we have never talked. One of them is God.

"I am almost ashamed to admit this to you, but I have not spoken to him about that which means so much to me. We did not start well, and because I was raised at the abbey, I feared he would think me a religious zealot. I was not controlling my anger at that time, and I thought somehow that if he knew the stand I took in Christ, the seeming contradiction would cause him to shun all I believe."

Joyce smiled at her in true compassion and said, "Thank you for being so honest with me, Megan, but I must tell you, Bracken's lack of faith in Christ has little to do with you. You see, he has never hungered."

Megan stared at her.

"Think back, Megan. Think back to when you knew you wanted Christ as your own."

Megan was reflecting now.

"There had to be a hunger, Megan," Joyce went on, "or you never would have reached out."

A minute or two of silence passed before Megan recalled in a voice of wonder.

"I was desperate. My family did not know what to do with me, and there were days when I knew the nuns were ready to lock me away forever. There was such a void inside of me that I felt hollow all the time."

Joyce nodded and continued softly, "This is what I speak of, Megan. Bracken has experienced no such need. Not even when his father died did his heart feel the need. He is a devout man in many ways, but a personal relationship with God's Son does not seem to fit into the plans he's made for his life.

"I have such hope, Megan, that your marriage to him will make a difference. I am not telling you that your sins do not matter, but do not be afraid to be yourself with Bracken. He is a most compassionate man, and we have talked at length about what I believe. Your own story would be new to him, but I have told him what Scriptures say concerning Christ."

Megan drew a great breath. "And what of your other children, Joyce? Where do they stand?"

Joyce smiled. "You know Stephen and Brice well enough, I think, to see that they believe as Bracken. The girls know Christ, both Kristine and Danella, but of my sons, only Giles."

"I am sorry he will not make the wedding."

"So is he. But his term as squire is most important for his upbringing. It is what his father would want."

They were quiet for a time.

"Has it been very hard?" Megan asked, referring to Greville's death.

"At times," Joyce admitted. "When Danella was wed and then had the baby, I missed him so much. When I came to Christ, I wondered if he'd ever made that choice. And now, I know he would have been so proud of Bracken and would have adored you as I do."

Both women stood and hugged. Megan praised God for Joyce's words. She was so wise and caring, and Megan thought of the different women of the Bible that she had admired over the years—Sarah, Ruth, and Priscilla. She shared her thoughts with Joyce, and the older woman only smiled in humility.

The conversation then turned to Derek, and both women wept over his newfound knowledge.

"He told me a man in London spoke with him," Megan said. "And it was just as you've said, he felt an emptiness deep within, and he cried out to God to fill that void."

"Louisa told me that she was shocked speechless when he shared."

"Yes," Megan agreed. "She was most upset, but I believe God used Derek's conversion to reach her."

"It's just a matter of time, Megan, until they all know. I believe this with all my heart."

Megan sat quietly, because in truth she did not feel quite so sure. She prayed then that God would increase her faith.

When they exited the room, they walked together to the great hall for the midday meal. Both knew God's peace in the way His hand had moved in their lives, and both prayed that their lives would continue to touch those around them in a positive way for God.

VINCENT, ANNORA, AND COMPANY arrived late that very evening. Darkness was swiftly falling as they rode through the gates. Megan, whose day had stretched on without end, swiftly changed her plans of retiring and made her way to the great hall.

Not many people were up and about, which suited Megan. The greeting she shared with her parents was subdued. Megan felt helpless as to how to make it easier, but when she suddenly noticed the fatigue in her mother's face, she knew she could at least offer hospitality.

"You've come far," Megan spoke softly while under Bracken's watchful eye. "Would you like some refreshment, or would you rather be shown to your room?"

"I will retire," Annora replied stiffly, and Megan, after a hushed word from Bracken, led the way, leaving her father in her betrothed's hands.

Megan had chosen a resplendent group of rooms for her parents that included two large bedchambers and a small salon. Megan hoped that such an act would please her parents and make them feel welcome at Hawkings Crest. Indeed, Annora prowled the premises for just a moment, and Megan held her breath.

"Everything looks well, Megan."

"Thank you, Mother," Megan returned softly, trying not to

betray the rush of emotions within. She continued to watch her mother. She knew Bracken wanted her right back downstairs, but something in Annora's demeanor caused her to linger. Megan knew she'd chosen wisely when Annora suddenly stopped and faced her nervously.

"I feel I must apologize to you, Megan."

The young woman's heart leapt. Could her mother actually be sorry for what she had done?"

"As I'm sure you have noticed, Marigold is not with us," Annora went on, and Megan knew keen disappointment. "I am sure she is not feeling well right now; she is not acting herself." Annora's voice now grew very agitated.

"We had words, the first ever, and then she said she wasn't coming to your wedding. I'm sure she'll be very sorry later, and I do hope she will have a change of heart and arrive before the ceremony."

Megan stood mute for a full minute. In truth, she hadn't even missed Marigold. She realized now that she would have been surprised if the older girl had walked in, but this was the last thing Megan could say to her mother. Megan felt pity of sorts for Annora's belief that Marigold was acting out of character. Megan thought her sister's actions were completely in keeping with her personality. The small redhead now wildly searched her mind for some suitable comment.

"'Tis all right, Mother," she finally replied. "I am just pleased that you and Father have come."

"Are you?" Annora's brow arched.

"Yes."

She *was* pleased that they had arrived. She was going to say more to reassure her mother and try to remove the frown from her face, but there was a great pounding on the door.

"I wish to be alone!" Annora's voice rang out to the intruder.

"Is Megan in there?" Bracken's voice thundered from without.

"It's Bracken," Megan said, and moved immediately to the

door. He came in uninvited, his gaze fierce as his look encompassed both mother and daughter.

"We are trying to have a private conversation."

"I can believe that," Bracken said ruthlessly. "In here... where no one can stop you."

Annora's gasp echoed in the room, and Megan reached for Bracken's arm.

"Please, Bracken—" she began, but he cut her off.

"No, Megan, I will not leave. You still bear the scar from her last attack. I will not leave you alone with this woman any longer."

There was nothing else Megan could say. She turned to see that all color had drained from her mother's face.

"Is it true, Megan?" Her voice was a hoarse whisper. "Have I scarred you?"

Megan's hands moved helplessly in front of her. "It's very slight, Mother. I think it will fade."

Annora plucked a torch from its wall sconce and approached. She moved to Megan's side, and her free hand balled into a fist as she took in the tiny white line on Megan's otherwise flawless cheek.

Her hand then reached for Megan's arm. It was the first time Megan could ever remember her mother touching her in gentleness.

"Forgive me, Megan."

"I do, Mother." Moved by her mother's first apology, Megan could not take her look of anguish. "We shall put it behind us. Why don't you rest now."

Annora nodded, and Bracken reached for Megan's arm. They both bid Annora a good rest and left, closing the door behind them. It was a very silent couple that walked toward Megan's chamber. Neither spoke until they stood just outside the portal.

"Are you all right?"

"Why shouldn't I be all right?" Bracken wished to know.

Megan shrugged. "You seemed terribly upset."

Bracken took Megan gently by the shoulders. "I was the one who saw your cut, swollen face, Megan. I was the one who witnessed your tears in the chapel. Your mother may have many fine qualities, but she has a violent temper, and for that reason alone I do not trust her."

Megan could only nod. It was true.

"How is my father?"

"I think he wished you to stay and speak with him."

"I'll plan to see him tomorrow. In many ways," Megan continued, "you have ruined him for me."

"What do you mean?"

"I mean that I always thought his care of me was the best, but in truth he never did what needed to be done. He removed me from Stone Lake because he had no control over my mother, but my father should have done everything to keep us together as a family."

Bracken was very pleased by her words. He'd believed for many weeks now that her home had been nothing short of chaos, and it was good to see that she was now realizing how unhealthy it had been. Bracken believed their own home would be as it should, one of warmth and caring.

"What will you say to him?" Bracken finally asked.

"I don't know, but just as I said to my mother, I wish to put it in the past and go on. Bitterness will do no good."

"He deserves your bitterness." Bracken's voice was uncompromising.

"Oh, no, Bracken." Megan caught hold of his sleeve. "Bitterness only destroys the vessel that contains it. Bitterness accomplishes nothing."

"You sound like my mother."

Megan removed her hand. "We have much in common."

Bracken nodded, his black hair gleaming in the light of the torch on the wall. "You share the same beliefs."

"Yes. I'm sorry I didn't tell you before."

Bracken only stared, thinking it made no difference.

"Do you think you can sleep?"

"Yes," Megan answered, but wished he hadn't changed the subject. She debated what to say next but waited too long.

Thinking she was tired, Bracken said, "Goodnight, Megan. I'll see you tomorrow."

"Goodnight, Bracken."

They parted, Bracken with his thoughts and Megan with hers. Bracken truly did not see that Megan's faith would be a hinderance to him, although he could not see the need for himself. He felt he was man enough to let Megan worship as she wished.

Megan's thoughts were entirely different. She prayed that Bracken's present belief in God would grow and that he would hunger for something much larger, something so huge that it would swallow him whole and at the same time make him more of a man than he ever dreamed.

"Did you sleep well?"

"Yes, Father, and you?"

"Fine."

For all Megan's good intentions of putting the past behind, the morning had not started well. Annora had slept in and broke the fast in her own room, but Vincent, having met Bracken's family, asked Megan if he could see her alone.

They decided on a walk outside the castle walls. Even though her father would be with her, Megan told several people where she would be. As had become the norm, Arik was close by.

They had walked along with few words. Vincent did not know what to say to this daughter who had changed so much, and Megan had told herself she was not going to apologize. She had done nothing wrong, nor was she bitter, but Megan also knew that if Vincent's conscience was bothering him, it would be no help to pretend that nothing had happened.

"I spoke briefly with your mother last night."

Megan nodded.

"She did not realize she'd struck you so hard."

Megan did not nod this time, but still said nothing.

"Megan, what has happened to us?"

Megan stopped and faced him. It was an honest question and deserved an answer, but the words were not there. Megan's hands moved helplessly before she said, "I do not know how to explain, Father, but I do know the changes are good. I do not wish to be as we were," she admitted.

"It's Bracken, isn't it?" Vincent burst out with such vehemence that Megan's eyes widened. "You can't believe the things he said to me. If you were not to marry him, Megan, I would make life miserable for him." He raked a frustrated hand through his graying hair. "If there were only some way that I could get you out of this."

At one time Megan would have thrilled to his words, but no longer. She had never seen him like this.

"Father, what did he say to you last night?"

"Not last night!" Vincent was still very agitated. "Before you left Stone Lake he told me I didn't care for you, and that I couldn't control my wife!"

Megan only stared at him. Vincent froze.

"Megan," he whispered, his voice raw. "Do you share his feelings?"

Tears filled her eyes. "I do not know how I could think otherwise. You never tried to stop Mother; you just always sent me out of her reach."

Vincent's heart literally pained him over Megan's words. He could hardly breathe with the intensity of it. It was all so true. He had a wonderful relationship with his daughter as long as his wife wasn't near. And he had a tolerable relationship with his wife as long as he did what she asked and kept Megan clear of her. He had never cared enough about Megan to fight Annora. He thought about his daughter often while she lived at the abbey, but only visited her when he had other business in town.

Weeks earlier, when he'd come to Hawkings Crest to check on her, it was the first time he had gone out of his way on her behalf.

What kind of man was he? There were names for his sort, Vincent realized, and years ago he'd nearly beaten a man for calling him such. He saw now that he should have listened. Much would have been different.

"I hate this strain between us, Father," Megan now said. "But I do not want to be the recipient of Mother's cruelty any longer. I have tasted otherwise, and I do not want to return to my old way of life. I don't know if you can still care for me, but I am afraid that things will have to be on our terms—Bracken's and mine."

Megan didn't know where she found the courage to speak so, but God blessed her honesty. Vincent's arms came out, and he enfolded Megan gently against him.

"I am so sorry, Meg, so sorry to have let you down."

Megan did not tell him it was all right, but she hugged him back tightly and prayed silently.

"Your mother has long been in control," Vincent admitted when they stepped apart. "Now Marigold has hurt her, and I wonder if she'll be ready to listen to reason."

"She is so blind to Marigold's true nature."

Vincent nodded sadly. How many times as a child had Megan suffered at her older sister's hands? Marigold would commit some crime and then see to it that Megan took the blame and was beaten by Annora. And all her father ever did was send her away. Vincent's eyes closed.

"Are you all right, Father?"

"I am not sure. I think I will stay here for a time and then try to talk with your mother."

Megan nodded. "I do not have high expectations for her, Father," she admitted. "But things do not have to be strained between us. You can come here as often as you like, with or without Mother. I know Bracken does not trust her, but as long as we're at Hawkings Crest, I think he will agree."

Vincent saw then that a miracle had taken place in his daughter's heart. She was talking submissively about Bracken. He was still choking on the words the young lord had shot at him, but if he put his pride aside, he could see that Bracken was quite possibly the best thing to ever happen to Megan.

Megan did leave him then, but she was not heavy of heart. He needed time alone, and Megan wanted the quiet of her room to pray. Arik escorted her back, and when Bracken spotted them returning he immediately approached.

"Are you well?"

"Yes," Megan told him.

"And your father?"

"He wanted some time alone. I told him that he and my mother would be welcome at Hawkings Crest, but it would have to be on our terms."

Bracken smiled. He liked the word "our" on her lips. While he stood quietly, simply watching her, Megan suddenly reached out and smoothed her fingers across his eyebrows.

"What was that for?"

Megan blushed, regretting the action. "They were a mess. Don't you ever brush them smooth when you see to your hair and beard?"

Bracken's smile grew, and Megan, wishing to hide her embarrassment, tilted her chin and flounced away. Bracken watched her go. This was going to be some marriage, and with the wedding the following afternoon, he could hardly wait to begin.

Twenty-Seven

THE WEDDING WAS SET FOR 3:00 on the afternoon of September 20, 1531. The entire castle was aflutter, but the bride, dressed in a gown of exquisite styling and fabric, was remarkably calm.

Louisa had made the garment using her purchases from the village. Slashing the skirt front and sleeves, she had taken the cream satin and lined it with a deep green satin before lacing it with gold braid. The neckline was fashionably square and trimmed with the same gold braid. Stiffened with flour, Megan's small headpiece was made from the cream satin as well, and set perfectly atop her head of rich red curls.

Megan was ready by 2:00 and had enjoyed visits from Richard; Derek and Stephen; Louisa, Joyce, and Kristine; her father; and finally Brice. Megan knew her mother would be coming as well, and if anyone could make her nervous, it was Annora.

There was a sudden knock at the door, and Megan held her breath as Helga answered. Annora swept inside, and just as Megan had believed, a dress of light blue velvet hung from her lovely, slim form. Annora stopped cold upon spotting Megan's dress, and she tried to dismiss Helga with a jerk of her head. That faithful servant looked to Megan, who nodded but asked her to return shortly.

"How dare she," Annora began, but Megan cut in respectfully.

"This is my home, Mother, and these are my servants. How dare you." It was all said so softly and without a trace of anger that it totally disarmed Annora.

She stared at Megan for several seconds and then quietly asked, "Where did you find the material?"

"From a woman in the village. She said she bought it from Elias the peddler."

Annora had nothing to say, and Megan voiced a question that in her mind had to be answered.

"Did you hate me so much, Mother, that you would sell my dress fabric?"

"Oh, Megan." Annora's voice sounded desperate. "I did it in a burst of anger. I don't hate you; I just don't know how to be a mother to you."

Megan's heart was sad, believing Annora hadn't even tried. Annora would have done anything for Marigold and certainly must have thought she'd been a good mother to her eldest daughter.

"And now it seems," Annora admitted softly, "that I have not known how to be a mother to Marigold either."

"What do you mean?"

"Your father and I talked at length yesterday. He told me that from now on things would be different. When I fought him, he told me that some of Marigold's activities have been reported to him. Do you know of what I speak?"

"No," Megan told her honestly.

"Well, the details do not matter." The older woman was obviously embarrassed to repeat them. "It seems she is going through a phase of," Annora searched for the word, "rebellion."

Megan stayed quiet for only a moment. "'Tis no stage."

"Why do you say this?" Annora asked, her eyes begging her younger daughter not to destroy Marigold further.

"I know not of what father speaks, but many was the time I was punished for Marigold's deeds. She has never cared about anyone but herself. You are the only person she has not fought with for the whole of her life."

"How can you say this? Marigold is as sweet a girl as God ever created. You are but jealous." Annora's eyes begged Megan to admit it this time.

Megan smiled sadly. "I was at one time, but no longer. Now I pity her."

Annora looked positively crushed, and Megan marveled that she had not grown angry. Megan hated to have these words on her wedding day, but she somehow believed that when her parents left in the morning, she would never see her mother again. She was nearly certain of it when Annora turned away, defeat enveloping her. However, she surprised Megan when she stopped at the door.

"It was wrong of me to sell the fabric, but I am glad you found it." Annora finally looked at her. "It's beautiful on you, Megan."

She left before Megan could frame a reply. When Bracken and Helga entered the room a minute later, Megan was still standing like a statue.

"Are you all right?" Bracken demanded as he stopped just inches before her.

Megan looked into his eyes. "My mother said I looked beautiful." Her voice was that of a child's, breathless with wonder. Bracken smiled tenderly. How long his little Megan had waited for such approval. He had known it all along.

"She is but learning what I have known for many months."

Now it was time for Megan to smile. Bracken offered his arm.

"Come, my dove. Come below and marry me."

Megan didn't need to be asked twice. Placing her hand on his arm and holding her head high, she walked beside him down the great stone staircase to the crowded hall below. All whom she loved were gathered there, and just minutes later she and Bracken were joined as husband and wife before God and England.

The festivities that followed were of the richest kind. A banquet was laid out and music played. There was laughter and dancing, and Megan noticed at one point that Joyce and Louisa had even managed to wring a smile from her mother.

The hours flew. Megan and Bracken were together at times, but often as not they were separated by the crowd. Megan had just finished a dance with Kendrick when Louisa captured her.

"You must be growing tired. Come upstairs and freshen up."

It was just the rescue Megan needed. Her feet were beginning to ache, and the noise was giving her the start of a headache. Louisa chattered as they climbed the stairs, and Megan took almost no notice of where they were going. Not until Louisa stopped outside a strange door did Megan balk, but by then Louisa had hold of her hand and nearly dragged her over the threshold.

Megan stood in shock. It was her room, but it wasn't her room. She had never been in this chamber, but all of her things were beautifully displayed and laid out—the tapestries, bed hangings, everything. Megan stared at the bed. It was a suspended canopy bed, draped in a soft yellow cloth. Her own rich counterpane lay smooth on the mattress. Megan didn't know when she'd seen anything so wonderful.

She would have stood for some time, simply taking in the wonder of it all, but something or someone pounded at the door. Megan started.

"What was that?"

"Only some of the servants securing the door."

Megan looked at her in confusion, and then her face cleared.

"I forgot about Bracken's plan for my sleepwalking, but where do I get out?"

Louisa pointed to a closed door, and Megan laughed to see Joyce standing nearby.

"I didn't even see you."

"I know." Joyce came forward with a huge smile. "That door is to Bracken's room and his dressing area. Then behind you," Joyce let her turn, "is the doorway to your salon. The only door into the passageway is through Bracken's dressing area, which means if you start to prowl you'll have to go past Bracken, then Lyndon, and quite possibly Arik."

Megan laughed and commented that she would have to look around, whereupon both women laughed.

"Later, Meg," Louisa said. "Bracken awaits you."

"Oh." She had been completely unaware of the time and only just now did she understand the purpose of Louisa's spiriting her away.

The older women helped Megan from her gown and saw her into a lovely night garment, also tenderly sewn by Louisa's capable hands. Joyce brushed her hair, and then both women hugged her and took their leave through Bracken's room, leaving the door open behind them.

Megan stood still for only a moment before her curiosity got the best of her. She approached the door and peeked inside. Leaning against the bedpost, Bracken stood and simply watched her. His beautiful, dark wedding coat was gone and he wore only shirt, trunks, and hose.

"Are you going to join me?" He sounded so amused that Megan came forward. The room was shadowy, so she could make little out.

"Louisa said we were coming upstairs to freshen up," Megan began when she stopped a few feet in front of Bracken.

"Do you feel refreshed?"

"Yes, but neither your aunt nor your mother mentioned that this was all a plan for my husband to steal me away."

Bracken's beard split with a grin. "Forgive me?"

"Yes," Megan told him and smiled in return.

"We are both strong-willed, Megan," Bracken surprised her by saying. "We both like to have our way."

Listening keenly to his serious tone as well as his words, Megan nodded.

"We have quarreled and we will quarrel again, but I want our differences to be put aside in this room. When we come to this room, I want our troubles and disputes to be left at the door."

"Yes, Bracken," Megan told him, thinking they were wise words.

Not knowing how she would respond, Bracken was warmed tremendously by her agreement, and he stood staring at her for just a moment, his heart swelling with love as well as pride that she was finally his. A second later he reached for her, and Megan came gently into his arms.

The following day was busy. It began with a huge meal to break the fast, and then came Vincent and Annora's departure. Megan was not certain how they would part, but it was better than she had hoped. Her father hugged her and thanked her warmly, and her mother, although reserved, did thank her for Hawkings Crest's fine hospitality. Annora was not a woman easily pleased, so Megan took this as high praise.

Midmorning saw everyone in various pursuits and pastimes. Megan and Kristine were playing a game, and most of the men were at the archery butts. Bracken and his mother found themselves alone in her salon in the tower.

"It was a wonderful celebration, Bracken."

"Yes, it was," he agreed. "I'd like to repeat it, only I wouldn't want to go through the waiting again."

Joyce smiled contentedly. "Just remember to court her, Bracken."

"Court her?" Bracken frowned. "What are you talking about?"

"I'm talking about wooing your wife."

"Why would I do that?"

Joyce sighed very gently. He really didn't know. He had spent so much time running Hawkings Crest that he had taken very little notice of the ways between men and women. Joyce was proud of the fact that her sons were not rakes or libertines, but Bracken was so unknowledgeable that it concerned Joyce. At a time when Bracken should have been observing his own parents' love, he was a fatherless young man running a huge keep. Joyce prayed and answered him gently.

"Bracken, I am only suggesting that you continue to do things that let Megan know you care. I know that Megan would never be unfaithful to you, but you can make her much happier in your marriage if you let her know she is loved and desired."

Bracken still frowned at her, and Joyce knew she would have to let the matter drop. Megan's face from that morning swam before her eyes. The younger woman's smile was bright, and her eyes were at peace, but her cheeks had been so pale. Maybe in time, her words to Bracken would take on more meaning.

WINDSOR CASTLE

"You say Marigold is here?" Henry asked of James Nayland.

"Yes, my king. She arrived yesterday."

"Yesterday? Was that not Bracken and Megan's day to be wed?"

"Yes, your grace, it was."

Henry frowned, and James waited for the storm, but the king remained calm.

"The wedding did take place, did it not?"

"Yes, my lord, just as scheduled, and in less time, I might add, than the six months you allotted."

Henry was silent for several moments. "Are the rumors still coming in concerning Marigold's association with young Kirkpatrick?"

"Yes. She has been careful, but a few have seen her."

"I must tread with caution where Lord Kirkpatrick is concerned; I want to do everything possible to keep his alliance."

"Because of his wife's connections with Spain?"

"Yes. See to it that Marigold is at my table tonight," Henry now told the loyal counselor. "She hasn't graced our courts with her fair countenance in several months, and I wish to visit with her."

Hours later Henry had his wish, as Marigold, a vision in black, sat beside him at the head table. They had talked of many things over the course of the meal, but Henry now mentioned the wedding.

"Why didn't you attend your sister's wedding?"

"I will." Marigold didn't even hesitate. "It's next week."

"No, Marigold, it was yesterday."

She really could do the most amazing things with her eyes, but Henry was not fooled.

"Yesterday? Surely you jest, my lord. I am certain my mother said next week."

"No," Henry said with a shake of his head while pretending to be absorbed with his food.

"I'll have to send word of my regrets." Marigold's voice was a study of contrition.

"Why didn't you want the man yourself?" Henry asked, knowing that James Nayland, from a nearby seat, was hearing all and watching very carefully.

"My sister's heart was set on him." Again her voice was regretful.

"Well, she's a lucky girl. I have great plans for Bracken of Hawkings Crest."

"Oh?" Marigold tried for casual interest, but couldn't quite pull it off. Henry had to fight a self-satisfied smile.

"Yes. He's an earl now, but I have better for him."

So as not to turn his head, Henry only glanced down out of the corner of his eye. He could not see the beautiful blonde's face, but the hand, tightening to white around her goblet, told him all he needed to know.

Twenty-Eight

IT WAS VERY HARD FOR MEGAN TO SEE Bracken's family leave, but the time had come. Unbeknownst to her, the family had discussed leaving in stages, but when all was said and done, it was decided that a mass exodus was best.

Megan knew she would miss them all, but Louisa's absence was especially going to pain her. She had been with them at Hawkings Crest for so long that Megan found herself asking just how she was going to handle her departure. If the tears clogging her throat were any indication, she was not going to enjoy it at all.

She was in deep conversation with that very woman as Bracken, just yards away in the courtyard, spoke with his mother and brothers.

"Plan to come again in the spring."

"Megan's birthday," Joyce guessed correctly.

"Yes," Bracken went on. "We will have a tourney and celebrate my wife's eighteenth year in a style befitting her."

No one could stop the smiles over the way Bracken had said *my wife*. It was a delight to watch his love of her blossom. They talked on for some minutes while Louisa and Megan had their own time.

"You'll come again soon?"

Louisa hugged her. "Of course I will. You could come to see me as well."

Megan's eyes widened, and Louisa laughed. It was clear that the younger girl had never considered this.

"Oh, Megan," Louisa now turned earnest, "I can't begin to express what you have done for me."

Megan smiled. "Not I, Louisa; God alone."

"Yes," the new believer agreed. "God alone. I like that, Megan. I will remember to walk with God alone."

Megan had to hug her again.

"I still have so many questions," she told Megan after a moment.

"And you will find the answers, Louisa. Of that I'm sure. And don't forget Derek. He will be searching as well."

As if he'd heard his name, that young man joined them.

"I can see that Mother is going to cry halfway to London." Derek's voice was light, and Louisa teased him right back.

"Oh, I don't know; I might cry all the way."

Derek gave her a comical look of horror and then thanked Megan solemnly.

"I hope you will visit often," she told him. "And bring your mother."

"I will plan on it," he said and bent to kiss her cheek.

The others gathered now, and soon all were exchanging last-minute hugs before riding on their way.

The courtyard seemed empty without them, and Megan's heart was heavy. In truth, she wished she could go to her room and have a good cry.

The idea was tempting, but Megan suddenly remembered that she had lost some of her privacy upon her marriage. Having to enter through Bracken's room was at times something of a hindrance.

"Will you be all right?" Bracken asked of her when the dust of the inner keep had begun to settle.

"I am not sure," she answered honestly.

Bracken put a gentle arm around her shoulders, but when

she stiffened he immediately withdrew. It was clear that she wanted to mourn their leaving on her own. Still, he cared and wanted her to know this.

"I shall be at training fields if you need me."

"Thank you, Bracken," Megan told him, and watched as he turned and walked away in the morning sun.

The first day of November was upon them when a missive came from London. The king wished to see both Bracken of Hawkings Crest and his bride of six weeks. Megan nearly panicked.

"Why would he wish to see us? We have done as he asked."

"Megan," Bracken tried to reassure her. "There is nothing to fear. As you stated, we have done as he asked; he merely wants to see us."

"But Bracken, he's the *king*."

"He is but a man, Megan, and no one to be feared."

She tried to calm the frantic beating of her heart, but it was with an effort. The missive asked that Bracken present himself in one week, which left Megan little time if she had nothing appropriate to wear. Megan turned suddenly from her husband and started away.

"Where are you going?"

"To check on my clothing." *And yours!* Megan suddenly thought. She turned back. "Have you something to wear, Bracken?"

He hid a smile. "I'm sure I have several suitable choices."

Megan nodded absently and continued on her way. Bracken said something, but she didn't attend. It was all too sudden.

However, as Megan climbed the stairs a bright spot appeared on the horizon. Louisa lived in London, and Bracken was sure to plan a visit.

⚜ ⚜ ⚜

Megan had been to London many years ago and had enjoyed it immensely. She thought she might enjoy it once again, but her nerves were so rattled that she saw little as they rode toward the king's residence after a long day on the road.

Megan had never known such disappointment as to find out that they were expected to stay at Windsor Castle. Bracken promised her a visit to Louisa's before they returned to Hawkings Crest, but Megan, wishing she could see a familiar face, felt very let down that it could not be sooner.

The castle was grand, but Megan felt little elation as they entered. She was tired and dirty, and more than anything desired a bath and bed. She knew that her servants felt the same way, and if it had been possible to give a magical blink and be back at Hawkings Crest, Megan would have done so.

"Good evening, my lord. Good evening, my lady," a guard intoned as he met them in the vast foyer. "I will show you to your rooms. The king dines in an hour and requests your presence."

Bracken nodded, having clearly expected this, but Megan could have wept. With the late hour, it was inconceivable to her that the king had still not eaten. She and Bracken had not taken refreshment either, but Megan was too tired to care.

Gaining their rooms took some time as they walked down one massive hallway after another, but they were finally in their own suite. Helga was unpacking for Megan, but Bracken soon joined them and dismissed Megan's faithful lady with a nod.

"Will you be all right?" It seemed this was all Bracken asked her of late.

"It seems that I have little choice to be anything else."

"On the contrary, if you are not doing well, I will make your regrets to Henry."

"You can't do that!" Megan was horrified, and Bracken actually laughed.

"Megan, he is no monster. Indeed, he is a man who likes to

have his way, but if you are tired he will understand."

Megan stood and tried to reckon with all that had occurred. She drew a huge breath and let it out slowly.

"I will join you. I am tired, but not overly so, and I do not think I will sleep at all if I must wait until morning to meet the king."

Bracken smiled at her pluck but wasn't at all surprised. The Megan he knew rose to every occasion. "I'll call for you shortly."

"I'll be ready."

Thirty minutes later Megan was as good as her word. Her wimple in place, she was a vision in navy blue and gold when Bracken came for her. Since she'd taken some time to pray, her face was serene. She took Bracken's offered arm, and fortunately for Megan, he began a conversation meant to soothe.

"I really preferred it when you wore your hair down."

"You did? You never told me that before."

"I'm telling you now."

"Well, I'm a married woman now. It's not proper for my hair to hang long."

"Says who?"

"Well," Megan faltered. "Everyone."

"Umm." Bracken sounded clearly skeptical. "I guess I'll go along with it while we are here, but I am the final say at Hawkings Crest, and when we get home, you can do away with your wimples."

"Why, Bracken, that's outrageous! It's not proper, I tell you."

"And who says we need to be proper all of the time? It's probably 'everyone' again."

Megan smiled at his teasing, not realizing that he was quite serious about wanting her hair down. Indeed, it was a good thing she did not know. It would have left them arguing when they reached King Henry's massive dining hall.

"The Earl and Countess of Hawkesbury," the footman announced in a thundering voice as Bracken and Megan stood on the threshold.

As they stepped forward, Bracken felt Megan's hand tighten

on his arm, and he spoke to her in a soft, reassuring voice.

"You will do me proud, Megan. You have nothing to worry about."

"What if I say the wrong thing?"

"You won't."

He sounded so confident that Megan felt reassured. Her chin rose slightly as they walked across the huge tile floor, and when she saw a group of women watching her handsome husband with appreciative eyes, she smiled with great pride.

Henry was in a group against one wall, and Bracken moved slowly in that direction. It had been years since they'd seen one another, but Henry recognized him. Bracken knew some pride of his own when Henry broke away and came toward them. Megan curtsied low, and Bracken bowed when the king stopped a few feet before them.

"Welcome, Bracken," Henry spoke, his voice deep and resonate.

"Thank you, my lord. If it please your highness, may I present my wife, Lady Megan, late of Stone Lake."

"Hello, Megan. Welcome to Windsor Castle."

"Thank you, your grace. I am honored at your hospitality."

The king smiled. He had heard that Marigold's younger sister could not hold a candle to that blonde beauty, but Henry found her lovely and very charming. It passed through his mind that she might also be as deceitful as Marigold, but then he warned himself not to judge too swiftly.

"I would like to meet with you tomorrow, Bracken."

"Yes, my lord."

"Afternoon. Two o'clock."

"Certainly."

With that, the older man moved off. Megan stood in shock.

"That's all there is to it?"

Bracken's grin was lopsided. "Well, that's all there is for you. I must still meet with Henry tomorrow."

"Are you nervous?"

"No. Curious, but not afraid."

Megan was amazed at his calm. She did not know what she would have done without him.

They circulated some, and Megan met other lords and ladies, but it wasn't long before they were seated separately for dinner. Megan found herself seated among men and women she did not know, but who had obviously been to court before.

Megan did a lot of smiling and nodding, but because she was not comfortable with the way they mentioned different people who were not in attendance and systematically tore them apart, she didn't have much to say. It was one of the longest meals of her life. An hour after the meal ended, she had still not seen Bracken.

But God was taking care of her. Two older women had come to speak with her. They were not among the women she had dined with, and Megan found real companionship with them. One was Lady Noella, who was Viscountess Dinsmore, and the other was Lady Evadne, wife of the Duke of Ellsworth.

They seemed genuinely interested in her, and within moments Megan was confidently sharing with them. She soon learned that both were old enough to be her mother, but it didn't seem to matter. They chatted freely and without restraint, and Megan detected no malicious intent in either woman.

Some 20 minutes later the threesome, who had been speaking near one of the hearths, moved from the heat. That was when Megan heard the voice. Her footsteps lagged, and she finally came to a halt.

"Megan?" Lady Noella spoke. "What is it?"

"That voice," Megan said.

Both women stared at her. The room was so noisy that it was barely possible to make out any one voice, but Megan looked certain.

"What voice?" Lady Evadne asked.

Megan's head turned slowly until she spotted a tall, well-built, dark-haired man just a few feet away. Megan stared at him, listening to his every word as though mesmerized. She was suddenly back in the forest on that awful night she had been ambushed.

We lost men tonight over a trunk full of homespun rags! There's nothing here but some good horse flesh. Let's ride.

"That's him," Megan said, her voice still soft.

"Who, Megan?"

"He's the one." Megan's voice was louder now. "The man who helped kill my father's men and steal my father's horses."

Everyone within ten feet of Megan stopped and stared. Megan took no notice. She was still watching the young lord when he turned cold eyes in her direction and stared at her. A shudder ran all over Megan. She wanted to cry Bracken's name, but she was too frightened to move or speak.

The crowd that had grown so silent all began to speak at once. The noise was so overwhelming that Megan began to tremble from head to foot. A moment passed, or maybe an hour, Megan couldn't tell. She felt a hand on her arm and someone calling her name, but everything was receding.

Megan slid into unconsciousness long before she realized that the hand holding her, and the voice calling her name belonged to the one she had wanted to call for just moments before.

Twenty-Nine

MEGAN MOVED HER HEAD TO THE SIDE to avoid the smell that burned her nose, but still it persisted. She gasped and tried to speak, and suddenly the air cleared. With her head pounding, she attempted to open her eyes. They drifted open very slowly, and she took a moment to focus. When she did, she found Bracken leaning over her, his face harsh with concern.

"Bracken!" Megan gasped weakly, her small hands fisted into the front of his shirt. "He's here! The man who attacked us in the forest. He's in the dining hall."

"Hush, Megan," his voice soothed. "You've had a long day."

"No, Bracken, no." Megan's voice was turning desperate. "I swear to you, it's him. He's here."

"Megan, Megan." Bracken's voice was pained. "You're overly tired. Now try to rest; try to calm yourself."

He didn't believe her...wouldn't even listen to her. Megan began to cry, and Bracken, feeling very helpless, gathered her against him and let her sob. Megan continued to try to reason with Bracken but didn't realize that she was speaking only in her mind. He didn't answer her because he couldn't hear her, and Megan was growing weaker and more lethargic by the minute.

She was nearly asleep when she heard Bracken talking to Lyndon.

"What is it?"

"Henry wishes to see you."

"Now?"

"Yes."

Bracken placed Megan gently against the pillows and began to rise, but she suddenly gripped him with a strength he didn't know she possessed.

"Don't leave me, Bracken. Please, don't leave me. That man is here, and I beg you not to leave me."

Bracken hesitated. He'd never seen her like this and was seriously considering refusing Henry.

"I'll stay with her, Bracken." Lyndon's voice came low to his ears, and Bracken knew he could trust none better.

"I must go, Megan, but Lyndon will be with you all the time."

"Bracken."

"Shh," he hushed her again. "I will return as soon as I am able and come directly to you."

Miraculously, Megan calmed. She knew in her panic she had not been trusting God, but now it was time. Megan wished Bracken did not have to leave, but she would accept the situation.

Bracken saw the acquiescence on her face and rose. Megan sat up, and although still shaking, walked with him to the door. They did not exchange words before he left, but Bracken looked deeply into her eyes before opening the door and stepping without.

"Tell me about the incident of which your wife speaks."

Bracken answered his king quietly, telling him in detail of the attack in the forest, as well as the report that the same attackers had been seen near the home of Black Francesca.

James Nayland was nearby, taking in every word as well, but neither he nor Henry gave a flicker of recognition. They had been given secondhand news of all these events, and some that Bracken was not aware of, but neither man let on.

"Young Kirkpatrick denied ever seeing your wife and has now left. He was very insulted," Henry said at last.

"Yes, my lord."

"Can you control your wife or not, Bracken of Hawkings Crest?"

"Yes, your grace, I can. I am most sorry for the incident."

Henry stared at him, his expression giving nothing away.

"We will not meet later today as planned." They stood now in the wee hours of the morning. "Come to my chambers tomorrow morning. Ten o'clock."

"Yes, my lord."

Bracken was shown out, but neither Henry nor James Nayland made a move to retire.

"He tells the truth," Henry stated.

"I believe you are right, my lord."

"The girl, Megan. Is she all right?"

"She is resting but very upset."

Henry nodded. "For a time I thought she might be of her sister's ilk, but I think not."

"I quite agree with you, my king. I believe Megan sincere in her outburst."

"I hate to do it, but if there is one more charge against young Kirkpatrick, I'll give him the boot, his father's connections or no."

James nodded. "I can't see as you have any choice."

"I thought you would see it that way. Go to bed, James. I'll see you at noon."

"Goodnight, Henry. Sleep well."

The faithful servant and friend left on silent feet, but even if he'd stomped away, Henry would not have heard. He was deep in thought with the task of weighing two men in the balance, and it was nearly an hour later before Henry made his choice and sought his own bed.

❦ ❦ ❦

"I wish to try to explain to you."

"There is no need," Bracken told Megan the next day as they sat together for their noon meal in the private salon in their suite.

"Yes, Bracken, there is. I am calm now, but I don't think you understood."

"Megan," Bracken jumped in, "I understood everything. You saw the man that attacked you in the forest and stole your father's horses."

Megan could only stare at him. "If you understood, then why didn't—"

"Because you were my only concern at the moment. You were hysterical. There was nothing I could do about Roland Kirkpatrick, so I just—"

"Is that his name?"

"Yes, but as I stated, you were my concern. I also knew it was only a matter of time before Henry would wish to see me."

"What did he say?" Megan looked uncertain for the first time.

"He wanted to know what you were talking about and then asked me if I could indeed control my wife."

Megan's eyes dropped, and she blushed to the roots of her hair. Bracken didn't try to lessen her embarrassment but let the full import of her actions sink in.

"Kirkpatrick was highly insulted, and Henry did not seem overly pleased with the whole incident," Bracken told her softly. "I understand you're upset, Megan, but it seems nearly everyone in the room heard you accuse the man."

"But he did it." Megan thought this explained all.

"Be that as it may, you insulted the man. I believe you, and somehow I think Henry does as well, but what if you'd been wrong? Think of the shame. We've drawn enough attention to ourselves as it is."

Bracken's last words were voiced in irritation, and Megan

became a bit testy herself. They continued to eat, but now there was a strained silence between them. After a time, Megan spoke up, telling Bracken in very few words that she wanted to be alone.

"You'd best ready yourself for your meeting with Henry."

"That meeting is canceled. I am to see him tomorrow morning."

Megan looked as frustrated as she felt. "What are we to do around here until tomorrow?"

Feeling put out with his wife, Bracken stood. "I don't know about you, but I am going to the archery butts. Windsor's targets are some of the finest in the land."

"And what of me?"

Bracken speared her with a glance, knowing he was being ruthless. "We are delayed here, Megan, because of your outburst. Do not vent your wrath on me for something you have done."

Megan knew he was right, but her pride rushed to the fore. "Very well, I shall take a walk on my own."

"I shouldn't do that if I were you."

"Why? Is Lord Kirkpatrick still here?" Megan's face had become fearful, but Bracken hardened his heart against all compassion.

"No, but the entire castle is talking of you, and I should think you would want to lie low, as it were."

Knowing he was being unfair but feeling very frustrated in the whole ordeal, Bracken turned away. It was amazing how easy it was to take things out on his wife. Had he been home, he would have pursued Roland Kirkpatrick to the ends of the earth seeking answers, but this was Henry's domain, and he was not at liberty to take the law into his hands or even to begin an investigation.

Of course, one could learn many things just by walking the hallways and grounds of Windsor Castle. Bracken had spoken the truth to Megan about visiting the archery fields, but he did not intend to take a direct path there.

❦ ❦ ❦

Megan retired to her room and spent the next hour in prayer. Bracken's words had been right, but his delivery of the message was one of the harshest she had ever received. Megan was wrapped in pity for some time.

Many minutes passed before Megan realized the embarrassment she had caused her spouse. They had been invited as guests of the king, and Megan had spouted off after dinner like a servant girl.

Hot tears filled her eyes as she confessed her sins to God and made an effort to give the whole ordeal over to His care. Megan longed for her copy of the Psalms and Proverbs, but she had feared bringing it from her room at Hawkings Crest. Instead, she stopped and dwelt on a few of the many verses she had already taken into her heart. She found the most comfort in the first few verses of Psalm 27.

"The Lord is my light and my salvation; whom shall I fear? The Lord is the strength of my life; of whom shall I be afraid? When the wicked, even mine enemies and my foes, came upon me to eat up my flesh, they stumbled and fell. Though an host should encamp against me, my heart shall not fear; though war should rise against me, in this will I be confident...For in the time of trouble he shall hide me in his pavilion; in the secret of his tabernacle shall he hide me; he shall set me up upon a rock."

Megan asked God to score these verses into her heart so that her words and actions would be changed forever. She so wanted to leave a godly impression with those watching her in this place, and even though she knew they thought her a hysterical young female, she determined to leave a better last impression than she had a first.

Megan had just come to this resolve when Helga asked if she would see Lady Evadne, the Duchess of Ellsworth.

"Of course, Helga. Please show her into the salon."

Megan took a moment to check her appearance and then

worked at not showing her embarrassment as she joined the duchess.

"How are you, Megan?"

"I am doing well, my lady; thank you for asking." Megan's cheeks were slightly pink, but the other woman didn't seem to notice.

The duchess laughed softly. "Please call me Evadne. I tell you, Megan, sometimes I am very dull."

The younger girl stared at her.

"I just figured out that you are Megan—Louisa's Megan!"

"You know Aunt Louisa?"

"We've been friends for years. She could hardly wait to tell me of her conversion. Had I realized it last night, I'd have told Noella. She would have been thrilled as well."

Again, Megan could only stare. They had both been so kind last night, but it had never once occurred to Megan that they shared a faith in Christ.

"I didn't realize," Megan finally said. "I'm sorry to say that Louisa never mentioned you."

Evadne smiled. "She never said anything about Elly?"

"Why, yes, she did."

"That's me. She's never called me Evadne. We met shortly after I became the Duchess of Ellsworth, and the name Elly started as a joke. Now it's all she ever calls me."

"You're Elly?"

"Yes."

Megan couldn't stop her smile. "She's talked of you repeatedly, telling me how thrilled you were going to be when she told you of both her and Derek."

"And I *was* thrilled, as you can well imagine, but right now, my feet hurt."

Megan gawked at her.

"Oh!" the younger woman finally cried. "Where are my manners? Please sit down."

They both landed on the settee in a gale of laughter and talked for the next two hours. Megan had never met such a woman. She reminded her greatly of her mother-in-law, and Megan was like a sponge whenever the older woman talked. At one point Evadne questioned her about the night before, and Megan felt free to explain. Evadne promised to pray that God's will would be done.

The time was growing late when Evadne asked Megan how she enjoyed marriage. Megan did not take offense; she was glad to share with someone.

"We had words this morning over the incident last night, but most often Bracken and I get on very well. We have our times of trouble, but in truth I love being married to Bracken. He is beyond kindness to me."

The duchess studied her face. Uncertainty appeared momentarily in Megan's eyes.

"There is something you don't like, isn't there, Megan?"

Megan's face flamed, and her eyes dropped. "I can't speak of it, Evadne. It's a sin for me not to be content with my lot."

Silent for some moments, the older woman placed her long, tapered fingers beneath Megan's chin and raised the girl's eyes to her own.

"I will not press you to explain, Megan, but if it's what I'm thinking of, you're wrong. There no sin in such pleasure. Do not settle for endurance. 'Tis something to be enjoyed."

Megan's blush only deepened, and Evadne could tell that her words had not been taken to heart. The older woman determined to pray.

"I really must be going."

They both stood.

"I can't wait to see Louisa and tell her of your visit. I am sure Bracken plans for us to go there."

"Oh, Megan." Evadne's voice held regret. "Louisa and Derek left just last week for Joyce's home in the north. I know she planned to stay for a time."

Megan surprised her with a smile. "Then I am especially glad that God gave me this time with you. It was just what I needed."

The two embraced.

"Take care, Megan, and go with God."

"Thank you, Evadne. You will never know how you have blessed my heart."

They parted then, and when Bracken returned an hour later Megan was still on a cloud. She told him of their meeting, and Bracken was truly pleased for his wife. Still, he knew that the news he must share would remove some of the sparkle from her eye.

Just before he'd returned to their room, a missive had been delivered to him from James Nayland. It seemed that Megan was expected to attend Bracken's meeting with the king as well.

MEGAN COULD EAT NOTHING the following morning, but she felt no hunger, only fear, when she eventually stood outside Henry's chambers. When they had left their rooms, Megan found dozens of speculative eyes resting on them. It was almost more than the young countess could take.

She had tried to give herself and the situation to God, but still her stomach clenched. The apprehension was not just for herself, but Bracken. He had proven himself a loyal lord, and now Megan, in a moment's time, had evidently ruined his reputation. She felt more grief for that than anything else she'd ever done.

Bracken had not laid such a claim at her door, but it was the truth. He had been very kind to her when he'd returned yesterday, and they had spent a pleasant evening in their own rooms, but Megan knew well what she had done.

"His royal highness, King Henry, will see you now."

The footman seemed pompous enough to be a king himself, but Megan took little notice. Bracken stepped back to let her precede him and within seconds they stood before England's king.

"Come forward."

The two approached, and Megan found herself under Henry's close-eyed scrutiny.

"I hope you will grace my court often, Lady Megan, but it is to be hoped that you will learn to control your tongue."

"I am sorry, your grace. It was very foolish of me."

Henry nodded and felt solid confirmation that Megan was nothing like Marigold. That blonde creature would never have admitted to a wrong. An instant later he transferred his attention to Bracken. Megan was forgotten.

"I have some lands for you, Bracken of Hawkings Crest. Are you up to the added responsibility?"

"Yes, my liege. I accept them with humble gratitude and the hope of serving you better."

"Very good. I also have a new title for you and anticipate that you will continue to serve me well as the Duke of Briscoe."

Bracken's head bowed. "This humble duke thanks you, my king, and offers his sword to defend your crown as you rule England, the greatest country in all the world."

"It is good," Henry's voice rang out. "Journey home safely now. I will like as not send for you soon."

Bracken and Megan bowed their way from the room, and a moment later the footman announced their presence into the hall.

"The Duke and Duchess of Briscoe."

Megan's hand rested calmly on Bracken's arm, but she could not for the life of her understand why. Bracken had been made a duke! It was all too fantastic to be real, but the fact that he had not been rebuked caused her no end of relief.

Megan realized then how proud she was of her husband. She had never heard him talk as he had to King Henry. Where had he learned to say all the right things?

The same eyes studied them as before, but this time Megan took little notice. She was too busy working through all that had just occurred. They were back at the rooms before Megan even felt her feet on the floor, and once inside Megan could only turn and stare at her husband. Bracken stared right back, his face solemn.

"Were you surprised?"

"Yes," he admitted. Indeed, his voice sounded like he was trying to take it in as well.

"I am very pleased for you, Bracken. I thought Henry might banish you from court because of me."

"Oh, Megan, why did you not tell me of your fear?"

She shrugged. "I thought you would only say 'twas my fault, and that would be true."

Bracken shook his head. "It was unfortunate, but not that severe. And also keep in mind—Henry does not do things impetuously, Megan. His plans for me were most likely settled long before now. Do not forget that I rode into battle for him over a year ago. He does not forget such things."

Megan nodded. "Nevertheless, I am pleased for you, Bracken. You will serve well the title of duke."

"What of yourself, Megan? You are now a duchess."

Megan shrugged. "It was you I cared about."

Bracken was very moved by her words. He would have shown what was in his heart, but the situation was not private enough; they could be disturbed at any moment. Unfortunately for Megan, it never occurred to Bracken to just reach out and touch her hand or gently kiss her lips. And just as unfortunately, it would take some time for Bracken to understand that this was the very reason she stiffened at his touch.

Megan spent her first Christmas at Hawkings Crest alone. Bracken had been called to Henry in the middle of December. The king, weary to death of losing men, money, and time, sent Bracken and several other lords north. As emissaries of peace, they rode out with a full battalion of men to the Scottish border.

Still just a bride, Megan stayed at home in the country. Many young women in her situation would have gone to their parents' home, but even though Megan had heard from both her father and mother, she did not feel welcome at Stone Lake

Castle for a prolonged stay. Also, the fact that she didn't know when Bracken would arrive home caused her to stay put.

This did not bother her. She had many things she wished to do in Bracken's absence, and the castle spent one of its busiest winters with Megan at the helm. Louisa came for a visit, staying for almost a month. While she was there, a group of knights stopped in long enough to deliver a letter to Megan. They had seen Bracken, and although he didn't know when he would be able to come home, he had wanted them to bring word to Hawkings Crest.

Megan waited until she could find time to go to her room and be alone to read her letter. It was very short, and Megan could see that he'd ordered a scribe to write it, but it nevertheless touched her heart.

> Megan,
> I am well. Thinking of you. If you are with child, please take care. Will be home soon. Act in wisdom.
> Bracken

Although it was short, the letter meant a great deal to her. She was not with child, and for the first time Megan wondered just how disappointing that might be to her husband. Every man wants sons to continue the line, but not every man receives his wish. Her father was a fine example of that. Vincent's only brother was dead. Megan assumed some distant cousin would take Stone Lake Castle on her father's death.

Who would inherit Hawkings Crest if there were never a male heir? One of Bracken's brothers most likely. Megan would like to present Bracken with a child; indeed, she was sure it would make him quite glad. If only it didn't require...Megan refused to finish the thought.

You are positively wicked, Megan, she told herself. *How can you expect Bracken to see you as a godly woman if you act like that? If you can think of nothing better to dwell on, you had best get back to work.*

❧ ❧ ❧

Bracken's back ached some, but the castle was in sight, and that was all that mattered. A night here at Wyndmere, as a guest of Lord Trygve Osborn, and then tomorrow he could ride for home.

The men had never met before Henry's call, but they had been together in the north country for over 12 weeks, and there was little they hadn't shared. Bracken found Tryg, who was ten years older, to be a man of his word, a mighty warrior, and a lover of all that was right. Bracken had come to admire him greatly.

Being to the south now, since they had just reported to Henry in London, and being just a day's ride from Hawkings Crest, made it difficult to stop over, but Tryg pressed him and Bracken agreed. It would be good to sleep in a bed and sup from a table and trencher.

They rode side by side through the massive gates, their men stretched out behind them. All the keep seemed to cheer over their lord's arrival. Trygve was the Marquess of Overton, and he had shared with Bracken many times about the loyalty of his servants.

Trygve had also shared about Ann. The men were dismounting in the inner bailey when a woman came running, and Bracken knew it was she. She was tall, slim, and blonde, and in a moment she had thrown her arms around her husband. Trygve swung her around with a great laugh, and when they stopped, he looked down only at her. Bracken watched unashamedly as Ann's hands tenderly cupped her husband's face and she reached up on tiptoe to kiss him.

"I missed you so," she said.

"And I you."

"I love you, Tryg," she said, and kissed him again.

Bracken turned away then and did not hear his friend's reply. He didn't have to take his imagination far to know that his reception from Megan would be vastly different. She ran

Hawkings Crest to perfection, and he knew she would do anything he asked, but she was not an affectionate woman. Indeed, he was finding, quite the opposite.

"Bracken," Trygve now called to him, his arm still around his wife. "Come, meet my Ann."

Bracken came forward and was rewarded with her warm smile.

"You have ridden far, Bracken, and I am glad you have taken time to stop before going home."

"My men and I appreciate your hospitality."

Ann smiled again. "I will go now and see to your needs." She smiled at Bracken and then said to her husband, "The children are anxious to see you."

"We will be right along." He watched her go and turned back to Bracken with a huge smile. He threw an arm around the younger man's shoulders and urged him to the house.

"Come, Bracken, come and eat. Before you know it the morning will be upon you, and you can go home to Megan." Out of pure contentment, Trygve gave a great shout of laughter. "Then it will be your turn to be greeted as I have been."

Trygve happened to glance at Bracken's face then, and what he saw stopped him short. It was gone now, but he had very definitely seen a hardness in Bracken's eyes.

"Did you fight with Megan before you left?"

"No." Bracken faced him, but his body was a bit stiff.

"What is it then?"

"I don't know what you mean."

"Yes, you do. I said you would be greeted as I was, but that's not so, is it?"

"You overstep yourself, Tryg," Bracken warned.

"Nay, Bracken, I do not." The older man was not easily intimidated. "We have shared nearly all and learned much from each other in these last weeks, but each time we spoke of our families I sensed an emptiness in you. Do you love your wife?"

"Yes," Bracken answered without hesitation.

"Have you told her?"

Bracken frowned. "I protect her and provide for her. I tell her in a thousand ways every day."

Trygve shook his head. "'Tis not the same, Bracken. A woman needs to hear."

"That's ridiculous!" Bracken disdained. "She is not an affectionate woman; it would change nothing."

"Bracken, you are wrong. Do you court her? Do you romance her?"

This was the second time someone had advised him to do such. His mother's words seemed so long ago that he had completely forgotten about them. Still...

"You do not know her—" Bracken began, but Trygve lay hold of his broad shoulders.

"I do not need to know her to know *about* her. Ann and I knew each other two hours when we became husband and wife. I found her beautiful, so 'twas no difficult thing. I learned later that it was torture for her. For months she froze at my touch.

"Then she began to grow thin and depressed. It took some time, but I finally understood that it's different for a woman. I began to bring her flowers, hold her hand, and even kiss her without expectations.

"She began to return my embraces, and even conceived, and now, Bracken, I am greeted as you saw. We have been married ten years, yet I still court and romance her. In return, she longs for my presence."

Bracken stared at the older man. It had never once occurred to him that Megan was responding to his treatment of her. He thought now about the way she hugged his family and even the children who lived at Hawkings Crest. She was certainly affectionate with them. He was doing something wrong—quite possibly everything.

"I do not wish to pry into the most private part of your life, Bracken, but what I have told you is true."

Bracken finally nodded but didn't speak. A part of him still wanted to deny all of this and lay the blame at Megan's feet.

"Come along," the older man continued. "We will wash and

eat, and you can think on what I've said. 'Twill be no embarrassment for me should you want to discuss this again."

Bracken thanked him sincerely, and the men walked toward the high, stone edifice. Wyndmere was a fine home, a showplace, but Bracken took little notice. His heart was completely centered on the little redhead awaiting him at Hawkings Crest.

STONE LAKE

"Why, Marigold." Annora's voice held surprise at the sight of her oldest daughter but no particular pleasure. She hadn't been home for months, and even though Annora had worried for her, she had also enjoyed a better relationship with Vincent than she'd ever had in her life.

"Hello, Mother." Marigold's voice was very sweet, but for the first time Annora did not respond in kind.

"Where have you been?" Annora wished to know.

Marigold hesitated. Her mother was not happy with her, and this was something new. In truth, she was only home because she needed money, but that wasn't going to work if Annora was vexed with her. A new tactic was needed.

"Why, Mother, did you not receive my letter?"

"No." Annora's voice was cold.

Marigold's sigh was deep. "No one is dependable these days. I wrote telling you I was spending the winter in France. I hope you weren't worried."

"Not overly," Annora said, suddenly realizing it was the truth. Again this perplexed Marigold.

"Oh, Mother," she remarked, as though she just had a thought. "You're not still upset about my missing Megan's wedding, are you?"

"No, Marigold, I'm not." This, too, was the truth. "Megan has done well for herself. I am quite proud of her."

Marigold nearly panicked. Her mother had never in her life had a good word for her younger sister. What in the world had gone on? For the first time Marigold saw that she'd been away too long.

"Whatever do you mean?" She asked, just managing to keep her voice light.

"Oh, hadn't you heard?" Annora's voice was triumphant with genuine pleasure. "Bracken's been made a duke. Your sister is the Duchess of Briscoe."

Under the guise of adjusting the hem of her gown, Marigold managed to duck her head and turn away. Her face was a mask of rage. She didn't speak until she had her voice under control.

"Well, now, isn't that grand! Maybe I should go and visit to extend my apologizes and then my congratulations."

Marigold turned with a smile, and Annora, still wanting to think the best of this selfish child, was swiftly taken in.

"Oh, Marigold, that's a wonderful idea. I know they would love to have you."

Marigold nodded serenely before the conversation went to general topics. Annora's heart was filled with well-being over Marigold's benevolent attitude. Marigold's heart was filled with hatred, first for Henry, the man who had increased Bracken's title, and then for her sister, that redheaded cow who had been lucky enough to land on her feet.

Thirty-One

BRACKEN DID NOT LEAVE WYNDMERE as early as he had expected, so he and his men did not gain Hawkings Crest until sometime after midnight. Bracken bathed and called for Megan in the night, but they did little more than greet each other. Megan wished they could have visited, talked of his trip, and discussed whether he was home for a time, but Bracken fell asleep very swiftly and she returned to her bed.

The hour was late before Megan rose the next morning, but even when she moved silently through Bracken's chamber she found him fast asleep. Indeed, the day was long spent before he rose, and by that time Megan was out in the keep, going about her chores for the day.

Bracken, a little embarrassed to have to hunt for his wife on his first day back, attempted to find her by casually searching on his own. In truth, this was no difficult task. He loved Hawkings Crest, and a stroll through first the castle and then the keep was a pleasure.

Bracken had not been out ten minutes when he saw that Megan had been busy in his absence. There was a freshness in nearly every room of the castle. The rooms were not only clean, but Bracken spotted new wall hangings and rugs everywhere. He smiled when he thought about what she might have spent, but it did not concern him.

From what he could tell, Megan was nowhere in the castle, so Bracken took himself outside. Here, too, things looked changed for the better. Always neat, there was a new cleanliness to every corner of the inner bailey. But something wasn't right. Bracken was walking around in an attempt to put his finger on what was different when he saw that the byre was missing.

He shook his head slightly, but his eyes were not playing tricks on him. Bracken was walking slowly toward the location of the old byre when he spotted the new one. Duke and duchess had talked of the need for a new byre, but he never dreamed Megan would have one built on her own. It was a fine structure, both in design and function, but anger was swiftly filling Bracken and dampening his appreciation for the improvements.

Without caring what people thought, Bracken began asking everyone within sight where Lady Megan had gone. Even at that, it took some time, but he eventually found the way.

"Here, Noleen," Megan instructed from her place outside the castle walls. "Return to the castle with this basket."

"Yes, my lady," the servant girl replied. "Do you need more?"

"No, I think this will do."

Megan smiled at her, and Noleen moved away. The duchess went back to gathering herbs, leaves, and bark, but a moment later she heard Bracken speak to Arik and turned with a smile. The smile swiftly died as her husband neared; she saw that he was coldly furious.

"I could not find you," he began. Megan stared at him a moment. He was livid. Megan frowned. She thought they were far beyond this point in their relationship. Nevertheless, her voice was very repentant.

"I'm sorry, Bracken. I told several people where I was, but I see now that I should have stayed until you were awake."

"It seems that you have been very busy."

Normally Megan would have smiled at this, but it seemed he was not pleased by her efforts.

"It was a long winter, and I took advantage of your absence to see to some things."

" 'Took advantage.' " His anger seemed to be growing. "You have stated that accurately. You wait until I am gone and then order the building of a new byre."

Thinking he was still tired from his trip, Megan blinked at him and said slowly, "We discussed all of this, Bracken, and made plans to build it just after the new year."

"I did not want the byre where you placed it." He was not even trying to be reasonable.

Megan was becoming angry herself. "It's in the very place we discussed."

"While I was away I decided it was best to build the new one in the original location."

"While you were away? Why did you not send word?" Megan demanded.

"Because I didn't think my *wife* would go behind my back."

Megan had never been so hurt in all of her life. He had said the word "wife" in a way that made Megan feel as if she were repulsive to him. And what in the world was this really all about? It was inconceivable to her that he would really be so angry about the byre, but she could think of nothing else.

Husband and wife were still glaring at each other when Clive appeared in the clearing. Bracken, not knowing if an emergency was afoot, diverted his attention.

"What is it?" Bracken demanded.

The boy answered timidly. "I'm sorry to disturb you, my lord, but Lady Marigold is here."

"My sister?" Megan's mouth nearly dropped open.

"Yes, my lady."

Megan was so surprised that for a moment she didn't know what to say. In truth, her sister terrified her. Bracken had said a long time ago that he would never let her be hurt, but one look at his still furious face told her she would gain no support there.

Megan knew she would have to face Marigold alone. She squared her shoulders and turned to Clive.

"Please see that Lady Marigold is made comfortable and tell her I'll be along shortly."

Bracken had not said anything during any of this, and now Megan was too upset to even look at him. She gathered the piles she had been sorting into the basket and lifted it by the handle. Without a backward glance, she moved toward the castle, Arik falling in behind her.

"Megan!" Marigold exclaimed with every semblance of delight as soon as the young duchess joined her in the great hall.

"Hello, Marigold."

"That is all? Hello, Marigold?" In a cloud of scent, the older girl then moved forward to give Megan a hug, and although Megan returned the embrace, she was not at all easy.

"My goodness, Megan," Marigold exclaimed after she'd stepped back to inspect her. "Being a duchess must agree with you. You're nowhere near as fat as you used to be."

Megan barely managed a smile. It had always been this way. Marigold complimented her constantly, but in such a backhanded way that Megan always felt as if she'd been slapped.

"Mother wrote that you had not been home lately." Megan was desperate to change the subject.

"No. I wintered in France. I wrote Mother, but you know how forgetful she is; she probably mislaid the letter."

Megan didn't know any such thing; her mother was very organized. But the women had now taken seats near one of the hearths and Megan remained quiet, her mind wandering to the long afternoon that certainly lay ahead.

"I'm sorry to have missed your wedding, Megan. Did Mother explain how ill I was?"

"No. She led me to believe that you simply chose not to

come." Megan's voice was calm, but she always grew very tired of Marigold's lying ways and was not going to allow them.

Marigold looked at Megan in surprise. "It would seem that the kitten has grown claws."

"No, Marigold, I am not being catty," Megan said gently. "I just wanted you to know that I know you're lying."

Marigold threw herself back against the seat.

"Oh, come on, Megan," she said in disgust, all sweetness gone. "You sound like an old woman."

"I do not enjoy lies, Marigold, and I'm not going to pretend otherwise."

The older sister eyed her disdainfully. This wasn't going to be any fun if Megan insisted on being so forthright. As usual, Marigold had another tactic up her sleeve.

"Well, enough talk about us. Where is that delicious duke of yours?"

"Bracken is in the keep. I imagine he will be along shortly, but I fear he's not in a good humor."

"Lovers' quarrel?" Marigold's eyes were huge, her voice sweet as honey. Megan was not fooled.

"No," she told her shortly, and then asked if Marigold would like a tour.

That took the next two hours. By the time they were finished, Megan felt like a limp rag. Marigold had been ready with a compliment for nearly everything she saw, but each one held an underlying criticism. By the time they parted in order to ready themselves for the evening meal, Megan was shaking all over.

Relaxing some while Helga was doing her hair, Megan tensed all over again when she heard Bracken enter his own room. She need not have worried. He was there for quite some time but did not seek her out. Megan could have wept. What a terrible homecoming. She had missed him so much and worked so hard to please him, and all it had gotten her was his wrath. Now Marigold had come to Hawkings Crest, and Megan felt utterly defeated.

She and Bracken hadn't even talked! It could be that he

would be leaving again soon. If Marigold tarried, they would have no time together at all. On the way downstairs, Megan determined to put her own hurt aside and do what she could to repair the damage. However, one look at Bracken's stony features told Megan that Bracken was not ready to forgive.

This was proven when the evening meal followed the day's pattern of being long and difficult. Bracken did not say five words, and Marigold chattered away until Megan had a headache, something Marigold was aware of and enjoyed immensely. Marigold had seen few keeps as grand as Hawkings Crest, and her fury over her sister's good fortune knew no bounds. She could see that Bracken's men were all captivated with her, and whenever that happened Marigold was in her element. The only problem was Bracken himself.

Why had she not noticed when Bracken was at Stone Lake Castle that he had grown into a man of tremendous size and fine appearance? Marigold found him very handsome and desirable. Some of his men were as well, but if she was really going to score a conquest here and hurt Megan in the process, it would have to be the lord himself. However, every time she looked at Bracken, Bracken was looking at Megan, who was not even aware of his scrutiny.

That things were not well between them right now was obvious, but Bracken still had no interest in Marigold. It galled that slim blonde to no end to sit with a man who found her fat sister more interesting. She would have to think of something.

She had entertained thoughts of being the duchess herself, but it didn't look as though Bracken would actually send Megan away. This meant that her stay at Hawkings Crest would have to be cut short. Maybe she could think of another way to disrupt things. Then when she left, she would at least know there was disaster in her wake.

For the next two nights, Megan walked in her sleep. She did not get even as far as the passageway. Lyndon woke her the first night, and Bracken the next. It was the only time her husband had spoken to her. Megan was beginning to grow frantic. It would seem that Marigold's visit was going to stretch on indefinitely, and Megan knew that until she left, things would not be resolved with Bracken.

She began to ask herself questions. What had Bracken seen and experienced while he'd been away to make such a radical change in him? He said the byre angered him, but Megan had the distinct feeling that there was something more. She continued to pray and try to reach out to him, but by Marigold's fourth night at Hawkings Crest, Megan was exhausted and completely defeated. She knew she was being a poor hostess and, indeed, Bracken frowned at her quite fiercely; nevertheless, she went to bed early and slept through the night without waking or walking.

The next morning Bracken was up early, but not out of his room. He sat for many minutes and thought about his actions of the last days. He could honestly say that right now he hated himself. Why was he treating Megan as though she were a disobedient child? Why had he not taken Trygve's words to heart and come home to woo and court her? Bracken shook his head in disgust. Why had he reacted as he did?

Bracken suddenly stood. He didn't know if it would ever happen again, but he must go now and try to make repairs. He would start by apologizing for the way he had behaved. Megan was not in her room, so Bracken continued on to her salon. She was there, still in her dressing gown, the Psalms open before her.

"Good morning, Megan," he said civilly.

"Good morning, Bracken," Megan replied, trying not to

overreact. It was the first time in months that she had heard the normal sound of his voice.

"I have come about last night. I am sorry."

Megan smiled sweetly. "'Tis all right Bracken. I'm sorry I turned in early, but in truth I was so weary."

Bracken frowned. "No, Megan. I'm talking about in the night, when you came to me."

Now it was Megan's turn to frown. "I did not come to you in the night."

"Of course you did."

Megan stiffened and shook her head. "What game is this you play?"

"No game." Bracken frowned in return. "You came to me in the night. In my anger I sent you away."

Megan's eyes could have swallowed her face.

"I would do no such thing."

Bracken hesitated. This was quite true. He had been very surprised. "Could you have been asleep?"

"You know me well enough to know I would not—awake or asleep."

Bracken stared at her. "But your voice. I heard you."

Megan froze and then said flatly, "My sister."

Bracken shook his head. "The voice, it was yours."

"Think, Bracken." Megan sounded impatient. "You have commented yourself on how much we sound alike."

"But I was so certain 'twas you."

"Oh, come now, Bracken!" The last fragment of Megan's tolerance was gone, and she was now in high fury. "Do you mean to tell me you do not know my generous curves from those of my slim sister?"

"I did not touch the woman in my bed!" he thundered. "And how would she get in?"

"I wouldn't know." Megan's voice was cold.

Bracken looked desperate. "We shall ask Lyndon. Come with me so you can hear his reply."

Megan dutifully followed, her body stiff with outrage.

"Lyndon," Bracken called to him when they reached the antechamber, but the young knight did not stir. Bracken shook his shoulder.

"Lyndon."

Still nothing. Bracken placed his torch in the sconce on the wall and carefully turned Lyndon's head. He lifted his one eyelid and stared for a moment. Lyndon never stirred.

"He's been drugged."

Megan's hand went to her mouth. "Will he be all right?"

"I don't know. Return to your room whilst I find Arik."

The next hour was nightmarish for Megan as she sat in her room. Could Marigold really have gone this far? Each time Megan asked the question, her mind gave her an unqualified yes. She made herself dress and ready for the day, and a short time afterward Bracken came for her. Lyndon was sitting up on the edge of his bed.

"Lyndon, are you all right?" Megan asked, her voice tearful.

"Yes, my lady. I'm sorry I let you down."

"No, Lyndon, it was not your fault."

"She asked me to have a drink with her."

"Who?" Bracken wished to know.

"Lady Marigold. I sat with her, but then felt very tired. I dreamt she came to my room but wouldn't let me kiss her." Lyndon realized to whom he'd spoken just then and blushed. He turned tortured eyes to Bracken.

"I'm sorry."

"It's all right, Lyndon." Bracken's voice was compassionate. "Sleep some more. I will wake you later."

Arik remained with Lyndon while Bracken and Megan went back to Megan's room. They stood quietly for some time before Megan spoke.

"She must leave," she said, and then held her breath. She did not know what she would do if Bracken argued otherwise.

"Yes," Bracken agreed. "Will you tell her, or shall I?"

Megan's chin raised with determination. "She is my sister; I will do the task."

Thirty-Two

MEGAN FOUND HER SISTER IN BED. For the sake of privacy, she had given her an elegant suite of rooms in the tower, but she now felt not the slightest compunction about walking in uninvited.

When Bracken had questioned her about talking with Marigold, she had not understood that he would not accompany her. Nevertheless, she now stood over her sister like an enraged warrior, waited for her to awaken, and then spoke with calm force.

"You will leave here today, Marigold. Your lies will not work here, nor will your deceit. Bracken is well aware of who came to him in the night, and you will leave Hawkings Crest now."

Marigold only smiled and stretched like a spoiled cat. "Did Bracken tell you how much he enjoyed himself?"

Megan didn't so much as blink. "Get out, Marigold. You have one hour."

With that she walked away. Arik was waiting for her, something Megan was very pleased about as she was shaking so violently that once on the tower stairs she tripped. Arik's great arm alone kept her from going headfirst down the full length.

She continued on to the great hall and ordered food for her sister's entourage. She would never send them away hungry, but this way she would not have to share one more meal in her sister's company. It was more than an hour before Marigold made her appearance, and Megan could see that she was not ready for travel. Bracken was still nowhere to be seen. Megan once again had to handle the situation on her own.

"Is there something wrong with your hearing, Marigold? I told you to leave."

The older girl's look was wounded. "But I didn't think you really meant it. Why, Megan, we have barely had time to get reacquainted."

"I will not have you living here trying to seduce my husband. Now leave."

The hall had strangely emptied, save Arik who stood behind Marigold. Neither girl really took notice of him. Marigold continued her sweet act for several more minutes before the real woman came to the surface. She snarled at Megan in a way that made her feel frightened, but the younger sister held her ground.

"I can see that I will have to order your things packed and have you removed bodily."

"You wouldn't dare," Marigold retorted, her lip curling.

"Just watch me," Megan told her.

Marigold's small bosom heaved. "You little fool," she spat. "He asked me to come to him and expects me again tonight. He told me that I'm the most beautiful woman he's ever seen and that you repulse him."

Megan sadly shook her head. "You've told so many lies, Marigold, that you have begun to believe them yourself. I find I am not angry with you—I pity you too much for that."

Marigold's open hand struck Megan's cheek. It was not a hard blow, but Megan hadn't seen it coming. Her head was tossed to the side. The younger woman was just reaching for her cheek when Marigold let out a bellow that brought Megan's head around fast. Bracken, as well as much of the castle, came running to see that Arik had come forward and quite literally lifted Marigold by her upper arm. Marigold screamed in agony until the huge man shook her like a rat. When at last she hung limp and silent from his huge fist, he spoke to Megan in that rusty voice.

"Go to your room. I'll see to this."

Megan didn't hesitate. She heard Bracken's voice somewhere behind her, but she nearly ran from the hall without looking at anyone.

Megan would have given anything not to have it come to this point, but she hadn't known what else to do. She told herself she was not going to cry, but the effort caused her to stand trembling alone in her room for an hour.

It was at that time that Bracken came. Megan turned from the window to watch him approach, but when he tried to take her into his arms, Megan stumbled away.

"Don't touch me, Bracken." The tears would hold no longer. "I can't stand for you to touch me until I understand what has happened between us."

"Megan." Bracken's voice was pained and he tried again, but still she resisted him.

"No, Bracken, I mean it," she cried. "You said you would never let me be hurt again, but now something has made you hate me, and until I understand I don't want you to—"

She stopped when he pursued her into the salon. Megan tried to evade him, but Bracken caught her in his arms in just seconds. Megan cried and shoved against his chest, but to no avail. Bracken lifted her high in his arms, sat in a large chair by the fire and placed Megan in his lap. Megan worked with all of her might to get away from him, but he would have none of it.

She eventually cried against his chest until she lay spent and silent. The past days, the morning's ordeal with Lyndon and then Marigold, and the torrent of tears, had all worked their way. Megan could not have moved if she tried. Bracken dipped his head to see if she slept, but only found her staring vacantly across the room.

"Your sister is gone," he began softly, his heart beating under Megan's ear. "I sent Arik with you and did not accompany you myself because I feared I would strike Marigold. Now I wish that I had. Arik is at this time berating himself for not seeing her intent. He blames himself that you were hurt."

Bracken dipped his head again. Although Megan had not moved, there was now a tiny spark of life in her eyes.

"I have much to tell you, Megan, but not now, not while you are worn and upset. I want you to go to bed. When you awaken, we'll talk."

Bracken dipped his head one last time, and this time Megan looked at him. Bracken held her eyes for the space of several heartbeats before leaning forward and pressing a kiss to her forehead. He lifted her then, walked into her bedchamber, placed her on the bed, and bent over her.

"I'll send Helga to you. When you have rested and feel better—maybe after you have had a hot bath—then send for me. I wish to speak with you."

Megan managed a small nod, and Bracken stood a moment longer.

"As for the charge that I hate you, Megan, nothing could be further from the truth."

With that he was gone, and moments later Helga appeared. She helped a silent Megan from her gown and settled her comfortably back in bed. Even after her mistress slept, Helga sat nearby sewing and keeping watch over her charge.

Megan awakened feeling much better and was greatly refreshed after her bath. She did not send for Bracken as he'd directed but sought him out herself. He was at the new byre. When Megan learned of this, she was tempted to return to the castle but made herself carry on. She found Bracken walking through the byre inspecting every square inch. Megan stood for a time and watched him, but as soon as he noticed her, he stopped what he was doing and approached.

Dark eyes searched her face for signs of fatigue or pain, but he must have been satisfied with what he saw for he nodded slowly and said, "Will you walk with me?"

"Certainly."

They were quiet until some distance outside the walls, and then Megan said softly, "I am sorry about the byre, Bracken. 'Twas never my intent to deceive you."

"I realize that, Megan. I completely overreacted."

"So, you're not angry?"

"No. I did think it would be best to leave it where it was, but I can see now that our first location is a fine one."

Megan was so relieved that for a time she fell silent.

"When do you go again?"

"Go again?"

Megan looked at him. "Yes. I was under the impression that you would only be home for a short time."

Bracken shook his head. "I know of no such plan. I will be here."

Megan nodded.

"Does that disappoint you?" Bracken tried to hide his dread of her answer.

"Oh, no, Bracken." Her eyes were wide. "I missed you."

"I missed you also."

Again they fell silent. To be parted from a new spouse for weeks was no easy thing, but to return as they had, under such stress and strife, was very difficult indeed.

"I'm sorry about your sister."

"Thank you, Bracken. I fear she will never change."

"She is a vile woman."

Megan had no choice but to agree.

"I am glad you are nothing like her."

"She told me that you asked her to come to your room."

Bracken turned and gripped her shoulders. "Did you believe her?"

"No," Megan said softly. "She has always been full of lies, and I know you would not do such a thing."

Bracken nodded and dropped his hands. Her words relieved him greatly.

"Was it difficult, your being away?" Megan asked.

Bracken began to share, his voice a bit quiet because he just realized how little they had talked, but he did tell Megan where he had been and the way they had lived. Bracken told how he had managed to visit his mother. He'd even seen Danella and her family for the first time in more than a year. Megan listened in silence to every detail.

"I met a man," Bracken finished by saying. "His name is Trygve Osborn, Marquess of Overton. We worked and lived together all the time I was away, and I have come to greatly admire him. We spoke much of our families, and he said I was not treating you well."

They had seated themselves under a tree now, and Megan's eyes rounded. "But, Bracken, I do not know such a man."

"I know, but he says he does not need to know you to know that I have treated you poorly." Bracken hoped she would understand his meaning from these few words, but her look was as innocent as a child's.

Bracken cleared his throat. "He and his wife, Ann, have been married for over ten years, but he also said that for months after the vows were spoken Ann would freeze at his touch."

Bracken watched Megan's eyes drop and her face flame. He opened his mouth to tell her he would try to be more understanding in the future, but she rushed in.

"I'm sorry Bracken. Before we were married, I just didn't know anything about the ways between a husband and wife, and ofttimes I am still not sure."

Bracken's pledge was momentarily forgotten. He stared at her bent head.

"Megan, what do you mean, you didn't know anything?"

"I just didn't. I think most girls talk to their mothers, but I was not with my mother, and the nuns never taught us. I am sorry I did not know and that I am still so ignorant."

Bracken felt pain wash over him. She had been so innocent.

In truth, he was no more experienced than she, but he had had some idea of what marriage would bring.

"Oh, Megan," Bracken said and reached for her hand. He felt her stiffen and watched as her eyes flew to his. He knew in that instant he was going to have to show and not tell her that he was ready to change. He could give her a promise right then, but without proof of his actions, she would never believe.

Bracken continued to hold her small hand as they talked, but Megan never did relax. Still, Bracken ignored her tension and kept his touch very light and tender. He wasn't a man given to praying, but this was enough to make him want to drop to his knees and beg God to help him show Megan what was in his heart.

Thirty-Three

BRACKEN WAS BEGINNING TO FEEL like a spy. Since he had talked with Megan more than two weeks ago, he had worked at understanding women in general in order to gain a clearer picture of his wife. He had never studied the creatures before, and he was finding them fascinating. His greatest discovery was that they were so emotional. Bracken was a man of deep emotions, but he did not, as a rule, allow them to control him.

A few days past he'd watched a servant in the keep scolding a female underling concerning her shoddy work. What the servant said was true, but Bracken watched in amazement as great tears filled the young woman's eyes and she went back to her task sniffing and blowing.

Bracken could only shake his head. It caused him to think about his own sisters and how remarkably different their interests had been from his own as they were growing up. Some of it had to do with age, but most of it was because of their gender. Bracken found himself asking why God hadn't created women to be a little more like men.

It was at the moment that Megan sought him out, and Bracken found himself very thankful that they were so different. She had a question for Bracken, but he was so preoccupied with the woman herself that he could barely answer. Even without touching her, he knew her skin was like warm satin. The green velvet of her dress made her eyes the color of the forest on a spring day. Her sweetness and the very sound of her voice were like a web around him. He had managed to reply, but Megan had stared at him rather strangely.

Even though he desired to do so, Bracken had still not begun to show Megan his affection during the course of the day when she needed it most. Still, he was learning plenty. Fortunately, for Bracken, spring was around the corner, and love was in the air. It was affecting the whole castle.

Right now he was watching Stafford and Pen. The two had been married for six months, and Pen still eagerly ran to embrace the young warrior every time she saw him.

He witnessed as Stafford placed an arm around Pen's waist and with his free hand tenderly stroked her cheek. Even from a distance he could see her eyes soften before she placed a hand on the back of Stafford's neck and brought his lips down to hers. They kissed briefly, and when Pen turned away, Stafford gave her a playful smack on the seat. From where Bracken stood he could hear the girl's laugh. Bracken then turned to find Lyndon watching him as he studied Stafford.

"What is it, Lyndon?" Bracken's voice was curt, but Lyndon couldn't stop his smile.

"Bracken, what are you about?" he asked good-naturedly.

The duke hesitated. Lyndon had recently become betrothed; maybe he could help. He also knew Lyndon would never gossip the matter over the entire keep.

"What do you do to make Gabriella know that you love her?"

Lyndon, seeing his sincerity, thought a moment.

"Sometimes I take her flowers from the meadow."

Bracken snapped his fingers together. "That's it! Tryg said something about flowers. I'll do it!"

Bracken walked away then, looking more like a boy in love than a seasoned knight. Had he looked back, he would not have found Lyndon laughing, but instead would have seen that his friend's eyes were filled with fondness and admiration.

❦ ❦ ❦

Megan was in the kitchen working over some of her herbs when Bracken found her. She was measuring, pouring, and working so intently that it was a moment before she noticed him.

"Oh, Bracken," Megan smiled. "I didn't see you."

"These are for you."

Megan stared at the bundle of purple flowers in his hands. Some were a bit smashed and the stems on others were broken, but they were pretty nonetheless.

"Thank you, Bracken." Megan's voice spoke of her confusion. "I don't recognize what herb they are. Were they for something special?"

"Nay," he shook his head. "Just for you. For your bedchamber or salon."

Megan looked at the flowers and then back at her husband, her brow still knit with bewilderment.

"Bracken," Megan began. "I still do not—"

He cut her off. "I was only thinking of you and wished for you to know it."

Bracken watched as understanding dawned. The transformation was amazing.

"These are for me?" Megan's eyes began to glow. "You gathered these for me?"

Bracken cleared his throat, now wishing they were alone. "Yes."

"Oh, Bracken," was all Megan could say as she smiled up at him with shining eyes. "They are splendid flowers. Indeed, they are most wondrous. I'll go right now and put them in water." Megan turned away but came right back.

"Your brows are mussed," she explained seriously as her soft fingers smoothed over his brow. As she turned away, Bracken pulled the wimple from her hair. He did this often, and normally Megan would have complained, but so taken was she with the flowers she didn't even turn. All those in the kitchen who had witnessed the scene smiled as Bracken then made his way outside, a huge grin parting his beard.

By evening, the flowers seemed to be the talk of the entire castle. Megan heard little whispers here and there, but it was some time before she understood it was the flowers from Bracken about which they were speaking.

"You should've seen 'im a grinnin' after 'e 'anded 'em to 'er," Megan heard a woman say who was setting up for the evening meal. "It's spring all right. I tells ya, 'e's in love."

Megan did not let on that she'd heard—it was all too fascinating to stop. The other women all agreed and Megan listened for a few minutes more before moving on in great thought.

Bracken was acting oddly, but Megan didn't really think that spring was involved. In fact, when Megan stopped to think on it, Bracken was coming for her less and less. With the thought came regret that she'd shared her true feelings with Bracken a few weeks back. She must have said something to make him think he was upsetting her.

In truth, the physical side of marriage was not something Megan enjoyed, but that was life; some things were pleasure and some were duty. Megan wasn't certain, but it seemed to her that only women of loose morals found pleasure in such union. However, Evadne's words at Winsor Castle still came to mind: "Do not settle for endurace. 'Tis something to be enjoyed."

Megan resolved to talk with Bracken. She never wanted him to think she was angry with him, and she did so want a child. The thought of bringing this up to Bracken caused her face to heat on the spot, but she knew it must be done. Megan could have used some time to calm herself, but Bracken suddenly appeared at her side. She watched his mouth open and shut as he changed his mind about whatever he was going to say. Megan stood quietly as he then took in her pink face.

"You're blushing."

Megan shrugged uncomfortably. "'Tis nothing."

Bracken looked unconvinced, and Megan cleared her throat. "May I speak with you after the meal, Bracken?"

"Certainly." He watched her a moment. "Are you sure you don't wish to speak now?"

"It can wait."

"All right. In my chamber then?"

Megan shook her head. "You do not want us to quarrel there."

Bracken's brows winged upward. "You're planning an argument?"

Megan looked helpless and finally admitted, "In truth, Bracken, I am not sure."

Bracken weighed her words a moment before nodding and wisely let the subject drop. She was becoming quite anxious, and he needed to show her that he was more than willing to abide by her wishes.

The meal was plentiful that night and enjoyed by all, but both duke and duchess were preoccupied; Megan, with regret for setting up an audience with her husband, and Bracken, with speculation as to what she might say. Indeed, he didn't intend to wait long. As soon as Megan was through, he asked her to join him in the war room.

Megan agreed readily enough, but it took a moment for her to get started. She paced the room some and then started to sit on a chair. Bracken motioned to her, however, bidding her to join him on the long settee. Megan did so, but she was clearly not relaxed. In fact, when she began to speak, it was with her eyes on a distant spot across the room.

"Have I angered you, Bracken?"

"No," he answered as he studied her profile. "Do I seem angry?"

"Not exactly," Megan said softly. "Just different."

Bracken had hoped she would notice, but it was supposed to bring pleasure, not confusion.

"This is a problem?"

Megan knew then that she was not explaining herself well. She made herself shift so that she could face Bracken and look into his eyes.

"Since we talked outside the walls, Bracken, you do not touch me as much."

Bracken leaned forward so his face was on her level. He whispered, "You could touch me."

Megan looked horrified and would have moved from the settee, but Bracken gently captured her hands.

"Nay, Bracken, I could not!" Megan's voice was breathless as she pulled to free her hands. "'Twould be a sin."

Bracken's smile was very tender, but he did not release her. "Oh, my little Megan, no, 'tis not a sin. My mother is a woman of God, like yourself, and I know she delighted in my father's touch."

"But, Bracken," Megan knew she might hurt him, but it had to be said, "with her commitment to Christ, she is different now. I do not think she would feel the same way."

Bracken only smiled. "I know all about my mother's belief, Megan, but it was her who told me to court you."

"Court me?"

"Yes. She said to woo my wife gently. I did not fully understand her at the time, but now I see that this way you will know what is in my heart, and our union will bring happiness to you."

Megan was more confused than ever. She so admired Joyce and would have loved to talk with her. Could Bracken really be right? Is this what God had for her? Megan felt something stir within her. Bracken had been unspeakably tender with her in the last two weeks, and it seemed she cared for him more every day.

Megan was still thinking on all of this when Bracken pulled her close. Megan held herself still as he put his arm around her, but there was nothing to fear. Bracken began a gentle dialogue, meant to soothe and make Megan feel cherished.

"I'm planning a tourney."

"You are?" Megan's voice was slightly breathless with her anxiety.

"Um hmm. Next month. In honor of my wife's eighteenth birthday."

Megan turned her head to look up into his face, her apprehension forgotten. He was serious!

"Bracken, why did you not tell me?"

"I just did. All of my family is coming; yours, too, I hope."

"Oh, Bracken," Megan's joy was so complete that she laid a hand spontaneously on his chest. "You are too good to me."

"You are my wife, Megan," he replied, staring down lovingly into her eyes. "How else am I to treat you?"

Megan could only smile in absolute serenity. After kissing her gently, Bracken pressed her head onto his chest. Megan was uncomfortable at first, but soon the beat of Bracken's heart came to her ear. Suddenly she was back atop his horse, Warrior, safe in his arms as they returned from the Stone Lake abbey. It wasn't long before she had relaxed completely. They talked for another hour, and when they finally rose to take the stairs, both were bathed in tenderness and contentment.

Thirty-Four

BRACKEN'S TREATMENT OF MEGAN over the next week was unlike anything she'd ever experienced. Something wonderful was happening between them, and Megan had never known such joy or peace.

"Come to me, Megan," Bracken had bid one night early that week. The day had been long and Megan was tired, but she complied. When she had joined him, however, he had simply put his arms around her and pulled her close. After a moment, Megan had said, "Bracken, are you angry with me?"

"No."

Still he did not move beyond settling her a little more securely beside him.

"Are you certain?"

"Yes, I'm certain. Go to sleep, Megan."

"In here?"

"Yes, Megan," Bracken had answered, and she did not miss the laughter in his voice. It had done nothing to help her relax, but she tried to do as she was told. It had been a busy day, and after a moment Bracken's heartbeat came to her ear. Megan sighed hugely when she heard that sound, and although Bracken had never let on, he felt her relax against him. Within ten minutes she had gone to sleep.

Bracken then relaxed as well and thought about his relationship with his wife.

At one time all I did was take from Megan. I never knew how remarkable it would be to give to my wife.

On this contented thought, Bracken had joined Megan in sleep until morning.

Now some four weeks later, things were still going well. Megan's birthday was upon them, and she had the entire castle cleaned and ready for their expected guests. Bracken's family had sent word of their arrival, and the day had finally arrived. Megan was so excited that she could hardly remain still.

"By the time they arrive, you're going to be dead on your feet," Bracken warned her, pulling her close for an instant. Warmly accepting Bracken's embrace, Megan only smiled, smoothed his eyebrows, and sailed on her way.

Joyce, Brice, Kristine, and Giles arrived together, and within the hour, Stephen had come with Louisa and Derek. Megan's head felt as if it were spinning. She was in conversation with Kristine and Giles, whom she had just met, when Joyce grabbed her eldest son's arm and pulled him from the group.

"You did it, Bracken. I can tell by the way Megan looks at you that you did it. You're courting her."

Bracken only smiled. "I want to laugh when I think of how confused I was by your words, but then I met Tryg." Bracken went on to explain to his mother, and her eyes were shining with tears of happiness when he finished.

"It's a miracle, Bracken. I have prayed so long and so hard."

Having heard these words from his mother many times, Bracken simply hugged her, and Joyce was pleased that he did not question her. In truth, she had been very worried over their marriage.

Not many months past, Louisa and Derek had come for a visit. It was at that time that Derek shared with his aunt and mother that the Scriptures said a believer was not to marry an unbeliever. Joyce had felt as if the very ground had been snatched from under her. She saw herself sitting with Megan in her room at Hawkings Crest and telling her how excited she was that Megan was marrying Bracken. Joyce had been so sure at the time that this would be Bracken's turnaround, and then Joyce learned that the union had not even been God's will.

This news drove Joyce to her knees as nothing had ever done before. She prayed for days. Her heart was so burdened for her son and Megan that she could hardly function, but then the Holy Ghost moved in her heart. Joyce finally came from her knees to see that God's hand had still been there. He had not lost control of the situation.

She began to pray for Bracken in a new way. She asked God to show her son how to treat his bride. She knew without the indwelling of God, his change would not be like her own, but she did believe with all of her heart that God could work in the heart of any man.

She also prayed for Megan. Joyce was certain of one thing—had Megan known that it was against God's Word to marry an unbeliever, nothing whatsoever could have induced her to do so. Joyce prayed that God would show Megan how to respond to a sin committed in ignorance. She also prayed that as Bracken became more tender, Megan would be more receptive. From what she had seen in the first few minutes of her arrival at Hawkings Crest, God had answered her prayers with a resounding *yes*.

The only thing left to see to was choosing the correct time to tell Megan. Joyce felt that to leave someone in ignorance was a sin as well. Telling her would not change Megan and Bracken's situation, but it might that of the next generation. Joyce felt this was of the utmost importance. She was still praying about the matter when the group headed en masse for the castle to refresh themselves and partake of the noon meal.

"Is something wrong, Megan?" Bracken asked his wife the next evening.

Megan stared at him. It was nearly inconceivable that she should not have married this man, but Megan wanted above all else to be a godly woman, so she had taken Joyce's news as best as she was able. She could see, however, that it must be affecting her, or Bracken would not have noticed. Now, how would she tell him what was on her heart?

"I try to study in the Holy Scriptures every day," she began. "And I love my quiet times spent with God."

Bracken nodded. He had seen her reading often.

"But not everything I read or learn of is easy to take. Ofttimes I am convicted of sins that I was not aware of." Megan hesitated, praying that she would not have to tell him that their union had been wrong. As it was, Bracken's mind was elsewhere, and his question rescued her.

"If you want to do something, Megan, then do it. Your faith is your choice."

Megan gently shook her head. "I must take the Scriptures in their entirety, Bracken, and not pick and choose what I wish or what suits me."

Weighing her words, Bracken stared at her, his eyes narrowing.

"I thought God wanted us to be happy."

"He does," Megan said. "And happiness is mine—so are joy and peace—as soon as I obey."

Bracken shook his head, and Megan said, "So you mean to tell me that your father only enforced half of his words?"

"What do you mean?"

"I mean that if your father instructed you to go hunting in the forest and then to take your catch to the kitchens, it would be acceptable and obedient to hunt and then leave your game with the guard at the gate?"

"Of course not," Bracken told her.

"So it is with God, Bracken. He wants all of His instructions obeyed. If we only obey half of His Word, we sin."

This was new to Bracken, and again his eyes narrowed as he thought. Finally, he said, "But I am no child in need of a father's training, and neither are you."

Megan smiled at him with understanding, his point well taken, but still she said, "I will always be in need of my heavenly Father's care and teaching. And I think if you will search your heart, you will see that if your own father were still alive, you would consult with him on many things. It is the same with me and God."

Bracken's face showed understanding for the first time. No one had ever compared God the Father to his earthly father, a man Bracken missed very much indeed. It made perfect sense.

But suddenly Bracken had more spiritual matters to think about than he was comfortable with. For years he had tried to tell himself that there was no difference between his mother's faith in Christ and his own belief in God. However, when he was being very honest with himself, he had to admit that the changes in his mother, the lack of fear and overriding sense of peace he witnessed each time they were together, had little to do with the passing of years and steps toward maturity.

Likewise, both Louisa and Derek had changed, and in his heart Bracken knew why. He had never known Megan before her conversion, but Bracken understood that the reason she gave of herself so freely to him was because of God's work in her life. Still, Bracken was not convinced that he needed to make this step.

Wasn't his keep in fine shape? Didn't he treat his wife and servants with respect and caring? Didn't he have the king's approval and land and wealth to last him out and hand down to his seed? Why did he need to become religious? It still did not make sense. Rather than work it out, Bracken sought to change the subject.

In her wisdom, Megan let the matter drop, but she praised God that they had talked of spiritual matters as they never had before. She truly saw it as a step on the path to a new life in Christ for her spouse.

Vincent and Annora arrived the next day. Annora did not go so far as to embrace Megan, but this meeting was vastly different from the one before the wedding or the departure thereafter. Vincent did give his daughter a mighty hug, and as most of the guests were outside preparing for the tourney and the great hall was rather empty, Megan sat by the hearth with her parents for a visit.

Vincent opened the conversation with a painful subject.

"Has Marigold been back?"

"No," Megan spoke with relief. "And after the incident with Arik, I do not expect to hear from her."

Vincent was silent for a moment.

"What is it, Father?"

Annora spoke up. "Marigold was at Stone Lake just days ago. She was asking for money. When your father refused, she became enraged. When she learned we were coming here for your birthday, she began making threats against you. Your father told her to leave and not return. We came as soon as possible."

Megan stared at them, not at all surprised. Marigold was certainly capable of all they had related and more.

"I'm sorry, Mother," Megan told her softly.

"'Tis not your doing, Megan. I can see now that your sister has played your father and me against one another for many years."

"I did not want to send her away, but I cannot trust her at Stone Lake any longer." Annora nodded in agreement with her husband.

There was something urgent in both their manners, and both looked a little shaken. From what they had said, Megan was still not certain that it was all that great a problem; it sounded like idle talk from an angry woman.

On the other hand, she did wonder if maybe she should inform Bracken. As though her thoughts were a plea, Bracken entered the hall and came across to them. He sat with them, and Megan quietly explained what Vincent had said.

Bracken's eyes studied her before he said, "You are not afraid?"

"No, Bracken, in truth, I'm not. I know she is capable of nearly anything, but I am so protected here."

Bracken nodded and reached for her hand. He then turned to Vincent and Annora.

"We thank you for coming, not only for this news, but for the celebration as well. I will inform my people of these threats, and special care will be taken during the tournament."

"My men know as well," Vincent put in quietly.

"Mother," Megan said then, "you must wish to freshen up. May I show you upstairs?"

When the women had gone, Bracken also seemed ready to leave, but Vincent detained him.

"I do not wish to upset Megan on her birthday, but there is more."

Bracken sat and regarded the older man with interest.

"I have never seen such a look of madness in a woman's eyes."

"Marigold?"

"Yes. She said that Megan was nothing but a cow and didn't deserve you. She said she would be the Duchess of Briscoe and would see to it that Megan suffered well before she died." Vincent leaned forward now, his face fearful. "I urge you Bracken, do not let Megan out of your sight."

The words were still ringing in Bracken's ears some 20 minutes later when he went looking for Megan. She was just coming from her mother's room, and they met in the wide passageway.

"Is your mother settled?"

"Yes, but she kept looking at me oddly. In truth, Bracken, I feel sad for my parents that it has taken them so long to see Marigold's true nature."

Bracken only stared at her.

"Bracken, what is it?"

It was only right that she should know so that she could move with caution, but as with Vincent, Bracken had no desire to frighten her. He sighed very gently and reached to smooth her cheek with the backs of his fingers.

"Your father feels that Marigold is going mad and truly fears for you because of this."

Megan stepped a little closer to her husband, and Bracken put his arms around her. Megan spoke with her cheek laid against his hard chest.

"You won't let her hurt me, Bracken." It was a statement.

"No, I won't, but you need to walk with caution."

"During the tourney?"

"Yes. I believe your father thinks she might try something."

Megan tipped her head back. "I'll make sure you or Arik are close by at all times." Megan put her cheek back to Bracken's broad chest, and a moment later felt him pulling off her wimple.

"Bracken!" she scolded and reached for his hand, but it was too late—her hair hung in a red mass down her back.

"I've told you many times," Bracken said without apology as he held the wimple behind his back, "I want to see your hair."

"But my mother is here," Megan complained while attempting to smooth her unruly curls. "What will she say?"

"It matters not." He was unperturbed. "Just remind her that she is at Hawkings Crest and can go without her wimple as well."

Thirty-Five

MEGAN HAD NOT ATTENDED a tournament since she was a young girl, so the following days held a great many surprises for her. Competitions at the archery range and all swordplay would take place on the actual day of Megan's birthday, and the following day would mark the wrestling matches and the javelin throw. The last day would end with a jousting competition.

The opening of the tourney started with a parade of the knights whose castles had answered the invitation. The men were in full pageantry dress as they paraded proudly onto the jousting field. The colors from six other keeps joined those of Hawkings Crest, Stone Lake, and White Hall, Joyce's family home.

Megan was in the stands with all the other ladies. She watched proudly as Bracken, sitting atop Warrior and as the host of the games, rode proudly in front. Lyndon and Kendrick were just behind him. Megan's pride grew as they circled the practice field that had been splendidly laid out for this occasion, and it tripled when she heard two older women talking behind her.

"My room is so comfortable and clean."

"As is mine. So roomy."

"Marcus and I had to share a room with four other couples at the last tourney we attended, and we did *not* get the bed.

"Dreadful."

"That isn't the worst of it. The men in the room snored so loudly I hardly slept all night; Marcus was the worst."

Megan heard both women laugh softly, but she did not turn around. A swift shift of her eyes told her that her mother-in-law had heard as well. Joyce reached for Megan's hand and squeezed gently. Megan had all she could do not to laugh.

By the final day of the tournament, the knights of Hawkings Crest had more than proven their worth to all present. They had won the archery competition hands down, and Arik had taken on all comers, sometimes two at a time, in the wrestling. There was only one knight, a huge, bald-headed man, who caused Megan worry.

His name was Sir Rodney of Helt, and he'd beaten Bracken when they wrestled and nearly outthrown him in the javelin. Today it was time for the joust, a sport where a man could be accidentally killed, and Megan knew some very real fear as the men paraded in once again.

She managed a smile as the knights from Hawkings Crest were once again the first in line, but her heart was beating with trepidation. She calmed some when she saw Bracken headed her way. Horse and rider were in full armor, and Warrior pranced with anticipation. Bracken reined him in with a sharp word, and within moments he stood before the grandstands as though made of stone.

Megan stood and Bracken held out his halberd. She pulled the scarf free that hung from her waist and sported the Hawkings Crest colors, and then tied it onto the end of his lance. His head dipped in her direction, and his eyes twinkled. Megan beamed at him and thought her heart would explode with love.

She sat back down and tried to calm herself, but it was all moving so fast that Bracken and Sir Rodney faced one another before she felt ready. Oddly enough, it was her mother who noticed the strain on her face, and in a gentle voice was able to calm her daughter's fears.

"Your father says he's not seen many knights with Bracken's strength or power. Fear not, Megan."

"Thank you, Mother," Megan told her and was sharply reminded of a conversation with Bracken just the night before.

"I'll pray for you during the joust, Bracken," she had told him.

"I have my armor and a strong horse, Megan," he reassured her. "There is no need to pray."

"I will pray anyway," she had said. "The Scriptures say, 'There is no king saved by the multitude of an host; a mighty man is not delivered by much strength. A horse is a vain thing for safety; neither shall he deliver any by his great strength. Behold, the eye of the Lord is upon them that fear him, upon them that hope in his mercy.'"

Bracken had looked at her in shock for many minutes before finally saying, "This is in the Holy Bible?"

"Yes, Bracken, in Psalm 33. I can show you."

He shook his head. "There is no need. I believe you and beg your forgiveness for my arrogance. I would indeed desire your prayers."

Calmness now covered Megan as she prayed for Bracken and each man participating. She knew that he might not come away whole, but the tourney was in God's hands and Megan knew she would not find peace in any other place.

Megan paced the rug at the side of her bed and stopped every few seconds to stare in the direction of Bracken's room. The light from the torch on the wall cast shadows on the floor, but Megan took little notice.

You could touch me, had been Bracken's words to her many

days past, but Megan had not as yet made a move to do so. However, she was so proud of the way he'd beaten Sir Rodney of Helt that the desire to be with him was overwhelming her. Her only hesitation now was that he might already be asleep. A sudden thought came to mind, and Megan moved to light a candle. Once lit, she shielded the flame carefully with her hand and walked quietly into Bracken's room.

As Megan hoped, he lay on his stomach. She also took note of the fact that his head was turned away from her. Because he was a light sleeper, she knew Bracken was aware of her presence, but he didn't speak even when she set the candle down on the small table by the bed and climbed up to kneel beside him on the soft mattress.

Bracken's heart was pounding in his chest as he felt Megan settle on the bed. He had known it would only be a matter of time before she came to him, but right now it felt like years since Bracken had begun his tender assault on her. The desire to roll over and sweep her into his arms was almost overpowering. He forced himself to exhale very slowly as her small hands reached to rub his bare back. He wanted desperately to respond in such a way that Megan would not be fearful, but would instead know just how welcome she was.

After a moment he simply said, "That's nice."

"I thought you might be sore." Megan's voice was a little breathless, and for the world Bracken would not have told her that his vassal had given him a complete rubdown.

"It's kind of you, Megan."

They were silent for a moment, and then Megan spoke quietly, her hands having no real effect on his muscles but tremendous results on his heart.

"I was proud of you today, Bracken. You fought so well that I had to confess my pride that you belonged to me." She heard him chuckle and smiled as she continued to rub.

"Does one area of your back hurt more than another?" she asked solicitously.

"You're doing fine," Bracken told her, a smile in his voice.

They fell silent for a time; indeed, Bracken was nearly asleep when Megan spoke.

"I have news for you, Bracken."

"Hmm?" Bracken murmured, thinking she could tell him the castle was under attack and he still wouldn't be able to move.

"I am with child, Bracken."

One second Megan was rubbing his back, and seemingly an instant later her head was on his pillow with Bracken bending over her, the candle held high so he could see her face.

"Is it true, Megan?" He felt as if he'd run for miles.

"Yes," Megan said as she tried to see his face. "I waited to tell you because I felt a need to speak with Louisa. She confirmed my suspicions."

"How long?"

"Just a month now. The baby won't be born until December."

Bracken's huge hand sought her stomach and spread over the fabric of her gown. Her abdomen was still flat, but it wasn't hard to envision her swollen with his son. His eyes sought hers.

"Oh, Megan," Bracken breathed. "Are you all right? Do you feel ill?"

Megan shook her head no and smiled. "I am a bit tender, but all else is well."

Bracken's look became almost fierce. "We will not lie together until after the child is born."

Megan chuckled softly and her fingers stroked his beard. "Oh, yes, we will, Bracken. You are overreacting."

Bracken captured the hand at his face and pressed a kiss to the palm. "We will turn your duties over to others," he stated emphatically. "In fact, Louisa is already here, and we will simply ask her to stay until the child has come."

Megan shook her head, and Bracken frowned. "That is out of the question, Bracken. A woman needs great strength to have a child. If I lie about until my pains begin, I will not have the endurance."

Bracken sighed deeply. He wanted to coddle this woman,

and she would have none of it. Indeed, she very logically destroyed all of his arguments. However, he was going to lay down the law on some things.

"Megan," Bracken began, but the diminutive redhead cut him off.

"We can't argue in this room, Bracken," she took great delight in telling him.

"We're not going to argue," Bracken informed her. "I'm going to tell you a few facts, and you are going to listen and obey."

"I'll argue with everything you say," she promised.

"Then we'll go into your salon for this discussion."

Megan feigned a huge yawn. "I'm much too tired to move," she told him with a dramatic sigh.

Bracken tried to hide his smile but failed miserably. Megan grinned unrepentantly and spoke invitingly.

"Come, Bracken, lie down and put yours arms around me. I am weary, as are you. The entire castle will surely know of this news tomorrow, and we will both need our rest."

Bracken could find no argument for that and did as Megan asked. Megan was asleep in less than a minute, but Bracken took some time. He was calmly going over in his mind all the changes he would lay out for Megan in the morning.

Bracken had searched for 20 minutes the next day before finding Megan in the creamery. She and Eddie were in close conversation, and he waited with barely concealed impatience for their conference to end. That Megan was very aware of his anxiety was quite apparent when she finally approached him and stood smiling up at him.

"Did you need something, Bracken?" she asked sweetly.

"We will talk, Megan," he said, telling himself to stand firm.

"Of course, Bracken. I must go to the byre and then—"

"The war room. Now."

"As I was saying," Megan said swiftly, "the byre can wait."

She sailed ahead of him, and the castle folk, who had heard the news just as Megan predicted, smiled as they watched them depart.

An hour later Bracken was finishing.

"Half of your duties will be delegated. It is still my desire that Louisa stay, but if you will not have that, then you will do as I ask."

"But, Bracken, there is no purpose," she tried one last time. "I am perfectly able to continue in *all* of my duties."

"My mind is made up," Bracken said, pinning her to the settee with his eyes. Megan sighed but did not comment.

"What goes on in that head of yours, Megan?"

The beautiful green eyes narrowed. "I was thinking that mayhap it's time for Henry to call for you again."

Bracken's own gaze narrowed in order to cover the laughter lurking in the depths of his eyes. He slowly shook his head.

"I do not plan to let you out of my sight."

Megan smiled then. She knew he had spoken out of concern for her, and, indeed, he was acting so adorably that she could hardly fault him.

A month later, Megan's thoughts were not so benevolent. Bracken seemed to dog her every move, and there were days when Megan wanted to run and hide. When she thought she could stand it no longer, he seemed to ease up. Maybe it had taken that long for him to see that she was going to be fine. Whatever the reason, the duchess was thankful.

Megan would have been surprised to know that much of Bracken's attention, and then the lack thereof, stemmed from the fact that he had just received word that Marigold was now back in France.

"Helga, what did that woman say to you?"

The faithful servant bit her lip, but she knew it was no use. When the Lady Megan used that tone, she could never deny her. The women were coming from the archery butts, where they'd been watching the men practice. Megan had noticed several women coming to speak with her personal maid. Helga seemed to grow more agitated with every step, and Megan had to question her.

"Helga?"

The older woman wrung her hands. "It's just more of the same, my lady."

Megan nodded and did not comment. For over a week now there had been news in both the keep and the village that Roland Kirkpatrick was back in the area. Word was out that he was still angry with Bracken over what had happened at King Henry's court.

Megan had spoken with Bracken each time she became worried about the situation, and each time he had reassured her. But now her fears were returning. Telling herself she must try to reason with Bracken once more, Megan dismissed Helga and made her way toward the castle.

"Bracken," Megan said to him as soon as she had found him in the war room. "There is more word from the village."

"Megan," Bracken replied patiently. He had been out earlier and heard the news as well. "Are you thinking about Roland Kirkpatrick again?"

"Yes, Bracken. Your lack of concern—"

"I am concerned," Bracken cut her off, "but I'm not frightened as you seem to be. I will protect you. When I come face-to-face with the man, I will confront him."

"It's not me I'm worried about."

"Megan," Bracken stressed the words again. "Henry has given me leave to handle this as I see fit. I do not fear Roland or the situation."

"What if he seeks you out first?"

"So be it. He's not going to take me by surprise, Megan. I am able to deal with this." There was amusement on his face as he spoke these last words, and Megan knew more frustration than ever.

His lack of concern was maddening to her. She wanted to stay with him in the war room until she had talked him into taking immediate action, but knew it was of little use.

"I think it's time I make a visit to the village," Megan said to Helga once she had gained her chamber.

Helga knew that tone and said in a voice breathless with fright, "Oh, my lady."

"Not today," Megan told her as if this would calm all of the servant's fears. "Tomorrow, Helga, and I shall need my cloak."

"What was Lady Megan about today?"

Bracken shook his head over Lyndon's question. "I was not able to speak with her. I left word of our going with Clive."

Lyndon could see how this would be true. Bracken's decision to go to the village had been rather sudden, and he had only planned to be gone for a portion of the day. Indeed, it was good to see Bracken relaxing again. Many in the keep had chuckled over his hennish care of Megan, but Lyndon knew that when God willed and his own Gabriella carried his child, he would be just the same.

Bracken, Lyndon, Arik, and Kendrick, along with several other knights, arrived in the village just before noon. They made their way to the pub, and after being served a noon meal of pork, coarse bread, and ale, began to listen and observe. It wasn't long before they learned that Roland was out of the area that day. Bracken felt their trip had been a waste of time.

They were just leaving when Lyndon heard of a small fair going on at the other end of town. For amusement's sake, they made their way in that direction. The first cart, filled with apples, was run by an old woman with a humpback and a filthy face. The men, all but Arik, sauntered past her without a second glance.

Bracken noticed the way the huge man stopped, but thinking he was in a mood merely left him and traveled on.

He learned little else about Roland that was new at the fair, but he was no longer sorry they had come. Bracken was well respected in the village, and this was proved to him by how many merchants approached and told what they knew. Some, he was sure, also did this for Kirkpatrick, but for the most part they were a loyal group.

The men made their way back out of the fair and met Arik at the edge. He was just as they'd left him, parked at the old woman's stall, his arms folded across his broad chest.

"What troubles you, Arik?"

The giant did not answer or even look at him.

Bracken glanced around in frustration and then scowled at the old woman who let out a coarse bark of laughter over absolutely nothing. She didn't seem to notice the look but pottered around in her shuffling gate, adjusting her fruit for better display.

"Arik," Bracken went on patiently, "if you've news, tell me. If not, let us return to Hawkings Crest."

Arik looked at him this time, staring down into his eyes silently before slowly shifting his gaze to the old woman.

Bracken was swift on the uptake, and he moved casually over to inspect her stand. She had little, but he wasn't really concerned. He stood in front of her cart, and she stood at the rear. With his eyes on the fruit, he spoke softly.

"I've coin for more than fruit, if you have it."

When the old woman didn't answer, Bracken shifted his eyes without moving his head in order to look at her. His eyes grew in utter disbelief when blackened teeth peeked out at him through a crooked grin and one lid dropped over the most beautiful green eyes in all of England.

The desire to grab the Duchess of Briscoe and run with her on the spot nearly got the best of him. Bracken started toward her, but stopped when she dropped her gaze and began to sing in a hoarse voice and putter with her fruit. A swift look around told Bracken that the fair had suddenly become crowded. To take her now would cause an incredible scene.

Bracken turned back to Arik, his body stiff with rage.

"I will see you back at Hawkings Crest," he spoke through clenched teeth. "Come to me the moment she is safe."

Arik nodded calmly, and Bracken forced himself to walk away without a backward glance.

MEGAN PACED THE CONFINES OF HER SALON and tried to be calm. She had confessed her foolhardiness to God the Father, but she had yet to speak with her husband. She knew he was aware of her presence because she had seen Arik talking to him, but he had not yet chosen to make an appearance.

When she finally heard his door, she froze in her place and waited for him to appear. Megan's heart sank at the sight of him. She had been home and cleaned up for over two hours, but he was still furious.

"I'm sorry, Bracken," Megan said softly when he stopped in the doorway, but he did little more than glare at her.

"It was unwise of me," she continued. "I was worried for you, and I simply did not think. I have dressed that way many times before, and I knew there was no better way to gain information."

It was the worst thing she could have said. Bracken was suddenly swept backward to the agonizing time he had rushed to find her before the marriage. On the way to Stone Lake they had talked with Elias the peddler, only to be told that they'd given an old beggar woman a ride and had certainly not seen Lady Megan. To think that she had dressed that way twice made Bracken more angry than ever.

"How you could do such a thing in your condition is beyond me," he said between gritted teeth. "I am so angry right now that I can't even bear to look at you."

Bracken turned away before Megan could make a sound. She didn't know when she'd been so crushed. Tears filled her eyes and spilled down her face. She knew well that she had done wrong, but if he could just find it in his heart to forgive her, Megan would press on to do better. As it was, Megan didn't want to press on at all. She sank into the nearest chair and sobbed, her heart feeling like it was going to break in two.

Two days later Bracken had still not spoken a word to her. He took his meals in the war room and avoided Megan at all costs. Her hurt and humiliation were beyond description, but she didn't know what to do. At one time Bracken had told her to grow up. If Megan had thought it would do any good, she would have searched him out and said those exact words to him.

He was acting like a child in a tantrum, but telling him such a thing was impossible for more than one reason. He seemed determined not to let her near him. He ate alone and was always gone from his bed long before Megan rose. If Megan started toward him in the keep, he would turn away. It shamed Megan to be ignored, so she stopped trying. His men seemed just as vexed with her as he, and Megan was beginning to feel desperate. She finally approached Arik, her heart in her eyes.

"Arik, I feel a need to see the meadow. Will you go with me?"

He nodded without hesitation, and the odd couple made their way out the gate. Arik was very soothing company. He said nothing, and Megan was left alone with her thoughts as she walked among the beautiful wildflowers.

"For a man so concerned about his baby," she said to God, "he seems to have completely forgotten I am even with child. I have told him I am sorry, Lord, and now I know not what else to do. It was wrong of me, and I know that sin has its consequences, but this is too much. It is his anger and pride that stand in the way of our reconciliation.

"His anger makes me feel lonely and cold inside. If this continues, I feel I would do better at Stone Lake, but I don't wish to leave. What will I do if he never forgives me?"

The thought made tears pour down Megan's face. With her back to her protector, she cried for several minutes. She was still deep in her misery when Arik's voice surprised her.

"Rise, Lady Megan."

Megan started violently and then followed Arik's gaze to see men approaching. She did not know them, and they were dressed in rags, so she swiftly did as Arik bid. Megan dashed the back of her hand across her eyes and spoke with only a slight sniffle in her voice.

"We have no coin to give you. If you have something to sell, you'll have to go up to the castle."

They didn't seem to hear her. They came in closer...not speaking, and acting oddly. Arik stepped partially in front of Megan, and the young duchess' brow rose when the men were not deterred. Most men were petrified of Arik. It was at that instant that Megan noticed others coming in from behind them.

"Arik?" she said fearfully. The big man drew his knife. Upon seeing it, Megan's heart suddenly rocketed with panic. She was too terrified to even scream, but Arik grabbed her arm and moved Megan so none could advance from the rear. The men came in closer, and Megan saw that more approached from the woods, seemingly dozens of them.

Had Arik been alone, he would have stood and fought, but his only concern was Megan. He turned and began to run, nearly dragging her with him, but the men were soon on top of him. He sent Megan on with a hoarse shout to run and a shove that nearly sent her to the ground. But Megan had gained only 50 yards when some of the men caught her. She fought as well, but there were too many.

Seeing Megan with men surrounding her gave Arik renewed

strength, and the dozen men attacking him with clubs flew everywhere as he dislodged their relatively small bodies in order to get to her. Megan was still struggling herself, and just as Arik gained his freedom, she watched a tall man come up behind him with a huge cudgel.

Megan found her voice now in a full scream as the club hit Arik alongside the head, not once but twice. Watching in horror as the big man's legs buckled, Megan screamed again. A hand was clamped over her mouth, and an angry countenance suddenly appeared in her face. Megan stared in terror at Roland Kirkpatrick's furious eyes just before a cloak was thrown over her head.

The horseback ride was the longest of Megan's life. The cloak had been removed, but a cloth had been tied tightly across her eyes, completely blinding her. Her hands were bound in front of her, and she had long since lost the feeling in her fingers.

Just when Megan had lost all track of time and direction, her horse stumbled and she fell. Her numb hands grabbed desperately for some hold, but found none. Megan fell hard onto her shoulder, much as she had months before while riding in the processional from Stone Lake. However, this time Bracken was not there to take her atop Warrior.

Rough hands lifted her and tossed her back onto her horse, but they let go before she had her balance. Blinded, and with numbed fingers, Megan could find no hold, and she was knocked unconscious when she fell off the other side and landed on her head. She awoke, feeling quite ill, to the sound of angry voices.

"She's no use to us dead!"

"What do you want me to do?"

"Be more careful, you fool!"

Megan recognized Roland Kirkpatrick's voice, but for all the anger, Megan was lifted gently.

"Now hand her to me," Roland ordered, and Megan felt the jostle of arms as she was settled across his saddle. The horse had no more moved when Megan felt a hot rush that made her heart sink with dread. The need to relieve herself was almost unbearable, but it was not the same. Megan knew she was losing her baby.

"Oh, Father, please, no," Megan whispered tearfully.

Roland naturally misunderstood her. "If you do as you're told, you have nothing to fear. Just sit quiet now; we'll be there soon."

Megan tried to stem her tears, but they seeped out anyway. It was all her fault. She had gone to the village and caused Bracken's anger, which had put her in the meadow. It was too late for regrets, but Megan felt them nonetheless.

"It's not time yet," Roland tried to reason with her.

"I want her dead, do you hear me, Roland! Dead! If you won't do it, I'll see to it myself!"

Megan listened with dread to the sound of her sister's voice. It never once occurred to her that Marigold was behind all of this, but when she could make her mind concentrate, it made perfect sense.

How foolish she had been. She had heard Roland's men talking. All the intrigue surrounding Bracken and Roland was really over her. Had Bracken known this? Is that why he'd been so furious? Megan pushed regret aside. She had apologized to Bracken, but he had rejected her. She had tried to bridge the gap between them, but he had been unwilling. At some point she had to stop thrashing herself for the sins of the past.

It looks as if they plan my death. Perhaps this is what it's going to take, she prayed in her heart. *Bracken will surely be in*

pain over my loss, and perhaps this will bring him to You, Father God.

Megan was warmed by the thought. It helped, since she felt with a certainty that her baby was gone. It also helped to lay still. In the six days she'd been in this rundown castle, there had been much blood and no one to help her in any way.

Marigold and Roland's voices were fading now. Megan wasn't certain if they were moving away from her door or if she was falling back to sleep. They had fed her and given her water, but she was still so weak. Megan was still wondering why that would be when she drifted off once again.

"A week, Lyndon. My wife has been gone a week, and I am no closer to finding her."

This was very true. With Lyndon always at his side, Bracken had followed the trail of Megan's abductor, but it had led nowhere. From there they had searched and questioned everyone within miles. There were still no leads. Now the two men stood in the war room. Lyndon, nearly as torn up over Megan's loss as Bracken, said, "We will find her, Bracken. I know this. I feel it."

The duke turned tortured eyes to his friend. "What have they done to her?"

"Don't think about it, Bracken; it will distract you. Just concentrate on finding a way."

Bracken nodded. They were words he needed to hear. If he thought overly long on Megan or the baby, panic would set in and then he would be of no use to anyone. In order to keep the anxiety at bay, Bracken found himself trying to pray.

I will make amends, God, if you will but spare Megan. I have wronged her, and I will make repairs if You will but give her back to me. The thoughts had no more formed when Kendrick came to the door.

"Lord Vincent has arrived." The loyal knight was breathless with excitement. "He brings word."

❧ ❧ ❧

"You should have kidnapped a maid as well, Roland," Marigold said bitingly. "Megan looks worse than ever."

Roland looked at the madness in Marigold's eyes and then at her pathetic sister and asked himself how love could drive a man to such an act. The stories Marigold had told him concerning her evil sister, Megan, had made him hate the girl, but then he watched the small redhead fall from her horse twice and never utter a sound. To protect his investment, he had taken her atop his horse, but then he had told her not to cry and she had quieted swiftly.

Not until they arrived at the castle did he realize how tightly her hands had been tied. He released her and then watched as she shook all over with pain when the blood rushed back to her fingertips. Still, she did not utter a word. And then, when he'd finally removed her blindfold, she'd blinked, focused on him, and spoken only four words.

"Please, let me go."

Roland had actually considered it. He was a man who had little care for his own life, so Bracken's wrath did not disturb him, but he knew if this woman was his own and someone had taken her, he would be crazy with grief.

He made himself leave the room before he could relent. At the time Marigold had not yet joined him, but he knew that to let Megan go would send Marigold into a frenzy. After she arrived, Roland wondered if it really would have mattered. She was more agitated than ever.

It wasn't enough to have Megan kidnapped with a plan to ransom her, Marigold had wanted the younger girl humiliated. She had demanded that Megan be paraded naked through the castle before all his men. Roland's stomach rolled when he thought of how close he'd come to agreeing.

He'd gone to Megan's chamber, and holding a sword at her chest, told her to rise and undress. In order to go through with it, he had forced himself to ignore her white face and violent trembling, but when he'd seen the dark spotting on her shift, he relented, telling her to dress again. Turning, he swiftly exited the room, thinking as he did that he would rather face Marigold than force this on Megan.

He didn't see Marigold for more than an hour, but he needn't have worried. By the time he came face-to-face with her, she had completely forgotten her orders.

Now it was the following evening. After bringing Megan into the great hall for dinner, Roland thought she looked paler than ever. Something deep inside of him told him he was not seeing a woman in her monthly flow, but something much more significant. He had to remove Marigold from the room and find out.

"Why aren't you eating?" Marigold asked Megan, her voice now as sweet as a child's.

"I'm not very hungry," Megan told her sister kindly, and Roland knew then that Megan recognized her sister's madness.

"Why not?" The older woman frowned, and her voice changed, causing Megan to pick up her fork. Roland watched her hand shake.

"Well, I guess I'll try a little."

Marigold smiled as if all was well in the world and then began telling Megan and Roland about the different men who had loved her.

"Of course, Bracken does too, Meg. I'm sure it will take some time to get used to the idea, but then it really doesn't matter since you'll be dead." Her voice was as sweet as that of a young girl in love for the first time.

The sound of it chilled Megan to the bone. She watched as Marigold went on eating, but she felt so ill that she had to lay her fork down. She felt Roland's eyes on her and glanced at him before swiftly reaching for the utensil to spear a small carrot slice. Roland hated the fear he saw in her face but knew he deserved it. It was impossible for her to know that he himself had never killed anyone in his life.

"I want something sweet," Marigold suddenly demanded like a spoiled tyke.

"Very well," Roland said smoothly, now seeing a way. "Let me return Megan to her room, and you and I shall retire to the fire with tea and dessert."

"Why are you taking her up?" Marigold's harsh voice was back. "You have men for that."

"I wish to see to it myself. After all our hard work I do not want our prisoner to escape."

Marigold's laugh was hard. "She's not bright enough for that, but suit yourself. I shall be waiting."

Roland took Megan's arm and led her from the table. He had no reason to be harsh with her, but he rushed her along until they were out of the great hall. He didn't speak until they were back at Megan's room. Roland opened the door and allowed her to precede him. Megan, thinking he would shut her in and leave, turned in fear when he stepped in behind her.

"Are you with child?"

Megan was so stunned by the question that she did not at first respond.

"I must get below. Answer me at once. Are you with child?"

Megan turned her face away and spoke just above a whisper. "There is no need to concern yourself. What's done is done."

Had Megan been looking, she would have seen the way Roland's hands balled into fists of anger and regret. He didn't speak but stood still a moment before turning to join Marigold below.

Thirty-Seven

"HOW DID YOU LEARN OF THIS PLACE?" Bracken whispered to Vincent as they stood outside the rundown keep that sat halfway between Stone Lake and Hawkings Crest. Vincent had come to Hawkings Crest with news that he knew of Megan's whereabouts. It was late at night, but they had ridden out so swiftly that the men had not even had time to speak.

"Marigold was reported seen here."

Panic clawed at Bracken's throat as he grasped the older man's arm with incredible strength.

"Marigold is behind this?"

"I fear so." Vincent winced at the younger man's hold, but understood. "For a time she covered herself well, and her mother and I relaxed, but the lies about France have now come to my attention. We will recover Megan," Vincent added and watched as a look of steel entered Bracken's eyes.

Within moments they had the castle surrounded and all moved in for an attack. The castle defense was feeble at best, as Roland had not done a good job of arming the keep. He had less than a dozen guards, and they seemed totally unprepared for an attack. Few lives were lost as Bracken's men broke through the door. In less than 20 minutes Bracken stood in the great hall, his sword and shield making him appear larger than ever.

He didn't move a muscle when he saw Roland and Marigold by the hearth. It looked as if they'd both been up all night. They stood at the same time, and still Bracken did not move, not even when that lying wench ran across the room and threw herself at Bracken's chest.

"Oh, Bracken!" she cried dramatically. "You've come for us. Roland kidnapped us both and has already forced himself on Megan. It was my turn tonight, but you have spared me."

Bracken did not even look at her. His eyes remained on Roland, who seemed amazingly calm. Bracken knew by just studying the man that Marigold's words were all lies. Roland had not touched Megan, and Marigold was up to her usual deceitful tricks. Bracken moved her aside with one arm. Marigold put on a lovely display of hurt and rejection.

"Bracken?" Her voice was pained. Then her father entered behind him.

"Father!" Marigold screamed in outrage and began to back away.

"Halt," Vincent shouted as he came toward her, but Marigold turned and ran. The older man pursued his daughter, but Bracken turned back to Roland.

"Where is she?"

Lyndon and Kendrick had flanked and grabbed Roland, but he still managed to motion with his head to the upstairs.

"If she has been harmed, you'll die."

Thinking of the lost child, Roland wanted to say, "Kill me now," but refrained.

Bracken swung away, and in minutes stood outside Megan's door. He smashed the lock and moved slowly inside. The room was dim with only one torch burning. Bracken found Megan sitting on the side of the bed. She looked pale but unharmed, and Bracken was so relieved that for a moment he could not move. Even when she smiled and spoke, he could not propel his feet forward.

"You came," she said softly, her voice so full of wonder that Bracken's joy deserted him.

"You doubted?" he frowned.

Megan gestured helplessly with her hands. "You were so angry, Bracken, and although I knew they planned to ransom me, I wasn't certain if you would—"

"Of course I came," Bracken cut her off, feeling very hurt and wanting to lash out in return. "You carry my son."

The change in Megan was frightening. The light left her eyes so rapidly that Bracken blinked. He watched as she turned her face to the wall.

"Then you have wasted your time." Her voice was flat, and Bracken felt a fear so great that it robbed him of breath. "I fell from my horse. There has been much blood."

Bracken discarded his sword and shield to cover the distance between them in only a few strides. He went down on one knee before Megan, and although still feeling breathless, spoke earnestly.

"I did not mean that, Megan. It's you I've come for. I am sorry about the babe, but truly, it's you I want."

Megan turned dull eyes to his, her voice utterly emotionless. "It's all my fault. I have lost our child. The blame surely lies at my door."

"No, Megan," Bracken began and touched her for the first time. Her skin was so hot and dry that alarm slammed through him all over again. He could feel his emotions spinning out of control and shook himself in order to keep his head. He could tell her the way he had yearned for her every moment she was gone; indeed, he'd nearly been out of his head. But Megan was ill, and right now she needed his cool logic.

"Come, Megan, we're going home now."

Megan didn't even look at him as he rose and lifted her, nor did she speak. Her lack of response concerned him more than anything. What had she been through in the last week?

By the time they gained the great hall, Vincent had Roland bound. He was still being held, but when Bracken stopped with Megan in his arms, he was allowed to approach. Roland stared at the duchess, and Megan sighed gently.

"I am sorry for the loss of your child."

"You do not hate me, Roland; I know this to be true. Why then, why have you done this terrible thing?"

Roland turned his face away in shame. "There are times when love drives a man to foolishness. I am just such a fool."

"Marigold," Megan stated, and Roland turned back to see her shudder.

"She will bother you no longer."

Megan took in the grief in his face, and her heart sank. She was terrified of her sister, but she did not hate her or wish to see her dead. However, the look in Roland's eyes told her she was not going to gain her wish.

Bracken, seeing the alarm on his wife's face, lifted her a little closer to his chest and moved to the door. Megan spotted her father in passing, and although he gave her a tender look, she also read the mourning in his eyes.

"Bracken?"

"Hush, Megan," he told her. "Until you are home and safe, I refuse to discuss it."

Megan had little choice but to comply, but the sky was swiftly growing light, and there was no missing the covered form at the bottom of the great stone stairway that led to the keep. Megan's hands fisted in Bracken's coat as she saw the wisps of blonde hair at the edge. Bracken turned her away as soon as he was able, but Megan had already begun to tremble all over.

"How is Arik?" Megan asked some 30 minutes into their journey.

"He will be fine. He wanted to join us, but for once I had my way."

Megan didn't comment, but Bracken could see that she was well pleased.

"We are moving very slowly," Megan then said.

"Yes."

It was fully daylight now, and although Megan felt bruised, cold, and achy, she was anxious to be home.

"Why?"

"Because you are not well."

Megan did not answer for a time. "It's very cold for June."

"It is not cold at all; Megan, you are ill."

Megan stared up at him in surprise, and for the first time noticed the perspiration beaded on his forehead.

"Why don't you remove your coat?"

Bracken finally looked tenderly down at her where she lay wrapped in his arms and coat, but didn't answer. Megan suddenly realized she was shivering against him and felt foolish.

"Try to sleep," Bracken told her softly, his look loving.

"I am not sleepy."

"All right." Bracken's manner was indescribably congenial. "Then tell me how often you dress as an old woman and go a wandering."

Megan heard the laughter in his voice but was afraid to believe her ears. She lay staring up at him in wonder until he glanced down. Megan watched one lid drop as he winked at her and still felt amazed. She lay contemplating the change in him until she remembered her child.

"I am sorry, Bracken, that I lost our baby."

"There will be other children, but there is only one Megan."

Megan's mouth opened in surprise at his compassionate tone as well as his words, and when he looked down and smiled at her in complete tenderness, Megan came undone.

She turned her face into Bracken's chest and sobbed. He did not try to hush or calm her but left her to her grief. Less than an hour later, she fell fast asleep.

Bracken, so certain that arriving home would fix everything, knew deep pain when Megan remained unwell. Her body burned with fever, and although Bracken had expected delirium, he was disappointed. Disappointed because anything would have been better than her stillness. She was sleeping round the clock, and there were times when her breathing was so quiet that Bracken was certain he had lost her.

He was rarely gone from her side. When he did leave, the only one he trusted in his absence was Helga. He'd never seen a woman so upset, yet able to cope, as Helga was. She had come to love her mistress unreservedly, and Bracken trusted her above all other servants.

The physician had come several times, and although he'd been very solemn, each time he seemed content. However, not until the third day, when Louisa unexpectedly arrived, did Bracken begin to feel hope. There was a slight stir at the door and suddenly Lyndon was there beckoning to him with an anxious hand. Bracken moved into the passageway and immediately took his aunt into his arms.

"How did you hear?"

"I didn't—" Louisa admitted, "not until I arrived. But for some reason I felt compelled to come. May I see her?"

"Certainly, Louisa, and then I must speak with you."

The woman studied his haggard face for a moment and then nodded. A minute later they stood by Megan's bed.

"Megan." Bracken's voice was a caress. "Aunt Louisa is here to see you. Please wake up."

Megan's hand moved slightly on the counterpane, but she did not waken.

"Megan," Louisa tried.

Still nothing. The two stood by her side a moment longer, and then Bracken led his aunt from Megan's room to her small salon.

Louisa studied him as he closed the door, understanding his need to be near Megan without disturbing her, but when the job was done he did not speak. Louisa continued to watch as Bracken paced the room like a caged animal. It took some time for him to speak, and when he did, Louisa had to hide her astonishment.

"I need God, Lou. I need Him now."

"What do you mean, Bracken?"

"I mean, I need His help, and I don't know how to ask."

Louisa took a deep breath and then slowly made her way to a chair. She took a minute to think and pray before asking Bracken to join her. He sat across from her, his desperate eyes pinned to her face.

"If you want God right now because you want Him to do something for you, then I am afraid I can't help you."

Bracken's shoulders slumped. "Then you don't think He can heal Megan?"

"Oh, Bracken," Louisa spoke with a surety. "I *know* He can heal Megan, but it may not be His will to do so."

Bracken frowned at her.

"Dear," Louisa continued patiently, "God is not like some magical stone we can pull out of our pocket to use when we have a want or need. You can call out to God right now, and He will save you, but that does not guarantee that Megan will live."

The large man's hands clenched in pain. His eyes closed for an instant. When he spoke, Louisa heard the desperation.

"The thought of her dying destroys me, Louisa, but even if she lives, I don't think it will fill this emptiness I feel inside. I want to be changed—I want to be a better man—but I continue to make the same mistakes over and over."

Louisa smiled gently. "The changes God makes are very real, my dear nephew, but you will still sin again and again. However, the hopelessness will be gone. For every sin there is forgiveness, and fellowship so sweet that I cannot find the words to describe it to you.

"But, Bracken," Louisa warned him again. "I mean it when I say there are no guarantees. You must come to God His way, through His Son, Jesus Christ. You cannot come with the intention of bargaining on your own terms."

Louisa had never seen Bracken's eyes so impassioned as he looked at her, his upper cheeks were flushed with the intensity of it. She had prayed for just this time every day since she'd understood her own need, but never did she dream that she herself would be involved.

"Show me the way," Bracken pleaded with a low voice. Louisa did so with joy. She explained the way of salvation to her nephew and then asked if he wanted to be alone. To her surprise, he wanted her there and he wanted to pray out loud.

Tears poured down Louisa's face as she listened to Bracken's confession. The words were humble, but she heard the confidence in his voice as he prayed, knowing he was being heard. When he raised his head, he did not smile, but his broad chest lifted in a great sigh of relief. Neither one could speak, and for just a short time they sat in silence.

"I'd best return to Megan," Bracken said at last.

"Yes."

He stood to go, but paused. "Louisa, is it wrong to ask God to heal Megan?"

"No, Bracken, as long as you are ready for His answer, yes or no."

Bracken nodded. He started away again, but paused once more. This time he returned and pulled Louisa from her chair. He gave her a hug so tender that her tears began again.

"As I sat by Megan's bed I literally begged God to spare Megan so she could tell me of Him. Then He sent you. I do not know if this is a sign that I shall lose my wife, but you are here and for that I thank you, Louisa."

Bracken did leave then, but his aunt couldn't follow. She sank back down in her chair and had a long cry. She cried with joy over Bracken's conversion and also petitioned God on Megan's behalf.

Thirty-Eight

ANOTHER WEEK PASSED BEFORE MEGAN opened her eyes, but by that time the entire castle was aware of the change in Bracken. He had never been a cruel lord, but the serenity that now surrounded him was unmistakable to all who had contact with him.

Bracken had known the most amazing peace since his conversion. He had not even entreated God concerning Megan's recovery, but prayed, "Thy will be done; Thy will be done," each and every time he knew anxiety over her condition.

Just minutes before Megan awoke and called his name, the physician had finished checking her. He had been most thorough in his examination, and upon leaving he'd given Bracken a very hopeful report. The young duke's heart was near to bursting as he sat back beside the bed and watched Megan stir.

"Bracken?"

"Yes, Megan." He tried to keep his voice quiet, but hearing the sound of hers made this a chore.

"Is Marigold really dead, Bracken, or did I merely dream it?"

"She is dead, Megan; I am sorry."

Megan nodded weakly. "I feared so. I have long prayed for her, but Marigold never had love for anyone other than herself. How are my parents?"

"I believe they are doing well. They were here to see you."

This news caused Megan to try to lift her head. "They were here? Who saw to their comfort?"

"Louisa."

"Louisa was here?"

"She is still here and longs to see you."

Megan managed a weak smile, and Bracken beamed at her.

"There is something different about you, Bracken, or do my eyes deceive me?"

"No, Megan," he told her warmly. "There has been a change."

"Then you have forgiven me about the baby?"

"There is nothing to forgive."

Megan now stared at the canopy above her, her eyes sad. "I dreamt of the baby often, Bracken. I heard you speak to me, and I wanted to wake and talk with you, but I knew as soon as I left my dreams that my baby would be gone."

"No, Megan, the babe is not gone. He lives strong within you."

Megan turned to look at him, hurt etching her every feature. "Oh, Bracken, do not tease me so. My heart can't take it."

Bracken bent over her, his face now so close that she could feel his breath on her cheek. He had not planned to tell her this just yet, but her dreams had left him little choice.

"I would never be so cruel, Megan. I tell you true. You have lost some blood, but our babe is made of sterner stuff." Tears filled Bracken's eyes before he finished. "You will still be a mother before Christmas."

Megan could only stare at him, her mouth opening and closing with no sounds issuing forth.

"I didn't want to tell you because I feared it would overly excite you."

"Oh, Bracken, are you certain?"

"Yes, my love." With that he drew the covers back. When Megan's torso was uncovered, Bracken smoothed the fabric of her nightgown and took both of Megan's small hands and gently laid them on her stomach.

"In time, Megan you will know for yourself. The babe moves strong within you even now, but he's too tiny to make his presence known. I feared I would lose you, but God has other plans. He has given me both my wife and my son."

"Oh, Bracken." Megan searched his eyes and saw the truth within the peaceful depths. "Please hold me."

Bracken moved to do so but murmured, "I don't want to hurt you."

"You won't. I just need to touch you."

She felt bruised as Bracken's arms surrounded her and lifted her to his chest, but Megan had never known anything so sweet. She managed to put her arms around his neck and lay content for several minutes.

"I am so tired," she admitted at last. Bracken placed her back against the pillows.

"Mayhap you should sleep for a time."

"I don't think I have much choice," Megan murmured sleepily and her lids grew heavy.

"Bracken," she managed before slipping away. "Does my mother know of the baby?"

"No. No one save the doctor."

"Send word to her, Bracken. She has lost Marigold. Maybe knowing of this child will help the pain."

She couldn't say more, but Bracken sat beside her for a long time after she slept. Barely able to talk, but still thinking of others—this was his godly wife. This was a woman in whom God had worked. For the second time that day, Bracken cried. He had cried when he told Megan she was going to be a mother and again as he thought about what that meant for him. His father was dead many years now, but he finally had a heavenly Father to show him how to get the job done.

"I brought you some fabric, Megan," Annora told her daughter. "You'll need some new gowns once you start increasing."

"Thank you, Mother. Was the trip very hot?"

"Dreadfully, but this news of your baby is more important."

Another week had passed. Megan was sitting up in bed, waiting patiently while Annora displayed the cloth. She beamed at her mother when she saw that all the colors were perfectly suited to her. Her mother, however, was wearing black these days, and Megan hurt with the reminder.

When Annora declared that her daughter had had enough company and began to gather the fabric in order to leave, Megan asked the question that had been on her heart since her parents had arrived.

"How are you, Mother?"

To Megan's surprise, Annora sat back down and stared at her.

"I see her everywhere. I hear her voice in yours, and each time I think of her the memory mocks me. She was a fake, but I saw only what I wanted."

"Oh, Mother." Megan's voice was compassionate. "Don't torture yourself. It's over."

The older woman turned her face away. "When I think of the plans she had for you, I feel I almost hate her. You must feel the same way."

"No, Mother, I don't."

Annora stared at her incredulously. "Megan, how can that be so? How can you be feeling anything but hatred toward your sister?"

"Because I always saw her for who she was. What she did was reprehensible, but Marigold had always treated me badly."

"It was not the same for me." Annora's voice was sad.

Megan nodded, well aware of the blow her mother's pride had taken concerning her oldest child. As Megan watched her, she saw Annora's chin rise as though ready to do battle. Megan tensed, but it was not for her.

"I shall never forgive her," the older woman stated, her voice now strong. "Dead or not, her evil acts will always live in my heart. I think in time you will feel the same."

"No, mother," Megan told her gently. "It's over for me and will remain so. I have forgiven Marigold just as God forgives me when I sin."

Again Annora stared at her. "How can you even compare the two?" she asked. "What is it that causes you to treat the situation with such compassion?"

Megan tried to explain, but as soon as her voice became fervent in mentioning Christ's saving blood and the fact that all people sin, her mother cut her off.

"I am upsetting you, Meg. I shall check on you later."

"Don't go, Mother," Megan entreated her, but the other woman was now standing.

"Yes, Meg, it is time." The older woman's movements had become very agitated.

"All right." Megan's hands were tied. "If you should decide you would like to discuss it, I will be here."

Annora paused in her flight, her movements almost awkward. She came swiftly toward Megan and bent to kiss her temple. The older woman then left before Megan could say any more.

"She did not wish to speak of forgiveness, Bracken," Megan spoke from her place in the courtyard as her parents rode away. "I tried several times, but she was closed to the subject." Megan turned to look at her husband. "She will find no peace as long as she hates Marigold. I know this for a fact."

Bracken's arm went around her, and he navigated her back to the castle. "We will continue to pray. God willing, you will gain another chance to speak to her before her heart grows overly hard."

"I could write to her. Maybe I should do that now."

"I'd rather you rested now. Write your letter this afternoon."

"Bracken?" Megan asked conversationally. "Do you plan to treat me as a child until the baby is born?"

"Am I treating you as a child?"

"Did you know, Bracken, 'tis rude to answer a question with a question?"

"Did I do that?"

Megan had to laugh, but she still agreed to go to her room and put her feet up for a time. Having been up and around for only a week, she was tired enough to fall asleep, but just as she was dropping off, the baby moved for the first time. Megan didn't call for anyone or move from her bed, but thoughts of sleep were miles from her mind.

Autumn was upon them when Bracken watched an old woman shuffle across the inner bailey. Her head was uncovered, showing her very gray and wispy hair, but within seconds Bracken was back at the village standing at the old woman's apple cart. He told himself it couldn't be his wife, but he began to look for Megan anyway.

This wasn't hard to do because someone, usually Arik, watched her constantly since the kidnapping, but Bracken heaved a great sigh of relief when he spotted her waddling her way from the kitchens. It was beginning to look as though she was going to be as wide as she was high. Bracken had not known many expectant women, but he was quite certain that Megan's middle could win a prize.

The dresses Megan and Louisa had sewn just two months before were now being taxed to the limit, and the baby was not due for two months. Bracken felt pained when he thought of how far she had to go.

"Have you eaten something that disagreed with you, Bracken?" Megan wished to know as she neared.

"No," he said honestly. "I was contemplating how much larger the baby would grow before December."

Megan sighed, rubbed her stomach, and pulled a face. "I look horrible."

"I didn't say that, but you do look uncomfortable and your time is not yet near."

"Which," Megan stated emphatically, "is a kind way of saying I look awful."

Her face was so humorous and adorable that Bracken laughed.

"Ah, Megan," he said on a sigh. "I do love you so."

Megan froze in her place. She stared at Bracken as though seeing him for the first time.

"Are you in pain?" he asked anxiously. "Should I send for Helga?"

"You told me you love me," Megan said in a voice of wonder.

"Of course," Bracken shrugged. "I say it often."

"Nay, Bracken, you do not. This is the first."

"I do say it, Megan; in a hundred different ways I say it. Every day I provide for your needs and see to your comfort. You have clothing, food, and loyal servants. I touch you with tenderness and respect, and when you cry my arms are waiting to hold you.

"I do say it, Megan," he concluded. "You have not been listening."

Megan stared at him. "I find no fault in your care of me, but a woman likes to hear the words."

"It cannot make that much difference," Bracken replied, trying to dismiss the subject, but her eyes were so full of yearning and hope that he had a hard time looking away from her.

"I am not good with words," he tried to explain, but Megan gave him no quarter.

"I need to hear only three."

Bracken glanced around swiftly and suddenly grabbed Megan's arm and pulled her into a dim corner of the passageway. He took her face between his hands and looked into her eyes.

"I love you, Megan."

The round redhead sighed with unbelievable pleasure. "And I love you, Bracken of Hawkings Crest," she whispered.

He bent and kissed her, and Megan's eyes closed in bliss. He was right, he did "tell" her everyday that his love was constant, but there was something very special in hearing the words.

The baby suddenly kicked between them, and Bracken's hands immediately dropped to Megan's stomach. He had felt the movements often, but the look of delight in his eyes never waned.

"Perhaps it will be sooner than we think," Megan whispered. "I am so large that maybe my dates have been wrong."

"Perhaps. We will pray for God's timing and be patient."

Megan loved it when Bracken spoke of God with such submission. When his arms came around her, she lay her head on his chest and sighed with contentment.

You have given me so much, heavenly Father—more than I ever dreamed. Please bless this child in my womb. Help us to show You to him.

Bracken's thoughts were much the same, and for a time the world ceased to exist. Duke and duchess would have stood holding one another for quite some time, but there was a sudden commotion coming from the great hall. Several servants passed, and someone said the names Lady Joyce and Lord Stephen.

"Oh, Bracken." Megan grabbed his arm in excitement.

The duke needed no other encouragement. He took Megan's small hand in his, and they made their way out to the great hall to greet his family.

"I WAS UPSTAIRS WITH MEGAN WHEN Vincent pursued Marigold. She ran through the castle and then out to the front steps. He never laid a hand on her. She fell down those high, stone steps and broke her neck."

"She was so evil," Giles commented softly, a frown knitting his young brow.

"Yes," Joyce agreed, her heart going out to Bracken and Megan.

"What has happened to Roland Kirkpatrick?" Stephen wished to know.

"He is in the Tower awaiting his sentence. I do not believe things will go well for him."

The family was gathered around the hearth in the war room, and for a moment they were silent. Bracken had been relaying the events of the past months. Megan had written concerning some of them, but Joyce was naturally interested in the details.

"Tell us the rest Bracken," she entreated after a time.

"We took the journey home very slowly. When we arrived, I felt certain that all would be well. This was not the case. Megan lay sleeping for days, and at times she grew so still that I feared I would lose her."

Bracken reached for Megan's hand, and continued with his eyes on his mother.

"I have never known such fear. In the past I have made vows to God, but always on my terms. This time I only asked God to spare Megan because I knew she could tell me how to find Him. The hole in my heart went on without end. I have never known such desperation. I wanted for the first time to have a relationship with God's Son, and I had no idea how to go about it."

"And then Louisa came," Joyce filled in, her heart in her eyes. Bracken smiled as well at the remembrance.

"Yes. I asked how she had heard of Megan's illness, but of course she hadn't. I know now that God sent her when I needed her most."

"And what did she tell you?" Stephen asked. He still believed as Bracken once had, that God had no real place in his life. Keeping this in mind, Bracken answered gently.

"She was not easy with me. She told me that there would be no bargains, no guarantees. Louisa said my submitting to God would not spare Megan. God could still decide that her time on this earth was over."

"And yet you still believed?" Stephen seemed fascinated.

"Yes. It sounds cold, but I knew that not even Megan's spared life would fill the emptiness I felt within. I had run from God for years. It's a wonder He did not give up. I knew that it was long past time for me to surrender."

Bracken turned then and looked at Megan, his hand still holding hers. "God has given me my wife and my child, but of more importance is what He did for my spirit."

Megan smiled tenderly into his eyes. She had longed and prayed for this without really thinking how precious it would be. The change in him was so dramatic. Their life was not perfect, but when God spoke through the Holy Scriptures about new life, Megan had only to look at her husband to know just what He meant.

The warm fellowship of the group was interrupted when Stephen suddenly stood. Megan had been so intent on Bracken that she had not noticed his discomfort. Without looking at anyone, Stephen wordlessly walked from the room. No one spoke for a time, but then Bracken broke the silence.

"He will come," the older brother spoke with confidence.

"Yes," Giles agreed, a smile on his face. "He fights as you did, Bracken, but as with you, it is just a matter of time."

Bracken reached and clapped Giles on the shoulder. "It's good to have you here, Giles. Maybe Mother would agree to your staying for a time."

The younger man's eyes lit up, and he turned to Joyce. "Mother?"

"I don't see why not." She smiled at him. "It will be quiet with Kristine at Danella's—she is expecting again—but I shall survive."

"It's settled then," Bracken announced and stood. "Let us go and see how you're doing with your archery."

Bracken's hand dropped for a moment onto Megan's shoulder, and then the women watched them move away. The conversation waned after that, but neither woman cared. Feeling tired of a sudden, Megan was content to doze. Joyce, after her long journey, wanted to sit quietly and pray.

Megan's first pain hit her in the kitchens. A month had passed. Stephen had moved on, but Joyce was still at Hawkings Crest, and Giles was also in attendance. No one noticed the duchess' sudden look of shock or the way she held onto the edge of the table with a white-fingered grip. After a time, she stood erect and rubbed the dampness from her upper lip.

The next contraction was over 20 minutes later, but it lasted much longer. and Megan was thankful that she'd taken herself off to be alone in her parlor. She panted for a time afterward and debated calling for someone. The thought of lying in bed, as she was sure everyone would insist she do, was not to be tolerated.

Feeling fairly well, Megan forced herself to rise and go about her business. In no time at all, she grew fairly adept at turning away from the people around her or sitting down when she felt a pain coming on. She was not one given to moaning or crying out, but some cramps taxed her to the limit of her self-control.

Hours had passed when Bracken sought her out. He was slightly preoccupied, so although Megan had just had a contraction that flushed her face and beaded her brow with moisture, he didn't notice anything amiss.

"I am going hunting. The hour is not early, but with the light snow from this morning, the timing is good."

"I'd rather you didn't, Bracken," Megan said unexpectedly.

The duke blinked at her. "What did you say?" His voice told of his incredulity.

Megan sighed. "I'm sorry, Bracken; I just wish you could be home right now."

He studied her intently for a moment, first her eyes and then her swollen stomach.

"Your pains have started," he stated seriously, his voice low.

"Yes," Megan admitted.

"'Tis too soon," he said, as if to reason with her would make them go away.

"They have come," Megan told him logically.

"When?"

"Hours ago."

Bracken bent promptly and lifted her in his arms. Megan protested and tried to gain his attention, but they were at the bottom of the stairs before he listened to her.

"Please, Bracken."

"Please what?" He stopped and stared down at the round bundle in his arms.

"I do not wish to go to bed. The pains started around 20 minutes apart. Now, hours have passed, and they are still some ten minutes apart. I cannot lie in bed for hours, Bracken, or I will lose my sanity."

The indecision was clear in his eyes. Good sense told him to take her right to bed, but eyes humbly entreated him and told him to listen to her words. He stood for long minutes and then slowly lowered Megan so she could stand.

"I will abide by your wishes—" he began just as a pain hit her. Bracken forced himself to stand helplessly by as Megan held onto his arm with strength that only severe pain can bring. She panted as it subsided, and Bracken felt breathless himself when he spoke.

"Please let me take you up, Megan."

The small woman emphatically shook her head. "I tell you true, Bracken, it will be hours yet. Let me stay active."

His great chest rose in a heartfelt sigh. "As you wish. I will be at your side at all times, and I will have Helga ready our room, but for the time I will do as you ask."

More hours passed, and still Megan felt no real urgency. To Bracken's chagrin, his mother agreed with Megan's handling of the situation. Joyce stayed close herself, but she did not urge Megan to alter her plans.

The evening was growing long when Megan's demeanor changed. She sat quietly through two more very close contractions before speaking to her husband.

"I wish to go upstairs now, Bracken."

The young duke heard her, but for a moment he could not react. He had watched the intense pain these last spasms had brought, and for a moment he was paralyzed with anguish for her. She had shown the qualities of a knight the way she suffered without complaint, but watching her, there was no disguising the misery.

"Bracken," Giles said, shaking his brother's arm. "Help her."

Still the older man did not move.

"Bracken," Joyce now tried. "Megan is ready to go upstairs."

Joyce and Giles shared a look and then glanced at Megan. They found her looking oddly at her husband. She stared at him for the space of several minutes and then spoke gently.

"I need your help, Bracken. I know that the day has been long, but if you could only get me to our bedchamber, I will give you your son."

The word *son* seemed to snap Bracken out of his trance. He

moved swiftly then, but with extreme gentleness. He lifted Megan as if she herself were the child and bore his precious bundle carefully to her bed. He bent over her once she was settled but had to wait while she gripped his hand for another pain. When it subsided, he whispered, "I'm sorry."

"It's all right," Megan smiled at him in love. "I understand." Megan stroked his beard until another paroxysm gripped her, and Bracken moved to allow his mother and Helga access.

The remaining time was not long, but to Bracken it felt like hours. It was just before midnight when from his place in his wife's salon he heard a baby cry. He had been trying to read Megan's copy of the Psalms and Proverbs. He now set that aside and stood but could move no further. The door was open, and he heard his mother praise God in a loud voice, but he couldn't make himself walk in.

I have a son, his heart kept repeating. *I have a son.* It never occurred to him that Megan might not be safe, but not until Joyce called to him could he propel his body forward.

He walked into the room on shaky legs and found little light and even less activity. Megan lay still, her eyes on his as he entered. Joyce sat on a chair near the bed, a small parcel wrapped in her arms. Helga stood on the opposite side of the room, her eyes suspiciously moist.

"How are you?" Bracken asked when he stood by the bed.

"I am well. What do you think of our baby?"

Bracken turned to bend over his mother. He smiled.

"He's not very big, is he?"

"*She*, Bracken," Joyce told him, and watched his look of astonishment.

"She?" Bracken turned just his head to ask his wife. Megan nodded with a sleepy smile.

"I know 'tis not what you planned, but she is all ours."

"She?" Bracken now asked of his mother. Joyce chuckled.

"Take her Bracken; hold her," Joyce urged. "You will not yearn for a boy."

It was the best thing Joyce could have suggested. Bracken

took the baby in his hands, awkwardly at first, and then moved her with confidence into the light. Her face was bunching up to cry, and Bracken chuckled low in his throat.

"Not only have you given me a daughter," he lovingly accused Megan, "but I find the first time I hold her that she is a termagant."

Megan laughed as well. "Is she not beautiful? I think she has your chin."

The baby let out a wail then, but her parents ignored her.

"My chin? You've never seen my chin." Bracken's bearded face was still turned to Megan.

"But I can tell," she stated with complete confidence. "Will you bring her here?"

Joyce and Helga exited quietly when Bracken put their daughter in the crook of Megan's arm and sat on the bed beside her. They looked at her for long minutes and then at one another.

"What shall we call her?"

"I don't know, Bracken. I had only a boy in mind."

Bracken troubled his lower lip.

"Gwen is a pretty name."

"She doesn't look like a Gwen," Megan told him, her eyes on the baby. "How about Ursula?

Bracken's nose wrinkled. "I knew an Ursula once. She was an old hag."

And on the search went. It was a ridiculous time of night to be discussing names, but more than an hour passed before it occurred to them that a name did not need to be decided upon immediately. Bracken sought his bed with the intention of sleeping through the night. He might not have bothered had he known that the matter would still be decided before morning.

Somewhere around 3:00 A.M. he woke to the sound of the baby crying. When he got to Megan's room he found the baby lying comfortably at her breast. Bracken stretched out carefully on the bed to watch. Megan's eyes were closed when it came to him.

"Meredith."

"What?" she blinked, and then frowned at him.

"Meredith. Do you like the name Meredith?"

Again Megan blinked. "I do," she said with some surprise. "Indeed, it's a wonderful name."

Bracken nodded, well satisfied. "It will be so. Meredith of Hawkings Crest."

"Do you think she'll be Mary or Edith?"

"Meredith," Bracken stated firmly, and Megan agreed. A moment later she looked down to see the baby staring right at her.

"Did you hear that, my darling? You're our little Meredith. Isn't that a wonderful name?" Megan pressed a soft kiss to her daughter's brow and glanced up to find Bracken's eyes on her. She thought he would have been watching the baby, but in the dim light she could see that he studied her intently.

"I love you," he said with sudden tenderness, causing tears to rush to Megan's eyes. "And I have loved you since I stood in the Reverend Mother's office and knew that I would storm the abbey if that is what it took to get you back."

"Oh, Bracken," Megan whispered. "I never knew."

"'Tis my fault. For far too long I was afraid to let you know you were in my heart."

"It's good to know now."

Bracken leaned to kiss her, and when he moved they both saw that the baby was asleep again. Bracken tenderly lifted little Meredith, and when he was on his feet, called for Helga. When both infant and servant were gone, Bracken went back to the bed.

"Will it disturb you if I join you?"

"No," Megan assured him. "It's lonely in here."

"It was in my room as well."

Megan moved very carefully as she was still quite tender, but a few minutes later, her head was pillowed on her husband's chest, his arm wrapped securely around her. She lay very still as the beating of his heart came steadily to her ear. Megan had worked at not holding onto Bracken's life too tightly, reminding herself always that he belonged to God, but at that moment, she found herself praying that she would hear his heartbeat for years to come.

Meredith needs us both, Father God, she prayed silently. *If it be Thy will, may we raise her together and show Your love to her and to all who may follow.*

Megan then smiled at her own prayer. Meredith was just hours old, and here she was praying for more. What must she be thinking? Megan found it was not a hard question to answer. She was thinking of how much God had already given them. He was sure to have much more in mind, much more indeed.

Epilogue

HAWKINGS CREST
OCTOBER 1542

WORD OF BRACKEN'S ARRIVAL CAME to Megan, and she swiftly passed baby Gwen into Helga's waiting arms. She spoke a word to the other children, who obediently remained upstairs, their beautiful dark eyes watching their mother exit.

Megan ran downstairs to the great room, but Bracken was not fast enough and Megan met him in the keep. He put an arm around her and swept her into the newly built chapel. When he found it empty, he pulled her up against him and found her lips with his own.

"I missed you," he said when at last they could speak.

"And I you. Bracken," Megan could wait no longer, "is it true?"

Bracken's eyes closed in agony. "Tis true. Henry has found Catherine Howard guilty of misconduct and had her executed."

Megan let her head fall forward against his chest. "This is the fifth wife, Bracken; how much more will our king demand?"

"He is obsessed. There is already talk of Catherine's replacement."

Megan moved to look at him. Her eyes were sad. Bracken reached to touch her cheek.

"How are you and the children?"

"We are well."

"How about young Stephen's touch of flu?"

"He is also well. If activity means anything, he's a specimen of health."

"I saw my brother Stephen in London. He talked of coming here to visit."

Megan shook her head. "He's not been, and I can't say as I'm sorry." Her tone was teasing. "He spoils the children terribly when he's here, especially young Stephen when the other children are not looking."

"Now I wonder why that is." Bracken drew the words out, and duke and duchess smiled at one another.

They both loved remembering the birth of young Stephen, now eight, and the rebirth of the older Stephen. Megan had been far along in the pregnancy when they'd made a trip to Stone Lake Castle. Stephen had accompanied them.

It was not the best time to go, but Megan's mother had just given birth to a baby daughter. Because Annora was doing so well, Vincent had begged them to come and meet Megan's baby sister, Mercy. Vincent and Annora had named her such because of the mercy God had shown them in the way He worked in their lives and marriage. It was on the way home from Stone Lake that Megan's pains began. Stephen had never been so frightened in all of his life as Bracken and Helga prepared Megan to give birth in the forest.

Bracken and Megan were confident, calm even, but Stephen nearly came undone. Megan did not understand what was so frightening, but when Bracken left them for a time, Stephen began to talk.

"What if you die?" There were tears in the young man's voice. Finally Megan understood.

"Then I'll live forever with God," she told him serenely.

"Oh, Megan." Stephen's tone was tortured. "To have such assurance must be a wondrous thing."

"You can have it as well, Stephen."

"Nay, Meg, not I." His look was heartrending.

"Yes, Stephen, you. Trust me. I would never lie to you."

The words were a turning point for Stephen. He respected Megan as he did few people. He was ready to listen for the first time, and by the time Megan's baby was born, Stephen was a new creature. It was simply a normal course of events to name the child after Bracken's brother.

"And what of little Arik and Gwen?"

Megan pulled a wry face.

"Arik has it in his head that he must have a sword for his fourth birthday next month, and he can talk of little else. Of course, big Arik is encouraging him in this pursuit. Meredith has experienced a growth period and is almost as tall as I am. Gwen has a tooth in her mouth and is still spitting up all over me on a regular basis."

Megan was smiling and Bracken laughed at his wife's description of their brood. He had been away for only a month, but so much had occurred. Indeed, not just in his family. England itself was changing before their very eyes.

"Come, Bracken," Megan now urged. "The children are most anxious."

He did not need to be asked twice. Within minutes Bracken's children were swarming him, and he held and kissed each one in turn. He couldn't stop staring at them. They *all* seemed so much taller and more grown up. He had two hours with them before the time grew late and they were ushered off to bed with promises of a special outing in the morning.

Bracken then ate a hasty meal and rushed to be alone with Megan as soon as they were able. They sat before the fire in the bedchamber for many minutes, not speaking but getting silently reacquainted.

Finally Megan said, "What is to become of us, Bracken? In truth, I am frightened."

"There is no need. God makes kings, Megan, and He is still in control of England. The monasteries have been dissolved, and Henry's push to restore what he calls the true church of

England is crushing many innocent people beneath his political heels, but our God is the king of the universe."

"Then you are never afraid, Bracken," she stated, her face turned up to see him.

"I would be a fool not to be alert, my love, but I fear not for tomorrow. Has God not proven to us repeatedly that He will see to our every need? Has God not proven His love over and over?"

"Yes, Bracken, He has. I am not trusting."

"Then I will pray that your trust increases."

Megan smiled at him again and put her head back against his arm. He never made light of her shortcomings or rebuked her harshly, but with love and tenderness led the way by word and example.

"You've grown rather quiet," Bracken commented.

"I was confessing my sin of faithlessness and then thinking about the future."

"Worrying?"

"No, not this time. This time I must leave it with God. This time I must trust completely."

Bracken turned her so she was in his arms and he could look down into her face. "In the Holy Scripture a dove is at times the symbol of peace. You're my dove; did you know that, Megan?"

"Oh, Bracken." Her eyes sparkled at his praise. "I love you so."

His head lowered to better place a gentle kiss upon her lips, but he stopped to say one more thing.

"There are no guarantees concerning tomorrow, Megan, but believe as I do, my dove. God alone holds England in the palm of His hand, and as long as He gives me breath I shall be here for you."

"Thank you, Bracken."

"For what?"

Megan smiled, thinking that God had outdone Himself the day He had created her knight, but she didn't answer and Bracken knew that enough had been said. The duke's head lowered once again and this time he kissed his precious wife so tenderly that words were no longer necessary.